UNBOUND CHAOS

THE UNBINDING CHRONICLES: VOLUME I

J. NEFF

EDITORS: J. M. NEFF, MARIKO IRVING
COVER ART: EMILY VERKAMP

A project of this magnitude is not realized overnight. Ashley Shackelford created the persona of Dalyn Tyrdrac in 2005 when we first began experimenting with Dungeons and Dragons (3.0) while we were college students. He is also the first person to say "Hey, what if Dalyn was dumb enough to fuse with the arcane somehow?" His question broke magic as we knew it in the world that we were building together.

Time, however, only seems to accelerate as a person grows older. I continued world building after college, finding myself brought back to Espa almost two decades later when I sat down to write a novel as a joke. When I began *Unbound Chaos*, I was freshly finished with my PhD, and I was no longer intimidated by a text in the tens of thousands of words. I told my wife, Janell, that it was finally time to write a fantasy novel, and she challenged me to try it. I wrote the first five or so chapters and she began reading as I continued writing. Her feedback, encouragement, and determination to keep me writing resulted in the volume you now have in your hands (or are viewing through your digital reader).

Furthermore, the story and content of this book draws inspiration from the thousands of experiences that have filled my heart with a love of stories. It's easy to make the connection to Dungeons and Dragons, but other influences have given me the ideas to keep this story moving: video games like the Final Fantasy series, Secret and Trials of Mana, Kingdom Hearts (actually, if it's a SquareEnix title, its lingering influence can be easily spotted), and the Breath of Fire series by Capcom; cartoons, animé, and manga ranging from *Avatar: The Last Airbender*, *FullMetal Alchemist*, *Fairy Tail*, and *Black Clover* inspire a lot of the philosophical questions posed by this narrative; finally, the works of fantasy authors like R. A. Salvatore, Margaret Wise and Tracy Hickman, Lewis and Tolkien, and mythologies from all over the world fueled my inspiration to put these adventures into words.

Finally, my friends, Cory, Casandra, Emily, and my brother

James have created and played numerous tabletop roleplaying sessions with me, helping shape the ideas for characters. The details of those characters created the foundation for the personalities within this growing series. Janell played with us, too. She created a character by the name of "Elmadyn" that you may see very soon!

I hope you enjoy Miranda's adventure as much as I enjoyed writing it. I learned much about myself through this journey, and I hope you will take away something precious to you as well.

WEST E...
[DRAIKIN PENINSULA]
FARZG ESTATE
OSGOOD
[THE LICHWOOD]
Osgo...
THE ASTRAL SPIRE
[MAMMOTH MOORS]
[TOLIN FORE...]
SHESTER
NORTH TIMBYL
LODAN
[GULF OF NOCTURNE]
ALABASTER
[ZENITH PLAINS]
OSFER
Alabaster
THALISTON
[EZDELL HILLCOUNTRY]
THE SHINDOR OCEAN
[ERMEN MOORS]
[SELLAN RANGE]
DEVITUS
Claston
ARGENTUM
CLASTON
NULODIA
K'TAL H'YUCK
FT. CUNNINGWORTH
GLERN
LANCETHINA'S ESTATE
BERITON
ACERO
MYSTALON
[THE TYMBYRWYLDE]
MT. EMBER
TANLIN FALLS
CARULUS'S CAMP
PORT UNDINE
SEA OF UNDINE
N
CHYU'TAÏ OCEAN
TOBIT
TIBOT
IGNIA SEA
SOLAR SEA
C...
SCALE: 100 MILES
[THE ISLES KNOWN FOR NOTHING]
YENDRALIA

Vernum
Summer
Autumn
Winter
EQUINOX
SOLSTICE
SOLSTICE
EQUINOX
REPLENISHING
GROWING
FLOURISHING
HARVESTING
FALLOWING
RESTING
WARMING
FESTIVAL
FESTIVAL
"the thing that is in Balance"
ANNUAL CYCLE
RSPA
the

Annual Cycle of Espa

Winter

101 Days. Solstice, 3 Months
- ❖ The Fallowing – 40 Days
- ❖ Winter Solstice – 21 Days, Two Full Moons that overlap on the third hour of solstice
- ❖ The Resting – 40 Days

Vernum

103 Days. Equilibrium, 3 Months
- ❖ The Warming – 40 Days
- ❖ The Celebration of Equilibrium – 23 Days With 3 Days of equinox
- ❖ The Replenishing – 40 Days

Summer

101 Days. Solstice, 3 Months
- ❖ The Growing – 40 Days
- ❖ Summer Solstice – 21 Days, Two New Moons that overlap on the third hour of solstice
- ❖ The Flourishing – 40 Days

Autumn

103 Days. Equilibrium, 3 Months.
- ❖ The Harvesting – 40 Days
- ❖ The Celebration of Equilibrium – 23 Days With 3 Days of equinox
- ❖ The Festival – 40 Days

Weeks in Espa are five days long. The solstice and equinox months have holidays that add days to their respective weeks.

TABLE OF CONTENTS

Chapter 1
The Examination

iranda gripped the hilt of her sword with an anxious tremble even though the expression in her cold blue eyes could pierce the hull of an adamant juggernaut. Invictus, a strict but just god, demanded that all his clergy pass a trial by combat before being accepted as an acolyte, the lowest official rank in his church. While she had trained physically and mentally for today's exam, Miranda's confidence and faith found themselves in a dance with doubt, the source of which stemmed from the visiting examiner. High Priest Gaius Carulus, known for his unrelenting scrutiny and judgment, had traveled a great distance from the largest port city in the kingdom to administer the exam in Devitus, the last pocket of civilization on the borderlands between the Kingdom of Alabaster and the wilderness of the Trollcrag Mountains.

The frontier town of Devitus served as a buffer for the "civilized" peoples of Alabaster, including numerous farming villages scattered across the fertile river valley of the Starlock

River that flowed to the east. It emptied into the Nulodian Sea over two hundred miles away from the fortified walls of Devitus. The frontier town sat on the eastern reaches of Alabaster's borders, with the sparsely populated central Trollcrag region to its east, home to a few giant clans and various sects of druids. The city of Nulodia rested over the delta, where the Starlock River spilled into the Nulodian Sea. In that city, the High Temple of Invictus served the metropolitan population of the region. Primarily concerned with law enforcement and the succession of nobility, the priests of Invictus were known as the keepers of law and order, a duty not to be taken lightly as the forces of chaos always seemed ready to encroach on the progress of civilization.

Miranda thought that perhaps this was why High Priest Carulus was so strict on admitting acolytes to the Path of the Sword of Justice, those who have been welcomed into the folds of Invictus, the keepers of the law and protectors of order. After all, keeping the forces of chaos and disorder at bay could be dangerous work. An unprepared acolyte could easily and quickly become a dead acolyte. She stood with two other would-be acolytes in the courtyard of the small church dedicated to Invictus, accompanied by their mentor, Bishop Thomas Selasine. Bishop Selasine stood tall at six and a half feet, a human man of imposing stature, his broad frame accentuated by the full-plate armor worn by higher-ranking church members. A vicious scar on the right side of his face was partially covered by an eyepatch that undoubtedly hid the evidence of a severe injury the bishop had taken in an altercation unknown to Miranda. His black hair, twisted into the braids typically worn by those of the faith, spiraled down the front of his armor, tucked underneath the flowing beard that made Selasine seem as wise as he was intimidating. He had broad features and a wide nose, and the wrinkles of middle age encroached around his forehead and eyes.

Though it was only a matter of moments after the three had been summoned, waiting on the high priest felt like watching an hourglass with an infinite amount of sand count the moments, never moving closer to the designated time. When the high priest's vanguard arrived, Miranda felt excitement and uncertainty in her heart. To make things worse, she had many questions about the high priest. She wondered why he would travel so far to oversee the entrance examination of three inconsequential acolytes that served the last community in civilized lands. Perhaps he had other business in the area, but that thought only helped to fuel Miranda's curiosity and doubt.

"Adûnzha," Bishop Selasine hissed, a command in an old language meaning roughly "at attention" in the common tongue. Miranda and the other two examinees stood straight as commanded, their shield hands gripping the hilts of their swords as dictated by church protocol. The vanguard entered the church courtyard, a regiment of at least twenty mid-to-high-ranking priests and paladins bearing the standards of the church and the high priest. While the priests made their way on foot, the paladins entered the courtyard mounted on the blessed horses that found their way to their masters at the direction of Invictus himself. They shone a deep, royal purple in the sunlight, one of the holy colors of the church. Behind them, a rearguard blocked the main entrance to the church's courtyard as High Priest Carulus entered atop a white warhorse, the magnificent beast adorned with gold and purple plate armor. Since the paladins of the order were the only ones to receive a blessed mount from Invictus, the clerics often purchased thoroughbred warhorses to accompany their more martially inclined brethren.

Carulus strode up to Bishop Selasine and the would-be acolytes, his eyes exploring the small stone chapel and the modest garden in the courtyard. Finally, he turned his attention to Selasine, who waited quietly in the full Invictus salute. His shield hand was pressed to the hilt of his sword, the other to his chest with his hand open, palm up to the sky. Miranda knew the bishop would hold that salute until the high priest addressed him. Since she and the others were not yet members of the Path of the Sword of Justice, the official clerics and paladins of Invictus, they were not allowed to engage in the formal salute. Carulus dismounted his horse, mirrored Selasine's posture, and commanded, "We harvest the bounty of law."

Selasine shifted from his salute to simple attention and replied, "Peace and prosperity, the blessings of the Sword of Justice." Miranda felt a tingle run down her spine. She had rehearsed the salutes with the bishop hundreds of times, recited catechisms daily, and had been preparing to engage with other members of the church as appropriate to the hierarchy. This was, however, only the second time that Miranda had ever seen another clergy member other than Bishop Selasine. Six months ago, a paladin passed through Devitus on a quest and sought worship and meditation at the church. Miranda had only been studying and training with the bishop for about six months at that time, so she was oblivious to some of the intricacies of the church's ceremonies. This time, however, she was keenly aware of what was expected of all parties involved, the phrases that would indicate rank and expectations, and the salutes and bows that would seem esoteric to anyone outside the church hierarchy.

"At ease," the high priest commanded. Bishop Selasine, Miranda, and the other examinees relaxed their posture, releasing their grip on the hilts of their swords. Miranda knew that, at this point, the examination had begun. The high priest would scrutinize every move, response, and decision made by the candidates. She began trying to predict what the high priest would say to them so that she could respond with the correct phrase or catechism. She tried to maintain a cold, neutral expression, but the high priest seemed to catch on to her anxiety without much effort, his expression sadistic as he began to greet the candidates.

"Your name, peacekeeper?" the high priest said to one of the young men waiting with her and the others.

"Justin, sir." He seemed uncomfortably stiff in his posture as Carulus examined him. He had dark blond hair that was well-kept, and he had a handsome but young face. He stood just short of six feet tall, and his frame was athletic. He would make a fine cleric or warpriest, Carulus thought. He stepped toward the three candidates and turned his gaze to Miranda.

"And you, peacekeeper?"

Her blue eyes shimmered in the light of the late morning, sparkling with excitement tempered with nervousness.

"Miranda, sir," she replied, her body instinctively as stiff and attentive as Justin's. Her red hair was tied back into a tight ponytail that hung midway down her back. Carulus's eyes lingered on her. She was beautiful with sharp features and lovely cheeks. Her eyes, however, glowed sapphire blue in the morning light. Carulus nodded in approval; she also looked as if she would make an excellent cleric. After a moment that seemed to last an hour, the high priest resumed introductions.

"And you, peacekeeper?" his voice repeated.

The third candidate stood confidently and replied, "August, sir." Almost as tall as the bishop, August seemed a good candidate for paladinhood under the church's guidance. Though his frame was not as wide as Selasine's, he would still make an imposing sight for those who challenge the law. His features seemed chiseled from stone, and a well-kept, short beard adorned his wide jaw. His hair and eyes were brown, giving him a rugged look. Carulus gave an approving nod and turned his attention to Selasine.

"Which one is the healer?" the high priest asked, catching the bishop off guard.

"The healer?" Selasine replied, his eyes quickly scanning over his pupils. "They have all proven themselves capable of treating injuries with the blessings of Invictus. I am afraid—"

The high priest interrupted him. "The one that saved that family after their home had been burned. I have heard the rumors, Selasine. Six months ago. A miraculous healing. One of your students shows great promise."

Bishop Selasine's gaze locked with Miranda's. "If that's the case, then Your Holiness is looking for Miranda."

An ambitious smile stretched across the high priest's lips. He was not imposing like the bishop but rather a half-elf standing around five feet tall. He was not dressed in armor like his regiment but in ceremonial robes of purple and gold. The scales of justice adorned the front, which was the holy symbol of Invictus. Raising his hand in an open-palmed gesture toward Miranda, Carulus recited the opening line of the Catechism of the Peacekeeper to her. "Creation finds itself on the precipice between law and chaos."

Her heart skipped a beat. This was the first direct test

applied by the high priest. Swallowing, she replied in a confident voice, "Those who find refuge at the feet of Invictus welcome order into their hearts." Her voice was melodic and sweet, but it still carried her conviction with force.

The ambitious smile twisted into something more sinister as his eyes narrowed, and his gaze moved to August. "Those that embrace order are protected by the Sword of Justice."

Without hesitation, August replied, "Those that are protected by his holy might rejoice, for the hour of delivery is upon us."

Satisfied with August's response, the high priest turned his attention to Justin. "Deliver them from chaos and shield them from anarchy," the high priest prompted with the penultimate line of the catechism. His eyes, still narrow, scrutinizing the candidates, peered at Justin expectantly.

"And may we, peacekeepers, stand firmly at the precipice, keeping the darkness at bay," Justin replied.

With an excited clap, High Priest Carulus snapped his hands in front of him. "Well, Bishop Selasine, it seems that your peacekeepers have a firm foundation in the tenets of the faith. But do they have the traits necessary to serve the Sword of Justice as acolytes?"

This change of direction was as much a test for Bishop Selasine as it was for his pupils. Selasine replied, "May Your Holiness test them in their strength and resolve. Let us hear the voice of Invictus and obey the will of order."

Miranda's head swirled. That phrase served as a harbinger for the most brutal part of the examination: a trial by combat. While she understood the necessity of using violence in some cases, she would rather resolve issues without fighting. It saddened her that some people would engage in violence instead of listening to reason. Still, she had not taken much time to size up the high priest's entourage, but she assumed that some of his well-trained paladins would serve as the combatants in a duel-type setting with the candidates. She mentally kicked herself for waiting so long to consider their role in this exam, even though it had only been moments since they had arrived. Returning her attention to High Priest Carulus, Miranda felt her stomach drop as she heard the proposal emerging from his lips.

"These candidates have been trained, but they have yet to face the forces of chaos head-on. Instead of a traditional duel, I propose that they accompany our regiment. We make our way to the lair of Erk the Pirate Lord. His wicked ways have wrought havoc upon the Sea of Undine, and the King of Claston has requested this scourge be dealt with." Carulus clasped his hands together, his face beaming with pride. This unorthodox approach was not unprecedented in times of war. Still, it seemed strange that three acolyte candidates from the most rural part of the kingdom would be conscripted to accompany a trained regiment on a life-or-death volunteer mission.

Miranda could not hide her expression, confusion wrought with a shred of terror. Pirate Lord Erk was notorious for targeting the richest vessels in any body of water for hundreds of miles. Rumors of the might of his pirates reached far inland, some of them suggesting that even the cabin boys on his ship could slay dragons. Having newly established acolytes along for such a journey would only serve as a detriment to the entire battalion, or so Miranda thought. Bishop Selasine thought the same and immediately objected in violation of church protocol.

"Your Holiness, have you gone mad?" Selasine exclaimed, and it was the first time Miranda had seen him lose his composure.

"Watch your tone, bishop," Carulus sneered in return. He approached Selasine and leaned close to him, hiding his words from the examination candidates. "That family was dead; we both know that. The girl is special. We need that kind of healing on this mission."

A grim expression overtook Selasine's face. A successful move against Erk would undoubtedly be an extraordinary legacy, one that Carulus could not resist once the request had been made and approved officially through church channels. These actions would probably be sanctioned by The Council of Four, four powerful clergy chosen by the avatar of Invictus to lead the church. Clenching his teeth, Selasine replied with more of a growl than words, "If these children are summoned to such duty so early in their walk with the Sword of Justice, then I demand to join your battalion as an auxiliary and as their direct commander." Carulus was well known for his attention to the church bylaws and regulations. The bishop knew it was better to insert them as volunteers than conscriptions, and his demands perfectly followed protocol. He saw his peacekeepers as his children, and he wanted to control the terms of their assignment in the mission.

Carulus's eyes twisted with anger, but he allowed his thoughts to process Selasine's demands before responding. He then spoke in a voice loud enough so that the examinees could hear his words. "Your resolve to defend the law from chaos is commendable. With your guidance, these young acolytes will shine as beacons properly equipped against anarchy." Miranda's eyes widened in shock. That line was almost the same catechism used to congratulate the mentors of newly welcomed acolytes. Did this mean Carulus admitted them to the flock before the trial by combat? "Be sure to make your preparations with haste; we set out for the Undine Coast at dawn. Ensure that each acolyte is properly equipped and understands the mission at hand." Turning to the candidates, the ambitious smile returned to his lips. "Congratulations and welcome to the Path of the Sword of Justice, acolytes. May Invictus guide your hand against chaos at every turn."

Without another word, the high priest returned to his horse. His silver hair, also twisted into the braids worn by members of the faith, bounced on his shoulders as he leaped into the stirrups, slinging his legs over his horse. The high priest was not a young half-elf by any means, but he was still spry and able to mount his oversized horse without issue. The collection of clerics and paladins that had accompanied him on this journey were ready at a moment's notice. They followed their leader into the town of Devitus, presumably to also make last-minute preparations for the journey to the Undine Coast.

Miranda, Selasine, Justin, and August watched the others depart. Selasine's grave expression made Miranda's stomach sink further. She knew that pledging to the clergy of Invictus could be dangerous, but she could also tell that the high priest's orders were unusual. Then again, sages had designated this era as the most chaotic in history. Though the gods still walked among mortals, the very fabric of magic itself had unraveled a century before. Common people with no magical aptitude suddenly could wield powerful magics. In contrast, ancient and well-studied wizards could not even conjure small quantities of flame. To make matters worse, individuals like Pirate Lord Erk had built their enterprises utilizing the anomalies in the fabric of magic. The Church of Invictus was the most prominent force that had stood firm against chaos for the last century. Miranda thought that perhaps this mission was pivotal to stem a new wave of chaos, much like the one stopped by the church one hundred years ago when magic unraveled.

Selasine gestured to the church building. "We have much to discuss." The three acolytes followed their mentor into the old structure. Miranda wasn't sure how old the little church might be, but it always seemed quaint and beautiful. She grew up in Devitus as an orphan taken in by the monastery of Lexcord, a goddess dedicated to building a strong society focused on helping those in need and protecting the innocent. Miranda didn't remember her parents very well. Still, somehow she felt like she could see the faces of her mother and father in the mosaics and the stained glass that adorned the main chapel. She was only four when they passed, remembering her father's radiant red hair, much like hers. She could also remember her mother's voice, perpetually singing a lullaby. The only thing she knew about their end was that they were likely killed in an accident involving mysterious powers related to the instability of magic. Between the monastery of Lexcord and the Church of Invictus, Miranda grew up as a young woman of great faith. Today, however, she found that faith put to a different kind of test than she expected.

The small chapel contained a wooden statue of the avatar of Invictus. Around it were chairs, mats, and benches in orderly semicircles extending from the altar toward the entrance. While most laypeople would only visit the Church of Invictus to address grievances between themselves and other townsfolk, the frontier community of Devitus had a sizable number of casual worshippers that did not pledge the Path of the Sword of Justice, the well-studied and arduous path of the priests and paladins of Invictus. Bishop Selasine served the community for almost two decades, assisting the militia in defending the town, handling civil disputes, and being an ever-present force for order. In return, the community brought their thanks, alms, and other tithings to help Selasine maintain the church. Though Devitus's location did not yield extraordinary wealth, the people were bonded together by common struggle. The townsfolk included Selasine in their number as a welcome member of the Devitus community.

Miranda slid into a bench near the idol of the avatar of Invictus. Bishop Selasine was strict regarding church protocol and liturgy, but he was very casual and relaxed in most interpersonal interactions. Strategy meetings were more like conversations, as Selasine would consult all his pupils before advising them on a course of action. She pulled her legs up to her chest as she sat, visibly reacting to her anxiety over the situation. For today's exam, she had worn a steel chain skirt with leather trousers and a scale mail that was a little large for her. The metal in her armor clinked as she rocked nervously on the bench. Becoming an acolyte like this didn't feel right; it didn't follow the rules. Isn't that everything that Invictus stood for? Following the rules?

Bishop Selasine slumped into the bench beside Miranda. Justin and August sat on a bench behind them, leaning forward to listen to the words of their mentor. Justin, a young human man of eighteen years, seemed to be as concerned as Miranda. While strong in his own right, his true strengths lay in his cunning and strategy rather than brute force. He took the planning part of missions very seriously. The bishop let out a swift sigh before beginning, "As you can see, not everyone in the service of Invictus is motivated by order for order's sake."

Justin chuckled, but August and Miranda remained silent. After a moment, Selasine reached over and tapped on Miranda's knees in a gentle, comforting way. "Relax, Miranda. Don't let the high priest get to you. If I didn't think you were capable, I wouldn't let the high priest take you with him." He felt his stomach drop. He knew it would be significantly dangerous, but he trusted the structure of Invictus's law. He wanted to protect his acolytes, but he knew all too well that the world was riddled with violence and conflict. He hoped this would allow them to see that reality without witnessing the frontline horrors of war. Miranda let down the weight of her legs with a heavy forward falling motion, almost tumbling into the floor. Listening to what the bishop said, she took a moment to ponder. Maybe her fears of facing real chaos were imaginary, especially if Bishop Selasine had faith in her.

"Yes sir," she said, feeling strength through his reassuring chastising. "So, I'm guessing what the high priest whispered to you is a secret?" she continued, her sapphire eyes locked onto the feet of the idol in the center of the chapel.

Selasine shook his head. "Not a secret." He turned his torso to look behind him at Justin and August. "Go down to the cellar behind the chapel. You'll find an armory of sorts. Gather up two sets of armor for yourselves; you'll need it. There's a display in the back of the armory with a battlemail that will fit Miranda perfectly. Bring it back with you too. Understood?" The young men nodded and stood to leave. Miranda also started to stand, but Selasine raised a hand to gesture for her to wait.

"Sir?" she retorted, hoping he would want her to help her brethren.

"Not a secret." His eye narrowed. "I need to ask you some questions about that night."

Justin and August made their way to the instructed destination. Miranda kept her eyes fixated on the feet of the statue of Invictus.

"Miranda. I can tell you're upset over how the high priest welcomed you into the flock."

She blinked for a moment and sat, rocking on the bench. "Yeah. It didn't really follow the rules, you know?"

Selasine let out an amused laugh. "Of course, it followed the rules, child. The only rule is that you be recommended by an established clergy member for admission to the Path of the Sword of Justice. There's a great difference between law and tradition. The trial by combat is merely a tradition."

Miranda's eyes finally left the statue's feet. Looking at Selasine, she asked, "So Invictus will accept a cleric that didn't face a trial by combat?" She felt tears of relief pushing their way to the surface but fought to maintain her composure.

"Miranda, I think it's clear that the Sword of Justice accepted and blessed you beyond measure before you even came to me for guidance." Selasine's expression became serious. "Remember the burned home?" Miranda nodded in response but said nothing. "Please tell me how you healed that family. What prayers did you recite? Did you use a power from beyond the divine?"

The truth was that Miranda wasn't even sure what happened that night. All she could remember was praying to Lexcord and Invictus for the strength to heal the family, which worked. About six months after beginning her service as a novice peacekeeper, she was summoned to help fight the fire with Selasine and other townsfolk. When checking the smoldering rubble, Miranda was the one who found the family trapped by the collapsing frame of the house. She tried the only thing she could think of, the healing prayers that would channel the spirit of Invictus into her and allow her to cure wounds with the assistance of her divinity's essence.

Relaying her encounter to Selasine only left him with more questions. "If that's the case, Miranda, it sounds like you passed your examination months ago." The bishop sighed. Miranda knew that he was fifty-three years old and was especially wise. She was worried that what she had done troubled him.

"Bishop?" she asked in a small voice.

He inhaled deeply, shaking his head to reinvigorate his countenance. "Yes, Miranda?" he replied, raising a hand to stroke his long black beard dotted with varying strands of gray.

"I know that sometimes violence is necessary to protect the ones we hold dear. Why is it necessary to take military action against a group of pirates that are not attacking our kingdom? Are not the laws and enforcement of those laws the responsibility of a sovereign kingdom like Claston?" she asked, prodding at the nature of the mission Carulus summoned them on.

Selasine's face broke out into a broad smile. Miranda's natural response was to smile as well; seeing her teacher pleased filled her with pride. "You have to understand, dear. Carulus is a different kind of priest than I am. Warpriests serve the church in a specific way. We are called on in times like these when somebody like Carulus needs an army. We bless and heal the church's troops while they fight the enemy.

Carulus, however, is a bureaucrat. He's more concerned about the law's wording than the law's spirit. If he thinks something will benefit him and it fits within what the law dictates, then he will use it to enrich himself."

Miranda perked her head to the side, the bundled ponytail behind her swinging from the momentum of her sudden head movement. "What does that have to do with whether or not this mission is a good idea?" she giggled a bit. "I'm sorry. You know it frustrates me when people dodge questions."

Selasine rumbled out a laugh and wrapped his arm around the girl. She was a person who thrived with affection. Her performance in training sessions always improved if August gave her an encouraging bump with his forearm. She would often hug August, Justin, or Selasine if she got excited or needed to get their attention. He attributed it to her status as an orphan. He worried the monks caring for her during her childhood weren't tender enough for parenting. He should have been more insistent on adopting her instead of letting the monks at the monastery take the responsibility. Part of him, however, was grateful that the monks had taken such good care of her. She was a kind, sweet young woman whose main objective always seemed to be making peace between people. She served under him for almost a year as a peacekeeper, a deputy agent of the church that could enforce laws and resolve disputes based on the edicts of Invictus. She embraced that role so wholly that he thought she should have been taking this test almost ten months ago.

Tearing himself from his thoughts, he finally addressed her question about the necessity of violence against Erk, "I don't have many details about the official situation. Carulus is the type of person to keep that information secret, too. Based on rumors, Erk was a minor pirate, taking hostages and plundering with little violence. About ten years ago, though, he started killing more people in a crusade against the king of his nation, Claston." Selasine shrugged. "Violence might be the only way to teach them a lesson. I can't say for sure, but I just want to go along to make sure you three acolytes are safe."

Miranda let out a deep, contented sigh. She felt safe with the bishop. As an orphan, Miranda was taken in by a group of monks that worshiped the goddess Lexcord, a deity of justice and right. Her heart was pure, and her love for her worshippers was immense. The monks taught Miranda to love life and avoid violence until it became a last resort. The summer after she turned nineteen, they suddenly sent her to train with Bishop Thomas Selasine of the Church of Invictus, Lexcord's deific brother. The god Invictus's concern was more on the proper descending of nobility and enforcing the laws of society. Though he was justice incarnate, not all lands embraced his teachings. One of the fundamental philosophies of Invictus was that all life is sacred, including the lives of the poor and the evil. Kingdoms like Claston did not have the church's full support in maintaining their autonomy as they continued with unjust practices such as slavery and serfdom. Nevertheless, Bishop Selasine took her in as a pupil nearly a year ago. Since then, she felt like he had become a father figure to her. She was afraid to tell him that, though, as she would worry that it would be an undue burden. The stoic asceticism of the monks taught her to fight her emotions in most cases. Even with such rigorous discipline in her early years, she had never fully learned to control how her feelings twisted her face. She had to keep her expressions in check if she wanted to hide her emotions. It was difficult, and she didn't try to fight it frequently.

Miranda smiled at him. "Thanks, Bishop Selasine," she concluded as a loud rattling sound clanged from the church's nave. The two turned around to see Justin and August returning with piecemeal chunks of armor and a beautiful battlemail strapped firmly to a mannequin. Selasine laughed, "You didn't have to bring the whole armory up, boys!" his tone nurturing and understanding with just the slightest hint of condescension.

"You know I tried to tell him. We could just try on the armor down there, take what fit, and bring up this dress thing," August replied, looking at the mannequin in disbelief. Selasine had stood up, walking up the center aisle of the church's sanctuary. Miranda scurried off the bench behind him, the chain skirt and scale mail she was wearing clanking loudly as she rattled behind her mentor.

Justin protested, "We still needed the bishop's approval on everything we take out of there. Just because he let us go down there doesn't mean we could take whatever we wanted. Those swords weren't on his list, and you had no business going through them," the young acolyte scolded his peer.

August shrugged and looked at Bishop Selasine, "Hey, I thought magic weapons might help regardless."

Selasine winced internally. Those weapons honestly belonged to somebody else, but he was sure that person would have been okay with the acolytes borrowing them. He didn't want to press the issue but agreed with August's sentiment. Moreover, he didn't want to bother with the moral questions. His acolytes wouldn't see any fighting if things went according to his plan. Carulus had demanded them for healing; in his mind, that was their only responsibility.

"Well, let's see what fits, kids," Selasine ordered, looking at the scattered armor. Miranda's armor was the most obviously complete set. The armor on the mannequin seemed elegant but imposing. There were several pieces, including a large breastplate that shimmered with a blue hue. This likely indicated that it was made of mithril, a metal so incredibly light and durable that it was sought worldwide. The battlemail also included shoulder plates, a ring mail that ran down underneath the breastplate, and a beautiful golden mesh long skirt made of an unknown metal. Though the color of the skirt seemed similar to gold, the fine mesh made of almost imperceptible rings was much sturdier than the soft metal. Miranda tapped on it with her fingers, the metal so stiff that she thought it would break the hand of somebody striking it with full force.

"Wow," she marveled at the battlemail. Her shimmering blue eyes seemed watery in the light in the church's nave. To be fair, she was in a deep state of awe. The armor was more beautiful than any armor she had ever seen. She could not tell where it came from but felt incredibly excited to see it.

"Not to be long-winded, but this belongs to you, Miranda," Selasine smiled. His dark eye sparkled with joy as Miranda was astounded by the armor. He only knew it once belonged to her mother, Lady Reshiria Hyacinth. She was known around Devitus as "The Queen of the Arts." She and her husband,

Philotrax, had arrived in Devitus a little over twenty years ago, and Reshiria gave birth to Miranda in their estate on the outskirts of the city to the west. She was a displaced noblewoman who met a tragic fate with her husband. While she was alive, she patronized the artists of Devitus religiously. She could have easily spent a million gold coins doing so in the short four years they lived in their humble region. He was not surprised that Miranda's mother's armor was so elaborate and immaculate. It shimmered in the afternoon light radiating through the church.

Miranda's eyes widened, "Bishop!" she gasped. "Is this the armor you always told me about?"

Selasine nodded in return. August laughed as he teased, "All this time, I thought you were just telling her fairy tales."

Selasine wrinkled his nose, "August, I've told you not to tease Miranda when it comes to matters regarding her family. Remember that the humbler our beginnings, the higher our achievements."

August's cheeks flushed, immediately regretful. "Woah, no, I didn't mean to—" he blustered. He didn't make the connection that the armor would have been part of Miranda's inheritance until after he had made his comment.

Miranda giggled. August was a genuinely sweet person. Over the last year, he had started to feel like a big brother to her. Again, she buried those sentiments to avoid complicating their relationship. He always picked on her, although Selasine often scolded him for taking things too far. She had rarely been distraught by August's pranks and ribbing, so she thought sometimes Selasine seemed a little overprotective toward her. "It's okay, August. I'm just surprised you could carry as much as you did," she teased.

August's face recoiled sarcastically. "Well, it was certainly more than *you* would have carried up."

She shrugged and smiled. "Of course! I wouldn't have carried anything. I would have convinced you and Justin to leave so I could put on the battlemail. Then I would have left this training junk in the basement, along with you two. You'd still be on your own with Justin, though. I agree; it's good to get the bishop's approval for what you take out of there."

Justin pursed his lips, "Hey, now, don't push me under the chariot. I'm just following protocol. War Requisition Procedure Three Hundred Ninety through Four Hundred. The commanding officer of a regiment has final approval over battle-related provisions. Furthermore, they have the final say in the requisition and distribution of armor and weaponry." He gave a smug glance at Miranda.

Her lips twisted to the side in a smile as Selasine corrected him, "In that case, you'll need to take this armory to Carulus and get his final approval. He is, after all, the commanding officer of this expedition, according to the law," the bishop's gruff voice scolded him in a playful tone. He chuckled as he spoke, but then he noticed something resplendent on the floor. He suddenly crouched to pick up a pair of gauntlets that August and Justin had brought up. He had not really noticed them before with all of the things stored in the cellar. They were made of mithril, much like the breastplate of Miranda's battlemail. The forearms had widely protruding sapphire blades built into them, providing an additional defense against enemies in close range.

"Miranda," he said gently to get her interest.

She immediately turned her attention to him, a firm, "Sir?" she piped and stood in the attention stance, her shield hand on her sword hilt and her posture straight.

Selasine laughed. "At ease, Miranda. Here, take these gauntlets too." He picked them up and pitched them to her gently. She caught them, her reflection visible in the pure mithril metal.

"Apologies, bishop," she whispered with a delay, staring at the sapphire blades protruding from the back of the forearm. "They're hypnotic," she mumbled, shining the gem blades into the light.

He smiled, "Yeah, and they might save your life sometime."

She winced and returned her attention to the present. "Oh yeah," she mumbled. "I didn't really want to think about how sharp they are. They're just beautiful," she continued in a slow murmur.

Selasine placed his hand on her shoulder and Justin's, who was adjacent to them. "Listen. Whatever it takes to keep you children safe, there is no expense too great. By law, we have every right to take what is necessary to fulfill that mission. So, Justin, don't be so pedantic. August, don't tease your peers. And Miranda," he grumbled. "Please, believe in yourself. Carulus will test you based on what happened that night. I know you have it in your heart to do what needs to be done." With his encouragement complete, he turned to the pile of armor on the floor.

"On the other hand," he groaned. "I guess we better figure out how to get these boys armored too."

***

Invictus, the god of justice and law, stood gazing over a swirling mass of clouds. In times of peace, he found much time to observe and admire creation. His sister, Lexcord, joined him sometime later as they pondered the tragedies and joys of humankind and elvenkind. In this primordial place, they would only be spiritually present with mortals, and from here, they could hear the prayers of their followers.

Granting those prayers was as simple as channeling their divinity to their most devout followers. Most prayers were for healing or protection, although sometimes a priest would call for a smiting, a prayer that could only be answered for experienced clergy. Today, however, Invictus and Lexcord heard a familiar voice that they could not place. The swirling clouds before them seemed agitated, and as they swirled faster and faster, both Invictus and Lexcord were confused. The primordial essence of this place could only be swayed by the gods or by the most powerful mortals using incredible magics. Magic, distinctly different from the divinity of the gods, was much less predictable. With the broken condition of magic in the current world, it was enough to cause both divinities concern. For a moment, Invictus felt uneasy. Lexcord motioned to the primordial clouds, "Brother, look."

A clear image of a young woman with crystal blue eyes and beautiful red hair appeared in the clouds before them. She had the lifeless body of a child and mother in her arms and a hand placed on the burned chest of an adult human man. She was crying, reciting the prayer of healing that a cleric of Invictus would use.

"Restore to order what was damaged by chaos," she kept repeating, tears streaming down her cheeks. Invictus looked into the image before him, his heart moved by the woman's fervor. He closed his eyes and channeled his divinity to her but to no effect. It was too late to heal these mortals from their injuries and would require greater divine power than her body could channel.

"The spirits of these mortals have departed," Lexcord said, somber. She, too, felt moved by the girl, but the gods could not intervene.

An unseen, booming voice echoed in that primordial place. "I don't know if you can see what is happening but look at the magic stirring within that girl. See how it has collected in her body? It's overwhelming!"

Invictus cast a glaring stare around him but saw no source of this new, imposing voice.

A bright, purple light emerged from the girl's body as the burns on the family's body began to mend. Wisps of smoke began to draw out of their lungs, congealing into a great ball of blackness that dissipated in the light coming from the girl. Moments later, the child and woman began to breathe, coughing abruptly. The man came to as well, shouting as he awoke. The girl with the red hair did not seem to notice the light that radiated from her, but she continued to pray fervently. The survivors waking caused a commotion, and a face familiar to Invictus appeared in the projection in the clouds. "Thomas," Invictus mumbled, feeling his follower's faith surging at the sight of the family, rescued from the edge of death. The gods, however, were more perplexed than before.

Invictus and Lexcord traded glances of disbelief. The unseen voice laughed. "I see that there is still one that can bend the arcane stream to her whimsy."

"Who are you?" demanded Lexcord. In fact, the two gods could not tell if the source of the voice had been in the primordial place with them or if the voice was nothing more than the will of magic itself mocking them for their helplessness.

"Just somebody who can see the magic and how it flows through our universe. It's like a stream of sorts, and its flow is connected to every living thing. I don't know how she stores magic like that, but that makes her special," the voice replied. It seemed to carry a casual tone even though the voice was loud and commanding.

After a moment, the gods realized the presence with them had left. They were not sure exactly what had transpired. As the primordial place returned to its normal balance of prayers and visions, Invictus gripped the ornate hilt of a sword fixed in a scabbard on his belt. Lexcord grimaced, knowing that her brother had already decided.

"I'm going to the mortal realm." His tone was matter-of-fact, stating something already known to them. His sister nodded in agreement.

"I'll watch over you from here," she replied, returning her attention to the swirling clouds that served as their spiritual compass over the mortal world.

Thomas Selasine sat in the study of the small church, pouring over a dusty tome titled *Siblings of Order: Chronicles of Lexcord and Invictus*. He was searching for a clue as to how the girl Miranda could utilize healing magic of the highest order just the day before. A monk in the Order of the Hammerfist brought the girl to him around six months prior to yesterday. Her kindness and empathy prompted the followers of Lexcord to put her on a path of study that would lead to less violence but required great wisdom, which the girl had for her age. With proper training and experience, she could adjudicate matters deftly as a Judge or an arbiter for Invictus. But the day before, she had healed a family that had presumably died after their house caught fire and collapsed on them. Thomas, Miranda, and several townsfolk combined divine prayers and water to extinguish the fire. Before it was entirely safe, Miranda ignored protests and went inside the remains of the house first. She found and healed the family before anybody else could catch up to her. Thomas was perplexed by this event.

The door to the study blew open suddenly as if an intense gush of wind had filled the church, nearly flinging the door from its hinges. Loose scrolls and papers fluttered in a whirl around Thomas. The burst of air snuffed out the flame flickering at the end of the candle he used to read. He looked up from the tome, his eye fixed on the door now barely visible in the moonlight. He did not feel tense or fearful but curious about what divine event might have brought upon this occurrence. Standing, he asked in a hushed tone, "Is someone there?"

Hearing no response and no other activity in the building, Thomas made his way from the study into the chapel. Standing in front of the wooden statue of the avatar was a familiar face to the bishop. The avatar of Invictus gazed up at the statue of himself, his earthly form aglow with the sheer might of his presence. "You know, in the cities they have marble and granite statues dedicated to me," he commented, his voice deep and commanding. The deity was six feet tall with broad shoulders and warm, black skin. Tightly woven braids of brown and gold cascaded down his shoulders in front and behind his radiant, silver armor. The scabbard of an ornate longsword protruded up from his belt, and his left hand rested on the hilt as he addressed the bishop.

Thomas started to bow with reverence, but Invictus raised a hand, using his divine power to prevent the towering man from lowering himself. "My apologies, my Guiding Sword. We are a poor province and wished only to honor you with a trivial idol."

Invictus shook his head. "Don't apologize, faithful one. I was going to say. Even though they have great statues and elaborate temples, I always feel more at home with worshippers like you, Thomas. This is simple. This is beautiful. I am greatly honored by you and those you care for in my stead."

Selasine felt his heart ready to burst from his chest. The god of order, the Guiding Sword of Justice, law incarnate, knew him by name and deed. "You honor me beyond my merits," he replied, knowing that he would have collapsed in disbelief were it not for Invictus holding him upright with his divine will.

Invictus again shook his head and, in a stern voice, chastised his follower, "Do not doubt yourself, Thomas. Your work to bring order to the frontier is one of my favorite tales. You do us both a disservice if you cannot see or acknowledge the impact you have made. Humility is admirable, but overdoing it is dishonest." With a somber voice, the divinity added, "Besides, your service to me has cost you dearly. The greatest honor a mortal may bestow upon the divine is that you still follow me."

Thomas smiled, "This is my chosen path, and you are my chosen god. To what do I owe the honor of a visit from Invictus himself?"

The god looked at Thomas carefully and began to approach. The light radiating from him lit the chapel as if it were daytime, causing long shadows to cast off of the idol, the benches, and the chairs in the small sanctuary. "It seems you've been privy to strange events lately involving a young woman new to my service."

Thomas gulped, realizing the very incident he was researching could have brought personal attention from Invictus. "Yes, Miranda. Bless her; she cried out hard enough to bring you here in person!"

Invictus, normally of blasé humor, laughed, his divine voice echoing off the chapel walls. "Absolutely she has! But not perhaps for the reasons you might expect." His face snapped back to the normal, stoic expression that had been memorialized countless times in the idols of his avatar worldwide. "I saw what happened from the primordial place. The healing."

Thomas calmly nodded. "Yes, we have been extra thankful for your mercy. It's not normal for someone so inexperienced to bring out the strongest aspects of the Sword of Justice."

Invictus breathed deeply. "That's the thing, my friend. I didn't do it."

The words echoed in Thomas's mind. The implications were too complex to make immediate conclusions. Still, if the avatar of Invictus denied his involvement, then there was no doubt: Miranda had access to healing power beyond that of the average cleric. Taking a moment to contemplate why Invictus would come to address this in person, Thomas suddenly became fearful. "My lord, does this mean she is guilty of blasphemy?"

Invictus tapped his fingers on the hilt of his sword, "No. The girl recited only the healing prayers common to novice priests. It seems that the will of the universe itself, the fabric of magic, or some other entity was inclined to answer the desires of her heart." Both Thomas and Invictus knew that the fabric of magic unraveled nearly a century ago, but healing magic was usually outside the capabilities of even the most powerful wizards. Only the gods could intervene and undo what man or nature had done in violence. There was almost no way this was connected to The Unbinding, the word historians used to describe this time of unprecedented magical chaos.

"My lord, was it possibly the Silver Maiden?" Thomas asked, inquiring about Lexcord.

"She was by my side in the primordial place when it happened. If we had channeled the power to bring back the dead through that girl, she would have been a fourth casualty last night. My faithful servant, can you take me to the girl? Do not tell her who I am." With his request in place, Invictus's appearance changed abruptly from that of a god in the flesh to a humble paladin dressed in plate armor with features so average that it was unlikely anyone would remember his face. The sanctuary fell immediately dark, only the bright winter moons' light giving the room a faint glow.

"In the barracks, my lord." Invictus already knew the way but allowed Thomas to lead. "Please forgive our indulgence, but my students have converted the old barracks into more comfortable living spaces for themselves."

Expressionless, the transformed god nodded. He followed Thomas through the courtyard to a long barracks-style building pressed against the courtyard walls behind the chapel. Three sections of the building were lit by torch or candlelight. At the same time, the rest were dark and reflected only the silvery light of two brilliant full moons that marked the deepest part of winter. The two approached the lit room in the middle of the three. Thomas rang a small bell hanging outside. A shuffle of activity rattled from within the room. A moment later, the door opened to reveal a girl with shimmering blue eyes who looked somewhat surprised to see company at such a late hour. "Yes, bishop?" she mumbled, taking a moment to rub some sleep out of her eyes.

"I know it's late, but there is somebody here to meet you

and your brethren," Thomas replied, hoping that by including his other students in the meeting, Miranda would be less suspicious.

The girl turned her sapphire eyes to the mysterious stranger, who seemed very underwhelming for a paladin bearing the symbol of mighty Invictus. She gave a sweet and welcoming smile, her red hair wild from likely falling asleep during her studies. She had worn a wool robe to answer the door, as the winter air could be brutal this late at night. "Hello, traveler," she greeted pleasantly.

Invictus smiled in return, recognizing her from his vision in the primordial place. "Hello, peacekeeper." Using the power inherent to his divinity, he scanned Miranda for any sign that she was influenced by demons, spirits, or other gods, an examination that yielded no additional information about the girl. The only aura radiating from her was the familiar spirit of his sister Lexcord and, with it, the same love and compassion that would be expected from the Silver Maiden, a beloved nickname for the goddess. Though the girl before him had sworn her faith to order and justice, the kindness in her heart was so similar to that of his beloved sister that he felt fraternal feelings toward this mortal. Her features were sharp and pretty, and her messy red hair was radiant in the moonlight as it reflected shimmers of crimson and silver. "I am a mere paladin passing through on a quest seeking refuge and meditation. It's good to see brethren this far in the wilderness."

Miranda's eyes blinked with wonder and curiosity. "Is that so?" She paused, allowing a moment of silence brief enough to avoid awkwardness. "Please, allow me a moment." Closing her door, she went back into her room. Invictus traded a glance with Selasine, stoic. There was a ruckus behind the door, and less than a minute later, Miranda threw open the door to her room and began rushing toward the stone church house. "Come on!" she chided as she entered a side entrance that Selasine knew led to a small kitchen.

Before Selasine could redirect or object, Miranda began preparing food for their guest. Sticking her head out of the kitchen window, she shouted at Invictus and Selasine, "Hey, tell Justin to get in here! I need him to cut the vegetables!"

Invictus smiled at Thomas. "She has a bright energy about her. She reminds me of my sister."

Thomas sighed gently under his coarse beard, attempting to reply sarcastically, "The Silver Maiden with red hair? Isn't that blasphemy?"

Invictus laughed. "Rouse the others. It looks like we're having a late-night meal."

Chapter 2
Departure

The acolytes spent the rest of that afternoon preparing for their long journey to the Undine Coast. After sorting out their armor, Miranda went to the church's kitchen to look over what dry goods they had for travel. The kitchen was small and practical; it seemed like the original architects had not anticipated the fervor with which common people would follow Invictus. Given that his purview was law, order, and justice, people in a rural frontier town embraced those values strongly to maintain peace in their settlement. Still, Miranda and Justin had spent much time in this small kitchen, preparing meals for the three peacekeepers, now acolytes, that reported to Bishop Selasine.

She stared blankly into the pantry, a wooden cupboard built to the side of where a stove had been installed. She chewed on her lip nervously, a habit that she had given up on breaking years ago. She wasn't sure what would be good to take on such a long journey. Honestly, she had never traveled so far away. She was excited to see the world outside of this little river valley. But she did not want to starve while off adventuring, either.

Selasine knew exactly where he would find Miranda as he entered the church from the side door that led directly into the kitchen. He smiled, watching her stand vacantly in front of the pantry. He cleared his throat as he entered, getting her attention.

"These provisions would last us another month if we could take the whole kitchen," she said absentmindedly.

The bishop laughed. "Well, that's out of the question. Here, come with me. There are foods that are meant for travel," he ordered, motioning for her to leave the kitchen with him. The sun descended in the northwest, casting an orange glow over Devitus in the peak summer light. It was currently the month of The Flourishing when most temperate crops reached a blossoming peak. Selasine and Miranda left the church building together. They exited through the main gates on the west side of the church complex, the same gates that had been blocked off by Carulus earlier that day.

Selasine led Miranda from the church down the dirt road directly to the center of town, where the marketplace was located. She followed behind her mentor, waving at the townsfolk as they passed. Many of them would stop and offer a brief blessing to the bishop and his pupil, thankful for their continual, watchful eyes over their settlement. Miranda had been training with Selasine for nearly a year. August and Justin began their work as peacekeepers weeks before her. The peacekeepers were a welcome addition to the bishop's entourage. August was known for his strength and handiness. Justin was an incredible problem solver, and he never forgot a face. Miranda was most well known for her insatiable desire to be helpful. Every project in town that needed an extra set of hands could rely on Miranda to help out, even if she had no idea what she was doing at first. However, she was a quick learner, and the townsfolk came to appreciate her efforts. This earned her a reputation for being like her parents, although she did not remember them well. The townsfolk always compared Miranda's helpfulness to her parents' efforts to restore the Church of Invictus's grounds and gardens.

As Selasine and Miranda neared the marketplace, a hollow wicker ball rocketed toward the pair. Instinctively, Selasine reached out and snatched the ball out of the air, smacking against his hand with a loud pop. A voice warned, "Now you're going to get it! You almost hit the bishop with the ball!"

Selasine tapped on the hollow ball meant to be knocked around with sticks. Most children used this inexpensive toy to practice the motor skills necessary to be sharp with a sword or club one day. The game usually consisted of knocking the ball into the air with a stick and not letting it return to the ground. Selasine was an experienced swordsman and, according to the children, a veritable god when playing the game. He tossed the ball high into the air, loosened a strap on his belt, and removed a scabbard. He handed the sword inside to Miranda, a common longsword with an unassuming hilt and cross guard. Selasine smacked the ball back into the air using the scabbard, using his precise control and awareness to continually bounce the hollow ball. He approached the kids playing in the street with the ball steadily clacking off the tip of his scabbard. "Somebody lose a toy?" he asked, giving a playful but menacing glare at the children. They all tried to point fingers at each other, generating an incomprehensible din of accusations and "not-me" protests.

Selasine couldn't help but laugh, spoiling the confused worry of the children. They then stood, fascinated with how easily the bishop balanced the bouncing ball on the end of his scabbard. "Woah, you're really cool, mister bishop," one of the kids commented.

Selasine smiled broadly, casting a glance at Miranda. "Catch," he warned as he changed the angle of his scabbard so that the ball would bounce toward the child who had spoken. Excited, the kid used both arms to catch the lightweight toy, immediately tossing it back into the air. The kids, five in total, rushed back into the street, swinging their sticks wildly, putting in too much effort to hit the ball.

Miranda's face was lifted in a sweet smile, her most common expression. "Justin will scold us for playing instead of focusing on the mission," she teased.

Selasine's lips also twisted into a smile, his whole beard

moving with his jovial countenance. "I'm sure he would, and we would deserve it. But," he gestured to the children playing in the street, one of them now dominating the game and the others cheering her on. "It's important not to forget why we do what we do, Miranda. These simple, quiet, peaceful moments for children like these are the reason we fight against the forces of chaos."

She inhaled deeply, the thick summer air full of floral scents. The Devitan River valley was easily identifiable on a map, but the population density paled in comparison to cities far to the west like Nulodia, the port city, or Alabaster, the capital city of this kingdom. This small town of about five thousand people was the only place she had ever known. Though she was an orphan, the monastery of Lexcord and now the Church of Invictus were both home to her. She thought about the bishop's words as she soaked in these last moments of small-town life before departing on her first, real adventure. Finally, she replied with a catechism that had a similar message, "Times of peace and prosperity flourish when the faithful are diligent. Chaos ebbs and flows like the tide; may our children know days without struggle."

Selasine's expression stayed tied up in his smile. "Plus, an old man has to be good at something. Even if it's just playing ball with the local kids," he teased.

Miranda's smile melted into a neutral expression. With his role in her life, he had become a fatherly figure to her. He would make an excellent dad to any young person, she thought. She was sure Selasine had a family once, but she didn't know what became of them. She had very early memories of meeting his daughter Telisi when Selasine brought her to the monastery. The churches of Lexcord and Invictus often worked together closely, so it was not a surprise to see Selasine frequently at the monastery in her early years. It seemed that Telisi quit coming to play with her around Miranda's ninth birthday. All this time, Miranda had not asked about the girl, nor did she want to. She had a sixth sense about people's emotions and feared that asking the bishop questions about the past would be painful or worse.

They arrived in the marketplace as the sun began to settle

behind the rising ridges northwest of Devitus. Selasine approached a vendor that Miranda had visited many times, Dokash the Hunter. He specialized in wild game, dried meats, and nut and berry mixtures that were almost as good as sweets. August complained that they were too sweet, and Justin considered sweets an indulgence detrimental to discipline. Miranda would always shrug happily as she took their extras whenever the bishop had given them bags of mixed treats.

Dokash was an orc, a powerful, beautiful race of humanoids with features reminiscent of swine. Their pressed, flat noses were excellent for sniffing out game while hunting. Their elongated ears helped them detect threats long before they could be seen. They grew easily seven feet tall, and their muscular physique made them quite capable of fighting. Like elves and humans, their skin tones could range drastically from extraordinarily pale to pleasing tones of ebony. Their teeth grew like a boar's, and the men often polished and took pride in their tusks. Dokash's skin was dark and sandy, likely due to his time outdoors, and his tusks were well-honed.

Dokash was getting ready to close up for the evening when Miranda and Selasine approached. As the orc saw one of his favorite customers approaching with his pupil, Dokash paused and waited to greet them. "Bishop Selasine, Sword of Devitus," he beamed as the two neared. "Had to bring the girl out for a snack?" His voice was boisterous and friendly.

Miranda giggled. "Not today, master Dokash," she replied, the blue in her eyes twinkling in the twilight.

Selasine laughed heartily, "Not today, but the next twenty. For four people."

Dokash wavered with surprise. "Eighty days of provisions? Bishop, that's a tall order."

Selasine's head bounced with a simultaneous nod and shake, understanding the size of the order for a town with limited resources. "How about I buy what you've got, then, and I'll harass the high priest for the rest."

Dokash gave a snort similar to a short laugh. "I'll see what I can do. It'll probably take a while to round up everything I have left and prepare it for travel. If you've got something else you need to take care of in the meantime, I can deliver your supplies to the church. When are you leaving?"

Selasine grimaced. "At dawn, most likely. I would like to stay and help you get everything ready. I'm kind of particular when it comes to travel."

Dokash clenched his fists. "You got it. Will you be helping too, Miranda?" the orc asked her, looking at her through his light blue eyes.

She paused for a moment, then her expression became one of surprise. "Bishop, if we're going to be gone for a while, is it okay if I go up to the monastery and say goodbye to the headmistress?"

Selasine turned to face Miranda suddenly, the monastery about a mile outside town to the north. "Take the guys with you, but you're right. It's a great idea to say your farewells, even for short trips or adventures."

Miranda's smile was unrestrained. She hadn't been out to the monastery in a couple of months. She was not the only orphan the monks had in their care as she grew up. Many of the orphans cared for by the church grew up and they joined the church to continue the cycle of helping unfortunate children who had been abandoned or lost their parents. Actually, she had considered that path herself. However, the headmistress rejected that idea and sent her to train with Bishop Selasine. Miranda loved many of the monks for their wisdom and kindness, but she was especially close to the headmistress.

"Thank you, bishop!" she replied, turning away from Dokash's supply store and trotting back to the church quickly. There she found August and Justin arguing about which wagon they would take.

"I'm just sure he's going to want the smaller, covered wagon," August insisted.

Justin shook his head. "We need the extra space in the uncovered wagon. If we need shelter from the sun on the way, we can take parasols," the acolyte replied.

August's face twisted in horror. It was almost as if Justin announced that he was an undead creature, like a skeleton or zombie. Miranda burst into laughter, listening to her friends discuss the matter as she approached.

"See, that is the worst idea I've ever heard, and Miranda agrees. She's laughing because parasols are the absolute worst fashion accessory ever invented," August replied sarcastically, watching Miranda walk toward them. The churchyard was rather sizable. Inside the gate was an expansive courtyard with several gardens, some of which had been remodeled and reinvigorated about twenty years ago. Selasine told Miranda that her mother, Reshiria, had spent so much money and effort remodeling the little church and its humble grounds. Behind the church was a barn, a stable, and a barracks turned into lodging for the three acolytes. Though August's family was local, Justin's family lived in the countryside, and Miranda had no known family. It was easier for their duties as peacekeepers if they simply lived on the church grounds in town.

Miranda let out a soft warning gasp, "August! What's wrong with you? Parasols can be nice. Just pair it with a summer dress, and nobody will question mister macho on his quest to save the world from umbrellas!"

August's complexion went white as he started to sputter. Justin laughed, his soft but confident voice echoing against the buildings around them. They were gathered outside of the barn where Selasine kept the carts. They had rolled out two options: a small, covered wagon that would barely seat the four of them and a large, uncovered wagon with more space than they needed. She pursed her lips. "Hey, I was just with the bishop, and he ordered eighty days of food from Dokash. We're probably going to need the big one."

Justin punched August in the arm. "See!"

August simply laughed, accepting he had been outvoted by his peers. "Fine, I guess I'll ask the bishop if I can borrow his parasol," he grumbled, picking up the hitch for the larger wagon.

Miranda raised her hand quickly, "Um, hey guys. Can I ask you for a favor?" her voice was somewhat timid. It wasn't that she was uncomfortable with Justin and August, but she always hated the feeling that she would be asking too much of somebody. Traveling a mile outside town this late when they had a journey to prepare for seemed like a lot. The sun was deep into its descent in the northwest, indicating that it would be dark soon.

August put the wagon down, stood straight, and looked at Miranda curiously. Justin turned his attention from the carts to her and said, "What can we do?"

"Well, since we're leaving so quickly, would you two be willing to escort me to the monastery so that I can say goodbye to the headmistress?" She looked at the ground as she asked, poking the toe of her leather boot into the dirt nervously.

August smiled broadly. He could see how uncomfortable she was asking. Though he had a robust family, he was the youngest of all his siblings. In a way, Miranda and Justin were his chance to play big brother, being a half year older than Miranda and a year and a half older than Justin. "No bandit attacks in nine months, no magical beasts this close to town in the last year. The roads are safer than ever, but I bet the bishop still wants us to go," August added, trying to make it sound like an ordeal.

Miranda's face flushed, "I don't want to be a burden. I can help with the preparations if we don't have time."

August approached between her and Justin, standing over her and Justin by a full head. They were close enough that he could wrap his arms around them simultaneously, embracing them somewhere between a hug and a headlock. "The only reason the roads are so safe is because of us, you dummies. Come on, let's go see some monks!"

Miranda beamed with happiness, "Thank you, August!" she piped in sincere gratitude while she struggled to get out of his grasp. She wrapped her fingers around his wrist and clamped on a pressure point, pinching the nerve in his hand and making him recoil quickly. He let Miranda go but kept Justin firmly locked under his arm.

"Yeah, don't mention it," he grunted as Justin elbowed him in the stomach to no avail.

Justin struggled a little more, trying to keep August engaged. Justin tried to make it a contest of muscle, which he would never win against August. They wasted another precious minute wrestling while Miranda watched, giggling. She hoped that they would still have this much fun with every moment on their journey.

"That's really not cool," Justin complained, running his fingers through his hair after they broke apart.

August tapped his temple sarcastically, "Every moment is training. Right?"

Justin wrinkled his nose. Technically, that was correct, so there was no need to argue. He reached into the covered cart and procured a torch. "We had better hurry. If we make it back before the bishop, all the better."

Miranda watched with wide eyes as Justin pulled some flint from one of his pouches and lit the torch effortlessly. She knew how to do it and had her own flint, but she was still new to adventuring. She was still building her basic survival skills. Watching others do what was necessary with so little effort filled her with admiration. She strove every day to be a little more like these three people she had come to love so dearly.

Torch in hand, Justin started toward the church gates. The three of them did not stop for armor, but they made sure they had their weapons. The odds of an attack on the little road out to the monastery were very low. For starters, Selasine and his peacekeepers had kept it free of highwaymen for the last year. Additionally, the monks of Lexcord were well-trained fighters that would suffer no nonsense. A person would have to be a fool to challenge both groups.

The walk out to the monastery could easily take fifteen minutes. As they departed, Miranda wanted to know how her fellow acolytes felt about their journey and destination. "So, do you think it will be a hard journey?" she asked as she and August followed a couple of steps behind Justin, still holding the torch.

August shrugged nonchalantly. "Seems like there is a road that goes east out of Devitus and turns southeast about five days in. Five more days on that road will put you in the Western Trollcrags, full of trolls and giants. Lots of caves in those mountains. We'll probably get attacked by one of those hybrid animal monsters, like a bear and a horse combined."

Miranda's eyes widened in the torchlight, and she tried to picture the abomination August just proposed. "Won't there be an entire army with us?" she replied, still imagining.

Justin waved the torch in the air as they walked, "Yes,

Miranda. We'll be safe from horse-bears, which don't exist, by the way." His tone was more confident than condescending.

August protested, "Hey, just because you haven't seen it doesn't mean it's not real!"

Miranda giggled again. Justin's overly rational nature always made August rant about the most entertaining things.

Justin gave a slight grin, "Okay, that's fair. But don't you think if horse-bears were out there, some military would have figured out how to weaponize them already? It'd be a well-known fact worldwide and a common entry in creature compendiums."

"What in the Abyss is a compendium?" August snapped back.

Justin and Miranda afforded a laugh at his expense. With a haughty posture, August walked with exaggerated motions, "Well, if we do run into a horse-bear, I'm going to tame it and ride it all the way to the beach on the Undine Coast."

Miranda squealed with excitement, "Oh yeah! The coast! This means we're going to get to see the ocean!"

August and his family, a clan of merchants, had traveled around a lot. In his early life, he visited Nulodia and Alabaster, even having traveled as far as Claston, the kingdom on the other side of the wilderness of the Trollcrags. He would normally be dismissive of such fantastical views of seeing the world, but the genuine care he held for his friends superseded his cockiness, "We should get to see the ocean, and I know you'll love it. It's so relaxing to just lay on the beach and play in the sand."

Justin, like Miranda, had not been very far outside of Devitus. "Always plotting your next diversion, August?" he asked.

Miranda huffed, "Hey! I want to relax on the beach too! Wouldn't it be fun to build sandcastles together?"

August nodded in the torchlight, "See, that's what I'm talking about. Go on an adventure, beat up the bad guys, then hang out at the beach like the heroes we are! It's part of the compensation for being a hero. Leisure time."

Justin rolled his eyes but couldn't help but smile as well. "It is written that a soldier of Invictus must set aside a day of rest and a day of worship. Okay, fine, Miranda, we'll build sandcastles. But!" he paused. "Only if you both have the required catechisms for acolytes memorized before we get to the coast."

With their company, the mile to the monastery seemed like an inconsequential distance to Miranda. To the north of Devitus, this ancient, white marble complex consisted of a primary hall running north to south with eight wings running east to west, each branch containing different types of rooms. The dormitories for the monks were located in the northernmost branches, and the headmistress would likely be in her study at the northern, far side of the main hall. By the time they arrived, only enough sunlight was left to make out the forms of the mountains surrounding them in the valley.

Justin placed his torch in a brazier on the porch that opened in front of the main hall. A series of marble steps welcomed anyone to this place, leading up to the stone porch constructed around the front of the main hall and wrapping around the first two wings, breaking away to the east and west. A marble colonnade marked the path to the main doors, with gigantic, bronze statues of Lexcord placed as decorations to the right and left. The summer air had cooled to a comfortable temperature, and birds and insects filled the evening air with busy sounds.

August motioned his head toward the main doors. "We'll wait for you here. Hey, I know you'll be pretty sentimental, but we've got to finish prepping for the journey. How quick can you make it?"

Miranda's lips pursed, and her eyes narrowed, indignant. "Well, I didn't plan on taking all night." She turned to walk into the monastery's front doors, stopping to cut her head down and back toward her friends, "I'll keep it short, though. I've never had to give the monks a farewell. I guess I understand why some people say they hate goodbyes, yeah?"

Justin elbowed August. The bigger acolyte grunted, surprised. "Hey, what was that for?"

Justin shook his head. "Take all the time you need, Miranda."

She smiled. "Thanks guys, for seeing me up here and for

seeing me home. I'll be quick!" she finished, turning into the open doors of the monastery. She found herself in the familiar main hall, a dull, brown rug running the length of the hallway. The floor underneath was cobbled stone; she had many memories of running down these hallways as a little girl. Her flying adventures were ended more than once by the uneven stones that paved the way through this reverent, quiet building.

At this hour, Miranda knew most of the monks had retired to their quarters for meditation and prayer. She would have loved to see some of them but knew her time was too short. She passed the first wings, the kitchen on the left while facing north, and the dining hall on the right. She wasn't sure which wing she caused more trouble in as a child, but there were plenty of stories she could tell about either side of the hall. Like that one time, she ran through the kitchen and tripped into a bag of flour. She might have been seven, but she couldn't remember clearly. All she did remember was pretending to be a ghost until Mother Alma, the head of the kitchen, dumped a bucket of water on young Miranda. She smiled at the memory.

As she progressed down the corridor of the main hall, she looked over the paintings that lined the walls. She saw them many times as a girl but didn't fully appreciate them until she was a teenager. Around that time, she found a story of Lexcord battling a great evil, so she begged the headmistress to explain the paintings. They told a story about Lexcord and her conquest over the dark forces of Hoxark, Lord of the Abyss. The series of paintings were beautiful, and Miranda often pictured herself traveling to the far-away locations in the paintings. Lexcord faced the forces of evil in the mountains, the forests, the beaches, and the plains. Miranda's eyes filled with excited tears; tomorrow, she was leaving for one of those beautiful places she had only ever seen through paintings like these.

Her pace quickened as she passed the next wings, a library on the left and a chapel on the right. If anybody was not in their dormitory, they would certainly be in one of these rooms. There was an ivory idol of Lexcord in the chapel, and the monks often spent time there in prayer. Unlike the Church of Invictus, there were never any pulpits for delivering homilies and sermons in Lexcord's places of worship. The goddess thought it was more important to act rather than pontificate. Miranda spent countless hours in the library on the other side of the main hall. Once the monks taught her how to read the common language, she became an avid reader. Her favorite stories were histories and epic plays. That's how she found the story that she connected to the paintings. She smiled slightly as she slipped past the archways leading to those wings. The tears in her eyes grew heavy; nostalgia and a bittersweet goodbye intermingled.

She didn't have many memories of the next two wings; they were both arenas and obstacle courses designed to facilitate training for the monks. She had proven very early on in life that she was too clumsy to ever hope to be a graceful, well-honed monk. Her accidents in the kitchen and dining hall alone were enough to bar her from entering the training rooms without assistance.

As she approached the final wings, she spotted a pair of monks chatting in the main hallway. She slowed her pace a bit, hoping not to attract attention to herself. Her chain skirt seemed to clink louder thanks to the silence here, though, and Miranda knew she would attract attention just from her noisy approach. The dorm hallways met here, and a lounge was set up in the common area outside the headmistress's study. The monks of Lexcord were committed to mastering all disciplines, which sometimes required intense study in the evenings. It seemed some people learned better while studying together. Miranda had overheard so many conversations here it caused her memories to overflow.

"I'm not crying!" she insisted in her mind. As she passed, the chatting monks were not bothered by her presence, engaged in a deep, hushed conversation. This lobby was a large area, and small staircases raised up from both sides in the back of a rotunda going up about a half-floor. At the top was an ornate door that opened to the headmistress's study, the chief monk in charge of the monastery. Miranda ran up the right-side staircase of the rotunda instinctively, her orphan dorm having been down the east dormitory wing. Each step up made her feet feel heavier. She did not want to say goodbye. She approached the door, pausing before she pulled the cord that would ring the bells throughout the study and the master suite within. She could see the light under the door; she knew the headmistress was definitely awake.

Miranda tugged the cord. She heard a faint tinkling bell and a deep, bellowing creak as the wind blew through the ventilation of the old marble building. She used to fall asleep to that sound.

The door popped open, "Yes, yes, what is it so late into—" a voice began.

There stood Miranda, a smile glued to her lips but tears running down her cheeks. "It's just me, headmistress!" she replied quickly in a hushed tone. Her voice broke a bit as she spoke. She was overwhelmed with emotions and embarrassed at her failure to keep herself within an acceptable boundary of expression.

The headmistress, an elven monk about two hundred years old, looked up at Miranda with a surprised stare. The headmistress stood average for an elf, around five foot three. Her muscles were easily visible in the casual robes worn by the monks. The garments flowed loosely around the arms and legs, helping the wearer maintain maximum mobility. Miranda reached out to hug the headmistress.

The elf returned the girl's embrace, letting out a deep sigh of concern. "Is something wrong, Miranda?" the headmistress asked, her voice soothing.

Miranda shook her head, her ponytail wagging behind her. "No, I just came to tell you I'm going on my first adventure. We're leaving at dawn tomorrow, most likely. I just wanted to—" she choked up, unable to finish her sentence.

The headmistress broke their embrace and took the girl's hands in hers. "That's wonderful news! I had hoped your studies were going well with the bishop." She patted the girl's hand in hers.

Miranda sighed deeply and sniffled as she inhaled. "Going so well that I'm officially an acolyte now!" she replied, trying to sound happy, but the tears caused the ends of her words to crack slightly. She didn't understand these emotions, which is why they were so difficult to control. It was a new feeling.

Maybe it was a deep appreciation for how the headmistress cared for her? Maybe it was a fear that she would never see her again? She couldn't say, but it was a stronger emotion than her resolve could resist.

"Congratulations, my child. I knew that the brother of our Silver Maiden would be the best teacher for you. You are a wise, beautiful young woman. The world will listen to you for many reasons. Your power resides in here," the headmistress said, pointing to Miranda's head. "Use those smarts, child. Your intuition, trust your instincts."

Miranda beamed, her tears slowing. "Thank you, headmistress. For everything." The headmistress always wanted her to follow her mind, but more often than not, Miranda found herself guided by her heart. She knew she had to find a balance between the two, but her heart still jumped ahead of her thoughts.

The headmistress patted her on the arm, giving her a soft smile. "You'll do great, Miranda. Just remember, your mind and heart must always align," she commented as if she could read the girl's mind. "Stay fervent, my dear."

"You already know, don't you?" Miranda said, following her question with a deep inhale.

"Of course, dear. Those that walk the Path of the Sword of Justice are a dramatic lot. This high priest, I don't particularly like him. He follows the code of Invictus to the letter, but I don't trust *his* heart," the headmistress replied, shaking her head vigorously. Her warm orange hair, tossed with intensity, tied into a ponytail like Miranda's.

Miranda nodded, feeling the warning in the unspoken words. "I'll do my best to make you proud," she replied, her voice still wavering.

Her former teacher and mentor, the headmistress, hugged her again. She was the first to realize Miranda responded well to affection and positive reinforcement. She hugged the beautiful little orphan daily as she saw the girl in the halls of the old monastery. Selasine was right to blame the monks for how she craved affection, but not for the reasons he thought. The headmistress felt sad, however, as she worried that Miranda's destiny might be more than she ever realized. "My dear, can you wait here for a moment?"

Miranda blinked, lingering tears chasing their predecessors down her cheeks. "Of course, ma'am."

The elf did not close the door as she darted back inside, her nimble, bare feet scampering across the huge study at a surprising speed. She went to a trunk and opened it, digging around for something. Miranda watched through the partially ajar door, breathing quietly, almost like a little girl again, spying for information in the evening after curfew. A moment later, the monk returned with a small, elaborate container.

"Here's a box with some jewels and trinkets your parents had intended for you to have. I was safeguarding this until your twenty-first birthday. However, good judgment says I should give it to you now. Don't let those Invictus rituals let you forget how to think for yourself," the headmistress cautioned as she handed Miranda the ornate box. It fit easily in two hands, a beautiful teak container inlaid with gold and bronze. The logo was not a crest but a symbol Miranda had seen earlier that day. The same pattern on the box was evident on the mithril breastplate of the battlemail the bishop gave her earlier.

Miranda's mouth was pulled into a distinct round shape, unaware that her parents left her any wealth other than the estate. Even then, she had seen the estate many times, Selasine checking on it every few days with her. However, almost everything inside was covered, so Miranda did not know what was really in that place. "What's in here, headmistress?" she asked, bewildered by this unexpected gift. She no longer had tears in her eyes, her countenance now surprised.

"Mostly beautiful jewelry that you can do whatever you choose with. There are some other trinkets in there; you might play around with them and see what you think about them. Trade them, wear them, and use them as you see fit." The headmistress smiled as she made sure Miranda had what was rightfully hers.

"Thank you again. For everything," Miranda repeated, hugging the monk again.

"See you soon, Miranda. I don't say goodbye," the headmistress said with a smile.

"Then I won't say it either. See you soon, headmistress,"

Miranda replied. She knew the headmistress was a person who didn't like goodbyes. But now, she realized that there was a way to part with a friend that was a promise to come back. She decided to always say 'see you soon' instead of goodbye.

When she exited the monastery, Justin and August were discussing places to hunt along the journey to the Undine Coast.

"The heavy deer population over there has enabled a wyvern infestation in those parts of the Trollcrags, though," August complained as Miranda approached.

Justin replied, "True enough. I think it would make sense to keep a modest wyvern population in that region. Their parts are so useful in alchemy and in creating antivenoms. As long as people know there are wyverns in that region, they'd save more lives than they would take."

August laughed. "That's a chaotic position, Justin. I didn't know you had it in you."

Justin's eyes widened, but then he noticed Miranda emerging from the monastery. "Oh, hey, she's back!" he sputtered, interrupting the intellectual conversation that August accidentally started.

"That's done," she sniffled, a smile on her lips. She was sad, but she was excited. She was thrilled. She was ready for the next chapter. Her first adventure might not be legendary, but it would be the start of her legend.

August smirked as Justin took the torch and headed back to the south. "So, Justin is talking about turning to the dark side."

Miranda's eyes widened, "What? Justin?!" she exclaimed.

"Are you serious, August?" he burst into laughter. "No, I just said having a place to harvest wyvern organs was actually a good idea. Nothing more, nothing less."

Miranda pouted playfully, "Yep. There it is. Justin of Chaos. What a shame."

Justin growled, waving the torch as they finished their walk in mostly silence.

Upon their return to the church, they found Bishop Selasine and Dokash out by the barn. In the short hour that the acolytes had been gone, their mentor and the best local hunter had prepared the uncovered wagon for travel. Justin gave a smug look to August but said nothing.

Miranda broke away from the other two, sprinting to the barn. Her eyes were still red and a little swollen as she greeted the bishop and Dokash, "We are back, teacher," she stated, the short run across the churchyard not winding her at all. Part of the peacekeeper's training was maintaining physical fitness to the utmost degree.

Selasine nodded, focused on pulling the crates piled in Dokash's cart into his own. Without a word, Miranda began helping the bishop, surprisingly strong for her demeanor. The other two acolytes quietly joined in, assisting with loading and organizing the cart. There were even barrels of potable water that Dokash had prepared for travelers leaving Devitus on longer journeys. They were particularly heavy, Dokash the only one strong enough to lift those barrels on his own.

Selasine wiped the sweat from his brow. The summer night was alive with the sounds of nature, the spolflies particularly loud tonight. They made a distinct, buzzing sound that signaled the height of summer. With a stretch, the bishop looked at the cart. "Well, as far as provisions go, we are secure. You three need to get to your rooms and get some rest. Make sure to pack your tunics and casual clothes, and make sure your armors all fit," he commanded.

The three acolytes stood at attention and replied in unison, "Yes, bishop," Justin, the only one remembering to include the salute, sword hand to the sky in front of the chest.

"Very good, Justin," Selasine laughed. Miranda's eyes shot wide in horror as she realized her mistake. Her sword hand snapped up instinctively, having practiced the salute numerous times. "Dismissed, acolytes," the bishop concluded, pointing to their dorms.

They walked across the courtyard to the barracks that had been refitted to serve as dormitory-style rooms. Three sections of the old military housing were partitioned, one for each of the three acolytes. Miranda's room was in the middle. She opened the door to her space, an everburning candle the only light in the room. She paused and looked at her friends as they entered their rooms, "Hey, don't stay up late worrying, okay?" she asked.

Justin nodded, a smile on his lips. "Goodnight, Miranda. Goodnight, August," he finished as he entered his room and closed the door.

August lingered, looking at his friend, a half-moon rising out of the north over the ridges and mountains behind the monastery of Lexcord. The world of Espa had two brilliant silver moons, but at the peak of summer, only one would be visible. The second would return to view as the world cooled for the winter. The current moon's silver beams cast an eerie glow over the courtyard behind them, the reflected light making Miranda's red hair seem luminescent. "I've traveled a lot but have never been nervous about a trip. I'm worried, but probably not for the reasons you think," he replied after a brief moment.

Miranda shook her head. She told herself not to worry as much as the others. "The bishop will be with us. And we'll be together, fighting against pirates!"

August laughed. "Healing. We'll be healing people who got hurt fighting pirates."

She smiled, feeling reassured. "Healing. We can't worry because people are depending on us, right?"

The other acolyte only smiled, nodded, and entered his room. As he closed the door, Miranda heard him grumble, "Without a doubt. Goodnight, Miranda."

She took a deep breath, entered her room, and looked around. After Justin and August brought the armor up from the cellar under the church, they placed her battlemail in her room, still on the mannequin. The mithril gauntlets that Selasine gave her were placed on a table in the center of the room. Miranda usually used that table for her studies but did not need to study tonight. Using the light from the everburning candle, she lit a couple of more candles to help her try on the armor.

At first, it looked a little small. As she slid the breastplate over her head, she realized that she was either underestimating the size of the armor or overestimating her own size. It fit perfectly. The bands that ribbed around her body underneath the breastplate and her torso were almost as flexible as leather, but they were also harder than mithril. She could feel the straps on the back of the armor that helped her tighten the breastplate and ring mail comfortably. She then stepped into the golden-ringed skirt, the intricate metal mesh as fluid as fabric but harder than steel. It was pleated and layered strategically to give maximum mobility and protection. It was long, hitting Miranda's legs mid-calf. She found a pair of armored boots that would protect her feet on the battlefield in her closet, and the mithril gauntlets with the sapphire blades fit perfectly. She adjusted her outfit, finding her mirror to take a look.

Looking back at her was a resplendent warrioress, somebody she had never met. The logo etched into her breastplate was barely visible in the candlelight, but it caught her memory when she noticed it glinting in the dim light. She reached into her pack, withdrawing the box of jewels the headmistress gave her. She confirmed that the two logos were the same. At first, she thought the lines were abstract and fluid, but upon closer examination, she could clearly see the forms of two serpents intertwined. With a contemplative look, she unfastened the ornate gold latch on the box and opened it.

Inside, she found the most opulent collection of rubies, sapphires, diamonds, and pearls. Many were inlaid into rings, earrings, necklaces, and other jewelry Miranda was not certain about. There was also a small ivory ocarina, a radiant tiara, and a jewel-encrusted music box. She pulled out the small toy, absentmindedly winding it up. To her surprise, the device began to play a melody, functioning fine after over fifteen years of being forgotten.

Miranda's lips pursed further, examining the music box carefully. Many of these trinkets had some visual element to accompany the music, like carved men and women dancing or a carousel with magical horses. This music box had no diversions beyond the music, just a beautiful jewel-covered exterior and a haunting lullaby that Miranda thought felt familiar. It was hard to remember her parents' deaths happening around her fourth birthday. She felt a comforting presence as she listened to the melody; her breathing slowed, and her eyes closed. She felt like she could see a beautiful woman with blue hair, but it was only the image created in her imagination while looking at the stained glass of the church, she thought.

After a while, she removed the armor, which fit better than she could have hoped for. She sorted through her casual clothes and undergarments, taking several pairs of cotton-lined chainmail that served as a last line of defense under the rest of her armor. She put a couple of tunics and several garments into her travel bag. She checked that she had rope, grappling hooks, flint and steel, candles, torches, a few vials of inks and acids, and other typical items that were useful on adventures. She double-checked everything. She felt ready to go.

She slid the box of jewels into a strongbox hidden under a floorboard under her bed. She kept the key to it on the chain she wore around her neck that held her holy symbol of Invictus, the scales of justice. She had not decided what to do with these extraordinary pieces of jewelry, and she would worry about that when they returned. Before sealing it away, however, she took the music box, which fit easily inside the palm of her hand. She placed it into her adventuring pack, wrapped up with a bundle of cloth. She felt drawn to it and wanted to take it with her.

She set her pack by the door and changed into her night robe. Blowing out the candles and whispering "dark" to the everburning candle to make it extinguish, she tucked herself into bed. She suddenly realized how tired she was, but her brain had been moving quickly all day. She had no time for thoughts as sleep washed over her minutes after she laid down.

The three acolytes woke up at their usual time, an hour before dawn. Instead of training and catechisms today, Selasine met them in the courtyard of the church with a wagon and horses. He acknowledged his pupils with a nod as they approached.

The three of them were already armored and ready to travel. For the first time, they spent most of the morning braiding their hair into the style common for the clergy of

Invictus. "We braid our locks because there is strength in solidarity. A single cord of rope is easily torn, breaking under small stresses. Many cords braided together make a stronger rope. There is order in the braids, and so we braid our hair to signify our unity." Miranda had heard the lecture perhaps a dozen times. Her thick red hair cascaded down the front of the breastplate of her battlemail, providing a colorful contrast to the mithril that shone a silvery blue in the early morning light. She had tied her hair into a long braid, much like the bishop. August and Justin had opted for a braiding style closer to the high priest's, dividing the hair in half and braiding separately. Miranda thought they looked like a force to be reckoned with, four soldiers of Invictus ready to fight against chaos.

"The Sword of Justice reveres the harmonious music of the morning," Selasine said a moment after his nod to greet his pupils according to protocol.

Miranda finished the catechism as expected, "The awakening dawn a paragon of order and beauty." Her voice was musical as she recited catechisms. She smiled brightly, the anxiety from the day before gone. Justin and August traded glances as she approached, the battlemail an intimidating and beautiful carapace that would keep their friend safe. August had chosen a suit of full plate mail bearing only the insignia of Invictus on the breastplate. He had spent many months training to acquire the strength necessary to move nimbly in the heaviest armor imaginable. Made of well-tempered steel, the armor was lighter than it looked.

Justin, however, had opted for a suit of chainmail supplemented by a breastplate that also bore the insignia of Invictus. Alone, he would have made an imposing figure, wielding a longsword, the chosen weapon of his god. Standing beside August and Miranda, the trio looked like a battle-ready team shrouded in the blessings of Invictus. Selasine smiled, his uncovered eye sparkling with pride.

The night before, Selasine had carefully reviewed his plan to supplement the primary force led by High Priest Carulus. This morning, he shared his plan with his students: stay out of the way of the primary fight, tend to the injured, and detain any pirate deserters that cross their path in the aftermath. He privately reasoned that if it was healing that Carulus sought, then that's what his team would do. Combat was a likely occurrence, if not an inevitability. Still, those fights would be relatively controlled if Selasine could intervene. The threat to his pupils would be much less significant with him nearby. Besides, he was confident that August would have no trouble in a fight, and with Justin and Miranda supporting him, he could stand toe to toe with even experienced pirates.

The only thing that troubled Selasine was the uncertainty of the uncanny magics that the pirates may wield. After the fabric of magic unraveled a century ago, the majority of common people found themselves able to wield various types of magic: moving walls of stone, conjuring water or light, or even the ability to summon animals or elemental creatures. Others still found themselves blessed or cursed with the ability to wield great destructive magic: fireballs of intense heat, bolts of lightning, and even the power to extinguish life with just a word. Some criminals in the underbelly of civilization took special deliberation to recruit like-minded individuals with destructive powers, providing a magical edge to their organizations. Pirate Lord Erk was among the most successful of these groups, naming themselves "The Unbound Pirates."

With that in mind, Selasine considered the powers held by the three acolytes. August could call upon his uncanny magic to increase his speed. Justin could make his skin as thick as stone. Miranda, however, did not seem to be able to call upon the arcane to assist her in any way. This was not necessarily a problem, as many people never found an uncanny connection to the arcane. He didn't consider the miraculous healing six months ago an arcane event, but if that was truly her uncanny magic, then it only added to the group's potential. Selasine was confident that all of his students would play a different, integral part in supporting the battalion leading the raid against Erk.

Selasine's little group climbed into the wagon. August joined the bishop up front. Miranda sat in the back, legs hanging off the uncovered wagon loaded with provisions, spare weapons, armor, and clothes. Justin chose a spot somewhere in the middle, but Miranda did not pay much attention to the others. She stared at the little church building as the cart lurched into motion. The feeling in her gut caused memories from last night to surface, pleasant memories of the monks of Lexcord that raised her in the monastery right outside of Devitus. She realized that, although she was an orphan, she had never felt truly alone. The monks had served as a community to take care of her in her younger years, and this last year with Bishop Selasine made her feel like she had discovered a place to belong. Swimming through those memories, she thought it funny that she was never scared of the things that scared most children: the dark, spiders, scary sounds, and creepy cellars never bothered her. Now, at twenty years, she realized that her fears had more to do with what resided inside her than outside: helplessness, lacking strength or experience, and disappointing those she cared about. As the cart left the courtyard of the church grounds, passing under the lone arch in the small wall surrounding the complex, Miranda's thoughts wandered back to the day the monks brought her to Selasine to begin her studies for the priesthood. Her formal training with the bishop began a year ago, but she had known Selasine since early childhood. Though he was imposing and seemed harsh, Miranda first noticed how caring he was, thanks to the warmth of his smile. She always felt safe with Selasine at the monastery. After entering into tutelage with the bishop, she felt safer having him close by. For a girl without parents, she felt lucky to have so many others who worked hard to keep her safe and make her a strong young woman.

Miranda was yanked out of her contemplation quickly as the wagon suddenly stopped. She had been so lost in her thoughts that she missed the half-mile ride from the church close to the center of town to the city gates on the east side. She turned to face the front of the cart, seeing that she grossly underestimated the number of brethren that accompanied the high priest. Initially, she thought it seemed like he brought a small, elite squad, but a veritable army stood before her and outside the city gates. She stood in the back of the cart and quietly exclaimed the casual curse favored by those on the Path: talirix volïs—Unhallowed Chaos. Selasine did not seem surprised and turned to the two acolytes in the cart.

"This is the power of order mobilized to stop chaos," Selasine said with a half grin. Miranda knew that the bishop was an experienced warpriest, having participated in campaigns against several uprisings and criminal enterprises throughout his service to the Sword of Justice. When he told stories of the mobilized forces of the church, Miranda's imagination had never managed to capture the magnitude of what he meant. This was what he always meant when he said you could smell the army before it came into sight. Miranda estimated that there were hundreds of horses and more than one thousand soldiers, most of whom were human or elven, with the occasional giant, dwarf, or orc who had pledged themselves to the service of Invictus.

Miranda's heart began to beat quickly with anticipation. "Will we be marching with them?" she asked, turning her eyes back to the bishop.

"No," he replied, his voice low. "We'll be marching with the high priest." A smug, satisfying grin rested on his lips, and his beard and eyepatch made him seem more piratelike than priestly.

Miranda noticed the irony and suppressed a giggle. In her experience, Selasine solved more disputes using diplomacy and tact than by force. If the high priest demanded to bring Selasine's students, the most logical way to make this valuable for the acolytes was to accompany them in the company of His Holiness. This was very much what she would have come to expect from her mentor. However, she didn't have much time to contemplate the situation as Carulus appeared atop his warhorse.

As far as the church hierarchy was concerned, Carulus would have outranked Selasine significantly. Individuals interested in joining the Path of the Sword of Justice usually began as non-sanctioned peacekeepers deputized by a priest or paladin. After being recommended for admission by another clergy member, peacekeepers could become acolytes in the Path of the Sword of Justice. From there, acolytes had many directions they could choose, including the path of the arbiter, a cleric specializing in resolving civil disputes according to the law, a path Selasine thought was perfect for Miranda. Selasine had chosen the path of the warpriest, a heavily armored beacon of strength and hope on the battlefield. Opposite Selasine, Carulus had chosen a more political route as a bureaucrat. Both routes could potentially lead to the high priesthood, but being a bishop in a community hundreds of miles away from the epicenter of civilization made it difficult for Selasine to be recognized for his contributions to Invictus's cause. A bishop was a regional cleric with responsibilities in their community, but a high priest could find themselves called to duty worldwide. Even though Carulus outranked Selasine greatly, Miranda found it interesting that the high priest would let the bishop make demands.

The small army had already begun to deploy. Mounted units flanked the ground troops. The administrative battalion, Carulus's personal guard, took a position in the middle of the marching order. Selasine, Miranda, Justin, and August rode behind the high priest's entourage in their humble uncovered wagon. As they exited the town and waited for their place in the marching order, the acolytes rearranged the provisions in the cart so that they could sit near the front. Miranda was anxious and excited about the journey as she had never left the Devitan River valley. She couldn't help smiling all morning as this was her chance to see the world outside her frontier town. Their destination, the Undine Coast, had a reputation for being one of the most beautiful regions in the world. She felt safe enough since her only job would be to heal injuries. Perhaps after all the fighting, the four of them could enjoy the coastal region for a day. She still wanted to swim in the ocean and build sandcastles with her friends and mentor.

Selasine drove the cart with August sitting beside him. Miranda and Justin sat somewhat comfortably on crates behind the driver's bench. Justin looked at Miranda as they began moving behind Carulus's division. With a sarcastic grin, he reached into a pack he had brought, withdrawing a white parasol. He opened it and rested it on his leg, the canopy above blocking out the morning sun.

August gave Justin a long, defiant stare, followed by an eventual shrug. Miranda and Justin laughed, and Selasine looked perplexed at his acolytes. The hour after dawn was spent before they had reached the gates, and it took another two hours to begin moving. Now that they should have been on a steady march, Miranda was confused when not even an hour into the journey, Carulus's battalion stopped. Selasine slowed his horses, stopping as well. They sat for almost an hour before the high priest's group resumed their march.

Miranda was puzzled as to why the leader's battalion was among the slowest moving. She leaned forward and asked Selasine, "How long will the journey take at this rate?" Selasine's stoic expression broke into a smile. After knowing Miranda for so long, she still voiced complaints couched in the politest way possible. Her question indicated that she understood the high priest was inefficient in matters of logistics. "Ten days, acolyte. We should be able to make this journey in ten days. Seven, if somebody would get their act together, but that's not our cause to worry about. Just enjoy the countryside and the mountains." Miranda replied with an understanding nod, turning her eyes to the natural wonders of the Devitan River valley.

She had seen these sights plenty on walks and rides through the countryside. The valley was flanked by two large arms of the central Trollcrag mountains on the north and south sides. The Starlock River that flowed east carved the valley here over the course of millennia. After marching all day, they stopped atop a ridge overlooking the valley. Devitus could be seen in the distance, the volume of lights increasing as darkness fell. Miranda stood near the edge of the ridge, gazing out over the valley. Her eyes were wide with a sense of wonder; her imagination had never considered the possibility that even her home was unimaginably beautiful.

August noticed her admiring the countryside and approached her. "What do you see, Miranda?" he asked, touching her shoulder.

She looked up at him, her eyes sparkling with awe. "That's where we live! I never knew our town was so pretty from so far away."

He smiled at his friend; her sheltered view of the world seemed so pure. He moved the hand from her shoulder to around her, giving her a loving squeeze. "You know, if you had not pointed it out, I would not have even thought about it. We're off to make war, and you can still see the beauty in what we're fighting for."

Miranda remembered what the bishop told her yesterday while playing with the children in town. She leaned into the hug that August was giving her. "If we lose sight of that, then what are we fighting for in the first place?"

He laughed in response, agreeing with her. Justin's voice nudged both of them, "So, are you two here as tourists or as soldiers?" he interrupted.

August turned around, his hands immediately tossing into the air. "Hey, it's a beautiful night; we can just camp under the stars!"

Justin made a disgusted face. "Ew. Insects. Vermin. Predators. Unexpected rain showers. There are literally a thousand reasons to pitch a tent," the smaller acolyte chided.

August shook his head defiantly. "You want to put in an hour's worth of work just to get six hours of sleep if you're lucky?" he laughed.

Selasine immediately canceled the argument, "Acolytes!" he commanded in his gruff and authoritative voice, causing them all to stand at attention out of sheer habit. "Quit wasting time and help me get some tents set up," he ordered, the three of them quickly complying. Each put up a small, personal tent over their bedrolls. The military tents were bigger and took far too long to erect for just an overnight rest. In a way, August got his wish to sleep under the stars, and Justin got the shelter and privacy he demanded. Miranda thought it was a great compromise and tucked the reality away as a metaphor for explaining compromise to townsfolk with disputes.

They nestled near Carulus's encampment, and the center of his battalion was practically a mobile pavilion. The four of them would not have to worry about guard duty, as the high priest's soldiers had it entirely under control.

The journey would take them another two hundred miles to the southeast. On their second day, Miranda took more time to observe the army of the high priest. She was pleased that she was not the only woman making this trek, as Carulus's troops were an evenly divided mixture of men and women, humans and elves. The women in the army filled various roles, from warpriest to paladin to healer. As the march halted at the end of the second day, Miranda tried to catch a glimpse of the healers to gauge their habits and behaviors. Many of these healers were elves trained in natural and divine healing, and their battle preparations included brewing healing potions, preparing spices and herbs to alleviate pain, and reciting prayers of protection to Invictus. On the third night, one of the healers took notice of Miranda's curious watching.

"Are you in need of healing, girl?" a soothing, melodic voice rang out as Miranda watched from the far side of a campfire. She observed as two healers added reagents into a brewing potion.

Miranda looked around for the source, checking behind her. There she saw an elven woman with beautiful golden braids pulled toward the front of her face rather than behind her. Miranda did not have time to think, quickly responding, "No, ma'am, I am uninjured."

The elven woman stepped toward her with a carefree bounce. She reached out and took Miranda by the hand. "Then come, share your heart with me."

Miranda was speechless but gripped the elf's hand firmly and followed her to another campfire. As they approached, the elf gestured to a large rock nearby where they could both sit comfortably. Miranda complied, taking a nervous seat. The golden-haired elf slid on the rock beside her, reaching into a pouch on her belt. "You have a pure heart, child. What is your name?" she asked. She withdrew a leaf from the pouch and placed it in her mouth.

Miranda was slightly puzzled by the elf's choice to have a snack in the middle of a conversation. "I'm Miranda," she replied, leaving it at just her name.

"No titles or family names or points of pride?" the elf replied cordially. There was no trace of the leaf, probably already swallowed and gone.

"None that really mean anything. I just wanted to learn how to help like the healers do," Miranda replied, distracted. How did she eat the leaf so fast?

"Very well, then. I am called Maréli," she said. "I can teach you what it is you wish to know."

Miranda's unsure face broke into a happy smile. "Oh, can I learn how to make healing potions?"

Maréli gave an aloof shrug, "Can you recite the prayers of healing?"

Miranda sat up straight and said the prayer loudly, clutching her holy symbol. Since there were no injuries to treat, nothing happened.

The elf laughed enthusiastically, "Well, that answers my question. I can tell you've had a little . . . experience when it comes to healing," Maréli replied as she reached out and touched Miranda's braided hair.

Miranda gave an affirmative nod but also thought back to the night of the fire. "Actually, there was one time that I accidentally brought a family back to life after they had passed in a fire," she mumbled, feeling Maréli's eyes searching her soul.

The healer's eyes seemed to fill with a sorrow of sorts. "You poor darling, your heart is so pure but your destiny so dark," she commented, making Miranda pause. Maréli retook Miranda's hand, "Come, girl. I want you to report to my encampment every evening for the rest of this journey. We will teach you the ways of the Healer of Invictus, and you'll be able to save far more people than you will ever fight."

Miranda was unsure what to do with Maréli's cryptic words, but she immediately agreed to train with the healers. She was so excited to learn something new and helpful that the dark destiny comment slipped completely from her mind. Throughout their journey, Miranda learned how to brew healing potions and began working on her own batch to share with her fellow acolytes.

While the marching army kept highwaymen and raider bands at bay, the front guard was accosted by various magical beasts looking for a meal. The experienced healers that had been teaching Miranda made sure to prevent casualties before the real fighting began. Even Miranda had an opportunity to offer healing prayers for the injured, an exercise that she felt would prepare her for bloodier experiences as a battle healer.

The day before they arrived at the designated location on the Undine Coast, Miranda wanted to be with Selasine and the other acolytes for the last camp hour before time to rest. She left the healers and returned to her own encampment.

Selasine, who encouraged the young woman as she spent time with healers in other battalions, greeted her with his powerful smile. "Miranda!" he bellowed, causing Justin and August to turn their attention as she approached their small camp area. She had not been present with them during downtime since the first night of the journey, often returning to her tent late into the night. Only the night watchmen had seen her in camp over the last several days. Still, with the healers making their final preparations for tomorrow's operation, Miranda returned to plan with her small group.

Due to the toil of travel, preparations, and post-battle healing, Miranda's battlemail needed a polish. Throughout the journey, she changed her hair from the traditional braid pulled to the back of her head to two long braids pulled to the front of her face. They rested just alongside her temples, keeping her hair barely in her peripheral vision. They swayed with every movement she made. Most healers wore this style to distinguish themselves from the fighters who braided their hair to the back. Selasine could see the exhaustion in her eyes, but mirth and excitement still sparkled behind those crystal blue orbs. "I brought healing potions," she said, her voice soft and tired.

"If things go right, we won't need those," August replied.

Miranda took the vials from a pouch attached to her waist, a leather bag one of the healers gave her to keep the potions safe. "Right," she said singularly, having not really thought about how close to the fighting they would be.

Selasine shook August's shoulder. "If things go right. They never do. Thank you, Miranda." He extended a hand to accept the product of Miranda's preparations. "Make sure to keep a couple for yourself." August and Justin both took one as well.

The exhaustion in her body could not keep her from smiling. Selasine's pride in her efforts over the last week made all the difficulty worth it. She might have never really known her father very well, but moments like these are why she felt so much like Selasine was a surrogate father to her. His kindness tempered with sternness had shaped her into a disciplined and caring peacekeeper, now an acolyte of the same faith that he lived to the fullest every day. She wanted to be like him, and she wanted to make him proud.

They spent another hour or so discussing their plans for the next day. Reconnaissance troops had already begun scouting for inland pirate activity near the estimated location of Erk's lair. The Sea of Undine sat between the steep rise of the southern Trollcrag Mountains and the fertile plains of Claston, an autonomous elven kingdom in the far east. The mountainous west side of the sea provided numerous caves and gullies to hide ships, treasure, and maybe even entire towns from the watchful eye of Claston's naval forces. Selasine's "battalion" was to meet with the high priest tomorrow afternoon. Until then, they had no responsibilities.

As the camp grew quiet, the four bundled under their tents and settled in for the night. Miranda's heart thudded with nervousness, a feeling that tomorrow would be a turning point in her service to Invictus. If she could keep the strength to heal countless wounded, maybe the church would send her on more missions. She could see the world and help people along the way. Though it saddened her that the people making decisions had chosen violence as the solution, she understood that the forces of chaos did not often understand a message unless it was painted in their own blood. Erk had killed and robbed countless innocents. This was his reckoning. Miranda was at peace with that, thinking of her mentor, her parents, the monks at the monastery, and all of these people she had met only recently. She could make a difference.

That night, Miranda slept peacefully for the last time.

Chapter 3
Unreasonable Expectations

At about noon on the day of their arrival near the Undine Coast, the high priest welcomed the four from Devitus into his command tent, already set up with a war table that doubled as a dining table. Right now, it was arranged for a strategy meeting. Carulus stood with one of the army's commanders, and a roughly built model of the base camp occupied a small section of the table. Other models had also been built, including pirate encampments, docks, and boats placed where they made logical sense. Large mountains divided the models representing the army of Invictus and those representing pirates. Selasine greeted Carulus with the standard salute, left hand on the hilt and the other palm in the air. Carulus gave him a casual wave, never looking up from his table. Miranda, Justin, and August did the same as they entered the command tent, only to be ignored.

"Reporting for duty, Your Holiness," Selasine interrupted.

"Yes, yes, good." The half-elf high priest scratched his silvery braided hair in contemplation. "This area here," he said, gesturing to the model of the base camp. "This is where we expect the first wave of the injured to be returned."

"Wave?" Selasine asked, perplexed. "I know it's a large-scale operation, but isn't that so we don't miss any of the major pirate encampments? Do you have numbers?"

"Five thousand, give or take. The vermin have built their own ecosystem in the caves in the mountains." Carulus sneered at his planning table.

Miranda did some quick calculations. The army she traveled with was no more than fifteen hundred strong. With the rumors of the strength of Erk's forces, she became increasingly concerned, but she gripped the holy symbol of Invictus hanging from her neck. Through this, she could channel the divinity of the Sword of Justice and do her part to quell the chaos.

The commander beside Carulus instructed, "The healers have already prepared the triage. We'll need you amongst the hospital tents immediately. I've received word that the first wave of casualties are coming from the caves. Booby traps, as expected." With a unified salute, Selasine and the acolytes left the command tent for their post.

From what Selasine could decipher, the forces of Invictus would begin rooting out the pirates entrenched in the cave networks on the eastern side of the Sea of Undine. With enough pressure, the hope was to scatter the pirates and cause them to flee into the ocean, where a sizable naval force from Claston would be waiting to demolish them. Since the cave network along the coast was complex and confusing, the holy forces of Invictus would be at an initial disadvantage due to the terrain, but their superior faith and training would turn the tide of the battle. Plus, with healers at the ready, a fifteen hundred troop force could easily take an opponent thrice its size in this kind of skirmish.

The church's base camp was a hastily constructed siege camp built by a siege engineer team that worked under a different administrator than Carulus. The high priest's pavilion sat directly in the center of the camp. Most of the soldiers pitched tents south of that central location, but the four from Devitus camped between the high priest and the healers on the north side. They passed by their tents on the way to their assignment.

Arriving at the hospital tents, an elven woman with golden hair stood on a raised platform looking at the palisades that marked the outer reaches of the base camp. The palisades were constructed on the east side of the camp, the same side as the mountains. Two wooden gates were built into the temporary wall, one on the north side close to the healers and the other closer to the south side near the troops' encampment. The terrain here was hilly and difficult, indicating their proximity to this particular arm of the Trollcrag mountains.

Miranda took a deep breath and rushed over to the elf. "Maréli!" she said in a greeting, gripping her sword with her left hand and turning her right palm to the sky in front of her.

"At ease, Healer Miranda," the beautiful elf replied, her braids dancing in the gentle breeze. Maréli, the chief healer of the Nulodian Temple of Invictus, invited Miranda to prepare with the other healers. Though it did not carry a specific military ranking, Maréli had the ecclesiastical authority to designate any church members as healers.

Selasine overheard the exchange and could not help but smile. "You couldn't make it just a week as an acolyte?" he said in jest to himself, proud of the speed with which Miranda impressed one of the most powerful healers in the entire church structure.

His doting thoughts were quickly interrupted by a wailing voice. As all hands came on deck at the hospital camp, a small group of soldiers appeared at the palisade carrying a stretcher. On it were three men, carried by two dwarves. Though they made up such a small part of Invictus's followers, the dwarven regiments of the church were notorious for their efficiency. After bringing the men to triage, one of the dwarves grunted up at Maréli, "Too bad about the dispeller. Don't think he'll make it." He then stomped off to continue his duty of retrieving the injured.

Miranda blinked for a moment. "Dispeller?" she asked out loud to herself. Selasine and the other acolytes caught up to her and Maréli about the time the dwarf gave his lamentation.

Selasine tapped Miranda on the shoulder, causing her to jump with fright. She made no sound but quickly turned her attention to her mentor, a hand instinctively ready to draw her sword. Selasine shook his head and raised his hand. "Dispeller. It's a special role that dismantles magical traps. Especially important when you're dealing with unknown and uncanny magics."

Miranda nodded in understanding but became very concerned, "Does that mean the healers can't help the dispeller?"

Selasine shook his head, "Just because that one lacks faith does not mean the healers do. They are more capable than any healers in the world. Do not fret," he comforted her.

Miranda seemed relieved, returning her attention to the palisades as more dwarven carriers brought in stretchers with injured clergy. The group of four found a triage tent and began working to diagnose and treat the injured. Their injuries were relatively straightforward: punctures from spike traps, broken bones from falling rock or log traps, crushed ankles from pit traps. Most of these wounds required only a brief, simple healing prayer to fix. However, some unlucky individuals took significant damage from the traps. After healing these early, light injuries, the troops would regroup and head back to the caves in small battalions.

Miranda quickly had a harrowing realization. "Our soldiers aren't even fighting yet," she whispered.

Justin overheard her and gave her an encouraging pat on the back. "Don't sweat it; we can handle this!" he said, smiling to reassure her. He had helped Miranda heal the last couple of injured that passed through their tent. She tried to force a smile, but she had a grim feeling that the fighting would be much worse.

She was, of course, correct. After about three hours of healing minor injuries, the paladins, clerics, and soldiers brought for triage had more severe wounds. Miranda saw fire and acid burns, victims of electrification, and dismemberment. Her healing prayers would help ease the pain, but they could not restore their bodies to the point where continuing to fight would be feasible. Other, more experienced healers saw the gravest of injuries, including the first wave of deaths. A few of the clerics present could undo the work of chaos to the point that those who departed could return to life and potentially fight again. However, the toll of combat and resurrection would significantly fatigue both the healers and fighters.

Miranda kept her focus and continued healing the injured until her body weakened. Repeatedly channeling the divine power of Invictus was taxing. By mid-afternoon, she could barely recite the words of the healing prayer. She was not alone; other clerics began to drop from exhaustion, their efforts expended on continual waves of injured. Whatever uncanny magics these pirates had accumulated posed a particularly threatening combination that resulted in large casualties and significant wounds.

Then the truly terrifying injuries began to emerge. Miranda saw lifeless bodies with all the moisture sucked from them, among others who showed no physical signs of injury but had left the mortal realm nonetheless. Her healing prayers were utterly ineffective, and she felt ready to collapse from the exertion. Her vision began to blur, and she remembered only the outstretched hand of one of the desiccated corpses, seemingly trapped in the throes of a warning gesture. Were the forces of chaos truly this terrifying? Were they capable of such great destruction that an elite force of Invictus's strongest troops could not stem the tide of chaos?

The world around Miranda began to swirl. She had healed thirty? Thirty-five? She had lost count, but maybe that meant she had made a great difference. She stepped a little way out of the tent to breathe deeply. Her body could not continue, and she fell to her knees, the long skirt of the battlemail flattening against the ground, glinting gold in the late afternoon sunlight. Before darkness could overtake her, a familiar voice echoed through the hospital camp. "Rally, Invictus's chosen! The forces of chaos seek our destruction, and you are the last bastion of hope for the faithful!" Through blurry vision, Miranda could see Carulus meandering among the tents, raising his voice to inspire his healers. The high priest continued to give a rallying cry, but the way he walked through the hospital camp seemed very uninspiring. His hands were firmly clasped behind his back, his posture slouched forward a bit. A sickening feeling began to swell in Miranda's stomach.

Carulus's wandering seemed aimless, but Miranda's clarity of thought began to return. He walked in circles with each pass, closing in toward the center of the healers' camp. The exact center, though? Not quite, it seemed. She was bothered by his directionless gait. Justin, August, and Selasine continued working with the injured. Her mentor was too occupied with serious injuries to check on his exhausted pupil. She could see them working diligently in the triage tent, which had a roof covering the beds, but only one side was walled. That was okay, she thought; the others needed him more. She took a deep breath and prepared herself to stand when she realized the high priest was standing directly in front of her.

"This is why you're here, child." Carulus seemed harsher than usual, his ragged, aged features exacerbated by the stress of the battle. There were easily one hundred men and women in the hospital camp with grievous injuries that would not allow them to battle again any time soon, if ever. His piercing golden eyes stared down at her, and she could not meet his gaze. She realized that the high priest was the source of the uncomfortable feeling in her gut.

She tried to look up at him but hid her tired eyes with a quick glance away. "Yes, I am here to help. I can help." She kept repeating it aloud as much to herself as to the high priest.

His voice sounded sterner and gruffer than before, more serious than even during their first meeting during the acolyte test. "No child, not just your prayers. You're a miracle worker, blessed by the Sword of Justice."

Miranda's breathing began to accelerate. "W-what?" she replied in disbelief. She realized that this was the moment Selasine had warned her about. Carulus seemed overly interested in the accidental healing that Miranda had done six months ago. She tried to remember what she felt that night but couldn't. She only remembered praying, and the high priest's continued insistence filled her with anxiety.

"Help our troops the way you helped that family! Call upon your innermost strength and work a miracle beyond our understanding!" he ordered, unclasping his hands from behind his back, raising his palms to the sky in a grandiose gesture that seemed so theatric that it made Miranda feel even sicker.

"I'm sorry, Your Holiness, I—I don't know how," she replied, lowering her head in shame. Carulus looked down at her with disdain, watching her fiery braids droop in defeat.

"You can, Miranda, you have to! Without you, this mission will be lost! We need your incredible power!"

The sinking feeling in her stomach spread through her body, her extremities turning cold from fear and helplessness. Tears started to swell in her eyes as she felt true despair for the first time. She looked up through her tears directly at the high priest. "I can't, sir; I don't know how to do anything but pray!" The melody in her voice was frantic and desperate.

A sneer of rejection twisted Carulus's mouth into a sinister visage. Selasine looked out from the triage tent and realized what was happening. He began approaching, angry with himself for not noticing Miranda's depleted state sooner. Carulus turned to her mentor. "I guess the rumors were not true, bishop. The promise shown by your student was a lie that will kill hundreds this day. Remember, her failure is your failure." With a dismissive shrug, the high priest started to walk away.

Miranda pushed herself up and gathered her strength, her flowing tears turning into sobs of shame and anger. Angry that she could not reach the power that once blessed her and the people of Devitus in such a way that brought out smiles and tears of joy. She had healed numerous people of minor injuries, but the family in that burned house was the only time that she brought mortals back from the brink of death. Her shame turned into additional rage, upset that someone so respected in the church would base a battle plan on such a flighty rumor. His expectations were neither fair nor represented order in any sense. A righteous indignation burned in her chest as she forced herself to her feet.

Miranda's exhaustion, combined with the weight of her battlemail, was too much, and she started to fall. Carulus's back was turned to her, and the world spun up directly at her vision. A strong hand under her arm rescued her from the tumble, Selasine's firm grip helping her steady herself. After the scathing rebuke the high priest had given them, all she could do was fling her entire body against her mentor, her head resting on the breastplate covering his chest as she started to cry uncontrollably. Why would the high priest blame Selasine for this? It was her failure to reach the power within her. She clung to her mentor, who embraced her, holding her with a nurturing tenderness, letting her emotions run. She started to try to articulate her thoughts, but the only sounds she could make were sobs.

At that moment, another wave of injured and dead began to pour into the camp. Carulus stretched out his arms, still choosing theatrics over reason. "All of this could have been prevented if you had taught your student how to reach the power inside her, Thomas." Seeing a new tragedy unfolding before her, Miranda's emotions became muddled. Her heart remained firmly lurched in her throat. She couldn't even remember her prayers. The only thing she could remember was the face of a traveling paladin with whom she had the honor of celebrating a meal as he passed through Devitus on a quest.

That unassuming face lingered in her mind for no explainable reason. Those emotions that were tearing her apart began to seem distant. Even though Selasine was right there holding her, his embrace began to fade from her mind. She felt something putting her at ease as a warmth started to flow through her body. Her tear-stained cheeks sparkled in the waning sunlight as she felt herself press away from Selasine, standing upright.

Miranda felt like she had a second voice speaking in her mind. She felt calm with a resolve similar to how she felt on the night of the fire. She began to repeat the basic healing prayer. "Restore to order what was damaged by chaos." Selasine reached out to try and stop her, but he stopped abruptly as he noticed a light, faintly purple aura beginning to surround her. She repeated the prayer again, louder.

"Restore to order what was damaged by chaos!" she said again, more confident and increasingly indignant. The aura around her began to glow brighter. She started to repeat the prayer in a frenzied tone, her words getting closer together.

Carulus turned around, his arms still outstretched. He saw the aura growing around Miranda, his look of disdain replaced by the ambitious smile he had the day he met the girl. "Yes! This must be it! Behold the power of order!" he crowed.

Miranda fell to the ground again, slamming her fists against the earth as she continued chanting the prayer. Her body felt light, and her mind was barely present as the intensity of the aura around her became blindingly bright. Selasine tried not to look away, but he averted his eyes instinctively. Justin and August had stepped out from under the triage tent, curious about the piercing radiance filling the camp. They, too, had to cover their eyes. Carulus watched with smug accomplishment as the light from the girl's body began to envelop the entire base camp. A shrill but faint sound pulsed with the radiant glow, echoing against the side of the mountains that housed the den of Erk's pirate army.

After what seemed like hours in Miranda's mind, she stood up easily, feeling reinvigorated. The light was gone. A din began to rumble in the section of the base camp dedicated to treating the injured. Those who were dried husks a moment ago found themselves completely healthy; those who were dead without injury began to awaken. Missing arms and legs were grown back, burns were soothed and left no scars. What had been a horrifying scene only moments before was turned into a celebration as even the healers found themselves with new strength.

Miranda blinked in disbelief, her eyes filling with tears again, this time tears of relief. It worked? The prayers worked? She thought she might have been dreaming. Did the high priest know it would take equal measures of cruelty and despair to bring this out of her? Did he blame Selasine so that she would take it personally and fight for her mentor? The sounds became overwhelming with the word of this miracle passing through the base camp like a flame to dry wood. The world spun briefly, and Miranda's only words were, "I did it. I—I did it." She turned to look at Selasine, eyes wide with surprise. "Bishop, I . . . I did it." The excitement in her heart could not be relayed by her words. Half of what she wanted to say, she could not. She realized that her body had just expelled a substantial amount of energy. She went from refreshed to exhausted almost immediately. This power inside her was something different than Invictus's blessings. Overwhelmed by her relief from the situation and the intensity of the power that had just been discharged from her, she smiled at Selasine as she collapsed unconscious into his arms. The wise bishop held his pupil before lifting her and checking her vitals. Her hair had lightened to a faint pink color, but other than that, she seemed fine.

"Still breathing, *mahalàkhas*," an old language exclamation of joy. Selasine cast a vengeful stare at Carulus, who was still celebrating the miracle.

"Look, Thomas! You've stumbled upon a great gift! Wake her! We'll need another miracle like this by dawn!"

Selasine's eye narrowed, and he drew his sword, hoisting Miranda over his left shoulder. "Touch the girl, and I'll bring the wrath of Invictus down on this entire operation, fool."

Carulus's eyes widened in disbelief and anger. "You dare—"

Selasine cut him off. "Yes, I dare, how dare YOU." If Miranda had been awake, she wouldn't have recognized her beloved bishop at this point. "This plan was nothing short of a stream of madness pulled straight from the bowels of Indervill itself!" Such a rebuke carried significant weight in the folds of Invictus, as Indervill was the god of chaos. Known for its unpredictability and lack of form or substance, Indervill was a boogie to those who revered the path of law and order.

Carulus, megalomaniacal in his own right, realized he had no recourse against the bishop. If word reached the Council of Four that he planned to defeat five thousand pirates with only fifteen hundred soldiers while relying on the miracles of a young woman who had barely found her way into the church, his entire career would have been for naught. He manipulated the paperwork appropriately and legally but was absolutely sure of his calculations. Still, the archbishop who had appointed Carulus already had doubts about the girl's usefulness. He resigned to let the matter rest until she was ready to continue. "Yes, yes, Bishop Selasine. We need to let the girl rest. Perhaps I have been overly ambitious and must pay penance to our Sword." His words seemed genuine, but Selasine could feel the hollow echo of insanity behind them. Carulus made haste to the command tent, and Selasine sheathed his sword.

A host of confused but elated clergy surrounded Selasine and Miranda. Murmurings of "miracle girl" and "sent by Invictus to save us" began circulating through the crowd. Selasine hoisted Miranda over his shoulder with one arm and used the other to point at the mountains. "You have a mission, don't forget that. Focus on our objectives, and later we can discuss the miracle you've witnessed here today. Go, and do not dawdle! Now is not the time for speculation, only action. The forces of chaos are nigh!" Justin and August looked at each other with a smug exchange. Their lowly-ranked bishop was a better leader than the high priest. And everyone knew it.

Selasine took Miranda to her tent to set her down to rest. She breathed peacefully, her sparkling blue eyes closed in repose. The pink tint to her hair was starting to darken back to its normal crimson richness.

****

Dread Pirate Lord Erk looked at the enemy base camp through his spyglass. The bright light disoriented him and his officers watching the enemy's movements. "What in the Abyss was that?" he spat at his first officer, Jax Slicer.

"Dunno cap. Seems like they really have the gods on their side. Maybe we should retreat?" he replied, unamused and melancholy.

"Gods, my ass. That was something beyond the gods. Just look." Erk shoved the spyglass in his hand.

Jax grunted. He took a moment to soak in the scene and piece together what had happened. "She undid Drymouth's magic. Was that what that light was? What a pain."

A cunning smile cut across Erk's face. "Definitely a pain. We can't stay here, though. Let's mobilize a full retreat, especially for the people. Drymouth can hold off the enemy."

Jax sneered. "Drymouth is exhausted though."

Erk shook his head. "Doesn't matter. They'll never be able to clear the caves before he's had time to rest. Besides, do you think she's the one The Master is looking for? If she can heal wounds to that extent, maybe she could —" he said, his thoughts trailing into silence.

Jax snorted. "Yep. We need that power."

Erk nodded. "Send Apocalypse and Shalo. Under cover of darkness. Get her. Have her back at *The Nebula* before we depart tomorrow. Evan needs her," he said with impatience.

Jax gave an evil grin, his rotten and missing teeth adding to the sinister nature of his countenance. "Got ya, cap. And lemme guess. Not a hair damaged?"

Erk gave him an approving nod. Jax was his first officer because he could read Erk's mind. "Don't fail me. Don't fail The Master. Don't fail my brother." The two of them glanced back at the small cave entrance behind them. "And I mean it. Not one hair."

Chapter 4
Lost Treasure

elasine did not really sleep. He drifted in and out, feeling a restless rumbling behind his eyes. Asking Justin and August to take turns watching over Miranda was the most he could do, exhaustion gripping his body and anger fueling his anxiousness. The high priest had much to answer for, but the core mission was of singular importance. The way Carulus abused his pupil made his blood boil and ate away at his ability to sleep. Still, in those fleeting moments of darkness, Selasine tried to rest.

***

Thomas sat on the front porch of his cottage in a wooden rocking chair. He could smell the stew his wife, Iria, made with the small game he hunted early that morning. The early spring wind spoke to his very will: it was time to plant new crops. As he wrestled with the decision to plant more grain or legumes in the upcoming growing season, a din of thundering footsteps scuttled throughout the cottage behind him. He was suddenly pulled from his thoughts as a small girl of around four years burst from the house, running directly toward him and jumping into his lap without an invitation.

Thomas gave a low rumbling growl and scooped the girl into his arms. "You have to charge with meaning! Otherwise, the monsters will eat you!"

The girl gave her scariest roar back. "But daddy, I'm the monster!"

Thomas roared with laughter. "Then you're the cutest monster to ever walk the planes!" He hugged the girl tightly before a light pierced his vision.

***

"Sir?" a voice beckoned from the flap of his tent.

Stirring for a moment, Selasine reached for his sword. "What is it?"

"There's a direct attack on the base camp," the voice replied. Selasine recognized it as the commander advising Carulus earlier in the day. "All battalion commanders are being asked to respond," he continued.

"Numbers?" Selasine started to get up, sliding into his armor quickly, though it still took about five minutes.

"Just one. It seems to be a commanding pirate officer. Wielding uncanny magic."

Selasine sat for a moment in silence. "What kind of magic?"

"Explosive bursts of fire. He disabled an entire battalion with a single blast."

Cursing under his breath, Selasine finished donning his armor and weaponry. He began to pray to Invictus for strength, protection, and general enhancements to his body. It was time to make a statement that the pirates would understand.

Selasine found himself at the palisade a few moments later, sword in hand. His body shimmered with the protections that Invictus bestowed upon him. The wooden palisade overlooked a small forest that had grown on the mountainside, hiding the caves that spread throughout the spiring mountains above. In a clearing below, Selasine could see the lone pirate whose body glowed with intense heat in the darkness of the early morning. "Has he made demands?" Selasine asked the commanding officer who accompanied him.

"None so far, and any attempts at an approach have only caused him to grow angrier and more explosive." The commander begrudgingly confessed, "Carulus said you were the most experienced warpriest in our number, and he has faith that you can put a swift end to this."

Selasine cracked his elbows with anticipation. "I'm getting too old for this," he commented as he began to walk down the forest path toward the clearing. As he approached, he could feel the temperature around him rising quickly. The heat generated by this lone pirate was incomprehensible—how could one person's uncanny magic be so powerful? It reminded him of an old friend who could control the power of heat. This phenomenon seemed similar, but the impact of the magic was very different. With that in mind, his own uncanny magic would not be especially effective in defeating an enemy that could simultaneously attack in every direction.

When Selasine arrived in the clearing, the pirate gave him a sadistic smile. With a growl, the heat and pressure in the area seemed to absorb into the pirate's body, resulting in an explosion a moment later, blowing nearby trees down and nearly pushing Selasine backward. However, the divine shield surrounding his body protected him and allowed him to push forward toward the enemy.

Selasine's brow furrowed with determination as the enemy gave a second blast of fire, pushing Selasine backward and knocking him to the ground. Selasine prayed again for the speed and precision to reach his enemy. As he felt the empowerment of Invictus, Selasine rose, uninjured and determined as he felt Invictus's empowerment.

"You're strong," the pirate commented, sending a third burst of pressure and heat. The divine shell surrounding Selasine began to crack, but thanks to the speed enhancement, Selasine quickly closed the gap between them. Making a swift jab with his sword, Selasine struck the pirate's bicep, slicing it open and causing the pirate to howl with pain. Trying to take advantage of the opening, Selasine struck again, missing exposed flesh and finding only chainmail under the pirate's clothing.

"You idiot!" the pirate exclaimed, absorbing a new volume of heat.

Selasine could smell sulfur in the air and heard a popping sound close to the pirate before the explosive blast followed. Selasine felt his divine protection shatter under the weight of the burst. Selasine changed the direction of his prayers without showing the fear he felt. "To purify what has been sullied, Sword of Justice take the air away from this place. Suffocate the chaos with your righteous fury."

Invictus granted Selasine's prayers as a whirlwind forced all the air out of the clearing. Almost immediately, both men in the clearing felt their bodies screaming for air, triggering the instinctive response to gasp. Selasine stifled the urge to panic, keeping his composure so he could finish his bloody task. While the undisciplined pirate panicked, clutching his throat, Selasine began to wail against the pirate's body with his sword, some of his blows striking true. Within moments, they could feel the rush of air returning to the clearing, allowing them to breathe again.

Looking down at his chest, the pirate could see that he had been mortally wounded as blood soaked his tunic and poured through his chainmail generously. Rolling his eyes, he tried to suck in a lung full of air but found his lungs filling with blood. Unable to speak, he clenched his fists and pulled the heat into himself again. Selasine began to withdraw, but the explosion came with even more force this time, blasting him into a tree. He lost consciousness immediately.

***

"Daddy, look!" The girl, almost ten years now, had been learning to fashion garments out of various fabrics. Today she stitched some old flour bags into a summer dress, a practice common among poorer townsfolk. Her black hair was braided and pulled back, a sign of Thomas's conviction and faith being shared with his daughter. Invictus had blessed them, he thought to himself. Especially him.

"How beautiful," he said, smiling. Iria approached him from behind and slid her arm underneath his, clasping it to her. He looked down at his wife, a beautiful elven woman with jet-black hair. Since The Unbinding began around ninety years ago, unions between elves and humans had increased. Elven nobility had relaxed the laws restricting such unions, especially because some of the inherent magical powers of the elves had begun to wane thanks to The Unbinding. Many feared that the magic that allowed elves to live for centuries would expire and that the lifespan of an elf would eventually shorten to that of humankind. While a minority of traditionalists objected to the lack of evidence, the growing unity between humankind and elvenkind swayed the opinions of most nobles. What was the difference between them now other than the sharpness of their features and the shape of their ears? Thomas was glad because he loved his wife and daughter with all the strength that Invictus could give him. It was time to retire from the church and live a simple life. Another warpriest could easily replace him in the church. Nobody could ever replace him in his family.

"Telisi, tell your father how many tries it took." Iria looked up at Thomas with adoration in her eyes.

"Just one, daddy. I did it right this time!"

Iria laughed. "Well, one try this time. We're out of extra fabric now," she said, letting Thomas know that he needed to pick up some next time he went to the market over in Devitus.

He nodded. Looking back at his daughter, something felt wrong. He felt a pressure build in his chest, and his breath became short. Iria's face began to blur, and Thomas began to hyperventilate. Telisi was no longer standing before him but a girl with flowing red hair. Miranda seemed out of place in this memory, bringing Thomas's mind back to the present.

He could swear he heard her voice. "Bishop!" she said, panicked. "Please, help!"

***

Selasine awoke suddenly, clutching his chest. When he impacted the tree, he broke some ribs, but two healers were standing over him, chanting prayers of healing in quick succession. No evidence of the pirate's body remained. Perhaps the last blast obliterated his own body as an attempt to take Selasine with him out of the mortal realm.

He gasped for air as the prayers repaired his body. "Mir..." he said, the vision he had while unconscious sending him into a panic. "Miranda. Where is Miranda?"

The healers looked at each other, giving a gentle shrug. "We don't know, sir; we came with the commander."

Selasine stood up, an anxious tremble in his hand. Feeling no signs of his injury, he began sprinting toward the camp. "Miranda," he murmured to himself.

It took only a minute to get back to the girl's tent. He found Justin outside the tent, lying on the ground. "No!" he hissed, rushing to his student. Blood had soaked the young man's tunic, a single slice wound across his throat.

"Order, grant your faithful the blessing of another chance. A life ended too early is the work of chaos; let us set the universe to right in the Path of the Sword of Justice." A sparkling light covered the two of them, and the wound on Justin's neck closed. Color returned to his cheeks, and he started to breathe. Selasine collapsed to the ground, but his desperation fueled his strength, allowing him to crawl into the tent's opening.

There were no obvious signs of a struggle, but the tent was otherwise empty. Miranda was not resting in the pallet where Selasine left her.

"No! Miranda!" the bishop said, agonized as the previous prayer had drained him completely. He couldn't keep moving, and his mind faded from consciousness again.

***

Thomas could feel the temperature dropping far too quickly as he approached his cabin. He had spent the day traveling to Devitus, picking up supplies for the upcoming planting season. The evening air could be crisp this time of year, but this sudden drop in temperature felt abnormal. At this rate, the temperature would be unbearable without a healthy fire in the hearth. He needed to get home and make sure everything was in order.

As his cabin came into view, the frigid temperature began to solidify the moisture in the air. Nearby flora had frozen solid with icicles hanging from their leaves. Thomas's battle-hardened instincts sent a shockwave of worry through him. Something was not right. The cold around him felt so brutal that he could swear his blood was freezing. He quickly recited a prayer of protection, his mind trying to piece together what was happening.

Abandoning the hand-drawn cart behind him, Thomas rushed to his cabin door. He could barely turn the front door handle, the metal burning his hand from the cold. He had only ever felt a cold this intense once in his life, almost sixteen years ago, on a campaign against a group trafficking prohibited magic items in Nulodia. The church's success against that group dealt a serious blow to organized crime in the city. The cold forced him to squint, and Thomas began to panic. There was no way this was possible.

He opened the door to his home and found a tall individual sitting at the kitchen table. This man looked to have ancestry among the frost giants. A long white beard draped his face, and white flowing hair spilled down his back. His eyes glowed a harsh purple color giving him an otherworldly look. It was him. One of the ringleaders of the group that Thomas had personally helped defeat. Eldon Farzg, The Frozen Death. His natural, frost giant magic allowed him to drop the air temperature around him without significantly affecting his own body. He was also able to wield magically conjured ice with lethal efficiency.

"Thomas. You look cold," Farzg said with a blank, expressionless taunt.

Barely able to speak due to the cold, Thomas reached for his sword. "O-out of here, Farzg."

"Tsk. You won't be able to defeat me again, Thomas. You don't have your fiery friend with you. That's too bad."

"H-how d-dare you m-mention her. W-what are you d-d-doing here?" Thomas inquired, the frigid air causing his teeth to chatter and his words to sound broken and stuttered. His body was starting to succumb to the cold.

Farzg tilted his head to the side. "Just tying up loose ends. You took everything from me. My business. My fortune. My prestige. My brother. It's your turn to know loss, Thomas."

Farzg's words caused a righteous fury to burn in Thomas's heart. "No," he muttered, the cold causing his breath to form a distinct cloud of condensation that promptly froze, forming ice crystals in the air. His body could not bear the cold anymore, and he collapsed in the doorway to his house.

Farzg stepped over the warpriest as he lay on the floor, desperately trying to crawl. "I guess my work here is done. Your god won't help you this time." Farzg bent down. "And the worst part about it? I don't like violence. It's a good thing freezing is a peaceful way to leave this mortal realm. Goodbye, Thomas."

***

Selasine opened his eye, still lying on the floor of Miranda's tent. Current events and memories swirled together, and as he came to, he shouted, "Telisi! Iria!"

August heard the voice in the tent and burst inside. "Miranda?" he inquired, only to find his mentor lying on the floor of the tent. "Where is Miranda?"

Unable to process his emotions, Selasine's face flushed with anger. "The high priest! Check with the high priest!"

August furrowed his brow. In the commotion created by the pirate with explosive magic, he had been unable to keep track of the comings and goings of others in the camp. With a nod, August rushed across the encampment, bursting into the high priest's command tent without regard for protocol. Carulus sat at the war table, staring at the models. With an enraged visage, August demanded, "Where is Miranda?"

Carulus looked distant, trapped in his thoughts. "I don't know, acolyte." His eyes never left the war table. With a burst of anger, August snatched the high priest out of his chair by the collar of his ceremonial garb.

"Where is she? Whatever is happening here is your doing, blasphemer," August roared, his anger overwhelming him.

Carulus refused to meet his gaze. He calmly pushed against the young man with his hands, an unseeable strength allowing him to free himself from August's grasp. "I know, acolyte. This is my sin to bear."

The hypocrisy and callousness derailed August's righteous anger, turning it into indignant fury. "Can't you see, it's not your sin to bear! Miranda is the one who is missing because of you! Where is she?"

Carulus finally met his eyes. August, imposing and much taller than the high priest, towered over him. The half-elf's golden eyes glinted in the torchlight, the sun not yet peeking over the horizon. "If I knew where she was, acolyte, I'd retrieve her myself. We need her. The church needs her."

The abject futility of this line of inquiry made August huff. He turned away from the high priest and stormed out of the command tent. Jogging back to the acolytes' encampment, he found Selasine sitting upright, checking Justin's vitals. The boy was breathing but still unconscious. The bishop looked at his pupil with hope. It was quickly dashed by the feral expression that had twisted August's rugged face into something terrifying. The acolyte could only shake his head, his anger stymying his words.

At that moment, Maréli approached the three, realizing Justin was injured. She knelt beside Selasine and Justin, whispering some prayers that were no longer part of the liturgical traditions. She tilted her head, looking at Selasine, "What happened to the boy?"

Selasine let out a deep sigh. "Sliced throat. Looks like it was done stealthily. I got to him in time to bring him back; he couldn't have been gone long," he replied.

Maréli's face became grave. "And Miranda? Where is she?"

Selasine shook his head, exhaustion clouding his thoughts. "I'm not sure. She's not in her tent."

The chief healer frowned. "Even if this was somebody in the church's doing, they wouldn't have done that to the boy," she reasoned.

Selasine pressed his hands to the ground and stood up. He gripped his sword firmly in his hand. He thought back to yesterday and realized that the brilliance radiating from Miranda could have been visible for miles, maybe even across the mountain. Furthermore, the caves pouring through these mountains could give the pirates any number of points from which they could observe what was happening in the base camp. As his thoughts began to solidify, his face began to contort with anger and worry. "The exploding pirate. He was a distraction. Erk did this. That's why they tried to slay Justin with impunity. They must have realized what happened yesterday and who we can thank for the miracle. Miranda was helpless after yesterday afternoon. If my instincts are correct, they took her."

August reached out to help prevent his mentor from falling

after a sudden, lurching motion forward. "Why would they take her and not just kill her?" the acolyte questioned, fearing for his friend.

"They want her power. It's a hallmark of chaos. Power for power's sake. We have to get her back." Selasine disappeared into his own tent. Emerging a moment later with two adventuring packs, he shoved one into August's hands. "We have no time to waste. We have a better chance to find her if we go together and we go quietly."

August nodded, looking sad at Justin as he rested on the ground. "Can we at least spare a moment to put him in the tent?" the young man asked. Selasine nodded, grabbing Justin by his shoulders. August lifted Justin's feet, and the two placed him in the tent, covering him with a warm blanket.

As they exited the tent, Selasine's heart was heavy for the acolyte he had saved. "Be with him, Sword of Justice. Be a light to guide his path and shower your blessings upon him," he prayed, looking back at the tent where Justin rested. "Please be okay, Miranda," Selasine whispered, gazing at the mountains opposite the camp.

***

Thomas awoke, his extremities numb and his breathing shallow. The early spring air seemed crisp and warm compared to the cold coursing through his veins. Unable to stand, he dug his fists into the floor of his cabin, forcing his body to move. The exertion started to warm his muscles, but the lingering pain from the cold made each inch agonizing. "Telisi, Iria, please. Can you hear me?" he called out to his darkened home. Farzg's chill had extinguished the flame in the hearth and any candles or torches that might have been burning otherwise.

Night had fallen over the little cottage in the woods, just a couple of miles outside of the fortified walls of Devitus.

"Yulesta, yolasha," Thomas cried, elven words for wife and daughter.

After an eternity of crawling, he found himself in his bedroom. From the floor, he could see there were two people in the bed. It took all of his strength to bring himself up to the bed, confirming that Iria and Telisi both were lying there, Telisi wrapped in her mother's arms.

"Iria," Thomas choked, using the last of his strength to pull himself into the bed. Reaching out to her, she felt unbelievably frigid. "Iriliandria, wake, please. Yulesta." His extremities had begun to feel sensations again, but Iria's skin was so cold that he couldn't touch her for long. "Warm her, please, Invictus, help." Reaching for his holy symbol, his fingers could not feel it in his hand. "Telisi, yolasha, please wake. Daddy is home. I brought you some sweets from town, they're sweet, just like you. You can have an extra today if you wake up, yolasha. Please, please." His heart couldn't bear the reality. He squeezed the holy symbol of Invictus so tight in his hand that it pierced the skin of his palm. "Please, Sword of Justice, lend me your strength. What chaos has wrought, let it be undone." It seemed that his prayers fell on deaf ears.

Thomas spent the night holding their frozen bodies in his arms, unable to pray or speak. The tears he shed could have filled the ocean.

Chapter 5
The Face of Chaos

iranda's eyes crept open, finding herself in a cave lit by two torches. As she came to her senses, she realized she had been unconscious on an unfamiliar table. She sat up, still in her battlemail. Her braids had frayed and begun to come loose. Brushing the stray hair out of her face, she looked around. This particular cavern seemed to be an opening point for a tunnel that ran through the mountain. She was alone in the cave. "Hello?" she said in a hushed tone. Her voice echoed off the wall back to her.

"Good, yer finally awake. I got tired of carryin' ya," a disembodied voice spoke out.

Her hand went for her sword but only found the scabbard on her belt. She gave a panicked look around the room. "Who is there? Show yourself!" she demanded in an attempt to sound intimidating. The melodic nature of her voice would not have bothered a wild deer.

"Relax, lass. Not gonna hurt ye." A man materialized out of

thin air, a pirate roughly the same height as Miranda. His head was wrapped in a black turban, and a scraggly black and graying beard hung from his chin. He looked very unkempt, and an unwashed smell permeated the air as he appeared. "Call me Shalo; I'm here to get ye through these caves without killin' yerself."

Miranda blinked in confusion. "Wait, how did I get here? Where are we?" she asked as she slid her legs over the side of the table. The golden skirt of her battlemail dropped around her legs as she stood, giving a meshy-sounding clink as it rattled against the table.

"Yer in the gambling parlor, girl. Well, one of 'em. We've gotta go meet with the cap'n." Shalo scratched his beard, looking toward one of the tunnels that led out of the cave.

Using what she knew about the pirates, Miranda could piece together that she was in the cave network underneath the southern Trollcrag range that extended into the Undine Sea. "How did I get here?" She stood up, fear clutching at her chest.

"You had a nap after the light show yesterday. I jus' carried ye along while Apocalypse kept yer church friends busy." He scrunched his nose. "Well, most of 'em anyway."

Miranda stood, feeling vigorous and energetic after her brief, miracle-induced coma. "Where's my sword?" she asked, looking around the dimly lit cave.

The pirate tapped the scabbards attached to his belt. "I've got it, lass; ya won't be needin' it down here. Don' worry; the cap'n wants ya safe and sound."

Miranda began to size up the situation, but, realizing she wasn't immediately in harm's way, she relaxed. Her holy symbol still hung from her neck, comforting her. She could still channel the power of Invictus if things turned dangerous. Plus, she still had on her gauntlets with the sapphire blades. She had at least one line of defense. She found the cave's darkness unsettling, and being alone with a strange, smelly pirate only made it worse. His odor reminded her of garlic. "What does the 'captain' want from me?"

Shalo shrugged. "Dunno, don' care. Yer a pretty lass; he might want to make you his sea witch. Ya got some kinda power, too; it seems like I dunno much. I jus' follow orders."

Miranda tilted her head, her front hanging braids emphasizing the angle of her posture. "Uh, sea witch? Power?" She let out a sigh. Of course, it was the power. Carulus wanted her for that power. Now the pirates she came to help destroy wanted her for the same mysterious power. "Does he know I have no idea how to control the power?"

Shalo laughed. "I dunno, ya have te ask him. If ye get a move on, we can get there in an hour."

Unsure of what might happen if she went with Shalo, she felt very certain of what would happen if she didn't. She had seen the injuries inflicted by the traps that littered the caves. She knew that some of the pirates possessed terrifying uncanny magic. But right now, she only had a single pirate standing between her and freedom. Well, a single pirate and no idea how to get out of these caves. She bit her lip while she considered her options. "Hey, Shalo?"

Not expecting such a gentle, casual use of his name, he turned to face Miranda. "Wut?" he replied in a guttural way.

"Thank you for showing me through the caves. I'll trust you to get me to the captain safely."

Gratitude? Shalo couldn't make sense of what he just heard. He kidnapped her, killed the priest guarding her tent, and possessed her only weapon. "Uh, right. Jus' followin' orders."

Shalo made good on his promise to keep Miranda safe as they moved through the caverns. He showed her how to recognize the traps that the pirates had constructed throughout the cave network. She couldn't figure out how they worked, but she learned the signs to look for to avoid them. After half an hour of traversing the underground terrain, the two found themselves in a wide cavern with many tunnels extending from different directions and heights. Before they entered the cavern, Shalo gave a warning gesture to Miranda.

"Careful, lass. This one can lead ya into the Underrealm. Sometimes we get, uh, visitors."

Miranda looked into the tunnel, curiosity sparkling in her bright blue eyes in the torchlight. "Visitors?" she asked, trying to peer into the cave before her.

"Nasties from the Underrealm. They get hungry 'n come up

this way if they can't find anything below. Be alert."

Miranda gave a soft, whimpering request, "Can I have my sword?" The music in her voice expressed her fear and uncertainty.

Shalo narrowed his eyes. "Course not, lass. Yer my prisoner!"

She looked into the cave with numerous tunnels, a gut feeling telling her she needed her sword. She whispered a prayer and clutched her holy symbol, causing it to light up brighter than a high-quality torch. Holding it up to the cavern, they could see small, mushroom-shaped figures skulking around, diving away into the shadows when Miranda shined her light in their direction. "Are you sure I can't have my sword?" she insisted.

With a grumble, Shalo reached for one of his scabbards and withdrew her sword, passing it to her. After he gave it to her, he immediately dissipated into the air. Miranda looked around in a brief panic, but she quickly realized that his uncanny magic probably allowed him to fade in and out of sight. The magic was so effective that his odor disappeared with him. Shining her light into the cavern, she gripped her sword. She could see where many of the mushroom-shaped figures had tried to hide in the darkness, perhaps planning an ambush. The tunnels loomed especially dark, and the stalagmites scattered throughout the room gave the assailants plenty of hiding places. If Shalo was to be believed, Miranda thought she could rely on his support in a skirmish. She was, however, unsure of his combat ability. He was strong enough if he had carried her from the base camp to here. If these mushroom-shaped creatures attacked, she would soon know. Her thoughts were interrupted by a whisper.

"Meet me in the middle o' the cave." Miranda hoped that Shalo's invisibility would give them an edge if they faced any danger.

Miranda started into the cavern, the shadows bending away from her glowing holy symbol. The long outlines of the stalagmites were slightly unnerving, and the looming mushroom-shaped figures could scatter behind them easily. They appeared individually to be no larger than a small dog, with at least a dozen of them diving behind stalagmites every time Miranda pointed the light in their direction. Gripping her sword in hand, she found herself chewing her lip in anxiousness. She had fought magical beasts and bandits alongside Selasine and the other acolytes, but Selasine was a gifted warpriest. He would prepare himself and his pupils with divine enhancements that made fighting safer. Plus, Selasine would be the one to always kill the beasts, anyway. Thinking on that for a moment, she clutched her holy symbol again. She whispered, "Please, Invictus. Protect us from harm and guide our hands against chaos." A swirl of light surrounded her body, and she could feel the familiar sensation of Invictus's strength coursing through her. It wasn't as strong as Selasine's blessings, but she could feel the difference. Invictus had answered her prayers, making her feel bolder and more prepared.

As she neared the center of the cavern, she realized that the mushroom-shaped shadows were closing in on her. She hoped that Shalo had stayed close by and that perhaps his invisibility would allow him to make a surprise attack. The patter of footsteps behind her interrupted her thinking. Shining her lit holy symbol around her, she realized she was surrounded. These strange mushroom-like creatures were no longer afraid of her light. She readied her sword as the creatures stalked toward her, and she noticed that under each mushroom cap, she could see two black eyes and a small beak centered beneath them. Their legs and arms looked like separate fungal growths that had burst from the mushroom's stalk, but their short length made the creatures look almost silly as they scampered toward her slowly.

Then, Miranda realized what made these little things dangerous. From about twenty feet away, the mushroom creatures lowered their heads and pointed them at her. A visible burst of spores rushed at Miranda, and before she could react, the spores dissipated and scattered around her. The protection granted to her by Invictus shielded away the cloud that certainly would have been unwise to inhale. Miranda charged forward, hoping to startle the small creatures and return them to the shadows. She brandished her sword, making a side-to-side chopping motion with the tip angled at the ground to slash at the tiny creatures. To her surprise, the creatures did not retreat and began to cluster together to stand their ground.

Maybe eight or nine were in this group as they closed into the same space. As Miranda found herself within striking distance, she made a concerted effort to swipe at their mushroom caps. Before she could, however, a shrieking, terrifying sound began to emanate from the cluster. Their small beaks resonated together, making an amplified, distressing noise. Miranda instinctively covered her ears as the divine barrier did not seem to affect the sound. The sound rattled her brain so much that she did not realize a separate cluster of mushroom creatures had also begun to screech behind her. After a moment, the shrieking lessened, and she readjusted her grip on her sword, giving a mighty swing. As her blade connected, the shrill cries turned louder. This time, the divine protective shield around her activated, blocking a sonic wave of force that surely would have blasted Miranda. As a result of the intensity of the shockwave and Miranda's inexperience with the protection prayer, the shield shattered, leaving Miranda to her own defenses. Fortunately, her strike swept through the fragile creatures and sliced through many of their soft caps. With her second swipe, she targeted the creatures she did not hit with her first swing. The onslaught of sound ceased almost immediately.

Miranda gave a brutal kick to scatter the creatures, hearing an organic crunch as her metal boot connected with the spongy flesh of the fungal beings. The injured and surviving creatures scattered toward the shadows, having underestimated their prey. Miranda took a moment to catch her breath, turning around to see Shalo collapsed amidst another cluster of mushroom creatures. His invisibility did not protect him from the spores, and they had caused him to fall asleep, rendering him vulnerable to the otherwise unthreatening beasts. Acting on instinct, Miranda charged at the fallen pirate, noting that the creatures had already begun to tear away at Shalo's flesh with their beaks.

By the time Miranda could scatter the feasting creatures, Shalo lay in a growing pool of his own blood. His vital signs were positive, but he was unconscious. Miranda checked his wounds. For their size, those mushroom creatures could deal substantial damage in a short time to a victim made helpless by their spores. With a quick healing prayer, she stopped the bleeding. Running her hands along her belt, she found that Shalo had not taken the pouch with the healing potions and supplies. Opening the bag, she rummaged through for a vial of chemicals that could be used to rouse victims of magical or trauma-induced sleep. Holding it under his nose briefly, Shalo started to gag and cough, waking him. Miranda noticed that his skin now glowed a tint of orange, an unsettling sight in the dark cave. She wondered what effects the spores would have long-term.

"Damn these beasties, lass. Mushbeaks, the worst kind," he said as he regained his faculties. Without a word, Miranda continued to work on the pirate's injuries, using some bandages from the pouch to wrap some of the deeper wounds that had barely closed after her initial prayer. She applied a balm that lessened the pain radiating from the bites, and a second prayer to Invictus gave Shalo the fortitude he needed to stand. "Guess I'm lucky yer favored by the gods, ya see?"

Miranda giggled. "Maybe they would favor you too if you gave them a reason to."

Her suggestion was so sincere that Shalo didn't know how to respond. A moment passed as he took some time to consider all the dressings she had put on his wounds. Miranda would have loved to have found her way back to the bishop and her friends, but she could never let a person die when she could have helped. Even though she knew it meant staying with this pirate a bit longer, she genuinely hoped he was not in pain from his injuries. "Ya sure made quick work of these bites, lass," he commented, hardly able to tell that moments ago, he was well on his way to bleeding to death.

She nodded. "I hope you can't feel them now; they looked pretty deep. If you need more pain reliever—"

Shalo interrupted her. "Nah, lass, 'tis not my first brawl with the little beasts. I inhaled some spores while I was sneaking around and passed right out. Glad I gave ye back yer blade." Miranda grimaced, expecting that he would demand she return the sword. Instead, he continued, "With yer skills as a healer, cap'n is really gonna like ya. I 'preciate ya myself, savin' yer own kidnapper like that."

Miranda shook her head. "I couldn't just let you die. Plus, I need your help to find the way out of here."

Shalo thought for a moment. "Ye didn't have to patch me up so well, though; I feel like a new pirate!" He checked his footing and their surroundings. After he was sure of himself, he walked to one of the tunnels, beckoning for Miranda to follow. He pointed to an etching in the rock that led into the tunnel, directing Miranda to look. "That symbol there, that's the mark that'll help ya get through the caves." She took note of the etching, two cutlasses roughly scratched into the rock with a chisel or some other tool. This information might have helped those first waves of clergy as they explored the caves, she thought. However, she was not able to relay that information to anybody. For the moment, she could only bide her time and absorb as much information about the pirates and the cave networks as possible.

Miranda wondered why she had not seen any other pirates in the caves. The fighting had been fiercest in the afternoon the day before. Perhaps it was enough to prompt the pirates into retreating? She had no way of knowing where she was relative to the church army. Her helplessness made her uncomfortable. She followed Shalo in silence for a while longer until they emerged from the cave network on the coast of the Undine Sea. The sudden shift from the darkness of the caves to the bright daylight of early afternoon made Miranda shield her eyes with her hand, resting it above her brow. The mountains behind them spired upward, making a tall ridge of peaks that sliced the land and the sea into two parts firmly separated. Miranda knew that her friends were on the other side of those mountains. She whispered a prayer on their behalf.

Palm trees littered the mountainside on the coastal side of the caves. The distance between the cave and the sea was barely half a mile, the white sand glowing in the afternoon sun. Miranda saw several ships waiting in the depths of the sea in front of her while smaller craft dotted the beach as groups of pirates loaded supplies and loot to take to the seaworthy vessels. Perhaps the attack had worked, and the pirates were attempting to escape? She knew their retreat would lead them into a trap as the naval forces of Claston were waiting further out to sea. At least, that is what Selasine told her.

Shalo walked several paces ahead of Miranda and kept gesturing impatiently to her. His hurried beckoning became more frantic as he led her toward the beach. Other pirates began to notice them, drawing their weapons when they saw Miranda dressed in her battlemail. For the first time, she realized how recognizable her armor made her and the danger that could pose. Fortunately, Shalo's company made the open hostility short-lived as he rebuked them with a single-hand signal. Miranda had to hustle to keep up with him, as Shalo seemed to be running. Training with Selasine made it easy to keep up with the pirate, but she didn't quite understand Shalo's hurry.

A short distance north on the beach, Miranda could see large docks built out into the Undine Sea. A complex of shanties spread out near the docks, making a small seaside town that would have been quaint and welcoming were it not for the presumably vicious residents. Miranda tried to take in as much of her surroundings as possible but feared what might happen if she did not keep close to Shalo. As they neared the docks and shanty town, Miranda could see pirates hurriedly loading goods onto the anchored ships. Shalo beckoned again, stopping and turning to face her. "Quick lass, yer 'bout to meet the cap'n."

Despite Shalo's insistence, she slowed her pace, her eyes looking to the crowds of pirates moving frantically on the docks. One figure stood out as well-dressed, but his height allowed him to hide easily in the crowd of other pirates. This individual seemed to notice Shalo's hurried approach. Miranda could swear he was meandering slowly toward the stairs down to the sandy beach. The well-dressed stranger stood at the top of those stairs that led to the docks, Miranda and Shalo approaching from the bottom.

Miranda looked upward at the stranger, presuming that this was the captain. He seemed to be a handsome elf approaching middle age and looked to be almost a foot shorter than her, even though he loomed at the top of the stairs. Golden hair spilled around his shoulders from beneath a tricorn hat, with an elaborate red jacket draped around his frame. From the bottom of the stairs, Miranda could see his gray eyes analyzing the two of them standing in the sand. His features were elven and sharp, but Miranda thought he had a handsome, kind face. She felt no malice, even as his lips drew into an evil smile.

"The girl with the red hair. The miracle worker," the elf said, all of his attention focused on Shalo and Miranda.

"Aye, cap'n," Shalo shouted, gesturing to the stairs and looking at Miranda. She followed his cue, and her eyes locked with the captain's cold stare. Her countenance was expressionless; she was a captive, after all.

"It seems she's armed, Shalo. Why didn't you take the girl's weapon?" the captain asked as Miranda neared the top of the stairs, Shalo only two steps behind her.

"Tell ye the truth, cap'n, this lass saved my life from the shrooms in the labyrinth," he held up his bandaged arms and pointed to the evidence of his injuries. "I didn' dare let her go unarmed when ye wanted her unharmed."

The captain tilted his head as he and Miranda stood face to face, and he peered up at her with scrutiny. Her battlemail glinted in the afternoon sunlight, reflecting mithril and gold hues around her, making her seem more serene and mystical. Hiding her emotions, her lips were pursed into an interrogative note as she returned the pirate captain's stare. He finally spoke directly to her, "So, you saved Shalo from mushbeaks and followed him here willingly?"

Miranda's lips relaxed into a soft smile, and she nodded, her loosened braids bouncing on the breastplate of the battlemail.

The elf smiled broadly, extending an arm to take her by the hand. "Dread Pirate Lord Erk the Radiant at your humble service."

Miranda, not quite expecting the elf that stood before her to be an infamous pirate, stretched out her arm as the pirate captain lifted her hand to his lips and kissed the armored gauntlet on her hand. She felt enthralled by how he carried himself with confidence and poise, and her trepidation about meeting him melted under the warmth of his smile. Realizing she had yet to honor her part of the social contract of introductions, she took a quick breath. "Oh, Miranda. I'm Miranda, Acolyte of Invictus."

Turning his head to the side slightly, Erk's brow raised. "Just a role in the church? No family name? No origin story?" he replied, dubiousness evident in his voice.

His insistence caught her off-guard. "My parents' family name was Hyacinth, but I was orphaned before I was old enough to remember them very well," she replied, her eyes cast off to the side with a bit of shame.

Erk still had her hand in his, and he clasped it, gauntlet and all, sweetly between his palms. "Do not be ashamed of your background or family name, Miranda." His voice was rich and comforting. Miranda knew she should have felt something gross, unsettling, or otherwise revolting from someone with such a nefarious, chaotic background. Instead, she felt like her heart was stuck in her throat and that her ability to rationalize was swept upside down.

"Well, Dread Pirate Lord Erk—" she started to speak.

"Please, call me Erk. I want you to think of me as a friend. I am a deadly friend, which means I'm an even deadlier enemy. But please, not so formal."

Miranda lost her words. What in the world was going on? Was he using enchantment magic to sway her will? Had she been drugged? Or was this vile example of baseness capable through chaos truly this charming? She mentally screamed at herself to say something.

"Okay, Erk. Thank you for welcoming me," she said, her voice unintentionally inflecting so her statement sounded like a question.

"Shalo!" Erk commanded, his voice deep and authoritative now.

"Sir," he said, half at attention, distracted by some baubles he had pulled from a pouch.

"See that Miranda will stay in the dressing room on The Neb. Tell Jax I set you to it if he complains. Tell him I'll put his tongue in that jar in my lavatory if he complains again."

This time, Shalo replied more enthusiastically. "Sir!" and he marched away toward the docks.

Erk turned back to Miranda, whose expression had gone from bewilderment to confusion. "I know the notice is short, my dear, but we must depart for our next adventure soon. I hope that you'll be our guest on the voyage." His eyes cut severely, and then Miranda understood. The tone of his voice, his demeanor, and even his appearance seemed to change as he turned his back. "Otherwise, you'll be along as our prisoner, and that never goes well for a pretty lass at sea." Erk felt his stomach drop. He turned his back because he couldn't stand to see her reaction. It didn't feel right to threaten the girl. There was somebody in his life that would kill him without a second thought if they found out he had said something so perverse. He really didn't relish his title as a Dread Pirate Lord anyway, but in his heart, he knew that violence had the potential to make solutions to his current problem much easier. He had a reputation to live up to and a goal to realize.

Miranda gulped, gripping her holy symbol out of nervous habit. She thought, "So, is this the true face of chaos?" The question echoed in her mind. She could see the pirate's body language. It made her more curious than terrified, and she was incredibly terrified.

***

The primordial place was special for many reasons. While in this place, the gods were omnipresent but not omnipotent. To use the full extent of their immense power, they would have to descend upon the mortal realm, the center of existence. Invictus stood in the primordial place, with yellow, gold, and gray clouds surrounding him. A series of prayers had been bombarding his divine consciousness since yesterday. His followers seemed gripped in the throes of war, something he had experienced many times over his godhood. This time, however, the prayers were strange.

"Find Miranda," he heard at the end of one of the prayers. He knew that name, but in the primordial place, it could take time for his sentience to catch up to his ruminations.

Two other things made the primordial place special: here, the avatars of the gods could not fight with each other, and in this place, it was almost impossible to channel all of their divinity through mortals. Thus, the gods would be limited in the prayers that they could answer. Invictus felt a familiar presence in the primordial place with him. He ignored it at first, listening to the prayers of his followers instead.

The familiar presence spoke with the voice of a small child. "Chaos, havoc, and winds of change. Dance on the graves of those who took our names. What say you, interloper?"

Invictus's mind was pulled away from the numerous voices whispering in the clouds. His eyes narrowed with disdain. "Indervill. To what do I owe the displeasure?"

Some swirling clouds rushed together, forming a physical representation of Indervill's avatar. In this particular moment, it manifested in the form of a lamia, the head, and torso of a beautiful woman fused with the tail of a mighty serpent. Its eyes were black and hollow, but a closer look would reveal stars and galaxies ripped from existence by the forces of chaos. Its voice now spoke polyphonically, several different voices layered for an unsettling effect. "Haughty and prideful, too stubborn to see when things are out of your control. I win this time and taunt you, I must. Can you spare a coin for the poor and feed your own children? Maybe you haven't seen what I have."

Invictus tried to ignore Indervill, returning his mind to the prayers of his followers. There was an increase in specific prayers for the girl Miranda, and they started to echo more loudly in his mind. Nevertheless, chaos embodied continued to chide and provoke him.

"Like two children at play, but I have the toy. You want to play with my toys but do not want to pay the price. Mine, mine, mine. And you can't catch me. I'm too fast for you." At its best, Indervill spoke in riddles, but at its worst, its ramblings were incoherent. Invictus didn't have the time to try and decipher the meaning until he remembered the miracle Miranda had manifested when she resurrected that family.

"The girl is not a plaything, you realize?" Invictus replied sternly, solemnly.

"Toys and trains, blocks and stains. Stains of blood, the color of her hair, for where she treads, all will know suffering and chaos. Those faithful to entropy more so will it than those that cling to the lie of order. Build your illusions, brother, but don't cry when your castle of glass shatters around your knees!"

Invictus inhaled deeply, concentrating. With enough effort, the clouds around him swirled and twisted into a vision. Before him, he could see Thomas Selasine and one of his pupils skulking through a dark cave with minimal light. Their expressions were serious; Invictus had a feeling that Indervill's rambling had something to do with these two. With such focus, Invictus could hear their prayers more clearly.

"Light of Lexcord, Sword of Justice, guide us against the forces of chaos. Let us find Miranda and bring her back from the grip of uncertainty. Shine a path before us so that we, agents of order, may right that which has been wronged."

Invictus smiled as he stretched his presence throughout all of reality. From the primordial place, he could sense all of his followers. The one that these two men sought, Miranda, was close to their location but still far away. Invictus channeled his divine power into the mortal realm, using that energy to light a path through the darkness for his followers.

Invictus turned his attention back to Indervill. "Nobody wants to play with a child who treats others like objects. You will see your error, eventually."

Without more taunting, Indervill seemed to recede into the primordial place, having finished its game with the god of justice and order.

Chapter 6
Flower Petals

elasine held up his torch, trying to pierce the darkness before him. He and August had identified a smaller network of caves near the base camp that would have been quick access for someone to have infiltrated the palisades. If one of the pirates had taken Miranda, these caves would have been a likely first destination. There were no eyewitnesses, however, as nobody in the base camp noticed suspicious activity regarding Miranda's tent until Selasine had found Justin, swiftly assassinated in silence.

There were plenty of traps, but Selasine identified a key flaw in Carulus's plan. The traps were intended to inflict injury on large numbers. With enough of these small booby traps, even a sizable force could lose morale and strength. Erk's pirates had probably realized that their greatest threats would send large numbers, and the traps in the caves reflected that. Plus, moving through the cave network in smaller numbers would make it easier to avoid these traps altogether, an advantage that would keep large forces of interlopers from making their way under the towering mountains. Furthermore, if the pirates needed to flee the beach, they could escape to the countryside under the mountain. It served as a brilliant buffer against the forces of order.

That realization made Selasine curse himself. Carulus's plan was doomed from the beginning, and Miranda was now paying the price for his poor planning. While the Path of the Sword of Justice favored large-scale, government and church-sanctioned action, enforcing order was not limited to a marching army. Carulus should have sent a small, unnoticeable force to target key individuals within Erk's hierarchy instead of a grandstanding invasion of the entire region. None of that mattered at this point, though. Selasine's only goal was to make sure Miranda was safe.

Selasine's internal dialogue was interrupted by the sound of a trap springing. August had enough time to shout a warning as he felt his foot pull a tripwire. A large rock dislodged and rolled between them, crashing into a larger boulder nearby. At best, a group could have interrupted the boulder as it rolled toward them somehow. At worst, scattering troops could have caused enough chaos for somebody to break their leg trying to escape. Since it was just August and Selasine, the boulder rolled harmlessly between them. Selasine couldn't help but give a helpless sigh, frustrated with the lack of reconnaissance conducted by the high priest. The only information he even considered to take Miranda on this doomed expedition was the rumors of her ability to heal injuries that she shouldn't have been able to.

As they traversed the caverns beneath the mountains, August tried to maintain a crude map to help prevent them from moving in circles. It seemed to work at first, but eventually, some of the tunnels led to caverns identical to the ones they were in previously. Selasine's compass did not function well under the mountain. After a couple of hours of moving through the tunnels, he and August had lost their sense of direction. The only thing that could convince them they were moving forward were traps that had not yet been activated.

They eventually found themselves in a massive cavern with

numerous tunnels extending in so many directions that Selasine felt his heart sink. He and August stood in the center of the cavern, evaluating their options and checking the cave for activity. There was a noticeable puddle of blood in the center of the cavern. Bending over to look at it closely, August gave Selasine a concerned look. "It's fresh. Well, recent enough that whoever bled here is still feeling it."

Selasine's heart sank further. Could this be the result of Miranda trying to make an escape? Had she escaped and gotten lost in the caverns? The blood did not hint at whom it belonged or where that person might have gone. Selasine took a moment to analyze the cavern. In the torchlight, he could barely discern that another scuffle had happened about thirty feet from the pool of blood. He approached the scene, noticing a few slain mushbeaks, their mushroom caps sliced wide open, exposing their strange fungal brains. "August," he whispered gruffly, trying to get his pupil's attention.

The young man joined his mentor as they analyzed the scene. "Looks like it's not just pirates that we need to worry about here," August commented, gazing at the corpses.

"That means if Miranda is okay, she might not be for long. We have to find our way through here," Selasine replied, feeling the urgency of their task. That urgency spiraled into desperation as he counted tunnels. There were at least eight ways to leave this cavern, maybe more if the holes in the ceiling and floor led to other tunnel networks. He sighed with frustration, refusing to give in to the seed of hopelessness in his consciousness. He whispered a prayer to Invictus for guidance as he and August returned to the center of the cavern.

A sound from one of the higher tunnels caught their attention. Selasine drew his sword and withdrew a sizable shield from his back. He handed the torch to August, preparing to deal with any threat. His blade was an ornate, magical sword that emitted a red hue. The shield was a steel kite that was particularly light for its size. August took the torch from his mentor and readied his sword. With the torch in his left hand, he could not wield his shield, but he hoped he would not need it.

A flitting sound filled the air. August held up the torch

higher, and he and Selasine could see a stream of shadows pouring out of one of the tunnels about thirty feet in the air. "Brace yourself," Selasine warned. The shadows began to fly into a different, ground level tunnel.

August nodded and gripped his holy symbol. "Sword of Justice, lend us your aid. Fortify us against the onslaught of chaos and let us lay low the enemy," he prayed. A brilliant flash shone from his holy symbol, covering them in a faint, purple aura.

The shadows continued to surge out of the tunnel. Their swooping path led them almost directly overhead Selasine and August. A moment after August finished his prayer, an unseen force suddenly slammed into him, knocking him back a few steps. Whatever it was, he felt claws trying to grab him, but his plate armor kept them from piercing his torso. He then felt a searing pain in his right arm. Examining it in the torchlight, the creature's talon must have torn into him, causing a serious injury.

"August!" Selasine shouted, swinging his blade through the air a moment too late to strike whatever had hit the acolyte. Before he had time to redirect, a similar force slammed into the bishop.

The acolyte recognized what it was this time. "Giant bats?" he asked out loud to confirm.

Selasine reacted to the force with a fierce jab from his sword. A loud screech indicated a true strike. The bishop replied, "Looks like it; keep your guard up. They'll strike from the air, confusing us for food. Give back as hard as they give, and they'll tire," he instructed. The giant bat remained skewered on his sword. Its body was at least four feet long, and its wingspan was incredible.

The pain in August's arm made it difficult to wield his weapon. He could feel the warmth of his blood pouring down his arm. The injury was probably worse than it felt. His eyes skimmed the upper reaches of the large cavern. The shadows were still spilling from the upper tunnel to the different one on the ground level. Based on the estimated time of day, the acolyte assumed the other tunnel did not lead outside. The commotion in the caves over the last day must have confused the bats, and now they were looking for a meal anywhere they could find it. August sheathed his sword and crouched down. The pain was starting to get to him.

Selasine noticed his pupil's condition and rushed toward him. He freed his sword from the dead bat. In their initial attack, the assailants had knocked Selasine and August about fifteen feet apart. As the bishop approached the acolyte, another bat dove at him. It drew up short when Selasine readied a deadly counter, the bat recognizing the threat these two posed. August's blessing on the two of them was working. It would keep weak-minded foes at bay as long as the two of them could see their assailants.

In the meantime, August took out the healing potion Miranda had given him. He felt so stupid for his condescending remark when she offered it to him. Playing big brother was a fine line to walk, but, as usual, Miranda's wish to be helpful was about to pay off. He drank the contents of the vial, his wounds sealing and healing rapidly. The bishop reached him just as the bleeding stopped.

Selasine was about to sheath his sword to pray for August's wound when he caught another bat diving to attack. Even though August was already crouching, Selasine still yelled, "Duck!" August dove to the ground. The swooping assault was too fast to stop, and the bat impaled its own face on Selasine's sword, which was in his outstretched arm. A spray of blood filled the air, but then the bat's limp body fell on August.

"Talirix volïs!" the acolyte cursed as the weight crunched down on him. The pain from the gash was starting to subside, so he pushed the bat off him. August had dropped the torch, causing it to dim. In turn, the fluttering sound overhead seemed to redirect.

As August lay on the ground, the bishop asked him, "Are you alright?"

The acolyte nodded. "Thanks to Miranda. The healing potion," he explained.

Selasine gave a half smile, "As I said, things never go according to plan. We must get out of this cavern; we can't afford to stand here fighting with vermin all day."

The bishop crouched low to the ground with August. The

bats seemed bothered by the light. After waiting on the ground with the dimmed light, almost motionless, Selasine heard August have an excited realization. "Aha! Bishop, can I put out the torch?"

Selasine looked at his pupil in disbelief. "What? Why?"

"They seem drawn to the light. Maybe it will buy us a few moments."

The bishop looked up at the shadows, still pouring from the cavern. His instincts told him it was worth a try. "Let's see what happens," he finally commented. He had another trick up his sleeve in case they needed light quickly.

August lowered his torch to the ground, putting it out with the fine dust on the rock floor. His request began to make sense in the lessened light. The sound of the bats in the air continued, but the dive bombing attacks ceased.

Suddenly, Selasine thought he could discern a faint glow on one of the paths through the cavern. "August! Look!" he whispered. Before them was a trail of glowing flower petals, clearly leading to one of the tunnels that egressed from the cavern. Feeling a surge of faith and hope, the two began to follow the petals in pitch black. After their eyes adjusted to the darkness, the petals glowed brightly enough to light their way, highlighting the path beneath their feet. After following the tunnel for a distance, they came to another, much smaller cavern. This room was well lit by torches and bore the effects of its pirate inhabitants. Mugs rested on a large table, and barrels of some kind of beer or mead sat on the ends of the tables. Maps and tapestries had been haphazardly hammered into the rock walls. "I think we're on the right track," Selasine whispered, certain that this would have served as some kind of choke point had the church's army identified the correct tunnel. The two proceeded cautiously, weapons at the ready instead of torches.

The tunnels seemed bizarrely quiet, especially as the evidence of the presence of pirates began to increase. Had Carulus's prediction that the pirates would flee come to pass? Selasine cursed again, realizing they would take Miranda with them if they had her as a captive. Surely Carulus would have to pay for his short-sighted plan. But he could worry about that later. If his speculation was accurate, they had very little time.

Any time the path diverged, Selasine and August could find the glowing flower petals indicating which way they should go. The remaining traps in the tunnels were adorned with the delicate petals, giving the two enough warning to avoid them. It took them only fifteen minutes to traverse more caverns than they had in the preceding six hours. Surely it was approaching noon by now. Selasine imagined the high priest's reaction to an abandoned cave network, simultaneously giving him a justified laugh and a disillusioned sigh. When the flower petals stopped appearing, Selasine and August could make out the bright sunlight at the end of the tunnel they were in. They both approached the exit cautiously, trading a knowing glance of preparedness.

The sunlight washed over them, warming their spirits as much as their bodies. As their eyes adjusted to the brightness, they saw that Selasine's speculations seemed accurate. Several skiffs and lifeboats littered the coast, a beautiful white sand beach that stretched northward. The immediate coastline was completely abuzz with activity as pirates and common folk loaded possessions and other goods onto the crafts. Fortunately for August and Selasine, they could stay relatively hidden among the palm trees that dotted the side of the mountain that overlooked the beach. Getting a bearing on the cardinal directions using the sun and the estimated time of day, Selasine looked north to see a village of sea shanties and docks nestled into a well-protected bay on the coast.

Selasine nodded toward the village, and August followed with his eyes. The shanty town also looked bustling. It was maybe a mile away, but a set of stairs leading up to the docks and shanties sat only half a mile away. A knot immediately formed in Selasine's throat as he observed the scene. He could see Miranda at the top of the stairs and a short-statured human or an average-sized elf standing face to face. The shorter figure wore a red jacket that was bolder and more elegant than the average pirate garb. Miranda was easy to spot due to her battlemail.

"There!" August exclaimed, losing his sense of stealth as he saw his friend. His arm extended, pointing directly to their goal.

His error had immediate consequences. A group of pirates on the shore heard the shout, but they did not seem to be able to pinpoint the source. He and Selasine immediately sought cover behind trees and shrubs that littered the mountainside. August's face burned with shame, realizing his mistake. Anyone approaching the caves would have to climb a steep hill, giving the two clerics a high ground advantage. The pirates, unwilling to abandon their current task, gave a cursory look up the hillside. Seeing nothing out of the ordinary, they dismissed the noise as unimportant.

Unfortunately, when the pirates abandoned their search, Selasine and August could no longer see Miranda or the person in the red coat. Selasine knew August would be unnecessarily hard on himself, so he gripped his pupil by the shoulder. "Inexperience is no reason to blame yourself. At least we know she's still okay for now, right? Let's put that enthusiasm to good use and get her out of here." Selasine tried to force a smile, and August continued to look at the ground. Then, with a narrow gaze, he looked at his mentor.

"Sir. You have an eyepatch," August murmured, his brain ahead of his words.

Selasine's head tilted to the side, not expecting his pupil's words. "Yes, I do."

August then started to smile. "It's the perfect pirate disguise!" The young man's demeanor shifted quickly as a plan formed in his mind.

Selasine's nose wrinkled in debate. "Disguises? Deception for personal gain is a tenet of chaos." His eyes lit up after he recited the rule. "But in this case, it's not for personal gain! August, you're brilliant."

The two of them turned their attention to the caves behind them. Maybe they could find enough in that final cavern to dress as pirates to locate and extract Miranda from the shanty town. As they returned to the entrance from which they emerged, they felt a surge of excitement. Miranda was okay, and they felt like they were very close to the end of this extended nightmare. Even in disguise, however, they knew they would need to avoid any undue attention. A hasty disguise could be a death sentence for both of them.

Back in the cave, they found tunics, hats, turbans, and a few accessories like seashell necklaces and earrings. Selasine and August put together outfits that they thought made them look menacing. Unfortunately, they didn't have a mirror to check the solidarity of their disguises. To cope, they checked each other's outfits and helped one another look as pirate-like as possible. They prayed for safety and returned outside. Behind them, however, they could hear the din of soldiers moving through the caves. Perhaps a contingent of troops had found the correct path? They didn't have time to stay and check, and even if they did, they did not want to be caught by Carulus's troops while dressed as pirates. As such, they came running out of the cave. As they did, they passed by a lone pirate who was now watching the cave.

This single pirate was barely over five feet tall and looked malnourished. Selasine and August only afforded him a glance as they rushed past him, running down the hillside toward the beach. In passing, Selasine noticed his features looked ragged and disheveled. His shoulders slumped forward, and he wore a gray tunic that covered most of his gaunt frame. The most striking feature, however, was his eyes, which appeared to be sunken deep inside the man's skull. The pirate made no effort to stop Selasine and August as they ran by, giving them hope that their disguises were working. Furthermore, they suspected an onslaught of Invictus's faithful was hot on their trail, meaning others could deal with this strange pirate.

Selasine and August slowed their pace to a casual walk to avoid attracting the attention of other pirates. It only took them a few minutes to reach the stairs that ascended to the shanty town on the hillside. They now stood in the last place they saw Miranda. Taking in their surroundings, their fear of discovery eased as they stood easily within viewing distance, the pirates around them not giving them a second glance. Selasine furrowed his brow. "I wonder if the five thousand 'pirates' includes all these commoners?" he grumbled quietly.

August joined Selasine in examining the crowd. Though numerous pirates hastily made preparations to sail, both clerics quickly realized there were at least two or three commoners for every sailor or pirate in the crowd. They seemed panicked, trying to assist the pirates in prepping the numerous vessels at the docks to sail. Actually, it seemed that most of these people were in the process of being uprooted. Selasine had seen it before: peasants, commoners, and serfs fleeing the impending conquest of a mobilized army. He began to further question Carulus's motives in this ordeal.

Turning to August, Selasine spoke in a hushed voice. "I think Carulus overestimated what we would be dealing with here. Most of these people are common folk; there's no way there are five thousand pirates here," he spat. August nodded in agreement.

"They're on the run," the young acolyte replied. "That means we have to hurry. They'll take Miranda right out of port and into the trap set by the Claston navy." Selasine gave a swift nod in reply. The two joined the ebb and flow of the hasty crowd. Although August and Selasine were very tall and imposing, nobody in the crowd seemed to acknowledge their presence. Selasine breathed a sigh of relief as they looked for signs of Miranda in the crowd.

It wouldn't have been difficult to spot a girl with red hair in a radiant battlemail in a crowd like this. The lack of visual clues prompted Selasine to adopt a different strategy. He looked at his immediate surroundings and found a crate full of netting and rope. Picking it up, he walked purposefully. August followed suit, taking a different crate filled with sundry items. At this point, a passerby objected, "Hey, that's not yours!"

Selasine, in the worst possible pirate voice imaginable, replied, "Yarrr, it be fer yon captain." August cringed; so did Selasine, wondering why he didn't speak plainly.

Surprisingly, the ruse worked. The passerby added, "Well, you'd better hurry and get it to *The Nebula* before he raises the anchor. They were ready to go an hour ago."

Afraid to ask for directions, they rushed off into the crowd. They hoped they were headed in the right direction. Looking down toward the docks, they could see vessels of various sizes moored. As they examined the boats, they noticed a particular ship that overwhelmed any of the others present in the bay. An exquisite galleon, replete with three towering masts and six or seven decks adorned in gold and gemstone, caught the attention of many onlookers in the harbor as it started to push out to sea. The people and the pirates began to chant, "Long live the Captain! Long live the Captain!" Selasine looked at August, his eyes wide with horror. Was this the influence of Erk and his numerous followers? Did these people really trust and honor a nefarious leader that attracted the attention of Invictus's military might? Selasine suspected that some details were missing in the story of Erk.

It didn't matter, though. As Selasine began to turn his attention back to his immediate surroundings, he realized that a group of armed pirates had formed a semicircle behind himself and August. "These are the ones?" a brutish-looking pirate with a shaved head asked a commoner. The same commoner that had told Selasine to get to *The Nebula*.

Selasine gave a quick look to August. August's eyes looked ready for a fight as anger pulsed through his body. Selasine felt anger, too, knowing that Miranda was likely on that beautiful ship making its way to sea. Now, however, was not the time to brandish steel with abandon. They were outnumbered significantly, and further missteps could prove deadly. Selasine's warning glance set August at ease just enough to try and talk their way out of their current predicament.

"Is there a problem?" Selasine asked pointedly to the pirate with the shaved head.

"Those goods, you were supposed to take them to *The Nebula*?" he returned, a menacing cutlass in his hand.

"I thought so, but it looks like the captain has already set for the open sea," Selasine replied, feeling trapped between his deception and how bad he was at lying.

"Anybody working on the captain's crew would've known he wouldn't stay long with those fanatics coming through the caves. Or are you just incompetent?" the pirate retorted, attempting to provoke.

Selasine choked his pride to reply, "Of course we're incompetent! Can't you see we missed the departure?" his face honestly twisted with anger and embarrassment.

The pirates started to laugh and put their weapons away. The pirate with the shaved head took a step forward. "An idiot is a king on the open sea. Here, put those supplies on our ship," he said, gesturing to a different vessel anchored at the docks. "You can sail with us. I'm sure the captain will be glad you didn't desert." The look in his eyes screamed suspicion, but Selasine understood. In a culture built on plundering, there was no true code of law to protect life or property. This pirate had every right to be suspicious of him, just as Selasine was of the pirate.

Selasine hesitated for a moment. Committing to sailing with this group of pirates would possibly help them reach Miranda, but he didn't like the waiting game. He feared how the captain would treat Miranda on the voyage. Not knowing the destination made him even more uneasy. Still, perhaps this would be an opportunity to learn more about these pirates, their objectives, and why Carulus insisted on an all-out war with a poorly understood enemy.

Taking a deep breath, Selasine gave a nod. "Right away," he replied in reluctant compliance, adjusting the crate in his arms.

"Shame our first meeting was commandeering goods for the captain. I'm sure he had good reason," the pirate replied, insincerity dripping from every word. Selasine realized what kind of game he would have to play to keep August and himself safe on this journey.

"Absolutely a shame. Call me Thomas, boss. This is August. We're pretty handy in a fight," Selasine informed the pirates, walking toward the indicated ship.

The pirate wrinkled his nose in nonchalance. "I'm Gurd, captain of that vessel, *The Water Sprite*. This here is my first mate Chaz," he said, pointing to a pirate dressed in leather armor that looked more like a dancing uniform.

"We'll get to know you on the voyage then. Say, how do I know you'll take us back to the captain? Do you even know where he's headed?" Selasine asked with feigned distrust.

Gurd's eyes narrowed with even more suspicion, commenting, "You miss your departure and then want to interrogate us?"

Selasine tried to backpedal. "Oh, nothing like that, captain. I just don't want to try and chase *The Nebula* only to end up somewhere else. The Captain would have our hides doubly so."

Rolling his eyes, Gurd replied, "We're headed for the Isles Known for Nothing, just like everyone else. Should be safe from the fanatics until we can regroup and get our families resettled."

August had heard the name of those islands in many stories. They were infamous for being a magical place only findable by pirates seeking shelter from the law. He thought it ironic, then, that he and Selasine would be representatives of that law they were trying to hide from.

Selasine forced a laugh, "Well, I'm glad we're on the same page. We'll earn our keep on the way."

Gurd's harsh lips twisted into a piercing smile, "You'll do that and more; no stowaways allowed."

August and Selasine took their stolen goods onto the indicated ship. They could see *The Water Sprite* painted proudly along the bow of the ship. This wasn't the best idea they had ever had, but it also wasn't the worst outcome considering everything. Assuming Carulus's story to be accurate, a navy sent from Claston would likely be waiting for the pirates in a blockade in the central part of the Undine Sea. With any luck, they could catch up to Miranda while *The Nebula* stood off against that navy.

The Nebula was comfortably out to sea by now, and it seemed like the deck of that marvelous vessel was glowing in a purple light as brilliant as the sun. Recognizing it, Selasine set his cargo down on the deck. He and August waited for further orders in stunned silence. Miranda's healing gift currently belonged to Erk.

***

Drymouth stood silently at the entrance to the cave. Suddenly, two large pirates burst forward from the cave, sprinting down the hill behind him. If Erk's predictions were true, the fanatics would find their way through the caves any hour now. Those two must have been trapped between the invaders and the escape. "Better hurry; it's time to go," he said out loud, mostly to himself. He then sighed. He and Jacques stayed behind to "send a message," as Erk put it. Jacques's uncanny magic would let them join the captain later, teleporting them safely to the deck of *The Nebula*.

The enemy began to emerge from the cave minutes after the pirates ran past him. Seeing a lone pirate, the clerics and paladins formed a line in front of him. One of them demanded, "Surrender your weapons; you are to be arrested and interrogated. Resistance will only result in further bloodshed!"

Drymouth rolled his eyes, which already looked lifeless. "Let's get this over with," he mumbled in a voice nobody else could hear. His deep voice dragged out each word with a dry intonation. He stretched his gaunt frame as the enemy surrounded him, approaching him cautiously. Suddenly, one of the clerics shrieked in terror.

"It's the one! Run!"

The sudden break in discipline caused the enemy to hesitate. Drymouth flashed a sadistic smile as he said, again mostly to himself, "Too late." He opened his mouth, his tongue hanging out listlessly. As he inhaled, the front line of fanatics around him began to charge at him. That would be their last mistake. The uncanny magic began to work inside him. As he inhaled, he rapidly sucked the moisture out of every living thing within one hundred feet. The air filled with a sickening gargling sound as Drymouth breathed in deeply. The palm trees nearby instantly withered, shrubs crumpled, but its effects on humans and elves were the most horrific. Their skin began to shrivel tightly around their muscles, and their eyes liquified and joined the vortex of moisture spiraling into Drymouth's maw. After a single inhalation, the immediate surroundings were devastated. The members of Invictus's clergy immediately slumped in various states of death or agony. Those that survived wished for death, and Drymouth was glad to grant their wishes as he began to inhale a second time.

In less than a minute, at least a dozen corpses surrounded Drymouth in front of the cave. From the sounds coming from the cave, word had reached the others that he was waiting outside. He shrugged and mumbled, "This endless, agonizing thirst." He walked toward the entrance of the cave, licking his dry, cracked lips.

"So, you're the one responsible for our holdup on the first day," a voice boomed from the entrance of the cave.

Drymouth looked at the opening in the side of the

mountain. It stretched fifteen feet into the air, letting in enough light so that he could see a lone paladin standing there, a massive two-handed sword gripped in his hands. His armor shined tones of silver in the sunlight. Drymouth shrugged, "I guess I am, but you started this." His words were only audible to himself. Closing the distance, Drymouth inhaled again, snuffing out the plant life around him.

"Not going to work on me," the paladin taunted as the new vortex of moisture bubbled from all around him in a spherical shape, an invisible, protective barrier surrounding him. He charged at Drymouth without warning.

"This is bad," Drymouth mumbled to himself. Unarmed, unarmored, and unconcerned, he stood in place, accepting his fate.

The paladin's charge was interrupted as an unseen pirate appeared suddenly beside Drymouth. Cloaked in black and red, the newcomer gripped Drymouth's arm. The paladin did not hesitate and descended upon the two, his mighty sword lifted into the air. Before it could connect, Drymouth and the other pirate dissipated into the air, a circle of light forming quickly beneath them and taking them away instantly.

They reappeared an instant later on the deck of *The Nebula*. Drymouth almost looked disappointed that he had survived. "Guess that's enough for now. I'm full," he said, but not even his teleporting companion could hear him. He looked at his surroundings, seeing the pirates working to turn the sails precisely, catching a steady wind that buoyed the massive vessel out to sea. Something seemed out of place, though. Though Drymouth looked like the avatar of death, he possessed a sharp intuition. Looking to the upper deck, he saw Dread Pirate Lord Erk standing at the helm. Instead of his first officer today, a beautiful young woman stood beside the captain, red braids cascading down her radiant armor. Drymouth didn't really care much for the politics of the pirates. They simply helped him find relief from this endless thirst. If there had been changes in the upper workings of the pirates, that would change nothing for him. His job would be the same: consume.

Drymouth felt a jarring sensation in his gut. Normally,

placating the thirst brought him a measure of comfort. However, it felt like the urge to consume would eat his own flesh. So be it, he thought. It would finally be over. His vision blurred as he collapsed onto the deck. He could see his crewmates looking at him, but their faces made no sense. As he could feel death tugging him away from the mortal coil, he noticed that the girl with braids was now bent over him. Erk was by her side, standing with a clear smile on his lips. Through his distorted senses, he heard Erk say, "It's going to be okay, Evan."

Evan. Drymouth hadn't heard that name much in thirty years. The captain was probably the only person left that remembered that name. The rest of them had been consumed by the malady that made Drymouth insatiable. Or so he assumed. "It's okay, captain; please just let me die," he murmured, barely able to feel his lips. By then, the pretty girl was muttering some phrases. It sounded like they rhymed. Her eyes were a beautiful blue and looked like pools of pure, magical water. They could quench his thirst. He opened his mouth to drink, but his throat was too dry to breathe. His heartbeat slowed. He had imagined dying as a peaceful relief, but this was euphoric. A bright light started to glow around his body; the only thing he could see was the girl. Was she an angel? A goddess? It didn't matter. Those blue eyes would finally quench the thirst, even if she was the reaper guiding him to the other side.

Two days later, Evan sat up in his bed. He didn't remember getting there; he only remembered dying in that girl's arms. "The curse nearly claimed you finally," a voice chimed nearby. Recognizing that voice, Evan turned to see Erk sitting beside him.

"Am I dead?" he asked, not expecting a response.

"Not now," Erk said with a laugh.

"But the thirst. It's . . .," he couldn't finish his sentence.

"Gone?" Erk prompted. "It's no wonder. You even look your old self."

Evan moved, his muscles responding well enough. He had sensations in his body that he hadn't felt in uncountable years.

"By the gods," he muttered, his voice real. He found a mirror near his bunk, looking with wonder. He was a bit taller than Erk at almost five and a half feet. His body was incredibly muscular, proving he had trained continually in his youth. His face was handsome, sharp elven features making his countenance seem a little long with a broad but pointed nose. His gray eyes were full of tears of joy. "By the gods, I'm whole again. I'm whole!" he started laughing. Laughter felt wonderful, he thought. It had been even longer since he could muster a laugh. "How? Erk, how did you do it?"

Erk shook his head. "Don't thank me, Evan. Thank the girl."

Evan could not remember anything from his last moments except that girl's eyes piercing through the veil of reality and ripping him, body and soul, back from the Abyss. Her fiery hair filled his vision with warmth, and the sincerity in her voice gave his tired soul a longing to live. "The curse is gone?" he exclaimed, touching his hands all over his body, savoring the sensation he felt for what seemed like the first time.

"It seems Miranda healed your affliction and restored your body to before the curse began. You're back in action, brother." With a teasing addition, "I swear it's like the last thirty years didn't happen. You're a total war machine."

Evan looked at Erk, a smile of genuine gratitude. "Can I meet her? I owe her a debt of thanks."

Erk nodded, "She's in Naomi's dressing room, resting. She's been asking about you every hour since you fell unconscious. I'll bring her to meet you when she wakes. Even then," he started, his voice trailed off, abnormal for somebody as confident as Erk.

Evan looked at his brother with concern. "What is it?" he asked as he draped himself in a robe that Erk had brought from his personal garments.

"We will all owe that girl a debt before her work is done. I already owe her much; she's brought my brother back to me. But the longer she is with us, the more I care for her. She can heal more than just your body. It's like she's so pure and so sincere that she heals something intangible."

Evan touched his chest, now muscular and whole instead of the sunken, decaying flesh of his cursed body. "You think she can heal the body and the soul?"

Erk shrugged. "I think you're living proof that she heals the body." The pirate lord stood to leave, adding, "And after only two days, I think I'm becoming proof of the latter." The two of them sat silently for a moment before Erk swallowed deeply. The words in his heart got caught in his chest. "She reminds me of sister," he continued. "Iria."

Evan's face lit up at the mention of their sister. "Oh, brother, please tell me you've heard something from her?"

Erk shook his head. "I haven't. Please, rest, brother. I'll bring Miranda once you're both awake," he ordered, quickly slipping out of the cabin.

Evan nodded, letting out a deep, disappointed sigh. He really didn't want to rest anymore. He wanted to meet this Miranda. Patience was never one of his strengths. He looked around his cabin and found a book to read. "Why not?" he chuckled, reading to distract himself from the wait.

Chapter 7
A Moral Question

 iranda knelt with Evan in her arms, trembling. The morbid husk had changed from a ghastly sight to a handsome elf with features similar to Erk. When he suddenly appeared on the deck of the ship, he collapsed, and, acting on instinct, Miranda went to treat his injuries. After her prayers were ineffective, she began to call on that force within her that Carulus had driven awake and aware. Praying to whatever listened beyond the gods, she begged for healing, peace, and comfort for this disheveled soul. In a brilliant flash like what she had felt before, the light of the universe seemed to pour from her body, enveloping the elf and healing him. Erk knelt beside her, together on their knees, the man's healed body resting unconscious in Miranda's arms.

Erk smiled sweetly at her, saying, "Thirty years ago, the King of Claston placed a curse on my brother. He was doomed to become one with his Unbinding, a horrific spell that dries everything and everyone. It began to dry him from the inside out, and what you saw before was all that was left of him. Miranda, my dear, you've been with us for less than an hour and given me something that no other priest, cleric, or holy man has been able to in three decades."

Miranda looked from Erk to the elf she had just healed. He looked serene, resting in her arms. "Is this your brother?"

Erk nodded. "My little brother Evan. We were both born before The Unbinding. We've seen many tragedies over the last century. You have healed the biggest wound in my heart through these long, anguishing years."

Miranda felt dizzy, so she gently sat Evan on the ship's deck. She used her hands to support herself on all fours, a wave of nausea and exhaustion shaking her to her core. Erk reached out and touched her shoulder, "Are you alright?" he asked gently.

Miranda shook her head, her braids flailing. After a moment, the sickened feeling began to ease. She opened her eyes to see Erk still by her side, and several crew members stood nearby, watching in disbelief. Erk extended a hand to her and stood up. "Come, dear, let's get you some rest." She nodded in compliance, and Erk helped her rise, stabilize herself, and led her to some sort of cabin, a small but elegant room about fifteen feet to the left of the captain's quarters underneath the upper deck. As Miranda went inside, Erk closed the door.

"Shalo," he said, the trickster nearby but invisible.

"Sir?" he piped in response.

"Nobody is stupid enough to bother Naomi's stuff on a normal day. Don't let new circumstances change that. And if anybody is stupid enough to try? You know what to do, Shalo," Erk said in a voice loud and menacing enough for the word to spread to the entire crew.

Shalo nodded to himself, replying, "With pleasure, cap'n."

*

Miranda opened the door to the guest cabin after a couple of hours had passed. As she started to step out, she thought she tripped on something, but it was Shalo standing dutifully between her door and the ship's deck.

"Ay, lass, yer on me boot!" he shouted in surprise. He

appeared quickly, his distinct odor swirling into existence simultaneously.

"Shalo!" she squeaked in response, a half-shout that turned to a giggle as she untangled herself from the pirate. He turned to face her, a wide smile brimming under his unkempt beard.

"Well, if it isn't the sweetest healer this side o' yon Rift! How did ya rest, lass?" he said, his eyes sparkling with genuine joy to see her.

Her lips turned into a slight smile, Shalo having served as her guardian twice now. In her mind, he was the closest thing she had to a friend on the ship. "I feel much better, thank you."

Shalo gestured for Miranda to follow him. *The Nebula* was a massive ship by any standard. Shouting from the top deck to the upper deck was futile unless the sea and the wind were calm. Today, they were neither, as the shores of the Undine Coast grew smaller looking out from the stern. Shalo took Miranda to the upper deck where Dread Pirate Lord Erk stood looking off the stern, and an incredibly tall pirate that Miranda had not seen before was manning the wheel. "Uh, cap'n?" Shalo grunted.

Erk did not react. He was looking through a spyglass at the growing distance between *The Nebula* and the sea shanty town they had left behind. "It looks like we'll all make it alright," he told his ephemerally visible friend.

"Yus, cap'n. And this one is alright, too," Shalo replied, his comment finally tearing Erk's attention away from the spyglass.

Erk turned to see Miranda and Shalo standing behind him, the girl's cool eyes wide with wonder. She seemed enthralled looking out over the water, her braids whipping wildly in the wind. Her mouth rested slightly open, but she also gripped the railing fiercely. She had never seen such a sight, and her heart soared with a feeling of freedom despite her apparent captivity. Erk saw the look on her face but the fear in her body.

"Relax, Miranda. Unless the water is choppy, it's not likely anybody will be thrown overboard," the captain said to her, reassuring.

Miranda inhaled the salty air deeply. She loosened her grip on the ship's railing, daring a look over the side of the stern.

She quickly pulled back, the massive galleon's upper deck at least forty feet above the rushing water. Turning to Erk and Shalo, she couldn't hide her smile as the beauty of the Undine Coast lingered in the distance. Erk's face beamed joyfully, watching the girl's innocent reaction to the environment.

"What do you think?" he asked in a gentle tone.

She didn't respond immediately. She soaked in the view momentarily before looking at Erk and Shalo. "It's more beautiful than anything I've ever seen!" she exclaimed, her whole body enthusiastically responding to her elated feelings.

The pirates laughed, endeared by her honest, unfiltered reaction to the open sea. Erk offered the spyglass to her, extending his arm with the tool lightly gripped in his fingers. Miranda's shoulders and chest inflated as she excitedly took the spyglass with a gentle pluck. She pressed the viewing end up to her right eye, and an audible sound of bewilderment escaped as she soaked in the zoomed view of the coast. "The sand is so far away now. I wanted to build sandcastles once I got to the beach!" she commented as she observed the far-away white sand.

Erk tilted his head and contemplated Miranda's reaction for a moment. "Miranda, are you hungry?" he asked, considering the events of the last day. She nodded absentmindedly as she peered through the spyglass again. Shalo took the cue and scampered away to take orders to the kitchen. Erk watched the young woman as she slowly lowered the spyglass, a tear forming in her eye and running down her gentle cheek.

Miranda cried silently, unwilling to let her sadness take control of her body. Her bottom lip shook momentarily before taking a deep breath; she closed her eyes and shook out the last of the tears. She had thought of Selasine, August, and Justin. She wished they were here to see this beautiful scene with her. She rehearsed Selasine's lecture in her head, "The beauty of nature is composed by the order inherent to all things," his voice almost real to her. Then, she pictured August complaining about the boring liturgy, urging Selasine to let him fish for the afternoon instead. Justin, quiet and contemplative as usual, would sit in meditation as long as there was a comfortable warmth from the sunlight. He would have been happy to train, too. August wouldn't have taken it seriously enough, though. And she would have bounced between all three of their paths, finding the beauty in being happy, alive, and together. Right now, alive was the only thing she had.

Erk watched as Miranda silently mourned. As a notorious pirate, he had a reputation for callousness and cruelty, especially after somebody had made themselves a threat to his agenda. In his heart, he was especially protective of "his people." Still, different sources would claim Erk had no real loyalty to anyone or any cause but his own. If those on the side of law and order were to be believed, Erk would have felt no empathy in this moment. Erk would have agreed with them. But he felt something stir within him as Miranda, so full of hope and kindness, a true miracle worker, suffered inside. Erk had to confront the reality that Miranda's tears fell because of something he had done. Naomi was going to stab him at least once for kidnapping her. He felt like he deserved it after watching her cry.

The feeling that crept up in his chest was one that he had not felt since before The Unbinding sent his world into absolute chaos. He wanted to reach out and hug Miranda, but he didn't. He couldn't. This was his doing. He and his men were to blame for this sad moment, forever crystallized inside the tears of a girl that had done nothing but be born with a gift. Erk knew this feeling but couldn't remember what it was called. Guilt? If he opened that door, the last one hundred years, and especially the most recent ten, might easily overwhelm him and end everything he had worked so hard to accomplish.

"I know I've done you harm, Miranda," he started with a lecture, but the sadness in her beautiful blue eyes turned sharp to anger impossible to conceal. Like blue daggers swiftly flying through the air, her eyes cut straight to his gray gaze that reflected no emotion. How appropriate, he thought, making the analogy of daggers in her stare toward his own. Naomi's favored weapon was a throwing dagger. He could feel them in his heart.

In his mind, Erk, a master at manipulating people, felt the

sudden regret of miscalculation. He knew the girl would be resentful, but he misunderstood her cycle of emotions from elation to sadness. A direct approach to her feelings would not work on somebody so candid in their negative emotions and carefree with the positive. Control over anger, spite, and sorrow was something Erk admired in others. Normally, people tempered enough to hide their true feelings were capable of cold calculations and strategic "business" decisions. To see such anguish and rage expressed in a contained, gentle way made Erk's heart race with indecision. Something in his mind *wanted* Miranda to see him positively. Perhaps it was her gift? Gratefulness for using her miracle to heal his brother? Maybe he feared Naomi's response, and that exacerbated his guilt? He thought people should be disposable, but he could never relegate Naomi to that. Nor would he do that to this Miranda. Her spirit was too bright to cast aside so easily. Gathering his thoughts, he continued, "Have you ever known somebody to do something wrong for a cause that they thought was bigger than themselves?"

The philosophical question made the malice in Miranda's glare vanish, making her immediately pensive. She thought about Selasine, who managed never to compromise his morals or his code. She thought about August blowing off lessons in favor of leisure. She thought about Justin, who tried to follow Selasine's example without fail. But then, she thought about Carulus who whisked her away to an invasion hoping she could save troops that he carelessly threw into the deadliest of tasks. Was his heart set on a goal bigger than himself? Was this what Erk meant by his question? She furrowed her brow as she calculated a response. "Yes. I suppose that's why the high priest that attacked your base forced me to come with him. He had heard about the miracle I had done by accident and gambled on that rumor," she replied, cutting her eyes to the ground.

This information surprised Erk. "You mean, he had no idea you did not understand your gift?"

She nodded, "I tried to tell him. He wouldn't listen, but thanks to him, I feel like . . .," she trailed off for a moment. Erk let the silence sit, watching her think. "I feel like I know how to reach inside and call for that power now. He did something irresponsible, but I guess in the end, it worked out? I reached that power just in time to heal your brother." Her eyes widened as she remembered. "Oh, how is Evan? I meant to check."

Erk's face twitched at the sudden change of direction in the conversation. "Oh, he's resting in his cabin on the first deck," he replied. "Did you want to see him?"

Miranda nodded, her gaze leaving Erk for the pirate at the helm. "If that would be okay," she added, realizing she might not be allowed to go below deck.

"Of course, I am sure that seeing him would benefit you both," Erk replied.

Before Miranda could reply, Shalo came up the stairs to the upper deck, panting from his hasty run below to the kitchen. "They're workin' on some food for ye, cap'n. Told 'em for cap and his guest," he reported, standing at attention.

Erk nodded, "Thank you, Shalo. Miranda, I would very much like to continue this conversation with you. Would you join me for a meal in the captain's quarters?"

For the first time in the last day, Miranda realized she had not taken the time to eat or drink anything. Furthermore, she thought eating with Erk would be her best chance at getting a decent meal. Plus, the closer she got to the captain, the more likely she could gather information that might help the cause of order. She forced a smile to reply, "Of course, captain. I would be honored."

Erk returned a genuine smile, "Very well. Please, take some time to change into something more comfortable and enjoy a bath before we dine. I've arranged so that the dressing room will have everything you need, and if you can't find what you want, don't be afraid to ask."

Miranda breathed deeply. It sounded like a dream, a pirate captain ready to give anything she could ask for. The one thing she really wanted was the one thing she knew he wouldn't grant her: to let her return to her friends so they could return to the sleepy town of Devitus together. She started to feel like they would never go back there, just the four of them. Erk turned to leave the upper deck, heading for the captain's quarters below. "I'll send for you once everything is prepared. Shalo, you know what to do."

The pirate's turban bobbed as he nodded, "Aye, cap'n." Miranda saw his gesture before he made it, having spent the most time with Shalo since she awoke that morning. The sun was headed for the northwestern horizon, the evening settling upon them as *The Nebula* charged through the churning water of the Undine Sea. She followed Shalo back to the "dressing room," a small cabin off to the left side of the captain's quarters. He unlocked the door for her and waited outside. A small window in the door let her watch the pirates working on the deck, their movements rehearsed and habitual. Looking outside, she noticed a wooden latch that slid out horizontally, closing the window. She could see Shalo standing guard at her door, a job he seemed to take with a surprising degree of sincerity. She slid the window shut, taking a breath before she turned around.

Feeling at ease, Miranda looked around the room. It seemed like it had been specially prepared to serve her, and Erk spared no details. It was filled with numerous effects that were especially luxurious. A bed rested against the wall to the left of the door, covered with a lush blanket made of some kind of silk. A wardrobe full of beautiful dresses sat next to it, and a wool rug covered the floor, hiding the wood of the planks that made up the deck. In a corner opposite the bed sat a large metal bath and a vanity adorned with gold and silver, and a mirror set into its center. On it rested various makeups and perfumes that were popular in the cities. Miranda did not know much about those things, as the monks in the monastery did not teach her about makeup or perfume. They always instructed her that the beauty of one's heart is more important than appearance. She was still trying to wrap her mind around what that meant now that she'd seen a few hearts that did not match appearances or reputations.

Miranda sat in the small, ornate chair in front of the vanity and looked at herself in the mirror. She looked as rough as she felt. Her braids were unraveling, and her face was smeared with dirt and blood. Her battlemail could have used a polish even though it was still resplendent. She loosened her braids, finding a beautiful comb on the vanity she used to smooth out her tangled hair. The deep red tones of her hair had dulled as it became dirty throughout the journey, the battle, and her trek through the cave. She unfastened the belt holding her scabbard and pouches tight to her side, placing it on a dressing table beside the vanity. She unfastened the bindings of the long skirt of the battlemail, letting it drop to the carpet with a soft metallic clink. It took a little work to loosen the straps of the breastplate on her own, but she'd rather not look for help undressing on a ship full of pirates. Her undergarments were a fine chain mesh lined with a warm cotton layer that kept her skin warm and provided additional protection.

She dropped everything on the floor in front of the mirror. Her blue eyes flickered in the candlelight that supplemented the waning natural light from outside. She looked the same underneath the armor, her body muscular and well-trained. She looked at the beautiful red hair draped around her shoulders, her skin a light sandy color that seemed to glow in the candlelight. Turning from her reflection to the bath, she dipped her fingers in the already drawn water. It was warm and comfortable, and a faint floral scent wafted off the top of the water. She stretched one of her long legs over the side of the tub, her muscles tensing and relaxing with the temperature change. She eased into the water, immersing herself completely in the warmth.

The soaps and scents that Erk had left by the bath for her were far too powerful for what she was accustomed to. In the warmer seasons, she would normally bathe in the river that flowed through the valley where Devitus was located. In the winter, Selasine arranged for his pupils to use a simple bathhouse in the city, a unique feature for a town so small. Normally the soaps she used had only a hint of smell to them, but these were too much. She used them conservatively so that she did not overwhelm her senses. She relaxed in the water for a while, watching the sunlight fade dimmer still.

While resting in the bath, Miranda had plenty of time and silence to fill with her thoughts. Nothing about this journey had gone according to plan except the trip from Devitus to the Undine Coast. She wished that somebody would explain her strange gift to her. So far, she had only used it to heal people, but for some reason, she felt there was the potential to do more with it. She couldn't say why she thought that, but a nagging voice told her that she should try other miracles. The three times that her gift had manifested, she felt weak and empty afterward, even though all instances had given others cause for celebration. After saving the family in Devitus, she slept far past her normal waking time the next day. After the miracle in the base camp, she fell unconscious for almost an entire day. After healing Evan, she needed to nap from afternoon to evening. Something within her fueled her gift, and it took time to recover. Despite how taxing it was to use it, she started to imagine all of the tragedies she could prevent with such a powerful gift. She prayed to Invictus for guidance in finding the utility behind this power within her, the holy symbol and strongbox key still resting on the chain around her neck as she indulged in the warm water for far too long. It should have lost some warmth by now, but the bath seemed enchanted. It was warm and just as clean as when she had gotten in. She stretched, her arms spilling out over the sides of the tub. She found herself wishing she had something like this back in Devitus.

Sliding out of the bath, Miranda used only one of the many linens readied for her to dry. She combed out her wet hair, glistening cleanly in the candlelight. She rummaged through the wardrobe, looking for something comfortable. She felt safe in her armor, but it had felt burdensome and heavy before she took it off before her bath. The dresses here looked like they were made for royalty in various colors and styles. Many of them were somewhat immodest, speaking to their role in parading the "assets" of noblewomen whose only value to their families rested in their ability to improve family status through marriage. Miranda felt lucky that she didn't have those burdens and could enjoy the freedom offered through service to the Church of Invictus. Her mind lingered on that thought for a moment. Though transactional marriages were allowed in the Kingdom of Alabaster, Miranda thought about the unfair nature of the practice. She imagined being betrothed to a stranger, making her sick to her stomach. Then again, she understood that her unique circumstances had probably saved her from such a fate. From what she understood, she was technically of noble birth. Everyone close to her always told her how beautiful she was and that she would make a great wife one day, but she didn't understand what they meant. Selasine had even hinted that a couple of older gentlemen in town had sent the bishop marriage proposals, promising to care for Miranda and her estate for the rest of their days. She was glad Selasine had given the men a resounding 'no' in response.

Miranda shook herself out of her thoughts. She pushed the corsets and ballgowns onto one side of the wardrobe. There's no way she would wear those, even if that's what Erk had ordered. She chose a knee-length royal purple dress with poofy sleeves and a plunging neckline. It was one of Invictus's colors, even though it wasn't as modest as she had hoped to find. Part of the struggle was that most of the clothing was far too big for her. Shoes of various sizes and styles littered the drawers of the wardrobe, and Miranda chose a simple pair of black leather boots with a raised heel. The makeup was the only thing she wanted to play with that was outside her normal routine. She had seen noble women in Devitus that used varying types of makeup, using colors and lines to distinguish their eyes or hide blemishes. It also seemed that elven women were more commonly concerned with making sure makeup matched societal expectations, but Miranda wasn't sure what those expectations even were. She messed around with the powders and pigments, settling for two blue stripes curving down her cheeks to her jaw. It was reminiscent of the warpaint used by warpriests in the service of Invictus, representative of how she felt as a captive left in a room of luxury. She forewent the jewelry left for her, but she did fix the beautiful comb into her hair.

Miranda stood and looked at herself in the mirror for a moment. She looked and felt different, the purple dress hugging her muscular figure. Her blue eyes sparkled in the candlelight, and she felt confident. She stared at herself, trying to keep her mind calm and distracted from the things that would have been painful. She liked the makeup. It made her feel intimidating but still pretty, something that she hadn't considered about herself until this moment. She could thank the liturgical schedule of her training for her muscular physique, which included both recitations and physical training. After all, the clergy of Invictus could be required to outmatch lawbreakers in a physical confrontation, and they needed to be in top fighting shape at all times.

Enraptured by her thoughts, Miranda felt herself ripped from them when there was a loud knock at the door. Turning from the mirror, she moved across the room, opening the small window. She saw Shalo and another pirate talking there and opened the door slowly. Shalo turned to greet her, "Miss Miranda, yer dinner . . .," he began, but he seemed unable to finish his sentence.

The pretty girl in the flashy armor had totally transformed. Her hair seemed longer now that the braids had been smoothed into the rest of her hair, and her dress accentuated the strong body underneath all of that armor. Blue stripes called attention to her beautiful eyes, a cold gaze that could pierce through a person's heart. The pirate with Shalo stared in stunned silence before muttering something about "getting back to duty," then turning and walking away.

Shalo swallowed hard and restarted, "Miss Miranda, yer dinner with the cap'n is ready!"

Miranda smiled at him, "Lead the way, friend."

Shalo's cheeks burned red underneath his beard as he led the striking beauty behind him fifteen feet away to the door of the captain's quarters. Like on many ships, the captain's quarters rested beneath the upper deck. However, *The Nebula* was so large and magnificent that it also had two cabins beside the primary lodging for the highest-ranking person on the ship. Right now, one of those cabins belonged to Miranda, the other presumably to Erk's first mate.

Shalo rapped at the captain's door. After a moment, it opened, but there was nobody immediately present. For a moment, Miranda wondered if Erk could also turn invisible until a voice from within called out, "Please, enter." Shalo pushed the door inward to open it the rest of the way. The room was so well lit that Miranda thought it was daytime inside the captain's quarters despite the sun waving its last goodbyes on the horizon, bathing the sky in deep tones of purple and cerulean.

The first thing Miranda noticed was the smell: the rich aroma of unfamiliar food mixed with subtle floral fragrances. Miranda followed Shalo into the captain's quarters, seeing Erk sitting at the head of a dining table dressed in his formal captain's jacket, a striking red garment adorned with black leather and gold metal accents. He wore no hat in his cabin, his golden hair cascading around his shoulders. Shalo waited impatiently for his captain's commands, but Erk allowed the silence to grow for a moment. Upon seeing Miranda, Erk smiled, but Miranda did not notice. She was far too distracted by the globes, maps, chests, and wardrobes that seemed to overflow with gold and objects stolen from vessels targeted by the pirate lord.

Erk gestured to the seat at his left, "Please, Miranda, join us." Us? She thought. Miranda then realized that the ship's first officer had been standing quietly off to the side, obscured by an ornate room divider haphazardly placed without making a clear division between the open space and a space of privacy. Jax Slicer stepped out, an unusually tall human, standing even a full head above Bishop Selasine. While Erk did not look or seem like a traditional pirate, Jax was a pirate through and through. He had an eyepatch over his left eye, a leather tunic to shield him from the oceanic elements, and a bushy beard that only created an elongated illusion of height and width for the already sizable man. Before she could finish sizing up the first mate, Erk added, "Shalo, you, too, are welcome to join us if Miranda does not mind."

Miranda looked at the pirate she had healed and who served as her guide through the caves before they set sail. The look in Shalo's eyes was one she had seen before, a hopeful gaze waiting on Miranda, the gatekeeper, to open the gate in his favor. She could tell this was a special moment for the pirate, even though he ranked highly in Erk's forces. Excitement stirred in Miranda, knowing that welcoming Shalo to their meal would be a kind gesture and cement their relationship as one of mutual benefit.

Miranda's eyes met Erk's as he waited for her to respond. Feeling the pressure of his judgment, she cocked her head to the side to reply, "Of course, Shalo is my guardian on this voyage. I would be glad for him to stay and dine with us."

Shalo's eyes lit up with joy. He said nothing, perhaps due to protocol, but Miranda could feel his gratitude without words. Following Erk's direction, Miranda sat at the table with Shalo on her left, Jax joining the captain on his right. The meal before them was not a spectacular banquet, but it was more than the average sailor would experience at sea. Dried meats had been beautifully prepared on platters of varying kinds of metals, and there were many types of vegetables boiled into soups and broths that would be easy to preserve and prepare on longer voyages. The cutlery and dishware were assembled from so many varying sets that none of it matched. On the surface, it seemed elegant, but it was ultimately what Miranda might have expected from a feast with pirates.

In a down-to-earth fashion, Erk stood and served himself, which prompted Jax to do the same. Miranda hesitated to join, so Shalo took her plate and gathered a variety of dishes to try before preparing his own. After each of his guests looked prepared to eat, Erk ceremonially greeted Miranda and the two pirates with them. "We hold this meal in honor of our esteemed guest, Miranda, the miracle healer. After blessing us and my brother Evan with an unbelievable healing, it is the least we could do to show our gratitude and sincerity," the pirate lord lauded, the room staying awkwardly silent. "Let us partake," he concluded, and Jax and Shalo immediately began to feast.

Miranda slowly began to pick at her food when the conversation started. Erk ate conservatively between questions. With a calm smile, he asked, "Miranda, why did you join the Path of the Sword of Justice?"

Miranda stared at the dried pork on her plate covered with a sweet gravy. Letting her eyes meet the captain's, she replied, "I am pursuing the path of the arbiter. I want to help people and find ways to resolve conflict without violence." Her eyes returned to her meal.

Erk nodded in detached amusement. "And how are you preparing to deal with cases where a plaintiff may not be satisfied with your ruling?"

Miranda had not truly thought about the heavy weight that arbiters of Invictus carried. She tilted her head back and forth momentarily, responding, "I would hope that the rule of law would help an unhappy person see reason in a case like that."

Erk took a moment to savor a broth made from carrots and turnips. Her youth and inexperience clearly directed her answer, so he wanted to reply carefully. "The law dictates that sons inherit their father's lands after his death. They'll receive it in equal parts. This is not disputed." Miranda nodded in agreement as Erk continued, "There was once a farmer with two sons. One left in pursuit of his own path, abandoning his family and farm. The other stayed and helped his father diligently through the years. After the father's death, both sons laid claim to the lands. The law says this land should be divided, despite the first son's absence for many years. By virtue of his birth and nothing more, he is entitled to those lands. And, on the contrary, his brother, who had spent so much toiling on the land, must now share the land he once farmed with his brother, who had contributed nothing. What do you think of the situation?" he finished, placing his tongue between his teeth in a contemplative challenge.

Miranda's eyes narrowed in thought. "Is the question of resolving this based on the fairness of the law? Does the brother that stayed object to his brother receiving his inheritance because he did not stay and farm with the family?" she asked, unsatisfied with the nuance in Erk's hypothetical situation.

Erk nodded, adding, "Should not the work and effort contributed by the brother that stayed be rewarded?"

Miranda paused before responding, "Duty and law are intertwined, but the law protects the brother that left the farm. Suppose his quests and adventures yielded him nothing. In that case, his family has worked to ensure he has something to return to as a safety net to prevent another person from destitution. Would the brother that stayed rather see his brother a beggar than receive an inheritance?"

Erk had never heard the morality of the second brother in the question examined. In most cases, people were quick to side with the brother that stayed, his hard work earning him a greater share of the inheritance. Erk thought carefully, realizing that Miranda could see through the trap inherent to such questions of law and morality. "Your insight speaks to the nature of mortals rather than the nature of the law. What is more important? The heart of humankind and elvenkind? Or the laws that bind us together?"

Miranda answered without hesitation, this time with a catechism that addressed this very question, "Beings of good heart need no laws; beings of no heart cannot be bound by laws. It is the essence of balance and the emergence of natural order that law binds our inclinations to do others harm. In this, morality and the law intertwine, each guiding the other toward the goal of righteous order." She felt a tremble rising in her voice as she neared the end of the recitation. At this point, she felt Erk had done more to test her faith in Invictus academically than Carulus.

Erk tilted his head to ponder for a moment, impressed that Miranda was so prepared to confront these questions. Her poise under scrutiny definitely needed refinement, but her commitment to her ideals was irrefutable. He took another minute to enjoy the banquet before them, pondering alternative scenarios that could highlight the flaws inherent to a worldview that revered law and order above all else. The scenario of the two brothers was weak, anyway. Instead, he decided to get to the heart of who he was, beginning a new line of questioning. "What happens when the law neglects those that need protection the most?"

Miranda's skin paled slightly as she confronted the question in her mind, calculating a response that reflected the values she had acquired while living at the monastery of Lexcord. "The law itself should be unbiased and fair. If the law has failed to protect anyone, it's because the hearts of mortals have forgotten the spirit of the law. When an evil ruler sits in charge of the law, their very nature invalidates the laws they write. When a person of dark heart twists the law for their own benefit, they've broken the sacred contract between all life that binds us together." She thought of another catechism to add, an excited perk in her tone that made the music in her voice sound happy. Erk took a surprised breath as what she said was a familiar catechism to him. "The peacekeepers must be ever watchful of those who would use the law to defile the peace. In those cases, the moral decision is to fight against the wicked despite the laws that have been perverted for the desires of the depraved."

Erk's visage twisted into a most excited smile as he replied, "So, you understand the intricacies of navigating between what is legal and right. In that case, let me tell you a story about a young elf betrayed by the very law he once swore to uphold." Miranda's eyes lit up with curiosity, and her jaw relaxed as the promise of a story was usually a prelude to an interesting lesson. Selasine told many stories, so she wondered what kinds of stories a pirate might tell. Erk's eyes returned to his meal, "I know this story well. Because it's my story."

***

Gaius Carulus held a correspondence in his hand. As one of the twelve high priests of Invictus, he received numerous appeals and requests for help. This one, however, was different. This was a report about a girl in the outer provinces of Alabaster, the frontier town of Devitus. Earlier this month, he had heard rumors that the bishop stationed there, Thomas Selasine, had taken a promising pupil under his tutelage and made her a peacekeeper. He furled open the scroll to reread it.

> "Your Holiness: If the rumors are true, then it is without a doubt that this girl's miracle from last month is a portent of things to come. The family should have died in the fire, but they live thanks to her healing powers. This girl is an asset to the church. Please see that she is brought from the outer provinces to Nulodia or the capital city. Have her serve some time with Maréli and refine her powers. In Order and Justice, Archbishop Renault."

Carulus rolled up the scroll. Perhaps an asset such as this could be tempered more effectively in the fires of combat instead of under the safe tutelage of the healers. The King of Claston, an independent elven kingdom far to the east, was still sending daily requests for assistance in quelling the activities of a notorious pirate lord, some Erk the Radiant that specifically targeted nobles loyal to the king and royal vessels leaving Claston's ports.

Up to this point, Carulus was not highly concerned with the activities of pirates in the Undine Sea. While the Church of Invictus would normally respond to such requests, he considered this a conflict between subject and king. According to the requests sent to Nulodia, where Carulus presided as high priest, Erk had been exclusively targeting the vessels of the king and the aristocracy of his kingdom. Claston as a kingdom, however, was primitive compared to Alabaster. With serfdom and slavery still being legal constructs under the rule of King Claston, Carulus had all but ignored his requests up to this point. Devitus, however, would be on the way to the Undine Coast. He could certainly mount an effective attack against the pirates nestled in the numerous coves there, and with the wrath of the church, it would be child's play.

Carulus demanded a scroll and a quill from his assistant to write back to the archbishop, one of the Council of Four. He thought that a counterproposal would be his best course of action. If the girl could accompany them to eliminate the pirates, she could demonstrate her gifts on the battlefield and grow stronger. Furthermore, this would be an opportunity to take a well-deserved administrative vacation to the Undine Coast.

A month passed, however, and it became evident that this Pirate Lord Erk was not a small threat. In only the last year, he had amassed support from thousands of disaffected serfs frustrated with some decree made by the King of Claston. Carulus again had to acknowledge that, within the purview of the church, conflict between king and country could only be resolved through mediation, which the King of Claston refused. Nevertheless, Archbishop Renault had approved his plan to take the girl on any "minor" excursion. All that remained was to find just cause to declare the pirates an enemy of the church. Carulus knew he could get a sizable force of warpriests or paladins. Putting down a massive rebellion and finding a girl capable of working miracles in the church's name would certainly put him on the shortlist to be appointed to the Council of Four. The achievements would speak for themselves!

Unfortunately, Erk's forces continued to grow. Rumors of the reaches of his cruelty and might began to seep into the far corners of even neighboring kingdoms. Carulus finally found his justification: if this force continued to grow, it could easily spill over the borders between Alabaster and Claston. The high priest began putting together his formal request for an army. He figured four months would be sufficient to finish the paperwork, raise the army, and march to their destination. Twenty-five thousand serfs and five thousand pirates hardly made a force that could stand up to the church. What had King Claston even done that would spark a widespread rebellion like this? Carulus doubled the number of reconnaissance troops he would employ as they prepared for battle against the pirates.

But only a month before the expedition, the archbishop personally came to visit him. Renault was a half-elf like Carulus, and together they championed causes that continued integrating humans and elves into a harmonious society. Renault stood in the high priest's study, pouring over the documents summarizing the expedition, the objectives, and the agreements between King Claston and Carulus.

Renault kept reading, giving approving nods as he double-checked the documents that had certainly already been checked dozens of times. As he reached the end of the summary, Renault curiously tilted his head. "The girl from Devitus is still listed as an asset in this battle plan?"

Carulus took a deep breath, expecting this question to resurface in the final once-over by the Council. "Yes, archbishop, I believe she will be an asset. I heard personally from Thomas Selasine that she showed great promise as a healer and possibly an arbiter. If she does well, I may encourage Selasine to put her on the path of the Judge rather than –"

"No, no, Carulus, I don't think we know enough about the girl to take her on an expedition of this size. Perhaps we should wait to test out her gifts in a more controlled environment," the archbishop replied, his gaze never leaving the paperwork.

Carulus furrowed his brow, bothered by Renault's position on the subject. "Of course, archbishop. I did weigh the dubious nature of this 'miracle' against the number of troops I would need to defeat Erk. I can go without her, but I will probably need another thousand troops, paladins especially."

Renault squinted, skimming over the requisition requests, the troop numbers, and intel on Erk and his forces. "You really think the girl makes a thousand-man difference?" The archbishop suddenly had a dreadful feeling. "If so, why did you leave her in Devitus for these months? She could have been training with Maréli this entire time," he admonished.

Carulus lowered his head in deference. "Forgive me, archbishop. As I researched the rumors, I stumbled upon ancient tomes that told of a power beyond imagination. The ability to become one with the arcane much like we as priests become one with the divine. According to what I theorize, this girl's power is outside of the realm of our regular training."

The archbishop's face twisted in annoyed frustration. He knew that Carulus was an impeccable bureaucrat and that he had probably checked protocol and bylaws thoroughly before concealing this information from him. Furthermore, since the girl was properly listed in the battle plan, Carulus's thesis held merit with the high paladins that certify the troop and supply requisitions. Nevertheless, the Council of Four should have cleared such wild theories. Renault realized they needed some revisions to the rules regarding what the generals could authorize on the Council's behalf. "I see you've gone to great lengths to prove the weight of your theory to the generals, then. I have no recourse to stop your plan. Realize this means that your success is assumed, and there should be no complications," the archbishop warned.

Carulus felt a malicious disdain swirl in his mind. His nose twitched irreverently as he calculated a sarcastic yet orthodox reply. "Well, archbishop. I, too, trust the authority of the high paladins. I trust you, who appointed them, as well," he retorted, the sneer evident in his voice.

Renault turned to leave Carulus's study. "Very well. I'll make sure to expedite your requests." Carulus's mouth twisted into a sinister smile, feeling like he had won. Renault shut the door behind him, letting out an exasperated sigh. "Well, I guess I'll mobilize a pegasus battalion to keep tabs on the operation.

Damil will be perfect for that." He snatched a deep purple stole from around his neck, a gesture of derision, questioning his own recent appointments to high offices. The next month was going to be a nightmare of paperwork.

Departing from Devitus took far too long. Selasine and his pupils had the right to form their own battalion, but four troops could hardly supplement a division. According to what Carulus had read, however, if the girl's power was what he theorized, she would do well to stay with those she knew for now. He knew he would have to push her to a breaking point to let that power take over when no options were left.

The journey to the Undine Coast would take around ten days. Carulus didn't mind the trip so much as the continual reports he would have to send back to Nulodia and the capital city. He felt that the archbishop would be watching this endeavor with close scrutiny. As his personal guard marched at the center of the army, he could closely watch the girl. Throughout the journey, he was pleased to see Maréli also noticing the girl's penchant for healing. This was the training that the archbishop wanted for the girl, and thanks to Carulus's stubbornness, she could receive her training on the way to their destination. It would only be a matter of time before the forces of Erk had met their reckoning, and Carulus would finally be rewarded for his brilliance. This couldn't be more diligently organized.

Not even a day into fighting, Carulus celebrated success. His ploy of putting too much pressure on the girl worked. He was thrilled with the results that he achieved on this journey. The girl's gift unlocked just as he suspected: when she had no other options. Certainly, it must have activated the first time she felt despaired that her healing prayers did not work on the family in the burned house. Today that despair was their ally. Selasine was not pleased, but the bishop would soon understand this was good.

Carulus's intelligence warned him that one of the pirates possessed overwhelming power. Known as "Drymouth" to his comrades, the pirates gave him a massive berth. His uncanny magic was nearly impossible to fight against as it drained the moisture out of the environment. Drymouth's handiwork made up most of the early casualties in the assault, but the girl easily undid the pirate's insidious work. As he imagined the assurance of a quick victory, a commotion outside his command tent tore him from his thoughts. He went to the entrance and glanced outside. The commander in charge of his troops was nowhere to be seen. Stepping out into the warm night air, Carulus felt something was terribly amiss. Catching a battalion of paladins heading for the palisade, he inquired, "What's happening?"

"Your Holiness! A single enemy has approached the palisade and demands a challenger," the battalion sergeant replied, rushing his men to the palisade that overlooked a forest clearing that led to the caves. Carulus's face twisted into annoyance. He wasn't surprised that the pirates would attack under cover of night, but they only sent a single pirate to challenge the fully mobilized might of Invictus? This was an insult as much as an attack, and Carulus returned to his tent to prepare a strategy for the next day, the girl's incredible power ever-present in his mind.

Within the hour, however, one of the young men that had accompanied Selasine and the girl burst into the command tent. He shouted that Miranda was missing and wanted to know where she was. Carulus felt his entire essence screaming with frustration. A single pirate attacked the base camp, and now the girl on whom his entire plan was based was missing? He ignored the young man as much as he could, dismissing him. Surely the girl would turn up after the chaos caused by the lone pirate settled. He thought about making a prayer of penitence for his harsh dismissal of the young man, but he did not even touch his holy symbol.

Carulus sat in contemplation until dawn. The most recent reports showed that his troops had found their way through the cave network and were ready to storm the beach where Erk's ship and troops were located. The girl was missing, and at least one pirate had attacked the camp undetected. Resistance from the pirates in the caves had all but evaporated in the last six hours. It seemed that they were withdrawing, which fit into the plan. The high priest cursed himself for leaving the camp exposed enough that the girl could go missing at such a critical point in the operation. He had only one choice. He sat down at his strategy table and began penning a report.

"Archbishop. Your wisdom has proven beyond mortal understanding once again. The miracle girl is indeed powerful, but more powerful than we imagined. She may have fallen into the hands of Erk and his pirate kin. We will attempt to extract the girl, but she is far too dangerous to be left in the hands of the enemy. As such, I will take any measures necessary to ensure the safety of the clergy engaged in this operation. It pains the heart of Invictus, but if the girl's gifts are turned against the church by the pirates, then she will be dealt with as a weapon rather than as one of the faithful. Bishop Selasine, furthermore, has disappeared without leave and should be considered in violation of the tenets of his faith. The rest of the attack has had the desired effect. The pirates are now to be dealt with by King Claston's naval forces. In Service to Justice, Gaius Carulus, High Priest of Invictus."

He stamped the correspondence with his seal and called for a messenger. Upon the messenger's arrival, Carulus slipped the scroll into the messenger's palm, muttering, "Make sure that the archbishop gets this, and quickly. We may have little time to respond to the threats now before us." The messenger nodded and complied, hurtling off through the camp with his singular purpose. Carulus closed his eyes. "What a disaster," he said to himself, defeated in his apparent victory.

Chapter 8
Two Days at Sea

elasine and August stood on the deck of *The Water Sprite*, each holding a different rope. Their strength helped them easily align the modestly sized ship's sails. Between their efforts and the expertise of the navigator they knew as "Jim," *The Water Sprite* surged through the Undine Sea at an incredible rate. Supplemented by a young, human couple with uncanny wind magic, the small ship tore a path directly for the Isles Known for Nothing.

The ship's captain, Gurd, had not taken his eyes off August and Selasine since the ship departed. They were certainly helpful on their first day at sea, but something continually felt wrong to Gurd. He had never seen them in Port Undine, the temporary name for the shanty town that had popped up in the well-defended bay they now fled. Their common language accents seemed odd, and they definitely did not have a maritime background. Still, they were exceptionally helpful and eager.

Selasine, however, was disturbed by what was going on around him. He expected *The Water Sprite* to be a pirate vessel, but this ship seemed more like a passenger ship. Entire families were present, including women and children. Many of the "pirates" were married, and their families accompanied them around the ship, helping carry out the necessary duties for sailing. This situation did not sit well with Selasine. Still, at the very least, it enabled him and August to maintain a safe distance and degree of anonymity.

Still, Gurd did not trust them. He had invited the two onto his vessel so that he could keep an eye on them, especially because they claimed to have been part of Dread Pirate Lord Erk's crew. There's no way two individuals so out of place on a ship could have been under the employ of the captain, and Gurd knew it. He felt a bit guilty for putting his men and their families at risk by inviting these strangers aboard, but he also had a duty to the pirate lord that had stood against the evil king for the last century. Two, strange warriors would be at a major disadvantage at sea. Gurd planned to use that to extract the information he wanted from them.

Selasine and August proved most helpful in belaying and jibing the sails, their strength unquestionable. The two of them managed to keep *The Water Sprite*'s direction true while they were on deck, and they were remarkably good at following orders. As their first day at sea ended, Gurd personally approached Selasine on the deck.

"Guess we need to see about your sleeping arrangements," Gurd said as he approached, Selasine and August panting and sweating from adjusting the sails to keep up with the wild winds that ripped down the Trollcrag mountains and out to sea. Normally such a voyage could take a couple of days, but thanks to their efforts, *The Water Sprite* was well ahead of the other ships making this journey.

Gurd showed Selasine and August down to the bottom deck. Opening the door to a storage room, Gurd wrinkled his nose at the damp, dusty smell. "Seems like this spot is free," he mumbled, the darkness of the bottom deck making him seem like a sinister pirate instead of the caring captain that Selasine and August had witnessed all day. Selasine could feel that there was more to Gurd's story, and the two danced around their palpable distrust of each other. Selasine and August looked into the storage room, sizing it up quickly. There would be enough room for them to lay out their mats and get some rest.

Gurd decided that he would begin to pry apart the holes in these strangers' stories. He began his interrogation in a way that he thought would be simple enough, asking, "So when did you two join the captain's crew?"

Selasine shook his head once, more to himself than to Gurd, "Hasn't really been that long," he replied, hoping to use it to explain his and August's greenness in navigation.

Gurd stared without emotion, the lack of light making his face seem like stone. "Is that right? 'Coz he's been docked in Port Undine for the last month," he replied, using the implausibility of Selasine's suggestion to demonstrate his doubt.

August tried to force a chuckle, "Guess we just lost count of how long it's been." The young man's heart raced, assessing the situation for potential danger.

Gurd sneered slightly, "I know you aren't who you say you are. I don't know who you are or where you came from, though, and that's what I want to know."

Selasine's eye narrowed, the movement barely visible. "Well, captain, I'm certain you're not a pirate. You have the demeanor of an experienced sailor, but there are women and children on this ship. I'm here to discover why those fanatics attacked commoners and peasants. And I'm here to see that those responsible will be held accountable for their crimes," Selasine replied, hoping that a kernel of truth blended with Gurd's perspective would deescalate hostility.

Gurd lit a match he had tucked away in his pocket and used it to light a small candle. The aura of light made the sailor look closer to a pirate than his shaved head and fashion choices. "So, you're an outsider, just like I thought. You're right; most of us aren't pirates. That still doesn't tell me much about you, though," he redirected, clarifying that he wanted information about his new "crewmembers."

Selasine thought a prayer to Invictus, a prayer of guidance and discernment. Though his mind was exploring his options in this scenario, his heart encouraged him to be forthcoming with information that may put Gurd at ease. "Port Undine was attacked by a high priest of Invictus out of Nulodia. His official story was that the King of Claston had been begging the church for help for months now and that the attack would be carried out against pirates. I'm not with that high priest. I'm here to see why the high priest lied and said he would be warring with pirates, not commoners and sailors," Selasine finished, hoping this information would not result in hostility.

Fortunately for Selasine, Gurd had heard enough information about the situation with the church that this aligned with what he knew. The captain immediately looked at ease, the tension from his suspicious gaze melting into the candle's light. While they were among the sea shanties and things were happening fast, Selasine did not have a chance to examine Gurd. Almost six feet tall, the 'pirate' with the shaved head was stocky and strong. His clothes looked nice despite being ragtag, and his face was dotted with scars and piercings. He could blend in as a pirate in any port easily, but the gentle nature of his eyes contradicted that rough exterior.

Gurd's relief changed his entire demeanor. "Have you found the reason the fanatics attacked us then? We've always heard that Invictus is a god of law and order. The only intervention they have offered for the last hundred years is arbitration, which the king refuses," he said in almost a plea for somebody to listen.

Selasine did listen, and it greatly affected his spirit. "I have heard that the king refuses arbitration, but I do not understand why. The church could have helped him put the kingdom at rest so long ago," he lamented.

"The king is unwilling to budge on the decree," Gurd replied, but his statement seemed incomplete.

Selasine prodded for more information, "Which decree exactly?"

Gurd looked concerned that Selasine asked about the decree. August set his pack down on the floor and found a crate to sit on, Gurd watching him until he stilled. "Anyone found guilty of using their uncanny magic will be cursed to have that magic consume their bodies and souls. The king has forbidden anyone but himself and his chosen from using those powers, even if they were to be used for good. History showed us how violently he put down the first groups that wanted to use their powers for personal gain. Nobody understands why he came for the simple folk that just wanted to use our powers to make life a little easier for our families," he summarized for the outsiders.

Selasine's brow furrowed. He had heard about the unrest and the rise of Erk to interkingdom infamy in recent months but had never heard of a law forbidding the use of one's uncanny magic. It seemed draconian and impossible to enforce. "How does the king enforce his decree, then?" Selasine asked, the civil unrest in Claston starting to make sense.

Gurd grimaced as he replied, "Everything from secret police to public spectacles in which the king curses those found guilty. In most cases, it's a horrifying execution. I had a friend whose only power was to create light, and after being cursed, he burned bright like the sun until there was nothing left, not even a body for his widow and children to mourn."

Selasine realized why the church had been so slow to respond. Such a law would never be deemed just by the Council of Four, and any rebellion, as a result, would be considered a lawful rebellion. "I guess that means that Erk has been leading the pirates to weaken the king's resolve?" he continued.

Gurd nodded, adding, "We have much to thank the captain for. Mostly our freedom, our lives, and the lives of our children. Nobody is exempt, and the king's curse is too much to resist."

Selasine felt a swell of anger inside. For Carulus to have organized the attack on Erk, he would have had to have used a certain amount of deception to get the army approved by the Council and the high paladins. His face was twisted into a scowl, and the candlelight from Gurd made the lines in his face seem deeper. He replied, "A grave injustice has been done here. The high priest that attacked you and your people must be exposed for his deceit, and the true nature of this conflict must be brought to the church."

Gurd's expression became hopeful, "Does this mean you

have a connection of authority with these fanatics?"

Selasine nodded. "I serve as a bishop to Invictus in the frontier between Claston and Alabaster. Everything that has happened here is an affront to the law and the church. I swear to you, captain, by my faith in the Sword of Justice, that I will right this wrong. I am at your full disposal and will aid you in appealing to the church."

A few moments of silence passed. Gurd and Selasine looked at each other, and August rested comfortably on the crate he had chosen. Gurd finally mumbled, "Well, now that I know who you are, why don't I make sure you have more comfortable lodgings." August breathed an audible sigh of relief while Selasine remained resolved.

"Our thanks, captain," Selasine replied.

"Gurd. Just call me Gurd, holy man," the sailor added, beckoning for Selasine and August to follow him.

Leading them up to the second deck, Gurd showed them the primary crew's barracks. Hammocks were tied between the beams of the ship with mats and cushions strewn about. Every sleeping area had a trunk, but many were wide open with garments and belongings strewn haphazardly nearby. "We refit the ship's cargo hold to carry families as units, but I've still got a crew of my own to take care of too. There are probably two hundred of us here, mostly women and children. I hope you don't mind staying with the crew,"

Selasine shook his head, "It's not a problem at all. It's an honor, actually."

Gurd grunted in agreement. "Well, I'll let the men know. You two get some rest; we'll put you back on the sails tomorrow. I'll introduce you to the captain once we reach the Isles Known for Nothing."

The night passed without incident, although Selasine felt as if he slept on high alert. The rest of the crew gave them a wide berth, but the barracks seemed to be where the sailors would end up after they had too much to drink in the dining cabin. August slept lightly, stirring anytime a drunken sailor stumbled to one of the hammocks. Selasine was afraid to sleep, as the last two days' events had awakened memories he had long buried. Iria and Telisi lingered fresh on his mind, but now they were accompanied by Miranda. Selasine blamed himself for everything that had happened up to this point but resolved that he would not lose Miranda. His heart could not stand to lose another child so dear to him. In a fit of dozing sleep, Selasine realized how much the girl had put his heart at ease over the last year. Telisi would have been about the same age as Miranda now. Honestly, the little girls got along well the few times their paths intersected at the monastery. For all the talk about the miracles that Miranda had worked, Selasine only now realized that just teaching and mentoring the girl had helped wounds in his soul start to heal after a decade of anguish. That was a miracle that had nothing to do with unknown powers. Her kind spirit, full of hope, had eased a suffering that no prayers could ever touch.

Selasine awoke suddenly to August's hand on his shoulder, a grave look in the young man's eyes. "W-what is it?" Selasine sputtered, coming out of his sleep, disoriented.

"Commotion on deck," August replied, his eyes trained on the door. "I heard shouting for the women and children to get below deck."

Selasine listened as the din of chaos spread throughout the cabins. He quickly readied himself and headed for the deck, his pupil immediately behind him. As they emerged into the morning sunlight, the sailors had readied themselves in battle positions, looking out to both starboard and port. A voice bellowed from the upper deck that Selasine recognized as Gurd's.

"We're surrounded, but don't let that discourage you. We'll protect our families and our freedoms; use all of the powers at your disposal!" he encouraged, the sailors gritting their teeth and preparing for an assault. But from whom? Selasine wondered. What enemy? He did not see other ships as he looked around in confusion, but a flurry of motion caught his eye. He cursed under his breath when he realized the situation.

"Invictus, guide our fates," he whispered, motioning for August to follow him up to the upper deck. Captain Gurd stood at the helm, sword drawn in his left hand, right hand on the wheel. "Captain!" he shouted, feeling the pressure of the impending attack.

Gurd nodded to Selasine, both of their expressions grim. Selasine reached inside his armor to pull his holy symbol free. "Captain, if you let me handle this, I can promise there will be no casualties." Gurd hesitated, but that hope he felt last night bubbled inside his emotions.

"Very well, then. What do you need?" Gurd asked.

"Pull our colors from the mast and raise up something purple. Anything purple," Selasine replied, his anxiety increasing as the motion out to the port side intensified. It quickly became apparent that a dozen warriors mounted on pegasus were approaching *The Water Sprite* at an intense speed. These elite troops would waste no time obliterating their targets, so Selasine hoped this was only their first examination of the vessel. About two minutes passed, and Gurd's men brought several silk shirts and trousers that had been hastily tied together. They were all mostly dull shades of purple and blue. As the first riders made an observational pass over the deck, the sailors began changing out the colors. The paladins above made no attacks but stayed safely out of the range of crossbows and pistols. Selasine sighed in a moment of relief. "They were counting us, preparing a strategy. Maybe testing for uncanny magic. Please, hurry with the colors."

Gurd's men raised the 'flag' as instructed, which caused the activity of the pegasus battalion to shift slightly. After a few moments, one pegasus rider approached the starboard side of the ship and shouted, "Who among you claims to walk the Path of the Sword of Justice?"

Selasine could feel the anger from last night swelling in his chest, but he tried to maintain his composure. He stepped toward the side of the vessel, returning the call, "Bishop Thomas Selasine of the Devitan Frontier, thrice honored warpriest, titled Shield of Alabaster, Wilderness Warrior, and Judge of Hearts." It had been so long since Selasine gave his full ecclesiastical title that he almost stumbled over the final part.

In an unexpected response, the pegasus rider returned to join the others. After an uncomfortable moment, Gurd leaned toward Selasine, "What happens now?"

Selasine stood, bewildered. "I'm – I'm not really sure. He was supposed to identify himself in return. That wasn't supposed to happen."

After approximately ten tense minutes passed, a small detachment of riders began to approach from the starboard side, Gurd hissing, "Stay alert, but non-threatening, men." The order resonated well with the sailors, hoping to avoid conflict.

The pegasus were graceful creatures, but their flight could be awkward to an untrained rider. Selasine knew these paladins were among the most respected fighters within the church, doubly so while in a saddle. This ship of common people would be slaughtered in minutes if the paladins did not recognize their error and attacked. Five riders were present as the small contingent approached, including a paladin that Selasine recognized.

The riders approached close enough to confirm Selasine's identity visually. The one Selasine recognized broke away into an aerial gallop toward the upper deck. Gurd's men tensed, but Selasine gave Gurd a cautionary gesture.

"Thomas? Thomas Selasine?" the rider said in a questioning voice as he descended onto the upper deck, Gurd's men standing as far back as possible to prevent provoking the paladin.

"Damil Starstorm, by the Sword, it's been at least five years!" Selasine exclaimed, a smile gracing his lips for the first time in two days.

The paladin dismounted his pegasus, and the two men embraced each other. Damil was somewhat smaller than Selasine, approximately the same height as August. He had an elaborate helmet adorned with purple and gold plumage, and the design of the scales of justice tempered into the crest. His hazel eyes sparkled in the early morning light as he greeted his friend, his chiseled, handsome face twisted up into a broad smile.

"Thomas! What on earth are you doing cohorting with pirates? The high priest had declared you a deserter, but it looks like you were—" he paused, looking around at Gurd's men timidly holding their weapons, staying far back. "Not even captured; wow, what is happening here, Selasine?"

Thomas's face dropped. "Please, Damil, listen. These aren't pirates. They're common folk. Peasants. Serfs. Sailors. They are being pursued by the King of Claston for daring to use their uncanny magics. This is a legal rebellion according to the tenets of Invictus. We should have had no business in this affair beyond arbitration."

Damil scratched his clean-shaven chin, his plate armor reflecting tones of orange and yellow as the sun began its ascent through the sky. "How did you learn of this?" he asked, evaluating the fact that Selasine's description of the pirates made much more sense than Carulus's.

"There's women and children below deck, Damil. Carulus has a lot to answer for, but there's no time. I need a pegasus. We need to catch up to their leader, Erk," Selasine continued, his excitement to see his friend obscured by his desperation to save Miranda.

"You're pursuing the girl, aren't you?" Damil asked, a bit of hesitation in his voice.

"Yes, this is my fault, and I ought to set it right. I can confirm that she is on Erk's ship, and their destination is the Isles Known for Nothing. I don't know how I will get her to safety, but I know they've taken her. That's all I need to know to pursue," his voice breaking with a sudden wave of emotion. "She's on their headship, *The Nebula*."

A pained look of compassion filled Damil's eyes. He thought of Telisi and Iria, and the paladin understood how excruciating this uncertainty was for his beloved bishop. "Thomas, I—" he started but stopped to gain his composure, the tragedy in Selasine's past still moving him to tears after a decade. "*The Nebula* broke the blockade this morning. It seems the girl's powers are capable of more than healing."

Selasine squinted with a dubious and suspicious scowl, "What do you mean more than healing? Miranda has no idea how to use the power; there's no way she could weaponize it. Even if Erk forced her to use it, she'd turn it on herself before she used it to cause harm. I'd stake the memory of my wife and daughter on it." His face was red from this sudden and unexpected revelation.

Damil realized that he had accidentally painted it like a violent event when in reality, there were no casualties. "No, no, nobody was hurt. Like, literally, nobody was hurt. The report I heard before we dispatched is that a bright wave of light covered all of the ships in the blockade, and the next thing anybody knew, they were all back at the navy yard in Claston. Messenger hawks and riders have been all over this side of the Undine Sea trying to communicate between Carulus, the King of Claston, the admiral of their navy, and myself. If I didn't have my gift," he paused, pointing to his head, "If I didn't have this, then I'd probably think the entire navy was sunk too."

Thomas nodded, remembering that Damil could communicate with limited people over large distances through a telepathic link. Wizards used that type of spell to coordinate experiments, conduct research, or play the esoteric strategy game Xanadu with each other without needing to be physically present with their colleagues. Using his uncanny gift, Damil became a master of reconnaissance for the church and was eventually promoted to High Paladin of the Pegasus Division.

"What of *The Nebula*, then?" Thomas asked.

"Out to sea. None of us have been able to locate it," Damil replied, glad his friend had calmed somewhat.

"All the more reason to take me with you, please; you know I can fly," Thomas pleaded.

A sincere look of sadness filled Damil's eyes again. "I would without a moment's delay, but—" he hesitated again, something that used to drive Thomas crazy. "I have orders to bring you straight to the archbishop."

Thomas shook his head in objection. "I will not give up on Miranda, and I will not report for deserting an army that should have never been raised. Send that message to the archbishop with that gift of yours."

Damil gave a shy grin, "He thought you'd say something like that. Believe me, Thomas, the archbishop wants the girl back as much as anybody. We need a concrete plan. The only reason we approached this vessel was its lead on the rest of the fleet, and since the blockade had been broken, we thought it our best chance to figure out what happened. Finding you along with these people is a stroke of luck."

Selasine frowned. "We can plan from here, though. We're closer to her here; leaving isn't logical."

Damil shrugged his head toward his shoulder, "Well, the

pegasus will need to rest, and this vessel isn't prepared to care for thirty of them, let alone all hundred of us." Selasine's eye widened in shock. Only one of the Council could dispatch an entire battalion of pegasus. This was not Carulus's doing.

Thomas let out a swift breath. Damil was starting to listen to reason. "But it could support two or three, yes?" the bishop asked. He thought there would be no way Damil would leave behind two pegasus, but he might be willing to ride with him. August had never trained on flying mounts, so Thomas knew it would be dangerous to bring him. Even though he sincerely hoped to fight by his friend's side again, leaving August behind was not an option either. He had already failed two pupils and was unwilling to let that happen again.

Damil twisted his lips in thought. He closed his eyes and lowered his arms to his side. Taking a deep breath, he seemed to start mumbling to himself. Thomas recognized this as Damil's uncanny magic. Most likely, he was communicating with the archbishop, a valuable gift in time-sensitive situations. After a few minutes of an incoherent, one-sided conversation, Damil slowly opened his eyes, giving an encouraging look to Selasine. Then, he began to speak calmly, "The archbishop doesn't quite know what to make of the situation. But he's given me permission to leave you two pegasus. With that in mind, I don't quite know what to make of the situation either." Damil reached out and placed a hand on Selasine's shoulder. "There was a day you would have chased after me with such fury, remember?"

Thomas smiled again, a flickering memory of the love he and Damil shared for each other in their early years with the church. With a nod, Selasine took Damil's hand in his. "If you were in danger, I still would. But these days, it looks like you're the one rescuing me," he added with a bit of a laugh.

Damil's smile melted into concern. "I don't leave my beauties with just anyone, Thomas. Take good care of the pegasus, and please, for the love of Invictus, take care of yourself too."

Thomas nodded, the promise reflected in his eye. "There's no chance that you're staying with one of those pegasus, is there?" he asked, remembering fondly the days they fought side by side, inseparable on and off the battlefield.

Damil shook his head with a sad smile, "I'm afraid not. We'll keep looking for *The Nebula* ourselves, but I feel you'll get there first out of sheer determination." He squeezed Thomas's hand as it still rested in his own. "I'll be back with your pegasus," he lamented, releasing himself from their clasped hands, mounting his pegasus, and taking off, the sound of hooves clacking on the deck and wings swishing through the air.

Within the hour, Damil had returned with a couple of other riders. To prove his point about the followers of Invictus, Selasine asked Gurd to bring some of the children up from the lower decks to see the magnificent animals as they paraded them on deck. Gurd, feeling as if his ship had suddenly been seized, complied for many reasons. Primarily, he knew the children would be fascinated by such a fantastic sight on an otherwise boring journey. He was also grateful to Selasine for intervening against the pegasus regiment. Gurd could now see the size of the heart of the man he invited onboard under suspicious circumstances. He wasn't sure how this man was connected to Erk, but Gurd wanted to help.

The pegasus were gentle animals, and the children aboard *The Water Sprite* loved seeing the majestic creatures as they circled the ship and landed on the deck. As tension on the deck dispersed, it became clear to Damil that Thomas was right. As previously reported, these were not vicious pirates but disaffected people displaced from their homes. It's no wonder Erk had such a reputation with the people. In their eyes, he was a hero standing against tyranny.

After bringing the spare mounts to Thomas and August, Damil returned to the saddle of his own pegasus. He looked down at his old friend, holding the reigns of the winged beasts tight in his hand. "Thomas," Damil started.

Thomas looked up at Damil; the gratitude was immediately apparent. "I'll never be able to repay you for this," Thomas said in a low tone.

Damil smiled, "It's not a transaction, my dear. You could, however, come visit me in the city when all of this is over. We don't have to pick back up where we left off; we can start over.

Together."

Thomas's breath slowed, memories of the past fighting for their time to replay. Telisi's and Iria's faces flashed in his mind, Miranda facing unknown danger, his old companion saving him in his moment of need. It almost felt like too much, but he knew he didn't have time to confront those memories right now. "When this is over," he said, finally. With that, Damil and his cohorts launched off the deck of the boat, the children around them letting out gasps of elation as the beasts circled the masts, gaining momentum.

The pegasus battalion headed north toward the bay once housing Port Undine. Selasine approached Gurd, the reins of his borrowed mounts in hand. "How far to the Isles Known for Nothing? I don't want to burden you with the care of animals," he began.

Gurd nodded in agreement, "I understand. The voyage could take us another ten days. If the winds are favorable, maybe seven." Selasine knew that the pegasus could fly that distance in a tenth of the time.

"It's settled then; we'll be moving out as soon as possible," Selasine added.

That second day at sea, Selasine cared for the pegasus while August helped the other sailors maintain the sails. With a good rest, they could fly straight to the Isles Known for Nothing, arriving ahead of Gurd and possibly even Erk. Selasine sat quietly on the top deck with the pegasus, a makeshift stable constructed from crates and other readily available resources. The air was warm, and the wind soothing. Selasine finally found a moment of peace, closing his eyes to rest. For the first time in a couple of days, he felt hopeful. The memories that washed over him were fond and comforting, smothering the nightmares screaming so loudly since this all began.

***

Nulodia was a thriving city of commerce on the far western shores of the Kingdom of Alabaster in the fertile Starlock River delta. The Grand Cathedral of Invictus was located in the temple district of the large city, serving as law enforcement and legal counsel for the substantial population of the Nulodian region. The laws of Alabaster were aligned with the church's tenets, and the King of Alabaster relied heavily on the clergy of Invictus to support his rule.

Thomas reported to the barracks of the church as required. He handed over the paperwork given to him by the bishop of his provincial church, which identified him as a peacekeeper ready to stand for the acolyte test. With his strength and build, Thomas would make an excellent warpriest. Fortunately, due to the church's efforts, war was not a likely endeavor for church recruits in this part of the world, but warpriests still supplemented law enforcement divisions throughout the kingdom.

The sergeant ensured everything was in order and told Thomas to report to the courtyard one hour before dawn. He would face his test alongside several other peacekeepers. That next morning, Thomas reported, fully dressed for battle. Among the others lined up there, he noticed another tall young man that had traveled from outside the city to join the Path of the Sword of Justice. He smiled at Thomas but said nothing, filling Thomas's stomach with butterflies. Something about this other person made Thomas feel drawn to him.

They both passed their test and became acolytes to train under one of the high paladin's regiments. Later that day in the cathedral dining hall, they sat across from one another.

"So, did they make you recite all of the catechisms, too?" the handsome man asked Thomas, causing him to turn red with nervousness.

"Well, I could barely remember my name, for starters," Thomas replied, staring at the food served to the trainees. It looked unappealing, but it smelled delicious. He poked at it with a fork as he spoke.

The stranger laughed a little more than Thomas thought he would have. Thomas looked up and saw his beautiful eyes gazing straight at him. "If that's the case, then I suppose you'll need some time to recover from your amnesia. That's unfortunate; I was really hoping to find out your name."

Thomas felt his heart leap into his throat and looked right back into the stranger's eyes. His sense of humor was just as cute as he was, making Thomas uncomfortable looking at him. His face turned even redder, and he couldn't really remember his name for a moment.

With a smile, the handsome stranger continued the conversation, "My name is Damil, by the way. I'll hang around with you until you remember your name, okay?" he said, a sly smile on his lips.

"If you make a promise like that, I can't promise I'll ever remember my name," Thomas added, the nervous feeling in his stomach swirling with an excitement he didn't recognize.

Damil smiled and continued to eat, choosing discreet bites from the food in front of him. Thomas felt himself starting to relax, getting more comfortable with this feeling. "If you want something to call me in the meantime, though, everyone around here seems to be calling me Thomas," he added, throwing a cheeky look across the table.

"Alright, Thomas. Until that real name returns to memory, it's just you and me."

Thomas and Iria's wedding was the most beautiful event Damil had ever seen. Five years ago, his promotion to the reconnaissance division had caused him and Thomas to drift apart. Thanks to his new duties, he had to sever the continual telepathic link he had with Thomas for the half of a decade leading up to that. It broke Damil's heart, but he knew it was for the best. It felt strange not to have his favorite person constantly in his thoughts; their minds intermingled. He loved Thomas with all of his entity, and though it pained him, he knew it was long over between them.

Damil sat in the back, trying to avoid being spotted. It didn't work, almost as if Thomas had telepathic powers of his own. Once the ceremony was over, Damil attempted to vanish without a trace, but as he reached the church doors in Devitus, he felt a familiar bear hug that immediately took him back ten years. A safe, happy feeling seeped through his mind, and he relaxed, waited for the squeeze to end, and turned to see his beautiful friend.

Thomas stood up straight, beaming with happiness. "Damil, you should have been at the front with the honored guests!"

Damil feigned a smile, today equal parts beautiful and

painful in his heart. "I didn't want to distract the groom," he teased.

The rare, boyish smile that Thomas returned was almost too much for Damil to bear. A second voice, just as sweet but much softer than Thomas's, joined the conversation. "Damil, darling!" He was nearly tackled by the bride, Iria, the beautiful elf even more elegant today. Her bridal gown was a luminescent purple, and her church insignia adorned the flowing purple train stitched in gold. Iriliandria Lancethinas, Lady of Flowers. Judge of Spades, Priestess of Peace.

In his usual humorous way, Damil laughed and commented, "It's your wedding, and here you are all fawning over me! Isn't there supposed to be drinks courtesy of the beautiful couple?" At this point, he knew he was caught and would stay way longer than he should. Thomas could see the pain in his smile, putting his own heart back up into his throat.

Iria grabbed Damil's hand and squeezed it, and she grabbed Thomas's as well. "There are drinks, and you have to drink them with us," she demanded, her radiant gray eyes piercing through the veil of her dress, telling Thomas and Damil that under no circumstances would she accept no for an answer.

Damil reluctantly joined the two at the head table, his mind desperately searching for a reason to leave sooner. Thomas had made quite a reputation for himself after leading a long investigation against a smuggling ring that had been plaguing Nulodia for decades. Damil, Thomas, Iria, and a fourth friend of theirs brought down the ringleader, Farzg. With Farzg's death, the organization broke apart and began cannibalizing itself. Shortly after, Damil and Thomas's lives took very different directions. He returned to visit his friend as often as possible, but their relationship just never felt the same. The love was still there, but a clear distance between them had begun to form.

The three of them celebrated together even after the rest of the guests had left. At some point during the night, Iria had fallen asleep in Thomas's arms, much like Damil used to do when they traveled together. With enough alcohol and happy reminiscing, it no longer felt painful. Iria was where she was supposed to be. As Thomas stirred, Iria awoke, and in a drunken, teasing warning, she grabbed Damil by the shoulder. "Hey, pretty paladin. Do me a favor. If something ever happens to me, you'll look out for this big oaf," she ordered.

Damil laughed, swaying under the influence, "Hey, vice versa, if something happens to me, you better—" he stopped, laughing. "You know, I just really miss those old times when it was us and Haelia?" he reminisced, gripping a nearby chair to steady himself. The three of them remembered the fiery hellspawn fondly, and she helped take down Farzg with uncanny magic that let her control fire. Being a hellspawn, a humanoid descendent of devils, made it hard for her to make friends and allies within the church. Iria could see her pure heart and was the best friend anyone could have hoped for.

Thomas stretched and let out a deep yawn. "If we can't go back to those days, then can tonight just last forever, us three here, happy, together?" he slurred out, standing with his bride in his arms.

Damil smiled and shook his head, "Duty still calls, old friend." Thanks to his moderation throughout the evening, he sobered more quickly than the others.

With a touch of sadness, they said their goodbyes. Damil's heart was full of joy now. Thomas and Iria's happiness was his happiness. He'd be back to visit as soon as he could, but he wasn't kidding. Duty could take him so far away that he might never see the two again.

As Damil approached the door to leave, Thomas shouted behind him, "Hey, Damil?"

Damil turned to look at his friend one last time for the next decade.

"I still don't know my real name," Thomas replied in a teasing, happy way.

With an evil grin, Damil gave a final attempt at a humorous reply, "Your real name is whatever that beautiful elf right there calls you when it's time for breakfast!" causing the three of them to burst into uproarious laughter one last time.

Chapter 9
Finite Fate, Infinite Faith

After eating with Pirate Lord Erk, Miranda could not get her thoughts to sit still. Upon hearing his story, everything Miranda thought she knew came crashing down around her. If she were to believe Erk, Carulus was responsible for laying siege to innocents, and she had unwittingly been a part of a plan that went against everything she thought she stood for. Furthermore, how could a king despise his own people so much that he would go to great lengths to increase their suffering?

She lay under the silky blanket staring at the "dressing room" ceiling of *The Nebula*. When Erk was a young elf, a sorcerer of great power fused his entity into the arcane stream, which caused the entire fabric of magic to unravel. As the chaos of The Unbinding followed, Erk and his brother Evan gathered people together for protection and cooperation, using their new, uncanny magics to improve their quality of life. The "king," however, had assassinated his brother to claim the throne just a few years before The Unbinding, and the chaos that ensued cost Erk and Evan their entire family, including their sisters and parents. Evan was cursed during a failed assassination attempt on the usurper. As a result of that curse, Evan had nearly perished, and Erk's desperation increased yearly. Miranda learned the current "king's" name to be Gelidor Claston, a follower of an evil god of corruption. Erk's fight would have been sanctioned by the church with this information. She felt they should have been helping the common people rather than offering arbitration.

With her thoughts swirling, Miranda laughed to herself in the quiet room. Selasine often taught stoically about fate and destiny, teaching that each individual is responsible for carving out their own path. With her strange healing gift, she wondered if fate would be so generous with her as to let her forge her own way. To make matters worse, she barely understood her gift. Erk seemed to think she could use it for more than healing, but she didn't know how. When she healed Evan, calling to that power seemed more natural than the two previous times it had manifested. She knew what she was looking for inside now, a second voice that radiated her deepest wishes and granted them with a spectacular purple light. She wondered if this was her uncanny magic even though it didn't fit within the current understanding of magic and what was capable with the arcane stream.

She closed her eyes, still unable to find rest. The silence was deafening and the darkness overwhelming. Erk indicated that the voyage to the Isles Known for Nothing could take another three to five days. He also wanted Miranda to speak with someone wise to the ways of magic once they arrived. In a way, she was excited to visit a legendary place like the Isles Known for Nothing. She was also afraid, but she tried to bury those emotions and let the warmer feelings drive her. Knowing that Erk had never meant her any harm was comforting. Still, intentions and actions could often have drastically different outcomes. She no longer felt like crying, but without Selasine, August, and Justin here, she didn't see much of a reason to smile either. She reached into the bag with her healer kit and withdrew the jewel-encrusted music box. She wound it up tight, and the haunting melody that played helped her find swift sleep, drowning out her thoughts, doubts, and fears with a nostalgic comfort.

A couple of hours before dawn, there was a knock on her door. She sat up in her bed, worried she might have imagined it. A moment later, there was another knock accompanied by Erk's voice, "Miranda, you're needed on deck. Please join us out here as soon as possible."

She stared blankly at the door, not responding immediately. She found matches by her bed, which she used to light a candle. She tucked the music box back into her healing bag. She gathered up her battlemail and spent the next few minutes preparing herself. She wasn't bothered by her lack of braids as she continued to learn the differences between traditions and law. However, she took a moment at the vanity to redraw the blue lines on her cheeks, giving her the look of a fierce warpriest. With a sigh of trepidation, she exited her cabin to look for Erk.

She found him on the upper deck, looking out at the water. He offered her a spyglass, and she took it, unsure what she was looking for. In the hours before dawn, the horizon was dark and infinite. She started to ask, "What am I looking for in the dark—" but then she could see it. Lights on the horizon were spread out at differing intervals. She grimaced, realizing they were likely approaching King Claston's naval blockade. "Nevermind," she mumbled and handed the spyglass back to Erk.

"These ships will destroy our families and our way of life," Erk added. "*The Nebula* can outrun them, but the smaller vessels will not be able to escape." He closed his eyes, and flames materialized around his wrists. "I could deal with the threat, but the people on those ships are also victims of the king's tyranny." He held a flame covered arm up, creating ominous shadows on the deck.

Miranda's heart did not sink this time. She knew that Erk was asking for her help, and based on what she had learned last night, she was willing to give that help. The problem, however, was that she did not know how to help with a gift she did not understand. "Right," she responded, looking back over the water, unable to see much with the naked eye. She clasped her hands to her chest and began to pray to Invictus, asking for guidance and protection.

The Nebula continued to the east for another couple of hours. The ships in the distance could be easily spotted as the sun appeared above the horizon in the southeast. Miranda figured there might have been twenty ships awaiting the refugees from Port Undine. She took a deep breath. She did not want to see innocent people demolished by this incredible show of force, but she also did not want to see the sailors from Claston struck down either. She wondered if the men and women on those ships knew they would be slaughtering innocents. She felt sorry for them if they were willing to blindly follow those orders. She had just endured a similar trial, letting Carulus manipulate her into using her gift in a way that led to where she stood now. She felt her resolve double as she closed her eyes and started to look for that second voice.

Miranda could hear the whispering in her spirit. She did not hear that voice the first time her gift manifested, but she could the second time. It did not seem to say anything coherent, but instead, it echoed the things she most desired in her mind. She felt like she could see and hear Selasine and the others; she could see the tiny church in Devitus and smell the countryside after a warm spring rain. Of course, that's what she wanted, or so she thought. Today, the only thing she wanted was to sail without bloodshed. She wanted more than anything to protect everyone involved in this massive miscommunication, and that is what she began to tell that second voice.

"Can we save them all?" she heard whispered loudly. She nodded mentally, but her body showed no such response.

Her thoughts screamed back to the voice, "We can, and we have to. We can save them all!"

On the upper deck of *The Nebula*, a purple light began to beam with Miranda as the source. Erk's face remained calm, emotionless as the girl began to glow. This could make all the difference. Today would be the day the king truly learned what he was against.

"Why do you want to save them?" the voices whispered. "They're here to do violence against innocents. Sink their ships, make them pay!"

Miranda mentally shook her head. "That is not the way of Invictus. Suffering begets suffering, and even though those guilty of great crimes can be punished, there has been no crime outside the king's actions. I am not the executioner. I am the protector," she felt herself responding, taking over that second voice.

The whispering faded as the light grew brighter still, swirls of white forming within the purple. Within minutes, Miranda looked like a beacon signaling to the entire world, the light extending into the sky beyond anyone's vision. She opened her eyes as she felt the power swirling through her body. It differed greatly from the feeling when she channeled the divinity of Invictus. She knew now what she could do. Her eyes glowed a bright sapphire color as the light that enveloped her reflected in them intensely. Eventually, Erk and the other pirates had to look away, but the light did not affect Miranda's senses. She stared out into the light, seeing the ocean and navy beyond. A surge of strength began to swell in her stomach, and she pulled the energy into the rest of her body with that center as her source.

As the power within her began to burst, she felt like she could replay the events of the last week in slow motion. She remembered Maréli's lessons, Carulus's provocation, and Selasine's anger at the high priest. She could see them so clearly in her mind, her mentor resting peacefully on the deck of a ship with a horse adorned with wings. She thought her vision strange but felt like she caught a glimpse of the future and the past. She dismissed those feelings as the energy reached her fingertips and toes, indicating that now was the time.

Something between the physical and the metaphysical snapped. Miranda screamed as her body responded to the energy swirling through her. "Everybody, just go home!" she shouted as the light pouring from her formed purple and white tendrils that started to lash out over the water, rushing over the thousands of feet between *The Nebula* and the closest ship. As the light made contact with the vessel, it vanished. More beams of light began to jet away from Miranda, each targeted at a single ship. After touching the ship, it would disappear.

Erk could hear a buzzing sound emanating from Miranda, but the light was too bright to watch. As the tendrils of light spurred across the water, he could hear the buzzing sound begin to pop, and he fought to open his eyes to figure out what this change in sound was. Opening his eyes but shielding them with his hand, he could gather that the light was moving across the water. He started to back away from Miranda, stumbling toward the stairs that led down to the foredeck of the ship. He hoped to see better with some distance between him and the spectacle before him.

His efforts proved fruitful as the intensity of the light began to lessen. He watched as each beam whipped out and touched an enemy ship, causing it to disappear. Erk's jaw slacked in bewilderment. Some of the lights went beyond the horizon, even. He observed in surprise until the burning light around Miranda began to fade. Thinking back to what happened to her after healing Evan, he looked back up the stairs, starting toward her in a dead sprint.

"Miranda!" he called out as he watched her body collapse onto the deck. Taking her in his arms, he inspected her for any signs of injury, but she only seemed to be sleeping peacefully as he held her. However, her hair had turned a vivid pink, which he thought strange. In fact, her body felt a little cold. She was still breathing strong, so he was only lightly perplexed. Erk sat her down gently, returning his eyes to the water. As the sun continued to rise from the southeast, the expanse of water in front of *The Nebula* seemed calm and empty. He reached for his spyglass, giving the water a close inspection. There were no signs of wreckage or evidence of a blockade. "It worked," he commented, his brain racing to understand what he had just witnessed.

Miranda awoke in the bed in the dressing room. The windows in the cabin let in the morning light, giving the room a peaceful glow. She was still dressed in battlemail, the metal cool against her skin. She sat up, her hair scattered wild on her face. "Pink?!" she shrieked. She felt like maybe it was the light, but she took a moment to focus on it. It had definitely changed colors. Brushing it aside, she slid out of bed, finding that the world around her felt like it was spinning. It took a moment for her equilibrium to return, but she willed her way through the dizziness. She hastily brushed her hair, anxious to get back onto the deck.

Miranda opened the door without warning, stopping abruptly as she spotted Shalo sitting outside on a crate he dragged over to make his guard duty more comfortable. He smiled broadly as the door opened, and Miranda emerged from the guest cabin, happy to see she was recovering. Her hair had darkened quite a bit while she rested. She looked directly at him, eager for information, "Shalo! What happened?"

The pirate bellowed a laugh, "Well, ya happened, lass. Buncha light, then, boom! The blockade was gone! Ya saved everyone!"

Miranda blinked in silence, trying to remember. She could see the tendrils of light in her memory, but it felt like that fleeting vision belonged to another person. She shook her head, "Where is the captain?"

Shalo pointed to the door to the captain's quarters. Miranda rushed over, catching the attention of the men working on deck. Before she could knock on the door, she could hear a commotion rising behind her. She turned around; a group of pirates waved to her, excitedly cheering. She paused, their cheers drawing attention from others nearby. Her mouth rested open, shocked. What was happening?

A voice emerged from the door behind her as it opened. "You've given them hope, Miranda," Erk said, catching her off-guard. She stumbled away in momentary shock, taking a few seconds to regain her composure.

"Hope?" she replied, still confused.

"Whatever you did, there's no sign of the navy that once waited. You've saved so many people from a tragic fate. And you're quickly becoming a symbol of hope to these men," Erk explained, gesturing his hand toward them.

Miranda looked out toward the pirates, feeling nervous and shy. She wasn't used to being the center of attention. She wondered how Selasine would respond. Her blue eyes shimmered as a tear formed, feeling relieved and overwhelmed simultaneously. She only hoped that nobody had been harmed by the light that lashed out at the other ships. "What am I supposed to do, captain?" she asked, an innocent plea.

"Wave!" he replied, taking her hand in his. He lifted their arms together, spurring a new wave of cheers from the pirates. "And don't forget to smile," he added.

Miranda couldn't smile, her lips drawn tight in surprise and contemplation. She held her hand up high with Erk's, trying to understand what he meant by 'symbol of hope.' With Erk's stature, it was not as high as she could have lifted her arm, but she was more comfortable with as high as he could reach. Just a couple of days ago, she was terrified of these vicious pirates and their capacity for cruelty. Now, they admired her, and she inspired them. Realizing how much her world had changed in such a short time, it did make her smile.

Erk watched as her face lifted with happiness, a gentle smile on his lips. "That's it, girl," he thought to himself.

The crew had demonstrated their gratitude long enough and began to resume their duties on the ship. The captain squeezed Miranda's hand before releasing it. "Come with me; somebody wants to see you," he ordered, heading for the stairs below deck. Miranda's gaze lingered on the men cheering for her, but she complied with the captain's request.

He led her below deck into a passageway with numerous doors. Erk stopped at the first door on the right and knocked. Miranda heard a voice inside that prompted Erk to open the door. She followed him inside the room, a small cabin designed to give a sailor more privacy and space. These rooms were probably reserved for the ship's officers. Thus, she was not surprised to see Evan sitting in a lavish chair, a book in his hand.

Erk broke the silence, "You're finally both awake at the same time!"

Evan looked up from his book, his lips twisting into a smile. "The healer!" he said, standing to greet them.

Miranda smiled in return, replying teasingly, "Miranda works too." Evan was average height for an elf, standing at a bit under five and a half feet. He had the same cascading golden hair and gray eyes as Erk. His features were sharp and handsome, a striking contrast to his previously emaciated appearance. His smile felt warm and full of gratitude.

Erk chuckled but did not speak. Evan looked to his brother, then back to Miranda, "Of course, apologies, Miranda. I owe you a debt of thanks."

Miranda started to object, "I am just glad you are better—"

Evan raised a finger, causing her to stop speaking instinctively. "Not just better, I'm whole again. The king took something from me so many years ago, but he also gave me something. While I was one with my power, I could see into the heart of the arcane stream itself."

Miranda listened, her head tilting curiously as he mentioned the arcane stream. "What do you mean?" she inquired, her imagination churning ideas.

Evan swallowed before continuing, "The fabric of magic itself. I could see it. It surrounds us; it flows through the air, through the ground. The essence of existence is wrapped up in the arcane stream and motivates all life. But right now, it is broken, fragmented. It clusters in places it shouldn't, especially in the bodies of humans and elves. When the usurper cursed me, he pushed my essence from the real into the arcane."

Miranda felt like she did not fully understand, but the way he described it so confidently gave her an image in her mind. "Can you still see it?" she asked, her curiosity working to make sense of Evan's experience.

He shook his head, "Not at all. I'm not complaining, though it feels like I can no longer reach the uncanny magic that once resided inside me."

Miranda's eyes widened in horror, "Does that mean I took your power from you?"

Erk frowned, but Evan quickly responded, "No, you didn't. The power was taken from me when the king cursed me. You simply pulled my mind back from inside the stream, leaving the curse and that godforsaken power there."

Miranda looked like she could cry at any moment. As a person who had spent their whole life unsure if they had an uncanny magic ability, she feared that losing such a power would be devastating to a person. She insisted, "Maybe I can try to fix your power?"

Evan again shook his head in objection, "At this point, I never want to feel that dryness again. After spending thirty years withering away under the weight of its power, I couldn't stomach it. Please, understand I feel nothing but gratefulness toward you, Miranda. Without that power, I can continue to live and fight alongside my brother."

Miranda's eyes still welled with tears. Erk watched stoically. Evan gave her a moment to process what he was saying.

"I'm just happy I could help," she whispered, two tears sliding down her cheeks. She closed her eyes and took a deep breath. She found these tears of relief comforting, warming.

Evan took a deep breath. "Miranda, when I felt like I was dying, I noticed something," he began to explain.

Miranda's composure was back. "What do you mean?" she asked.

Evan looked at the ground. "The magic of the stream. It fuels people's Unbinding powers. But somehow, it pools within you differently. It stays there; it doesn't just flow through you. If the arcane stream were a river, you would be a lake," he explained, trying to use an analogy that would be easily relatable.

"What does that mean?" she asked in bewildered response.

Erk interjected, "It means you are destined for amazing things, Miranda. If you can heal The Master, we may win this conflict with the usurper, and the people of Claston will be safe to live free of tyranny."

Miranda opened her eyes, the shining blue orbs bouncing from Evan to Erk rapidly. "The Master? From your story?" she asked.

Erk nodded, "He's in a similar situation as Evan. Except—" he paused, looking at his brother. "Well, he claims that he was the first one cursed by the king. His essence became crystallized and trapped in a gemstone. For many years we had thought our father was cursed first, but we cannot be certain. Still, we think your gift can restore him. If you'd be willing."

Miranda felt her heart rate increase. She wanted to help, but she was afraid. If they were relying on "The Master's" power, what if she restored him and he lost his power like Evan? She realized that this is what Erk meant by a symbol of hope. These pirates expected her to restore The Master, whoever that was. A terrible feeling coursed through her body. What if The Master causes more violence? What if she couldn't heal him in the first place? "I will try," she finally said, committed to helping. At first, Erk and Evan looked relieved, but Miranda continued, "I don't really understand destiny or how it works, and I'm a little scared of what will happen if I heal The Master. But, if my destiny is to help and heal, I'll keep healing until the kingdom is whole again." She let out a deep breath. Her fate may have felt limited, but her faith in building a better future overflowed.

And, to Erk, that is why this girl made the perfect symbol of hope.

***

Two days had passed since Justin had been slain and revived. Selasine and August were nowhere to be found. The bulk of the forces were now on the other side of the mountain, and the hospital camp was quiet. Justin had offered to help with the healing after he awoke, but Maréli refused, telling him to take time and recover. A brush with death was nothing to take lightly; she did not want the young man overexerting himself in such a state.

But at this point, there were no longer fighters to heal. It seemed that the pirates were retreating, and the mission was successful. The feeling in the base camp, however, was tense. High Priest Carulus had been silent, continually staying hidden in the command tent. The warm summer air was far more humid than Justin was accustomed to, and the boredom that plagued him added to the unseen pressure weighing over the camp. Trying to find an outlet, Justin approached Maréli, the most experienced person in the base camp.

"Chief Healer Maréli," Justin said as he entered the hospital tent where Maréli spent most of her downtime. Her eyes immediately cut upwards as she looked up from some scrolls on a makeshift table, evaluating his condition.

"Yes, acolyte?" she replied, the sharpness of her elven features exaggerated by the angle of her head as she looked up at Justin.

"I was wondering if there's anything I could do to help today; staying idle in camp is driving me crazy," he pleaded, feeling desperate.

Maréli tilted her head up to look more directly at the young man. "Of course, acolyte. Come," she gestured to the table.

Justin approached as requested, his eyes scanning the scrolls unfurled all over the table. The contents ranged from helpful reagents in alchemy to prayers intended to remove poison from the body. Unsure of what she might have been looking for, he waited quietly for her instructions.

"I need several things from around the forest here. I'm preparing provisions for the return journey. I think you're in good enough shape to scrape together some ingredients, don't you?" she instructed, her tone gentle and soothing.

Justin nodded and looked back at the scrolls. "Just let me know which ones and how many," he said.

Maréli grabbed a bucket beside the table and handed it to Justin. "I'm going with you; there's no need to bring the paperwork."

Justin followed her out of the tent and into the trees. The sun rested directly overhead, scattered and filtered by the palm and coniferous trees dotting the mountainside. As she collected ingredients, she started to inquire about Miranda.

"Did you know that Miranda had such a gift?" she asked, crouched over to inspect mushrooms while casually broaching a difficult topic.

"No, I had only heard rumors that she accidentally brought a family back from the brink of death. Selasine kept the matter very private and instructed us all not to worry," he replied.

Maréli's expression was cold and emotionless. Her eyes never left her task as she collected the mushrooms she had inspected, and then she began to check on some leaves from a nearby plant. "So Selasine didn't want to draw too much attention to the girl. I'm sure rumors like that grow with the distance they travel."

Justin winced, thinking that might be why they were

dragged away from Devitus. "I hope she's okay," he mumbled, sadness evident in his voice.

Maréli finally looked at Justin as she spoke, "She is. I can feel her heart from here. Whatever is happening to her now is likely taking her toward her destiny. A gift like hers has the potential to change nations."

Justin took a deep breath. Miranda wasn't a person who would want to change nations, though. She only wanted to be helpful. She was so caring and sweet, and Justin admired how gentle she was working as a peacekeeper. Even when met with violence, Miranda usually chose the swiftest, least violent way to subdue lawbreakers. Under Selasine's guidance and authority, she had already been working as an arbiter in a very unofficial capacity. She understood the laws well, remembered all the prayers, and had a heart for fairness and generosity. People occasionally came to the church at odds with each other, only to hear Miranda's lectures on the characteristics of those with good hearts. They often left in much better spirits, feeling that Selasine's rulings were fair in light of the girl's teaching.

"So, you think she has an important destiny?" Justin asked, hoping for insight.

Maréli returned to her foraging as she continued the conversation, "I know for a fact that she has an important destiny. But I know that you do as well, Justin. You and August are both tied to her by fate."

Justin gazed uncomfortably at the ground. "How do you know?"

Maréli smiled. "I'm a well-aged elf, acolyte. I've spent a century on both sides of the Unbinding. I know a thing or two about destiny."

Justin's mind fumbled. Did that mean Maréli was two hundred years old? There were a few elven families in Devitus, but Justin was not particularly close to them. Nevertheless, Maréli was the perfect teacher to help him learn the wisdom acquired over centuries, a key difference between humans and elves. "So, what should I do to help Miranda? How can I follow my destiny?"

The healer placed several more leaves, mushrooms, and

berries into the bucket. She carefully examined the flora, lamenting, "I can't find any torkoberry." Justin thought he began to understand how Maréli seemed so unbothered by the tension left in the camp. She had faith in Miranda and in her gift. That's why Maréli was one of the only ones who continued her duties diligently. She was at peace with her own destiny.

"I think I understand," he said before she addressed his question.

Maréli paused and looked back to Justin. "I knew you would understand. Miranda spoke so favorably of you. She really cares deeply for all of you. That's why she wanted to train with the healers on our way here. She wanted to make Selasine, you, and August proud. You're in her heart as a brother. If she can work miracles of this magnitude, you better believe that she will be coming to find you at the first opportunity she gets."

Justin smiled to himself, continuing to look at the ground. Most of the time, he and August treated her like a sister. They were overprotective of her when she first came to the church, but Selasine scolded them for that. August would try to play pranks on her, but they always seemed to backfire somehow. She was smart too, and Justin loved practicing catechisms with her. Her melodic way of singing the catechisms made them easy to remember. He missed her, August, and the bishop.

Maréli thanked him for his help. As they returned to camp, the sun was setting in the northwest. Justin had already decided he would not wait for Miranda to look for him. Instead, he would help find her even though his departure would be much later than anyone else's. He went to his tent to collect his things, filling up an adventuring pack with provisions, supplies, and clothing. The tension in the camp had reached a fever pitch as three battalions of troops awaited outside of the command tent. Fastening his pack, he crept out of his tent toward the command tent.

As the sun set, it cast an eerie light over the base camp. Foot traffic was almost non-existent, so it was easy for Justin to sneak close to the command tent. He tried to catch a glimpse of the assembled battalions, but it was still too bright for him to poke his head out from behind the tent. He attempted to listen carefully, but there was little activity inside the tent. The only sounds he could identify were the voices of soldiers in front of the tent, mostly expressing frustration with the waiting.

As the sun dipped below the horizon, darkness washed over the camp. Justin heard rustling inside the tent. To avoid being spotted, he stayed behind it, sneaking closer to one of the far corners before Carulus emerged out of the front. From there, he could hear the high priest issue his order, "You're being specially dispatched to find the girl. Remember, if she refuses to accompany you, she should be considered a dangerous threat to the church."

Justin felt a swirl of anger inside him. Selasine and August were most definitely off looking for Miranda. He wanted to help too. After the battalions saluted and marched into the woods, Justin followed behind them at a safe distance. Their torchlight lit the woods and mountainside, making them easy to locate and follow. He wondered where they were going as they did not enter the caves but headed south for the ocean. Justin followed them until dawn, feeling exhausted. There, those battalions waited on the shore, presumably for sea transport. Clutching his holy symbol, he whispered a prayer of guidance and luck. Going with them would be worth it if these people were looking for Miranda and their search was fruitful. He was technically an acolyte in the service of Invictus; there would be no reason they would not want him to come along.

He could never see Miranda as a threat to anyone, however, especially not the church. If they were to find her, he wanted to be there to protect her. She would trust him, and he could help keep her safe. This is what Maréli meant when she said that his destiny was tied to Miranda's. This is also what Bishop Selasine meant when he told his students that they were capable of forging their own fates. Right now, Justin knew that this was the path to take him where he needed to be.

Justin collected some firewood and approached the awaiting battalions casually, slipping among their numbers unnoticed except for a "Thanks, put the wood over there."

Chapter 10
The Isles Known for Nothing

elasine and August landed their pegasus mounts on a small rocky formation a significant distance away from what looked to be the largest island in an archipelago growing on the horizon since midafternoon. Holding a true course to the southeast, they departed *The Water Sprite* and carefully followed Gurd's "instructions."

"Just when you think you've nowhere to go. When it feels like all hope is lost. That's when you look for the Isles Known for Nothing. They appear to all travelers in the Solar Sea when all other lights have been extinguished," he told them as they departed. Technically, they had no other option but to look for Erk and Miranda on the Isles Known for Nothing, so the enigmatic message sounded true. Still, Selasine thought it felt like a riddle told by a mystic rather than a map to a concrete location. If all rational and supernatural reports were to be believed, they would arrive at their destination just by following a southeastern course.

The ride was difficult initially due to August's lack of experience. After getting used to the saddle, August felt confident enough to gallop through the air with Selasine. By the time they arrived, Selasine thought August should reconsider his ultimate goal in the church, aiming for Pegasus Knight instead of the other martial paths available to paladins. Still, they arrived at an island formation just in time, as their pegasus were exhausted. The sun burrowed its way into the horizon to the northwest, scattering the light across the islands in an ominous way. Neither Selasine nor August was sure what to expect, as the Isles Known for Nothing were a fairytale to most people. Sometimes it was portrayed as a peaceful settlement of the world's forgotten people, but in most legends, it was a haven for pirates. Based on the events unfolding due to Carulus's misunderstanding, Selasine considered that perhaps there was a balance between the myths and reality.

The small rocky island had no vantage points, and other small, mountainous islands obscured the contents of the central island. The two spurred their pegasus onto a larger island with a high standing ridge to try and gather as much visual information about the islands as possible. Winging their way to the top, Selasine and August could see a large, center island nestled into rolling mountains that jutted up from the sea. That central island was surrounded by an archipelago that looked to be home to countless villages and settlements. A mixture of mountainous and oceanside terrain would have made these islands an ideal place to hide, supporting the stories that suggested that the Isles Known for Nothing were the only place to outrun the law successfully. That same landscape looked equally dangerous as trying to escape the law in the first place. In the evening air, they could hear the loud sounds of tropical insects and birds, an organic cacophony representing the islands' natural diversity. The pegasus began to act agitated, a signal that the two needed to move on from their overlook.

As the darkness fell deeper, lights began to appear on the

islands. August and Selasine set their sights on the central island, which seemed much larger as they approached. The totality of the islands could have easily stretched out over forty miles, but the center of the formation took up more than a third of that distance. The mountains surrounding the island in the middle sheltered the rolling hills beneath from curious eyes. A large docking complex sprawled out of that island, cupping around it on the southwestern side where the land met the ocean. It was the only obvious access point to the city nestled underneath the mountains.

Selasine and August galloped across the tops of other islands as they approached the center. Many of them were covered by ancient, foreboding trees. It seemed that there were towns built into the tops of some of those trees, but they didn't stop to investigate. It took them another half hour to reach the central island from the smaller island with the rocky overlook, thanks to their mounts' exhausted state. The docks were very well lit, but the two attempted to approach from the least conspicuous direction. They planned to land near the docks that did not have many vessels moored, then attempt to blend in. Selasine had doubts about that plan, however, as their last attempt at pretending to be pirates imploded immediately. This time, however, they knew they were not pretending to be pirates; they were just two more people displaced by conflict.

The docks spilled into the sea on the southwestern side of the island. Selasine and August approached from the northwest and landed on the massive stone tide wall that overlooked the docks. Though the area was generally well lit, they found a cluster of unused docks near the end that did not have much foot traffic. They were near the edge of the tide wall on the north side, overlooking the ocean and steep hills that rolled down the mountains to the coast. Dismounting their pegasus, they took reigns in hand and began to walk southeast toward the main gate to the city glowing inside.

A yellow stone wall ran along the tide wall on the side opposite the ocean. It shimmered in the torchlight, glowing brighter the closer the wall ran toward the gates. Selasine led the way, hoping to avoid situations that might draw attention to the pegasus. As they walked toward the gates, they began to pass by people in the streets on top of the tide wall. None of them took clear notice of the two, and there was the occasional horse in the growing number of people. Selasine hoped the rag-tag nature of the island's inhabitants would keep them from standing out even with two massive, winged horses.

As the gates came into sight, Selasine breathed a sigh of relief. At first glance, it did not seem like there were any customs or inspection of goods coming in and out of the port. Furthermore, foot traffic was sparse near the gates. The atmosphere actually seemed relaxed, which was odd to Selasine. Living for so long in a port metropolis like Nulodia, he was accustomed to waiting hours to enter the gates after a return voyage. The laws in Nulodia were stringent regarding what could be brought through the port legally, and the customs officers took those regulations very seriously. As the two passed under the arch of the yellow stone wall, a voice greeted them in Khantongue, a language used primarily by wilderness peoples like giants and ogres.

"Marg'farked, ahlzbögendad?" the voice inquired. Selasine recognized the language, but he could not speak it.

In a surprising twist, August replied without hesitation, "MettosUndigne, fadwai noznogro peneeto." Selasine turned quickly to his pupil in stunned silence.

The same strange voice spoke in the common tongue, "So, only the boy speaks our language. Worry not; you're welcome here." A figure emerged from the shadows cast by the arch in the torchlight which dominated the port side. "Not even clerics of the Sword are immune to the Infernia wrought upon us."

Selasine sized up the interloper. He wore a brown cloak over a fine chainmail. He stood around six feet, a little smaller than August in stature. His face was round and charming, and as he approached the two, he seemed to have a bounce in his step. His lips were turned up in a genuine smile, his voice melodically fluctuating as he cooed, "Long many years since the beautiful pegasus graced the greens of Yendralia. Welcome they be once again, and the omens they bring!"

Selasine asked pointedly to August, "How do you speak Khantongue?"

August winced, realizing he had spoken before he thought.

"Dad used to hunt with the orcs up in the ravine. I grew up at the lodge; some of my best childhood friends were goblins."

Selasine pursed his lips in thought, realizing his surprise was misplaced. August's family, the Burchards, was related to nobility through marriage. Their influence in the Devitan Valley was substantial thanks to their role as merchants. It would make sense that August spent enough time hunting in the mountains with his father as a child. However, the younger children of such families often had to seek their own paths outside of their inherited trades. August was one of those younger children that pledged his service to the Church of Invictus in pursuit of glory, status, and revenge. Selasine knew the young man had lost a family member due to bandits, but he was unsure of the details. Khantongue, nevertheless, would serve any paladin well in dealing with wilderness peoples.

August turned his attention back to the stranger, "As I said, we merely seek refuge from the violence there. We await our comrades who will be arriving by sea."

The mysterious man's smile never wavered. "Here in Yendralia, you'll find refuge and so much more! Besides, the other Pirate Lords and Ladies anxiously await Erk the Radiant's return. Especially Pirate Lady Naomi! Your comrades will be celebrated for weeks!"

Selasine could not find an immediate reason to distrust the fellow, but experience made him wary of the overly eager stranger. "Could you point us to an inn with stables?" he asked directly, not wishing to prolong this exchange.

The man nodded, still smiling. "Check out the Silver Strand; it's in the lower district and as safe and welcoming as anywhere else!"

Selasine paused. Districts? Pirate Lords and Ladies? This society seemed to have some kind of structure that might be difficult for an outsider to discern. Rethinking his strategy, Selasine began to pry the man for more information. "How many districts are there?" he asked, estimating that the lower the district, the higher the poverty.

The interloper's eyes sparkled with excitement, his continual smile becoming somewhat unsettling by this point. "Three districts make up the marvelous city of Yendralia, the

City of the Invisibles. Those that come and go frequently stay in the lower district. We trade goods and supplies in the market district. But up there," he pointed to the hills that rolled up toward the mountainside that overlooked the rest of the island, "Up there, the Pirate Nobles of Yendralia watch over us and enjoy the fruits of their exploits."

August narrowed his eyes and asked, "That means Erk will be going 'up there' when he arrives, yes?"

The mysterious man nodded yet again. "Expect a huge celebration when he arrives. The pirate nobles are notorious for trying to outdo each other with their parties for every occasion. A most excellent spectacle of debauchery and festivities! You're in for a real treat here, strangers, and I think you'll love it so much that you'll never go back." Selasine's stomach felt uneasy. That would have sounded threatening if the stranger didn't speak in such a melodic way.

"So, to the Silver Strand?" August asked, looking back at his mentor.

Selasine nodded, "Thank you, stranger; your guidance has been most helpful."

The man replied, "Please, I am known as Cantalus, He Who Sings at the Gate. I remember every face that passes under this gate and listen for every fate that departs from these shores."

Selasine nodded, "Well met then, Cantalus. Thank you again." The bishop led the way into the city streets that stretched out from the gate and sprawled randomly through this lower district. August followed closely behind, their pegasus obviously ready for a rest.

Yendralia sprawled before them, climbing up the foothills of the mountains that sheltered this place. In the distance, a great fortress rose above all other sights in the city, a beautiful stone building that could withstand a siege for months. It had been easily visible since Selasine and August had passed under the gates and taken one of the winding roads into the lower district. The buildings around them were reminiscent of sea shanties, hastily constructed with whatever the inhabitants found available. Permanent buildings made of wood and clay were interspersed among the shanties, many serving as boarding houses for pirates in port, luxury inns and taverns, gambling halls, and brothels. The lawlessness of it all made Selasine shudder with discomfort.

The roads of the lower district were dirt roads beaten into the ground by frequent travel. There were no road signs to navigate the town, and people of all types loitered in the streets and in front of the shanties. Selasine and August could feel passersby watching them as they passed through the streets in the relative dark, and the torch lights inside the district were sparser than they were out near the well-lit gates. They realized they had no idea where to find the Silver Strand and that aimlessly wandering could keep them out all night. Selasine asked August, "Do you think we'll need Khantongue to blend in?"

August nodded, having overheard conversations as they meandered through the streets. "I'll get us there," he responded. As they passed by, a group of bystanders stood staring at the pegasus. August asked them in Khantongue where to find the Silver Strand. Selasine saw their gestures and confirmed with August which direction they should go.

"This way?" the bishop asked, his pupil nodding. They followed the directions shared by the bystanders until they found themselves in a cul-de-sac with a large wooden inn standing before them. A sign hung to the right of the door that read "Silver Strand" from top to bottom in bold silver paint. A beautiful wooden deck was built around the outside of the building. A couple of lean-tos pressed against the side of the raised deck, and people stood around outside in small groups. Off to the right, a large stable complex wrapped around the back of the inn. Selasine could see young men working at the stables, grooming and feeding the horses. He wondered where they had acquired hay on an island like this.

Selasine leaned toward August, "Do you think you can acquire our lodging and feed for the pegasus?" he asked, offering him a pouch full of gold coins.

August grinned as he took the coins from Selasine, "Of course, I can. Let's call it a debut for my heroics."

Selasine laughed, his student's casual bravado catching him off guard. August always seemed to stay cool in tense situations back in Devitus. The young man had a habit of choosing leisure over disciplined activities. Selasine knew those personality traits would make him stand out compared to paladins of normal, disciplined dispositions. August was strong and resolved, and his faith in Invictus was without question. It wouldn't hurt the paladins to learn how to lighten up. Damil was the last paladin Selasine had known with such a relaxed temperament, and he certainly wished the young man to have a bright and ambitious future like his former love.

August handed the reins of his pegasus to Selasine and turned to ascend the wooden staircase leading to the inn's door. Only two patrons were outside enjoying a drink on the patio, relaxing in the evening summer air. He entered the front door to the inn, which opened immediately to a roomy tavern, busy with the evening crowd. The aspiring paladin's large stature drew the attention of several patrons, but beyond that, August felt comfortable. With confidence in his stride, he approached the bar, where he could see a middle-aged man pouring ale from the barrels behind the bar. Maybe forty people were in the tavern, including the young men and women serving patrons. As August approached the bar, the man pouring beer gave him a welcoming smile, speaking in Khantongue, "Welcome warrior, how can I part you with coin today?"

August returned the smile, but his voice was stern, "A room and two stables might convince me to be generous."

The man nodded, "Without a problem, how long are we staying?" he asked in response.

August hadn't calculated the time necessary for *The Water Sprite* to reach the Isles Known for Nothing, and they had not spotted *The Nebula* on their ride over the ocean that day. To fit in, August replied, "Until the captain returns."

The barkeep stopped what he was doing and stared at August. With a suspicious look, he asked, "Which captain? This is a port, son; we see plenty of sailors day in and day out."

August amended, "Erk. Pirate Lord Erk."

The name caught the attention of some other pirates that were enjoying their swill at the bar. Two of them turned around on their stools to face August. Quickly sizing him up as a tough fight, they remained on their stools, but one of them interjected, "Another one of Erk's admirers?" bringing the conversation out of Khantongue to the common language.

August's face twisted in contempt. His mind raced for an answer to draw attention away from himself and Selasine, "Hardly. I'm just looking forward to the party, that's all."

The two pirates that had turned to face him started to laugh, August's confidence and quick wit allowing him to diffuse the tension. "Don't count on it, paladin. Dread Pirate Lord Erk has spent way too much time playing hero lately. Rumor has it that Dread Pirate Captain Zanfur is planning to challenge Erk for his seat at the Table of Lords," he said with smug derision and a little drunkenness.

August remained expressionless for a moment before he feigned a sigh of disappointment. He responded instead to the man behind the bar, cool in his tone, "Well, I guess if there won't be a celebration, then we'll just say five nights for now."

The pirates continued to watch August, taking a moment to look at each other. As August handed the barkeep some gold, they stood up. They waited for the men to finish negotiating until both were satisfied with the arrangement. August turned to leave, and the two pirates followed quietly behind him. As August descended the small wooden staircase leading from the deck outside, the two pirates leaped off the side. They hurriedly rushed up to August as he stepped off the bottom step.

"So, what's your business with Erk, boy?" one of them hissed accusingly.

August frowned. He should have known better than to start name-dropping in a tavern full of pirates. Though it led to some helpful information regarding Erk's rival, August was bored by the prospect of fighting everybody that didn't like something he said. "He's got something precious on his ship, and I'm just here to see that it makes it here safely," August replied with a truthful deception.

The confronting pirates seemed to salivate at this revelation, which August had predicted. Of course, they wanted more details on the treasure, one of them demanding, "What's this treasure like, paladin? It's not some boring church garbage, is it?"

August exaggerated as he replied, "Oh-ho, it definitely belongs to the church! It's not garbage, though; it's priceless. It's covered in mithril and gold with ruby-red pouring down from the top! You couldn't miss it. If you tried to steal it, you'd be in for way more than you could carry."

One of the pirates snorted and replied, "Well, it sounds like Erk could carry it just fine if he's bringing it to port."

August nodded sarcastically, "Oh, he had better carry it carefully. Since you two are planning on stealing it, right?"

The pirates' hands jolted to their weapons, one wielding a metal club of sorts, the other a short sword. August casually lowered his hand to the hilt of his sword, "Now, I don't have to fight you here. You see, I get paid if the treasure gets here safely. I get paid more if you try to steal the treasure, get away with it, and give me a cut. Right?"

The pirates looked at each other again, unable to resist the promise of a double-double-crossing. They "bribe" the paladin, steal the treasure, and vanish, never to be seen again. Then the paladin betrayed Erk for nothing, probably earning himself an early grave. They both gave the same troubling smile of agreement. "Well, Zanfur might like to know exactly what it is. You want to meet our boss?"

August gave a patronizing shake of his head, his voice feigning enthusiasm, "I don't know, I don't want to waste his time. I've just heard rumors that it's loaded with magical power, and if Erk gets it into port, nobody will be able to stop him. But," he leaned in close, "I just know that he might not bring it ashore with him at first. You'll probably have better luck stealing it from the ship after everyone disembarks." He shuddered inside; speaking in such a way felt very unnatural.

The pirates narrowed their eyes, their greed almost tangible, "So hit the crew while the boss is up at the fortress, paladin looks the other way, and we make off with the treasure."

August raised a finger in warning, "Well, you can't be sure the treasure won't be with Erk himself. You might have to keep your eyes on him."

One of the pirates furrowed his brow, "Wait, how big is this treasure?"

August gestured approximately Miranda's size, shrugging. "'Bout yay big, a little heavy with all that mithril and gold. You have to be careful, though; violence of any kind might damage the treasure, and if it even gets a single scratch on it, you'll both be as good as dead. And not by my hand either, trust me. There'll be a hunt for you to the ends of Espa. Remember, this belongs to the *church*," he emphasized with a raspy tone.

The intensity in their eyes made August uncomfortable. Nevertheless, he felt like his improvised plan was starting to take shape. The pirates relaxed a bit, releasing the hilts of their weapons, allowing August to do the same. The pirates seemed to have all of the information they wanted. One of them jutted his chin toward August, saying, "We'll see you the first night Erk is in port." They moved around August to go back up the stairs to the inn. August looked calm on the surface. On the inside, he was trying to calculate contingencies on what could happen if Zanfur bought the rumor, if they figured out that August meant Miranda, or if they got openly violent with Miranda close by. August trusted that if Miranda were okay, she would easily be able to care for herself if those two third-rate pirates attacked her or Erk.

August then looked into the cul-de-sac for Selasine. He spotted him by the stables, helping groom the pegasus. He figured the bishop was giving the stableboys a thorough explanation of his expectations and warning them that he would sleep in the stables with the beasts if needed. Chuckling to himself, he approached.

"What was that about?" Selasine asked, pointing back to the stairs of the inn.

"Tell me, bishop, is it chaos to turn your enemy against your enemy?" August asked.

Selasine stood upright by instinct, quickly saying, "It's one of the oldest acts of chaos in the Vexilatus."

August nodded, recognizing the Vexilatus as a catalog of specific acts of chaos and law. Acting in chaos required that paladins pay penitence in their prayers and actions. The Vexilatus described what must be done to atone in detail.

"Then I must pay penance, bishop. Do you know what I must do to make amends for turning my enemy against my enemy?" His voice was much different while formally addressing the bishop. He sounded authentic and sincere, calm even. This was the voice August was comfortable with.

Selasine paused momentarily, searching his memory for an answer before replying, "A prayer of penitence, and you must settle a quarrel between three people. Wait, August, what really happened up there?"

August sighed. The quarreling trio could take years to find and even more to solve. He shook his head, "Well, Bishop Selasine, I think I sewed a little chaos."

***

The Nebula crashed through the waters surrounding the Isles Known for Nothing at an alarming rate. Erk had not anticipated the swiftness or efficiency that Miranda's gift had when disposing of the Claston naval blockade. He had expected a prolonged standoff at best, but instead, she used the power within her to make it vanish. As a result, they were very far ahead of schedule, and a powerful wind out of the north added to their expedient arrival in the isles. The vessel approached from the north instead of the northwest, having sailed off course to deal with the blockade instead of taking a direct route.

Erk's calculations ceased when he saw Miranda ascending the stairs to the top deck. A smile broke across his face as she came into view, today wearing her freshly polished battlemail and the braids that indicated her status as a healer within the church. Her hair had fully returned to its rich shade of red, having turned pink after her miracle. As she joined him on the upper deck, he took another look at her armor, commenting, "That type of armor looks elven." He carefully examined the mithril breastplate and the fine golden mesh that made up the skirt.

Miranda's eyes dropped to examine what she could see of the armor she had worn since the beginning of this ordeal. "I'm not sure; it was given to me by the bishop of my church," she replied, unsure of its origins. "He told me it belonged to my mother."

Erk sniffed the warm salty air, looking back to the front of the ship. "Of course, it's no problem if humans wear elven armor. Their magical nature makes many things one size fits all. It's just a shame," he paused purposefully. After spending only four days with her, he knew she would jump to the worst conclusion. He wanted to assuage her worry before she had a chance to question the gift he intended to give to her. Her immediate reaction was an uncomfortable look at the ground, which meant his wish would be granted. He continued, "It's just a shame that the warrior wearing it doesn't also have an elven sword to complete the look."

Her eyes bounced from the ground to Erk, then to the hilt of her common sword. Though she took exceptional care of her armor and weapon, her armor was more recognizably unique. "Would it be wrong to wield something intended for use by another?" she asked, considering the implications of wearing the battlemail in a social context.

Erk shook his head. "No, ownership of material possessions is a fleeting construct made up by greedy men and women trying to cling to their control over this mortal realm through wealth. Just because it was made for an elf does not mean that it will belong to an elf forever." He gave her a kind smile, reaching to the scabbards on his belt. "For example, this sword." As he tugged the hilt, a blade coated in a subtle radiance emerged.

Miranda's eyes widened; the hilt and the blade were beautiful. It seemed similar to her battlemail, gold and silver metals shimmering in the light emitting from the blade. "Is this a sword that you acquired pirating the Claston nobles?" she asked, mesmerized by the sword's beauty.

Erk laughed, "I thought that would be your concern. No, my dear, this is an heirloom that belonged to someone very precious to me. My sister, Iriliandria. As I told you, she . . . well, she left Claston almost seventy years ago. We've not heard from her since. She left the sword with me, telling me she never wanted to be an instrument of violence again. I didn't blame her after everything we went through in those early years. You remind me of her in some ways. But I think you understand that sometimes violence is necessary to see your goals realized, especially when those goals protect the people you care for." He had withdrawn the sword fully from its scabbard, holding it by the hilt with the blade pointed at the ground. The silver handle was draped by a golden handguard twisting around like ivy growing from pommel to cross-guard. The broad, double-edged blade was about three and a half feet long, the radiance around the blade glowing tones of white and gold.

Miranda's eyes could not leave the sword. It felt familiar to her, but she couldn't figure out why. "It's beautiful," she whispered.

Erk's smile was evident in his words as he said, "And I want you to take it."

Miranda's gaze immediately shifted to Erk, who was looking intently at the sword. "You know I can't accept something like this," she replied, watching him cautiously.

His smile never broke, "That's why I'm not giving you a choice. This relic has sat in a chest accumulating dust for almost seventy years at this point. And now," his eyes shifted from the sword to Miranda's piercing stare. "Now it needs a new owner."

Miranda drew her lips up in contemplation. "Why? If what you say is true, then Iriliandria did not want to be party to any more violence. Wouldn't bringing the sword back go against her wishes?" she replied as she thought.

Erk gave an ambiguous shrug. "I'd say her wishes were that the sword be passed on to somebody more suitable than her. And if I give it to you, I'm confident that the violence wrought by the sword will be minimal. In a way, using her sword would be the most fitting fate for all of you. Her, you, the sword. The world will be better with this in your hands."

Miranda swallowed before extending her arm. "You are right; I would never wish to use something so beautiful for violence," she commented as she touched the pommel of the sword. It was a round pommel with a brilliant diamond encrusted in the center with ivy designs on the inlay around the gemstone. It reminded her of the sapphire blades fixed into her mithril gauntlets. Beautiful, but deadly.

Erk loosened his grip, giving it an insistent push to Miranda. "Which is why I know that this sword will never be used for anything more than protecting the innocent and the weak from their oppressors," he added.

Erk's logic made sense to Miranda. She had never considered herself materialistic, but part of her wanted to accept Erk's gift just because it was beautiful. Furthermore, it seemed to be a magical sword, which neither August nor Justin had. But Erk knew exactly how to make a convincing argument before speaking to her. In a way, she became concerned as she wrapped her fingers around the hilt of the blade, taking it from him. He clearly understood how to predict people's behaviors, and Miranda's conscience winced at the potential implications of being manipulated by Erk. She was not sure how to learn how to balance trust with suspicion, but she thought the pirate lord would be a great teacher. With that thought, she firmly gripped the sword, holding it up before her. Her crystal blue eyes shimmered, reflecting the magical glow of the sword. "Then, thank you, Erk," she murmured, still lost in the feeling that she had seen this sword before.

"We'll be making landfall around noon today. Take a last look around the dressing room for anything else you'd like to take ashore. There will be a celebration of sorts when we arrive, so getting back to the ship may prove difficult. We have more important duties, though, don't we?" he ordered, turning his attention back to the islands spread out before them.

Miranda hesitated, holding the exquisite sword in her hand. "Erk, can I ask you a question?" she began, timid.

He returned his eyes to the young woman. "Of course, I am at your orders," he replied.

"Why do you call it a dressing room? There's nothing but stuff for women in there," she asked, trying to piece something together to explain why Erk had a perfectly kept cabin full of luxury.

Erk laughed loudly, and his cheeks flushed deeply. "Apologies. I am betrothed to Pirate Lady Naomi, Queen of the Waves, Succubus of the Seas. While she has her own fleet of ships, she has traveled with me and my crew in the past. Anything that looks like it would be appealing or helpful to her ends up in there," he explained, smiling. "She has expensive tastes and an even bigger heart."

Miranda thought it strange that a notorious pirate would speak of betrothal and love. The surprises seemed never-ending. She removed her old sword from her scabbard and replaced it with the elven blade. The simple wooden scabbard was already dull, but it seemed to vanish with the resplendent hilt protruding from it. She nodded to Erk, "So, what should I take if it belongs to Pirate Lady Naomi?"

Erk smiled sincerely, "She would give you the entire room if she thought you wanted it. Please, just look around and see if there is anything you would like to take with you. Naomi will be madder at me if you don't. Everything she can't live without is on her ship," he elaborated.

Miranda's thoughts lingered on what Erk said about the sword. With a nod, she scampered back down the stairs to the guest cabin. Inside, she gathered regular provisions like candles, torches, and camping supplies. After collecting needles, threads, and buttons from a sewing box, she glanced at the ornate vanity. She gave herself a long look in the mirror. Just a couple of weeks ago, she would not have believed how far away from Devitus she would end up. Even a week ago, she had no idea how complex a lawbreaker could be. The differences between right and wrong were not always as clear as she had thought. With those feelings running through her mind, she looked down at the things on the vanity. She looked at the beautiful comb, a silver and sapphire tiara-style trinket that fit nicely into the back of her hair, pinning in tightly behind her braids. Erk's words echoed in her mind again, and she considered his practical philosophy. She slipped the comb into her hair and took the small makeup jar with the blue pigment. She tied everything up neatly into her pack and strapped it on her back. As she opened the door, she sighed with some measure of relief. She hoped she wouldn't have to see the inside of that cabin again, at least not as a captive.

Erk and Jax awaited on the upper deck at the helm. Shalo and Evan were also present but standing near the stern. Jax gently tugged on the wheel, and Miranda could feel the ship lurching at high speed. She gripped the railing of the stairs, feeling that fear from her first day on the ship returning. She stumbled up the remaining stairs, loosening her grip on the railing as the ship steadied moving forward. With a broad gesture, Erk motioned forward, "At last. Yendralia," he proclaimed.

Miranda's eyes followed his gesture. Before her sat a sprawling city nestled behind docks grander than those she saw in Port Undine. As the pirates began to furl the sails to bring down *The Nebula*'s speed, more of the islands came into view. The archipelago before her glowed with a natural radiance, hues of green and purple rolling up from the lush but rocky islands. A towering mountain range surrounded the city behind the docks, cupping around it like protective hands blocking out all intrusion. Miranda marveled at the beautiful spectacle that rolled out before her. Erk sighed listlessly, admiring the girl's appreciation for the world's natural beauty. He hoped their upcoming ordeals would not dampen that innocent, wonderous outlook.

Miranda took small steps with growing confidence as she approached the helm. Erk looked at her with a wicked smile. "I'm glad you decided to keep the comb," he said, his voice a bit more shrill than usual.

Her eyes widened as her hand reached up for it instinctively. "Oh, I . . . I just thought it fit me. And considering what you told me about the sword—" she replied hastily, a blush of embarrassment as she looked down.

Erk laughed and responded, interrupting her, "Yes! Yes, exactly. I'm glad you understand and have the wisdom to act accordingly. The comb suits you and your faith. Just like the sword. You need only be true to your heart and honest with those around you." He stepped toward her, reached out, and touched the plate of armor that cupped her shoulder in a protective carapace. "My gratitude for you only grows by the hour. I will do everything in my power to help you understand the gift you possess."

Miranda blinked slowly, recalling their conversations over dinner the last few days. Erk claimed he knew a mystic being who lived on one of the Isles Known for Nothing and wanted to take Miranda to meet them. She had agreed initially. However, Erk's natural tendency for manipulation had her on guard. Moreover, the pirate lord seemed to believe there would also be a conflict between himself and a different pirate once they arrived in Yendralia. His concerns about his rival made his plans to take Miranda to the mystic being ambiguous. She decided to just weigh each step along the way, carefully considering her options or the consequences. Right now, they simply needed to dock, make an appearance at a celebration, and retreat to the Fortress of Lords near the foot of the mountains surrounding the island city. She had to take those steps carefully, especially because she was isolated from everyone she fully trusted. At the very least, between Carulus and Erk, she was in touch with the mysterious gift inside her. Perhaps it could help her if she found herself in a situation that looked too problematic to solve with diplomacy. Part of her wondered if she could use it to find the bishop and the others and teleport herself directly to them.

Those kinds of thoughts troubled her. If she was honest with herself, she felt utterly lost. She had come to respect Erk's cause but couldn't fully agree with his methods. The fact that he was willing to go to such violent ends made her fearful. Many of her ideals and outlooks had changed. First, she thought that the King of Claston, Gelidor, was a much more terrifying person than who she initially thought Erk to be. Second, she worried about what would happen if, at any point, she felt that she could not or should not help Erk. She wondered what Selasine would advise her to do. As her thoughts swirled around this internal crisis, she could feel the ship dragging to a stop. She blinked, and her focus left her thoughts for her immediate surroundings.

A crowd gathered on the docks and the tide wall overlooking the port's ocean view. It was all built out of a beautiful yellow stone that glowed in the noon sunlight. Miranda looked over the crowds and let out a deep sigh. She had never seen so many people gathered in a single place, and the sight filled her with anxiety. Erk noticed her discomfort and reached out to touch her arm. "Miranda, do not worry. The officers will go ashore first and disperse the crowds. We will head to the markets to make our appearance. After that, you do not need to worry about the crowds."

She winced briefly. She knew she needed to learn how to control the emotions on her face. "I will follow your lead, then," she replied, relying on his apparent honesty.

As the crew of *The Nebula* lowered the gangplank and began to disembark, Jax, Shalo, and Evan went ashore with the men to draw the crowds with them. They showered the people with promises of riches, tales of bravado, and prospects of overflowing alcohol. As the crowds were easily swayed by such promises, they did not take long to disperse. The people of Yendralia followed the crewmates of *The Nebula* to the taverns and bathhouses. Erk, Miranda, and two other pirates waited for most of the crowd to disperse before approaching the gangplank.

Miranda had seen these other pirates working on the ship throughout their voyage. One seemed to be able to increase his strength at will, and the other seemed to be exceptionally quick while working on deck. She was impressed with their skills but did not realize that Erk had hand-selected them to serve as bodyguards. To be fair, however, Erk's personal bodyguard of choice had presumably been killed by Carulus's forces when Shalo kidnapped her from her tent. The thought that others were hurt in pursuit of her power frustrated her, but she didn't know quite how to express her emotions without troubling Erk. The pirate lord insisted that Apocalypse's gift would restore him, so he was not worried about whether or not he got killed. Nevertheless, this duo of pirates made a vicious pair, and Miranda was not surprised that Erk had replaced Apocalypse with these two.

Bongo and Royce, the strong and fast pirates, led the way down the gangplank. Miranda and Erk followed behind. As people from the crowd attempted to close in on the pirate lord and his guest, Bongo flexed his muscles and pushed the crowd back. Royce then worked himself into a frenzy, causing him to blitz around the area like a lizard darting off walls and roofs. The sudden movement was so intense that it frightened onlookers enough to begin dispersing the crowd.

Miranda followed Bongo and Royce as they cleared a path through the remaining crowd, while Erk followed behind after putting on the most ridiculous hat she had ever seen. It was an oversized tricorn hat with extravagant plumage adorning the base of the hat. The jet-black leather under the feathers stood out in the noon sunlight. She gave a judgmental sigh and asked in a tired melody, "So you said you wanted to be inconspicuous?"

Erk shook his head, his golden locks dancing around his shoulders. "Not entirely. They have to confirm it was us in the market district. This is the price of being a pirate lord. With every perk, there's always a price. Remember that."

She gave a hesitant laugh. It made sense that he would want a blend between undisturbed passage that onlookers could loudly confirm. "Yes, Pirate Lord Erk," she replied, her voice caught between a teasing prod and sincerity.

His face twisted into an annoyed visage, but the negative feelings burst into a hardy, authentic laugh. "So formal, Miranda?" he bounced back in a chuckle.

She gave an exaggerated nod. "I figured it would be prudent to give you the most honorifics in port, captain," she giggled.

Erk laughed in return, "Well, you've thought far enough ahead, haven't you?" he said, advancing his stride to catch up to her. "I do love formal introductions, but it felt strange to hear it from you."

Miranda smiled. As Bongo and Royce continued to keep the crowds at bay, she started to become concerned. "Are you still worried about your enemies in port?" she asked quietly.

With a smirk, he shook his head. "I wouldn't worry about that third-rate dread pirate on my worst day. Don't worry; we shouldn't face any confrontation. At least, not yet," he assured.

A single, paved road stretched from the docks directly to the Fortress of Lords. They found themselves alone as they followed it from the lower district to the market district. Erk furrowed his brow with anxiety. "Why is it so quiet, boys?" he asked Bongo and Royce.

Royce grimaced. "Let me find out, cap," he replied. Suddenly Miranda's casual watching could not keep track of the pirate.

"Where did he go?" she whispered quickly, but Erk gestured for her to be quiet.

"There should still be some crowd; we might be in danger," he replied. She noticed that his hand was fixed on the hilt of one of his swords. She, in turn, gripped the hilt of the new sword he had given her.

As they moved forward, Royce suddenly returned to the group's vision. He quickly warned, "It's an ambush, cap."

A couple of pirates not affiliated with Erk's men leaped out from an alleyway between an inn and a carpenter's shop. Miranda spewed out a quick curse, a darker prayer that would ask the invoker's god to hamper the efforts of another.

Invictus's power surged through her body, and a red halo surrounded the attacking pirates. Their sudden misfortunes became terrifying yet hilarious as they found themselves stumbling toward Miranda and Erk. One tripped over a barrel of harpoons, causing him to scream in horror. He did not impale himself, but it felt like a very close call. The other tripped over his own feet, falling face-first into a rainwater barrel. Bongo and Royce pounced immediately on the attackers as Erk grabbed Miranda by the hand. They started to sprint through the streets of the markets toward the Fortress of Lords.

As they neared the wooded approach to the fortress, a pirate stood in the road with a menacing stance. Behind him stood two winged horses mounted by shimmering warriors resting in war saddles. Erk took Miranda's arm with a sudden grab. "It seems like I was unable to keep my promise. We may be in for quite a fight here."

Miranda scowled. "I don't think we will have to fight, captain," she replied, looking hard at the warriors mounted on the winged horses. It reminded her of her vision of the future when she sent the blockade away.

Erk wrinkled his nose in confusion, "What do you mean?"

Miranda broadly smiled as she was sure of what she saw. "Because captain. Those two guys are some of the best friends a girl could ask for!"

Interlude
The Counselor of the Corrupt

On that first night together on *The Nebula*, Erk looked to Miranda. "Do you speak elven?" he asked his captive as they dined. She had impressed him thoroughly with her knowledge of the tenets of Invictus, and her heart was pure. She healed his brother, for which he could never repay her. He knew this girl was the missing link in his campaign against the usurper, Gelidor Claston.

Miranda shook her head, answering, "I'm afraid I only know a few words."

Erk smiled. "Very well. I only ask because the story of my journey would make more sense in informal elven, but worry not. I have told this tale in many tongues."

Miranda's eyes shimmered with excitement. She loved stories. She, however, had never heard a tragedy like the one Erk shared with her that first night, a tale that would shake everything she thought she knew about right and wrong. *The*

Nebula hurtled through the water, making the captain's quarters creak around them.

Erk took a moment to preface his story, explaining, "For this to make sense, please allow me to start at the beginning. The very beginning. My hatred for the king is founded in the very same virtues you believe in with all your strength."

***

"Erilkaiden, stop!" Iriliandria shouted.

"I don't wanna," her little brother replied. He was ten, but he was acting like he was five! Iriliandria was twenty-five; she was too old to be babysitting. If she had a choice, she'd rather be taking care of baby Evanthalus. Mom and dad always left the baby with Ara'Ilyvithia. This really wasn't fair. She was so ready to be thirty-six so that she would be the age of majority among elvenkind and could refuse such annoying tasks. Big sister Ilyia was thirty-five. Dad would probably announce her betrothal to Boscht of the Holia household soon. Though it seemed like an arranged marriage, Ilyia and Boscht were definitely in love. He had been wooing her for the last decade as her Dedicantae, an elven courtship expressed through absolute devotion to a person regardless of romantic feelings. Plus, unity between the Lancethinas family and the Holias would help strengthen their demands that the serfs of the kingdom be set free from their captivity to the land. They had seen the mercantile possibilities of a free society under the governmental structures of the Church of Invictus. Alabaster was a thriving kingdom, and Osgood, a human kingdom far to the north, enjoyed independence and prosperity under Invictus's teachings. In a sense, some of these newer noble families were missionaries for the cause of a liturgical monarchy. But right now? Iria couldn't care less about her duties to Invictus.

They stood in a citrus orchard, lemons and oranges growing overhead. The tropical climate of southeast Claston made for a favorable environment for the fruit. They even had a few yindai fruit trees, a core ingredient in many anti-aging balms that could bring back the beauty of one's youth. Solisberry, yindai, and eolnut trees were all sacred to elvenkind. It was fabled that the arcane stream itself passed through each of them. Regardless, Erilkaiden would not stop throwing the yinfruit at Iria, the small cone-shaped fruit ripe and bursting easily on impact. Her leather tunic was already drenched, and her little brother simply would not stop.

"Ha! Gotchya!" Erk shouted as he chucked another yinfruit from a scooping sprint, jumping in a spiral through the air to toss the fruit at his sister. It smacked her dead in the face, exploding with a squishing sound. It wouldn't have been a big deal, but yinfruits had a large pit in the center, much like a peach. The hard center of the fruit made an audible popping sound as it bounced off of Iria's left brow. It gashed her hard. Her little brother was deadly throwing fruit?! She would have been more impressed had it happened to somebody else.

"Talirix volïs! Erilkaiden, you brat! You've drawn blood!" she hissed as she drew the longsword from the scabbard on her belt.

Erk's eyes widened in fear. "No! Sis!!" he shouted.

"Bind that which sews chaos," she murmured, reaching up to grasp a holy symbol shaped like the scales of justice that hung from her neck on a shimmering mithril chain. A red aura wrapped around her little brother, dropping him to the ground from his spiraling ascent through the air. A trail of blood streamed down Iria's face from the injury caused by her brother's recklessness.

Erilkaiden looked up at his big sister, the red tendrils flashing hard as he tried to escape. He saw the injury he had caused her, and his stomach flipped upside down. "By Lexcord, Iria, I'm sorry!" he swore, the bindings squeezing with his breathing.

"I told you to stop five minutes ago. Not only is this goo hard to get out of my robes, but seriously. Those things hurt, Erk. You should think more about how you make other people feel with your actions," she scolded. "Besides, it's yinfruit. That's worth a fortune. And you're just throwing them like water bombs at a Festilvien," she continued, referencing the festival in honor of the king every year on his birthday. The water bombs were just toys meant to entertain children. The yinfruit, however, could fetch a few dozen gold each. "You're costing the family a fortune!" she scolded harder as she went.

Erilkaiden started to cry. "I'm sorry, yashirote, I promise!"

he begged, calling her the most respectful name for sister.

"Good," she grumbled, letting him out of the curse. The red, static bindings immediately vanished as she dismissed them. Erk ran to his big sister's side, looking up at her. She smiled at him. "Hey, you see what you did?" she continued with the lecture, pointing to the blood running down her face.

"I'm sorry, I really am," the young elf explained.

"You better be, Erilkaiden," Iriliandria swore back at him. She then gripped her holy symbol again, whispering a healing prayer that removed any trace of injury except for the blood that had dried on her face. She looked down at him, "I won't always be around to clean up your messes, Erilkaiden. You have to be more considerate; otherwise, you won't make any friends. You don't want to be the only elf with no friends, do you?" she asked, trying to get him to reflect on how he was acting.

"But won't you always be my friend?" he asked, still shaken up from having been bound by a divine curse.

Iria laughed, not expecting that question. "Of course, moshirin," she assured him, using the elven honorific for little brother. "Not all families are blessed to get along well, though. Our paths in life could be very different, and there may be a day when we part ways, never to be reunited. I don't want my little brother to be stuck without friends," she explained, hoping to get through to him about his reckless behavior.

"If that happens, then I'll be very sad," he pouted, looking at the ground.

"Don't be that way, Erk," she continued. "While I am here, I'll do my best to be your big sister and help you find the right path. But I want you to be able to find that path without my help. You are the only one who can understand what's in your heart. Like just now, why were you throwing the yinfruit at me even after I ordered you to stop?" she asked, prompting him to reflect.

"I don't know, it was fun," the young elf explained.

"That's not a good reason for doing something. You hurt me as a consequence of your actions. Promise me that you'll start thinking about why you do something rather than acting on impulse, okay?" she asked, her voice sweet and concerned.

"Okay!" he promised.

Iriliandria smiled. "Come, now. We have prayers to recite for your penance. We must go to the chapel."

Erilkaiden scowled, but he had already caused enough problems for today. He was still two birthdays away from beginning his magic training. Then he wouldn't have to do the silly church rituals with his sister. Mother was the one who was the priestess. Father was a wizard, which is what Erk wanted to be.

***

"Your focus is all wrong," Erilkaiden explained to his brother, Evanthalus. Now that Erk was thirty-six, he was considered an adult in Clastonian society. This also meant that he had earned the responsibility of helping Evan with his magical training. He was a decade younger than Erk, his age putting him near the end of elven adolescence.

"But I can feel the mana in me! I know it's there; it just doesn't shape how I want it," Evanthalus complained. They were standing in a burned field specifically designated on the Lancethinas estate for training destructive magic. Erk had watched his father burn this area with finely controlled fire magic. His finesse was unbelievable.

"Try this," Erilkaiden replied. He began the somatic element of the spell, turning his hands down and touching his fingertips together, leaving his thumbs straight out. He began to tap his fingers together in succession, starting from his pinky. As he did, he started to speak the incantation, "Ciere. Potestas. Ignis. Incendo." The older brother ignited a ball of flame in his connected hands and then turned them up in a cupping gesture. The fire orb hovered from his hands and moved with only Erk's concentration. "See? Make sure you begin the incantation with your focus on the fire. Then your spell will shape the mana you feel. You're just tricking the universe into listening to you. Most texts believe that the arcane stream flows through elvenkind with more generosity. Use that extra magic to fuel your wish to create the flame," he finished explaining.

Evanthalus closed his eyes. He perfectly repeated Erilkaiden's movements and words, and an orb of fire coalesced between his palms. It was much smaller than his brother's but hot in his hands. Fortunately, the mana in the spell granted the person holding the orb of fire a slight resistance to the element. Evan exclaimed with happiness, "Alright! I did it!"

Erilkaiden smiled at his little brother and dismissed his own orb of flame. "Amazing work, moshirin!" he added in his brother's elation.

Evan held the fire in his hands for about a minute, using his concentration to move it about. It would levitate to his will, and he could move it throughout the air just by imagining its course. He started to try moving it at different speeds, marveling as it swooshed through the air fast enough that inexperienced targets would have difficulty avoiding it. "Alright, I'm ready!"

Erilkaiden stepped into a deep stance, his thighs parallel with the ground, and his legs stretched wide. He sucked in a deep breath and pointed the palms of his hands at the orb of flame that his brother was moving through the air wildly. Erk lowered his index finger, then his pinky. He then raised them, lowering his middle fingers simultaneously. Then he clapped and chanted, "Oblitero. Destruo. Inanis!" A bolt of light shot out from Erilkaiden, and it started to chase Evanthalus's orb of fire. The light moved faster than the fire, overwhelming it with a glow. A moment later, the ball of flame collapsed, the light following it into nonexistence.

"Awesome!" Evan exclaimed. They had both successfully used a new spell in the same training session. Evanthalus was new to wizarding, having only mastered about one hundred simple spells. His older brother already had his three hundred spell pin, an impressive mark for a wizard under the age of fifty. They both had a new spell to add to their list of successful casts, Evan, the orb of fire, and Erk, the dispelling light.

"Amazing work today," Erilkaiden congratulated his brother.

They both noticed their older sister had been at the edge of the burned field. Iriliandria came running after the magic in the air settled. "Brothers! You must come quickly! There is news that the king's daughter Katherine has been accused of regicide. She would have been the presumed heir, and there are whispers that the church had a hand in this heinous act."

Evanthalus and Erilkaiden traded alarmed glances as their sister spoke. If the Church of Invictus was implicated in something so awful, then the royal family might retaliate against the Lancethinas and Holia families, two families dedicated to the service of the Sword of Justice within the kingdom of Claston. Father and mother might be in danger, they realized.

The three of them took off in a sprint toward the manor on their estate. The magic training field was about a quarter mile away, and they made the run in a little more than a minute. The three of them spilled into the back side of the manor, facing north. It was a rotunda with a grand porch and a recessed entrance to the manor. Grand glass walls overlooked the porch, reflecting a slight green tint. The glass cut the rotunda in half, leaving a sizable part of the outdoor porch covered by the rounded dome. The porch was enormous, stretching twenty feet from the top of the stairs to the entrance centered in the glass wall. Because their family had convinced the king to open trade with the neighboring kingdom of Alabaster, they had come into an enormous fortune based on those commercial exchanges. Their manor represented that, and sections of it were open to the public. The Lancethinas family's philosophy emphasized that the common people had a right to work closely with their leaders, and the people shared in the fruits of their unified efforts.

The entrance, built into the center of the beautiful glass walls of the rotunda, led into a grand parlor that was used to host parties and hold public meetings with the serfs and peasants that lived in these parts. As they entered, they immediately saw their sister Ara'Ilyvithia and her husband Boscht were present. Some of the mayors and representatives of the people were also present. This looked like a grave situation to Erilkaiden and Evanthalus.

"Everyone, please, relax," a booming voice called from the other side of the parlor. "Find a comfortable place to rest and wait for the second messenger." Iria, Evan, and Erk saw their father, Lord Elian Nel'fis Lancethinas, standing in one of the doorways to the rest of the manor from this large, open room. It stretched about one hundred and fifty feet across from east to west. The room was almost always open to the public, and there were numerous places to sit, tables and chairs for dining and collaboration, and even places to nap. There was a stage on the west wall of the parlor for performers and orators. The second messenger would most likely deliver his news from there, Erilkaiden speculated. The assassination of a king was usually unacceptable under the tenets of Invictus, and murder was always wrong according to Lexcord's values. Most elvenkind had a natural affinity to Lexcord, as she was an elven woman before she ascended to godhood. She was known to grant prayers to elves that were not even her clerics or paladins. He doubted that Princess Katherine would be capable of such an act as she strongly believed in the Silver Maiden. He had met her as an adolescent elf and had seen her several times over the last couple of decades. Erk was convinced that she had a pure heart.

The siblings approached their sister Ilyia and sat with her and Boscht. "How did your training go, brothers?" their eldest sister asked, deflecting from the obvious disaster unfurling around them. Iria was strict and smart, but Ilyia was sweet and meticulous. As a priestess, she had chosen the path of bureaucrat. She could recall the smallest details about laws, forms, and, unfortunately for Erk and Evan, anything embarrassing in their childhood.

"It was wonderful!" Evanthalus replied, enthusiastic. Adolescence for elves lasted from about thirteen to twenty-nine years. His youth and energy echoed throughout his words.

Boscht smiled at his brothers-in-law, "Still mastering spells?" he inquired. He was an accomplished wizard himself, having mastered over one thousand spells. He was eighty-one years old, twenty years Ilyia's senior. Adulthood for elves lasted until two hundred years old, when they would be considered middle-aged. By average estimates, elves could live to four hundred years old easily, so Lord Elian's children were still very young.

Erilkaiden nodded, "I managed to get the dispelling light incantation to inflect correctly. I should be able to recite it easily with a little study on days I need it." Remembering every spell without a daily study of the most important ones was difficult. Wizards kept spellbooks so that they could study the incantations and gestures required for spells on a daily basis. Nevertheless, a dispelling attack was very important for a wizard, and for Erilkaiden to have mastered it before age fifty was quite a feat. His promise was astounding, and Boscht, Ilyia, and Iria knew it.

They then began to discuss mundane issues, such as the weather and the affairs of other kingdoms and countries. Osgood, to the north, had successfully won independence from Alabaster. They petitioned the Church of Invictus for an independent state for the last five decades, and the church formally granted their appeals. They spent the next hour enjoying each other's company, even young Evan understanding that tonight's events could change the course of their lives. King Eisen Noldon Claston was young, only one hundred and ninety-four years old. Both the Lancethinas and Holia households had been working closely with the king to build a more just society for the elves and the growing population of humans within their kingdom. The greatest opposition to their cause came from the king's older brother, Gelidor Claston. First, he considered humans inferior, evidenced by their similarities to other primates. As children of animals, mankind had come to exist through natural processes and selection, breeding a race of resilient and capable humans with short life spans. According to their origin stories, elves were the descendants of the fae, races that included faeries, sprites, and leprechauns. The gods created those races with their own hands in Gelidor's mind, but humans, too, were favored by the gods. Most elves no longer shared the sentiments of the traditionalists. Nevertheless, Gelidor believed that humans should be treated as cattle or beasts. Second, he insisted on maintaining archaic societal structures like serfdom. He believed freeing people to make their own choices would prove bad for the kingdom and the people. He also despised any mention of the codes of Invictus or Lexcord. Their tenets made him uncomfortable.

Lord Elian left the grand parlor after he asked everyone to wait for the second messenger. About an hour into the Lancethinas children's conversation, Lord Elian entered the large room from the porch with a human charging in behind. The man looked somewhat frantic but carried several scrolls stamped by the king's brother, Gelidor. The messenger urgently approached the stage on the west side of the room, feeling the weight of his news pressing on the audience. The southeast corner of the kingdom had been growing in prosperity with recent royal decisions. Gelidor was not happy with this direction. For the king to be killed and Katherine accused was unbelievable enough. The Lancethinas were also concerned about the rumors that tied the church to the assassination.

The messenger began, "As Princess Katherine has not come forward to discuss the accusations against her, the king's brother Gelidor has taken up the royal mantle. From this moment forward, the princess is considered a fugitive of the kingdom and is to be arrested on sight. King Gelidor Claston will send an envoy to reconsider the roles that your family plays in this kingdom," the man looked terrified as he spoke. He understood the insistence of not hating the messenger in such a situation. "Please understand that His Royal Majesty assumes your assistance in apprehending the princess. Otherwise, your generously granted titles can be withdrawn by the new king. He would like your oaths of loyalty pledged in public by the end of the month."

Erilkaiden felt a burning fury in his chest. He had a feeling that something sinister had happened in the royal palace. Though Evanthalus was still fairly young, he, too, sensed the peculiarities of the situation. Iriliandria was certain that treachery had occurred.

"What does the new king demand in this oath?" Lord Elian spoke up.

"That you will support his rule with the same loyalty as that of his brother and that you will help him see to justice the perpetrator of his brother's murder," the messenger explained.

Erk frowned. Gelidor had worked up a scheme by blaming this on the princess and ensuring her disappearance. "That's a hefty promise," he commented.

Ilyia nodded in agreement, "It means that her fate would rest solely in the hands of Gelidor. There is no way that's a coincidence. We should be wary of a ruler who can be so shrewd. Invictus's code does not approve such regimes as lawful. The princess is more likely the rightful heir," she concluded, affirming what Erilkaiden was already thinking and Iriliandria was about to say herself.

From the east side of the room, a rich, comforting voice added, "As the High Priestess of Invictus, I cannot agree to such an oath. Our family and the people that dwell within these lands demand that a trial by the people be required to convict the princess of regicide before we support a change in succession." It was Lady Wailindis Lancethinas, wife of Elian and mother of Ilyia, Iria, Erk, and Evan.

With a fearful gaze, the messenger replied, "Is that what you want me to tell his majesty?"

"Indeed it is," Lord Elian asserted.

"May I have it in writing and signed with your seal, my lord?" he asked.

"Of course," the lord replied. One of Elian's staff was ready with his official scrolls and seal. He quickly penned his family's stance on the matter, he and his wife aligning in their convictions to the gods of law, justice, and good. Surely if Gelidor were a worthy king, he would let the processes of law bring transparency to his brother's assassination. Furthermore, they insisted strongly that the Church of Invictus would never condone regicide and denied all possibilities that the church could be involved.

Lord Elian spent the next several hours reassuring the people's representatives that he would do everything in his power to preserve the progress made working with King Eisen. Though Gelidor was a staunch traditionalist and believed that the right to rule was based on power instead of divine appointment, Elian was convinced he could work with Gelidor in the meantime. He had hope, and his children had faith in him.

***

Four years later, the Lancethinas household still held a place of prestige in the hearts of the people. They continually found themselves at odds with the new king. He had increased taxes every year since taking control of the throne, and he used the increase in revenue to begin building a large military. While Elian disapproved of the king's strategies, he agreed that a well-refined military could serve the kingdom by ensuring the safety of the common people from external threats.

King Gelidor and Lord Elian got along in matters of state even though the Lancethinas family had refused to swear an oath of loyalty to the new king. Though Elian insisted on increasing the manpower to look for the missing princess, Gelidor was content to begin ruling in his brother's place until the princess could be found and tried. He made minimal effort to find his niece, which was suspicious to Elian. As a result, he and his closest friend among the nobles, Lord Rostenanthalus Holia, began to look for evidence that Gelidor was to blame for King Eisen's death.

However, the events of that next year would turn the kingdom upside down. Rumors that circulated about the missing princess suggested she was adventuring with a notorious sorcerer named Dalyn Tyrdrac. Lord Elian appreciated Tyrdrac's mission as he paraded himself as an elf of the people. Rumored to be the descendant of the great silver dragon Tyrdrac, he wielded immense power. He claimed to be peeling back the veil of the universe to uncover the secrets of magic so that all people could reach it with less study and more efficiency. Elian watched the sorcerer's progress with great interest.

On a warm summer morning that year, Erilkaiden and Evanthalus were studying spells that could improve a wizard's resistance to weapons, especially bows and arrows. They had an assortment of arrows with blunt wooden tips wrapped in cloth, a longbow, and a crossbow. Evan practiced on the offensive first, letting Erk demonstrate the spells for him.

"Remember, aim for center mass," Erilkaiden explained to his brother. "The wooden arrows will hurt, but they should not be lethal if I fail to activate the spell correctly."

Evanthalus nodded and knocked an arrow into the longbow. He nervously drew the string back, the tension not a problem for his strength. At age thirty, Evanthalus was now a young adult elf and proving to be as equally deadly with steel as magic. Though it would be unorthodox to train in both the ways of the wizard and the warrior, Erk thought his little brother would be the best elf to change that paradigm.

"Ready, brother?" Evan warned.

Erilkaiden took a deep breath, began the gestures and the incantation, and let the spell flow from his memory. Though there was no obvious change, he could feel the mana within him bending to his spell. "Fire!" he ordered.

Evan aimed and let loose the wooden-tipped arrow. A loud crashing noise echoed across the field they were standing in, the same field where they practiced fire magic. The arrow exploded into splinters as it collided with an invisible barrier that had surrounded Erk. It was similar to the protective barriers conjured by their older sisters, but their protection came from the gods and was more holistic. This particular spell would only deflect arrows for a wizard.

Erilkaiden breathed a sigh of relief. "Excellent. It's becoming second nature," he commented, trying to maintain his composure. He had failed to cast the spell before and knew the pain of being struck by one of the arrows. Sometimes, he thought pain could make an excellent teacher. Iria would scold him for thoughts like that, though.

"My turn!" Evan exclaimed, excited for his try. This was his first attempt at the anti-arrow spell.

The bows and arrows were neatly arranged on a burnt stump. An empty pitcher also sat on the stump, a vessel to hold conjured water in case they got thirsty. Erk approached the stump and prepared a light crossbow with a wooden, flat-tipped bolt. A shot from this would still hurt, but it probably wouldn't impact enough through Evan's armor to cause more than a light bruise. Erilkaiden carefully prepared the crossbow to fire, putting the bow under his boot and pulling the string into place. He fixed the bolt against the string and unlatched the trigger safety. "Are you sure you're ready?" he asked his little brother.

"Absolutely," Evan replied, taking a position about fifty feet from his older brother. He began the spell, his gestures and words tapping into the arcane to bend the universe to his will. Something felt wrong, however, and the magic did not seem to respond even though he could feel it there.

Erk watched his brother, the somatic elements perfect and the incantation inflected as expected. This spell created an invisible barrier, so there was no visual confirmation of Evan's success in casting the spell. "Do you feel it? The barrier?" Erilkaiden asked.

Evan shook his head; his face twisted into confusion. "I can feel the magic, but it doesn't seem to respond," he explained.

Erk lowered the crossbow, "Try the spell again?"

Evan nodded and repeated the incantation and movements even more precisely than before. Still, he did not feel a change in the magic. "Hey, brother? Shoot at me," he ordered, growing frustrated.

Taking in a deep breath, Erk pointed the crossbow at his brother. "Brace yourself," he warned.

Evan stood tall and looked directly at Erk. "Ready!"

The twang of the string echoed in the field. The training arrow smacked Evan's chest with a thud, causing him to yell, "Ouch!" along with several additional swears in elven. However, it was not a serious injury, even though it stung.

"You must have missed something," Erilkaiden speculated. "Though I'm not sure what. Your execution looked perfect."

Evan nodded, his hand on his chest where the blunt arrow impacted him. "Seems like it; I felt like I did it perfectly," he objected. "I can feel the magic; it's just not reacting!" he complained again.

Erk licked his lips in thought, feeling a bit of thirst. "Let's take a break and come back to it. Here, I'll conjure some water," he promised. Conjuring water was one of the easiest spells for a wizard to master, and it was useful for long journeys and exhausting training sessions. He recited the simple spell from memory, the gestures involved so minimal that even children could use it at an early age. He blinked in disbelief as he pointed at the pitcher on the stump at the end of his spell. Nothing happened.

Evanthalus approached, looking forward to a breather. "Water?" he asked, following Erilkaiden's eyes to the pitcher.

"Let's try that again," Erk mumbled in annoyance. He repeated the spell, but it still did nothing. After a moment of stunned silence, he exploded, "Are you kidding me?! The mana flows through my body, and I've cast this spell a thousand times! What is going on?"

Evan, too, tried the spell. He felt a surge of magical energy within him, but it did not create even a single drop of water in the pitcher. "Something is wrong with my magic, too, Erk. I can feel it there, but it won't do what I ask."

Erilkaiden closed his eyes and began to concentrate on the sensation of the mana within his body. He focused on it so intently that he could feel the fabric of magic flowing through him. Instead of repeating a spell, he spent an entire minute mindful of the mana. After a few moments, Erk's arms began to glow as a magical fire ignited around his arms, stretching up to his shoulder. He, however, did not seem to move or feel the flames.

Evan shouted with surprise as the fire spread up Erk's arms. "Brother! You are combusting!"

Erk slowly opened his eyes, focusing on the magical energy swirling around his arms. "What is this magic that requires no incantation and only concentration?" he asked aloud, his mind reeling from what he saw and did. Such confusion caused him to lose focus, allowing the flames spiraling around his arms to diminish. He renewed his focus, and the fires grew in intensity. A light began to glow in his palms. Suddenly, the magic no longer seemed like a source of energy that he borrowed from the universe. Now it felt like an extension of his body. He poured all his focus into the fire, and the light began to glow brilliantly in his hands. The fires fueled the glowing ball that was reminiscent of a tiny sun. He recognized what would happen if he poured more energy into the orb.

"Brother?" Evanthalus questioned, drawing Erilkaiden's eyes from his arms to his brother.

"This is wild," Erk replied. "Watch this!" he commanded, raising his palm toward a different stump in the burned training field. Suddenly, a radiant beam shot out of the orb of light and remained steady as long as he concentrated on fueling it with the mana that flowed through him. After about ten seconds of exposure, the stump caught fire anew, and after thirty seconds, it had been rendered to ash. There was no trace of it except a smoldering hole in the ground.

Evan stood slack-jawed. Neither of them had ever heard of a spell capable of something like what they had just witnessed. They needed to report these anomalies to their father right away. Perhaps he would have answers.

As the two brothers walked toward the Lancethinas manor, Evan stopped walking suddenly. "Brother, run!" he exclaimed.

Erk turned to face Evanthalus, but as he did, he realized why his brother had told him to run. A terrifying haze had begun to emerge from Evan's body. As it grew, the grass and flora near him withered rapidly. Erilkaiden began to backpedal, staying out of the reach of the cloud that extended out about a hundred feet around his brother. After about a minute, the cloud began to swirl in a globe around Evan, eventually collapsing in on its density with Evan as the center point. The young elf felt invigorated as he absorbed the moisture extracted from everything around him. The grass and nearby trees had shriveled and turned black. Birds and insects lay on the ground, their bodies shriveled husks with no signs of life.

"By the gods," Erilkaiden swore. "Evanthalus, what happened?"

His younger brother shook his head in confusion, "I just kept concentrating on the magic I could feel within my body. I felt it swelling and growing, and after it passed the point of no return, I realized what it would do," he explained, shuddering with fear. "I worried what would happen to you if you stood too close. This power feels incredible," he commented.

Erk frowned. This defied logic. "Let's just get to father and see what he says. Perhaps we have some sort of magic-related illness causing the energy within us to misbehave. If anybody knows, father will," he promised himself almost as much as his brother.

They did not rush the rest of the quarter mile to the manor, and they entered the door to the pavilion carefully and as quietly as possible.

Iriliandria was in the parlor in a clear panic. She was dressed in her priestess robes, a deep purple smock, and a golden stole with pastel purple stitching. Her braided, black hair cascaded down her back. "Yashirote, what is wrong?" Erk asked as she paced back and forth in front of the door to an inner hallway leading to father's study. They approached her slowly, her body language more agitated than they had ever seen her. Her normal composure was disciplined and calm, but the way she paced now looked like something had unsettled her very foundation.

"Moshirin'thi!" she exclaimed, holding her hands to gesture for them to stay back.

The two brothers stopped in their tracks. "Iriliandria, what's wrong?" Evanthalus asked now, repeating their brother's question.

"Something unexplainable washed over me a few moments ago and now," she held her hands in front of her as a ball of electricity crackled into existence, much like the orb of flame that was a staple of young wizards. The electrical orb, however, was much more difficult to master and control, especially because its power could easily accidentally strike the wielder if they became too reckless with the spell.

"When did you start practicing magic!?" Erk exclaimed. Evan stared, amazed.

"Never!" she shrieked back as arcs of electricity began blasting out of the orb, zapping nearby metal objects like candelabras and metal furniture. From there, secondary arcs launched out, electricity visibly coursing through anything it touched. Erk immediately retaliated by reciting the incantation for the dispelling light and taking the deep stance necessary for the movements of the spell. The spell did not activate, and a stray arc of lightning blasted him as it bolted out of a nearby decorative suit of armor.

Iria's eyes widened in horror as she tried to dismiss the conjured electricity. It only seemed to react with volatility. She tried to regain her composure and concentration, telling herself that staying upset would only worsen the situation. Her wisdom was impeccable. She managed to reason herself to a point of control, finding the emotional and mental fortitude to dismiss the mana harmlessly into the air. "Moshirin, are you alright?" she gasped, rushing to Erilkaiden's side. His shoulder-length golden hair stood straight out in every direction, and his hands looked charred.

"I'm alright, sister; it was just a little shock," he responded, trying to hide his pain.

"Restore to order what was damaged by chaos," she prayed, and a healing light enveloped Erk for a moment. The pain from the electrical burn eased almost instantaneously. Iria reached out to hold his hand, a look of fear and concern in her eyes.

Erilkaiden snapped to attention. "Hey, your prayers still work," he commented. Iria nodded.

Evan spoke suddenly, "Father!" as Lord Elian emerged from the hallway leading to his study.

Their father had a grave, tired expression on his face. "Children, I could hear a disturbance. Is something wrong?" he asked, but his face seemed to know the answer already.

"My magic quit working!" Evan exclaimed.

"Mine, too," Erk added. "And that's not all," he said, looking at Iria.

She frowned and turned to face her father. "I found a power within me that does not come from Invictus. It's a powerful ball of electricity that behaves wildly when I conjure it," she explained.

Lord Elian took a deep, pained breath. "I thought as much. I noticed my connection to the mana severed a few moments ago. Then I received a terrifying premonition," he continued. He closed his eyes and began to chant. Erilkaiden and Evanthalus could feel the magic moving in the air but did not recognize the words of their father's incantation.

"Father?" Erk asked as his father seemed entranced.

Elian inhaled sharply, and his face twisted into an expression of agony. "This can't be!" he finally said aloud.

The parlor was empty at this hour, and nobody was expected to visit on this day. However, a crowd gathered on the porch where the Lancethinas family typically welcomed them. "It looks like we are not alone," Iriliandria said, her voice lacking the normal, concerned charm she usually spoke with.

Erilkaiden frowned. Something deep within him felt like this would tear his family apart.

That day, Dalyn Tyrdrac managed to fuse his life essence with the energy of the arcane stream. Due to his immense power, instead of simply destroying him, he became sentient within the mana that flowed through the universe. For everyone else, however, they found their relationship with magic completely changed. Wizards like Erk and Evan were limited to a single power that would manifest if they concentrated on the magic deeply. Others, like Iria, who had no magic before, also could use a single magical manifestation. They, however, had much more difficulty controlling their powers thanks to their inexperience with manipulating the mana that fueled their new gifts.

Within that week, civil war had broken out in every bastion of civilization around the world. Some, who were previously weak or powerless, suddenly found themselves capable of great feats and even greater violence. Some retaliated against oppressive governments. Some tried to overthrow legitimate, benevolent governments. Others used their powers to steal, kill, and wreak havoc without mercy. The people occupying the lands managed by the Lancethinas and Holia families bonded with their leaders and formulated plans to combat the machinations of chaos from both within and without. Because their families' dedication to the cause of Invictus had instilled in those people the values of law, justice, and equality, they chose to fight against chaos rather than propagate it.

Within the first five years, the kingdom of Claston saw numerous uprisings. Gelidor used those loyal to him to crush those rebellions without mercy. At first, Lord Elian tried to support the king with trained militias that took maximum advantage of their newfound powers. The king's policy of slaughtering his own subjects was too much for Elian. Both the Lancethinas and Holias quit supporting the king with troops. As a result, the king demanded that Lord Elian and Lord Rostenanthalus report to court for questioning. Their meeting was scheduled for the peak of summer in the fifth year of The Unbinding.

As the week of their interrogation arrived, they left their respective estates to travel to the royal palace in the capital city of Claston. The two traveled together, promising their families that they would be home within a week. They had frequently traveled to the royal city, so it wasn't the trip that worried Elian's wife and children. The king had demonstrated how merciless he could be, and going to him willingly would certainly be walking into a trap.

Elian, however, insisted that refusing to report would likely give the king the idea that the Lancethinas and Holias were conspiring against the crown. As such, he and Rostenanthalus committed to this course of action. The royal palace was a magnificent fortress built of marble and limestone. It was built on the high ground in the center of the royal city, and imposing walls surrounded the keep, defended by numerous towers built strategically along the outside of the courtyard.

As they approached the gate to the palace, they were stopped by the palace guard. "Halt, identify yourself," the elf demanded.

Elian sighed. This was a new face. The old guard knew Elian very well. "I am Elian Lancethinas, Lord of Southeastern Claston. His Majesty is expecting us."

His friend also spoke, "And I am Rostenanthalus Holia, Lord of the Eastern Reaches and into the mountains."

The guard was rather large for an elf. On closer examination, Elian realized this person was a half-elf, giving him a broader build like a human male. He was also five feet nine inches, an impressive height for elven ancestry. Elian thought it was odd for the king to employ someone he called "an abominable race born from the greatest sin against elvenkind." Lord Elian spent the last decade trying to reason the king from such a backward view. Lexcord herself blessed unions between humans and elves so much that certain rituals allowed the human partner to take years from the elven partner's lengthy lifespan, though such occurrences were rare. Elian wondered if the king had finally listened.

The guard turned to the portcullis that was lowered. Elian watched him call upon the magic inside him to cause his size and density to increase. He grew to ten feet tall, and his muscles bulged with strength. He easily lifted the portcullis with his oversized hand, permitting the two to enter. Elian had his answer. The king was recruiting based on the nature of one's uncanny magic now. That did not bode well for the kingdom.

They entered the keep of the royal palace, the central

corridor leading right to the king's public court. It stretched for six hundred feet, with numerous hallways leading to the rest of the complex. Elian and Rostenanthalus walked confidently toward the court, but the hallways were empty. No guards were present. No staff was in sight. As they walked under the archway that led into the king's court, their eyes followed a red carpet stretching from the doorway to the throne positioned on a dais against the far wall of the room. A marble colonnade with beautiful daylight torches lined the way to the throne. The two lords approached within fifteen feet of the king and demonstrated their deference with a knee on the ground and lowered heads.

"Good to see you, lords," Gelidor sneered at them.

"Your Majesty, we thank you for your invitation to court. We hope to clarify anything that Your Majesty wishes to know," Elian voiced, ignoring the king's sour demeanor. Gelidor was always condescending, so it was no surprise.

"Yes, Elian, you have much to answer for. Tell me, why did you cease sending troops to support my forces in quelling the rebellion in the north?" the king asked directly, a shrewd tactic to keep Elian from deflecting the issue.

Elian closed his eyes and found his wizarding voice. Ever since magic had broken, he began training as a priest of Lexcord to supplement the religious contributions of his wife and daughters. He carried himself differently in those endeavors, finding a gentler voice. Right now, however, he needed the authority he once had as an archmage, the highest order of wizards. "As we explained in our regretful declination, we cannot condone Your Majesty's use of wanton violence. As of now, one hundred thousand of your own subjects have perished in the last five years, most of those being peasants and serfs that demanded the king hear their grievances," his powerful voice echoed everywhere in the room. Many vassals of evil had heard that booming voice before finding themselves incapacitated. Elian continued with that overwhelming tone, "When the king would not listen, they began to act like children begging for their parent's attention. But instead of listening, His Majesty slaughtered them all without trial or accusations."

Rostenanthalus smiled. His friend was an incredible orator and had a genuine heart.

The king, a frail looking elf of about three hundred years, expressed his apathy through his dark, narrowed eyes. The pupils within seemed to consume his entire eye, giving him an eerie, black gaze. Elian always felt unsettled by his glare. White hair spilled around his aged countenance, which showed significant wrinkles as the king frowned and grimaced almost continually. His robes were a royal red with black and gold stitched into elegant patterns. The deriding tone of his voice made Elian twist his face into annoyance. "Very well, I suppose that is within your right as lords according to your little gods, correct?"

"Only when His Majesty acts unlawfully would we dare defy his will," Rostenanthalus added in response to the king's question.

The king scowled. "One does not have the authority to question the king because they prayed and studied. I am king by birthright and strength, and other gods favor me. Na'agamlor, The Shadowed One, guides my convictions." Without hesitation, Elian and Rostenanthalus snapped their eyes up at the king with an expression of horror. Na'agamlor was called The Counselor of the Corrupt by the followers of Invictus. His followers typically abused positions of authority and exploited systems and people to accumulate substantial wealth and power. However, they usually never declared their faith publicly. Doing so would cause law abiding citizens to distrust them, disabling their ability to maintain and abuse power. This was harrowing news, and the first time that either lord had ever heard of the king's choice in divinity.

The king continued ranting; his voice mid-toned and grating. "I am the one who writes the laws. Therefore I can never be guilty of breaking any. The kingdom must operate according to my will," he spat. Now Elian and Rostenanthalus understood.

"Your Majesty, we were unaware of your convictions as a follower of Na'agamlor. According to the law of Invictus, your philosophical alignment invalidates your rule. The Silver Maiden will rain judgment upon you," Elian responded in anger, his poise still that of the once powerful archmage.

The king's face twisted into a smirk. "Is that so, Lord Elian?"

Elian and Rostenanthalus stood, a sign that they no longer considered Gelidor the rightful ruler. The lords then reassessed the situation. The king had no guards posted in the room with him. They started to wonder if the king had an uncanny magic that made him confident enough to confront two of his well-trained nobles in such a perilous way. "In the name of Invictus, I demand you abdicate," Rostenanthalus asserted, drawing a magnificent longsword from its scabbard.

Elian's eyes narrowed with thought. A deadly confrontation with the king would cause even more upheaval in the kingdom. Rostenanthalus carried the rank of high paladin and had the full legal authority to depose a king by force. In doing so, Rostenanthalus would act as regent until an heir was chosen. That might create an opportunity for the cause of the people to find a voice. Elian considered the possibility that the king had a more powerful gift than his own. Once magic unraveled, the only spell that would still work for Elian was a spell that turned the wizard into a being of pure light energy. This gave him incredible strength, speed, and a body that would destroy anything that touched it, even weapons. Rostenanthalus had acquired the ability to stop time temporarily, another incredible gift that proved useful in saving lives in the recent upheaval.

"I will not abdicate, and I will not suffer your threats. I curse you both to lose your souls to the powers that brew within you," Gelidor hissed.

A red aura surrounded Elian and Rostenanthalus. They looked at themselves, then back to the king. A curse? Had he acquired an uncanny magic that would allow him to speak a number of terrifying words that would warp the universe to make his will a reality? "This is bad," Elian mumbled. He drew the war hammer from his side and approached the king on the dais, carefully walking up the small steps.

Rostenanthalus charged past, shouting, "In the name of the Sword of Justice, I smite you with the Light of Judgment!" In Elian's experience, a moment would pass after Rostenanthalus shouted, and several enemies would fall on the battlefield. He stopped time to smite several enemies at once. It was incredible to behold.

Suddenly, Rostenanthalus froze. The king began to cackle. "It works! Na'agamlor's gift works!"

Elian stopped himself from moving. Looking ahead to his friend, he could see that he was frozen in the middle of a sprint toward the king, his sword raised and ready to smite. No part of his form touched the ground, and it was unsettling to Elian. "What did you do? What is this gift you speak of?"

The king ran his tongue along his front teeth. "You see, I was unjustly denied the throne one hundred years ago. My youngest brother had no business being king at such a young age. My father insisted that I was unfit to rule and that Eisen would be the new king on his passing," Gelidor explained, feeling his heart race. He felt like he was finally in complete control of the kingdom. The mighty would fall before him now that Na'agamlor had blessed him with the power to curse people. In exchange, Gelidor promised The Shadowed One that the Kingdom of Claston would be a bastion for followers of the secretive, evil god.

Elian thought about the nature of curses. There had to be something he could do to break the curse. He started to pray, but then he felt a searing heat welling inside him. He used his experience with the mana to focus on what was happening. The mana pooled inside him, and his mortal body could not handle the growing pressure. He felt his essence start to slip into the arcane stream, his memories, his life, his soul all scattered to the inexplicable currents of ethereal magic that formed the lifeblood of the universe.

***

Erilkaiden awoke suddenly. Something felt wrong. The magic in the air had shifted dramatically. He scrambled out of bed and into the hallway of his wing of the manor and then into the main sitting room. Two guards stood at the entrance to his private lobby, one on each side of the door. "Young lord, does something trouble you?" one of them asked, a human who had settled in the southeast of Claston recently; he and his wife hoped to build a life together far from the persecution that caused their migration. His name was Edmon, and his wife's name was Maricely. She also worked on the grounds of the Lancethinas manor, the noble family ensuring they had opportunities to work toward a brighter future.

"Sorry to alarm you, Edmon," Erk apologized. Iria had taught him to consider the way his actions made others feel. Everyone was already on edge with the continual threat of rebellion in the kingdom. People had begun to call these new powers uncanny magic or "Profoundness" in the king's circle. Nobody was sure who they could trust anymore, making normal living impossible. Erk figured he could diffuse their worry, "Is there any news of my father?"

The young human stood at attention. "No, young lord," he replied.

Erilkaiden nodded, the answer that he expected. "Very well. I will see myself to the kitchen; I feel like I need a snack," he commented as he passed between them. In the central parlor under the grand rotunda, the day candle that had been burning since the previous morning showed that it was probably four hours before sunrise. He was not surprised when Iriliandria spilled out of her wing at almost the exact time as he did.

"No," she whispered loud enough that it echoed off of the glass in the empty parlor.

"Yashirote, why are you up?" Erilkaiden interrogated his older sister.

"I could ask you the same, brother," she said informally.

"Something unsettled me in my sleep. I'm not sure if it was a dream," he explained as they walked toward each other. Iria was about four inches taller than her brother; she still felt like his big sister even though they had become adults. "But now I am too worried to sleep. Father should have arrived at the royal palace yesterday. We've received no envoy."

Iria's face was grave. The low light of the everburning torches in here cast sharp shadows on their faces, enhancing the severity of their features. "I share your concern, moshirin," her formal tone returning. "Though it's only been five years, even I can tell something shifted in the arcane stream today."

There was a sudden racket outside the grand parlor. Iria

and Erk looked to see two elves had begun to bang on the heavy glass doors of the hall. "By the gods, aren't those the Holia children?" Iria whispered, recognizing them.

Erk ran to the doors and dismissed the magical lock from the inside. Despite all the chaos with magic, most magical items continued to work as intended. He had heard that some of them became unstable or more powerful, but Erk had not seen an example personally. As the doors opened, the two elves of the family their sister married into ran inside, clinging to Erk in fear. One was a boy and the other a girl, both in their teens. They were the twin children of Rostenanthalus, the younger siblings of Ara'Ilyvithia's husband, Boscht.

"Children, what's wrong?" Erk asked instinctively, wrapping his arms around them.

"They're all dead!" the girl, Amaranthia, cried. The young elf boy, Virtinthas, also had tears in his eyes, but his sister sobbed enough for both of them.

"Who?" Iria asked, rushing over to embrace the children with her brother. "What has happened? How are you so far from your estate so late at night?" she rushed with her line of questioning.

"Virt's uncanny magic lets him skip through the air. He saved us," Amaranthia tried to explain between sobs.

Erilkaiden imagined it was extremely difficult for Virt to use his uncanny ability while carrying his sister. He could walk on air as if it were solid, but he would have had to carry his sister in his arms to take her with him. It might have saved them from some immediate danger, but they probably would have made much better time on foot. It was a ten-hour walk between their estates, a two-hour ride if they had pushed their horses. "Start over, please, children. What has happened?" Erk asked, patient.

Virtinthas began to explain, "While father was away to speak with the king, the king's new militia attacked us at sunset. Mother was killed, Boscht, Ilyia, our servants, our friends, aunts and uncles," the young elf was openly crying now, overcome by his grief and his shock.

Iria clutched her chest. Time froze. To Erk, the world stopped spinning and lost all color. "Did-did you say that Ilyia is . . ." Iriliandria finally choked out, unable to finish her sentence.

"I'm so sorry," Amaranthia wailed. At that time, Evanthalus emerged from his wing. Erilkaiden was unable to move. Iriliandria looked at her youngest brother with the most pained expression.

"What is going on?" Evan asked, confused. It seemed that the shift in the mana did not wake him the way it did Iria and Erk. The sounds of their in-laws roused him instead, giving him a sleepier demeanor than his siblings, who had been jolted awake.

"Moshirin," Iriliandria said, her voice empty. Her heart had broken completely. "Oh, my dearest moshirin'thi," she said as she began to weep profusely, grabbing Erilkaiden with a massive hug.

Evanthalus approached, his drowsiness now replaced by a panicked look. "Oh no, what has happened?"

Erk started to explain, his voice monotone, "Ilyia, she was killed by the king's forces earlier this evening. The Holias, all of them present, but Amaranthia and Virtinthas escaped and managed to—" he trailed off. "No, mother! The others on our estate! We have to evacuate right away!" he shouted.

Iria and Evan became equally concerned. Erk put it together faster than the others. Iria was wise and could understand people, but Erk was analytical and had magnificent reasoning skills. It was part of what made him a talented wizard, even though now he focused more on honing his ability to fight while safely incorporating his devastating uncanny magic. They rushed into the main hallway of the manor, which was centered across from the entryway of the parlor. The main hallway had several chambers and closets, but they rushed past them into the front hall on the south side of the building. This room had two staircases on the sides that led to a door on the north wall directly above where they had entered the room. They ran to the staircase to their left as they heard shouting at the front hall entryway. It caused the five of them to pause as they turned to hear a brutal crunch at the magically bound doors. Erilkaiden snarled with rage. Evanthalus stood by his side. They gave each other knowing glances.

Erk spoke, "Go to mother. We will hold them off." Ever since magic had unraveled, he and Evan had been inseparable in their physical and fighting training. They were following a regiment more brutal than even the soldiers of Invictus. They had stolen the training routine of The Harbingers, a Lexcordian group known for their elite, insurmountable combat skills. There were less than one hundred in active service to the Silver Maiden. Nevertheless, their training was detailed in the tomes describing their combat efficacy.

Iria replied, "Right," having learned to trust her brothers when fighting over the last five years. She ran up the steps, the young Holias right behind her. There was a splintering sound as the front doors shattered under the weight of a heavy ram. There was a shrill, crackling sound as Erilkaiden fired a blast of intense sunlight into the doorway. The focused beam lit up the front hall as bright as day. It was an eerie but beautiful sight.

The king's forces shouted in pain as the hot light burned them through their armor. Even worse, it left their armor so hot that it would continue to burn them even after escaping Erk's beam. As long as he could maintain his focus, he could keep this beam trained on the door for several minutes, allowing Evan to prepare a desiccating ambush.

Evanthalus approached the entryway, which was down a twenty-foot hallway from the front wall of the main hall. It was wide enough that he had enough room to approach the door while staying out of Erk's attack. As he settled right next to the doorway, Erk let the light from his power diminish. He kept another charge ready in case Evan's ambush did not incapacitate enough of them.

As the light lessened, a wave of soldiers stormed into the manor. They thought they would have enough of a window to stop Erk from using another attack. They were not, however, anticipating Evan's sudden discharge of mana. He had refined control over his power so that his attack would only render elves and humans critically dehydrated. With a few days of rest and continual hydration, they would easily make a full recovery. They all collapsed in deadly thirst. Thirty people might have been in the hundred-foot radius around Evanthalus, including some outside caught in his attack. The ones outside the radius, however, began to shout. The unexpected efficiency of the brothers' attacks left the assailants reeling. Erk and Evan both heard distant voices coordinating around the front perimeter. The voices sounded like snipers positioning themselves around the estate, waiting for the family and servants to emerge. They must have been added to the forces when Amaranthia and Virtinthas escaped the attack on the Holia estate.

Just then, Erk had a dark thought. These were the same type of men responsible for the death of his sister, if not the same. What kind of justice could Ilyia have if a sick bastard like Gelidor manipulated the hands of justice? He's the very one who called for her murder. Erk began to channel the heat of the sun into his hands.

"Moshirote!" Evan shouted, the term of respect for elder brother.

As Erk felt his anger intensify, the orb in his hand swelled. It created a distorted radius, the heat even causing the moisture in the air to turn to steam. When his brother's voice reached his ears, it calmed him enough to allow the mana to discharge harmlessly. With the estate possibly under the threat of snipers, Erk thought his vengeance could wait.

As the brothers realized they had an opportunity to join their mother, they could hear the soldiers that were lucky enough to be far away from Evan's attack regrouping. The two of them ran up the east side staircase that wrapped around the round room, leading to the second level of the manor. They followed the long hallway on the other side of the double doors to the end, and they ascended another staircase on the left that led into one of the towers that spired above the manor. They saw their mother, sister, two younger in-laws, and a fifth elf as they entered a room at the top of the tower. He wore a bright red uniform, one of the servants of the Holias. He had a sedimentary build, his body soft, and his features especially round for an elf.

"Who are you?" Erk immediately interrogated.

"Please, forgive me," the new figure said with a bow. "My name is Jacques. I am a servant of the Holias." He then stood straight. "When the king's men attacked, I teleported away to alert everyone I could. I have been focusing on each member of the Holia household since the attack, and I finally found young Lady Amaranthia and Lord Virtinthas," he explained, his voice beginning to crack.

"What information have you been able to gather from your efforts?" Erilkaiden asked Jacques directly, feeling especially vengeful.

"The initial attack resulted in mass casualties. Lady Holia, Lord Boscht, Lady Ara'Ilyvithia, and countless peasants caught at the manor at the wrong time were all slain in the initial onslaught. I heard the commotion from the other side of the estate and tried to join my lady by her side. She had already left the mortal coil by the time I arrived," Jacques explained, the grief and terror causing his voice to shake. "They were merciless, and I had never seen the king's guards dressed this way. Instead of their normal, polished plate, they wore armor trimmed with black and a symbol of the scales of justice with a skull set into the breastplate," he continued, his entire body shuddering.

Iria's eyes widened. Erk and Evan looked at their older sister. Erk asked, "Do you know this symbol, yashirote?"

"Yes," she replied without hesitation. "That is the holy symbol of Na'agamlor, The Shadowed One and The Counselor of the Corrupt. If the king's men wear that symbol in any capacity, the situation is far graver than I anticipated. Father is in danger!" She finished with a frantic realization.

"Jacques," Lady Wailindis asked softly.

"Yes, m'lady?" he replied, bowing swiftly.

"Can you teleport to the royal palace?" she asked.

"I've done so on many occasions," he explained.

"Take me, then," she commanded. "Take me straight to the king's court, where my husband should be."

"Hai-rin!" Iriliandria shouted, using the formal word for mother.

Her mother gave her a stern look. She gripped her holy symbol and began to pray, "Sword of Justice, hear my plea. Shield myself and my companions from all harm as we seek to dispel the chaos that has manifested. We ask you, justice incarnate, to cover our bodies with your hands, our minds with your wisdom, and our souls with your righteousness." A fine, purple mist descended onto Jacques, Wailindis, and Iria, who looked at herself in disbelief.

"Mother?!" Erk exclaimed, suddenly worried.

Iria looked at her mother. "Please, don't do this!"

Jacques looked to Lady Wailindis for guidance. She ordered, "All three of us. You, Iriliandria, and myself."

The servant nodded his head and pressed his fingers together. A circle of light flashed underfoot, but smaller, brighter circles also formed underneath only the three requested by Lady Wailindis. In an instant, they were all gone. Erk, Evan, and the twins remained. They listened for the sounds of the attack, but the estate was quiet.

"Dammit, Hai-rin," Erk cursed. Evan looked at his brother, fear and uncertainty carved into his expression. Erk remembered Iria's teachings on the feelings of others. He had just lost his sister too, and possibly his father. "Moshirin, nes'ni," he ordered, commanding his brother to approach.

Evanthalus stepped forward, and Erilkaiden grabbed him with both arms. He embraced his brother, squeezing him hard. Though he was a young adult elf, Erk had trouble thinking of him as such. He was still that adolescent, boyish fighter mage with the power to change the world. Erilkaiden hoped the gods had chosen them for something great and that something would lead to the conclusion of this conflict. He let go of Evan and stood tall. "Moshirin'nides," he said. He let his little brother know he cared for him deeply and would do all he could to protect him from this chaos. The elven suffix 'nides was a powerful word that did not translate well to informal elven or common. It expressed powerful, unconditional love.

The four of them stood silently for five minutes, their worry beginning to run rampant. The lack of sounds in an estate under attack was especially concerning. It felt like immense pressure was waiting outside the building. Just as it became unbearable, a white light appeared underneath the four of them, and a moment later, Wailindis, Iria, and Jacques reappeared.

Erk nearly tackled his sister, and Evan grabbed for his mother desperately.

"By the gods, sister, mother," Erilkaiden practically wept.

"My children," Wailindis wailed. "It is true. Gelidor is in league with Na'agamlor. May Invictus himself smite this scourge. Never once in recorded history has a priest of The Shadowed One become a nation's sovereign. I am afraid the future of Claston is worse than that which we've seen in the unraveling of magic," she lamented.

"What did you see, mother?" Evan asked, finding his voice.

Wailindis closed her eyes. "The banner of The Counselor of the Corrupt sat behind the throne. Gelidor has truly turned himself over to evil intent, twisting the law to his whims," she cried. "I do not believe he attained this position without the assistance of dark clerics working behind the scenes to usurp the throne. Gelidor is far too foul to make long-lasting allies unless they, too, are bent to such a dark disposition," she explained.

"And what of father?" Erk asked, feeling his heart racing.

Iria started to sob. His mother, however, replied, "When we appeared in the court, Gelidor sat on the throne, laughing hysterically as we gained our footing." She paused to breathe, trying to speak more than cry. "We could see the frozen effigy of Lord Rostenanthalus just a mere foot from the throne. It hung in midair. It was the most unnatural, unholy thing I have ever seen," she could not keep her composure. She, too, was soon overwhelmed by her tears. "The king showed us Lord Holia's fate with sadistic glee. He no longer walks these mortal realms. Then," she paused, trying to find the words to continue. She was utterly incapable of speaking.

Erk started to tremble. Evan asked, "So, it's true then? The king has turned to darkness, and Lord Rostenanthalus has perished?" His heart was already breaking before there was any further elaboration.

Iriliandria nodded with grief in her beautiful eyes. "Father, too. Both slain by the king himself."

Erk's face turned hot red with rage. "Father?!" he clarified in a shouted question. "How?" His shaking worsened as he felt his heart sinking to the bottom of the Rift.

Iria tried to explain, "Gelidor has acquired a power that turns one's uncanny magic against them. For father, that meant—" she started but did not have the strength to continue.

"He burned himself into oblivion," Erk deduced. His father's power was so much more impressive than his own, the energy body making him nearly impervious. If his own gift was turned against him, then the young lord was sure there was nothing left of his father. Erilkaiden felt as if all the sounds around him were far away. His body felt empty and weak, and the thoughts in his mind blurred together in such a way that muddled vengeance with justice. How could Invictus and Lexcord sit by while something so monstrous was occurring? Erk started hyperventilating, prompting Evanthalus to place a hand on his shoulder. Evan was also crying.

Their mother continued, eyes filled with tears. "Tonight, the king has shown his hand. I am afraid that our suspicions about Gelidor were warranted. If only we had known. Na'agamlor. The Shadowed One. Gelidor has a dark heart and should not sit on the throne," she wept.

There was shouting in the stairwell of the tower. Gelidor's forces had regrouped and were now ascending to put an end to the Lancethinas and Holias. Erilkaiden, Evanthalus, and Iriliandria brandished weapons. "Wait!" Wailindis ordered. "Jacques, take us to the Holia estate. I will return with you to evacuate the servants and guardsmen."

"Mother, you can't! We can destroy these assailants with ease," Erk objected.

"Enough, mu-zim," Wailindis replied with a stern firmness in her voice, calling him the formal word for son. It was enough to snap him back to disciplined behavior. "I have lost two of my loves today. I shall not risk losing the rest. You will cease your quest for vengeance and join your siblings and the twins. Besides, you must secure the Holia estate for those that we rescue from here," she explained, shifting the focus of the rescue to the servants rather than making this seem like an effort to save Erk. Wailindis knew that her eldest son needed a meaningful role in this disaster. "Your work this night is not over."

Erilkaiden lowered his head in deference. "Yes, hai-rin," he complied.

Jacques motioned for Erk and Evan to come close. He

pressed his fingers together as they approached, causing a bright, white circle to open underneath them again. This time, there were no smaller circles. Instantly they were all suddenly present in the main parlor of the ransacked Holia manor. The scene was as gruesome as was expected. Iria, Erk, and Evan found their eldest sister slain at the king's orders. With each household's heads at the king's mercy, the royal forces attacked confidently and brutally. It made Erk curse the law and the code that had bound his father to such reckless behavior. Lexcord and Invictus were missing something critically important, and that was a refined, clear explanation of what to do when the law fails utterly at the hands of an evil interloper like Gelidor.

"This must end," Erk demanded.

His mother took her oldest son in her arms. She was only five feet tall, like Erk. She had the same golden hair and gray eyes as all her children, except for Iria, whose hair was black. "My sweet Erilkaiden, I'm so sorry," she wept for him. Erk was so close to his father. Gelidor had made an enemy that he did not understand. Lady Wailindis Lancethinas wept for her beloved and her children. Her strength as a High Priestess of Invictus was immeasurable. She could not foresee the depravity with which Gelidor had aligned himself. For The Counselor of the Corrupt to infiltrate its way to the highest level of government in a kingdom was unbelievable. Their followers twisted the spirit of the law into something vile for selfish reasons. They would answer for their crimes.

"Be careful, hai-rin," Erilkaiden pleaded. "I've lost two of my loves in this disaster as well. Please don't ask me to live without you, too," he spoke sincerely.

Wailindis looked at him with tears in her eyes. "I won't, son. The king was too busy gloating to destroy us. We are still protected by the might of Invictus. I promise, I will return."

Jacques and Wailindis stood close together, and her eyes lingered on her children as the two of them vanished. The Lancethinas siblings noted that Gelidor's forces had raided the compound to extinguish life and plunder property. For the rest of the morning, Wailindis and Jacques returned, bringing many of their household staff and peasants staying in the manor for many reasons. Jacques looked like he was about to collapse. About a dozen people had been rescued, but Erk noticed some missing faces. "Mother!" he asked as she and Jacques reappeared for the seventh time, unaccompanied. They appeared on opposite sides of the room, about five feet in the air, falling to the ground with a thud.

Jacques looked ready to collapse from using his uncanny magic numerous times in short succession. Additionally, his accuracy was starting to suffer greatly. Overusing his gift caused it to become unstable for a while, and he preferred to use it sparingly. This would certainly be the last trip tonight.

Wailindis looked at her son with even more heartbreak, understanding his urgency. He had taken a special liking to the young human hired to serve as his chamber guard.

"Mother, where is Edmon? And his wife?" he asked, completely lacking the emotional energy to process additional losses tonight.

"Gelidor's men raided the rest of the manor before coming to the tower. Many employees barricaded somewhere safe or stayed hidden until they saw my face. I'm so sorry, mu-zim, we could not reach him in time," she explained, her tears depleted. Only fourteen were accounted for out of twenty people that should have been present.

Erk added another line to the growing list of reasons why he would find a way to end Gelidor.

***

Iriliandria looked at Erk with sadness in her eyes. The last twenty-five years had been terrible. The usurper hunted their family with dedicated conviction. He intended to curse them like he had done their father and countless others over the last two and a half decades. Their efforts at mobilizing a resistance had been fruitless up to this point. Even Lady Reshiria, the only human with a noble title in the kingdom, departed some time ago. She had championed against the slaughter of newly almost-helpless dragons. Gelidor eventually threatened her as well, and she left the kingdom. Iria knew it was time to cut their losses and go.

"Erilkaiden," she began. They had just completed a mission in which they sunk two ships carrying siege weapons intended to help Gelidor continue to destroy the holdouts of rebellions in his kingdom. Both the north and northwest were in shambles, and discontent had spread to the southwest and southeast. At this rate, Gelidor would have no citizens left to oppress. The thought that such a vile elf could commit such atrocities broke Iria's heart. She could no longer survive without breathing the air of hope. The intense pressure on her heart made her desperate to seek a new path elsewhere, but her loyalty to her family and their cause kept her there.

But today, as she heard the screams of the sailors drowning mere feet away from salvation, something in her broke. In a way, the only path to prosperity under Gelidor's rule was to dedicate oneself to his cause. And to do so was a dark decision, but she knew that people's decisions had to be weighed with their experiences. Many of the humans in Claston had only ever known a time since The Unbinding, the official historical name for the era in which they lived. They needed salvation, not a violent end. And the elves, though they had the experience and wisdom of so many more lifetimes than a human, still had to secure the same basic resources to survive. She hated the elves that had chosen Gelidor's side but could not wish them death.

She pushed a magical blade in a beautiful scabbard into Erilkaiden's hand.

"What is this?" he asked.

"My sword," Iria explained.

"Why are you handing it to me?" he asked, confused as they stood at the crossroads between the capital city and the port city of Beriton. It was just the two of them.

"Because from this day forward, I swear to take the least violent route to solutions. I hope my children can know a world where violence is far from the only effective response to a crisis," she cried as she spoke. Her convictions helped her keep her words steady despite her tears. "Even in our resistance to the king, who is unlawful and must be deposed, I am watching my brothers lose themselves. I can tolerate the casualties of war," she lied, "but I can't lose my brothers." The truth was attached to her dishonesty, for which she would pray for penitence.

"Yashirote, you know that Gelidor left us with no choice,"

Erk tried to reason.

"No!" she exclaimed. "He did leave us a choice. He left us all a choice. We could have walked away from these lands and started over anew. We could have been a poor, farming family in a kingdom far away, but you know? We'd still be together. We'd still have each other. Father would be with us. Ilyia—" she choked, unable to control her emotions. She began to cry hysterically.

Erilkaiden's eyes filled with tears. She was right, but the number of lives they had saved probably equaled the number of lives they had taken since this ordeal began. He knew his sister could no longer carry on like this. Though his rationale was founded in a logical fallacy, he would not hold his sister to the same flawed standard as himself. They had worked so hard to stop Gelidor; he couldn't walk away now. Not especially after they had lost their father and sister in such a way.

Erk felt his heart breaking yet again. "Where are you going then, yashirote?"

"I don't know," she started. "I just know I want to go far away from here. This is a burden I can no longer carry," she cried.

Erilkaiden reached out and took his big sister into his arms. "Go. Find your place in the winds out there," he told her.

Iriliandria stood up tall. She tried to compose herself. "I can't. I would be abandoning my brothers."

With a deep breath, Erk objected. "You have to. If you can't stand to lose your brothers, you should know that your brothers could never stand to lose you, either. We may be required to operate outside of your moral code, possibly worsening as this conflict continues," Erk's tears had ceased, and he spoke frankly. "Honestly, I wish I could spare you any of this, yashirote," he lamented. "I wish I still had my yashirote'thi," he spoke in the plural, referring to Ilyia.

Iriliandria had been much closer to Ara'Ilyvithia than Erilkaiden or Evan. Still, she understood her little brother's heartbreak. He was much closer to their father than any of the other children. Erk's refusal to ignore his impulses would probably cause him much suffering. Still, Iria hoped one day it would lead to his salvation. She had taught him everything she could. She hoped the light within him would be as radiant as the light he could conjure with his uncanny magic.

Erk held a finger up before she could respond. "Your brothers only want to see a world where their big sister can find a happy life. If you think that world is beyond the sea, run back to the port and catch the first ship out of here. Chase your destiny, yashirote. We'll continue fighting for this world, but don't you think for a moment that you shouldn't follow your destiny." He put her sword back in her hands. "And take this. You may need to defend yourself," he insisted.

"No, brother. From this point forward, I will only use the powers Invictus bestows upon me to heal the injured and protect the weak. I put myself at the mercy of the gods. May the Sword of Justice guide me to a path where evil does not walk," she objected.

"Yashirote, you're being naïve!" he shouted.

"Moshirin, maybe I am," she retorted immediately. "If nowhere in the world is safe, then what is the point in living? I'm not naïve; I'm just too heartbroken to continue living like this. I have hope that somewhere my heart can find a place to rest, and I no longer need to hurt others just to survive," she started to weep anew.

Erilkaiden sighed deeply. "You won't stay to say goodbye to Evanthalus?" he asked, resigned.

Iria replied evasively, "You spoke of destiny?"

Erk nodded in reply, adding, "Do not run from it. Your heart knows best where it should be."

Iria grimaced. "It's calling me," she explained.

Erk nodded and squeezed his sister tight in his arms. "Then go to it. Answer the call. Invictus is wise, and you are among his most faithful." Tears streamed down his cheeks, wishing his sister a safe future. "I will tell Evanthalus I sent you away to a safer place. I will tell mother the truth."

Iriliandria's sobbing intensified. "Be safe, moshirin. Keep my other moshirin safe. Swear that you'll look after him always."

"As surely as the arcane stream flows," he swore with wizard slang.

She crinkled her nose in disbelief, "Magic is broken,

brother!" Her emotional state would not let her see the humor.

"My dear sister, I meant it optimistically," Erk protested her emotional response. "I know that magic is broken, but I hope to see it fixed within our lifetimes. It will flow right again. The Unbinding will end, and a new era of order will be ushered in. Gelidor will be helpless against the might of the arcane stream."

Iria's eyes widened with hope at her brother's words, but they were far more prophetic than he truly understood. The gods were certainly watching. She felt her worries ease. She knew that wherever she was headed, it would have a part in saving her brother from the darkness. The light of the sun glinting off the scabbard in her hand caught her attention. She forced it back into Erk's hands. Iria looked down at her little brother. "Please, keep my sword safe. I want you to gift it to a warrior or cleric worthy of its power. It is blessed with a holy light that extinguishes evil," she pleaded. "Violence may be necessary, but I can't be its author. Please, give it to someone with the strength necessary to wield it. My broken spirit cannot use it, even against evil incarnate."

Erk crunched his face in frustration. "Why won't you just keep it?" he begged.

Iria shook her head. "I can't take another life. I am forever overcome with guilt," she said with palpable sadness in her words.

Erk finally understood. His sister couldn't bear the weight of her actions in the kingdom. Though her power was great, her resolve to fight the king for either justice or vengeance was not as strong as his own. "Yashirote, if we part ways here, our paths will cross again. Our destinies are intertwined. I have no doubt," he reassured Iria.

She tearfully smiled at her younger brother. "May the Sword of Justice keep you safe," she said as she started to walk down the path to Beriton.

"May the Silver Maiden always light your path," he returned.

She cried countless tears as she made her way to her freedom.

***

"Evanthalus," Erilkaiden whispered. "Moshirin, you have to wake up."

Evan was trying to open his eyes, but he mumbled a response. "So thirsty," he grumbled. It took a few minutes, but he managed to open his eyes. He was in a covered wagon with Erk. But for some reason, Evan felt like his brother was on the other side of a veil. He was not sure if he could actually reach out and touch him. "Brother, water, please," he asked.

Erk tilted his head. "Are you thirsty?" he asked, handing him a flask. Evan had said something, but he couldn't quite understand it.

Evan replied, "Thank you, brother." Erk smiled at him. Then, Evan noticed particles of glowing light flowing through both of them. It looked like some kind of attack, and he panicked. He began to flail about, but the light followed him. Erk fell backward on his bottom. It flowed through him too. After the crash from Erk's fall, the wagon lurched to a stop.

"Dammit!" Erk cursed. "We're not quite home free," he spat.

Evan saw the sparkles of light begin to flow intensely through Erk, and they swirled within his entire body. Their colors changed from white, glowing specks of light to a radiant yellow and red, much like the sun's burning light. "What has happened, brother? Where are we?" he asked, but it seemed like his voice was drowned out by the sounds made by those particles.

Erk did not respond to his brother's question. "Mother didn't die for us just to get caught again."

Evan felt some sort of shock, but his body did not really respond. He didn't feel any grief. He wanted to be sad, but somehow his emotions were empty. "Brother, please, tell me what is going on!" he shouted.

Erk looked to Evan. His brother seemed especially agitated. "Don't sweat it; we'll be out of here soon." A moment later, the wagon opened from the back, and two soldiers dressed in the colors of Na'agamlor, black and gold, stood before them.

Before Erk could blast them with a beam of energy, Evan turned toward them, releasing his desiccating attack in a small cone in front of him. The soldiers dried so intensely that their bodies imploded, their flesh turning immediately into vapor and dust. The moisture in the marrow of their bones was sucked out with such intensity that it caused their skeletons to explode, splinters of bone raining on the ground and into the cart.

Erilkaiden sat in shock. Evan had never attacked with such intensity before! What had the king's curse done to him? He hadn't spoken a word since he awoke. Still, he seemed to be aware. Erk wasn't sure how much his brother could remember, but his attack helped keep their cover. "That works, too, moshirin. Well done, nice way to power up that attack."

Evan turned to his brother, and his mind told him to be horrified. Still, his body did not respond. Why in the world wouldn't his body respond to anything more than just moving around? He felt as if he were so thirsty that he could drink all of the rivers in the world faster than they could pour into the sea. "Yeah, don't mention it," he mumbled pathetically. Erk seemed to nod at him. Maybe his brother could at least understand him somewhat.

Erk stood and turned to the front of the wagon. "We just have to hope nobody on patrol notices that I'm not in uniform," he joked.

Fortunately, they were further away from the royal palace than Erk realized. They were already in the thickening woodlands that surrounded the capital city. Surely there would be numerous patrols and checkpoints on this path, so they went afoot when they had sufficient cover in the dark. Erk's uncanny magic also served as a torch to the elves' light-sensitive eyes by allowing the flames to form around his arms.

As they got some distance into a denser part of the woodlands, Erk stopped and sat on the ground, his back against a towering oak tree. He panted from the frenzied run from the wagon to the deeper coverage. Evan was behind him but did not seem phased by the half-mile sprint. He sat right in front of Erk, looking at him as if he were expecting a story as he did when they were younger.

"Can you remember what happened?" Erk asked.

Evan used his body to shake left to right in a forward

slouch. "No," he said, but he was not certain Erk could hear his words.

"I'm glad you can understand me, but if you are speaking, all I hear are mumbles. Some of your capabilities might have been damaged by the curse," he explained.

Earlier that night, they had executed an assassination plot against Gelidor. It had been forty years since Iriliandria departed for distant lands. Erk's recent attempts at gathering intelligence had yielded some obscure leads that pointed to a vulnerability in Gelidor's defenses. Now that the clergy of Na'agamlor had been openly welcomed into the king's dominion, he had quite a formidable personal guard. They relied on their uncanny magic to defend the usurper, and their methodical fighting capacity made approaching Gelidor directly nearly impossible. Erk, Evan, and Wailindis agreed that a covert operation had the best chance of success, even though the Sword of Justice would not have entirely approved of an assassination.

Evan tried to remember what had happened, but that part of his memory seemed empty. Erk mentioned a curse, so he wondered why that would be significant. "By Lexcord," he swore. "The king, he . . . he cursed me. Just like father. But father died! What am I still doing here?" he said aloud, unconcerned that Erk could not hear him. He continued observing the sparkling light, realizing it might be the key to understanding his current reality. He tried to remember what happened after the king's ambush began but could not even remember going into the royal palace at all.

Erk explained what happened to his brother, "We snuck into the royal palace through the sewage drains. Do you remember that?"

It did not sound familiar to Evan. He shook his body again to communicate a negative response.

The slow, wagging torso was unsettling to Erk, but he did not comment. "Well, that's how you, mother, and I ended up in the king's library in the middle of a trap. That information we got was planted by the Cult of the Corrupt. The usurper and his guard were waiting to ambush us there," he continued. He looked visibly agitated but nowhere near as emotional as Evan expected. Then again, Evan felt nothing either. No happiness, no sadness, only a thirst that seemed to have no end.

Evan asked, "How did we escape?" but his words were unheard.

Erk, nevertheless, seemed to respond to the question, "When mother realized what was going on, she channeled the pure divinity of Invictus into her body so that we could destroy the king. Her gamble was in vain; the usurper had already seen your power and knew to curse you as soon as the attack began," he started to hesitate, the emotion that Evan expected bubbling to the surface. However, Erk took a moment to compose himself. Then, with anger and spite in his voice, "Gelidor's curse can carry out its sentence quickly and with impunity. Mother used the entire divine essence within her to wipe out the usurper's guard, heal the curse on you, and cause the king to retreat," he continued, the disdain in his voice dripping thicker with every word. "I blasted our way out of that nightmare trap. I carried you in my arms, indiscriminately blasting anything that moved," he held a finger up. "It seems hotter when I shoot it from a focused point."

Evan shook again, expressing his discomfort with Erk's rage. "Don't give in to hatred, brother. Finding more ways to cause harm will lead you down a dark path!" he shouted as loudly as he could.

Erk watched in horror as his brother's body shook and mumbled loudly and angrily. There was something otherworldly about his movements and the sounds emerging from his mouth. "Moshirin! Calm, I am sorry. I found this supply wagon ready behind the castle, and I slipped us on board while the guards were making their final preparations," he tried to explain quickly. "I laid you behind some crates and hid, watching for some kind of inspection, but they rode out without even peeking in the cart. The resistance must be gaining ground in the south and is likely threatening to take the port. They seemed in a hurry," he finished.

Evan felt slightly bewildered that he couldn't remember anything Erk had explained. He knew he should remember, but he felt some of his memories had been erased. He realized he couldn't remember Erk as a younger elf. He was certain they had trained magic together before everything went to the Infernia. With a deep sigh, he replied, "Let's hope to Lexcord that the resistance can secure the port. That would severely damage the king's position."

Erk could tell his brother's response was positive, but he wasn't sure why. He looked the same, but he didn't feel the same. "Yeah, the rush on supplies to Port Beriton helped us escape the royal complex without issue. It would be great if the rebels took it. I've got a friend to make a deal with there," Erk continued.

Evan wanted to ask who and what kind of deal, but he didn't bother. He already felt slightly discouraged, thanks to his lack of true voice. He was glad his mind was still intact but quickly made this silent, magically powerful form feel like an Infernia. He wondered how long his mind could keep up with this torture. Finally, he tried, "How soon can we get there on foot?"

Erk wrinkled his nose. "We can probably get there on foot in about three days."

Evan felt a sense of relief. He hoped his brother's heart was so close to his own that Erk could understand him like this despite his words not reaching Erk's ears. "Then let's get a move on!" he insisted. He maintained that vigorous enthusiasm throughout his young adult life, and Erk thrived on it.

"Sorry, brother, I must rest. I do not know how the king's curse still affects you. Mother gave her life to see us to safety. She poured out her own essence to let Invictus take her over completely," he lamented. Still, there was not as much emotion as Evan would have hoped to see in his brother. He didn't fully understand why his mind knew it should feel something even though neither his essence nor his body felt the emotion. "Her sacrifice must not be in vain. If you would, please, take a brief watch for me. I'll be glad to return the favor after I awaken."

Evan sat watch for about three hours while Erk napped. He watched the sparkling light flowing through the corporeal world around him. As he observed, he realized it passed through the tree and Erk. Whatever that light was, it seemed to pass through all living things, even himself. However, as it passed through him, he could feel it carrying away his essence one fragment at a time. He wondered what would happen when the last of his essence was carried away into this stream of light.

After a bit, Erk awakened, still a little fatigued from the less-than-ideal sleeping arrangement. "Do you need a rest, moshirin?" the elder brother asked.

Evan gave his negative response shake. Erk began to worry that he was also losing his brother. Ilyia had been killed by Gelidor Claston's fanatical followers, desperate for power and control. Iria had fled the violence, her heart broken to pieces by the conflict she endured. Her soul was pure, and her strength great. However, her capacity for empathy always made her the most loving soul to grace elvenkind. This conflict was too much for her, and Erk did not blame her for retreating. He hoped that she was safe out there. His father had been destroyed by the usurper's curse, and his mother had just sacrificed herself to give her sons a chance to escape the trap laid by the followers of Na'agamlor. The only person Erk had left was Evan.

But now he was confronted with the reality that his brother bore a curse that seemed to resist the healing capabilities of a divinity's hands. His mother's decision to sacrifice herself must not have been for nothing. Erk was determined to see his brother healed.

***

Over the next thirty years, Erk spent millions of gold coins seeking a cure for Evan's affliction. Though he seemed to retain his cognizance, his little brother slowly withered away. His body began to shrivel and dry. His memories seemed to fragment and fade. It was harrowing to watch his brother waste in such a way. Still, a lot changed in those three decades as Erk became increasingly desperate.

That friend in Port Beriton secured Erk and Evan passage to the Isles Known for Nothing, an impossible feat for elves born in noble stations. Normally, the pirates there targeted noble and wealthy vessels that made significant profits by exploiting the weak. The dread pirates also had no trouble targeting the nobles of a kingdom simply due to their wealth. Nobility from many nations had been turned away from the shores of Yendralia, the bustling pirate city in the center of those islands. The god of the pirates, Cantalus, used his immense power to protect the island from those arriving in hostility. Many of those nobles came seeking retribution against the pirates that had simply corrected an imbalance of power. However, Erk and Evan truly sought refuge from violence and pursued a fate wrought with vengeance. Cantalus blessed them with entry.

Evan and Erk's immense uncanny magical powers helped them succeed in the pirates' and dread pirates' goals. Doing so led them to the most lucrative contracts, giving Erk the wealth he needed to both seek a cure for Evan's curse and purchase a ship in only five years.

For a while, they served as a captain and first mate in the fleet of Pirate Lady Naomi, a recent addition to the Pirate Nobles of Yendralia. Erk was a quick study and ready to captain his own ship within a week of serving on other ships, and his half decade of experience made him an adept captain when he acquired his own vessel. Pirate Lady Naomi preferred to hit slavers, and her efforts inspired Erk. To fund his search for a cure for Evan, Erk often worked independently as a pirate, targeting Gelidor's trade vessels. When he was not seeking wealth, he helped Naomi target slaving ships. His uncanny magic allowed him to sink the gunships of slavers from a safe distance. Naomi's crew would board the transport ships and save the women and children aboard, leaving the men and complete families to be rescued by assisting ships like Erk's. Naomi and Erk shared a strange chemistry. Though she was extraordinarily beautiful, Erk's detachment kept him from swooning over her as many people did almost immediately. He always seemed intense and hardworking, and he kept their relationship professional. She, however, couldn't seem to get her newest captain out of her head.

The Lancethinas brothers worked their way up from a humble galley to a magnificent galleon named *The Nebula*. There was an enchantment upon it that would always guarantee its course to a place of safety. Erk bought it from Pirate Lord Oniman so the old elf could retire. He traded the pirate lord one hundred million gold coins, about fifteen million gold coins in property, and a guarantee that Oniman would receive at least one gift from each of Erk's bounties or raids. Even after the end of the first twenty years, he had spent at least ten times that amount seeking a cure for Evan.

After acquiring *The Nebula*, Erk quickly found himself in the position of a pirate lord. Oniman's retirement created a power vacuum that saw four failed attempts at replacing the old sea dog. The last to try and replace him, Dread Pirate Lord Delidon, ran afoul of Pirate Lady Naomi and Dread Pirate Lady Lascha as soon as he arrived at the Fortress of Lords, the meeting place for the pirate nobles. After asking inappropriate questions at his first meeting, Delidon was later found choked to death on his own tongue, which had been magically inflated. Both Naomi and Lascha insisted that Erk be awarded Delidon's Lord Token. The other pirate nobles agreed.

After being pushed into the role of Pirate Lord Erk, he began to court Naomi in earnest. She was surprised by his first gesture, a flower delivery to her wing of the Fortress of Lords. Naomi had the skulls of one hundred slavers piled in front of Erk's personal quarters to indicate her mutual interest. The young elf immediately fell in love with Pirate Lady Naomi. Her ruthlessness against the forces of evil was so attractive to him that he knew without a doubt that Naomi was his other half. They worked closely together for the next ten years to promote each other's goals.

Meanwhile, despite Erk's efforts, his brother's condition had worsened to a horrifying degree. Erk was glad that he had found The Master when he did. They had raided one of the king's outgoing shipments of magical items, being sold to the distant kingdom of Gabah as an insurance policy that they would not set their sights on the easternmost peninsula of the Trollcrag continent. The kingdom across the sea to the east was building an empire based on trade and the military conquest of unwilling trade partners. For now, Gelidor was content to send shipments of magical items in exchange for food and supplies that kept his loyal followers fed. However, the rest of his subjects suffered from the famine created by an almost century-long conflict.

Erk found Gelidor's ships surprisingly easy to target. The

usurping king's gunnery ships were no match for Erk's long-range beam of light. The Master encouraged him to take more violent pathways toward his goals. He did so by sinking military targets without mercy. He could bore a hole into a ship's hull ten times longer than cannon range. *The Nebula* was huge, but it was also fast. Erk had assembled a mighty and effective crew, and their success propelled him to become the wealthiest pirate lord in the history of Yendralia. It pained him to use so much violence; he felt like Iria's eyes were watching him. His path had turned darker than even he expected. He supposed Iriliandria left because she understood that Erk may have had to take such a dark path to set things right.

The Master was an ancient soul that claimed he was once in line for the throne of Claston, but he gave up his right to rule in favor of seeking the esoteric within the arcane. When The Unbinding struck, he returned to put Gelidor in his place, but he was met instead by the usurping king's curse. The Master's incredible power allowed him to trap his own soul in a crystal to preserve its integrity until some sort of cure could be found for the curse. That was a crystal Erk stole from one of the ships bound for Gabah. When he touched the crystal, he was transported into a dimension where a strong elven paladin awaited him. He called himself Un'harzin, or "the bound one," an ancient elven reference to somebody bound in an everlasting, ethereal way. The paladin promised him assistance in defeating Gelidor. Erk felt this force of righteousness would be critical in defeating the usurper. Un'harzin had attained the rank of "Master" in service to his god, Pulhash. Pulhash was a hero of the common people, willing to go to any lengths to protect the weak and the innocent, including wholesale slaughter of evil forces. Though Invictus disapproved of Pulhash's methods, everything Erk understood meant that Pulhash was just a little too violent against the forces of evil. At this point, Erk liked the thought of finally extracting justice against Gelidor and his supporters. Erk called paladin The Master to honor his rank, and the pirate lord grew interested in Pulhash.

Still, The Master's philosophy seemed to be working. By escalating the violence against Gelidor's forces and allies, the king seemed to be struggling even harder to mobilize a resistance to Erk's changes in tactics. The Master had also taught Erk how to contact an ancient, eldritch dragon for wisdom and counsel. He went to ask the beast about healing his brother and The Master, and this primeval creature advised him to seek a force beyond the power of the gods.

Erk was determined to find a cure for his brother. And he hoped he could find a way to bring back The Master. His holy judgment upon Gelidor would be justice finally served, and those that followed dark gods that twisted the law would finally meet their destiny. He spent the next decade ruthlessly pursuing that goal.

***

Drymouth had drained the moisture out of at least one hundred enemies the day they escaped from Port Undine, but his thirst was greater than ever. He knew that he was going to succumb to that thirst. Erk, however, told him that a brilliant, purple light had foretold his salvation. One girl had been able to undo all of the damage he had done earlier with just a prayer and a beacon of light. He wished for that girl to come close because he was sure she could quench that thirst. He did not understand why and thought Erk should ignore the rumors. After thirty years, Evan could finally feel the last of his essence slipping into the void. Soon he would be at rest, and this unquenchable thirst would finally end.

Erk claimed to have seen the miracle with his own eyes. "If she can do something so great, why isn't there a chance she could heal my brother?" he explained to Apocalypse and Shalo. "And if she can heal him, I'm sure she can heal The Master." The pirate lord felt like he had finally located the missing link. Healing Evan would be a test of sorts. He only hoped that he could get the girl in his possession and that she could do for his brother what she had done for the followers of Invictus.

"Iria," Erk whispered to himself, looking out at the church's base camp. "What has become of the Sword of Justice you once served?" He then looked inwardly. "And what happened to you, Erilkaiden? Kidnapping a healer?" he questioned himself, letting out an exhausted sigh.

***

Miranda stared at the meal before her. Erk's story had moved her to tears numerous times throughout, and her heart broke for the pirate who had kidnapped her. She wasn't sure how much she could trust him, but he treated her like an honored guest ever since she healed his brother. She understood his perspective even though she didn't understand his actions.

Miranda replied with a resolved, tear-stained smile, "I will do everything in my power to honor your sisters and parents. Whatever I can do to help, in the name of Invictus, I swear that I will save as many lives as possible." Her voice grew in strength as she spoke.

Jax and Shalo continued to eat, having heard Erk's tale numerous times. The pirate lord smiled at Miranda's promise. "You've healed my brother. I owe you more than words can ever express. When we arrive in Yendralia, I will grant you your freedom if you ask. I do not want you to feel like a captive any longer, and I swear I will spend the rest of my days paying penitence for putting you through this ordeal." Erk inhaled deeply, sincerely.

Miranda turned her eyes back to her meal. "Thank you, Erk. And thank you for telling me your story." They finished their meal in relative silence.

Chapter 11
Reunion

elasine watched as two individuals emerged from the market district running toward the Fortress of Lords. He and August waited on their pegasus, blocking the road to the fortress on the hills above. With them, Dread Pirate Captain Zanfur stood, waiting for his opportunity to challenge Erk for his seat at the Table of Lords. Meanwhile, his men would be working hard to identify and steal the magnificent treasure that August had described only two days before. The initial reports were so promising that Zanfur himself paid a visit to the paladin and his mentor at The Silver Strand, and there they formulated a plan to bombard Erk with opposition from the moment he entered Yendralia.

As expected, the assault rooted out the Unbound Pirates' fearless leader as he made haste to the relative safety of the Fortress of Lords. With him, however, was a young woman whom Zanfur had never seen. Before he could question her role with Erk, August blurted out, "That's her, bishop."

Selasine nodded, fighting the urge to leap off the pegasus and run to the girl. Zanfur's eyes narrowed, wondering if this girl had anything to do with the church or the events in Port Undine. The holy men were certainly just as interested in her as he was in Erk. He cursed himself for not fully understanding what was afoot. Selasine replied to August, "Patience, acolyte. We do not want to alarm her or Erk."

Zanfur agreed silently. He only needed to issue his challenge to Erk. The rest would be up to the pirate nobles up the winding hillsides behind them. As Erk and the girl approached, their pace began to slow, and Erk reached out to tug the girl to a stop. After a brief pause, she began to run headlong toward Zanfur and his temporary bodyguards. The pirate reached toward the numerous scabbards on his belt until one of the holy men interrupted him.

Selasine announced, "Don't worry, captain, that girl won't fight if you don't."

Zanfur looked back at him, his sense of double-crossing on high alert. "You sure? She looks pretty intent."

As Miranda charged within shouting distance, Erk hot on her heels, she called out, "Bishop! August!" Selasine finally dismounted, tethering his pegasus to a nearby tree. August stayed in his saddle, watching Zanfur and Erk with mounting hostility.

Selasine could not spare a smile with the tension of the situation, but he called back to her, "Miranda! We're here!"

Zanfur trusted his instincts enough that he did not draw a weapon. He was not shocked when Miranda ran right past him into the arms of the massive priest that had helped arrange this confrontation. Their armor clanked together as she threw herself into his arms, which he promptly wrapped around her protectively.

Zanfur furrowed his brow and turned his attention back to Erk, who had stopped about ten feet away. He pulled all the disdain he could muster together to issue his challenge. "Dread Pirate Lord Erk the Radiant, Scourge of Claston, Brilliant Light of the Solar Sea. I challenge your right to sit at the Table of Lords and to govern the pirates of the Solar Sea. A fight between mortals for immortal glory and pride. What say you to the challenge?" The pirate sounded confident.

Erk rolled his eyes and reached into his jacket. "Is that really why you've gone to all this trouble to interrupt me?" he asked, pulling a small trinket from inside. "Here, take it. I have much greater issues to consider at this time. Now, leave us." Erk threw the token he had withdrawn at Zanfur's face, causing the dread pirate to instinctively snatch it out of the air.

Zanfur stood motionless, dumbstruck. Erk had literally just handed over his Lord Token. This trinket designated a captain as a Pirate Noble of Yendralia, the governors of the Isles Known for Nothing and the surrounding waters. Zanfur wanted this, but Erk's nonchalance made something feel amiss. He checked the token visually, and it seemed authentic. He pressed it between his teeth and bit down, the familiar softness of gold clinking in his bite. With this, he'd finally be welcomed at the Table of Lords. And he didn't have to fight at all! He started to laugh, holding the token in his fingers as he turned to gloat.

Erk had walked past Zanfur but stood a healthy distance away from Selasine. Erk watched as the bishop squeezed his pupil tight, his arms completely enveloping the girl as she clung to him. He could hear Miranda's tears of joy as a stream of incomprehensible words spilled all over the bishop's armor. The massive priest held his student tenderly, but he stared a storm of vengeance through his eye at the pirate. Erk and Selasine knew that the confrontation in front of them centered around Miranda, and they further knew that she would be upset if their first resort was violence.

August finally dismounted his pegasus and approached Miranda and Selasine, giving a pained smile to his beautiful friend. She nearly shrieked as she dove from her mentor to the budding paladin, "August!" He gave her an embrace as well, but Selasine's undivided attention had clearly turned now to Erk. Zanfur continued to linger nearby, realizing he was currently an onlooker to an ordeal much more significant than the challenge he intended to issue to Erk. As Miranda sobbed in August's embrace, Selasine reached for the hilt of his sword as a twitch of anger washed over his face.

Erk immediately spoke to diffuse the silent tension,

"Miranda has told me much about you, Bishop Selasine." The tone of his voice was neutral in an attempt to offset the potential for violence in this reunion.

Selasine sneered as he looked at the pirate. "If that's the case, then I'm sure you understand what I have to do," he replied, drawing his sword.

Miranda heard the metal of Selasine's sword ring as he slid it out of the steel scabbard on his belt. Immediately, she broke away from August and ran back to Selasine. "Bishop, I'm unharmed. Erk has treated me kindly despite everything else, please . . ." she pleaded as she assessed the situation. With a slow, blinking gaze, she asked, "But where is Justin? Did he not come with you?"

Selasine's anger slipped into his response, "You should ask your pirate friends where they would have left Justin had I not intervened."

Miranda's piercing blue eyes went to Erk, who stood motionless. "Did something happen to Justin?" she asked, her body language suggesting she was about to panic.

Erk shook his head and shrugged, "When I sent Shalo to take you from the base camp, we were still enemies at war. There could have been casualties on his mission; I'm afraid I know nothing more than that."

Selasine spat, "There would have been a casualty if I hadn't arrived when I did. Invictus spared him. Thanks to his injury, he stayed behind with Carulus's forces. He's okay now."

Miranda took a moment to absorb the information but could not respond. She felt so much anger at Erk and Shalo for concealing the circumstances of her abduction. She remembered Shalo mentioning that he had slain a priest in the process of abducting her. She finally made the connection that the priest was probably Justin and that Selasine had saved him with an advanced prayer. Her anger then melted to relief, knowing he was okay, thanks to her mentor. The rest of the feelings swirling within her were impossible to communicate. To some degree, she felt betrayed. She didn't want to cope with the reality that she almost lost a dear friend, that he almost died because of her. This wasn't fair, and once she heard those words in her mind, they began to echo. The second voice deep in her psyche whispered it incessantly, and Miranda narrowed her eyes with pain.

Erk noticed the change in Miranda's posture, and he watched as she drew her left hand up to her temple. His concerned glance caused Selasine to look at Miranda, her distress also obvious to him. "Bishop," she said, her voice weak and quiet. The whispering in her consciousness continued to thrash angrily, blaming Carulus for the beginning, Erk for the middle, and King Claston for the rest. None of this was fair, and it upset her greatly. She felt like she had started to lose control of her breathing.

The anger in Selasine's eye dissipated into fear and concern for Miranda. He reached out to touch her, but as he did, he felt a jolt of electricity rip through his body, causing his sword arm to go numb and bringing the bishop down to a knee. August lurched forward out of instinct, reaching to touch her shoulder. A searing heat overwhelmed his extended hand and arm, causing him to withdraw. Erk watched in confusion as Miranda's friends reacted in pain to her mere presence, but then it made sense. A piercing sound began to fill the air, so shrill that Erk had to cover his ears. Selasine and August backed away from Miranda, trying to plug their ears, their injured appendages throbbing with pain as the sound grew. Zanfur watched the spectacle, his jaw agape as three experienced fighters melted away from the girl in agony. Before he could react, the shrill sound reached his ears, causing him to let out a brief scream before trying to block the sound. Miranda's eyes closed as she touched her fingers to her forehead, the whispering inside her mind growing to a fever pitch.

"It's not fair; this shouldn't be happening. None of this should have happened. You should still be in Devitus with all of your friends close by. Nobody should have died because of you. Nobody should have almost died because of you. Is this what you wanted?" they whispered repeatedly in her mind, causing her to feel like her heart was sinking. This despair was similar to what she felt that day in the base camp, an overwhelming sensation of helplessness. She wanted to respond to the voices but could not form words. She wanted to cry but could not feel her face or her body. She inhaled deeply;

a burst of purple light surrounded her as she let out a terrified scream. The ground began to rumble violently, knocking Selasine, August, and Erk down. Zanfur's eyes widened as the ground below him began to shake, causing him to leap into a nearby tree in panic. As her emotions began to stabilize, the light around her began to fade. The shaking in the ground subsided, and Miranda slowly opened her eyes. The whispers were quiet.

It took a moment for her to realize that everyone around her had fallen helplessly to the ground. Miranda acted on instinct, sliding quickly to Selasine's side, who instinctively recoiled from her touch. Her crystal gaze filled with immediate sadness before realizing that whatever happened affected everyone around her. "Did I hurt you, bishop?" she asked with innocent concern and abounding fear.

Selasine shook his head, reaching out to touch Miranda's shoulder and finding it safe. "I can handle a shock or two," he replied, trying to play down the pain coursing through his body. He had been directly struck by lightning magic in the past, and it had never hurt with even half of the intensity as whatever just happened with Miranda. He did not, however, want her to know that.

She quickly turned to August, who had removed the armored gauntlet from his hand while resting on the ground after the brief quake. His arm was covered in severe burns, his face torn between pain and stoicism. "Oh no," she murmured, standing quickly and gripping her holy symbol. August tried to smile at her and make light of it, but the burns were deep. Miranda began to pray fervently, and the healing light of an answered prayer wrapped his arm in a soothing coolness. Within moments, he felt no pain and could see no visible signs of the burns. Miranda's non-miracle healing had also improved in just a few days, surprising August and Selasine. She carefully inspected his arm before speaking again, "I'm so sorry, August. I . . . I didn't mean—" she trailed off, ashamed and disappointed.

August slightly chuckled, "Hey, I've never met a priest that can burn a man to a crisp with one breath and heal him back to normal with the next." He gave her a teasing smile that he normally did when he had bested her in combat training. She scowled back out of instinct before realizing she forgot to check on Erk.

She stood suddenly and turned around, the golden pleats of the battlemail's skirt clinking with her change in direction. It took her only a step to realize that Erk was alright, watching as he stood up slowly and dusted off his jacket. She stayed close to August, looking at Erk and Selasine. Miranda's magical outburst had effectively nullified all of the tension between the four of them. The spectacle in front of them made them realize very quickly that Miranda had lost control of her gift for a brief moment. Erk suddenly felt thankful that Selasine was previously present to rescue Miranda's friend; if he hadn't been, the Isles Known for Nothing could have all been pulled into the depths of the ocean in the single moment that just passed. Selasine whispered a healing prayer for himself, easing the lingering electrical burn still stinging throughout his body. August stood up, replacing the gauntlet on his hand.

Erk approached within an arm's reach of Selasine and sat beside him on the road. The bishop's eyes were locked on Miranda as she stood beside August, his mind racing faster than his heart. The pirate spoke up, "As you can see, the high priest has awoken something in Miranda. Something that defies both order and common sense."

Selasine nodded in agreement but still refused to speak to Erk.

"While I will confess that I took Miranda under selfish pretenses, I quickly realized my error."

Selasine turned his eye toward Erk, remaining expressionless, waiting for Erk to continue.

Though Erk was typically the leader in conversation, he felt at odds with himself. He had as much to do with what had just happened as Carulus did. By asking Miranda to heal Evan and deal with the naval blockade, he blamed himself for Miranda's powers beginning to spiral out of control. He had not expected to find her friends waiting for them on the Isles Known for Nothing, but he was glad they were here. She needed them, and more importantly, she needed Erk.

"I think I know somebody that can help give us some

insight into Miranda's powers," the pirate lord continued.

Selasine sighed in frustration. His time on *The Water Sprite* with Gurd had shown him the true plight of Erk's followers. His anger over Miranda's abduction had fueled his hostility just moments ago, but her outburst had brought him back to a state of emotional neutrality. This wasn't a total loss. "What do you propose?" the bishop asked pointedly.

"That you, the acolyte, Miranda, and myself journey to the remote island of Olvidado. The sage Ezelbrecht lives there."

Selasine scanned his memory of the islands that made up this archipelago. He did not remember there being any significant outlying islands. "We have two pegasus; that should be enough to get to any island we need."

Erk nodded in agreement, "Except that the island is never in the same place. Ezelbrecht has made it nearly impossible to reach their location. We'll have to take a skiff and paddle through the reefs during low tide. If we're lucky, the fog will guide us to our destination."

Selasine's countenance drew up into contempt. "Do you really think it wise to chase nursery rhymes while Miranda's power spirals out of control?"

Erk expected the bishop to respond accordingly. "If you know a better way, I would be glad to hear you out. Miranda cares deeply for you, and as such, I hold your opinions in the highest regard," he replied, showing an unusual amount of deference. At this point, he knew that his pirating days were over. The key to winning this conflict lay in continuing to build his relationship with Miranda and her companions now. The lack of trust between them was understandable. He thought that even the most patient engineers could build bridges over canyons. This was his only way forward.

Selasine thought carefully about what steps to take. Ideally, he would have taken the girl to Nulodia for a thorough examination and rigorous testing under the care of the church. Then again, the high priest there was Carulus, and he had already wronged Miranda significantly. He had difficulty trusting Erk, but at this point, he felt he could trust the pirate more than the high priest. He grumbled a bit before finally replying, "So tell me about this Ezelbrecht."

Erk's face remained cold, but he smiled on the inside. "Ezelbrecht is one of the old ones."

Selasine's eye narrowed, "The old ones?"

Erk nodded. "An eldritch dragon."

The trio from Devitus all looked immediately to Erk for clarification. August interjected, "Wait, you want to take Miranda to see a dragon? What kind of dragon?"

Erk tilted his head down to the right. "When I was a younger elf, I came to the Isles Known for Nothing to escape the conflict with the usurper, Gelidor, who you know as the king. While here, I met Ezelbrecht seeking wisdom on defeating the usurper's oppressive regime. I took their advice, and I began to hit the king where it hurt most: his treasury. Recruiting pirates like Apocalypse and Jax helped me gain momentum, and what you see now is the empire built from Ezelbrecht's wisdom. I think Ezelbrecht would be a tremendous help sorting out Miranda's gift," he explained, leaving the air silent.

At this time, August realized Zanfur was still clinging to a nearby tree. With a sinister look, the acolyte walked over to him, almost fifty feet from the others. "So, you got what you came for, right?" he asked the "dread" pirate, who currently looked scared beyond his wits.

Zanfur grunted and slid out of the tree, looking back at Miranda. "Covered in mithril and gold, adorned with ruby. No, I didn't get what I wanted. And honestly, I don't want any part of it anymore. That woman is terrifying."

August laughed and gestured toward the three still waiting close by. "Well, now's your chance to take the treasure if you want it," he taunted.

Zanfur scrunched his nose and shook his head. "I suppose that clinging to a title like pirate lord will do me no good if I'm dead," he replied, sounding helpless.

August shook his head. "No, but if you get us a skiff, we'll take her away from here, and you can dine with your new colleagues in the fortress."

The newly-tokened pirate lord gave a sigh. "Fine, I'll see what I can come up with."

August turned away and began to return to Erk, Selasine,

and Miranda. Zanfur followed him at a safe distance.

Erk blinked in disbelief when his rival approached. "Go on then, Zanfur. The Fortress of Lords awaits," he taunted sarcastically, giving an exaggerated gesture to the road that wound the hills up to the fortified complex.

Zanfur shook his head. "Erk, who is this woman?" he asked, the bewilderment causing his voice to crack with uncertainty.

Erk smiled and looked at Miranda, who looked at Zanfur with a puzzled expression. "She's hope for the people of Claston and despair for anyone with true evil in their hearts. That's who she is," he replied proudly.

Selasine could hear the genuine way Erk spoke of Miranda to Zanfur. Just like Carulus, Erk had placed his hope in Miranda far too fast for his liking. Based on what Damil had told them just three days before, it was likely that Miranda was the cause of the blockade's mysterious transport from the open sea to the navy yard. Everyone expected far too much of the girl. And as the mysterious gift inside her grew, he realized how dangerous this would be. Especially for her.

"Erk, how soon can we start searching for Ezelbrecht's island?" Selasine asked, interrupting the exchange between pirates.

With a confident nod, Erk replied, "Right away, if you'll allow it." He was glad for a concrete reason to prolong his return to the Fortress of Lords. Besides, helping Miranda would be in the best interest of the other pirate nobles.

Zanfur tilted his head up. "I have a couple of skiffs down on the shore on the south side of the island if you'd like to take one," he added, feeling important.

Erk was quick to reply, "Yes, Dread Pirate Lord Zanfur. We'll gladly sail under your colors if you'd like." Erk gave a deep, reverent bow, the sarcasm palpable.

Zanfur's face twisted with frustration, "No, I didn't mean you had to sail with my colors. Just consider it my contribution to keeping that woman under control!"

Miranda's eyes examined the unassuming pirate. Nothing about him seemed exceptional; he had dark hair and eyes with an average build. He was taller than Erk at five feet but not quite as tall as Miranda at five foot nine. He had a well-groomed beard, which wasn't too out of place for a pirate captain. He wore a common black captain's jacket with a black tunic underneath. He wore as much jewelry as any pirate and a small hat that could be tipped to block out the sun if needed. She glared briefly before she added, "I have a name."

Zanfur gulped and turned his attention to Miranda. "Of course, lass, my apologies," he replied hastily, an obvious terror spreading through him.

Miranda's glare softened, "You can call me Miranda. May I know your name also?" she asked, that kind, endearing demeanor permeating every word she said now.

"Certainly, Miranda. I'm Dread Pirate Captain Zanfur," he proudly proclaimed, feeling the terror subside as Miranda's gentle nature allowed him to drop his guard.

Erk interjected, "I thought you were a pirate lord now?" his gall boundless.

"Oh, right, yes," Zanfur replied, his eyes darting to the ground.

Miranda took a step toward Zanfur, causing him to step back. She tilted her head, her braids shifting with the angle of her chin. "Don't be afraid, please. I promise it's all under control right now," she pleaded.

Zanfur's eyes widened, but he stayed put. He nodded and tried to stand straight.

Miranda's lips remained pursed inquisitively as she asked, "Zanfur, are you sure you want to be a pirate lord?"

The pirate shook his head, reaching in his jacket to fumble with the token. "No, I just didn't want Erk to be a pirate lord anymore," he replied, the honesty surprising.

Miranda looked at Erk, still sitting beside Selasine, who watched the situation intently. August stood nearby, a smug grin on his lips. She continued interrogating, asking, "Would you sink your own ships to keep them out of Erk's hands?"

Zanfur started to nod enthusiastically but quickly realized what Miranda was pointing out. "Wait, what do you want by asking all these questions?" he retorted.

Erk pushed his hands against the ground and stood up. He extended an arm to Selasine, offering to help him off the ground. The bishop cautiously accepted the pirate's assistance, standing with him. Erk responded before Miranda could reply, "She's calling you an idiot, Zanfur. But she's too kind to ever put it that way. The other lords will eat you alive if you go to that fortress. I mean, Oorzgo will literally eat you alive. The others it's just a metaphor. The trinket in your hand doesn't mean anything if you can't back up your words with actions and your actions with conviction. Be a pirate lord with the other seven if you want it so bad. You'll be dead before we're back from our quest, and I'll get my trinket back when Alaina finds out what kind of stunt you pulled."

Zanfur's eyes widened even more. "The Pirate Queen?!" he exclaimed. Erk nodded in reply. Oblivious, Zanfur continued, "Is she still alive?" he asked, confused.

Erk looked up to the sky in exasperation. "Of course she's alive, you nimrod. Give me that," he blustered, reaching into Zanfur's jacket and snatching the Lord Token. Zanfur's reaction was so slow that he slapped himself in the chest, trying to catch Erk's arm. "The first rule of being a pirate lord is that your life is only as safe as your information. Zanfur, I'm saving your life by stopping you from doing this. We'll take your skiff as a token of your gratitude, understood?"

Selasine felt an emotional paradox. While he reviled the elf for the terrible things he had done, watching him in his element was somewhat entertaining. If he could sway Miranda, then he was obviously capable of kindness and gentleness. On the contrary, he spared no details humiliating Zanfur to prove a point to his rival. Selasine gave a stern glance to Miranda.

"Acolyte, do you wish to accompany Erk to see Ezelbrecht?" the bishop asked, using her church title for formality's sake.

She smiled and gave a confident nod. "Yes, teacher, and I would be so happy if you and August would accompany us." As she spoke, Zanfur slumped in defeat, backing away in silence.

Selasine had figured that his presence on the journey was presumed, but he couldn't fault the girl for her politeness. Nor could he help but smile as he replied, "Of course, Miranda. The Sword of Justice guides our path,"

She started to giggle. For the first time in a few days, she had the privilege of reciting a catechism with her mentor. She wasn't expecting the giggle, but it took over her once it started. Slowly it escalated into laughter, a wholesome sound that was quickly contagious. August's smirk was accompanied by a low rumble that broke into a hearty laugh. Selasine chuckled to himself, reserved but responsive. Only Erk did not laugh. His lips were twisted into a genuine, happy smile, but he did not laugh.

Miranda's voice rolled from laughter into a delightful melody, her rich tone bringing out the most beautiful elements of the catechism. "The Sword of Justice guides our path! Let us set out with order in our steps and righteousness in our hearts. May Invictus shine his holy light upon us and pour out his judgment in abundance. Our steps forward bring the future, but our footprints are the evidence of our deeds. Silver Maiden, guard our hearts; Sword of Justice, guide our hands. Together we depart, and together we shall return," she beamed as she finished, her pretty face twisted into a sweet smile. Selasine's smile was relaxed and carefree, glad to see that nothing in this ordeal thus far had taken that beautiful spirit away from her.

August sighed happily, missing her floaty, soothing voice reciting catechisms and singing hymns. He had teased her in the past, calling her "Invictus's little songbird." Now, at this moment, he felt like the world would be hopelessly empty without that gentle voice. While she was missing, of course, he was worried about her. But only now did he begin thinking of what losing Miranda would actually mean. He almost lost the girl he thought of as his little sister, and his blood turned cold momentarily as he contemplated that fact. He knew what it was like to lose a sibling.

Erk clapped, breaking the clerics out of their thoughts. "Miranda, the song in your voice is beautiful and full of energy," he commented, pleasant and languid in how he spoke.

Miranda smiled at him, "I told you that I missed my friends. I guess what I should have said was that I missed my family. When you find something you didn't realize you had, wouldn't that make you laugh and sing too?"

Erk chuckled. "I won't argue, Lady Hyacinth," he retorted, subtly bowing.

Miranda scrunched her nose, "Now, who's the formal one,

pirate lord?"

Erk shrugged with a smile, "A quest begun with the Catechism of the Traveler. Are we not to pay our respects to all other formalities as dictated by the Sword of Justice?"

Selasine interrupted, "How do you know the scriptures, pirate?" his expression shifting to slight shock.

The elven pirate wiggled his fingers at Selasine. "My sister."

Selasine's head cocked upward in disbelief. "Your sister was a member of the clergy?"

Erk feigned a yawn. "It's not an exciting story," he said with a shrug.

Miranda's eyes widened. "Erk! Don't be coy! Iriliandria and Ara'Ilyvithia were both wonderful priestesses, and the brethren on the Path of the Sword of Justice deserve to hear their tale," she ordered.

She spoke in a way that Selasine had never heard, and it caught him so off guard that it took him a moment to realize exactly what Miranda had said. "Wait, Miranda, did you just say Iriliandria?" Selasine asked, recognizing the elven name of his late wife, whose common name was Iria.

Erk nodded to confirm, "Does my sister's name mean something to you, bishop? She is a cleric of Invictus, and so was Ara'Ilyvithia, my eldest sister. I had to listen to those catechisms for decades while Iria pledged herself to the Path."

Selasine's posture was tense, and he had difficulty responding. He realized that Erk spoke of Iria in the present tense. There were too many coincidences here. "So, you know the law by heart and choose to bend and break it as you see fit, then," he countered, saying something he heard Iria say word for word to someone who had abandoned their faith in Invictus.

Erk laughed. "You sound just like her." He raised the pitch of his voice to imitate his sister, "Dear Erilkaiden, your choices are leading you to a dangerous place," he patronized himself on her behalf. He felt his heart sink. He had gotten so caught up in the jest that he didn't realize he was thinking so freely and deeply about his sisters. He wasn't sure why, but he suddenly realized that Selasine's heart would have complimented Iria's in such a way that he felt like he could feel them both there, weighing his actions.

Selasine's voice broke slightly as he replied, "It sounds like your sister was a brilliant elf." His eye was turned sharply to the ground. Erk matched the description of Iria's brothers. In fact, Erilkaiden was one of her brother's names; Selasine had never considered that Erk could have been his common name. Still, he had golden flowing hair and sharp, gray eyes. This seemed like the cruelest joke straight from the bowels of Indervill. Iria explained that she had fled a distant war but didn't give him enough specifics. She always spoke fondly of her brothers, but she didn't mention that they had not also fled the unrest. She used such specific location and region names that Selasine did not realize she was fleeing a conflict in Claston. She refused to talk about that aspect of her past in much detail. Selasine was not surprised that he now found himself involved in a conflict that Iria had fled. He recognized that this might be part of his own destiny, something he had not even considered relevant in a decade.

Erilkaiden sighed. Miranda had seen Erk's heart as he told her the story of his family. She believed his story in spite of her doubts and worries about Erk. He loved his sisters, parents, and Evan more than anyone could imagine. She estimated that these emotions had been buried deep while Evan was wasting due to the curse. Now that he had been made whole, Erk's heart was free to feel again. Miranda, too, felt like weeping, but she then began to wonder why the mention of Iria's name made the bishop also emotional.

The pirate lord lamented, tears breaking up his words. "I haven't seen Iriliandria in about seventy years. She was smart enough to leave Claston shortly after the king began executing people with their very own gifts."

Selasine could not speak for the next hour, causing Miranda to worry more.

***

Indervill smashed its head against the clouds in the primordial place. The deity was currently vaguely humanoid. It whipped around its head harmlessly. "Betray me, you did! Betray me, you do! Not fair, not fair! It's a cheat, a trick, a scam. Can't you spare me some coin?" the god shrieked as it sprouted varying limbs that flailed in vain against the ever-swirling clouds. They swished and swooped back into place after the air came to rest in the primordial place.

A stern voice taunted him, the Silver Maiden Lexcord also present, "My brother is not really fond of pirates, you know."

Indervill sprouted hundreds of eyestalks that scanned the infinite space here. Clouds wisped to form Lexcord's avatar, a beautiful woman with traits and features reminiscent of elvenkind. Her silver hair draped her face with a pleasing frame and cascaded loosely down her back. She wore a silver tiara adorned with sapphires, the quality of which inspired legends among mortals. An ornate war hammer hung loosely at her hip, and on her back hung a tower shield perfectly fitted to shelter her from any onslaught, magical or physical.

"Shiny shiny, come to taunt, you win, you win!" the entity of chaos screeched. "You think it's over, you do? The madness we'll pass on and share it with you, too!"

Lexcord laughed. "Not taunting. You see, I was sad that Erilkaiden had lost his way. Of course, he despaired and spiraled into chaos. You were unrelenting in the trials you put on him."

Indervill formed a coherent avatar, this time a male centaur. "You smell like a spring rain, and you taste like bile. Why do you do this to me? Why am I the one you hate?" The centaur leaned closer, "Besides, the merchant did this to him, not me."

The Silver Maiden rolled her eyes, "You know, chaos is the shadow of law just like darkness is to light. You can't be surprised when compatible forces align, despite differing philosophies. You are no more merciful than The Counselor of the Corrupt in the way you treat mortals." Still, she could not refute her estranged sibling's logic. Na'agamlor had truly done more to Erilkaiden than Indervill. She did not truly consider the "merchant" a god. He was simply a human who became so wealthy through corruption that he bought immortality and omnipotence. Still, he could never buy his way into the primordial place. At least, he hadn't figured out how to turn his entrance here into a transaction. After thinking, she finished her rebuke, "Though you speak the truth, sibling, you miss the point. You could aid these mortals just like I do, but you choose to harm them in the name of your silly games. At least Na'agamlor's thirst for wealth is a tangible goal. You make no sense to god or mortal."

The centaur form stomped aggressively, "That's not what we meant. We do not blame the sun, nor do we blame the moon. We thank the sun, indeed, but we hate the moon. You can't fathom the depths of our depravity, can you? If you could, wouldn't you find me at home?"

Lexcord turned her attention to the swirling clouds and started to listen to the words and prayers of her followers. She inhaled deeply as a wind blew over her, her hair fluttering gracefully around her countenance. She closed her eyes as she took in the overwhelming sensations of prayers, supplications, curses, and lamentations. She heard prayers for forgiveness, atonement, and gratitude. She felt hearts lowered to the depths of grief and souls elated to the peaks of happiness.

"Indervill," she whispered. "Do you hear that? The countless souls whispering to me, people finding themselves through their dedication to my ideals? I can feel them with me, here, in the primordial place. And you know what? They are the reason I am here. I live for my believers. What do you live for, Chaos?"

The entity shuddered within itself. The ultimate taunt. Indervill could not forgive this. Why? It wasn't sure. "I live because you live. I thrive because you thrive. One step forward for you is one step backward for me. After all, I am the shadow cast by your light."

Lexcord frowned. When Indervill spoke clearly, it always spoke truthfully. "You know, you're not entirely hated. Without you, love at first sight would be a dream. Without you, nobody would know surprise and the joy that comes from that. You're not inherently evil; you just hurt many people when you don't have to."

The polyphonic voice of Indervill shrieked in reply, "Then why does it hurt, sister? Why does the entropy burn me so?"

She inhaled deeply. "Such is the injustice of existence. I'm sorry I can't save you, sibling, but I do not feel guilt in cutting off your limbs."

The entity of chaos huffed and vanished into the primordial clouds.

Chapter 12
Olvidado

iranda, Selasine, August, and Erk followed Zanfur's directions from the tide wall to the southern beach of the island. Due to the mountains that cupped around Yendralia, the beach's white sands sloped almost immediately upward into towering, rocky spires. Most sea traffic filtered in and out of the primary docks. The reefs surrounding the Isles Known for Nothing could be dangerous to large vessels trying to navigate the small islands. To move from island to island, many inhabitants used small rafts and skiffs to avoid the inflexibility of larger ships. During festivals in Yendralia, the waters around the large island would fill with these small crafts as people made their way to the central island to partake in the celebrations.

Though space on the beach was limited, some entrepreneurially minded individuals had set up various shops and shanties on the outer side of the island. Many specialized in fishing supplies, raft repair, and other sundry necessities for island hopping. Zanfur had directed August to a fishmonger that operated one of these businesses, and he had instructed the acolyte to give the man a passphrase that would tell the merchant everything he needed to know.

The four of them traversed the rocky terrain leading south from the tide wall on foot, Selasine and Erk having paid the proprietor of The Silver Strand a significant sum to keep the pegasus safe during their absence. Erk clarified, "If anything untoward happens to the beasts, then no amount of coin will spare you from the consequences of your neglect." Selasine felt the threat was credible enough that he did not need to worry about the pegasus. Still, flying horses would have made traversing this difficult path somewhat easier.

After climbing up a small rock face and descending a steep hill on the other side, the four found themselves among the sparsely populated outer ring of the island. While not officially a district of Yendralia, many of the same types of individuals plied their trades here. August spent a few moments scanning the shops and shanties until he saw the board he was looking for: "TeunTeun's Fresh Filets." He indicated with his finger which shop they needed and led the approach.

The shop was one of a few of the more permanent structures on the beach. A window opened for clients to speak to the owner about their fish needs. The wooden building had a porch built around it to lift the area around the shop off the ground. As the four approached the shop, they could see two people inside, busily dressing freshly caught fish. August stepped forward and said through the window, "The quick dagger comes calling."

To everyone's surprise, a gnome's face popped up from behind the counter. He had white, wild hair that frayed in every direction. He wore a green hat typical of merchants and was dressed in red, green, and gold silk. He was about three feet tall, standing at Miranda's hips. His skin was slightly wrinkled, and his bulbous nose seemed to be the center point of his face. His eyebrows were exceptionally bushy, an unkempt but unassuming sight. Miranda had never seen a gnome in Devitus, as they did not often venture out of their communities.

"Quick daggee ye says?" the gnome replied.

"Swift from the shadows, splashing into the shallows. Four birds spotted in the tree," August replied, hoping that he correctly remembered the elements of the coded question.

"Oh, 'zat so, eh?" the gnome replied, pulling himself onto the large counter under the shop window. "Call me TeunTeun, travelers. Who mights you be? Definitely not pirates, no, TeunTeun can see right through that. You tells, I sells."

August blinked incredulously for a moment. "Right. I'm August. The behemoth with me is Bishop Selasine," he began to explain, catching laughter from the gnome, a giggle from Miranda, and a shoulder punch from the bishop. With a smirk, August continued, "The red hair is Miranda, and you were wrong about the elf. He actually is a pirate."

TeunTeun's eyes widened as he saw Erk. "Oh my, my, my, goodness me! I paid too much protection moneys to Zanfur-gab, and now it's made ol' Erk-gab mad at me!"

Erk shook his head and gave a subtle smile. "No, master TeunTeun, nothing of the sort. We only need what the boy told you about in that moron Zanfur's secret code."

TeunTeun tugged at the long white beard that rolled off his chin, a look of relief on his face. "Well, if that's the way it's gotta be, no back-talk from me!" the gnome replied, sliding across the counter through the window and to the outside of his shop.

The gnome led the four of them behind the shop to an outdoor storage area full of barrels, rafts, rope, and nets. Miranda was perturbed by the haphazard nature of the storage area, the disorganized array making her skin crawl. The area was fairly large and spilled off the raised porch onto the surrounding beach. TeunTeun scanned over the junk and pursed his lips. "I could swear it was here, somewhere!" he mumbled.

Selasine stared directly at a couple of skiffs pushed up against the back of the building and stood up on their square sterns. Erk noticed them, too but did not pressure the gnome to select one of them. In fact, he was curious as to whether or not Zanfur's secret code would even work. Meanwhile, August carried on a conversation with Miranda in which he greatly exaggerated how he had roped Zanfur's pirates into helping him find her. TeunTeun suddenly exclaimed, "Oh, there it is!"

The gnome skipped over to the back of the shop and pushed one of the skiffs onto the ground. "I swear I left it underneath one of these," he grumbled as the small boat thudded onto the porch with a loud crash. Erk and Selasine recoiled, and the loud noise interrupted Miranda and August's conversation. TeunTeun began digging through some things left under the skiff, so the group approached carefully to see what he was doing.

"Hmmm," the gnome grumbled to himself. "Don't guess I quite remember what I was looking for. I could swear that four birds in the shallows was something over here, but it's escaped my memory," he commented incorrectly, indicating that he didn't remember the code either. He brushed his hand through his beard repeatedly. "Welp. Tell Zanfur I said sorry; I don't think I have it anymore."

August cringed in embarrassment for the gnome. Selasine and Erk stepped over to the skiff and lifted it. Erk assured the gnome, "This is what it referred to, master TeunTeun," holding the boat by the rim around the bow. The gnome looked at the skiff with disbelief. His round nose crinkled in thought.

"You know," TeunTeun replied, "I had a feeling it was around here somewhere. You're as smart as they say you are, Dread Pirate Lord Erk!" he lauded sincerely, causing Erk to smile.

"Your stewardship over others' property is commendable, master TeunTeun. We'll return it when we get back," Erk added, hoisting the small boat with little effort and Selasine's assistance.

TeunTeun nodded enthusiastically, happy to receive a compliment from one of the eight pirate nobles. "Always at yer service, m'lord!" he replied.

With a wave to the gnome, Erk and Selasine began to carry the skiff toward the water. Miranda and August caught up to the more experienced duo, finding a place to help them grab and carry the skiff. It was late afternoon, and the tide was pulling back into the depths. Erk instructed the others to place the skiff in the sand with its bow facing the water. He untied two oars that had been fixed onto the crosspiece of the small vessel. Then, he instructed Miranda and August to get into the skiff, setting them both near the stern. He pulled the boat from the bow, moving it toward the water. Selasine pushed from the weighty stern, and as their boots began to splash in the receding tide, they leaped into the skiff with Miranda and August. They sat on the bow bench, leaving oversized August and Miranda crowded on the stern bench.

Erk got the skiff into the open water using the oars and the withdrawing tide. Though the tide's retreat was quite gentle off this side of the island, a storm lingered on the horizon directly to the east, pushing choppy water as far as the Isles Known for Nothing. Selasine felt nervous on such a small vessel in the somewhat agitated waters. Unless Erk was secretly a triton, he felt confident that the pirate would manage the boat to the best of his abilities. August gripped the seat beneath him with a bit of anxiety. He still had on his plate armor, which surely would sink him straight to the bottom of the ocean surrounding the islands. Miranda, however, was more interested in helping Erk row the tiny vessel. For safety and logistical reasons, Erk insisted he take the lead this time but would love to teach her how to row on a less perilous voyage.

As the skiff slid over the tops of the low but frequent waves, Erk maintained the small vessel with incredible precision. Inside the boat, the quartet sat facing each other, Selasine across from Miranda and Erk across from August. By the time they had gotten well into the water, the sun had begun its ascent toward the horizon. The warm summer air felt chilly with spray from the rolling waves under the skiff splashing onto them. Water glistened on the metals of their armor, and it soaked quickly into cloth garments and tunics worn over the tops of their gear.

Erk pushed the oars forcefully, propelling the boat toward one of the outlying islands. As he moved the boat, Miranda began to ask some questions, beginning with, "Erk, did you tell anybody where we were going? Does the crew know where you are?"

Erk shook his head. "If I'm not at the fortress or on the ship, the crew knows they have unlimited leave. I trust Jax to secure

The Neb, so I'm not concerned. Besides, you've seen how opportunists like Zanfur work. I'd prefer to keep our mission a secret, even from our own people," he added, his wording intentional to make Miranda part of his crew.

Selasine stared at them as they talked, the suspicion in his eye relaxing somewhat. Clearly, they had spent much of the last four days together as they had a natural rapport. Miranda was not shy but could also be horribly awkward with strangers. At this point, Selasine's mind wandered to Erk's revelation on the path to the fortress. Erk claimed his sister's name was Iriliandria, which was also the elven name of his late wife. Physically, Erk could not have been more different from Iria; his hair was golden, and her hair was jet black. She was tall for an elf, and Erk was average height. She was, however, a cleric of Invictus, just as Erk had claimed his sister to be. In fact, Selasine met the beautiful Iria shortly after she arrived in Nulodia at the temple. She told him she was one hundred and twenty years old when they met, which would have aligned with Erk's timeline. Regardless of the facts, if Selasine's Iria was truly Erk's sister, Selasine had a duty to share the truth with the pirate lord. Selasine blamed himself for Iria's death enough. He thought it wise to settle everything with Miranda before trying to break such difficult ground with Erk. He had to let it rest for now.

Miranda then turned her eyes to Selasine and August, beaming with excitement. "I'm so happy you're here now, Bishop Selasine! Is this like one of the real adventures you told me about?"

Selasine's mouth twisted into a half-smile, "Not just like it, girl; it is a true adventure. I trust you've kept up with your prayers?"

Miranda nodded enthusiastically. "They were especially helpful when I was scared in the caves. Shalo wasn't much help fighting the mushbeaks down there, so I'm doubly thankful for the protection prayers."

Selasine nodded, but Erk raised a brow. The pirate inserted himself into the conversation, "Shalo said you healed him, but he didn't give many details about what happened beyond encountering the creatures."

While the skiff bounced across the waves, Miranda fully explained what happened in the tunnels beneath the mountains. Erk laughed at Shalo's misfortune, figuring that his invisible luck would have to run out eventually. Selasine and August were very impressed with how quickly Miranda thought to pray and fight the creatures, saving herself and the pirate from becoming fungus food. Selasine could not forgive Erk for everything that had happened, but it ultimately helped her grow. He was proud of his pupil.

As the sun set, the Solar Sea's waters turned from a deep shade of purple to a consuming blackness. The water remained generally agitated, and blind conditions over the water in such a small boat could prove deadly quickly. Erk began to fumble with a lantern that was attached to the crossbeam. Selasine merely gripped his holy symbol and said, "Daylight." A soft radiance glowed out of his holy symbol, surrounding the skiff with a light bright enough that the four of them felt like they were in a bubble of authentic daylight. Miranda marveled at this prayer, much different from the harsher, smaller light granted by her prayers. In fact, she still had to recite the incantation rather than simply calling the name of the prayer.

Erk gritted his teeth, "Well, that works much better than what I had in mind. Thanks, bishop."

Selasine's face remained stoic, but he fumbled his holy symbol between his fingers as he replied, "August is afraid of the dark."

The acolyte's face scrunched as he glared menacingly at the bishop. He probably would have elbowed him had they been close together.

Miranda giggled. Selasine and August had always picked at each other. It was always in good fun, and she felt like it seemed like a silly competition. In her imagination, Selasine was the father to the three peacekeepers, something she didn't realize was essentially a reality. That was until the bishop and her friend came to rescue her on horses with wings. It felt right in her heart to call Selasine dad and August and Justin her brothers. She didn't want to trouble them with those thoughts before, but now, after almost losing these people, she wanted them to know how she felt as soon as she could get them all in the same room. Her sapphire eyes shimmered with contentedness in the daylight prayer that her mentor had conjured.

Erk's eyes lingered on the holy symbol, and he thought it looked familiar. Instead of asking about it, he snickered at the familial banter. It caused comforting memories of his childhood to surface. Using the bubble of daylight around them, he continued to turn the oars with a rhythm that kept the skiff steady despite the agitated water. After a few moments of silence, Miranda asked Erk about Evan's condition. The pirate lord indicated he was as good as new since Miranda healed him.

The mention of Erk's brother was another confirmation to Selasine; Iria had talked a lot about both Erilkaiden and Evanthalus. She was fond of both of them, but she seemed to tell more stories about Evanthalus since he was so young compared to Erk. Evan was the most logical common version of Evanthalus, Selasine thought. He learned of the curse on Erk's brother, and even Selasine was moved by the selfless way Miranda healed his youngest brother-in-law. They moved silently for the rest of their journey, the splashing waves almost hypnotic. After about an hour of drifting in the churning water, the four could feel the summer air cooling rapidly. The storm on the horizon had slowly drifted over the Isles Known for Nothing. In between the push and pull of the waves, occasional rumbling thunder shook them with a sudden but gentle blast. The wind swirled angrily around them, enhancing the wet chill of the ocean air.

The dropping temperature and building humidity caused a fog to begin forming around them as they drifted in their limited light. The fog thickened so quickly that even Selasine's daylight began to lose its efficacy. As such, he protested their current predicament, "How are we supposed to make it in a fog like this?"

Erk nodded in rhythm with the churning of the oars. "The fog is part of the magic that protects the island. Ezelbrecht knows I'm looking for them. Otherwise, we could have been here for a few days," he replied, almost taunting Selasine.

After another half hour or so, the fog was so thick that they could barely see each other in the skiff. Nevertheless, they could feel the waves beneath them calming swiftly. As the boat slowed to a near stop, Erk began to pump the oars to drive the tiny vessel forward. The flat bottom crunched as it scraped sand. Erk leaned over, running his fingers through the sand, but he felt more water than earth. He sat still for a moment, the waves sloshing the skiff further onto an unseen beach. The summer air remained so cool that Miranda wished she had a dry, warm autumn cloak draped around her. After Erk felt more sand than water, he ordered the group, "Alright, hop out."

Selasine and August easily spilled out of their benches, standing and tugging the skiff out of the water. As Miranda and Erk stepped out of the boat, the pirate grabbed a rope attached to the tiny vessel and tied it to a small tree that was hardly visible in the milky fog that had enveloped them. The orb of daylight barely dented the cloudy swirls around them. The shadows beyond clearly indicated the landmass growing outside the light. Following the shadows, Selasine and company felt the soft sand turn to gravel beneath their boots. As the ground became firmer, the fog began to disperse. Selasine's daylight began to pour over the island around them. A rocky terrain funneled arrivers from the beach into a deep gorge. Around the landing point, a steep ridge of rocks stood firm against anyone landing anywhere but in the sand. Blackened, gnarled trees dotted the rocky juts that dropped slowly into the gorge. Miranda looked at the terrain with wonder, similar to what she had expressed when seeing the open sea for the first time. Erk and Selasine recognized that face, but only Selasine detected that something was different.

"What's wrong, Miranda?" Selasine asked suddenly, the silence becoming the norm.

She shook her head, "I'm sorry, I just . . .," she trailed off, a crash of thunder suddenly exploding against the rocky ridges and juts around them. "I can feel something terrible is here. Something hideously evil. Bishop, can't you feel it?" she pleaded. That look of wonder was also a look of fear, Selasine realized. She wanted to know what was here, but it scared her. He doubled his resolve to protect her.

Erk cleared his throat, grumbling as he said, "There is a

dragon here, remember? They are not the kind of dragon that is typically considered 'good,' but they are brilliant and wise. The Master was the one that introduced me to Ezelbrecht."

Miranda's face scrunched into a pained grimace. "Erk, you didn't tell me that the dragon's evil aura would be so intense," she nearly cried.

Selasine's eyes widened with fear. "Miranda, do you sense the presence of evil? I feel nothing," he added, concerned.

She nodded energetically. "I can't take it; it's so overwhelming. Please get me away," she shrieked.

None of the others could feel the tremendous evil present, which troubled Selasine especially. He should be immediately sensitive to the auras of people and other entities, a divine gift that August and Miranda should have been just now uncovering. Erk had visited the island many times before, but he was no longer delicately in touch with feelings and auras. Somehow, it seemed, Miranda's gift made her sensitive to something beyond their comprehension.

Miranda stood straight up and took a deep fighting stance. Selasine and Erk looked at her in disbelief as she inhaled deeply, giving a firm stomp on the ground. An earthquake began to rattle the ground beneath them, this one more controlled than the sudden rumbling in Yendralia. August lost his balance and fell prone, but Selasine and Erk kept their footing through the rumbling. A series of screeches emanated from the haunting landscape around them. She stood up straight before staggering.

Both Selasine and Erk rushed to her, August lifting himself off the ground. She didn't fall unconscious, but she did fall to her knees. Selasine felt his confusion swirling into an insistent question, "Miranda, what in the Infernia was that?"

She panted as she replied, "I . . . I'm not really sure. The evil here scared the power within me so badly that it started to happen again. I could hear the whispering voice inside me, but I listened to it this time. I didn't like what it said, but it caused the energy to build like it did earlier today. The only thing I could think of was taking all that energy and stomping it around us. I can tell that something is terrible here, but I know I don't have to be scared. Not if I'm with you, bishop."

August groaned, "Well, I guess this means you'll be winning our combat training in the future. Nyokto," he finished his sentence with a curse in Khantongue.

Miranda blinked slowly, looking at the descending gorge before them. "Whatever it is, it lives down there." The darkness beyond the daylight prayer loomed ominously below.

Erk shrugged, "Hey, I didn't give the wyrm a test or anything to find out if it was good or evil. I was in a pretty dark place, okay? I needed advice. I took their advice. And now, I think they can help you, Miranda." His expression was a combination of shame and helplessness.

She smiled, "No, I know they can. I've seen chaos on this journey so far. I think it's important for me to meet evil, too. I'm definitely scared. Will you three help me?"

Selasine gave a sympathetic sigh. "Of course, Miranda. Let's hear the dragon's wisdom and decide together."

Erk grumbled, "You mean you have to check it against some outdated code that doesn't consider the changes to our world over the last hundred years?"

Miranda twisted her neck quickly, casting a piercing glare at Erk. His face immediately contorted into an apologetic face. She snarked, "Well, at least we're taking time to collaborate instead of kidnapping people!"

He sank his head in honest defeat. "Nyokto indeed, you're not pulling any punches today, Miranda."

Miranda's spine felt a ping of regret. She had just smarted off to a superior! The monks in the monastery helped her overcome that habit a decade ago. Disagreement was not a cause to be rude. She saw his apologetic expression and immediately mirrored it.

Erk noted their mutual, contrite expressions and promised, "Miranda, whatever evil lurks down here is not ready for you. Please, I know Ezelbrecht personally. I guarantee they will not hurt us."

Selasine and August felt uncomfortable. Miranda nodded to Erk. "Let's see if we can understand what's happening to me."

A rumbling sound echoed from the gorge that sunk deep outside of the radius of light cast by Selasine's prayer.

***

Ten Years Earlier

Zanfur glared at Erk as his rival held a saber to his throat. He lay on the ground, helpless against the sharp point at his neck. "Bested again, Zanfur? Why don't you knock it off and just join my crew already? Your gift is brilliant." Erk retracted his sword.

Zanfur sat up and grumbled, "You just don't get it, do you? The only way to be a self-made man is to take one down and take his place!"

Erk rolled his eyes. "Is this a pride thing?" he asked, annoyed.

Zanfur gave an exaggerated nod, standing up. Everyone in the tavern had already returned to their drinks and distractions. This was the third time this week that Zanfur had tried to challenge Erk for his command of *The Nebula*. Nobody was sure why a captain was supposed to give up command of a ship if they were bested by a random interloper. Nevertheless, Zanfur had it in his mind that this was the way of Yendralia and the pirates of the Solar Sea. Moreover, nobody understood why Erk humored him so willingly.

Months passed, and Erk invited Zanfur to join *The Nebula* with his own ship, *The Silent Kite*. He wanted to encourage the young pirate to target the King of Claston's richest vessels. Perhaps, Erk thought, if he were to join a successful raid, it might give him the confidence to lead his own raids against the soft aristocracy of Claston's despotic, usurping king. As Erk approached him with the proposal, he tried to flatter the captain, "So, I wanted to ask you a question."

Zanfur tilted his head up to exaggerate his look down at Erk. "What is it, then?"

Erk openly smiled, "I am planning a raid against a merchant fleet returning to Claston this week. There will be tons of soft targets, but there'll be no way we could raid them all. I wanted a couple of smaller, faster vessels to join up with me. I'm not even asking for a cut. I just don't want these goods getting back to Claston. You're free to keep anything you plunder."

"This some kind of trap, Erk? You think I'm dumb enough to pit the Kite against the Neb?" he interrogated in return.

Erk's nose twitched impatiently. "No, Zanfur. We will have to sail together as allies, not try to sink each other. We're friends in this! I'm not challenging you. I swear, I just want some help doing as much damage as possible. And to make it worthwhile, you'll have the full protection of my crew and ship, and we'll share provisions if necessary."

"So I get to keep it all, huh?" he asked, calmer than before. Erk nodded in reply. "Alright then, when do we head out?"

A fortnight later, *The Nebula* crashed into open conflict with the gunnery ships of Gelidor's merchant fleet. Unfortunately for the Claston nobility in league with the usurper, their ships were far too small and easy to destroy by a galleon with the size and firepower of *The Nebula*. Zanfur and *The Silent Kite* slipped quietly past *The Nebula*, their plundering already beginning. As the night went on, blood ran thick on the Solar Sea as Zanfur's men slaughtered Gelidor's loyal merchants indiscriminately. Erk's crew followed their usual routine of using hostages to threaten violence, acquiring the goods, and leaving the ship otherwise unharmed.

It was too late when Erk realized what Zanfur was doing. Several merchant ships had broken away, surely privy to the events that had just transpired. Today, Erk would lose his reputation as the Kind Pirate. Now he was sure to earn the title of Dread. He had been naïve. He had been misled about Zanfur. Those who pointed him in this direction would pay. And since Zanfur had already stained Erk's hands with blood, he would feel no shame in ending his life.

Besides, it had been nearly a century since magic unraveled. Gelidor's grasp on the kingdom was unwavering. Perhaps it was time to change tactics. The Kind Pirate had no place in this kind of conflict. It pained him deeply, and he knew Naomi would be disappointed in his escalation of violence.

As such, he did not feel shame in deciding to end Zanfur. With Jax's help, Erk personally fired the cannon volley that sank *The Silent Kite*. Dread Pirate Captain Erk had a ring to it. Besides, it was time for a change of pace. Simple, non-violent piracy was not working. Sadly, The Master was probably right. Erk was too soft and too kind to carry out this kind of work or make this kind of change to the world around him. "Look what happened to Evan because of me!" he thought, screaming internally. If only he could find a way to free The Master from the gemstone. He could do what was necessary to rid the world of Gelidor's stain.

Erk shrugged to himself, his thoughts at war with one another. "You know, Iriliandria, I'm sorry I can't keep my promise. At this point, it doesn't matter if I do or don't. There are hundreds of elven nobles bloating in the water right now because I haven't been heavy-handed enough against Gelidor. That changes tonight."

He then said out loud, "Jax, go astern. Let's sink a few of those cargo ships for good measure."

Jax looked at him in disbelief. "Cap, you sure? Thought you only wanted to shoot the navy ships."

Erk gave an evil smile for the first time as a swirl of fire began to form around his wrists. "The usurper needs to understand that we mean business," he replied, his tone dark. Kind Pirate Erk was a thing of the past. Plus, worrying too much about the loot for himself would obscure his true objective. He realized that even his own mindset needed to change. Erk would carve out a name for himself that would strike fear in the heart of the "King." The flames on his wrists became beams of intense sunlight that he directed at a cargo ship. After a matter of seconds, the hole burned through the ship's hull, which assured it and its passengers a swift descent to the bottom. Erk turned his beam on another ship, the intense solar ray more effective than fire.

The survivors of that night spoke of a pirate captain wielding brilliant light, calling it a light of judgment. A minority faction of Claston nobles broke away from the king over this dispute, joining Erk in his crusade. And thus, the Solar Sea trembled at the might of Dread Pirate Captain Erk the Radiant for the next ten years.

Chapter 13
Ezelbrecht

The cool summer air blustered out of the gorge in gusts. The night sky seemed oddly dark as the companions could not see stars, clouds, or moons. The storm that had rumbled overhead earlier continued to shake the island with intense bursts of thunder, but the lightning was not visible. The sky simply seemed black and empty.

Miranda shivered in the waves of cold that radiated from lower in the gorge. Selasine had renewed his daylight prayer after they arrived on Olvidado. The light did not extend far enough for the group to see much further than a couple hundred feet out. The rocky gorge dove steeply toward the interior of the island. Erk had not been here in several years, but he remembered the unsettling ambiance well. In the past, he had been alone or accompanied by Jax. Watching Miranda's unfiltered reaction to the island gave him chills. The girl had proven how connected her heart could be to the world and the people around her. The pirate was shocked, however, that her immediate response was feeling so threatened that it caused her gift to surge out of control. If her reaction was so strong, he wondered what he was missing by his lack of spiritual and magical awareness.

Every few seconds brought gusts of wind out of the gorge, but every few minutes, a low rumbling sound echoed off the rock walls that grew higher as the four of them descended the path. Selasine and Erk stood in front, keeping a watchful eye forward. August walked close to Miranda, only a couple of paces behind Selasine. Though Miranda's initial reaction to the evil she felt here was panic, she had since calmed enough to traverse the gorge with the others. She became increasingly curious about the entity that Erk intended for her to meet.

As they found their way through the gorge, Miranda began to reflect on the last day's events. She had missed Selasine and August so much, and her heart was overflowing with joy to have them back with her. She had helped the bishop numerous times, apprehending lawbreakers and keeping magical beasts away from Devitus. This time, however, the quest centered around her, and she was not accustomed to so much attention. To further complicate the situation, Erk was the de facto leader in this endeavor since he was the only one who had ever been to this terrifying place. Suddenly, those exhilarating fights against magical beasts paled in comparison with such an ancient, mystical place like Olvidado. Miranda started to let go of her fear. Adventuring was dangerous, but it was also exciting. She could not help but walk with a timid smile, not for the danger but for the possibilities. She was in a place very few people would ever see, which was a priceless gift.

The landscape was nightmarish, thanks to the long shadows cast by Selasine's daylight. Erk's elven ears twitched with a warning as he noticed rustling in a cluster of thorny trees that had overgrown on a jut standing about forty feet over the main path. In the several times he had been to the island, he had never encountered any creature except for Ezelbrecht. Perhaps it was the additional visitors he had brought this time, or something had changed on the island. However, Erk was sure he heard something coming from the thorny palace above.

Erk hissed a warning to Selasine, "Be careful. I can hear something above," motioning to the growth on top of the rock outcropping. Selasine nodded, his combat instincts taking over. Miranda and August followed silently, maintaining high alert as the gorge's walls loomed higher with each step.

Moving stealthily through such terrain would have been impossible for such a group. Three of them wore armor that did not lend to quiet passage. Erk realized that his own stealthiness had likely gotten him to Ezelbrecht's lair unaccosted many times in the past. As Erk ruminated on those realities, August unintentionally stepped on a large, dry branch that cracked loudly.

Erk and Selasine reacted by immediately drawing their weapons and turning to face the young acolyte. Their eyes scanned for threats, but all they saw was an embarrassed August with broken wood scattered beneath his boots. Miranda looked at August from the side of her eyes, a teasing grin threatening to break across her face. Before she could smile, however, she noticed a dark mass suddenly drop behind her mentor and the pirate lord. Her crystal eyes snapped from August to this darkness, her own hand darting to the sword at her belt. She drew it forth, the magic on the blade swirling with excitement. Selasine saw the new sword, but now was no time to ask questions.

"At arms, men," Erk said, an unamused habitual voice taking over as he turned quickly to face the threat.

Miranda huffed as she gripped her holy symbol and immediately began to pray for protection. "Invictus, shield us from the fury of chaos, grant us your light, and curse those who would sully your legacy."

Selasine, who had turned around to confront whatever had landed behind him, heard Miranda use the combined prayer and curse. He had not taught her that. He became concerned but was more worried about the beast in front of him. At first glance, one would assume it was an enormous lion with its shoulders alone passing six feet in height. However, the sprawling bat-like wings stretching from its back made this creature truly terrifying. The wingspan nearly blocked the thirty-foot gorge. Selasine spat angrily, "Manticore."

Erk nodded. "Miranda, August, be wary of its tail," he warned. Miranda's curse caused a red aura to surround the beast as it snarled hungrily at Selasine, who was closest to it. Thanks to the shimmer from the curse, he could see it getting ready to leap before he needed to react. He prepared a counterattack rather than a dodge as the manticore's heavy body moved unbelievably quick for such a large creature. Selasine's blade struck the inside of its right foreleg, causing a spray of black blood as he slid forward, rolling to the ground to avoid being crushed or swiped by the beast. As he crouched under its chest, he recited the familiar shielding prayer he used to protect himself against Apocalypse.

Erk sprinted behind the monster quickly, preparing to force the creature to fight on all sides. The manticore let out an angry roar in response to Selasine's stab. Though the bishop had hoped to distract the beast, it lashed out against the next closest target: Miranda. Its paw was nearly as large as she was, and the beast lashed at her with claws extended. Despite the manticore's cursed aura, she could not react in time, taking the full brunt of its swipe to her torso. She raised her arms in a blocking motion, and the sapphire blades on her gauntlets pierced the pads of the manticore's paw, reducing the ferocity of the beast's attack. The battlemail prevented the razor-sharp talons from piercing her skin. The sheer blunt force of the swipe knocked her back at least twenty feet, the impact on the ground knocking the breath out of her.

August shouted, "Miranda!" as he rushed to place himself between the beast and his friend. The manticore retaliated by lowering its front legs and jumping quickly with its rear paws. The tail lashed over the top of its head, its appearance black and segmented like a deadly scorpion. Thanks to the red aura from Miranda's curse, August could parry the beast's attack with his sword. Activating his uncanny magic, his body seemed light and agile. He closed the distance between himself and the beast, striking at its face. His sword cut a gruesome gash across its left eye, more black blood spraying into the air. The beast roared with anger again.

Erk had given the creature a wide berth so that he could position himself behind it. As August began his onslaught against the creature's maw, Erk withdrew a dagger from his jacket. He was now armed with a sword in his right hand and a dagger in his left, both weapons swirling with a magical aura. He closed the distance between himself and the manticore and began his assault. Rushing up to the beast, he planted his sword firmly in the tendons in its rear right foot. The manticore responded with another horrifying roar and an attack from its tail. Using the dagger in his left hand, Erk swiped at the barb on the end of the tail, but he had underestimated the beast's size. Though he could deflect the force of the strike, the stinger nicked some exposed flesh on his neck, injecting just enough paralytic venom to cause the pirate to drop his remaining weapon.

"Erk!" Selasine shouted from underneath the beast, his experience as a warpriest keeping his attention divided between the enemy and his allies. As August used his enhanced speed to keep the beast swiping at air, Selasine rolled out from under the manticore, his eyes watching for the monster's tail. He withdrew his steel shield from his back, gripping it firmly. Then, he activated his uncanny magic, causing a dozen illusory images of himself to appear with his real body among them. They all followed his movements, being mere inches apart. A blur of Selasines began to rush toward Erk. He fended off numerous tail strikes by keeping his shield high, punishing the beast by repeatedly stabbing the tail as it struck at him. If the beast tried to sting an illusion, however, the mirage would simply dissipate into the air harmlessly, buying Selasine extra time to react. His defensive approach worked, and he arrived beside Erk quickly, whose body was almost completely numb. He seemed to be having difficulty standing and was experiencing a mild hallucination.

Selasine sheathed his sword and gripped his holy symbol. "Light of righteousness, Sword of Justice. What chaos has sullied, cleanse with your purity. Extract the filth from the blood, restore this body, and heal this mind."

A flash of purple light washed over Erk, instantly purging the venom and its effects.

Miranda sat up, the world around her spinning. She had never been hit that hard. Her body gasped for air, trying to find a breathing rhythm after having the wind knocked out of her when she hit the ground. She was almost certain she had cracked a rib as pain radiated through her chest when she managed to catch her breath. She felt a hint of vindictiveness and anger, an understandable response in lethal combat. Instead of letting her fear trigger the power within her, she gritted her teeth and stood. She gripped her holy symbol and began a new prayer. "There is peace in a just society. Allow me to be an instrument of that peace, Sword of Justice. Bind that which sews chaos and pour out your judgment tenfold."

August zipped just out of range of the beast's paw as it tried to latch onto his chest. In a way, its extra size worked against it, especially due to August's enhanced speed. Erk recovered his weapons while Selasine fended off the scorpion-like tail with his illusions and shield. Selasine heard Miranda's prayer as she spoke in a confident, bold voice. He raised an eyebrow as the cursed aura surrounding the beast intensified in brightness. Tendrils of red and white light emerged from the previously subtle aura, wrapping around the huge beast's body and limbs. Selasine marveled as that curse would have been advanced even for *him*. First of all, where had she learned that recitation? He had not allowed the peacekeepers to access the advanced library as part of protocol. Second, her faith must have grown over the last week to an extraordinary degree for Invictus to work his divinity through her so casually. He was intrigued about what she had experienced on *The Nebula*, especially considering Erk's sister was his late wife. If Erk had ties to such a powerful priestess sworn to non-violence as his beautiful Iria, then he likely had some scriptures on board his ship. Selasine wondered if this had been all part of a divine plan, as the coincidences were beginning to become alarming.

The manticore collapsed onto its side in paralyzed silence, a thunderclap echoing against the gorge's walls in place of the beast's voice. Its breathing was labored. Miranda then sat down, prompting August to turn and look for her. Rushing to her side and taking a knee, he asked, "Are you alright?"

She nodded, but her eyes lingered on the beast. Her lips were parted curiously as she observed the manticore. She was thrilled that she was successful in the binding curse on her first attempt. Now that the beast was no longer an immediate threat, she observed its features in the daylight radiating from Selasine. She had never seen a creature so large, as it seemed larger than the gryphons that the bishop, August, Justin, and she had rehomed earlier that year. She thought rehoming was a dishonest way to look at it; they destroyed their nest and kept the beasts from returning by putting up a punishing defensive fight. It was brutal, but at least they did not have to slaughter the magnificent beasts. The manticore was just as magnificent in a terrifying way, and the binding curse rendered it immediately helpless. She felt confidence welling inside her despite the pain coursing through her torso.

Selasine nodded to her, "That's one Infernia of a prayer," he commented. He moved to the beast's throat to put it out of its misery. Miranda started to stop him but realized this was the kind of predator that could not be reasoned with or redeemed. As Selasine plunged his sword into the manticore's throat, he winced as the black blood spewed out relentlessly. As the creature's life faded, its body dissolved into a black miasma, leaving no evidence that it had ever existed except for the pain in Miranda's body after being struck by the beast.

"Erk loaned me some of the liturgy that he used to study with his sister," she explained shyly. She winced as she stood, the pain in her chest red hot. She started walking toward the bishop and August.

As Miranda stood next to August, Selasine reached out and placed a hand on both of their shoulders. "Listen, children. You were both magnificent. Your aggressive attacks kept the beast busy, August. And Miranda, that binding curse would be a feat for even myself to use. I'm proud of you both," he finished, that fatherly smile that lit up Miranda's world on his face.

Erk joined them where the body had once been. His expression twitched as he tried to make sense of the situation, "Was that some kind of illusion?"

Selasine wanted to shake his head but remained motionless as he responded, "It surely didn't seem like illusion magic."

Miranda and August had never seen a manticore, so they had no frame of reference for how odd this conclusion really was. August asked, "Teacher, what do we do?"

Miranda turned her eyes to her mentor as he stroked his hand through his beard for a moment. "I guess the best path is forward," he replied, turning his attention to Erk.

The pirate lord nodded, looking down the increasingly difficult path into the gorge. "Just try to stay as quiet as possible. If anything else is out here, I have no predictions about the dangers," he cautioned as they restarted their trek.

Miranda was about to whisper a healing prayer for herself. The impact of the beast's claw had hurt much more than she anticipated, but the pain dissipated as she started to address it. She was unsure why, but she was certain it was connected to her gift. She didn't want to say anything; after all, they were here to understand her gift better. Perhaps she could mention it to Ezelbrecht once the group met them. Nevertheless, she was sure her body had healed itself from a moderate injury without her prayers.

After about six hours of traveling in silence down the rocky terrain, everyone but Erk began to look for the sunrise. The days in the summer were long and bright, especially in the Solar Sea. The pirate lord, however, informed the others that "The sun never rises on Olvidado. This is the Forgotten Island, forgotten by even time itself."

They eventually found themselves at the bottom of the gorge, the rocky ridged walls towering over a hundred and fifty feet above them. The same blackened trees and thorny bushes lined and obstructed the path before them, with a cave opening directly before them. The entrance to the cave was so dark that it consumed the daylight radiating from Selasine's holy symbol. It seemed like a black, gaping maw awaited the four as they reached the end of the gorge.

Erk did not hesitate to enter, but the others stood momentarily, absorbing the sights, sounds, and smells of the island and cave. August was the first to step forward behind Erk, Selasine extending his arm to Miranda. "Come on. Together," he encouraged.

She nodded, expressionless. She took her mentor by his hand as they entered the massive cavern. The fear inside her remained relatively calm as they entered the cave, but she knew it without a doubt: this cave was the source of the intense evil she felt as soon as they landed. Her awareness of it helped her avoid overreacting.

The cave was nowhere near as deep as they anticipated, opening immediately into a massive cavern that was easily a thousand feet around. The cave was lit by artificial moonlight as bright silver beams reflected off the stalactites and stalagmites that littered the cavern. Selasine's daylight prayer ceased to work as soon as he crossed the threshold to the cave, a sign that this place was so deep that even the divine dared not interfere.

The rumbling sound echoing throughout the gorge soon had an identifiable source. In the center of the cavern, a large reptilian form was curled into a crescent shape, with fantastic wings draped along the lower two-thirds of the beast's body. A long, menacing tail twitched on one end of the crescent, and the creature's eyes were closed at the other, its draconic face sleeping peacefully curled into the center of the beast's mass. Each deep, exhaled breath rattled the walls of the cavern, spreading the sound across the gorge.

As Erk entered the cave, he approached the dragon without hesitation. Selasine and August followed behind, but Miranda froze in fear upon seeing the beast. She heard the whispering begin, but she fought back with her own thoughts to silence them. There was no way that this dragon could be as evil as it felt, she thought to herself. Especially if Erk trusted them so much. That feeling inside her, however, remained close to the front of her mind. It was okay to be on guard but open-minded. She hurried her steps to catch up to the others.

As Miranda overcame her fear, she tried to look more closely at the legendary beast in front of her. Due to the dim moon-like quality of the light in the cavern, she could not tell what color the dragon's scales were. It was, however, massive. She estimated that the dragon's body alone would occupy as much space as the entire church complex in Devitus, church, courtyard, and all.

The deep breaths stopped abruptly as the dragon stirred. It lifted its head, the elongated neck stretching dozens of feet into the air as it awoke. It inhaled deeply, but then it stopped to sniff the air. "Erilkaiden, you've returned," it said in a booming voice that shook the cavern.

Erk stepped forward, fully bathed in the pale light. "I have, great Ezelbrecht. I come to seek your wisdom again," he stated.

Ezelbrecht sniffed a second time, "I assume that's your reason for bringing trespassers here with you then?" the dragon returned, its voice more controlled and focused in the space between itself and Erk.

"Indeed, wise one. I beg your forgiveness, but you are the only one I trusted with this matter," the pirate lord continued.

Ezelbrecht's draconic features snarled. "Your trust, as always, is misguided. I helped you rise against Gelidor simply because I owed Na'agamlor a debt of pain. Anything else that I do is a favor, Erilkaiden Thief of Light," the dragon warned.

Miranda had heard Erk called the "Radiant" but never a thief. It sounded so small compared to how the pirate loomed in her imagination before meeting him. She wondered how the dragon would have such a nickname for him.

"And for your guidance, I am willing to pay any price," Erk responded.

The dragon's eyes and maw twisted into a devious smile, "There are many things I could ask for, and you are so blindly willing to offer so quickly. This matter must be truly perplexing, then. By all means, then, share your plight with the immortal Ezelbrecht." Miranda shuddered. The dragon's smile was more terrifying than its snarl.

Erk nodded and turned to the others, gesturing for Miranda to step out of the cover of the various stalagmites throughout the cavern and into the pale light. "Ezelbrecht, I would like you to meet my friend, Miranda," he continued, his gesture growing impatient as she emerged.

The dragon watched as her red hair glowed in the silver light. Despite the poor lighting, her blue eyes were still bright and beautiful. She looked up at the dragon, the expression on her face scared. Erk held his hand out for her, and she took it in hers without looking toward him. Her eyes remained fixated on Ezelbrecht's and vice versa.

The ancient dragon exhaled a brief blast of air, causing Miranda's and Erk's hair to whip wildly around them.

Miranda's braids slapped against the mithril breastplate on her chest. Ezelbrecht then began to speak directly to her, "This girl. I feel like I have met you before, but you look to be barely mature for your species. I've lived for thousands of years and have never forgotten a face. I have seen yours, but I cannot recall your name. Who are you?"

Miranda's eyes stayed wide with fear and wonder. "I'm Miranda Hyacinth, Acolyte of Invictus," she replied, her humble name and title all she could offer. Not even a month ago, the most terrifying creature she had fought with was a gryphon, and even then, it was to ultimately save the beasts. Now, she stood before an ancient entity with immense power. Her life had changed so much. And she hungered for more, the call of adventure stirring in her heart. That sleepy town on the frontier was quickly becoming a distant memory.

Ezelbrecht lowered their neck, drawing close to the girl. They sniffed again, "I even know your scent, face, and presence. But your name does not match what I smell or see. Tell me, Erilkaiden, where did you find this ruby?"

Ezelbrecht was so close to Miranda that she could reach out and touch them. Her hand followed the whims of her heart, lifting slowly toward the dragon, who did not respond. Erk replied to the question while Miranda reached out, "She traveled far to fight against the pirates and our people on the Undine Coast. I found her there, and I kidnapped her because I could see she possessed a great gift. At the time, I did not realize what I had truly done, but we are here now with questions about Miranda's mysterious gift."

The dragon's tongue darted in and out of its mouth, shooting past Miranda and back as quick as lightning. Miranda's fingers made contact with Ezelbrecht's scales that covered the bottom of their incredible maw. A single scale was larger than her hand, and a gasp of amazement escaped her lips. "Wow," was the only word she could form. She felt her heart racing as she touched a living, breathing dragon.

Ezelbrecht did not react to her touch. They continued to observe the girl, noticing she did not seem to listen to Erk's explanation. The dragon's eyes blinked slowly, staring right into the sapphire orbs that shone in the false moonlight. A soft hiss emerged from the dragon's maw as Ezelbrecht analyzed the young woman before them.

"Miranda," the beast whispered.

"Yes?" she returned, mesmerized. Her hand still rested on the dragon's chin. The overwhelming sense of evil still weighed on her. Her imagination could have never dreamed of what she was experiencing now. An ancient being full of wisdom and malice sat before her, speaking her name.

"I can taste your fear, Miranda," Ezelbrecht commented.

With innocence in her voice and her mind far away, she replied, "And what does it taste like?"

Erk suppressed a laugh while Selasine and August looked on with dreadful concern and helplessness.

Ezelbrecht uncurled their body and stretched out their wings. Miranda stood patiently waiting for the dragon to return close by, this time relaxed and not eager to touch the beast. She asked a more serious question, "What is this gift within me?"

The dragon tilted their head. "Gift?" they asked, making a grinding motion with the bottom of their maw.

Miranda continued, "I have something in me that allows me to rescue the dead and the dying, but it does other things too. I'm afraid I will hurt somebody if I don't learn how to control it." She spoke so quickly that her words seemed to run together. "When I look for the power alone, I hear whispering voices. Sometimes the power acts on its own, too. I've already hurt my dear friends, and –"

Ezelbrecht interrupted her. "This sounds more like a curse."

Erk shook his head, "If it were a curse, a regular healer would have—"

With a warning roar, Ezelbrecht interrupted Erk. If Erk had towered over Zanfur in presence and power, Ezelbrecht did the same to Erk. "Foolish mortals, clinging to life and ideals with such fervor that you fail to see the obvious. Let me try this again," the dragon lowered their head to level their eyes with Miranda's. "Do you think anything 'good' has come of your 'gift'" Ezelbrecht asked pointedly.

She gazed back into the dragon's stare and slowly started to nod. "I saved an innocent family after they were killed in a fire," Miranda replied sincerely.

The dragon's eyes rolled to the side for a moment. "So, your gift allowed you to play god with the lives of mortals. Miranda, did that make you feel powerful?"

She shook her head insistently. "No, not at all. I was happy to see them whole again and to watch the little boy play with his parents."

Ezelbrecht swallowed, an incredulity building in their expression. "Well, how else does your gift work?" they hissed. "Can you show me?"

Miranda shrugged, unsure. "I'm afraid of losing control of it. I lost control earlier today and hurt my friends, but when we arrived here, I made the whispers stop. All of their anger and energy flowed through me, and I pushed it away into the ground."

Ezelbrecht raised a talon to their chin, emulating the gesture of deep thought; their voice, however, dripped with patronizing disdain. "So, you don't fully understand what it is, how to use it, or why it even happens in the first place. Erilkaiden, what manner of fool do you take me for?"

Erk gulped before he began his reply, "No fool at all, great Ezelbrecht. You are the only one I know that has knowledge of such things."

Ezelbrecht nodded their head, "Save the flattery, mortal. You see, there's a major problem with magic right now. I can help you." they took an oversized talon and pointed at Erk, the talon more than twice his size. "I can help you with worldly issues and advice. I cannot, however, use magic to diagnose a magical gift." Their eyes narrowed further, "Nor an incomprehensible curse."

Selasine and Erk traded troubled glances, and August stood uncomfortably nearby. He had been afraid before, but this was the first time he understood the true meaning of helplessness and terror. Miranda, however, remained calm, her blue eyes still wide with disbelief.

"I feel like I know you, too," Miranda whispered.

Ezelbrecht recoiled, their head rising up to full height. "Describe the feeling, girl," they commanded.

"I . . .," she stammered as she started. Unable to place the feeling, she closed her eyes and started listening to the whispers of that second voice. As they coalesced into a single, comprehensible voice, she continued, "Ezelbrecht the Gray, child of Gorthran, King of Dragons. You existed before magic and will continue to exist when its flame flickers out. You saw Gorthran shatter himself and become one with the arcane to counter the actions of Saraix, Queen of Dragons. Together their essence dances forever, seen by mortals only through the Dracon Wars."

Ezelbrecht froze. The silence in the cavern was tangible. Nobody moved nor spoke. Minutes passed by, the silence lingering comfortably. Miranda opened her eyes eventually and looked up at the towering beast. The dragon stared back at her, contemplating her response.

"Yes, child, that is me. How such a young mortal knows my true past is beyond comprehension. Perhaps you were right, after all, Erilkaiden. She is special," they responded with a dark tone.

Miranda did not respond; she only stared. Erk was noticeably lost in thought, August and Selasine daring to step out from the stalagmites into the dim light in the center of the cavern.

After a few more minutes of silence, Ezelbrecht lowered their neck again, pressing their nose close to Miranda. "I think I know how we know each other. Who are your parents, child?"

Miranda shook her head. "I only know their names, Philotrax and Reshiria Hyacinth," she replied, casting her eyes at the ground.

Ezelbrecht inhaled deeply and closed their eyes. "In ten thousand years, I've never been wrong. Erilkaiden, the girl's gift is neither a miracle nor a curse."

Erk snapped back to the conversation, a smug feeling in his chest for surprising a dragon as ancient as time itself. "What do you mean, great one?" he replied.

"You see, exactly one-hundred mortal years ago, Dalyn Tyrdrac the Silver inadvertently fused himself with the arcane stream that permeates this plane, the center of the universe. When this happened, the fabric of magic itself unraveled to make room for Tyrdrac's immense power. At that very moment, the wizards of the world lost their connection to the arcane stream, the unseen force that fuels their magic. Throughout the eons, it had many different names, energy, mana, ether, what have you," Ezelbrecht droned. "You mortals dubbed the calamity the 'Unbinding,' which is accurate," they said, patronizing. "Now that the stream is 'unbound,' energy collects in strange places."

Erk and Miranda looked immediately at each other. She blurted, "Just like Evan said!"

Ezelbrecht gasped. "Evanthalus speaks again? Surely he was cursed long before this girl was alive."

Erk nodded in deference. "You see, great one, Miranda's gift lifted my brother's curse. If your theory is true and these pockets of mana are collecting en masse in Miranda, that doesn't explain why she can heal with such spectacular ability."

Ezelbrecht snapped their maw, sending a shockwave through the cavern. "Foolish mortal, don't presume to know what I intend," they snarled, causing Miranda to tremble. Nobody reached for their weapons; a confrontation with this beast would only end one way. "It's not the what, anyway. It's the why."

Erk had never seen Ezelbrecht react this way to his theories and conclusions. He thought that he had a better rapport with the eldritch beast. Perhaps they were truly unhappy to see the pirate and his entourage. Erk wondered, "Is Ezelbrecht the one that sent the manticore?" That would explain the confrontation and the mysterious corpse but not how he brought his companions to Olvidado if Ezelbrecht did not wish to see them.

The cavern remained silent, none of the four wishing to incur another wrothful outburst from the old one. Eventually, Ezelbrecht continued, "You see, what's happening is excess energy is drawn into Miranda's body when she becomes stressed or upset. As I snapped at you just now, I watched as the very essence of this place began to funnel into her. I can see the arcane stream as it flows, the lifeblood of the universe. Even here, where the gods cannot see, the magic is still present. Now, hear my theory, Erilkaiden."

The pirate lord nodded but remained silent. The dragon smiled sinisterly, their maw opening just enough to flash rows of massive, deadly teeth in the pale light. "Philotrax and Reshiria were dragons, you see. At the moment of The Unbinding, they were the only two dragons that had taken a human form for whatever reason. When the magic went awry, they were unable to transform back. They lived out the next near century as humans but did not age. As a result, they had to move around frequently. I lost touch with them thirty years ago. The only thing I really want to know," Ezelbrecht tapped their chin, imitating human and elven speech patterns. "The only thing I really want to know is why they used those grotesque forms to create a child. And why did they pick an insignificant flower for their family name?" the dragon tried to feign a face of disgust.

Erk smiled. "Then, great one, did you recognize Miranda because her parents were those dragons?"

Ezelbrecht nodded, letting out a deep breath. "That explains her hair and her eyes. Philotrax was a remarkable red dragon; Reshiria was the most resplendent blue beauty. It's funny, Miranda. You're a human, but you're also a dragon."

She couldn't believe what she was hearing.

"The magic pools inside you because dragons are creatures inherently made from magic. After The Unbinding, we lost our ability to use our breath and innate magic, but the magic still pools within us; otherwise, we would die." The dragon paused, thinking. "Miranda is human and does not need the magic to live. But as a dragon, the magic swirls through her just like all of us. Her very existence is an anomaly that should not be a reality. Simply put, this girl has the powers equal to a god of magic. She does not need to study the arcane to tap its powers like a wizard. She does not need to hone her focus to unlock her powers like a sorcerer. She needs to draw the mana and shape it into anything she desires. This is why she can heal the dead and the cursed. Failure to put shape to her desires will backfire and create calamities with consequences as drastic as a war between the gods."

Miranda looked up in continued disbelief. "How can I be both human and dragon?" she asked.

Ezelbrecht sniffed the air and exhaled deeply, again, another gust of wind swirling in the massive, dimly lit cavern.

"Interesting. This is why I knew you, but I could not place you. You are neither a shard of Gorthran nor Saraix." The eldritch creature's eyes widened with a sudden realization. "You are the first dragon to be born without the essence of the Dragon King or Dragon Queen. Philotrax was a shard of Saraix, pure and kind. Reshiria was a shard of Gorthran, dark and cruel. Between the magic pooling in their human bodies and their newfound biological capabilities, they achieved the impossible. Mir'thax Toi'landra. Of fire and lightning. The first dragon created by mortals."

Everyone in the room focused their gaze on Miranda. Something like this seemed unbelievable. Erk realized his theory was right, then, that it would take someone with Miranda's personality and power to stop Gelidor. August felt lucky to have met, trained, and learned so much with her. Now she would always win in combat training. He looked forward to seeing what tricks she would learn with her gift. The girl he thought of as his little sister was extraordinary. Selasine's heart broke for her, knowing that Carulus's insidious attempts would only be the first of many to manipulate her power for some agenda. His attachment to her grew more defensive as he learned about his pupil.

"But, as I said, she is an anomaly. She should not exist. Even you priests should agree. She will only serve as an agent of chaos if her power is left to circulate. Lucky for you, I am here to ensure this abomination stays here on Olvidado. Surely she will live for millennia. It is safer to leave her sealed away in this place. Leave this place, Erilkaiden. I will care for the girl."

Miranda's eyes filled with tears immediately. Ezelbrecht's immense, immortal presence would be impossible to escape. In this domain, their will meant more than the will of the gods. She could not feel Invictus's presence through her holy symbol. Selasine's daylight prayer had ceased here. Even though she knew she was not alone, effectively, she was. Selasine and August would die trying to protect her if she objected. Erk would probably be killed, too, though she wasn't sure if he would flee or stay.

Just then, the whispers started in her ear. "It's not a whisper, is it? It's not a different voice at all." "Of course, it isn't.

It's my voice! It's the sound of the arcane stream." "Shape it the way you want. Take them all to the last place you were safe." "That's right! The beach! You can see it in your mind! That's where you want to go!" A brilliant purple light surrounded Miranda's body, beginning much brighter and more intensely than ever. Ezelbrecht recoiled quickly and perched their head, ready to snap. The light disoriented them so they could not carry out the attack.

The light filled the cavern and grew so bright that every entity present fell unconscious.

***

Reshiria sat in disbelief. Just a week ago, she was a magnificent blue dragon, a sight for all to behold in terror and awe. She could breathe fierce blasts of lightning that made humankind and elvenkind tremble before her in fear. And now? She was stuck as a human. She did not understand why the spell would not transform her back to her true form.

Initially, she had taken human form to manipulate the opinions of a noble elf with substantial land holdings in the mountainous region in the north of the kingdom of Claston. She thought a more suitable, seductive form would be more effective than using her combat prowess to impress her point upon him. Besides, substantial violence could potentially make her the target of bounty hunters. She wasn't afraid of such prospects, she simply found them hideously bothersome. Guarding her lair on edge for a few hundred years was not appealing.

Instead, a diplomatic approach would work much more smoothly and require significantly less effort on her part. Reshiria thought a few misplaced promises delivered with sugary-sweet words, batted eyelashes, and an elegant dress would keep this particular lord in her talons. She had used the form numerous times in the past to negotiate her desires.

But now she was stuck. She got what she wanted from the lord, but now she could not reach back into the arcane stream and revert to her original form. Perhaps she needed to rest. She had expended substantial effort maintaining this form for several days; maybe if she drifted off to sleep for a while, her magic would exhaust. Her regular form would be restored as the spell's magic ran out. Hopeful, she rested under a large grove of cedar trees she found on her travels. However, the nap did not have the desired effect. She sat there for hours, dumbfounded.

Within the next year, Reshiria had learned of her permanent fate. Not only were dragons separated from their innate magic powers, but their breath weapons had ceased to function. Some annoying mortal had wrecked the fabric of magic itself, and she was left to pay the price of his ineptitude. As a noble dragon, she found it excruciating to be trapped in this hideous human form. Fortunately, her draconic habits had prepared her to live the life of an extravagant mortal; her treasure horde proved more than adequate for her to live a life of luxury to which she was accustomed, even though she was in human form living in a kingdom primarily governed by elves.

After a couple of decades, rumors circulated that Reshiria had found the secret to eternal youth. As the humans and even elves around her continued to age, The Unbinding did not seem to affect her draconic longevity. She still looked like a youthful, beautiful woman. Of course, she hated her form, but at least the form she had chosen paid homage to her blue brilliance. The hair that draped her countenance was a subtle, deep blue reminiscent of the hues that signaled the coming of the night sky. Her eyes were glowing sapphires that could captivate mortals with their clarity and beauty.

As far as fates go, Reshiria realized she had been lucky to have been trapped in this weak body. When it became clear that dragons had lost their most deadly magics, ambitious treasure hunters began organizing hunts to eliminate the once untouchable beasts. Their hordes were divided, their eggs stolen, and their hides flayed and tanned for armor. Reshiria used her limited influence to prevent dragon culling in the northern reaches of Claston but began to worry that her lack of aging would make her a target.

Still, the political situation in Claston looked dire. Reshiria purchased a title of nobility from the king years before she was stuck in this human form. Using that position, she encouraged King Eisen and later King Gelidor to leave dragon hunting illegal, a law previously for adventurers' safety more than dragons. Now, she saw it as a way to save the lives of her draconic kin. Eventually, she realized that Gelidor was far too evil to honor his promises. About twenty years after The Unbinding, he encouraged dragon hunting by offering to only tax the hoard at half instead of confiscating all of it. When she asked him about this policy, he threatened to destroy her. She believed him.

She took several artifacts from her horde to arm herself appropriately, including an elegant elven battlemail made of mithril and golden adamant. The adamant rings of the chain mesh would be utterly impenetrable, even to the claws of a dragon. While not as strong as the adamant chain, the mithril breastplate was light enough that anybody could wear it. The adamant ring mail that underlay the breastplate together would keep her almost as safe as her natural scales. Furthermore, enchantments on the armor would protect her from magical attacks. She also took a collection of wands and scrolls that still worked despite The Unbinding. She hired mercenaries to serve as her guardians and set off through the wilderness in search of new lands and safety.

In the third decade of Reshiria's hell, she met Philotrax. She could tell he was a dragon like her from the moment his golden, fiery eyes made contact with her cool, electric stare. He had made a name for himself as a warrior in the kingdom of Alabaster, a progressive kingdom ruled by humans and elves, primarily. Using his timeless nature, he worked hard to build an incomparable physical body. He had turned this mortal form into a fighting machine that even dragons of old might fear. The fact that he was a dragon was enough to draw Reshiria to him, but his perfect physique and carefree attitude stirred feelings in her that were unfamiliar to her draconic form. She found herself thinking about Philotrax for prolonged periods. The fantasies that played out in her head ranged from her basest mortal desires to the lofty fairy tale endings she continually heard about for the last thirty years. She worried that her mortality was starting to affect who she was, and she was disgusted with herself.

Philotrax noticed her, too. His hair was a blazing crimson,

and he had grown it long and thick. He spent significant amounts of coin on having his hair styled in a way that was reminiscent of the spines that once ran down his back. His golden eyes were either welcoming or threatening. Reshiria's blue hair made her distinguished beauty even more irresistible to him. He had to know the truth about her; his answer was as he had hoped. The two of them, a red and blue dragon trapped in human form, bonded more over their experiences since becoming human rather than reminiscing about their draconic might.

One night, they sat in front of the hearth of Philotrax's estate in Nulodia. Reshiria, finding her mortal form somewhat cold-natured, had wrapped herself in elegant furs and sat close to the fireplace. She sat upright with her legs crossed and outstretched, the fire to her left side. Philotrax lay beside her, uncovered, his muscles glistening in the flickering firelight. The way he seemed to glow caused one of those new feelings to take over her. Her body felt as if it were on fire and that the only thing that would extinguish the flames was to feel his body pressed against hers, smothering it out.

Philotrax lay comfortable, his head on a pillow on the floor, angled to look directly into Reshiria's eyes. He had fewer objections about the aesthetics of mortal forms, but she was the paragon of immaculate beauty compared to everything he had seen in his centuries of existence. The way the shadows made her eyes flicker, he could feel her dark, sinister heart dancing behind those glinting sapphires. Her lips looked soft and alluring, and he sat up and drew nearer to her, buried beneath all that fur.

At some point in the conversation, they realized they were incredibly close, their faces only inches apart. Reshiria's heart stopped and then skipped a beat. The fire in her body felt hotter than any flame that Philotrax ever breathed in his draconic form. As his golden eyes drew near hers, their lips connected, neither of them sure which had pressed first. Their connection was surreal, and their mortal bodies had finally conquered their draconic minds. Reshiria gave Philotrax a silent invitation as the furs draping her shapely body fell to the floor.

However, their happiness and contentment seemed to be short lived. Reshiria knew immediately that she was with child. But the years passed, and she did not give birth. The child inside her grew for around fifty years, a typical incubation period for a dragon egg. As a result of her prolonged gestation, the two of them spent a significant amount of their draconic fortunes traveling as a pair of married nobles in disguise. They did not want to stay in one place too long to prevent suspicion.

Those wandering years changed Reshiria. Once an evil, domineering dragon, she was now a weak, cursed being. Her once non-existent emotions had blossomed, and she had learned empathy, caring, and love. Philotrax was the one who taught her what love meant to these mortals: the feelings in her body, the thoughts in her mind, and the fantasies of her heart all centered on this dragon who, like her, was trapped. He did not curse his fate as she did for so long. He gave her a reason to live, and she looked forward to motherhood.

Though Philotrax and Reshiria initially stayed close to Nulodia, they realized they needed to travel to more remote locations to avoid being recognized. They had been traveling through the frontier towns of Alabaster for over a decade when Reshiria's body finally succumbed to labor. In the remote town of Devitus, Philotrax had secured the services of a midwife, a cleric, and a doctor. She gave birth to a healthy baby girl, which was human by all evidence. At this point, the two dragons had given up on ever returning to their previous glory. Reshiria finally thought she understood mortals. Even the lives of elves were so short that fleeting happiness and peace were more priceless than jewels and gold. With this beautiful child, they could start over here in Devitus. If she grew at the rate of a normal human, perhaps nobody would notice that Reshiria and Philotrax did not age. Mortals were quick to see past anomalies if offered a somewhat rational explanation. At this point, they could blame their prolonged youth on The Unbinding, and it would be as much truth as deception.

They named their little jewel "Miranda," a humanized version of the draconic name Mir'thax Toi'landra meaning "Of fire and lightning." And as she grew, she possessed many of the same features as her parents. Her hair was a cooler crimson than her father's, but her eyes possessed the same shocking blue as her mother's. The people in the village of Devitus were eager to help these displaced "nobles," partially because the dragons used the last of their hordes to purchase land and titles from the baron. However, the people of Devitus were genuine, caring people. A century ago, Reshiria would have considered these insects as weak and foolish. Now, she understood why they worked so hard to build communities to stand against the forces of chaos that descended on humans and elves from the wilderness. She wanted to help build those communities, to contribute to a safe place for her little Mir'thax.

To bond more closely with the humans and elves that made up the population of Devitus, Philotrax began training with a group of monks that had built a monastery shortly outside of the fortified city that sat high in a valley between the spiring peaks of the central Trollcrag region. Reshiria had been working with two clerics of Invictus to remodel and restore an old church to a deity poorly understood by the more chaotic peoples. As a dragon with a penchant for cruelty and blood, she had slain many paladins and priests of this very god. She thought her labors would be seen as an effort to make amends. The two clerics had a beautiful daughter that was born about a year before Miranda. Reshiria imagined her daughter's future alongside this other girl, learning to craft and playing with dolls. For once, the future seemed steady, if not bright. Her heart had completely transformed over the last century. The dragon was gone.

Four years later, in the deep cold of winter, Reshiria awoke in the middle of the night. Her body had broken into a cold sweat, a terrible fever wracking her body. Philotrax stirred beside her, reaching out to touch her face.

"What's wrong, ivil'thax," he asked, his nickname for her meaning "beloved flames" in the language of dragons.

"I don't feel well, darling," she replied, the illness evident in her voice.

Philotrax left the comfort of their bed, lighting a candle on the bedside table. Their estate was humble compared to some places they had previously lived. Their remaining wealth would ensure that Miranda had a happy and secure home. Though their mortal forms were prone to common illnesses, neither had ever experienced such fever or trembles. Philotrax was very concerned for his wife. He chose not to reveal that he, too, was dealing with similar symptoms. His body was giving out. Being a dragon kept them young, but it did not stop the sands of time and the threads of fate from calling them out of the mortal coil.

He helped her draw a warm bath, calling their lone servant to bring in linens and herbs to treat the fever. He would have worried that, after all of this time, they had finally contracted the plague that kept mortals in constant worry for every cough and sneeze. He knew better, however, and continued to behave normally. He helped Reshiria into the bath, following recipes he learned throughout his journeys to make her bath comfortable and refreshing.

"Join me, love?" she asked as she sank into the water. He nodded and left the washroom to check on Mir'thax. He smiled as he looked into her room, her red hair tossed wildly about her face as she slept peacefully. He quietly walked over to his daughter and knelt beside her. He kissed her forehead and pressed his face against hers. She stirred slightly and opened her shimmering blue eyes. "What's wrong, daddy?" she murmured in a sleepy voice.

"Nothing, darling," he replied. He kept his composure remarkably well.

"Did you have a bad dream?" she asked, confused.

Philotrax chuckled softly. "No, Mir'thax. I just wanted to tell you that mommy and I love you."

"I love you too, daddy. And mommy." The little girl blinked gently, still half asleep.

Philotrax stood for a moment, watching his precious daughter sleep. Returning to the washroom, he undressed and slid into the large metal bath with his wife. He held her in his arms as they soaked in the herbs and aromas, bringing her fever down just enough to ease her pain. They dried themselves as Reshiria asked their servant to replenish the fire in the sitting room instead of returning to bed. They stood at Miranda's door as they waited, watching her sleep. When the fire was ready, they went to the sitting room.

The two stayed up late like those nights so many years ago in front of the fireplace, spending hours with their hearts and bodies connected in a way that would have been impossible had they not been trapped as humans when The Unbinding changed everything they thought they knew. Philotrax held Reshiria close, this time both of their exquisite bodies hidden under the pile of warm furs.

Though the fever had eased, Reshiria finally understood what was happening. She looked into the eyes of her love, the fire making those golden pools sparkle. "Eighty-four years trapped like this, fifty of them the happiest in all my centuries," she whispered to him.

A tear fell from his eyes. "Not yet, she needs us," he pleaded, his heart telling him their time in the mortal coil had simply ended.

"Do you think she'll understand?" Reshiria replied, feeling her heart break.

Philotrax's tears flowed freely. "The monks of Lexcord will make sure that she knows she was loved."

Reshiria began to sob uncontrollably. In over seven hundred years in this incarnation, this was the first time Reshiria had ever cried. It would also be the last. "The clerics of Invictus will make sure that all of this passes into her hands when the time is right," she assured herself as much as her husband.

Philotrax spoke no more, his body solidifying into a deep, red crystal as she watched.

Reshiria started to panic, tears raining out of her eyes. "I love you," she repeatedly whispered until her time came, crystallizing into a beautiful blue gem intertwined intimately with the sparkling statue of Philotrax.

The next morning, the servant sent for the baron and anyone who would listen. The beloved couple had been petrified in their sitting room, and nobody had a real explanation. Some theorized it was a magical beast, as the estate was not ransacked. Others thought it was perhaps a curse or an uncanny magic gone wrong. Their beautiful forms were tangled together, wrapped in each other's arms, Reshiria's hand pressed against Philotrax's face. Both clerics of Lexcord and Invictus tried to undo the petrification, but no prayers seemed to cure their condition. They theorized that this crystalline condition was something beyond regular petrification, and they had no answers. Eventually, the healers quit trying and contemplated how to resolve the aftermath.

Iria and Thomas offered to take the girl left behind. The monks of Lexcord insisted they were better prepared to handle an orphan. The people of Devitus decided to leave the statue of Miranda's parents at the estate, which was promptly boarded up and secured. Thomas Selasine would oversee the transfer of her parents' property on her twenty-first birthday or the day she married, whichever arrived first. As they checked the estate for things that would likely be stolen, Iria and Thomas took the resplendent battlemail, Reshiria's jewelry and magic item collection, and Philotrax's armory. He stored them in the old cellar beneath the church, which was still being remodeled. He gave the jewelry to the monastery's headmistress to keep it under more continual guard. They would keep these things secure until the girl needed them.

Thomas took one final look at the statue, two charismatic individuals who had greatly impacted their community. There was something special about them, and his instincts told him that the daughter they left behind would be special too. He clutched his holy symbol, praying earnestly, "As sure as Invictus guides my path, I swear that I will make sure Miranda has the future that you were working so hard to build for her here."

He could swear tears flowed from Reshiria's crystalized statue but convinced himself it was just a trick of the light on the gemstone.

Chapter 14
Betrayal

Belasine could tell that the light piercing his eyes was not Miranda's miracle light but the sun's. The sun! Just moments ago, he would have sworn that he would never see the sun again. He opened his eyes, staring at a beautiful morning sky with deep hues of blue. "Wait, is this the other side?" he thought. Sitting up, he found himself on the beaches of Yendralia. White sand spread out before him with tall purple mountains spiring behind. As he collected his senses, he looked around frantically.

August and Erk lay only a few feet away, still unconscious. A familiar, musical voice piped behind him, "I'm glad you're awake, bishop!"

He turned suddenly to see Miranda sitting on a grassy hill under a palm tree about fifteen feet away. He tried to get up, but the world around him spun too quickly, forcing him to stay planted on his bottom in the sand. "Are you okay?" he asked,

"What about the others?"

She smiled softly. "Everyone is fine, it seems. I'm so happy we made it out of there together. I . . ." she trailed off and looked at her other two sleeping companions. "I was so afraid of being alone again that all I could wish for was the last time we were safe. Apparently, this was the last time we were actually safe," she giggled as she gestured to the beach.

A moment later, August let out a groan. "Is this how it feels to be dragon food?" he rumbled, having heard Miranda's and Selasine's voices. Erk also stirred, brushing sand off his jacket as he sat up.

The pirate lord looked around, disoriented. "How in the Abyss did we end up back here? I thought for sure we were dead," Erk said, trying to piece together events.

Miranda's lips tightened. "I suddenly felt the mana flow into me when Ezelbrecht threatened to keep me. I was so scared of being alone there forever with that creature. The more they spoke of my power, the more I was sure I could at least get us back here safely. So I wished, and I kept wishing and," she smiled. "And we're all okay!"

As the companions woke up, they gathered close to Miranda under the tree on the hill. Since she was seated, the other three joined her cross-legged on the ground. She looked at peace, but the normal, innocent way she looked at the world was gone. Selasine could feel his heart grow heavy as he sat beside her and took her into his arms while she sat motionless. She leaned into his embrace but otherwise did not react.

"I am so sorry, Miranda. I did not know the truth about your parents," he began.

She breathed deeply, her radiant blue eyes looking nowhere. Her braids were severely frayed, strands of hair blowing carelessly in the wind and spilling around her shoulders. It was clear to everyone that taking Miranda to Olvidado was the right decision, but it was also a pivotal moment in her life. Three weeks ago, she was just a young peacekeeper working hard to help the people in Devitus with whatever trivial problems they had. Today, she had lost count of the people she had saved with the store of magic that built in her body, the arcane reacting to her draconic nature. She had also hurt her friends one more time than she had ever wanted to. She finally choked out, "I don't want this power." As she did, she began to cry.

Erk stared blankly at the ground. When he kidnapped Miranda, he was the Dread Pirate Lord Erk the Radiant, ruthless, cunning, and feared. In just a few days with her, Erk the Kind had returned to the peripheral of his mind. Now, he had to confront the guilt and responsibility he shared in this ordeal. Ultimately, it was probably good for Miranda to learn about the power inside her; however, Erk was sure there could have been a better way.

August was less interested in placing blame but instead wondered where they should go from here. "Bishop, what do we do now?" he asked, looking to his mentor for guidance.

Selasine sighed deeply, still holding Miranda in his arms. "Honestly, I'm not sure. This was only meant to be a brief excursion. Now we've become companions with the enemy we set out to destroy, and our little peacekeeper is more special than we could have ever predicted." Her tears stopped, her eyes focused, and she chewed her lip nervously.

"Bishop, I'd like to meet the one Erk calls The Master," she added to August's uncertain question.

Selasine winced internally. While he still held a measure of disdain toward Erk, he felt more like he understood the elf and his actions up to this point. Thomas was sure he would go to the same extraordinary lengths to protect those he held dear to him: Iria, Telisi, Miranda, August, Justin, and Damil. He would become the world's worst pirate if it meant he could have protected them from the beginning. As such, he nodded reluctantly, asking, "Where is this Master?" his eye looking directly at Erk.

"The crystal that contains his essence is in my study at the Fortress of Lords," Erk replied. "But if I go up there, all of Yendralia will demand a festival for my official return. We must move in secret if we want to be expedient."

Miranda stood up slowly, prompting Selasine and the others to join her on their feet. She shook her head, "You're right. We don't have time for a celebration. Every minute we wait, Gelidor is hurting more people. We need to find a way to stop him with the least amount of bloodshed possible," she planned out loud, including her friends in her thoughts.

"Miranda," Erk began, the coolness in her eyes soothing the burden on his heart. "This conflict was never your burden to bear, and I've pushed this all on you. I'm sorry," he continued, his eyes dropping to the ground.

She could hear the sincerity in his voice, and she could see the pain in his expression. In a sudden, unexpected movement, she flung herself into Erk, bending at her waist slightly to hug his shorter, elven form. She squeezed him tighter than anybody would have thought she was capable, her usual body language gentle and reserved. Erk's eyes opened in shock as the young woman began to rock side to side, not letting the pirate go.

She released him and stood up straight, her eyes shimmering thanks to tears that flowed from her eyes. Her voice, however, was strong and resolved. "I know, Erk. That's why I want to meet The Master. If he can stop this conflict, I want to help restore him. If he's not," she sighed as she thought. "If he's not, we'll have to find another way."

Erk blinked in disbelief, finding himself at a loss for words. Even with the power of the universe itself at her disposal, her kindness and concern for others never lost its priority. This woman was more remarkable than he could have ever known. "But why? Miranda, I would never reject your help, but you could easily walk away at this point."

She smiled at him and stepped back, the four of them now standing in a small square, facing each other. "When I was training with Maréli, she asked me if I knew my destiny. I said I wanted to help make the world a better, safer place. She told me she knew my destiny was to help, but in doing so, I would shed many tears."

Everyone waited a moment in silence. She continued, "Even though I would have never asked for this power, I have it. The facts will not change despite being afraid of what is to come. My destiny is bigger than myself. And I want to chase that all the way. I want to make my parents proud of me, and I want to make Bishop Selasine and my friends proud, too. Even you, Erk."

Selasine was already proud of her. Her resolve was the

most impressive display of force he had ever seen. He touched Miranda's shoulder, "Then that settles it. We will meet The Master, and then we will decide what to do from there," he added, looking to Erk and August for an agreement. The young acolyte smiled and gave a cocky nod.

The pirate lord silently agreed, still reeling from his moral and existential crisis. "Would you two like to retrieve your pegasus and meet us on *The Nebula*? I have a stable cabin that would be perfect for them. We can go up to the fortress under the cover of night. It will be less likely that anybody will notice us until we are close to the fortress," he asked and speculated.

August stood straight, "Don't get any ideas about setting out to sea without us."

Erk tried to force a smile, "I'd never make that mistake again."

Miranda giggled, breaking the tension. "Maybe we can celebrate on *The Nebula*?" she asked.

Erk's forced smile became relaxed and natural, "Whatever Lady Hyacinth desires, Pirate Lord Erk is glad to grant her."

With that decided, the four of them split up temporarily, Miranda and Erk returning to *The Nebula* with Selasine and August making a detour to The Silver Strand to take the pegasus from the stables there. No longer concerned with optics, the two clerics flew the beasts back to the docks, landing on the deck of *The Nebula*. Erk and Miranda watched them from the top deck. As they landed and dismounted, Selasine felt a familiar, sharp yet painless sensation wrack his brain.

"Th----s," he heard a voice. Selasine's face showed distress, causing Miranda and the others to rush to his side.

"Thomas," the voice echoed. The distress faded immediately as he recognized Damil's voice. He had not carried on a telepathic conversation in so long that he had forgotten what it felt like once Damil had initiated it.

Selasine closed his eyes, gesturing to everyone around him to be quiet. He opened his mind and directed his thoughts to Damil. "To what do I owe the pleasure, Damil?" His thoughts were pleasant and happy.

The high paladin's laugh could be felt through the telepathic link despite the lack of actual sound. "There's a pretty big problem brewing this way. Carulus has gone rogue. He is no longer complying with the archbishop and is threatening to sail his remaining troops into Claston. It'll be a slaughter if nobody can warn the king that it's not an invasion." Selasine's brows furrowed, causing his companions to grow worried.

The bishop thought, "From what I can tell, the King of Claston would slaughter them regardless of a warning. Is there any way you can stop the force from landing?"

"That's the problem. The last of Carulus's forces boarded some ships in the Undine Sea. Nobody knows where he might have gotten naval support. They certainly weren't church ships. I wondered if you guys had successfully retrieved the girl," the thoughts flowed between their minds as if they were standing face to face. Thomas frowned, and Damil could even feel it through their telepathic link.

"We found her, safe and two steps ahead of us. Turns out Erk is a pretty complicated guy. When I said this was a legal insurrection, I was right," Selasine's thoughts bounced back.

"That's most excellent news! So, I take it you've met the pirate then?" Damil detected Thomas's affirmative thought, much like a mental nod without words. "Is there any chance you could get your buddies to dig up some recon for us then?"

"What do you need to know?" Thomas thought in return.

"Who in the world supplied Carulus with ships?" Damil asked pointedly.

After a minute of silence, Selasine seemed to awaken from a standing sleep. As his cognizance returned, he looked at Erk. "It seems the priest that organized the whole expedition against you has stopped replying to orders from the church. Would it be possible to find out who supplied an enemy army with ocean transport?"

Erk nodded immediately. "We have many eyes and ears on the open water. Just ask me what you need to know, and I will see what I can come up with."

Selasine breathed deeply. He thought he felt like he already knew the answer. "We need to know who provided the high priest of the operation against you with naval support. They've apparently all boarded a few ships and are sailing toward

Claston."

Erk furrowed his brow. "I think I might already know where the ships came from. But I can confirm, also. Give me a bit. In the meantime, why don't we take Miranda's advice and celebrate our return on *The Nebula*?" He grinned deviously at the bishop.

Selasine grunted impatiently, "What are your thoughts?"

Erk gave a dismissive wave, "Anything I say at this point is just speculation. But if Gelidor and the high priest have been working together from the beginning, probably the usurper is still finding ways to support the high priest despite his lack of response to the church."

Selasine was caught somewhere between relief and worry. Somebody outranking the high priest must have given orders to abandon the mission, but only a member of the Council would outrank the high priest of the largest church in the kingdom. Technically, one of the high paladins could also call off the attack, but that would be unusual after they likely approved the operation. Either way, church forces sailing into Claston was troublesome.

Selasine gathered his thoughts and nodded approvingly, "Very well, I'll let you do whatever you need to do to get that information for us. In the meantime, let's focus on getting Miranda in contact with The Master and deciding where we go from there." He looked around *The Nebula*, impressed by the size of the ship. Most of the crew was ashore, but a small group of pirates had remained on board to take care of the ship while the main sailing crew was away. "Where are the stables you spoke of?" he inquired.

Erk nodded swiftly, then placed his fingers inside his mouth to whistle. The sharp screech caught a nearby pirate's attention, who reported, "Yes, cap!"

"Bishop, would you mind if Dezzo here took your pegasus to the stable deck? He'll groom them with the utmost care and ensure they have plenty of food and water. Plus, he'll protect them with his life, isn't that right, Dezzo?"

Dezzo looked to be Miranda's and August's age. At his captain's prodding, he gave another enthusiastic, "Yes, captain!" looking to Selasine and August for their approval.

Selasine reluctantly offered the young human man the reins to his pegasus, prompting August to do the same. Calmly and gently, the beasts followed Dezzo below deck, walking down an entrance Miranda had not explored in her time on *The Nebula*.

Erk straightened his hat and fluffed his jacket, "Well, with that handled, I'll see to investigating the high priest's army. Miranda, find Shalo and give him my orders: we celebrate on *The Nebula* until midnight. The festivities should provide additional cover for us to reach the Fortress of Lords without dealing with the attention." He knew he would have to arrange a public display of distributing the spoils of his recent plunders to the people of Yendralia. On top of that, they would have to arrange for Erk to deliver a speech. A small celebration on the ship would be much less involved.

Miranda nodded, her lips drawn tight in thought. After discovering what Shalo had done to Justin, her fond memories of the disappearing pirate eroded. Although she had a big heart with an immense capacity for forgiveness, she was not ready to forgive Shalo yet. If Selasine had not come to Justin's rescue, Shalo could have found himself on the wrong end of Miranda's anger. Besides, Shalo owed her his life thanks to her quick thinking in the caverns by the Undine Sea. Perhaps he could redeem himself, like Erk. After all, Erk's heart was true to his cause, and after hearing his story, she understood why he went to such cruel measures to fight for his people. In her thoughts, she realized it wasn't anger she felt toward Shalo but profound sadness. Fate and common sense would ease her resentment, she hoped. She resigned to treating Shalo cordially despite her confused feelings.

The problem for Miranda was finding a pirate who spent most of his time invisible. During their limited time together, Shalo spent most of that time watching her for Erk. She had not really gotten any information about his regular habits or responsibilities. Erk turned toward the captain's quarters and began to walk away. Miranda finally asked, "Do you know where I might find Shalo?"

Erk turned with a grin, "Check the bar 'Chummy's Slums' and buy a round for everybody in the room. You'll figure it out from there." He pulled a pouch off of his belt and tossed it to Miranda. "That ought to be enough to supply the bar all day. Just make sure you find him quick so that he can round up a celebration."

Selasine did not really want to spend much time in port. From what he had seen, pirates like Zanfur could be very unpredictable. August could see his mentor's discomfort and shared his sentiments. The quicker they fetched Erk's officer, the better. Erk had withdrawn to the captain's quarters as Miranda, Selasine, and August headed down the gangplank and into port. August asked a passing pirate for directions to Chummy's Slums, pointing him to an area more central to Yendralia's lower district.

Following the directions that August acquired, they found their way to a roundabout that was surrounded by bars and bathhouses. The foot traffic was heavy here, patrons slogging through a midday bar crawl. Selasine grumbled about the debauchery internally but led the group cautiously through the crowds. His large frame towered over most people here. They gave him a wide enough berth, allowing his pupils to follow close behind him. As they came around the roundabout, they saw a bar with a sign standing out front that read "Chummy's Slums." It was a wooden shanty-style building, similar to the surrounding architecture. It was fairly unassuming, and only the sign out front indicated what was inside.

Selasine opened the door and checked the room. It looked like a regular open tavern with a bar built in the center of the room. To the left side, a few tables were set up for the game of Xanadu. To the right, dining tables were neatly arranged. Despite its humble exterior, it was an ironically named elegant bar. He nodded to Miranda and August, leading them into the bar's dining area. There were a handful of patrons dining and drinking at the tables. A host approached, an elf in a uniform that seemed very formal to Miranda. The host bowed and said, "How can we serve you, friends?"

Miranda nodded to August. He said aloud in her stead, "A drink for everyone, on us!"

A few grateful patrons raised their glasses. Selasine would have never guessed that there was an establishment in this place that could remind him of the fine restaurants in Nulodia. It seemed strange to have such an elegant place in a den of pirates. It was also evident that higher prices attracted more exclusive clientele, making it a fitting place for a ship's officer to dispose of his higher salary. After a few moments, a servant brought out a tray of mugs, setting it on a table in the dining area. They began distributing the mugs, and some passing patrons grabbed a mug on their way by the table, giving August another toast of gratitude.

As the mugs on the tray diminished, Miranda watched closely at who had taken a mug. She was watching the tray so intently that she knew immediately what was happening when two of the mugs vanished into thin air. "Shalo!" she shouted and bounded toward the table with the tray of mugs. Several patrons looked confused as she nimbly weaved between tables, trying to get his attention. She spoke his name again, firmly and demanding. Not even a moment later, the pungent pirate appeared before her.

"Well, Miss Miranda! Was not expectin' ya to show up to a place like this!" he said, surprised to see her.

"I have orders from Erk, Shalo. Gather the crew; there will be a celebration on *The Nebula* until midnight tonight."

Shalo's eyes bulged, "Aye! Yer givin' orders on behalf of cap'n! Yer truly part of the crew now."

Miranda felt a pang of sadness, those feelings about what Shalo had done to her friend resurfacing as he smiled at her. She held her face expressionless, slightly colder than her usual demeanor with Shalo. "It seems so. We need the party so Erk can reach the Fortress of Lords without attracting too much attention. We may not have time for a festival, so it's best to move in secret," her voice was as gentle as usual, but it felt rehearsed as she spoke.

Shalo nodded, chugging the rest of whatever was in the mugs. "Alright then, back to The Neb. I gotta get Jax and Evan together on this," he replied, ready to go. They used the same strategy to navigate back through the crowds in the roundabout, Selasine parting the crowd. The entire trip to Chummy's Slums and back to *The Nebula* only took about an hour and a half. Shalo was nowhere to be seen, probably off rounding up the other officers. Selasine was uncomfortable that Shalo did not report to the ship with them but realized that Shalo probably better understood how to do whatever Erk wanted him to do. With a sigh, they waited for about another half an hour out on the deck when Miranda realized they could escape the sun in the dressing room of the ship.

The door to Naomi's space opened with a familiar creak to Miranda. She hated being here alone, but now that Selasine and August were here with her, she thought it a great place to hang out. After all, she knew the kitchen could take a while to catch up with the captain's demands. She started to realize that Shalo was probably in charge of the kitchen. "No wonder he smells like garlic," she thought to herself. She showed her companions into the room and immediately hopped on the bed and stretched out.

"Traveling with pirates has made you a little lazy, yeah?" August prodded as she wiggled on the bed, her battlemail clanking around. Selasine found a lounging chair close to the bath. He slid into it and let out a quick groan.

"You're one to talk, August. Wouldn't you rather be napping, hunting, or wasting time anyway?" the bishop retorted, chuckling.

August laughed, giving a quick sigh. "Of course, bishop. But even napping is outside what I would call a good use of time!"

Miranda grumbled in protest, "You know, there's not much to do when you're a prisoner on a pirate ship. I didn't have much to do besides nap and read *The Wrath of Justice* Erk gave me."

It made sense to Selasine, suddenly. *The Wrath of Justice* was an advanced text intended for those designated as either a Judge of Retribution or a Revenant of Justice, both elite divisions within the church hierarchy. Judges of Retribution were granted their title after arresting numerous lawbreakers. The Revenants of Justice carried out lethal missions of execution against serious threats. That's where she must have learned those prayers. Still, they were so advanced that he was surprised that Invictus would grant her such power. Then he worried. What if it was her gift and not her connection to the

Sword of Justice? He hoped that her faith and strength had grown enough to master those prayers and that his fears were misplaced.

Still, Miranda's comment was the perfect explanation to put August back into his relaxed element. Selasine chuckled. For somebody so casual, usually, he could be judgmental at times. That, and he tended to just say whatever he was thinking.

The acolyte smacked himself on the forehead in a gesture of shame, "Ah, dammit. You know, I didn't really think that through, did I?"

Miranda giggled. "No, you didn't, but it's okay. Bishop would never let me get away with napping if there was something more important to do, yeah?"

Selasine sighed deeply, his body finding a moment to sleep genuinely for the first time in days. He had hoped Justin found his way back to Devitus, but at least he knew he was alive. He was worried that Justin might have gotten caught up in Carulus's mission to sail straight into Claston. He doubted that he would be conscripted after a brush with death. His other two pupils were here and safe with him. He had much less worry than he had days ago, and sleep found him quite easily. Miranda, too, dozed off in the bed. August sat down against the bed, resting his head. He was not as comfortable as the bishop here. Something told him to stay alert and watch out for his friends.

Fortunately, August's mistrust was misplaced enough. Once Shalo had returned to *The Nebula* with the ship's officers, he found Miranda, Selasine, and August all sleeping in the guest cabin. He smiled, happy that the girl had found her friends. He told Jax, "So, I guess that means yer in charge of the celebration. I think I'm back on guard duty for these folks."

Jax rolled his eyes, "Yeah, somebody would be dumb enough to stir up that hornet's nest? No way you're gonna pin this whole celebration ruse on me. Besides, yer the chef. I got no business in the kitchen. Let 'em sleep. The cap'n will wanna see 'em if what you said was right. Let him wake 'em up."

Over the next few hours, the pirates pulled barrels of beer, ale, and wine aboard *The Nebula*. They advertised their party to the "special guest" crowd, including other pirate captains and their officers. As expected, many arrived under the pretenses of free booze and good music. Some of Erk's sailors were great musicians, and nearly all of Yendralia's party crowd knew it.

August jumped awake as footsteps thudded outside the door. He cursed himself for abandoning his duty to keep the others safe. A gentle knock was followed up by Erk's voice, "Hey, bishop? Miranda? August?" The others began to stir as August opened the door. Erk stood there alone, a grim expression on his face. "I've got some news about your high priest."

Selasine was quickly roused by the prospect. "What did you learn? And how?"

Erk tilted his head down just a bit. "I sent out some messenger hawks and had a friend send some mental messages around the Solar region. There's a huge contingent of paladins sailing on Claston naval transports. Looks like your high priest and Gelidor are working together directly now." With a grimace, Erk continued, "That means the Sword of Justice has unwittingly joined forces with The Counselor of the Corrupt."

Selasine frowned. "And you're confident in your sources?" his growing trust for the pirate evident.

Erk gave a humble nod. "I would have given you a warning was it doubted. Undoubtedly, the church is being transported by Gelidor's orders." He took a moment to consider the implications. Those paladins probably had no idea that Gelidor was religiously affiliated with Na'agamlor. "I fear for their safety, bishop," he concluded.

August stared at the ground. Miranda looked at Erk with a frustrated stare, not understanding why the high priest would be so misguided to align with someone as foul as the usurper. Selasine shook his head and grumbled, "Well, I'm not surprised. I've smelled this betrayal since he showed up in Devitus for the acolyte testing. I'm not sure what he's trying to do. But, Erk, I hope The Master can help us with this situation. I don't want to see lives thrown away for this huge misunderstanding."

Erk winced. "I hope your optimism isn't misplaced. I'm relying on Miranda's judgment to determine whether or not she should heal The Master." He looked directly at her, sitting upright on the bed, legs crossed into the adamant rings of the skirt of the battlemail. "I put you in danger on Olvidado while your instincts told you to run away. If you do not think The Master will be a force for good, I do not want you to proceed. I don't want to put you in harm's way again."

Miranda nodded, her face serious. August looked at his friend with concern, hoping he could help her shoulder this burden. She replied, "Thank you, Erk. I am confident that you now know that compromising your ideals for the greater good is pointless if you lose yourself and those ideals in the process. I know the good is still alive in you, and I believe in that side finding its home one day."

Her wisdom was so impressive for her age, Erk thought. He replied, "I think you're helping me call it back to where it should have stayed all along. I let Gelidor send me down a dark path, frustrated with a lack of results and my brother's condition. I won't let those same mistakes continue to dominate my path."

Miranda smiled, knowing that his words were genuine. "So, how is the celebration, captain?" she asked.

Erk chuckled. "Well, it looks like it's working. Tons of captains here, deep in their cups. They'll never notice us slip into the night and up to the fortress. That way, fewer chances of them demanding that I throw a celebration immediately," he replied. "This is, after all, what they wanted anyway."

Selasine hoisted himself out of the lounging chair. "Well, then. What are we waiting for?" he added.

Erk looked at the bishop. "Ready when you are. It's getting dark already," he encouraged.

Selasine grabbed Miranda's hand and helped yank her out of bed. The skirt of her battlemail rattled loudly as she stood up. "Let's hope we can end this quickly then," Miranda said, feeling as confident as she did when she defeated the manticore with a binding curse.

Selasine gestured to the others. "Wait a moment, please," he asked as he touched his hands to his temples. His thoughts reached out across space and time, only the name: "Damil?" The ether between them reacted, and his friend's thoughts replied.

"Thomas! Any news?" he asked, straight to business.

"Yes. It turns out that Carulus is working directly with the King of Claston instead of responding to the archbishop." His thoughts made Damil frown.

"I'll get word back to the archbishop then. You've got full permission to arrest Carulus on sight. On the order of High Paladin Damil."

"Understood," Thomas replied. He left the telepathic trance, everyone staring at him intently. He said out loud, Damil still listening, "Carulus is an enemy of the church and Erk's rebellion. He's to be arrested on sight."

Miranda laughed. "I want the honors," her normal, innocent teasing taking a darker turn.

Even Erk worried for Carulus a bit. Na'agamlor had twisted Gelidor into something far darker than anyone could have imagined. The overly ambitious priest might find himself a lethal end at the usurper's hands.

***

King Gelidor Claston crumpled the correspondence in his hand. "The entire fleet sent back here? Right in the port, not a scratch on anybody? No violence whatsoever? Are you sure this isn't a mutiny?" he growled angrily.

His advisor, Neiryin Asior, looked exasperated. "My liege, all reports clarified that the blockade was set appropriately. We think this may be connected to the power that the high priest said would serve as his secret weapon. It looks like Erilkaiden has gained control of that weapon."

King Claston nodded his head, his white hair bobbing around his face. "You are a fool, Asior. You speak as though you are worried that I am angry with this news. If I were, you would already be dead. This is a blessing." He raised a hand to scratch his pointed, aged chin. "You know, this means that the church is responsible for such a resource falling into the hands of a lawbreaker. They have no choice but to help me correct this wrong." His black eyes narrowed as he flashed a sadistic smile. "Invictus is willingly sending his faithful into the hands of The

Shadowed One. We should welcome them in style."

"What do you propose, my liege?" Asior asked.

"Invite High Priest Carulus to Claston with his forces. Send it by eagle; we want to ensure it gets there safely. We'll find that weapon and extinguish it. It is an affront to elvenkind," the king demanded. "The paladins on those ships will serve as hostages that we'll offer in exchange for the girl. That way, the church cannot protect her at the expense of many of their number. The law would misguide them selfishly. It is the easiest way to acquire the girl." He wrinkled his nose. "Do be sure not to include the darker details in your invitation."

Asior nodded in compliance. "At once, your majesty." He turned and sprinted away, ready to send the king's orders as he had dictated.

Carulus was glad to hear of the king's willingness to send naval support for his contingent of paladins. It seemed that the archbishop no longer thought that Carulus needed his troops. He couldn't be more wrong, Carulus thought. The girl was now in the hands of the enemy, and the forces of order were in danger. From what he had heard, she had ruined the naval ambush. He grew angry. She was supposed to work for him, not for the pirates. He grumbled to himself about traitors and loyalty.

"Your Holiness, shall we depart then?" the commander asked.

Carulus smiled. His commanding officer, Paladin Yolosqui Nohamar, had proven more loyal to his cause than he had anticipated. "Yes, commander. We march south to meet our transport. I'll send word back right away." He quickly scribbled a reply to the King of Claston.

"Your Majesty, we would be glad to unify ourselves with your forces. It appears the church administration does not want us to continue supporting your cause. However, I recognize the danger this weapon I have lost is beyond their understanding. I will rally my forces to you to protect you from the assault you anticipate."

He stuffed it in the scroll case attached to the eagle's leg, and it began its rapid return journey, blasting through the air at an incredible speed.

Gelidor Claston breathed a sigh of relief. Though the church had rejected his birthright as ruler of these lands, they at least finally recognized the danger Erilkaiden posed to law and order. A thousand paladins as hostages! Whoever was powerful enough to send his ships back to port was not authorized to use such a gift within his jurisdiction. He had to make sure that she was punished accordingly. He kept hearing whispers of this "miracle girl." Carulus planned to use her gift to destroy Erilkaiden. However, she turned her gift against the king; this could not go unpunished.

The king motioned for Asior to come closer. "This weapon Carulus spoke of. We are sure that it was her?"

Asior nodded. "Damil reported to the archbishop the same possibility."

"We no longer need the archbishop. Cut him out of your information."

"Are you sure?" Asior replied, stunned.

"Yes. You see, there seems to be a conflict of interest. The church wants to uphold law and order, but they do not fully respect our traditions. I fear they may have turned the weapon over to Erilkaiden to depose me." Na'agamlor's philosophy was to destroy those weaker than you that challenged you. Gelidor was convinced that these fools were much inferior to himself, and they were most certainly intent on his downfall.

Asior gulped. "Does that mean what I think it means, Your Majesty?"

"Yes," King Claston replied. "See to it that Carulus is arrested as soon as they arrive in port. Giving over such a powerful weapon is nothing short of an act of war. He will pay for his transgressions against the crown." Then, with his cruel smile, "And leave the rest of the paladins stranded at sea. Put some gunships on them. Sabotage. I want them to suffer in their own filth for a little while. Let them see why their path is misguided."

Asior nodded, "As His Majesty wills it." He sprinted off

again, thankful the king saw value in his gift. He could accelerate his speed at will. It made him a great messenger. Otherwise, he worried about his fate if the king cursed him instead. He didn't really like the king, but using his gift on the king's behalf put his family in a pretty secure position. That is if Asior could stay in the king's graces. He carried out his duty with diligence.

Chapter 15
The Master

rk draped himself in a dark, hooded cloak, removing his hat and covering his face. Selasine began a prayer, "Invictus, let our travels pass unnoticed. Keep our identities secret so that we can expose the forces of chaos from within," a prayer usually reserved for infiltrating the enemy and relying on accurate disguises. A shimmer of light hovered around the four of them, creating a glamor that would easily conceal their appearances from anyone not looking at them carefully.

Erk handed Miranda a cloak like his, "You might be the only person in port with recognizable hair. We best cover you up also."

She nodded, taking the cloak and draping it around her shoulders. She covered her hair carefully, tucking her braids behind her ears.

Together they emerged from the guest cabin, the deck of *The Nebula* now crowded with guests taking advantage of Erk's hospitality. The pirate lord's troubadours, including Evan now, were playing the accordion and various stringed instruments underneath the ship's main mast. Miranda saw Evan singing, still curious about the elf she had helped save from Gelidor's curse. She understood the things happening around her were far more important than getting to know people, but that didn't mean she couldn't at least wonder about their stories in the meantime. Between the cloaks and Selasine's glamor prayer, the four of them could slip quietly down the gangplank and into the streets of the port built on the tide wall of Yendralia.

Within a few minutes, they approached the first place that Erk was worried about, the main gate leading from the port to the lower district. August and Erk walked in front, Selasine and Miranda behind. As they walked under the gate, a familiar voice to Erk, Selasine, and August began to sing enthusiastically, "Adventures they've had right on our very shores, holy men adopting the habits and customs of pirates and pirates adapting the practices of holy men. Now they hail without wings, a journey on foot made in secret. Surely, a pirate lord would accept the traditions of his port and his people?" Cantalus sang as he emerged from the shadows, his round face grinning ear to ear, having seen through their disguises.

August barked in Khantongue, "Errvin gol'tdon, Cantaloos," his voice gruff but quiet.

"But when, if not now?" his melodic voice returned. "And with more guests than is typical of a lord retreating to the fortress. Serious business must be afoot," he finished in a spoken voice; passersby taking little notice of his interrogation.

"Cantalus, He Who Sings at the Gate. Perhaps we'll have a more interesting song for you to sing if you do not announce my return and let us pass undetected," Erk pleaded with the god of pirates.

"A mission carried out in secret, a most thrilling tale. But why, pirate lord? Perhaps all things revealed in good time, yes?" the bard still insisted on drawing attention to them.

August looked back to Selasine, whose brow was furrowed in frustration. Giving his mentor a devious grin, August turned to face the bard directly, stepping into his personal space. He, unfortunately, did not understand Cantalus's true significance to the island. "You see, this could be a matter of life or death. Drop the song and dance, bard, and let us pass quietly," August demanded, his voice threatening.

Cantalus's demeanor shifted so quickly that Miranda was shocked. He went from a carefree, singing jester to an imposing, deadly assassin in less than a second's notice. "You see, it's my only duty to keep track of who comes and goes from these gates, and the songs I sing weave their destinies," the bard explained, his hands resting on the hilts of a couple of exquisite daggers on his belt.

"Be that as it may, Cantalus," Erk interjected, "we simply do not have the time, nor can we afford the attention warranted by your wonderful music tonight. I assure you, the celebration following our ordeals will be so grand that you'll have to write a symphony to even describe it."

Cantalus's smile returned, his hands relaxing from his daggers. "So be it, then. Tonight, Cantalus will sing of the four passing in shadow. Tomorrow, their deeds are brought to light. Be careful; this journey may be your last," the words of his song fading as he turned back to the shadows.

Erk took a desperate look around. Cantalus was notorious for drawing crowds at the gate, especially when rebuffing people who honestly had no business in Yendralia. Erk knew that his role as the gate's guardian was not something to be taken lightly, something that he realized August and Selasine did not understand. "Did you have to threaten him? He's not a pushover; he was the first pirate lord. He is a god, literally. He just never leaves here for the primordial place."

August's eyes bulged as he glanced at all three of his companions. "Hey, how was I supposed to know that? The guy only sang to us when the bishop and I came through here a few days ago."

Erk's lips twisted into a sarcastic smile. "Your life is only as safe as your information here. Make no assumptions." August nodded in agreement, apologetic. Miranda had pulled the hood of her cloak even tighter around her face. Erk prodded them, feeling the moment had passed, "No worries, friends. Let's be on our way."

The foot traffic in the lower district was not overly dense in the outlying neighborhoods. Miranda, Selasine, and August followed Erk through several side streets and empty shanty neighborhoods to avoid attention. This time, the glamor prayer helped significantly, as Erk noticed dozens of people that should have recognized him. The people of Yendralia paid little attention to them as they journeyed through the city.

Approaching the market district was Erk's second fear. A fine, cobblestone streetway had been constructed from the ports up to the Fortress of Lords. That direct route would be impossible due to the possibility of being noticed. However, they would still have to use that path to enter the market district. While Cantalus did not watch this gate, vendors and barkers still watched traffic entering the district, hoping to make a sale. As they approached the main street from an alley, Erk motioned for the group to stop.

"This is a matter of timing, more than secrecy," he explained.

Selasine observed the street carefully, "What are we waiting for?" he asked.

Erk shook his head, "The one thing we've been trying to avoid: a crowd."

It made sense to Selasine and Miranda. Traveling too long with a crowd could expose them, but blending in with one briefly should help reduce excess scrutiny from onlookers watching foot traffic. Individuals or pairs seemed to move through the gates frequently, but those would not provide enough anonymity. After about a dozen minutes had passed, August started to grow impatient. "I should have brought a book," he mumbled.

Erk winced and gave him a gesture to be quiet. "Can you hear that?"

Everyone listened for a moment, the sound of music growing in the streets of the market district. From the end of the alley, the gates were about one hundred feet to the right. Vendors would mostly be trying to catch the attention of people entering the district. The chaos of a band in the street would make a perfect cover.

Erk motioned to everyone as he walked briskly out into the

open. They matched his pace, pulling their cloaks tight. As they entered the gates to the market district, they saw a parade approaching. An entourage of musicians loudly playing flutes and fiddles surrounded a palanquin. People in the streets stopped to watch the parade, waving to the entourage as they carried the covered platform, hiding the identity of whoever might have been inside. At the front of the parade, a beautiful blond woman was scattering rose petals about the streets.

Erk felt his heart soar and cursed himself at the same time. This was Pirate Lady Naomi's entourage. She was on her way to *The Nebula*, no doubt, to seek an audience with him. Well, honestly, probably to scold him. Or worse. The party made an excellent pretense of leaving The Fortress of Lords. Since Erk had not made his official return yet, he was presumed to be on *The Nebula* as host. It was unusual to spend two days in port without announcing his return, and Erk understood Naomi's probable suspicions. Everything happening with Miranda occurred so quickly that he did not think to send her a message at the fortress. Nevertheless, she was his beloved and closest ally among the other seven pirate nobles. He needed to get a message to her.

With Erk in the lead, the four marched straight in between the members of Naomi's entourage, who were dispersed in the streets wildly. The noise was jubilant and exciting, and Miranda wished she could dance with the parade dancers. They were dressed in fine silks, men and women dancing as couples and teams. Some stunts they pulled, like tossing dancers into the air, made Miranda hold her breath as she beheld the spectacle. She was so distracted that Selasine had to tug on her arm to get her to keep pace. There was no time to enjoy this wonder, she lamented. Armed guards surrounded the palanquin, Erk recognizing them as lesser captains under Naomi's service. He drew his cloak tight and began clicking his tongue in a series of long and short sounds. The noise was surprisingly loud and could be heard over the din of the street celebration. Erk did not stop walking.

Selasine listened, perplexed. After Erk made his series of sounds, a clicking reply echoed from inside the palanquin. Erk stopped several paces away from the covered platform, turning his back and clicking a reply. A voice from inside the palanquin ordered, "Stop. At ease." The captains placed the platform on the ground and took a step aside. Erk turned and sprinted to the curtains and dove inside the palanquin. One of the captains started to protest but was not quick enough.

Erk blinked, his eyes adjusting to the subtle light inside. There his companion Pirate Lady Naomi lay on a plush fur cushion, propping her torso upright with her arms. She was dressed in an elegant, somewhat revealing gown. Her silver hair was woven into an elaborate updo that glowed in the subtle light. Her skin was a radiant brown, accentuated by her bright hair. "Erk, my darling," she cooed. "I was just on my way to see you."

He put down the hood of his cloak. He beamed with happiness, Naomi the only bright spot in his life for the last two decades. "I figured you were, my love. It's good to see you," he replied, confirming his identity to her.

She now sat fully upright, speaking in hushed tones, "So why the secrecy?"

"For starters, I don't have time for the ceremony right now. I don't consider this an official return. I've just got something I need to retrieve from my study," he explained, not giving a full picture of his intentions.

Naomi drew a thin, stiletto-style dagger from a sheath well hidden in her gown. She pressed the tip between her teeth and bit down gently, the cold of her blade sending a mildly painful shock through her mouth. "So, you're not going to be at the party on your own ship?" she teased in an obviously fake, disappointed voice.

"Only time will tell if I make it back by midnight for the party," he warned.

"Fine. I'll let myself into the captain's quarters and have a private after-party until you return," she threatened. She batted her eyes at him.

"My current mission could be pretty dangerous. If you stay on The Neb, you might get swept up in what's happening. And I really don't have time to explain that right now. If you're okay with that, I don't mind if you stay. I'd actually love to have you by my side for whatever comes next," he cautioned. Under normal circumstances, Erk would have found her seductive games intriguing and fun. Today, he felt the pressure of the task before them. Nevertheless, Naomi's arrival at *The Nebula* would have exposed Erk's absence, which would be a headache.

Naomi was as mentally swift as she was beautiful. "Very well, I must return to The Fortress of Lords then. If I'm going to sail with another pirate lord, I need my personal effects. I didn't bring my pistols," she replied. In a loud voice, she shouted at her captain escorts. "Hey! Back to the fortress. I forgot something."

Erk's eyes widened, "Wait, my companions! They're out in the crowd here," he reminded himself, peeking out the curtain. After a few moments of scanning, he recognized them in the crowd, their desire to remain incognito making it difficult even for their allies to identify them. "Can the guards let them on as well?"

With some hand gestures, Erk got Miranda's attention first. She approached the palanquin, trying not to bump into anyone in the crowd. When she was within earshot, Naomi's voice sang, "Pretty girl with the red hair! Get on, captain's orders!" Miranda made a confused face but complied quickly. She almost tripped stepping onto the palanquin, but Erk helped her catch her balance. Miranda boarding the platform caused August and Selasine to approach. Naomi repeated her command, pointing from inside the curtain at the two. The captains carrying the palanquin called for additional carriers out of the crowd, and Naomi's servants were happy to comply. As August and Selasine boarded, they noticed the guards were purposefully ignoring them. Ignorance had as much value as knowledge in some situations, and it seemed to Selasine that not knowing who entered the palanquin might be in these people's best interests.

The eight foot by eight foot palanquin was suddenly very crowded. Naomi had large bundles of furs scattered about for laying comfort. With five people inside, it proved difficult for anybody to lie comfortably, especially with Selasine and August on board. Naomi gestured for them to sit, "Unless falling out of a moving palanquin is on your bucket list, I'd suggest you get comfortable." Her voice was deep and rich. Her confident presence and attire made August's cheeks burn. Erk was already seated, the others following his lead at her command. Once everyone was stationary, Naomi hissed, "Get a move on!" The palanquin lurched as about a dozen people lifted up on the support bars under the platform. Naomi did not seem to expect introductions, her eyes scanning her new guests. "Guess Erk the Radiant is still out there ruining all kinds of people's lives," she teased, dark but sincere. She saw all three of them bore the symbol of Invictus, and her heart caught in her throat. "Church people, really, Erk?" she said in a cheeky tone that it was hard to tell if it was a reprimand or an encouragement.

Erk nodded stoically as he looked at Miranda. "Miranda, this is my beloved Pirate Lady Naomi, Queen of the Waves, Succubus of the Seas, and Captain of *The Violet Blur*," he then gestured back to Miranda. "And, Naomi, this is Miranda Hyacinth, Acolyte of Invictus, daughter of Philotrax and Reshiria."

Naomi rolled her eyes and laughed. She looked at Miranda and grumbled, "Why does he think we'll understand all these titles and surnames? Look, I'm Naomi; just call me that. Tell me what to call you. That'll be simple enough."

Miranda smiled broadly; Naomi's attitude made her want to giggle. "I'm Miranda, then." Miranda realized quickly that this pirate lady was exceptional. The aura of good radiating from her was many times brighter than an average priest of Lexcord. Though she was wearing a revealing gown, it seemed less for others' viewing and more for her own comfort. Confidence, strength, and purpose beamed from this seemingly large but elven woman, and those characteristics helped her glimpse exactly what attracted Erk to her.

"Miranda, my dear. It's so nice to meet you. How did you end up traveling with Erk?" The pirate lady asked, her voice so rich and powerful that Miranda felt lost.

Erk winced. He worried that this would be where Naomi sent him to sleep in the depths.

Miranda responded, "About a week ago, the Church of Invictus began an assault against Port Undine under false pretenses. Our commanding high priest has now aligned himself with the usurper, and we are seeking a way to end the violence."

Erk breathed a sigh of relief. He had not asked Miranda to avoid the kidnapping conversation. Her eloquence and wisdom were straight to the point. In their brief time together, she also picked up on Erk's habits and mannerisms.

"Oh, how absolutely wonderful," Naomi replied. She then looked at Selasine and August. "And the meatheads? I'm assuming they are your bodyguards, darling?" she asked Miranda.

August started to object, "I'm August. Not really a meathead, though." His voice was a little pouty.

His protest elicited a laugh from Naomi. "No offense intended, August. Trust me, meathead is a compliment from me. Means I think I'd have to watch out for you in a fight." The way she spoke was so fluid and sweet that August blushed again.

Selasine finally added, "Bishop Selasine."

Naomi raised a brow, her elbows resting on her crossed legs. She raised her forearms to her chin, letting it rest as she looked at him. "So, you're in charge of these church people?"

Selasine shook his head, "Well, I'm Miranda's and August's teacher, but I don't have any more influence in the church."

Naomi shrugged. "I don't even want to try to untangle how Erk got himself mixed up with church people. But I do want to help Erk. So, when we get to the fortress, wait for all my servants to disperse while I prepare for travel. You can slip in through the kitchen on my wing, Erk. Nobody will notice." She bit the tip of her dagger again, Selasine surprised that he had just now realized she was armed.

Erk let out a sigh of relief. He was glad that his partner, a secretive, discreet pirate, would be able to smuggle them into the fortress without questions. Miranda watched out of the translucent curtains. She could see the market district fading to familiar hilly terrain. She saw this place only yesterday when the magic within her had gone out of control momentarily. This was the pathway up to the fortress. The final half mile was a well-manicured grove of trees that lined the path like decorative arches. She was grateful that she didn't damage this beautiful sight. A loud, grinding sound accompanied the opening of the gates that led into the fortress complex. The walls towered up at least fifty feet. Miranda was bewildered, Erk glad to see the wonder in her eyes again.

The march continued, Naomi's servants swapping out to keep the palanquin moving quickly. As they moved north, a direct approach to the fortress, Miranda was fully in awe as the complex spread out before them. A fortified keep sat in the center, with four even segments on each side forming eight wings that extended like a spider's legs from the keep. Their directions were primarily east or west, but even that impressive building paled in comparison to the beautiful palace towering behind the keep. On top of the far side of the palace sat a stronghold that spired up, possibly two hundred feet into the air. The entire complex was made of a beautiful black stone similar to obsidian, with golden accents built into the architecture. Erk and Selasine accidentally traded knowing smiles as they watched Miranda's reaction to the magnificent palace grounds, her eyes wide and lips gently parted in wonder.

As the palanquin neared the complex, it moved by the main building on the right side, passing beyond two wings connected by varying hallways. As they approached the third wing, the servants began to disperse into the complex, the hallways possibly containing living quarters or some kind of barracks. The palanquin ended up in front of the main door of the third northernmost wing on the east side of the fortress. Up close, Miranda could tell that there was a vast complex inside this wing.

Naomi stood, her dress billowing about her legs. "Remember, through the kitchen and straight to your wing." As she left the palanquin, her servants followed her into their wing's front door.

Erk waited until their eyes adjusted to the torchlight that kept the courtyards between wings lit. "Okay, follow me. Just walk with purpose. People will recognize me here, but news travels slower out than in. We're pretty well in the clear."

True to Naomi's instructions and Erk's knowledge of the palace, they entered through a kitchen into a hallway that seemed to stretch forever. Every hundred feet, there were exits into the courtyards. The hallways had many rooms built around them, quarters for the pirate nobles' servants. Miranda thought she was starting to understand the layout of the rooms, but then they stumbled into a large, dark room. It seemed massive. They turned immediately right and entered a different wing. There, she saw the rooms from before happening in reverse. She figured they had left Naomi's wing and entered Erk's. She was correct as, after they walked through a kitchen, they entered a grand hall that would have opened into the palace grounds from the front door of the complex. Since they had made a right out of Naomi's wing, Miranda realized that they had to be in the northernmost wing of the east side of the main fortress. She was momentarily sad that she didn't have a chance to see what was in the central keep of this complex in front of that magnificent onyx palace behind and above this fortified building.

"Home sweet home," Erk whispered as several magical candles lit around the grand hall of Erk's wing. Miranda had seen paintings of grand architecture before, but in front of her sat a dimly lit masterpiece. Marble columns stretched up to the roof in a pleasing order. The floor seemed to be a grand blanket of blended quartz and granite, sparkling in the candlelight with delicate designs etched into it. A beautiful marble staircase wrapped around the side opposite the front door. The kitchen entered the room between the exit on the right and the staircase on the left. "This way," he ordered, moving quickly up the marble staircase. Selasine, Miranda, and August tailed him close, not really trying to clutch their cloaks anymore. They entered a set of double doors leading into an ornate hallway with three sets of stairs on both the left and the right. The lavish purple carpet was pleasing, a look familiar to the clerics of Invictus. Candelabras kept the room warmly aglow, and Erk darted up the second set of stairs to the left. The others followed him, struggling to take in their surroundings. At the top of the stairs, Erk withdrew a key from his belt, unlocking the door before them. They entered the room, finding a massive study inside, the walls lined with books, astrological charts, and maps.

Erk skipped down a flight of twin stairs that led to a central chamber on a lower level. He slid across the floor quickly and sat in a chair with wheels affixed to the bottom. He gracefully rolled in the chair to the far side of a massive drafting desk in the middle of the room. Miranda, Selasine, and August descended the stairs to the center of the room. Magical torches sat in the walls, keeping the room dimly and safely lit. Miranda twisted her lips in thought; magical torches were a rare commodity this long after The Unbinding. The people that could create them were just as rare. She imagined that he had probably plundered them in excess from Gelidor's tributes to Gabah.

Erk bent under the desk, and Miranda noticed a couple of strongboxes beneath. Erk pulled out one that radiated an aura. Black wisping smoke permeated the air surrounding it, reacting gently to movement. Miranda had no feelings until Erk opened the box. She felt a warm presence wash over her even though the light bent to a violet aura that felt somewhat ominous. She approached the desk in the middle where Erk had opened the box. "I keep The Master's gemstone locked up here. If you touch it, you'll be able to hear The Master's voice."

Miranda scrunched her nose. "Is there any way you can introduce me? Can we touch the gemstone together?" she asked as she completed her approach. Selasine and August were immediately behind her, hustling in their heavier armor. She looked in the box at a massive shard of greenly tinted crystal. She could hold it in two hands as it would be difficult to carry. She looked at Erk for a response.

"I've . . .," he looked at the crystal, trailing off. "I've never tried bringing anybody besides Jax and Evan to meet The Master. They just touched the crystal on their own accord, and they were present with me. We can visit The Master's thoughts together."

Miranda nodded. "You go first, and I'll follow you after a minute, okay?"

Erk smiled, closed his eyes, and reached out to touch the crystal. His body stiffened as his consciousness slipped away. Miranda looked at Selasine and August. "I don't know what will happen, but I'm not really afraid. Please, don't worry, okay?" she warned.

Selasine let out a deep sigh. "I'm going to worry, and if you don't come out of there in just a few minutes, I will be right behind you. Got it?"

She gave a sheepish smile and shrugged. "This is why you're in charge, right bishop?"

He smiled. "Go figure this out, girl. I believe in you."

Her heart swelled. She knew she had made the bishop proud, and he trusted her to make good decisions. Plus, an awareness of this power within her made it easier to save herself and her companions in a dangerous situation. This was part of her destiny, and he was glad to witness it.

She reached out and touched the crystal and felt her consciousness being sucked inside. Her normal senses all failed her immediately. The world went black, and her body went numb. She heard nothing, smelt nothing, tasted nothing. After what seemed like an eternity, she felt her senses returning. Instead of manifesting in the way she expected, it felt more like she was watching herself from outside her body.

She could see Erk and watched her body approach the pirate lord. She didn't tell it to do that. Or did she? She wasn't sure, and her thoughts being disconnected from her body felt very disturbing. She heard Erk's voice, "Can you feel The Master's presence?"

She shook her head. He looked at her in disbelief. She had been so sensitive to the presence of Ezelbrecht that he was certain The Master would have elicited a similar response.

A gentle voice from the unlimited space around them spoke to them. "Don't fret, Erilkaiden. I am glad to meet another of your companions."

Miranda watched herself turn around, her perceptions opening as she did. She could finally see normally. Before her sat a strangely shaped human, his appendages much longer than expected. He levitated on an invisible cloud to further exaggerate his elongated legs and arms. Miranda had no feelings regarding this entity, but it was not how Erk had described The Master.

Erk gestured to the strange mental manifestation. "This is The Master," his thoughts rang out to hers. However, he sounded distant.

She observed what she perceived as The Master. "Why does

Erk call you master?" she asked, somewhat skeptical. She knew why, but she wanted to see the paladin that Erk had described.

The strangely shaped human stood, his image gently descending to the ground. A long beard unfurled from his chin, reaching down to his knees. As the image manifested, she could see him dressed in beautiful red royal robes. The whole illusion felt like it took hours to fully form in a way she could experience with all five senses. She no longer felt her consciousness and her vision break apart. She sighed in relief as she continued to orient herself with this plane of existence.

"You see, Miranda. The Unbinding broke magic as we knew it one hundred years ago. Almost everyone in the world awoke to a new power. Some of us were on the edge of attaining immortality. And many of us have, in some way or another, been trapped. The King of Claston sealed me in this crystal with his curse."

Miranda felt her internal resolve surge, demanding to understand this master character. She hated it when people tried to evade questions. "You didn't answer my question. I am not surprised that you already know my name, but I am annoyed because you haven't told me why your name is so revered."

The Master stretched out, his elongated arms and legs seeming to stretch on forever in this distorted reality. "I was the first person cursed by the King of Claston. My gift wasn't a new magical power. It was that I could simply cancel the magical powers of others. When the king made it illegal to use your Profoundness, as we called it then, I challenged his ruling with my ability to cancel magic. Our powers backfired together, and instead of cursing me, he simply trapped my essence in this strange dimension."

"That did not align with Erk's story," Miranda thought. Her thoughts echoed out loud in this place. She looked for Erk's presence but could not find it any longer. It felt as if he had been removed from this place. This frustrated her further, but she felt she was beginning to understand how this dimension worked. It functioned on expectation and feeling. To her, The Master might seem different. She knew then he was not what he claimed to be. She wanted to know who he was and how his agenda played into the conflict in Claston. It was the magic inside her that convinced her of this possibility. She could shape it to her will; why couldn't The Master do the same if he had such great control over this dimension?

Miranda tried to look around, but the scenery changed based on what she imagined. The only concrete images were this "Master." She noticed a flickering image of Erk had reappeared near him. The rest of this world seemed to bend and shift to her whim. She landed them in a beautiful field of flowers, the petals filling the air as deep, late summer winds rushed through the countryside, causing a rainbow of beauty to fill the air.

"I am the one who called Erk to this crusade, Miranda. And I'm the one who can help end it."

She gulped as she began to speak confidently, pretending to be in control of the situation. "Well, then, what is your name?"

The entity shrugged, the feeling hitting before the visual confirmation. "Erk heard of my rank within the Raiders of Pulhash. I am still that paladin, but I've begun to lose myself in this dimension. I've honestly forgotten my name. There have been a lot of voices whispering to me in the recent decades."

Miranda thought to herself for a moment. She found it strange that Erk would listen to the advice given to him by a person in such a bizarre dimension. She wanted to know more about what this entity had advised Erk. She probed further, "I have heard whispers too, but I'm afraid I don't fully understand their source." She did not lie entirely. The last time that she had activated her gift, the whispers made sense. But she did not fully understand whether the source was her imagination or the arcane stream. She wanted to know where the paladin Erk described was, but she suspected that it wasn't real. The truth was she wanted to know this creature's true identity.

The strangely proportioned man stretched, his arms covering all of the visual existence in this strange place. His voice replied, the sound reaching Miranda's ears before his lips began moving, "I can feel magic stirring within you. It seems drawn to you and passes through you like a river. Those whispers you hear, what do they say?"

She shook her head. She could feel Erk's blurry form watching her, remaining silent. She replied, "Well, it really depends on what's happening. They don't seem to say the same things every time. The last time I heard the whispers, I thought it might be my own wishes, but I don't think it was truly my thoughts."

The strange entity seemed contemplative. "You see, the arcane stream has a mind of its own. That's why wizards must practice spells to use incantations that manipulate the arcane stream to their bidding. The way the magic pools inside your body is likely the source of those whispers. The energy feeds on your emotions and whispers to you through the void," he responded, his voice and mouth still unsynchronized. It made Miranda uncomfortable, but her brain seemed able to make sense of this strange dimension.

She nodded, his explanation rational enough based on what they had learned from Ezelbrecht. She thought momentarily, letting the conversation change directions, "How are we supposed to stop the King of Claston?"

The being's elongated form was now wrapped around the imperceptible borders of this space. His stretched appendages grew in both density and size. "You see, Miranda, the king's gift is not a complicated spell. He places a curse on them that fuses their life energy with the arcane. A weak person will be immediately consumed by his gift. A person with a powerful life aura could survive, much like Erilkaiden's brother survived."

Miranda did not speak, but she became immediately concerned. Erk's mother had sacrificed herself to channel the pure divinity of Invictus. Her healing touch slowed the course of the curse until Miranda used her mana to pull his essence out of the stream. Whoever this was needed to be exposed outside of this dimension to reveal their true identity.

The strange entity continued. "Still, his feat seems unique among victims of the usurper. I once had a claim to the crown. I abandoned it for foolish reasons. Gelidor is unfit to rule a kingdom. The evil god of corruption brings out his dark nature." Miranda cringed with anger. She could tell this entity was reading her thoughts to say the most impactful things.

Regular people weren't this insightful; persuasive people relied on emotion more than articulated arguments. Whatever this being was, Erk and the world deserved to know.

The strange person's emotions seemed to also affect the environment. Though Miranda had chosen a field of flowers, as The Master spoke of Gelidor, the ambiance changed again. The beautiful floral field was interspersed with images of a horrifying dungeon. Instruments of torture were lined along the walls where this vision could be seen spliced between open fields of color.

"Is your life essence trapped within the arcane stream as well?" Miranda asked, her vision confused by the multiple realities happening in this dimension.

The entity became still. Miranda's perception of this place then firmly took hold. It seemed like The Master funneled his essence back into the man with stretched arms and legs, his grip on the dimension loosening as he shrank back to his relatively normal size. "I've been trapped here for one hundred years. I feel my life essence had long departed before I was cursed. In a way, only the arcane stream would sustain my life outside this realm."

Miranda would have narrowed her eyes, but this dimension made normal expression superfluous. "So does this mean you will die if I were to pull you out of this place?" She doubted "The Master's" explanation. From how Erk had told his story, it seemed like Gelidor's deal with Na'agamlor came a bit later than the beginning of The Unbinding. She started to hope her theory was correct. If she withdrew this entity from this protective dimension, its essence would disintegrate.

"It is quite possible that if somebody removes me from this place, I would simply cease to exist. But do not worry about those prospects. You see, I am resigned to my fate here inside this dimension of my own creation," he almost lamented, causing the fluid reality of this place to shift again to a dark cave with a fire pit dug into the center, a dim fire burning, shining light on the three of them.

Erk's presence grew as The Master spoke those words, and the pirate lord's voice added to the conversation. "I believe I may have found a solution to your imprisonment here, but there are still no guarantees." His voice was still weak, but Miranda no longer thought the twinkling image was her friend. She only wanted to yank this manipulative monstrosity out of this dimension and destroy it.

The fire in the cave flickered brightly. Miranda could feel The Master's curiosity increasing. "Oh, a solution? What have you found, Erilkaiden?"

Miranda saw straight through the lie. She stood tall, knowing this was her cue. "I have a unique condition, as you noticed. That magic flowing through me, I can apparently use it to bend the universe to my will." This was not deception for personal gain. Who was this terrible soul?

"So, you think there's a chance you could restore my earthly body?" the elongated man said. Miranda could feel his eyes on her essence. She tried to detect sensations of this being's intent, their very nature, but she was coming up empty. No good, no evil, just a silence where there should be sensations. Nevertheless, her intuition indicated that this entity was pure evil. The disparities between her experience and Erk's story cued her into the vile magic that constituted this creature's dimension. The silence spoke for itself. Good would have no reason to hide.

"I can try, but what would you do?" she replied. "I healed Erk's brother from the curse, and upon his return, he can no longer use his power."

"As I said, it's possible I would just cease to exist outside of this place. Those are risks that we must take to fight for what is right, aren't they?" he added, giving Miranda an uneasy feeling.

The being seemed resigned to an immediate doom outside of this dimension. She suspected the entity assumed the opposite would happen, granting it an advantage outside this strange place. "What do you think is right, then?" she asked, still trying to feel out this entity somehow.

"Well, to begin, the King of Claston has gone too far. He should answer for his crimes," The Master said.

Miranda could agree with the sentiment; however, he didn't even use the right title for the usurper. She knew without a doubt that this consciousness was reading her surface-level thoughts. She wanted to be angry on a deep level. She continued to entertain these thoughts, trying to learn about the very nature of this entity. "And?" she asked. "What about after?" her words seemed to echo in this strange reality.

"We will have no choice but to rebuild the world according to our vision. We may stumble at times, but we struggle our way forward. We are resilient, yes?"

Still unsure if she could even heal "The Master," she didn't need to weigh his words. It seemed he had a way of dodging questions, and she hated that. Erk's silence seemed different now as if he was simultaneously present and yet not present. Perhaps he was only present when The Master wanted him to be? Or maybe his ego was starting to break through this entity's control? This dimension had the same arcane stream running through it as the central plane of existence. She inhaled deeply, feeling the rich magic course through her essence and consciousness.

"I assure you, Miranda. If my earthly form can be restored, this conflict with the King of Claston will be solved within days. His curse on me was a fluke. It will never work again," the presence pleaded, sounding genuine enough.

Miranda had a sinking feeling in her stomach. Her power could be pretty unpredictable. Even though she could detect nothing from this entity, she thought it was probably the result of this strange dimension. Whoever this was, they seemed intent on sounding like they would be stopping the usurper. Though she did not believe the story articulated by The Master, she closed her eyes. She felt a righteous indignation to expose this false hero. She could feel the mana as it built inside her consciousness rather than her body. She then began to focus all of her thoughts on a single desire. Something crystal clear. For this dimension to cease and to free everyone in it. As her wish radiated through her essence, it mingled with the stores of magic pooled in her body. The false dimension began to dissolve, causing Erk's and Miranda's consciousnesses to be thrown back into their bodies.

The being within the crystal poured out into the center of the lower chamber of the study. A body began to form ten feet behind Miranda and Erk, still at the center table.

Miranda staggered backward from the crystal, barely able to orient herself with the prime dimension around her. Unintentionally, she stumbled even closer to the materializing creature, prompting August and Selasine to rush to her side. Before them stood a menacing, skeletal stranger. His elongated human body was just an illusion of the strange dimension, replaced by the reviling form of the evilest pits of magic. She suspected he was not as he seemed, and she was right. Erk, too, looked in horror as his mind had seen a completely different vision of The Master. While inside the crystal, he gave no indication that his corporeal body was a magically bound skeleton. The magics swirled within him, giving him an extremely imposing presence. Miranda had heard horror stories of these creatures that had all, thankfully, disappeared at the onset of The Unbinding. He hid his aura in that dimension because Miranda would never have agreed to release him had she known what he was.

Unwittingly, Miranda had unleashed a hideously evil lich from its own bonding crystal. This magical conduit allowed these dark creatures to practically live forever. It was a trick so complex that she was sure Erk could not have been a part of it. She choked back tears of anger as she demanded to know from The Master, "Now that you're here, have you remembered your name?"

The skull that constituted the lich's face twisted into a depraved smile. "Yes. My name is irrelevant, though. I will be the one that punishes you for your misdoings."

Miranda trembled with fear and rage. This was worse than The Master she expected, and she was sure Erk was also surprised. She had expected that she could immediately stop whatever emerged from the crystal if necessary. However, she realized that pulling this entity out of the crystal exhausted significant stores of her ether. She needed to absorb more mana from the stream to do something else fantastic. Her heart broke. She realized that her misunderstanding had put herself and her friends at risk. Selasine and August had drawn their swords. Erk's jaw rested agape. "This isn't what I expected, Master?" he asked as he drew his sword.

The Master turned a skeletal hand to Erk, open palm facing

the pirate lord. "You wouldn't have been foolish enough to free me if you had known the truth. Everything was hidden inside my crystal. You see, since I was a lich when The Unbinding happened, it simply forced my essence back into the crystal where I had left my life force centuries ago."

Miranda knew that all hope was lost regarding The Master, but she interrogated anyway. "How will you deal with the king?" she asked her hand on the hilt of her sword. August and Selasine stood close by, ready to strike.

"It's simple. I'll kill you and then him and take my rightful place. Then I will reshape the world according to my visions for the last century. A place of madness, true terrors to behold," the lich's skull facing Miranda directly, the permanent smile of death locked in its jaws.

Miranda's final insistence was more for her own sake, to build the confidence she would need to combat this evil. "Our only task is to stop the king," she added. "If he has to meet final judgment to stop him, then so be it. But the succession of heirs must be recognized—" she replied, but the lich interrupted.

"You foolish priest, do you not understand? The god you worship is young. I only respect the traditions of the ancient, the eldritch. I know secrets of this universe that go deeper than the Rift itself. I could feel the power within you; you have served me as just another pawn in my game. Now it is time for you to reap your reward. Then I will destroy Claston." Clearly, the entity from within the crystal had nothing but evil intent. "And after that, The King of Alabaster and of Gabah. I will control the world."

Miranda drew her sword, the magic around the elven blade swirling with great excitement, gold and white light flickering throughout Erk's study. "Releasing you was a mistake. May you pay for your deception!" She took a quick jab at the lich's rib cage, the magic surrounding the sword coalescing into a holy beam that should have surrounded the lich with its power.

However, a sinister light glowed within the empty eye sockets of his skull. The magic emanating from the sword was sucked inside the blackness that permeated his presence. Miranda felt a sensation unlike anything she'd ever experienced at that moment. The very life force within her seemed pulled into the blackness, a searing pain instantly spreading through her entire essence. She tried to scream, but the pain was so intense that her body would not respond. She realized what it was: the mana within her had been mercilessly torn out by the lich.

The Master spread his arms wide. "If you really need to know, girl, my name is Vortex. And I consume all that lives. Magic. Life. Nothing is safe from me. And since your life force is magic, you'll be even easier to dispose of." He began to whisper curses to unseen divinities, calling on otherworldly powers that Miranda didn't understand.

She tried to channel the mana within her body again. As it flowed through her, she felt the pain easing. Her essence was recovering. This was her chance to try out her power on her own terms. "I just want to put the lich back in his gemstone," she thought. She thought it, and she prayed it. Invictus listened, but he was confused. No prayer had ever put a lich back in a gemstone before. He, along with Erk, August, Selasine, and Vortex, watched as the study filled with a bright, purple light. The crystal in the box glowed responsively to Miranda's pleas, but the lich was unaffected. Her light faded as she did not have enough ether within her to force the universe to bend to her will.

Vortex stood tall, triumphant. "You can't just put me back. My essence is unbound, thanks to you, girl." The skeletal form grew in power the longer it remained in the central plane of existence. Miranda felt a familiar fear, like when she learned that Justin had been killed during her kidnapping. Not a fear of getting hurt, but the fear that others still would suffer for who she was. She overestimated her own ability. She felt her heart breaking again, seeing how the people she loved and had come to love were in danger due to her miscalculation. The ether flowing through her had to replenish before she could do something so incredible as force an ancient entity like this lich back into imprisonment. She would not give up. She fortified her resolve to fight.

It didn't matter, however, as his eyes flashed again, and he snuffed out the magic swirling within her a second time. This time she screamed in agony as she collapsed to the floor.

August and Selasine leaped forward, Erk stepping sideways to flank the creature. "Foolish mortals, bound to your ideals, never to rise above your short-sighted blunders. I don't think you fully understand; I could easily kill this girl," he hissed, malevolent. Squeezing his skeletal hand, the mana gushed from Miranda's body like water from a soaked rag. The tighter his hand drew, the louder her screams became.

August lashed out with a furious swing, gripping the hilt of his blade with both hands. As the weapon connected with the lich's skeletal body, the metal in August's sword began to hum. The sound was low-pitched at first, but it grew louder and more intense within seconds. After a moment, August's sword shattered. The permanent grin on the skull's face appeared especially wicked as the lich raised a hand and pointed it at August. "Pestilence, a prayer for the depraved. Sicken mine enemies. A gut-wrenching plague. May your bowels pour from your throat and your stomach burst with infection." Holding his broken sword in disbelief, August suddenly felt his stomach lurch. A horrible queasiness wracked his body, sending him to the floor.

Selasine, resolved, said a louder, more confident prayer. "May evil tremble in the face of justice. A judgment on your heart, brought by the might of Holy Invictus himself. Begone evil, never to return," he said, raising his longsword to the sky. A flash of lightning struck the blade, causing the bishop's body to be cloaked in a translucent suit of armor. His sword glowed a powerful white.

The Master's skull could express more than one emotion as the jaw and cheekbones shifted, reminiscent of a frown. Miranda lay on the floor gasping for air, and August had begun to vomit. Erk looked at the two young fighters in horror. "I called you Master because I thought you to be a wise person who followed a god similar to the one that my sister Iria revered. I had great faith in you, but you preyed upon my idealism and hope." Erk seemed to swell with emotion, the righteousness in his soul, the purity of his heart returning with a vengeance. "I had feared that you were not what you seemed. But this is worse than I could have ever predicted. I am prepared to dispose of you due to your deceit. May Invictus guide my hand, and may your sentience know judgment," he growled, indignant. A short sword flew out of a scabbard around his belt and plunged into the lich's spine, causing a distinct metal-on-metal grinding sound.

"You're not the only one I've had to deceive in my time, Erilkaiden, and you certainly will not be the last. Now, suffer for your naivete and gullibility," Vortex demanded as the skull's jaw opened widely. "Let me drink your life force, then. You're nothing more than a snack to the ancient evils within me."

Just then, a beam of light blasted the lich's body. Vortex howled in anger as the sensation of pain was something he had not felt in centuries. Turning to find the source, he saw Miranda, now on her hands and knees, looking at him with sheer determination. She closed her eyes again, feeling just enough magic swirl within her. She raised the sword Erk had given her and used it to shoot a beam of blinding white light at the lich. The second blast made the lich reel backward, howling again.

With contempt, he replied in a terrifying voice. "I guess I will just have to consume all the magic in this place to keep you down," he commented, placing his skeletal hands together. He began to chant and pray in a language that made Selasine's skin crawl. With the light surrounding himself and his blade, Selasine leaped forward at the lich, his sword crushing and splintering bones in the lich's ribcage.

The color in the lich's eyes turned from soft blue to otherworldly red. "You'll rot in the Abyss before I give up my chance to walk this plane again," Vortex warned, the colors flashing in his eyes, giving the illusion of a determined expression. This time, his anti-mana attack affected a much greater radius, sucking the light out of the torches on the walls, causing the magical weapons wielded by Erk, Selasine, and Miranda to temporarily lose their magical auras. The worst effect, however, was on Miranda. She started to scream again, but the sound was cut short. Her hair turned a snowy white color, and her body collapsed. Selasine could see the mana flowing out of her body and into the lich's aura.

In a fury unlike anything ever witnessed by gods, humans, or elves, Selasine's psyche snapped. He saw Iria and Telisi's lifeless bodies after Farzg murdered them. He could not lose another daughter. He refused to let this happen.

Invictus felt his very essence being yanked into the mortal coil.

Thomas Selasine's body began to glow a radiant purple. With a voice that seemed to echo thousands of other voices, the bond shared between souls pouring their faith into Invictus and, by extension, Selasine, he ordered, "Your days of lawlessness are at an end. Agent of chaos, this is your reckoning. With the authority of Invictus himself, I smite you into the next realm." Without another word, his sword also turned a brilliant purple. Vortex found himself unable to retaliate, the purity of the light stunning his body. As Selasine's sword connected, rivers of purple energy blasted wildly into the air, rising in myriad directions and then plummeting with extreme force into the lich. Erk heard his Master's voice, the familiar one he had gotten to know inside that gemstone, begging for his help.

Erk sneered, crawling over to Miranda and taking her into his arms. Her body was cold, and her hair a stark, bright white. She wasn't breathing, but her eyes were gently closed as if she were sleeping.

"Damn you," he growled angrily, picking up the sword he had given to Miranda. He ignored the brilliant lights from Selasine and Vortex, heading instead to the box where he had kept that crystal for many years. As he suspected, it was glowing as Vortex prepared to hide inside it again, waiting for uncounted years for another fool like Erk. As Selasine's smite obliterated the lich's body, the pirate lord began chopping the crystal furiously with the magical elven sword. Electricity arced out in every direction, shocking Erk repeatedly. But he continued demolishing the crystal, effectively destroying the magics that allowed the lich to stay bound to this realm.

"Damn you to the Abyss and back," Erk howled as he repeatedly struck the stone through the pain. Selasine stood motionless where he smote the lich.

As the magics in the crystal unraveled, Vortex felt his

consciousness departing the mortal realm. He had overplayed his hand and tried to fight while still weak. This was the fate of every lich who did not keep that ever-important card close to their chest.

At least, he thought, he was able to stop the girl.

***

Lexcord gasped and reached out to grab her brother's arm. They were there together in the primordial place. Moments ago, her brother was watching one of his paladins in battle. Suddenly, his vision was commanded by a different mortal. One of Invictus's most valued followers was in battle with a lich. The priest was in a library with three other mortals, two of them also followers of the Sword of Justice. As Invictus's vision was twisted against his will, the essence of his primordial avatar seemed to be sucked into the clouds around them. This meant the mortal world was trying to drag his avatar there. In very rare cases, calamities had unfolded so dire that a mortal could conjure the all-powerful mortal form of her brother. While walking among the mortals, the gods had to abide by the very laws of that plane of existence. In that prime plane, the center of the universe, the gods could have omnipotence at the price of mortality. While in the primordial place, they gained omniscience and omnipresence at the price of omnipotence. This was the way of the gods.

Lexcord worried that whatever was unfolding was one of those calamities that could pull Invictus out of the primordial place. If that was the case, she wanted to join him to end whatever great threat loomed over the central plane of existence. Before she could decide, his essence returned partially. Her primordial avatar shouted as he reconstituted, "Brother, what happened?"

Thunder rippled through the primordial place. Invictus's avatar seemed to blur and displace. Lexcord tried to touch his primordial form, but he was intangible. She cursed. This meant his essence had been divided between worlds. In short, somebody was borrowing Invictus's power but not his consciousness. This was a more frequent occurrence, as the threat needed only be dire enough for a mortal to be ready to sacrifice their own life essence to borrow the power of a god.

Lexcord thought intently about her brother's powerful presence in the mortal plane to conjure her own vision so she could watch the events unfold. She watched a vision in the clouds as this mortal, who she understood to be Thomas Selasine, channeled the power of his chosen god. His deeds were good, and his heart was pure. His past was filled with loss and sorrow. She understood his desperation, then, as the other mortals around him seemed to be on the verge of death in some form. A young man was suffering from a cursed contagion, an ancient prayer granted by the most primeval, unholy deities whose names were lost to the sands of time. Lexcord's essence shivered; she realized they were a significant danger if something was capable of such a dark curse. This being likely possessed powers beyond the most capable mortals' capacity to overcome and even those of some of the lesser gods.

She watched as Selasine wielded her brother's holy might to smite the ancient lich into oblivion as another mortal shattered the crystal which contained the life essence of the dark being. Then, she noted the fourth mortal here, a girl with icy white hair. She thought she recognized this girl, but something was wrong. Searching her unlimited understanding, she uncovered the memories of watching the girl bring a family back to life without any assistance from the divine.

A voice that boomed here half a month ago echoed its way through the primordial place. "I see that the arcane anomaly has had her essence expelled."

Lexcord winced, recognizing this voice to be associated with that memory. "What do you mean, interloper?"

"Hear, Silver Maiden. I mean no ill intent. It is I, Dalyn Tyrdrac, brain of the arcane. I am everywhere all at once; I am nowhere all the while. I make light of your deeds, but I have never had much respect for the gods. Sorry, I guess. You know, that girl has been making waves in the arcane stream. Everywhere she goes, it swirls around her, through her, and it expels out of her in the form of miracles beyond mortal understanding. And, based on your expression, I'm going to say beyond immortal understanding, too." The tenor of the voice was playful, but it was forceful and commanding as well. Lexcord felt unsure about the mixture of formal and casual speech patterns.

"Tyrdrac," Lexcord's essence mumbled. "You're the one who ripped open the arcane stream, aren't you? You're the mortal responsible for the chaos and death that followed in your foolish arrogance!" she shouted.

The booming presence seemed to sigh. "Yeah, I'm not really proud of that. I am hoping that girl right there is the solution to this chaos. The arcane dwells within her as her very essence. The problem is that it covers her mortal essence with a shell of sorts. Her mortal essence has been placed into some sort of stasis with the arcane energies completely drained from her."

Lexcord turned her attention back to the vision she had conjured. Thomas Selasine had used her brother's powers to demolish the lich and heal the young man from the ancient curse that wracked his body with a deadly illness. It's fortunate, she thought, that her brother's power dwelled within the man at this moment. Such a powerful curse would indeed need a god's unfiltered power to be lifted. As the priest turned his attention to the girl with white, formerly red, hair, Invictus's essence suddenly became whole in the primordial place.

His avatar shuddered for a few moments. "I hate when they do that. Mostly because it usually kills them."

Tyrdrac's voice echoed again, "Wait, he's going to die because he channeled too much of your energy? See, this is why I like you gods. The arcane can kill you for using it in so many ways you wouldn't expect; so many overly ambitious wizards meet untimely ends because of a miscalculation they made. Your people can just put it all on the line on purpose. Talk about commitment."

Lexcord's sentience experienced confusion. This Tyrdrac did not seem quite as vile as she would have anticipated. She could feel the goodness in his essence even though it seemed unwhole. She wondered what of his soul was missing and if that piece was what had been lost to the arcane stream. "That mortal will not die for this. I will not allow it. That ancient power was too much for any mortal to destroy. They surely would have risen to godhood within a century. I will use my power to restore the life he would have lost," Lexcord replied, defiant to Tyrdrac's sideways compliment.

"Ah, so it's his lucky day. Brother and sister are on the same job, and you get a second chance. Will you be so merciful if their destinies take them to a place where they must do this again?" Tyrdrac asked, incorrigible.

"Sister, Tyrdrac, the girl!" Invictus motioned to the vision that Lexcord had conjured. "What happened to the girl?"

"Relax, Invictus, her mortal essence is fine. It's just kind of sleeping for now. The mana that usually flows within her has been drained. Because it protects her through its own willpower, it took her consciousness with it. She's floating around out there, fueling people's powers that still have them," Tyrdrac explained.

"You're pontificating, dracolindin," Invictus complained, using a draconic word meaning "child of dragons."

"Well, I had to tell you so you can tell them down there. I can't really communicate with mortals. It would scramble their brains," the notoriously aloof sorcerer's voice still booming, sight unseen. It seemed like his voice was so powerful, but the way he spoke was so mortal that it pained Lexcord.

"What do you mean?" Invictus asked, his connection to Thomas lingering just enough to keep his body alive.

"They just need to take the girl to a place where the mana of the world pools and let the entire arcane stream run through her body. The bits that make up her essence will eventually come back together, and boom, she will be whole again. Back in action," Tyrdrac replied, his excitement reverberating around the primordial place.

Invictus felt antagonistic to Tyrdrac's tone. "You really have outdone every mortal in existence, you know," Invictus complained. "You ripped into the very fabric of the universe just for the chance to say you dined with the gods. And much to your disappointment, we don't have feasts here. Your hopes and dreams are spoiled, no doubt?"

The shrug could be felt much in the same way as the sigh earlier. "You know, I was trying to push the limits of mortal power, and I succeeded. The lives that have been lost, their blood is on my hands. But once this period of history has ended and the arcane is whole again, the world will need a person like me to help rebuild society. It's the only way to atone for my crimes against the world."

Lexcord frowned. While Invictus's work was primarily done among humans, elves, and occasionally dwarves, her work extended to all the peoples of the central, universal plane. Many others had suffered chaos and fear due to The Unbinding. He needed to recognize that his shortsightedness had been far more costly than he acknowledged. "You understand that the potential of your good deeds is severely overshadowed by the damage you've caused to reality itself?"

There was the sensation of a nod. "Yes, I know this. Which is why I must use the wisdom and power I've acquired by fusing with the arcane to prevent a new era of chaos from unleashing once the stream is whole again," Tyrdrac replied.

"So, you think you can repair the fabric of the universe then?" Lexcord asked.

"Yes, and I think that girl is the key. I can't explain it yet, but her unique qualities make her the perfect vessel for the arcane. You must let the mortals down there know she's still alive. From what they currently see, she's effectively dead. If they do any corpse-burning, that would be really bad. Her essence would have no body to return to. We'd be lucky if the power she holds would restore her body, but I don't know how that would work. And I really don't want to test it out."

The goddess of truth, beauty, and goodness and the god of justice, order, and law agreed. "Then we shall make our will known to our faithful. They need to go where the mana pools and take Miranda's body there. She is still alive and must be left whole to return whole," Invictus clarified with the arcane entity of Dalyn Tyrdrac.

Tyrdrac approved. "You know what, that is perfect. I wouldn't have said it in those words, but I'm sure your followers will expect you to speak a certain way. It's like a dress code but for your words. I like you, god and goddess, but you are far more uptight than is necessary."

The deities grimaced. He really wouldn't enjoy the dress codes. His spirit was rebellious, but his personality was fun. Invictus was generally stoic, and it took something exceptional to make him relax. Lexcord was relieved that the person who had ruined the world as everyone knew it was not a malicious person. Dalyn was fascinated that the gods and goddesses experienced true, genuine emotion. This is what it meant to dine with the gods.

Invictus reached within his consciousness and began to channel his thoughts to Thomas. Lexcord imbued those thoughts with her healing grace, restoring his life force enough so that when Invictus departed, Thomas would not perish. Invictus wanted to tell him the truth, but after his stunt against the lich, his divine energy could easily overwhelm the little life force left within him after Lexcord's intervention. These words would probably reach him in his dreams or through the dreams of the young men who were close to the girl. He wouldn't let anything happen on that plane that would do the girl any more harm. If there was a chance that she could repair the universe, she was a treasure beyond understanding.

Lexcord shared his sentiment. She channeled her essence deep within the mortal realm. She reached out to Erilkaiden and Evanthalus, specifically, two elves close to her heart that she knew were connected to Miranda. Invictus had her other companions within his folds. They would be more likely to experience the dreams intended for them and be able to remember them the next day. She hoped to improve the odds that the mortals would understand the situation, and Lexcord's special position among elves would allow her to reach them despite the condition of their faith.

Tyrdrac gave out a deep sigh of relief. "Look, I'm glad we can work together. I hope you realize that you can trust me. I really didn't intend to wreck the entire universe. To make it worse, I don't have a body right now. I'm one for theatrics, but even I don't like being a disembodied imposing voice. Just make sure they can find where the mana pools. Leave the girl there for a bit. Right? She'll get better."

Invictus breathed a sigh of uncomfortable relief. He was concerned about their divine message reaching their followers quickly enough. He was willing to go into the mortal realm to protect her at this point. He hoped Selasine would hear his voice and get Miranda to a sacred place. He needed to do some research himself. He began to dive into the information of the universe, and he went deeper than usual into the primordial representation of knowledge. Every discovery, thought, memory, or idea of consciousness was kept here in the primordial place in an infinite pool of green, viscous liquid. That pool of knowledge rested beneath the clouds that seemed to be tangible yet permeable at the same time. His avatar sank into the clouds and immersed in the green substance. He began to swim, focusing on the knowledge he needed. He kept repeating, "Where does the mana pool in the mortal realm?" As his thoughts echoed through this place, a vision coalesced in a bubble formed in this liquid environment. Inside, he saw a beautiful solisberry tree blossoming, the petals on the tree shining purple in the summer sun. Solisberry trees, however, were exceptionally rare. Their leaves were said to be made of the very essence of magic itself, and wizards used to seek them to enhance their arcane prowess. This tree sat atop a magnificent towering spire in the northern parts of the world. The mountains beneath this towering rock formation were covered with snow. Above this site, the stars seemed close enough to touch. Shooting stars blasted freely from this vantage, even the smallest specks of dust igniting visibly from there.

The god of justice whispered, "The Astral Spire."

Chapter 16
The Pirate Lords of Yendralia

rk carried Miranda in his arms, her cold, lifeless body limp. Selasine walked before him, his connection to Invictus feeling completely severed now. He felt extremely fatigued, as if he had nearly expended his entire life essence. Honestly, he was surprised that he still lived. Still, he was alive, and the only thing that interested him at this moment was figuring out a way to undo the dark magics that had rendered his precious acolyte's body lifeless. She had no physical injuries; surely, someone wise in the ways of magic would find a way to fix this. August walked behind them, still reeling from the curse that Vortex had placed on him. Selasine's healing touch had gotten him well enough to walk, but his vision was still blurry, and every few moments, waves of nausea wracked his stomach. He did his best to hold onto walls, railings, and tables to keep up with his mentor and the pirate.

Selasine descended a couple of flights of stairs and entered the main hall of the fortress. This place looked like a massive ballroom, with towering ceilings obscured by the darkness, stretching over fifty feet into the air. The windows were tall, gothic stained glass, the kind of artistic beauty that would have captivated Miranda for days. The moonlight that poured through them seemed especially eerie. Erk directed him down another flight of stairs that put them on the ballroom dance floor. The floors were marble, checkered tile that gave the illusion of a massive Xanadu board. In the center was a large, octagonal table. The pirate lord moved ahead of Selasine as they stepped onto the main floor of the ballroom, rushing to that table and placing Miranda on it. With a wild fury in his gray eyes, he said to Selasine as he ran toward the far side of the ballroom, "Just stay close to her; help is on the way."

Erk disappeared into the darkness. The everburning torches that sparsely lined the walls were not bright enough to keep such a massive, open room well lit. The beautiful, dark architecture of this building devoured even the brightest moonlight. It had not been an hour since they arrived at the Fortress of Lords, the night air still hanging thick over Yendralia. The bishop walked calmly to the table, taking Miranda's hand in his. He held it tightly, fighting back the urge to weep. He looked at the girl's lifeless face and felt his heart breaking. He could have blamed Erk for this, but he knew better. Miranda had made a decision in that crystal, one he didn't understand. Not even the Council of Four could have stood against the evil that was Vortex. Together, they had crushed an ancient wickedness, meaning that Miranda's legacy was already that of a magnificent heroine. But Selasine would not let her story end here. He couldn't bear the thought of a future without Miranda.

As the bishop stood with her, a loud, clamoring bell echoed throughout the complex. August, who was just now descending the staircase from the second floor overlooking the ballroom floor, looked around in the dim light, alarmed. Selasine noticed his confusion, trying to call out to him over the din of the bells, "Don't worry, I think Erk did that."

August stopped at the bottom of the stairs to sit, feeling a queasy sensation stop him in his tracks again. Selasine worried about him, too, because the full power of Invictus himself only managed to lessen the severity of the curse rather than curing it outright. As the ringing of the bells began to decrease, Erk appeared from the shadows again.

"What in the Abyss was that?" August called across the room, rising to his feet again, the bells still echoing in his nauseated brain.

"I've announced my official return. This should convene the pirate lords that are present," Erk replied, rejoining Selasine at the table as August walked over, lethargic.

Selasine nodded. He had never once aligned himself with pirates in his almost forty years of adventuring. At this point, with his connection to Invictus severed, he would take any help necessary to restore Miranda. In his mind, this was a fight much more significant than mere law and order against the forces of evil and chaos. This was about a man's ability to protect his daughter.

A few minutes passed in silence before a bright light emerged from the doors that led to Naomi's wing of the Fortress of Lords. As a handful of people entered, they brought brighter torches with them, placing them in the braziers to the side of the door to their wing. The new light brightened that side of the ballroom, making it much easier to see. Tall marble columns stretched into the darkness, the roof towering so far above that it was still invisible. The checkered marble sparkled white and black in the brighter light. From behind the entourage, Naomi emerged. She was now dressed in a chainmail corset with a captain's jacket draped around her shoulders. A tricorn hat adorned her head, her silver locks spilling down her shoulders. She wore a tight pair of leather pants with several belts wrapping around in expected and unexpected places. The three belts on her hips had several holsters, scabbards, and pouches. Four belts were wrapped around her thighs to support fine leather bandoliers full of stiletto-style throwing daggers. The hilts of several flintlock pistols protruded from the holsters on her belts. She looked ready to go to war.

As Naomi descended the staircase, another door to a

different wing opened. A massive figure crouched through the doorway, and as they emerged, they were easily ten feet tall. Selasine felt a moment of shock as he realized that this pirate lord was a cyclops. A single eye sat in the center of his face, but the inhuman maw was more disturbing. His jaw hung slightly in his relaxed state, revealing rows of cruel, sharp teeth. His head was shaved clean except for a greasy, dark green topknot. His ears were slightly pointed, and he carried a brilliant, massive torch in his oversized hands. Erk whispered to Selasine, "Great. Dread Pirate Lord Oorzgo. Not going to be helpful."

Oorzgo placed his torch in a brazier that sat on the rounded porch in front of the southernmost wing on the west side of the keep. He was dressed in a leather vest that looked like it could have weighed three hundred pounds. His pants were studded leather combat pants with pouches, pockets, and sheaths built into them. His size alone made him combat-ready with whatever he had tucked into the many hiding places in his pants. Selasine grasped that this was the kind of pirate he would enjoy bringing to justice.

Naomi approached the octagonal table, her expression shifting from casual to worried. "Oh, Erk, what happened to Miranda?" She rushed to the girl's side, placing a hand on her cheek, then on her neck. Naomi's expression became terrified as she looked to Erk for a response.

He shook his head as he responded, "Terrible, foul magic. She is not a normal human but the daughter of two dragons trapped as humans in The Unbinding. Magic flows through her body differently than ours. The Master was a lich all along, deceiving all of us. Our brave bishop here saved our physical bodies. I destroyed its soul. But not before," Erk paused, choked up by his anger and frustration. "Not before he managed to drain all of the mana from Miranda's body."

Selasine continued to hold Miranda's hand, and Erk shifted uncomfortably. August was sitting on the floor beside his mentor, actively trying to avoid vomiting again. The pirate lady pursed her lips, thinking, touching Miranda's striking white hair. She felt how cold the girl's body was. If she was dead, her body would have still been warm unless she had frozen to death. In that case, she'd be colder than she was. This was definitely a magical condition of some kind. She cooed, optimistic, "Well, it looks bad, but not as bad as I thought."

Erk leaned against the table, his face hovering close to the edge of the tall table without needing him to bend. Naomi towered over him at over six feet tall, taller than even August. Oorzgo descended the stairs as well, his monstrous expression obviously annoyed. "Wha's the meanin' of 'is," he grumbled, taking only a few strides to reach the table in the center of the ballroom floor. "Who 'at whi' haired girly?" he questioned, pointing to Miranda.

Erk said, "She's why I've announced my official return to Yendralia."

Oorzgo slapped his stomach, a haughty cackle as he retorted, "Now you's back, which means we's gonna fi-tuh'"

Erk frowned, "Don't bother, Oorzgo. I need the advice of the pirate nobles. I hope there are more here than just you two, no offense."

Naomi rolled her eyes but did not comment. Selasine realized that Oorzgo was too dense to interpret that as an insult. As the pirate lords congregated at the table, a voice responded to Erk's comment, "Never fear, Dread Pirate Lord Erk. Pirate Lord Ut'wah the Magnificent will vanquish your foes." Selasine helped August stand as the waves of nausea began to lessen significantly. They turned their attention to the southernmost overlook on the east side. There stood an orc of large stature. His skin was a rich obsidian hue. As a pirate, he was known for his shared tendencies with Erk. They both typically only targeted corrupt, wealthy institutions.

He bounded down the stairs gracefully, Selasine impressed with his agility. He wore a captain's jacket and a hat like Naomi. Black hair spilled out from under the hat, barely reaching Ut'wah's shoulders. Underneath his jacket, he had on sophisticated leather armor and chaps. An overwhelming sword was strapped to his back. Selasine's stature still seemed small next to Ut'wah, but he was not quite as overwhelming as the ten-foot cyclops. Ut'wah towered at seven and a half feet, the sword on his back easily six feet long. Selasine nodded with interest as he realized that the pirate had a holy symbol draped around his neck, that of his own god's sister, Lexcord. He wasn't surprised that some crusades called for a deity who was laxer with the rules than Invictus. Lexcord would certainly aid a pirate if his heart was pure and his quest one that helped the most vulnerable. Corrupt nobility, cutthroat merchants, and unjust magistrates often found their judgment at the hands of Lexcord's followers rather than those of Invictus. Selasine winced at the irony; there always seemed to be a priest of Lexcord nearby to clean up the messes left behind by the clergy of Invictus. In this case, it was both a systemic and individual mess: Carulus having started this whole ordeal with Miranda and Selasine allowing the girl to come to harm. Selasine would bear the shame and was glad to see a fellow believer in justice, even if their methods differed.

Selasine noticed that another door had opened, and torches had been placed in braziers beside the door to the third hall north on the west side. An elven woman a little taller than Erk descended the staircase that led to her wing's overlook. She wore black robes, and her hair was a purple so deep it looked like moonlit waves in the ocean. A broad-brimmed, pointed hat rested on her head lightly, and the robes billowed as she casually trotted down the stairs. Erk looked happy to see her. She spoke in a harsh voice, "Erilkaiden, you fool. A sea witch treasures her rest as much as her plunder. Why have you brought outsiders to the Fortress of Lords?"

Nonetheless, Erk seemed relieved. "Sorry to trouble you, Dread Pirate Lady Lascha. I have officially returned to Yendralia, and I seek the counsel of my fellow pirate nobles." Selasine tried not to judge based on appearances, but this pirate lady seemed to carry a dark aura. He was now further troubled by his lack of connection to Invictus. A simple prayer for knowledge could provide so much information on this dark character, but he couldn't even remember the words right now. It almost felt like the knowledge had left him when he lost his connection to his god.

"You've made assumptions again, Erilkaiden. What makes you think I even want to help a crusading whelp like you?" she scorned. Selasine then noticed a shadowy raven perched on the elf's shoulder. It blended into the darkness of her robes. It flapped excitedly as she taunted Erk, the bird nearly knocking off Lascha's hat. The pirate lady took a moment to correct it, then gave Erk an evil smile.

Erk sighed. She always used his elven name even though he insisted she shouldn't. He didn't understand, but he enjoyed the formality. It felt like she did not consider him an ally, which was probably for the best. Still, Ut'wah was wise and reliable, and Lascha's esoteric knowledge might prove helpful. "You are correct, Ashilascha. I have made assumptions. But the situation is dire, and any help you can provide will be greatly compensated."

Lascha's lips twisted from an evil smile to a curious, interested face. "Now you're speaking the right language."

Erk explained to the two new arrivals what he had described to Naomi. Ut'wah looked perplexed. He was also concerned about August. Though he was starting to feel much better, he still looked pale and ill. Ut'wah whispered a healing prayer that eased the nausea but left the lingering pain. He turned to Miranda and began to whisper prayers to Lexcord for information. He gripped his holy symbol, an elaborate war hammer trinket crafted in the style of the weapon favored by Lexcord's faithful.

"This girl is still alive, somehow, but her life force feels scattered," the pirate priest explained.

August winced through the pain, "Is there a prayer for something like that?" he asked Selasine and Ut'wah.

Selasine started to shake his head, and Ut'wah shrugged. Selasine spoke first, "Based on what Ezelbrecht and the lich said, her life force is somehow connected to the arcane stream."

Ut'wah looked deep in thought as Lascha interjected. "My understanding of the arcane is somewhat limited. The eldritch entities of this universe provide all power necessary to bend the waves and winds to one's will. Still, the arcane allows one to change reality itself."

The way she spoke was too ambiguous to guess the source of her power. Selasine cursed in his mind. Lascha waved her hand over Miranda's face, gliding over her chest, then back up. "She seems to be one with the universe," she commented. "You need to draw her essence out from within the universe."

Ut'wah agreed. Naomi added, "I told you, Erk. You should trust my instincts more." She grabbed his shoulder and pulled him close to her, a casual, gentle hug.

Erk grimaced but was pleased that most theories pointed to a solution, even if that still eluded them. Erk asked, troubled, "How do we gather somebody's essence and put it back?"

Nobody spoke immediately. Selasine, growing extremely weary, finally broke the silence, "Perhaps this is a topic best relegated to rested minds. If we are sure she is alive, we must make her whole again."

Erk was impatient and wanted solutions, but he also realized the stunt Selasine pulled earlier was a once-in-a-lifetime feat. August was in no condition to continue fighting for information, either. He had to see to a festival, anyway. Surely, the ringing fortress bell would rouse Jax, Evan, and Shalo. They would report right away, he was certain. He had missions for them. His own exhaustion was starting to catch up to him. His hands were blistered and aching from the electrical burns he endured while destroying the lich's magical refuge. Selasine was correct. The other lords and ladies could get back to their own diversions. He was fortunate that Ut'wah and Lascha were both here.

"Very well, my return is announced. I will retire to my wing while waiting for my officers to report. A festival will follow," Erk promised, his voice sounding monotone and withdrawn. Selasine wanted to be angry, but he could only feel sadness. Miranda sympathized with Erk so deeply. His story must have been one moving tale. Plus, Selasine still had questions about his sister. There were too many similarities for it to be coincidental. The bishop understood that Erk was simply too impatient to sit still. He, on the other hand, could barely keep his eyes open.

The other pirate nobles, satisfied, quickly withdrew to their respective wings. Erk showed August and Selasine to a series of opulent guest rooms in his wing, decorated with the finest silks, furs, and artwork. Selasine collapsed in exhaustion on the bed, asleep before he could change out of his armor. August kept a bucket close to his bed and fell asleep praying fervently. Erk sat at the small desk in his quarters on the floor above the guest rooms, having placed Miranda on a lounge nearby. He was honestly encouraged by the unusually cool temperature of her lifeless shell. Naomi's instincts were correct, and he would do well to listen to his beloved and closest ally. He hoped she would still accompany them on whatever the next step in this ordeal would be. He was certain that she would. One of the reasons Erk had fallen for her was her tenacity in fighting for an extremely noble cause. As a pirate lady, she and her fleet exclusively targeted slavers and went to great lengths to return freed people to their homes. She was extremely protective of the girls, and her flagship, *The Violet Blur*, was an all-woman crew. He estimated that her reaction earlier resulted from that protectiveness over any young woman in trouble. Her heart was so admirable, and he loved her dearly for it. Erk just wasn't sure what she saw in him anymore.

A half-hour passed, and nobody reported for duty. After an hour, Erk began to pace, worried about his officers. At the two-hour mark, there was a triple tap of something metallic on the door to his suite. He didn't bother to check who was waiting outside; he simply threw open the door. Evan and Shalo stood there, looking like they had just rolled out of the deepest sleep.

"Where in the Infernia have you been?" Erk cracked, his impatience tangible.

"Sorry, brother, I could hear the bells in my dreams but could not stir. I could see the strangest vision as I tried to tear myself from my sleep. I could see such a strange place, a tree among the stars," Evan complained and explained.

Erk tilted his head in curiosity. "A vision that held you captive?" he asked.

Shalo shrugged, "Me feelin's not quite the same, but I couldn't wake either. Ya know, I had a dream that we crashed ashore in the Glacier Gulf. It was eerie real, I tell ye. It's not sittin' well on me, even now."

Erk redirected the conversation, "Never mind that now. I've announced my official return. Take the chest full of platinum in the treasure hold. We will scatter it from the pavilion in the marketplace. Send word for me when everything is in place so that I can make an early morning statement."

Evan nodded; Shalo gave a salute. "Very well, brother. We'll see to it," Evan assured Erk.

Erk felt drained, but he could not rest. He started perusing the books on his shelf, beginning with dreams, specifically, the type capable of holding one's consciousness hostage. He poured through the tomes for two more hours before a messenger rapped his door and announced himself officially. "Dread Pirate Lord Erk, a message from Evan. All is ready for you in the marketplace."

He closed the tome and gathered his things. He slipped out the door, the messenger waiting to be dismissed. Erk locked the door tight behind him. He dismissed the messenger and went downstairs to the guest rooms, leaving a copy of his suite key tucked into Selasine's armor. This way, he could check on Miranda if he awoke while Erk was away. He hustled from the Fortress of Lords down to the marketplace with a swift stride. He found the pavilion, a central structure where speakers could address the crowds with plenty of room to gather around. There was a crowd even now, still an hour before dawn. News about the bells ringing at the Fortress of Lords traveled quickly. Erk muscled his way through the crowd until most onlookers recognized him. The people parted before him, giving him room to bound up the steps of the large pavilion. He stepped up to a platform, gesturing to Evan and Jax to begin.

The crowd grew quiet with anticipation. This pavilion was one of the most permanent constructions in Yendralia, made out of weighty granite. The sound emanating from the platform on the pavilion could echo easily with the right vocal projection. Erk spoke deeply and confidently, "Citizens of Yendralia, enjoy the spoils of your favorite Radiant Light. I wreak havoc on the King of Claston to retaliate for his misdeeds against the common people. Here, take what is your cut of the spoils. The finest platinum plundered from the king's treasure ships. May you gorge and feast and drink until the world turns black. Buy that thing you want; buy that thing you need. Those displaced by the usurper need your patronage. Go, spend. Remember, Erk the Radiant is your servant!" The crowd cheered as Erk's officers began to toss and scatter coins of platinum from the extravagantly sized chest. They tossed handfuls in the air and gave handfuls to people close by. Between the ways to share in the bounty, on average, people took a modest quantity of platinum before dispersing. In some ways, they realized that platinum's value would probably temporarily drop, but that did not concern them much. Some could spend their currency before the market had time to respond, so they left quickly.

Erk stepped down from his pedestal. He looked to his brother and Jax, "See to it that this is the wildest party since Naomi's return last year."

Jax gave an affirmative nod, realizing he would be the star of this party. Erk was likely caught up in something bigger than himself again. The first officer didn't mind it, as moments like these are why he became a pirate.

"Off so soon, brother?" Evan interjected.

"I have to help the girl," Erk barked, eager to return to the fortress.

"I owe her my life. Is there something I can do?" Evan replied gently. He wasn't sure what had happened, but he immediately worried for Miranda. She had saved his life, and he knew she was a pure, kind soul. He wanted to help his brother with the real issue, not throw a party.

"You spoke of a strange dream. I was researching messages through dreams, and your visions may have meaning. What was it that you saw?" Erk interrogated.

Evan shook his head, "Like I said earlier. I could see some sort of tower; it seemed made of natural stone but raised and shaped deliberately. As the dream carried me around, I could feel that this formation had an unbelievable height. I felt like I would fly away from the surface of our plane. When gravity failed me, I could see the top of that tower. On it sat a tree with the most beautiful purple blooms. I could see Miranda there, resting underneath the tree."

Erk breathed a deep sigh. "Why didn't you mention her earlier?" he responded anxiously, somewhat frustrated.

"Moshirote!" he replied, shocked at his brother's tense mood. "Calm down. It took a bit for the full weight of the vision to take root in my memory. Our main task was to get this done," he objected. "Please, brother. What is going on with

Miranda? Why is this dream of such interest to you?"

The pirate lord nodded. "Apologies, brother. Have you ever heard of a place like the one in your dream?"

Evan shook his head. "Nah, didn't seem possible or real."

Erk let out a deep sigh. "You've not given me much to go on, but I'll see what I can find. Evan," he began. "Miranda is extraordinary. She healed The Master, but he was a lich."

Evan's eyes widened, "Is that so?" He looked pensive for a moment. He had met The Master before as Erk sought a cure, but he had no memories that he could articulate of the strange dimension in the crystal. "Did the lich hurt Miranda?"

Erk nodded, his anxiety high. "He drained her essence, but she can recover. Please, follow me to the fortress. Stand watch over the guest rooms. Find me in my study if the bishop or the boy stir. They, too, were severely injured fighting that abomination. I will be reading." The resolve in his voice was the same as when he sought a cure for his brother. "Come, moshirin."

Evan nodded this time, following his brother to the fortress. Erk quickly tucked himself inside his study, researching symbols in dreams, including trees with vivid purple blooms. Evan hung out in the hallways beneath Erk's quarters to wait for signs of life. Evan himself dozed for a while in the chair at the end of the hallway when he heard the clicking latch of one of the doors. A moment later, August emerged from the room he had stumbled into with his bucket. "Who are you?" the young man asked.

"I'm Evan, friend. Brother of Erk. He's busy looking for clues about Miranda's condition," the pirate replied.

"Can I see her?" August asked, blunt.

"Of course," Evan replied, showing August to Erk's study up the stairs in the central corridor. The same place where a curse almost caused August's own body to destroy him. He shuddered, but he fought the trauma. They approached Erk, who had fallen asleep on the large central table in the study. Fragments of the soul crystal that Erk had destroyed were strewn about the room. Several books lay open underneath the sleeping pirate lord.

"Brother!" Evan whispered. Erk mumbled, but he did not

stir.

"Hey, Erk? It's me, August." Erk's hand wiggled and then flailed.

"He seems restless. This reminds me of how I felt when he announced his return, and I found myself trapped in my sleep," Evan explained, hesitating to wake Erk earnestly.

They waited for a few moments while Erk continued to sleep. August started looking over the books the pirate lord had strewn about on the desk. He started to see references to a pillar of light that used to guide ships in the northern oceans. He noticed recipes that involved a variety of blue and purple tree blossoms. He felt a shudder of familiarity run through his body and began to remember his own dream. He could see snow-capped mountains with a spire shining brightly above them. It reached so high into the heavens that it seemed otherworldly. August realized that Erk was already one step ahead of them. Surely the gods sympathized with their plight. August could feel the presence of Invictus flowing through him. A moment later, Selasine entered the study. The bishop did not look like he had rested, still drained from channeling the full force of the divine.

"Forgive me. I was too weak to resist the call of sleep. A lapse in discipline, nothing more," Selasine apologized as he approached August, Evan, and Erk at the table.

"Looks like Erk tired himself out, too," August mentioned, gesturing to the nearly comatose pirate lord.

Evan cleared his throat. "He seemed troubled by a dream that I had," he commented, looking at the books haphazardly open on the table.

Selasine gave him a curious look but recognized him thanks to Erk and Iria. He was likely the youngest of the Lancethinas siblings, Evanthalus. "Are you Erk's brother?" the bishop asked.

Evan gave a somber nod. "Evanthalus Lancethinas at your service," he replied. "And I take it that you," he pointed to the acolyte, "are August. And you are Bishop Selasine," he finished, only able to manage a half-smile.

Selasine scratched his chin. "Most certainly, we are. Well met, friend." He felt affection for Iria's youngest brother, as she always spoke kindly of him. However, Evan wasn't the one that kidnapped his pupil, so it was a little easier to feel positive, familial emotions toward him. Based on Erk's reaction to this ordeal, Selasine started seeing Erk's heart. These were his brothers-in-law, and it felt right in his heart to have met them this way. After a moment, he clutched the holy symbol that draped his neck, tucked away behind his flowing beard. Though faint, he could feel his god's presence again. He breathed a deep sigh of relief. He hoped his desperate move had not permanently cut the link between him and Invictus. "Was it a dream or a vision?" Selasine asked, returning the conversation to the matter at hand.

Before Evan could respond, Erk stirred a bit, causing the other three to shift their attention to the rousing pirate lord. Erk sat upright, staring at the books in front of him.

"Is it morning already?" Erk mumbled, wiping his eyes.

August chuckled, having said that before in much more unflattering circumstances. "The sun makes its journey through the sky," he commented, looking out one of the windows in the study at the morning light cast over the island. The illness in him seemed to have run its course. The divine healing provided by Invictus through Selasine's body had made the worst of it subside, and in the five hours after the battle, he had mostly recovered.

"What are you researching?" Selasine asked.

"Evan mentioned a dream earlier," Erk explained, motioning to his brother. "He could see Miranda under a tree with purple blooms."

Selasine tilted his head curiously. "And this was before he learned what had happened here?"

Evan nodded affirmingly, casting a pained glance to Miranda, whom Erk had brought from his private quarters to the study, placing her on a sofa butted up against one of the bookshelves. Selasine and August moved from the central desk to the sofa, rechecking the girl.

"Still cold," August mentioned.

Selasine felt his heart thumping with rage again. Her coldness reminded him of his previous failure as husband and father. He would not let Miranda meet an icy fate. The desperation swelled within him, but he wasn't sure where to begin.

"Do you think that his dream has significance, then?" Selasine turned back to the center of the room to ask.

Erk tilted his head down, looking carefully at Selasine. "Right now, every anomaly is worthy of scrutiny. Bishop, did you have any dreams? Visions? Any clues?"

"Nothing. I dreamt nothing," Selasine explained.

"Unfortunate. I thought maybe Evan's dream was a clue. Shalo also had a dream about shipwrecking in the Glacier Gulf. I wonder if the two dreams are connected," Erk questioned optimistically.

"Do you think that this is worthwhile? Should we seek the advice of another mystic or a former wizard?" Selasine inquired.

"That won't be necessary," he gestured to the books on his table. "It's been almost a century, but there was once a time that I bent the arcane to my own will. I used to be a wizard myself," the pirate lord replied.

"Is that how you're so comfortable in a library?" August asked, peering at the shelves, lost.

Erk nodded while Selasine stood in silent disbelief. This was another confirmation, as Iria had mentioned her brothers were wizards before The Unbinding. The timing couldn't be worse, but Erk and Evan both needed to know the truth about their sister.

"I had a dream," August added. "Do you think it would be helpful?"

Erk's attention snapped up from the books, "Was this the kind of thing that held you in your sleep against your will?"

August shook his head. "No, but it felt like some of the best sleep I've ever gotten."

Erk's lips twisted in thought. "Well, what happened in your dream?"

The young acolyte explained, "I could see snow-covered mountains and some kind of stone lighthouse. The lighthouse was taller than any building in the world. It seemed to stretch up to the stars."

Erk drummed his fingers on his chin. He started to worry

that this dream angle was too scattered to make sense of. He closed his eyes but could not remember if he had just had a vision or a dream. With Selasine already lacking any revelation, Erk now felt as if he were grasping at straws. Sighing, he closed the book in front of him.

August approached the table and took the tome that referenced the shining spire. "It was kind of like this, but way bigger."

Erk nodded, reading over the page. "That's the Astral Spire. It's famous for guiding ships in icy, northern waters. Nobody ever sails that far north anymore, though."

"Is it known for anything else?" Selasine asked.

"Not really, no. It's quite an enigma. I'm afraid these dreams might not be useful clues," Erk lamented.

Evan, who had been looking over the books on the table the entire time, asked, "What about Shalo's dream? He specifically mentioned the Glacier Gulf. That's in the north, the same as the Astral Spire, right?" he asked, not wanting his brother to give up.

Erk nodded, grabbing an older map from under a different book. "It is, but look," he pointed to the Glacier Gulf on the map, then to a mark that indicated the Astral Spire. "The two are almost fifty miles apart. Plus, there aren't many people in that part of the world. Who are we supposed to ask? I apologize for raising our hopes, but this does not seem like a fruitful inquiry. Let's find more books about magical conditions that cause a body to die without death," he ordered, collecting the books he had scattered about.

The four of them poured over every relevant title in the study. After about two hours of research, Naomi joined them, still dressed in her combat gear. As she entered Erk's study, he grumbled, "Who let you in?" Though he emulated a grumpy tone, it was obviously playful.

She grinned and held a ring of keys on one of her numerous belts. "My darling, you forgot that you gave me a key? I'm heartbroken," she said deadpan.

Erk wanted to smile but couldn't. "You wouldn't happen to have any titles relating to magical comas, would you?" he asked, frustrated.

Naomi gave a weak smile. Reaching into her pack, she withdrew a text titled *The Arcane Stream: Particles, Light, and Physics*. "If the girl's life essence is essentially magic, maybe there will be some clues in these texts?"

Erk exclaimed, "That's it! We've focused too much on the solution and not on the nature of the problem. Naomi, this is why I'm going to marry you," an encouraged smile back on his lips.

Naomi rolled her eyes, "I was just trying to be helpful, not propose again." She sounded annoyed, but she looked pleased.

The five of them spent the entire day reading and researching with the cooperation of the other pirate lords. They looked at every tome, scroll, and book they could find in the Fortress of Lords. Erk, in particular, seemed intent on finding answers and finding them now.

As evening set upon them, Erk called for a messenger. He gave orders for dinner to be served in the study. Selasine, a formerly studious pupil, agreed. August didn't groan, but he would have if the stakes were different. Evan and Naomi were concerned for Erk, as they knew he could be intense, but they had never seen him so determined in the face of futility.

Night settled over Yendralia again. Evan retired to his quarters, taking some books with him. August did the same. Miranda's body continued to rest on the sofa in the study. Naomi had fallen asleep on a different sofa, flanking the center with two sleeping beauties.

Selasine thumbed through a text about how the tides affect the flow of the arcane. "You really are concerned about Miranda, Erk. I can feel it."

The pirate lord let out a deep breath. "Yes. This is my fault, and I intend to correct my error. When I was a young elf, I began the study of magic, which was the norm for our family. The girls all grew up to be priestesses, and the boys all grew up to be wizards. I was almost forty when The Unbinding crushed everything I had worked for. It wasn't a total loss," he commented, holding his hand up and watching intense flames cover his hand. "I found that my ability to bend the stream had been replaced by the ability to concentrate the full fury of the sun's light. It was more powerful than any fireballs or lightning bolts I could use the day before. I was sad but not crushed,"

Selasine listened in silence, his eye intently watching Erk as he narrated.

"When I was seventy, my sister left Claston. She was broken inside by the cruelty of the war waged by the usurper Gelidor. She helped me hurt so many people, and even though they were servants of Na'agamlor, her heart still broke for them. I haven't seen nor heard from her since that day," the pirate lord continued, pausing momentarily. "Miranda gave me back my brother. I owe her my life. She even reminds me of my sister, some."

"Do you know where she went?" Selasine asked, interrupting.

"Iriliandria? No, sadly. She was convinced our family could find salvation in distant lands in the east or north. The rest of us that were left by then stayed to fight the usurper. Mother, brother, and I. We were too prideful to concede that Gelidor had won against us when he destroyed our family. We should have listened to her," he lamented.

"What happened?" Selasine asked, his heart hoping for answers.

"The 'King of Claston,' as you have probably heard him called, is actually a servant of Na'agamlor. He purged families like ours. Mother and father," he choked. "I had the power of the sun in my body. We tried to assassinate the usurper, but Invictus punished us for such underhandedness. Evan is the one that paid the price that day. When we discovered it was a trap, it was too late. My brother had already been cursed. In anger, my mother did what you just did fighting that lich. She sacrificed herself to save Evan and me. The king watched angrily, sending numerous elves to their deaths at mother's hand. She tried to break the curse on Evan, but it must have been too late. He nearly succumbed to that curse," Erk commented with another heartbroken sigh.

"How long ago was that?" Selasine asked.

"At least thirty years. Iriliandria had been gone for forty years at that point. I found myself in a dark place. My parents were gone. My oldest sister was long gone. My brother was in a declining state. I began using my Unbinding power as an asset to take what I thought I needed to make things right. I started to organize a pirating resistance against the usurper. That's when I uncovered the unfortunate crystal that contained the life force of Vortex. He used my own biases to manipulate me. He taught me how to manipulate others. He pointed me toward Ezelbrecht so that I could free him from his prison. He promised peace and justice if I could get him out," Erk admitted.

"What did he say to Miranda that convinced her to release him?" Selasine continued.

Erk shrugged, defeated. "That last time in the crystal, I knew something was wrong. I kept shouting to Miranda across the distance, trying to share my apprehensions. It seemed as if my words were sucked into a void. And when I did hear my voice, it did not say what I wanted."

Selasine let out a deep sigh. Erk shared as much blame for Miranda's condition as Selasine felt that he shared in Iria's murder at the hands of Farzg. "I can barely feel the presence of Invictus in my heart anymore. I fear I may have made a critical mistake," Selasine added, revealing this new weakness.

Erk's gray eyes stared at him, full of sorrow. "Add that to the list of transgressions that I will make right," the pirate lord replied, sounding determined.

Selasine smiled lethargically, but it melted into a frown of sorrow. "I understand your dedication to helping Miranda. It's no secret that I didn't trust you, but now I have more reasons than you know to ally myself with you," he continued, taking a deep breath. He knew the time for the truth was arriving. "I can tell your heart is not one of a true pirate. Otherwise, you would have already discarded her as a failed ploy."

Erk also took a deep breath as he responded earnestly. "I felt the light in me reawakened by her. I told her my story, and she listened with such prudence. When she levied judgment against me, I was offended at first. But her innocent, unbiased explanation changed my mind. I vowed to return to the days before I was designated a dread pirate."

"She has that effect on so many people," Selasine commented, his eye lingering on the girl, still lying on the sofa, her armor glinting in the torchlight of the evening.

"And we shall see to it that she continues to heal this world," Erk reassured.

A few moments of silence passed as the two continued researching diligently. Selasine did not want this opportunity to pass, so he broke the silence. "Erk," the pirate lord looked up, expectant. "This might be imprudent, but I need to know more about your sister."

Erk replied, surprised, "My sister?"

Selasine let out a diffusing sigh. "Iriliandria?"

Erk's expression shifted from shock to calm. "How are you so comfortable with her elven name?"

Selasine's eye filled with tears, "Because I loved somebody by that name with more strength than I ever knew I had."

Erk wrinkled his nose, a twitch of understanding and an internal, crushing feeling. "Iriliandria Lancethinas, Lady of Flowers? Judge of Spades, Priestess of Peace?"

Selasine cried more openly, "I have no doubts then. Iriliandria came to Nulodia around thirty years ago. She was the most marvelous healer. She refused to carry a weapon, and she refused to act in violence. We adventured together. She saved my life on more than one occasion."

Erk's eyes filled with tears as he asked the one question he wanted an answer to for the greater part of a century, "Where is she now, bishop?"

"We brought down a smuggling ring in Nulodia in our early adventures together. The mastermind behind their operations, Eldon Farzg, was presumably killed in the church's final raid against their compound. However, he was not dead. He returned for revenge against those of us who had a hand in his downfall," Selasine explained, feeling the weight of his words growing.

"And?" Erk needed to hear the truth.

"We married twenty-two summers ago. She gave birth to our daughter Telisi a year and a half later. We were happy and wanted to leave behind the life of adventuring for a simple, content life. Farzg found us in the early spring after Telisi's tenth birthday. He stole them from me," Selasine's hard exterior and stern expressions had all melted away. He sobbed uncontrollably, prompting Erk to place his head on the table and weep.

"Can the fates and the gods be so cruel?" Erk lamented.

"Edmi yulesta tek yolasha. Afirfin't lotz gerindalthus," Selasine cried in the elven tongue, 'My wife and daughter. Far too soon, stolen.'

Erk righted his posture, tears still flowing down his cheeks. "Your daughter, Telisi. Please tell me about my niece," he asked.

Selasine gulped, his body wracked with another fit of grief. "She had the same black hair as her mother," he began. Erk's crying intensified. Black hair was a rarity among elves. Traditionalists thought it to have been a bad omen or a warning of a tragic fate. Erk had hoped that, by sending Iria away, she could avoid that prophesied ending. It seems that she did not escape, and neither did his niece. "She was growing so fast. Her favorite story was when I rescued a herd of sheep from a wyvern that had strayed too far south into the Devitan countryside. Iria was teaching her to make garments. She was the best ten-year-old seamstress," he said, losing his words to tears again.

Erk looked at Miranda's comatose body in repose on the sofa. "I think I understand you, Bishop Selasine. And like me, you won't let it happen again, will you?"

Selasine nodded, clearing his throat deeply, causing Naomi to stir.

"As surely as their memories live in my heart, I swear it," Selasine added, the hardened determination evident in his voice.

"As I said, Miranda reminds me of Iria in some ways. Her honesty, her optimism," Erk added as Naomi returned to the central pit of the study.

The pirate lady looked at the man and the elf, who had clearly just been weeping together. "Woah. Looks like you uncovered something while I dozed, at least. I hope it's not what it looks like."

Erk shook his head, another tear squeezing out as he gestured to Selasine. "Naomi, I need you to meet Bishop Selasine, my brother-in-law."

Naomi looked at him incredulously, "I already met—wait, your who?"

Erk smiled. "My sister, Iriliandria? As fate would have it, she married this exceptional man," his arms still protruding in a gesture of demonstration.

Naomi looked puzzled, "What does this have to do with helping the girl?" Before Erk could respond, she put all the pieces together. She, too, had met Iria nearly thirty years ago, a secret she had hidden from Erk all this time. Erk's and Selasine's mournful expressions told her everything she needed, and her heart broke in silence. She would deal with her own feelings about this revelation later.

Erk stood up, laughing. "Absolutely nothing, on the surface. But underneath, I believe fate has brought us together. Come, bishop, Naomi. Let us get some genuine rest and begin anew tomorrow. If there are no answers in port, we will depart for the open sea."

"Where would we go?" Selasine asked.

"To the ends of the world if we have to. Into the Rift itself even," Erk insisted.

"Very well. I must see to my prayers if I am to restore my connection to Invictus as it is. Perhaps we already have the resources to figure this out. We just need time," Selasine replied.

Naomi smiled, "I've got my own crew to worry about. Guess that means I'll put Annaia in charge. This is an adventure I don't want to miss."

Erk smiled at her and took her by the hand. "Thanks, my love." He turned his gaze to the bishop. "I wish you a restful sleep, nulestotejin," he added, using the elven word for brother-in-law.

"Likewise," Selasine replied, gathering books to take to his room. He knew he would fall asleep reading and would not truly rest again until they found a solution.

***

Miranda felt cognizant but scattered. She was aware of her existence but not her location. Her senses failed her much like they had in the lich's dimension. This lack of sensation was not oppressive like in the crystal; she felt free. Her mind felt a rush of air, but when she tried to move her hands to touch her face, there was no response from her body. Actually, she realized she didn't have a body.

She felt the warmth of a fire. She saw a young man twisting her essence to light the flame on a torch. Suddenly, that sensation was gone. At another moment, she felt as if she had become water and was being poured from a vessel, only to have that sensation change to the sound of crackling electricity. She wasn't sure what was happening, and she grew scared. Whenever she felt her essence called to duty, she could see faces and hear voices, but then they would abruptly change. As her consciousness grew fearful, the people she encountered in this strange state seemed surprised. While she was scared, whatever they needed her for did not seem to happen as they expected. She tried to run away from the voices, but they called ever louder still.

She started trying to remember her past. She thought hard about how she ended up in this disembodied, wild condition. She could remember the lich. She remembered Selasine. She remembered Erk. She remembered August and Justin. Those were the faces and the voices she wanted to hear, so she focused on them intently. She got flashes of light to radiate in her consciousness but could not see or hear. Again, she felt her essence whisked away to activate an illusion and charm spell simultaneously. She felt like she was in two separate places for an instant but also like she was nowhere.

She wanted to cry, but there were no eyes for her tears. She wanted to scream, but there was no mouth for her to shout. Suddenly, there was the sensation of being lifted high into the air, stars materializing in her perception. She could see but still had no body with which to experience these sensations. A booming, imposing voice echoed in her consciousness, "Hey, don't be afraid, Miranda," the words comforting, but the voice loud.

"Where am I?" she screamed back through her essence. No words emerged.

"Well, you're kind of everywhere right now," the voice replied, still loud.

"How can I be everywhere? Where is my body?" she

replied, a burning sensation in her soul demanding answers.

"Right now, your body is," there was a brief pause. "Looks like a pirate is carrying you around."

"That's not what it feels like right now. I'm here with no control over anything!"

"Focus, Miranda. Use your scattered essence to reconstruct your memories," the voice cautioned.

She felt a pull back to the central plane of existence and found her consciousness fleeting in and out of the faces and voices of people again. Some used their uncanny gifts for practical reasons; others used them for theatrics or violence. Miranda's essence shuddered in resignation, realizing something had gone terribly wrong.

"Who are you?" she asked the voice as she felt thrown back into the stars. They were the only perceivable thing here in this strange place.

"I'm Dalyn Tyrdrac. I'm the genius who totally wrecked the arcane stream. I'm kind of stuck in here like this, too," he replied. "But if I concentrate hard enough, I can bring enough of my essence together to manifest a way to move through the stream as I see fit."

"Is that where we are? Like when Evan could see the stream?"

Dalyn corrected her, "Not exactly. Life essence and mana are similar in that they constitute something intangible but are very different. If a person's life essence is pushed across dimensions into the arcane stream, it will carry that essence away and scatter it within the stream of magic."

"So my life essence is lost in the stream?" she wondered.

"Kind of, but your life essence differs from a normal human or elf. Do you know the story of Saraix and Gorthran?" Dalyn asked, the tone casual but the voice still overwhelming.

Since she had no body to gesture with, she simply and loudly thought, "No!" causing her voice to boom through this ambiguous space like Dalyn's.

"Now you're getting it! Use that focus to hone your consciousness!" the voice laughed as if it was watching her.

"Aren't you going to tell me the story?" she replied, her presence becoming cohesive to her own consciousness.

"Of course, apologies," Dalyn replied. "At the beginning of time, Saraix, a goddess of great good, and Gorthran, a god of great evil, sought a way to influence the world for their causes. Unhappy with the limitations of the primordial place and the vulnerability they faced walking among mortals, Saraix found a different strategy. She had been studying the arcane stream, a power source different from the gods themselves. Mortals, too, had been learning to use this free-flowing energy to enhance their lives. However, bending this stream required intense study and understanding. Saraix realized that to protect mortals from the evil machinations of Gorthran, she would need to be ever-present with them. So she broke her essence up into millions of shards and cast herself into the arcane stream. Those shards? They would be born into the corporeal world as dragons. Beasts of great might that could defend the helpless. They were made of the very essence of magic and could draw on it at will, much like you, Miranda."

"What did the evil god do?" she boomed across space and time, unsatisfied with Dalyn's storytelling abilities.

"Woah, slow down. You'll get ahead of the story like that," he warned.

She hadn't been part of the arcane stream long enough to hide her thoughts. "Well, if you'd just get with the story, I'd already know!" she boomed with an immediate, "Oh, no. No, I mean, I didn't want to say that. I just wanted to think it. I'm so sorry," she backpedaled.

Dalyn's reply was sincere, "It's okay. I'm a sorcerer, not a bard. I'm not great at telling stories, but I am the only conscious company you'll have here. And you'll probably be here for a few days." After a pause, "Which actually might not feel like that long in here. Time flows differently when it's only your consciousness experiencing reality."

Miranda's awareness felt more sensations returning as she actively resisted someone trying to borrow her essence. This invigorated her; she could swear she gathered energy in a central location. She wondered if it were possible to create a projection of herself in this world-between-worlds. "Well, then, master sorcerer. Please finish your story," she chided. She would have giggled from embarrassment, having questioned his storytelling abilities unintentionally.

"Ah, yes. Well, Gorthran couldn't just let Saraix's essence walk among mortals unchecked. He also broke himself into millions of pieces and scattered himself into the arcane stream. From his essence were born dragons of evil nature. They were meant to plague mortals. And, thus, the seeds were planted for the Dracon War, the first calamity of this universe," Dalyn finished.

"That's an interesting story, master Tyrdrac. How does this relate to us?" she replied, her personality fusing with her consciousness, manifesting in using an honorific for the sorcerer of legend.

"Well, you are a dragon born with the biology of a human. Which, in my opinion, is the most fascinating thing. My great-great-grandfather was a silver dragon, and that's where I got my name. Tyrdrac," Dalyn explained, hoping Miranda would realize what he meant.

"So, if I'm a dragon, does that mean that I'm a creature made of magic?" she replied, somehow managing to tone the boom of her voice to something meeker and more appropriate for how she saw herself.

"Yes, yes, yes! See, since you are an *entirely* magical being created from the shard of a long-forgotten goddess, your body shut down when the lich purged the magic from it. You've returned to the essence from which you were born," he replied.

"Ezelbrecht said I'm not a shard of the Dragon King or the Dragon Queen. He told me I was the first dragon to be created by mortals. What does that mean?" she asked, her comfort increasing to the level that she thought she could smell and taste, though this dimension smelled and tasted like anything she thought of. She sought the scent of the Devitan countryside after a spring rain, almost forgetting that she was talking to someone.

"Wait, that's not possible. Or, logic would say. Dragons have descendants among the humanoid and fae races, but they are nowhere near as powerful as you are. If you are truly a dragon, you have to be a shard of one of the dragon gods. Unless," the booming voice paused. "Dammit all. This is bloody brilliant. Thanks to my mistake, an arcane impossibility has occurred. You're the result of my meddling, too. You seem like a nice young woman, and you're really pretty too. If we can get you back into your body, maybe you can come back and get me out of here? I'd love to take you out for dinner in the city," Tyrdrac prodded, almost in jest. He really considered himself a "lady's elf," and those habits shone through even in this state.

Miranda's accumulating consciousness giggled clearly. "Well, I can't take you up on that offer unless we find a way to get me back into my actual body. How would that be possible?" she wondered next.

"That's going to depend on your friends," he cautioned.

"I see," she replied, helpless. "So there's nothing I can do in the meantime?"

Dalyn, still booming loudly. "For starters, could you teach me how you changed your voice? I'm serious. I have scared the gods a few times just trying to be helpful."

As Miranda's focus in this place continued to clear, she began shaping the magic that she had begun to gather. She could fuse enough magical energy that she created a body out of pure mana. "Just focus your thoughts like you're casting a spell. I've never done anything but pray, but I know you're a sorcerer. You should be able to do it easily! Wish hard for what you want, and don't let anything else distract you."

Dalyn's voice continued to boom out, "Woah. Incredible. You have a body!"

Miranda's mana body responded with shock, "I know! It worked!" she practically jumped up and down. The control of her movement that she expected began to return. Though her physical body was limited, this new, magical body allowed her to make some changes. She gave herself a set of draconic-shaped wings, stretching out behind her as brilliant light. She left her hair braided, but unfortunately, her entire mass glowed with the pure energy of the arcane stream. The glowing body of energy did not render many details. Still, her braids made an obvious shape cascading in front of her face. She kept her mother's armor on, and it defined the silhouette of her glowing presence. She had grown fond of it over the last couple of weeks.

Suddenly her memories came flooding back to her. "I was

yanked out of my own body when the lich used that final attack," she realized.

"That was a nasty one. Vortex. He was a legendary wizard in my childhood. It goes to show no matter one's age or wisdom, the darkness is always waiting," he boomed again, trying to focus all of his concentration on his voice.

"How was a creature like that any kind of legend?" Miranda asked, her unity with the mana allowing her to inflect her voice now.

"I've been here for a century, and you're already better at this than me. This really isn't fair," he complained, ignoring the question.

Miranda's incorporeal manifestation giggled. "Have you tried concentrating on a singular desire yet?"

A moment of silence paused before there was a calm "No." It was followed by an immediate booming, "Oh, finally, I'm not shouting anymore."

"Yes, you are," Miranda indicated.

"Right," Dalyn said as his voice calmed again. "Sorry, I was excited that I made some progress."

Miranda stretched her wings out, magical shimmers trailing her like a sparkling toy, a magical or gunpowder-laden stick for children that spewed beautiful, bright, mostly harmless sparks once activated. Her body of light did not truly feel anything; it merely served as a conduit for her to perceive reality in a way that made her comfortable. With that in mind, she took off into the starry sky that she had been present since she could see, glowing brightly. She looked around and saw the physical world she knew beneath her. At this point, she wasn't sure if it was an illusion she had created or if this was the world where her regular body should have been.

"Where are you going?" Dalyn's voice chased after her.

"I'm going to find my friends!" she insisted.

"It's not that easy," Dalyn warned, but Miranda did not wait. Her magical body shot through the sky like a shooting star, intensely circling the planet far above.

"Woah," she marveled, looking at the whole of existence from so far up in the atmosphere. The entirety of their world was known as Espa. Very few souls had ever marveled at the twisted planet in its entirety. Defying all logic, Espa was a half-planet of sorts, with a northern hemisphere properly situated in space. However, the bottom half of the planet looked to have been a shattered mess. A deep rift of magma, metal, and magic on the lower side of the planet kept it bound in space and time. "Now this. This is more beautiful than anything I've ever seen," she murmured to herself.

A blob of sparkling light joined her in the high atmosphere above the planet. "Oh hey, you weren't kidding. I've been trying to do something like this for almost a hundred years. I'm glad you came to visit," Dalyn commented. "I mean, not the circumstances and all that. Sorry."

Miranda's luminescent body giggled again, the magic forcing the sounds to exist. "You're still not quite put together," she sympathized.

"Give me some time. Although, isn't reality spectacular from up here?" he added.

Miranda watched the churning southern hemisphere, primordial lighting frequently cracking in the eternally roiling nebula. In the northern hemisphere, she could make out distinct landmasses reminiscent of maps she had seen. "Can we go anywhere like this?" she asked.

"Considering that you've already upstaged my chance to share this experience with somebody new, I suppose that whatever whim you have next will probably be a lesson for me," Dalyn said, showing admiration in his voice.

Miranda's energy body flew in a beam targeted at the surface of Espa. As she reached the surface, she felt the mana inside her swirling, aching to meet the demands of people around her, drawing upon the uncanny magic inside them. Her increasing consciousness made it easier to ignore their demands and observe the world from this magical state.

She found herself in the courtyard of the church in Devitus. This was the last place she called home, so it was no wonder she ended up here. Though it looked like the world she knew, everything seemed painted with a deep blue hue. The colors weren't right. She could tell that it was daytime. She could see people in the streets, meandering about their daily tasks. She then thought about the people she knew in town; before she knew it, her magical essence was standing in the marketplace. The townsfolk moved about their business as if she were not there. She was imperceptible, she thought. She turned her senses up, focusing on what she expected to hear, but no sound penetrated the shell between their realities.

A moment later, an elven, shimmering shape joined her in the marketplace of Devitus. "Where is this place?" Dalyn inquired.

Miranda marveled at the people. She knew their names, their faces, and their troubles. She felt so relieved to see them. "This is Devitus. I grew up here in a monastery to the north," she explained as the two suddenly found themselves in the monastery's main hall.

"Just like that, and we move from place to place?" Dalyn asked, shocked.

"It seems like it," she murmured, her essence flowing down the monastery's main hall. She passed the kitchen and dining room, the libraries, and the training rooms, settling in the rotunda at the end where the two dormitory wings met. The building seemed empty, so she used her heightened awareness to look for the monks. She found several of them outside, sitting in a circle, meditating. They were dressed in silver and blue robes, the colors of Lexcord.

The two magic walkers found themselves outside with the monks but standing outside the meditating monks' circle. Curious, Miranda walked her magical body into the center and sat down. The monk she walked through suddenly opened her eyes, and she began to look around, confused. Miranda recognized the woman; her name was Emi. She had joined the monastery as an adolescent while Miranda was an orphan. Emi liked to fight, but after years of disciplined living, she honed her fighting focus into a strong faith in Lexcord. Miranda giggled to Dalyn, "This woman is my friend."

Suddenly Emi stood, crouching into a fighting stance, looking right at Miranda. Miranda stirred her essence and moved it from the middle of the circle, but Emi kept her eyes locked on the magical conduit. "By Invictus, Dalyn, can she see me?"

His own magical body shook its head. "I've been waiting

almost a hundred years to use my body language to make others feel inferior again. And by the time I get my hands back on that power, you're doing things I didn't even realize were possible. What is with you?" he teased.

"I'm serious, Dalyn; she can see me." Miranda's concentration frazzled, and she felt her magical body threatening to scatter.

"It looks like it. Or maybe she can just sense the high concentration of magic, which has put her on high alert," he countered, watching the young woman's concern.

"Of course!" she thought. She needed to remove herself quickly to not upset Emi and to regain her focus. With less than a blink, her mana projection suddenly appeared in a massive sitting room. She could not see the furniture; everything had been covered with sheets. A bright red rug was underneath the parlor furniture, the only color she could distinguish from the blue aura surrounding her vision here. Dalyn joined her instantaneously, still trying to twist his magical body into the right proportions.

Immediately, Dalyn cautioned, "Miranda, I don't think we're supposed to be here."

She shook her head, her mana braids still swinging as expected. "Nowhere is off limits for us like this!" Her voice was excited and enthusiastic, putting Dalyn's caution at ease. That date he had invited her on started to seem like something the elf would have liked, but he buried that thought. Using the incorporeal nature of her magical body, she decided to try walking through the walls of the building she was in. Of course, stepping through the fireplace of the sitting room took her outside to a huge yard with a grove of citrus trees. The blooms were colorful even with the blue tint of viewing them like this. It felt familiar to her.

She returned to the sitting room through the fireplace. She began using her heightened awareness to look through the sheets tossed over everything. She could see ornate, beautiful furniture underneath. A standalone cupboard made of beautiful mahogany, a chaise made of cherry and upholstered with the finest silk, and an antique lounge chair that looked to have seen better days were among the sights. Everything here felt so familiar. She realized she didn't have as much control over where they were as she thought. The church was home. So was the monastery. But why here?

"I think we should try to find your friends now," Dalyn insisted.

"I have to know why we are here, Dalyn," Miranda argued. The sitting room had a beautiful bay window off to the right of the fireplace, which sat on the north side of the building. The window had seating built into the sides for people to relax and enjoy the view of the countryside. In that space, Miranda could see something else covered by a sheet. It looked to be oddly shaped.

"Momma," she whispered as she felt the truth in her heart. "Daddy," she whimpered into the ether.

"Stay focused, Miranda. Maintain your form," Dalyn pleaded.

Dalyn's advice calmed her as she reached out with her entire essence and yanked the physical sheet off of the crystalized statue of her parents.

"What in the Infernia?" Dalyn boomed in shock.

"It's my parents. Philotrax and Reshiria," her essence reached out to touch the statue.

A strange sensation filled Miranda's consciousness. She felt the center of who she was at that very moment. Far removed from her body, the only thing she was certain of was that she still existed. Touching the statues had placed her consciousness into an overlap in the flow of mana. Inside the crystals, she could feel reserves of ether that overwhelmed her incorporeal senses.

"Momma?" she whispered again, using the tendrils of light that had become her hand to touch the statue.

She could see no source but felt a reply echo in the magic that held her together. "Mir'thax, why are you crying?"

"I'm not crying, momma, I promise," she lied. Tears of mana radiated from where she had formed the eyes on her energy face. She felt as if she was four years old again, and a cold winter night had descended around her.

"It's alright, now, Mir'thax. Daddy is here too," his voice causing a rumble in the magic, vibrating throughout the universe as far as Miranda could feel.

Miranda thought if she'd been in her real body, her heart might have exploded with joy. "I miss you," she cried. Though her emotions felt young, her thoughts had matured. One of her biggest regrets was that she was old enough to remember her parents but not clearly enough to articulate specific memories.

Her consciousness felt the psychic equivalent of a gentle palm on her cheek. The vibrations in her essence were those of her mother, "We were so wrong about the time we had left before the magic inside us became stale. I lived for many centuries looking for happiness, but I couldn't stay with it once I found it."

The mana streaming from Miranda's conduit's cheeks concerned Dalyn, but he could only hear Miranda's words. "Why did you have to go?" her presence choked out.

Philotrax's vibrations echoed through her essence. "As true dragons, the magic continued to flow through us after The Unbinding. But trapped as humans with no uncanny magic, we could not discharge it. Now we are again one with the stream, waiting to be born again when Saraix calls our names."

Reshiria responded, "And I hope to hear my name called for the first time by the Dragon Queen."

Miranda stopped, dumbfounded. "Mommy, daddy, I'm in the arcane stream right now."

"That's impossible, darling; you still live," Reshiria's voice echoed.

Dalyn didn't bother trying to perfect his magical features anymore. He thought about leaving Miranda alone, but this was the most interesting one-sided conversation he had ever heard.

"A lich drained all the magic out of my body, and the magic in me brought me here. Does this mean I died?"

Philotrax's voice laughed, "Of course not, Mir. You were born a human girl. The only thing draconic about you was your mother's pregnancy."

Reshiria's voice relaxed, "Fifty years is nothing for a dragon, but it truly takes its toll on a human's body."

Miranda didn't want to seem argumentative but felt she had more information than her parents. "Do you know a dragon named Ezelbrecht?"

Philotrax responded, "Of course, Ezelbrecht the Gray. The child of Gorthran, an entity of great evil. Born before time began. They cannot be understood by mortals."

"Well, they told me that I'm a dragon still. And I can bend the universe to my will with the magic that flows through me. I'm scared right now. I'm so scared, momma," as she choked, the mana began to flow from her eyes again.

Reshiria's essence seemed to caress her daughter's cheek again. "It's okay, darling. Do you trust your heart?"

"Yes," she mumbled.

"What's your heart telling you, Mir'thax?" she tenderly prodded her daughter.

"That I believe in my friends and everything is going to be okay," she cried.

"Then why are you crying?" Reshiria asked again.

"Because when they fix this, it means I'll go back to my body, and you'll be here again without me," she could feel her concentration slipping, her mana form beginning to unravel.

Her father's voice replied, "We're with you, Mir'thax Toi'landra. The girl of fire and lightning. Always."

Miranda cried harder, "But I can't always hear your voices! Please, come back to the mortal realm. I have so many stories that I want to tell you about my adventures and the pranks that August pulls on me." Her mana body had dissipated, and all that remained was a wisp that held the center of her consciousness, still a single tendril of light buried into the statue.

Dalyn remained still, quiet. Though not usually emotional, he found his essence was brought to the edge of magical tears.

"Sweet daughter, we would if it were possible," Reshiria's voice replied. "But our hearts and minds are beside you at every turn. We are so proud of the young woman that you've become. I can feel the size of your heart through the arcane stream. The world needs you more than we do. We will flow through the stream until our names are called; this is the only way."

The energies that swirled between these three entities resembled something beyond an embrace; they became a single essence for an instant. As they reconstituted their individual identities, Mir'thax replied sheepishly, "I don't care if the world needs me; I need you."

Philotrax's voice replied this time, "You need the bishop. And I can feel that he needs you too, but I don't know why. Your friends, too. Their names are imprinted on your very essence. We love you, Mir'thax. We love who you've become. And we know the world is brighter for having you in it."

"But daddy," she tried to argue. She could hear a familiar melody begin to play. The simple tinkling of a music box, a haunting lullaby that Miranda knew well. "I think I have to go now, daddy," she cried.

She felt their embrace again as the sound grew louder in her consciousness.

"Goodbye, Mir'thax," her father said, touching her cheek as her mother had done.

"Farewell, sweet daughter," her mother added, a pleasant pressure on Miranda's perceived forehead.

The last feeling her essence could muster was a heartbroken, "See you soon." At least she got to tell them goodbye this time.

Chapter 17
In Search of
Forbidden Knowledge

August nearly slammed into Naomi as he rushed into Erk's study the next morning. The young acolyte was dressed in a casual shirt and leather pants, his muscular frame seemingly as solid as the plate armor he had been wearing almost constantly for two weeks. Naomi repeatedly blinked as he bounded by her, book open in his hands. He hit the handrail leading down the steps to the center of the study with his bottom, sliding down the rail theatrically. Erk was at the center desk of the study; Selasine must have been in the stacks or elsewhere, as August did not see him.

Erk stood, a look of concern for August's wild enthusiasm. "August, do you bring news?"

August's face looked flushed and red. "It's here, it's all here!" he shouted. Naomi followed him into the center, maintaining a healthy distance.

Erk took the book out of August's hands and began reading. "The Astral Spire," the pirate lord murmured as he reviewed the content on the page.

August panted from excitement and his sudden outburst of energy. He was in the middle of grooming when he read in the book that, according to legend, a single solisberry tree bloomed at the top of the Astral Spire. "The tree with purple blooms from Evan's dream. The lighthouse in my dream. And then last night," he paused. "Well, it sounds weird, but I had the same dream again. Except, I remember more of it. We were taking Miranda there. To that lighthouse."

Erk's visage twisted into a curious face. He, too, had dreamed about the Astral Spire, but he was convinced it was because they had spent so much time discussing it the night before. After the emotional events of yesterday, he felt like the dream was invigorating. However, the shared dreams were not enough to answer his questions. "How can we use this information, August?" Erk finally inquired.

August pointed to some annotations in the book's margin, barely legible in the common language. He read them out loud, "A high concentration of magical energy in a single location is required to grow solisberry trees. These blooms will likely grow somewhere the entire arcane stream passes through at some point."

Erk tapped his chin. Out of the three sacred trees, solisberry trees were the rarest. The fruit that grew on the blooms of those trees used to be popular reagents for alchemical items that enhance a wizard's magical potency. He knew they were one of the possible trees in Evan's dream from the previous day but still wasn't sure how they could connect to Miranda. "That's a most excellent find, August. What does this mean for our mission?" he asked, hoping the young man had more explanation.

August nodded enthusiastically, "If Miranda's essence is magic, and all of the magic flows through this place, won't her essence flow through that place eventually?" He was not academic or articulate, but Erk realized he was smart. He was more than a battlefield brute; the bishop mentored some promising children.

Gathering his thoughts, Erk reached for a different tome, *The Dracon War: A Chronicled History*. He flipped through a few pages until he found a passage that stood out to him the day before. Erk read it aloud to August and Naomi, "Having shattered her essence and cast it into the stream, Saraix created the dragons of light, creatures of immense magical power. Their very life essence became that of magic, and the arcane stream flowed through them like a river."

"Remember what Ezelbrecht told her?" August added.

Erk nodded. "You're onto something with the flow of the arcane. But what does that mean for Miranda?" he asked, still critical.

The door to the study was still ajar from August's explosive entrance. Selasine stood in the doorway, his face pulled up into a smile. He, too, carried books he borrowed from the study the night before in his hands. "The Sword of Justice reveres the harmonious music of the morning," he announced to the study.

August saw his mentor in much better shape than the day before. Selasine looked refreshed and had a glowing aura about him. The young acolyte replied, "The awakening dawn a paragon of order and beauty!" It was rare that August would be the one left to complete the catechism. He had heard Miranda and Justin answer the bishop's greeting hundreds of times over the last year. The young man sighed, missing his friends. He wondered where Justin had gone after Carulus went outside the church's purview.

Bishop Selasine walked down the stairs that led to the central table. "Invictus has not scorned me," he began. "I feel his voice again, and I also had a dream. You," he said, gesturing to Erk. "You and your brother were with Miranda under the blooms of a solisberry tree. August and I fought with hordes of shadow creatures that sought to do Miranda harm," he continued.

Erk chewed his lip in thought. "Another reference to the solisberry tree," he commented, glad that August's research about the Astral Spire had yielded the reference to the rare tree. "Bishop, what do you know of this tree?"

Selasine crossed his arms, tucking the handful of books

underneath. "Only that its blooms are treasured by the faithful of Invictus. Their rarity and color make them prized possessions of the clergy," he explained.

Naomi shook her head, "Okay. So you put the girl under the tree, but then what?" she questioned. She wanted to be helpful and ensure their plan was refined and contained contingencies.

"Exactly," Erk replied, frustrated. "It's like we have all the puzzle pieces but no frame to put them together," he complained.

"The answers we seek are here," Selasine commented, withdrawing a small book from under his arm. The title on the tome read *Simulacra, Soul Prisms, and Magical Conduits.* "I suspect that Miranda's body works much like Vortex's prism. As long as there is a place for her essence to return, it will eventually make its way back," he explained, summarizing his research from the night before.

Naomi and Erk traded a glance. Erk inquired, "So even now, her essence is returning to her body, albeit slowly?"

Selasine nodded, "We will have to wait for the whole arcane stream to flow through her."

Erk finally understood. "That's why the solisberry tree at the Astral Spire is haunting our dreams. The mana flows to those trees as anchors, in a way. Right, August?" he asked, and the acolyte confirmed with an additional nod.

"We don't need to *do* anything because the stream itself will be the actor," Selasine suggested.

Naomi recognized the look on Erk's face. She knew what he was about to say. "We sail tonight, then," Dread Pirate Lord Erk ordered. He reached over to the desk in the center of the study and lifted his tricorn, black hat. He placed it firmly on his head, covering the top of his golden hair. "Let's get to *The Nebula*," he said with a smile.

August and Selasine looked at each other. "We'll bring Miranda to the ship right away," Selasine added.

Naomi tilted her head, her silver hair bending with the angle of her face. "Erk, darling, am I still invited?" she asked.

He smiled broadly, "Of course, my darling. Bring Rose and Hephaestia also, if you like." Selasine and August didn't recognize the names.

Naomi shook her head, "I'll have to leave them with Annaia, my first mate and a capable captain. She needs those two more than we will."

"What are we waiting for then?" Erk asked as he walked up the stairs to leave the study, turning.

August rushed up to the other side of the study to fetch Miranda. He held her gently in his arms, feeling a wave of excitement. "Good then, let's get to the ship," he said, eager to heal his friend. They didn't stop for August's armor; Erk promised he had a more promising plate mail on his ship.

The walk back to *The Nebula* seemed surreal. Only a few days had passed since August and Selasine arrived in Yendralia, and only three days had passed since their reunion with Miranda. So much had happened in that short time that Yendralia still seemed like a foreign place to the two men from Devitus. August carried Miranda's body, surrounded by a most intimidating entourage. In front of him, two figures of significantly different statures and of equally daunting presence: Selasine and Erk. Between the two of them, crowds dispersed out of their way quickly, the people of Yendralia waving and cheering to Erk from a distance. Behind him, a well-armed Naomi and Evan Drymouth, brother of Erk, ensured that nobody would accost this group, whether it be a mugger or a pushy salesman.

As the group arrived in the lower district, a crowd had gathered to throw flower petals in the street for their beloved pirate lord and lady. August looked at the woman in his arms, cold, lifeless. He whispered from his heart to hers, "Aren't the flowers beautiful?" She would have talked about them for the next six hours if she were awake. He hoped their current trajectory would put everything back right so she could annoy him by gushing about the most mundane things that brought her sparks of joy. He further hoped these trials would not have changed that sweet spirit that made her the most lovable person he had ever met.

Arriving at the gate to the port, Erk and Selasine traded knowing glances. There waited Cantalus in the center of the gate, that broad smile and round face waiting, knowing. Erk gave a cheeky smile to the bishop as they approached He Who Sings at the Gate.

"Hear, hear, gather 'round people of Yendralia!" Cantalus cried, his charismatic voice immediately attracting the attention of passersby. "Dread Pirate Lord Erk and Pirate Lady Naomi embark together on a quest of grand scale!" This quickly attracted a crowd, August giving a brief glance of worry. "A fair maiden trapped in the jaws of death, a young hero with great promise, the Shield of Alabaster and Judge of Hearts Thomas Selasine, the mighty and feared Drymouth, the scourge of Claston and radiant Dread Pirate Lord Erk, and the Succubus of the Seas, Pirate Lady Naomi: has such an ensemble ever departed from Yendralia?" The crowds cheered loudly for Cantalus as he began to sing. The melody was that of a haunting lullaby, which sounded familiar to everyone. "Six heroes departing, and many months shall pass before they return together. The cold of the north calls them away, a shocking truth still to learn. Their bonds forged in crimson, their destinies written in blood, their mission one of hope. As surely as the sun rises, they will seek that flower on the most perilous slopes."

Selasine looked back at Erk, smiling to himself. He now finally understood Cantalus's true purpose here. Besides kidnapping Miranda, these theatrics were the only true sign that Selasine had seen Erk was a pirate. Selasine felt forgiveness begin to creep into his heart toward the pirate lord. He was saddened that his brother-in-law had taken many wrong turns, but he no longer blamed him wholly for Miranda's ordeal. They shared responsibility, and together they would rectify this disaster.

The crowds saw them onto the tide wall overlooking the Isles Known for Nothing. Naomi stopped their entourage as they approached the gangplank to *The Nebula*. "Erk, my love. Please give me a moment," she requested as she bounded up the gangplank to the ship moored across from *The Nebula*. August and Selasine looked at the much smaller vessel. They could see purple triangular sails furled on the masts, the color so bright that it could be mistaken for a ship carrying the faithful of Invictus. Inscribed on the ship's bow, the words *The*

Violet Blur indicated this was Naomi's flagship. Selasine looked at August and grumbled, "How did we miss a ship with such bold colors?"

August shrugged. "I don't think we were really paying attention," he explained. Selasine agreed. Their only time on *The Nebula* was with Miranda, and they had spent most of that time napping.

After only a couple of minutes, Naomi returned. "My girls are ready."

Erk, a look of shock on his face, replied, "Wait, they're going to sail with us?"

Naomi nodded. "I decided on the way here. We're all coming with you. I trust Annaia and my crew will be assets on this voyage. Besides, who knows when you'll need a faster ship," she winked.

"Will your ladies have time to gather from port then?" Erk asked, concerned.

"Want to take bets on whose crew gets back first?" she challenged a wicked smile on her lips.

Erk vigorously shook his head. He knew better than to challenge Naomi on the discipline of her all-women sailing crew. Some of her lesser captains and servants were men, but only ladies were allowed to sail on *The Violet Blur*. It was strange to Erk, but most pirate crews were all men anyway. He then had a troubling realization. "Ah, Naomi, I had meant to tell you sooner," Erk began.

Naomi gave him a concerned look, "Yes, darling?" she antagonized, batting her eyes at him. August watched the exchange in disbelief as the normally confident Erk seemed flustered.

"We, uh," he stammered. "Miranda was using your dressing room as her quarters. She might have borrowed some clothes and makeup while she was . . . while she was sailing with us," he finally confessed.

Naomi scowled, "I thought I recognized that sapphire comb."

Erk tried to look Naomi in the eyes, but her gaze was so intense that his eyes danced to the ground, looking at the dock's planks beneath them. "So that was yours?"

She shook her head. "No, that was just in a bunch of 'girly loot,' as you called it, and stuffed it in my dressing room to 'sort through on my own time,' remember?" she scolded.

Erk immediately looked up, "Ah yes, that's right! Well, she liked the comb, and she took it. It was a big moment for her, you know."

Naomi smiled through a glare. August couldn't read her emotions. "Then, when we get her back to normal, I'll help her do her hair in a style that will work with the comb instead of those church braids." She dropped the glare when she addressed Selasine, adding, "No offense."

Selasine couldn't help but laugh. He was glad Naomi was coming along. She seemed generally helpful and madly in love with Erk. The bishop also suspected that, like Erk, she was a very unique pirate with a complex past. Furthermore, she had never acquired the title "Dread" like Erk had, a clue that she was at least less violent than her counterparts.

One by one, the companions boarded *The Nebula*. Erk immediately entered the captain's quarters, leaving the rest of them on the deck. A loud bell began clanging, similar to the one in the Fortress of Lords. A moment later, a different bell began ringing on *The Violet Blur*, their pitches and tones unique. Selasine suspected this announced the pirate lord and lady's official departure from the island, hence the ceremony as they headed to port. The bishop felt calm and determined, the former emotion having eluded him for most of the last few days and the latter the only one keeping him going. Those feelings belonged together for the sake of balance, he thought. He would pen a catechism about it later.

Erk returned to the deck, "Naomi, can we leave Miranda in repose in your dressing room?" he asked.

"Tsk," she shrugged. "It's not like I sleep in there anyway. Whatever you need to do, honeycomb."

Erk's eyes widened, his cheeks flushing. Selasine gave the most uproarious laughter that August had ever heard, causing the pupil to fear his teacher had gone mad. Evan looked amused but said nothing. With a second shrug, Naomi offered to carry Miranda. August could clearly see that Naomi was imposing as they walked. Now that she stood directly in front of him, he realized she was beautiful and massive. She was taller than August by at least a full head, and the sheer number of weapons draped around her body made her seem like a veritable war machine. "I'm heading into the dressing room as it is. You certainly didn't think a pirate lady would sail in her combat gear, did you?" she asked pointedly.

August was not accustomed to dealing with women as intimidating, beautiful, and comfortable with themselves as Naomi. Even the leather corset she wore under her jacket seemed more revealing than the typical dress for girls his age back in Devitus. His cheeks burned red as she towered over him, insisting she take the girl. August could only choke out, "But shouldn't somebody guard her at all times?"

Naomi's eyes drew up into a sadistic smile. She knew the effect she had on people. She counted her pistols and daggers, using exaggerated motions to emphasize all of her weapons. Her body twisted slightly as she revealed more weapons under her jacket, inside her corset, and tucked into her tall leather boots. August started to stammer, and the pirate lady let out a hissing laugh as she placed a finger over his lips. "It's okay, sweetie; if you wanted to watch me change, you could've just asked." She extended her arms under Miranda's lifeless body. August's cheeks burned redder than Miranda's normal hair as he complied, speechless. Naomi turned back one last time to wink at the others. "No boys allowed," she ordered, carrying Miranda to the door fifteen feet to the left of the captain's quarters. Since the door opened to the outside, everyone but Erk worried she would need some help opening the door. Instead, they stared in shock as Naomi blew a kiss at the door, causing it to open exactly as she wanted. Erk grinned as the rest traded confused glances.

"She can move things without touching them," Erk commented. "Just ask August."

The remaining men on deck began to laugh, except for August, who sheepishly lowered his head, his cheeks still flushed. "Yeah," he grumbled, causing another wave of laughter.

The next hour saw pirates scrambling to make their way

from Yendralia's various diversions to their respective ships. After the first thirty minutes, a pirate with a purple bandana tied around her flowing blond hair shouted over from *The Violet Blur*, "Erk, we're ready to go!" She was the same woman who scattered rose petals before Naomi's palanquin during the short parade.

Erk, Evan, August, and Selasine were all still working on deck, preparing to sail. As the woman called from Naomi's ship, Erk rushed to the port side of his ship, facing the starboard of *The Violet Blur*. "Thanks, Annaia! I'll let Naomi know!" he shouted back.

A familiar voice startled Erk from behind him, "Not much warnin' 'is time, eh, cap?"

Erk turned to see his first officer Jax. "Sorry for the rush, old friend. We're sailing to the north. We'll meet in my cabin as soon as we get anchors raised. I promise," he explained."

Jax flashed his wicked smile. "Sailing with the girls' club again?"

Erk nodded, a confident smile returned to his first officer, "Are you complaining?"

Jax shook his head. "Two ocean-worthy vessels, comin' right up, cap'n," he replied, not waiting for additional orders or assurances.

The latter half of the hour welcomed a handful of heavily intoxicated sailors to Erk's ship. Shalo was visible and herding them with a quirt. They stumbled aboard and immediately below deck. Shalo looked over August and Selasine; he had only seen them briefly when they were previously aboard. "Welcome, holy men!" he grunted at them as he boarded.

The two of them were busy tying knots in a length of rope. Selasine bent to work with the rope and looked over at the pirate that stood around Miranda's height. "Thanks, master pirate," he replied, trying to size up Shalo. His beard was scraggly, and his turban loose. Selasine detected a unique body odor after he approached them.

"You Miss Miranda's friends?" Shalo interrogated.

The clerics smiled. "Indeed, we are," Selasine answered.

Shalo's grin stretched from ear to ear, "Then yer especially welcome in my book," the pirate explained, excited. "She be one extraordinary lass, and I 'spect she's had a great teach. She always talked 'bout ya. I'm glad to meet ya."

Selasine gave a half-smile, rose to his feet, and offered his hand in introduction. "Bishop Thomas Selasine," he said as Shalo reached up and shook his hand. Selasine gestured to August, "This is August Burchard, my pupil and Miranda's friend."

Shalo furiously and excitedly shook Selasine's hand, glancing down at August. "What about the Justin character she always talks about?" Shalo asked, oblivious.

Selasine's expression dropped from pleasant to deadly. "He was slain by whoever kidnapped Miranda. Thank Invictus that I was there to restore him to life," he rumbled, sounding as dangerous as he looked.

Shalo turned ghost white. "So ya saved 'em?" he sputtered.

Selasine nodded. "In that case, there's no hard feelings between Erk and myself. My pupil survived, and Erk is diligently helping us work to save Miranda."

Shalo mumbled, "Thank the stars, then. Wait—What's wrong with Miss Miranda?" he said in a moment of realization.

Selasine shook his head, "It's probably best to consult the captain on that matter." He was exceptionally capable of reading body language. If this pungent pirate was indeed the one guilty of hurting Justin, then Shalo understood that Selasine was the one who kept Miranda from hating him forever. This pirate seemed to have a high opinion of her. Selasine was sure Miranda had won his admiration through her sincerity and kindness. He had heard how she healed the kidnapper after they faced mushbeaks in the caves near the Undine Coast. He knew Shalo was likely the culprit based on his uncanny magic alone.

Before they could continue, Erk's commanding voice rang out from the upper deck. "Raise the anchor, men!"

A second voice called out the port side of the upper deck, "Anchors up, Blur!" It was Naomi calling to her own ship. She had changed into an evening gown that glowed orange in the late afternoon light. It waved in the wind carelessly as she leaned over the railing.

From Erk's ship, August thought. Why doesn't she drive

her own ship?

By the time *The Nebula* and *The Violet Blur* had navigated their way out of the Isles Known for Nothing, the sun was dipping behind the horizon in the northwest. *The Nebula*, an incredibly huge galleon with tons of cannons and a massive crew, sailed in the lead. *The Violet Blur*, a swift caravel, darted in the wake behind *The Nebula*. Their silhouettes could be seen from the north side of Yendralia. There weren't many onlookers to watch them sail into the distance, but Cantalus stood on the sandy beach, watching them sail away. He smiled, still. There were no onlookers, nobody to listen; Cantalus sang to himself.

"Saviors of the kingdom, saviors of the world. Few have worn the mantle, fewer returned alive. Stay warm in the north, Yendralians." He continued to hum a happy tune as he walked around the northern beach, the sun finally dipping beneath the horizon and letting the waters turn dark. Cantalus had not sailed in over a century. Still, the entire island would need to mobilize to save the girl that would save their dimension. Magic needed the kind of healing that only Miranda could offer. Lascha and Oorzgo would comply with his orders.

***

Carulus stood on the upper deck with Captain Thilod'ni Silbiri, Thios in common. On the horizon, the high priest could see the port city of Beriton, one of the Claston Kingdom's more important cities. With a population of over twenty-five thousand, Beriton was the maritime capital of the kingdom, much like Nulodia was in Alabaster. Carulus eagerly awaited their arrival in Claston, his final play in the king's war against Erk. His decision to bring the girl against Erk was the correct calculation; however, he had not anticipated the depravity capable of well-organized pirates. The noon sun hung brightly overhead, the ship's masts barely casting any shadow.

Carulus and Thios conversed in elven as they crashed through the calm waters in the Bay of Beriton. Their journey had required them to leave from the Undine Coast five days ago, skirting a northeastern route directly for the southern coastline of the Kingdom of Claston. Carulus was pretentious, but he was not a fool. Sea travel was a miserable experience, but one that the high priest had to deal with if he were to have a chance at redemption in the eyes of the archbishop. His goal was three-fold: first, convince the king to assist him in utterly crushing the pirates in the Solar Sea; second, to have the church formally recognize the King of Claston's rule; and third, to recover or dispose of the girl who had complicated this entire mission. Erk would pay for interfering with a church operation. Unfortunately, there would likely be collateral damage.

"How busy is the port this time of year?" Carulus asked, calculating his moves once his battalions arrived.

"Busy enough; summer is the harvest season for the sweet and citrus fruits our kingdom exports to Alabaster and Gabah. Otherwise, it's mostly fishmongers and common folk. You shouldn't have any issues securing supplies as long as your coffers are deep," Thios explained.

Carulus furrowed his brow. Unfortunately, his coffers were no longer overflowing. The archbishop had withdrawn his support and even sent the high paladin of the church's pegasus division to arrest him! The audacity that a soldier could understand the consequences of a failed excursion better than a seasoned bureaucrat was a mockery of the law. "Actually, I hope to immediately mobilize my forces to report to the king in the capital city. Church politics have ensured that we will have difficulty carrying out our mission," the high priest elaborated.

Thios nodded, continuing, "King Claston has one-hundred thousand soldiers at his disposal and at least that many secret police operating among the common people. Remember, the use of your Profoundness is exclusively forbidden until you are formally authorized by edict of the king."

"You see, that's the very law that has created so much tension between our kingdoms. My Unbinding power is of little use, anyway. I am, however, an impeccable planner and 'profoundly' capable as a military commander," Carulus replied.

"Be that as it may, just make sure your men fully understand the king's position and the consequences for breaking the king's laws."

Carulus straightened his coat. "Make no mistake, we are here to solve the issues between church and king and the king and his people."

Thios nodded, silent. He already knew what would happen as soon as they approached the port.

The sun was preparing to dive behind the lower ridges of the Eastern Trollcrags as Thios's crew dropped anchor about a mile outside of Port Beriton. They had to await authorization to enter, so the captain told Carulus and his men to enjoy a day at sea.

Carulus sat bored in a cabin that had been specially prepared for him to conduct correspondence. He poured over his communication with the King of Claston so far. This entire ordeal had escalated into a nightmare for himself and the church. At this point, the king was convinced that now the church was conspiring against him with the pirates. Since the government of Alabaster was sanctioned by Invictus, the church and the government were intricately interwoven. A hostile act from the church could constitute an act of war, and losing the girl to the pirates certainly made the church's role in this suspect. Carulus cursed the search party and questioned why they were taking so long. The king wanted to speak to Carulus in person over the matter. The king's sudden change of tone concerned Carulus, and it drove him crazy being stuck on a ship like this.

He began to sort his thoughts, speaking out loud to himself. "The fighting was really only supposed to take three days maximum. The blockade was the insurance that this threat was dealt with. Why would the girl betray our plan so blatantly? I was counting on her to use her gift to help the church. If she could do so much more than healing, why didn't she use her immense power to escape? If you ask me, she's a traitor to the church and should be arrested. Still, I suspect that will complicate issues with Bishop Selasine," he grumbled to himself, and with a growl, he pushed several effects off his writing desk. "The archbishop fails to listen to reason, and the King of Claston is being secretive. If he blames me or the church for losing the girl, this could create an international problem. Why? Why did this happen to me? I had everything carefully planned. At this point, the best possible scenario is to catch the girl with Erk and slay them all. She will pay for her crimes with her life!" he shouted in the quiet cabin, a rage broiling inside him at an alarming level.

After his outburst, he had a moment of clarity. In his obsession with the mission, he realized that he had not prayed to Invictus in almost three weeks. He grimaced, gripped his holy symbol, and whispered, "Sword of Justice, I seek your counsel."

There was no response.

"Sword of Justice, it is I. Gaius Carulus, beloved of the Sword of Justice. Hear my voice."

His holy symbol began to vibrate in his hand. The strange occurrence caused him to break the thin silver chain holding the scales of justice in place around his neck. As he held it up in front of him, he could see that the scales on his holy symbol glowed, almost reminiscent of a set of eyes. "Sword of Justice?" Carulus mumbled, bewildered.

The holy symbol vibrated again, this time so intensely that Carulus dropped it. It continued to buzz with excitement for an entire minute, the high priest having never encountered such a phenomenon through experience or study. "What in the Abyss?" he questioned after the symbol finally stopped vibrating.

"Is Invictus ignoring you?" said a little girl's voice.

Carulus looked around with shock. "Who's there?" he asked, examining the tiny cabin. There was only room for a bed and a writing desk for him to pen his correspondence. It would have been impossible to have concealed a child in this room for their voyage. Carulus's eyes narrowed.

The voice continued, but this time it was that of an adult male, perhaps orc or giant. "It's just me, your friend!"

"I have no friends whose voices change so easily. Identify yourself," Carulus demanded, haughty.

A cloud of purple smoke emerged from the holy symbol, but the colors swirling in the smoke began to change, creating a rainbow in cloud form. "Don't worry, friend. Invictus is mad at you, but I like you!"

Carulus spat. "Indervill. Chaos incarnate. Why do you disturb me?"

Indervill used the wisps of smoke to create an illusory form. It chose to use Carulus's own face, but somehow the voice had reverted to the voice of a young girl. "I need your h-h-help. My brother and sister keep picking on me, and I am so mad at them!"

Carulus started to look disgusted, but his own countenance gazing back at him calmed him. "Invictus and Lexcord are picking on you? What do you mean?"

"We were playing, and I stole their new favorite toy. But then they stole it back from me. And THEN THEY BROKE IT!" the little girl shrieked.

Carulus looked around, alarmed. "They broke a toy?" he asked calmly, reaching out to feel that Indervill's chosen form was corporeal and not just an illusion. His fingers felt his own face, but he thought it strange that he could not feel the sensation of his touch.

"They took the toy far to the north. They won't let me see it or play with it anymore. They'll probably forget it there in the Glacier Gulf," Indervill complained.

"Why would you ask help from one of your brother's faithful? I have nearly fifty years of impeccable service to the Sword of Justice. I do not plan to betray my faith," Carulus asserted, indignant.

This caused Indervill's chosen form to twist and warp, looming larger now as Carulus's face began to burst from the cloud. As the cloud stretched, it started to peel back and form appendages, muscles, and features. Carulus stood face to face with a perfect duplicate of himself down to the last hair. He felt endeared to his own face, but before the comfort could wash over him, he felt an immense shame as he looked at his own naked form.

"Put this on, fool," Carulus scolded, handing a robe to the duplicate.

Indervill ignored him, but the voice changed. "They're gonna lock you u-up. They're gonna lock you UP!" The god of chaos bellowed in anger, the voice starting as a little girl but transitioning to the roar of a lion.

"What do you mean!? I plan to rectify the situation with the King of Claston and the archbishop. This will all be over soon."

Indervill giggled, a cacophony of voices present ranging from infants cooing to old men coughing their final laughter on their deathbeds. "Invictus doesn't want to play with you anymore, Carulus. But I do! You see, the king is a servant of Na'agamlor. The merchant, he can buy anything. Your life is worth nothing to him, and the merchant wants you dead. You're going to be executed for fun! But! They can lock me up in your place. And you can do something for me in the meantime!"

Carulus sat momentarily, his gut dropping to the bottom of the Rift. "This would indeed be a setback. What do you propose, Chaos?" the shunned high priest replied.

"I want that toy back. My brother and sister are taking it to the Astral Spire to fix it. I want it fixed, but I want it back! Please go get my toy!"

Carulus felt frustrated, as many did when dealing with the god of chaos. "What is this toy you speak of? How will I know when I have found it?"

He watched as his duplicate began to age rapidly, the polyphonic laugh causing Indervill's entire form to shake. Carulus watched until nothing but a skeleton was left. "You showed me the toy first! Miranda is what you called it! That's why I came to you! Can you get it back for me?" it asked, still speaking in a cacophony of voices that seemed suitable to the morbid appearance of this skeletal form.

Carulus's eyes twitched with madness and anger. "The girl! You said she had been broken?"

Indervill's skeletal form danced, waving its arms and wildly shaking its hips. "They broke it just to spite me. Sucked all the magic right out. Nothing left!"

Carulus's eyes narrowed. "So the girl is no longer a threat to the church?"

Another cloud of smoke swirled around Indervill. As the cloud dispersed, the full form of Carulus stood there, now fully clothed with the same robes the fallen high priest wore. Chaos replied in Carulus's own voice, "She's not a threat to anybody except YOU."

"Is that so?" the high priest sneered as he scratched his clean-shaven chin.

Indervill continued in Carulus's voice, "Oh! I have a better deal! I'll take your place in prison and give you some *incredible* powers. That way, you can get the toy back. And if you can't, DESTROY IT. If I can't play with it, neither can my brother and sister. Bullies."

Hearing it from himself made it a compelling argument. The fallen high priest nodded in agreement. "Very well. I will accept the freedom and the powers you offer in exchange for this task. If I can take her alive, I'll bring the girl back here to your avatar in Claston. If not, I will do as you say. I will destroy her."

Indervill adopted Carulus's ambitious smile. It fed off the increasing madness exuding from the high priest's words, behaviors, and thoughts. Chaos may have lost the girl temporarily, but it captured a critical piece of its brother's toybox. Even the Lord of Insanity understood the importance of timing. There was only one power that Indervill thought would be appropriate for this task.

"Thank you for your help in setting this injustice right," Indervill spoke, adopting Carulus's previous mannerisms and phrasing.

Carulus's consciousness felt like it was slipping away. He looked at his hands, and they began turning to shadows. He felt his heartbeat swiftly increase. He felt his muscles bulge and contract, then disintegrate into shadow. Suddenly, the power of Chaos flowed through him. Though Carulus no longer had eyes to close, he was aware of every entity moving around him on the ship. He could see all, hear all, smell all. He no longer had to move his body; he simply willed it, sliding along the floor, the wall, and the center of the room as a sentient shadow. He wanted to speak, and his words echoed all around him but only impacted the thoughts of others rather than producing a sound. "How can I fight like this?" he asked.

Indervill kept Carulus's ambitious smile on his lips. "You'll figure it out!" the high priest said to his shadow form. Gaius could no longer tell which one he was.

His shadowy body suddenly sprouted massive, spikey growths. They plunked firmly into the space around him, making loud stabbing sounds in the wood of the ship and repeatedly stabbing and killing his duplicate. Indervill's smile stayed on Carulus's face even in death. The corpse's eyes opened. "No locky locky if they find us like this!"

Carulus dematerialized and dropped through the ship into the darkness of the sea beneath him, his new body capable of moving through solid objects with ease. He swam with a singular destination: the Astral Spire. He didn't really think about why; he just followed the madness within him.

Chapter 18
Destiny

 ustin stood in the crow's nest of *The Valiant Sailor*, a ship on loan to High Priest Carulus on behalf of the King of Claston. The acolyte's ruse had almost fallen apart when the quartermaster discovered one more troop in the search party than anticipated. Using his knowledge of acolyte admission and church bylaws, Justin had convinced the quartermaster that there was simply a clerical error. He had only been recently admitted to the Path of the Sword of Justice by Carulus personally. Justin insisted he would be needed because he was personally connected to the girl they sought, and the unit commander agreed. With one more pair of hands and eyes, the commander set Justin to work on tasks that needed supplemental help. Justin was serving today as an extra lookout.

The search party boarded this ship only the day before. The King of Claston provided a skeleton crew to operate the ship, leaving many sailing responsibilities to the paladins and clerics on board. As they sailed southeast to go around the Trollcrag

Mountains that extended deep into the Undine Sea, they could see numerous ships making their way further southeast, many already vanishing on the horizon. The sun seemed paralyzed in the sky, indicating Justin's boredom. He would much rather be in an active role but didn't want to draw too much attention to himself by formally requesting a duty change. He wasn't confident the commander would even have the appropriate paperwork in a situation like this.

As the sun began to descend in the northwest, Justin noted they had cleared the western ridges of the Trollcrags that cupped the Sea of Undine to the north. He used a spyglass he had been given to peer in that direction. There he saw more vessels, most of them small ships. He knew he would need to identify numbers and types for his report to the commander. As he began to count, he felt the ship's course shifting hard to port. They would likely investigate these ships and check them to see if Miranda was on board. Justin knew in his heart that she was far from here, but that wouldn't make a convincing argument to the commander. Plus, he saw this as the perfect opportunity to gather information about the events that unfolded while he recovered from his brush with death.

Justin counted the vessels visible from his vantage point. There were seven that would be easy to reach. The larger craft would likely be checked first. After the ship completed its turn, Justin descended the mast to report to the commander. He found Commander Aguila on the upper deck, a human male with an earthy-to-red complexion. He was imposing like the bishop, standing at about six foot four and wearing the most radiant field plate armor that shone with a purple hue. He stood near the helm where the captain was busy driving the ship. As Justin approached, the commander gave him a smile. "Scout, report," he ordered.

"Sir!" Justin replied according to protocol. "Seven vessels spotted to the north, two galleys and a caravel. The rest look like fishing or small merchant vessels with no room for more than four to five passengers. They can barely be considered ocean-worthy, and their passengers are taking a great risk."

"Honestly, this sounds like riff-raff leftover from something bigger happening further north. Let's keep our eyes on the ships but not engage. Lieutenant!" he shouted.

A man who had been watching off the stern of the ship turned quickly and took a step toward the helm. "Sir," he replied. He looked about thirty years old and had a similar build to Justin. Braided brown hair spilled from beneath a golden sallet, standing just shy of six feet tall. He also wore field plate armor alloyed to glint purple in the sunlight, a sign that this lieutenant was a highly decorated paladin like the commander. An ivory scabbard rested on his belt, displaying an ornate hilt to a presumably magical longsword. However, the six-foot tower shield strapped to his back was the most striking. It made his stature seem immense even though he was of average build. In Justin's mind, paladins usually had intimidating physiques and overwhelmed the enemies of the law with brute force. The fact that a respected paladin with holy armor was roughly the same size as Justin shocked the young acolyte.

Commander Aguila addressed the lieutenant, "See to it that the ship's gunners do not fire needlessly at the passing vessels. There are galleys and a caravel among them; avoid engagement range. Our scouts and Pelscha will look for the girl visually and through magic. And take the acolyte with you. We may need to send word to engage quickly, and I want the gunners to know who he is. Make sure they know his face."

The lieutenant gave the salute typical of Invictus's faithful, shield hand to the hilt, sword hand palm up to the sky. "As Justice wills it, so be it," he replied and put himself at ease. He turned slightly to face Justin. "Your name again, acolyte?" he commanded.

Justin stood at attention, shield hand to the hilt. "Justin, sir," he answered.

"Aha!" Commander Aguila exclaimed.

"Yes, commander?" the lieutenant replied forcefully, snapping back to attention.

"The acolyte has greater discipline than any soldier I've commanded in a while. You might consider training him in the ways of the Shield Knights," the commander laughed. He then continued, "Be on to your task then."

The lieutenant bounded forward, darting toward the stairs

descending to the foredeck's lower part. Justin scampered behind him, quick to follow Commander Aguila's orders. The acolyte followed the lieutenant to the forecastle that led down to the first deck, then the second, where the cannons were located. Three gunners were on loan from the king; the rest were made of the clergy selected for this mission. The other clerics and paladins stood at attention as the lieutenant entered the gun deck, hustling.

"Lieutenant Gamnir, sir!" one of the paladins acknowledged with a swift salute. Justin was quick behind the lieutenant, standing at attention again after hearing the paladin's greeting.

"At ease," Gamnir ordered. "Commander wants us to avoid conflict if possible. The current course will keep us out of engagement range. However," the lieutenant turned to look at Justin. "Stay on high alert. We don't want to be taken by surprise. Be ready to fire and fight at a moment's notice. I or this acolyte, Justin, will bring the word if we must engage. Commander Aguila's orders. Understood?"

The paladins then saluted Justin, who returned the gesture crisply. "I am surprised that we have not met. Paladin Ekol at your service, acolyte," the lead paladin spoke.

Justin continued the introduction, "Justin Elzen, Acolyte of Invictus." Protocol dictated that no more titles were necessary, which was okay with Justin as he did not have any accolades or special rank yet. "I was dispatched as an afterthought," he explained, the honesty of his statement couched in his subtle deception.

"Very well, then," the lieutenant interrupted. "Now that pleasantries are out of the way remember the order. One of us will tell you to engage with cannon fire if necessary."

Ekol and the other clergy saluted again. Gamnir and Justin returned the gesture, and the lieutenant turned to exit the gun deck. Justin nodded to Ekol and followed Gamnir back to the deck. *The Valiant Sailor* was on a direct course north while the smaller vessels moved to the southeast. Multiple scouts had been positioned in the crow's nests to gather as much visual intelligence as possible. Justin looked toward the upper deck, then back to the forecastle behind him. He could easily reach the gun deck in about a minute from anywhere on the ship. Gamnir wandered off without additional conversation.

Taking a deep breath, Justin stepped over to the port side of *The Valiant Sailor* and looked toward the mountains that jutted up from the sea. The waves crashed hard against the mountains. Over time, Justin thought that part of the sea would be passable by ship or become new land. Erosion would wear the mountains down into the sea one day, or maybe the earth itself would continue to press up, towering ever higher with new coastal land surrounding it. He was blessed to see the beautiful mountain range, but sailing around it had increased the time it took to catch up to Miranda. As he gazed in a partial daydream, he noticed activity in the air as some kind of flying creature loomed in the distance. Withdrawing his spyglass, he tried to get a closer look. Through the device, he saw a creature with leathery wings that had wicked hand-like claws on the end of them. Its serpentine body had no arms, but it did have a fierce set of strong back legs adorned with sharp talons. As the creature flapped against its weight, Justin could make out a long, whip-like tail with a single barb attached to the end. Though he had never seen one in person, Justin knew what it was. "Wyvern," he hissed under his breath, lowering the spyglass. He began counting silhouettes in the early evening sky. When his count rose above ten, he became gravely concerned and immediately sprinted toward the upper deck.

Commander Aguila was busy conversing with the ship's captain when Justin appeared suddenly from the foredeck. "Acolyte?" the commander asked, surprised to see him.

"Apologies, commander," Justin exhaled as he came to attention. "Threat report!" he began as protocol required. "Wyverns spotted off port. More than ten. Possibly a code silver threat," he continued.

Aguila wrinkled his nose for a moment. To Justin, he seemed slightly larger than August. His braided hair was a beautiful forest green color in the afternoon sun. His suit of ornate field plate armor glistened as the evening sun shined, making a silver inlay with a symmetrical ivy pattern on the breastplate sparkle tones of orange. On his belt hung two scabbards, one sword for his left hand and one for his right. He matched Justin's idea of paladin perfectly. "Is that so?" the commander commented.

Justin offered the commander his spyglass. Aguila took it from him gingerly and stepped to the port side. He furrowed his brow as he could make out clear silhouettes of flying creatures. Raising the glass to his eye, he confirmed what Justin had reported. To make matters worse, their direction varied. Perhaps the increased activity in the area had agitated them. Maybe a greater threat had rooted them out of their hives. He turned to Justin. "Everyone's so busy watching for the girl on those vessels that nobody except you thought to keep looking for other threats. Not even myself. You've saved lives today, Justin. If those wyverns approach, we could be in for quite a fight. Acolyte!"

Justin saluted, his sword hand snapping so crisply that the commander remained silent momentarily. "Your form is impeccable, and your insight phenomenal. You are hereby recognized as the Watchful. A title awarded on the battlefield comes with an official promotion in the path you choose in the church. With your sharp mind, I hope you'll consider the Shield Knights." He reached into a pouch and withdrew a modestly sized badge, offering it to Justin, who took it in his palm-up hand without breaking salute.

Justin couldn't believe his ears. He had not even been an acolyte for a whole month! Justin was not expecting a battlefield accolade for the sheer luck of being the first person to notice an impending threat. He wondered what kinds of responsibilities the title might entail. Furthermore, he had doubts about his path within the church. Before any of this began, he was sure he would be a cleric on a path to arbitership, much like Miranda. After spending a day around so many interesting paladins, he wanted to know more about their paths. Nevertheless, he now outranked all acolytes, even August, if he hadn't somehow earned an accolade of his own. The thought made Justin snicker internally.

The commander's voice snapped him out of his thoughts. "Justin the Watchful. Alert the gunnery to fire scattershot at the wyverns if they approach. They are beasts with no intent but to kill. We shall not be made a meal."

Justin held the salute firmly until his orders were given. He replied, "Sir!" and immediately rushed to the gun deck. On his way down, he noticed Lieutenant Gamnir and a couple of other paladins with tower shields strapped to their backs. He had seen maybe six on the foredeck over the last day. It was difficult to distinguish between a couple of them as most of them wore the same golden sallet that Gamnir did. There could be more of these Shield Knights as the commander called them, but they may have had the same hair color and style. It had been difficult to tell them apart from the crow's nest when they trained sporadically on the deck throughout the day.

Arriving in the gun deck, Paladin Ekol was the first to notice Justin coming down the stairs. "Acolyte! Do you have news?" he exclaimed as the other clergy came to attention. The king's gunners looked uninterested.

Justin held up the badge that Aguila had given him. "Justin the Watchful, as per the commander," he corrected protocol requiring that battlefield promotions be recognized by all if verifiable by a token adopted by officers qualified to grant them.

"My apologies, Watchful," the paladin replied. A commendation was an impressive feat for an acolyte to obtain so quickly. This also meant that Justin now outranked paladins and clerics with no commendation. Ekol quickly snapped into a salute, and so did several other clergy members.

Justin also suddenly realized that he held rank. "At ease, paladin," he ordered. He was so glad that he had fully prepared mentally for this contingency. He calculated the probability of this happening once Carulus demanded their presence on this venture. Though it was deemed highly unlikely based on official records of church commendations and deeds, Justin acknowledged the possibility of receiving a commendation quickly amid conflict.

Ekol eased out of his salute, as did the other base rank clergy. "Are there orders, Justin the Watchful?" the paladin replied.

Justin nodded. "We may be beset by wyverns. If they come within range, you are to fire scattershot with lethal intent, understood?"

"Sir!" Ekol replied. He gave a new salute. Justin returned it and then relaxed, prompting the paladin to do the same. The gunnery crew began to organize for scattershot assaults.

Justin then returned to the foredeck. As he emerged from the forecastle, he could tell the commander had alerted the crew and the clergy to the potential threat. He could see the commander and the lieutenant on the upper deck looking off port still. He approached calmly, his hand drifting above the railing as he ascended the stairs.

"Justin the Watchful," Gamnir spoke. "Well done. There look to be two dozen wyverns. I triangulated the information we have with reports from other divisions. High Paladin Damil is in the region with a battalion of Pegasus Knights. Their activities may have disturbed this hive so drastically that they are migrating out of the region. That, or their hunting grounds are sparse thanks to the battle between Carulus and Erk's forces."

Justin nodded in response. "Sir, I await orders," he replied to the lieutenant.

The commander lowered the spyglass and looked at the young man. "This belongs to you, Justin the Watchful," he commented and returned the spyglass. "Based on the trajectory of the wyverns, we may have five minutes before they are within engagement range. Go with Gamnir. He will instruct you." Commander Aguila then looked to the lieutenant. "Put the Shield Knights in position on the port. Have Justin assist."

Gamnir and Justin both saluted. The lieutenant turned to walk down the stairs from the upper deck to the foredeck, reaching up to grip his holy symbol. Justin suddenly heard a voice in his mind. "Shield Knights! Assemble on deck." A few of them were already on deck, quickly making their way over to Gamnir. Within a minute, eight total paladins had approached the lieutenant, standing at attention.

"Justin the Watchful!" Gamnir shouted.

Justin, also at attention, saluted. "Sir!"

"Grab a shield. We need a tenth," the lieutenant ordered. Before Justin could object because he did not have a shield, Gamnir added, "You can find one on top of the forecastle."

Justin complied, running into the forecastle and up a

ladder that emptied at the top, a raised deck meant to serve as a defensive location against boarding attacks. He found several weapon racks loaded with polearms meant to defend the forecastle. Behind them, however, he located several shields propped against the foremast and organized by size. A couple of tower shields were in the stack, so Justin took one. It seemed surprisingly light. On closer examination, the metal reflected hues of silver and blue. "Mithril!" Justin whispered to himself. He found a large leather strap on the inside of the shield, and he draped it across his back, tightening the strap for comfortable carrying. At that moment, he heard a warning cry from the crow's nest, "The enemy diverges!"

Justin's head snapped to the port side. He no longer needed his spyglass to make out the forms of wyverns as they neared. At this point, the creatures were flying in several directions, with groups flying towards *The Valiant Sailor* and the other vessels fleeing to the southeast. Justin had a horrible, sinking feeling in his stomach. He hoped that whoever manned those other vessels was prepared for the onslaught. With little time to think or act, Justin looked at the deck from the top of the forecastle. The Shield Knights had taken up a defensive position on the port side, using their tower shields to create a barrier that extended the height of the port side by six feet. There was an obvious gap, and Justin knew that was where he was needed.

He took a deep breath. The drop-off of the forecastle was only about eight feet, so he carefully jumped down, rolling with his momentum. The mithril shield on his back clanked loudly against the deck as he did so, calling attention to him in the most dramatic fashion. Gamnir and several Shield Knights looked his way suddenly, causing the lieutenant to laugh. He then commanded, "Now we're talking. Take up position, Justin the Watchful!"

Justin complied, quickly slinging the lightweight shield from his back to his shield hand. He had trained with regular shields before, but this felt different altogether. He felt like there was an entire wall between himself and the enemy, and he felt his courage swelling as a result. The shield wall normally protected the deck from scattershot, gunners, and archers.

Justin analyzed the current situation, trying to understand the objective of forming a wall of shields against a flying enemy. Peering from behind his shield, he saw that five wyverns had detached and descended on *The Valiant Sailor*. His heart raced with excitement. This was his first real battle.

When the wyverns were only about two hundred feet away, Justin heard a series of loud explosions blasting beneath him. The sudden, deep booms shook the deck under his feet. Instead of startling him, he found that the sound renewed his resolve. Shortly after the explosions, two of the approaching wyverns released a sound somewhere between a hiss and a roar, the scattershot blasting them out of the air. The other three beasts quickly closed the gap between themselves and the Shield Knights and Justin. With determination now swelling in his heart, Justin pressed hard into the mithril shield as the half-ton beast flapped into range, using its long serpentine neck to strike at his shield before crashing into the wall of shields.

Justin was in the middle of the formation, with the two paladins beside him closing the gaps between their shields, making a three-person strong barrier to block the wyvern's body slam. The beast hissed and snapped rapidly, trying to snake its long neck between the shields. The rest of its body caught up to its neck, smashing into the three of them. Justin and his companions retaliated quickly with sword blows at its leathery, scaly body.

Scanning his mind for information, Justin instinctively shouted, "Tail strikes incoming!" as the wyvern's flexible, deadly tail whipped quickly over the tops of their shields, attempting to sting the defenders. Thanks to Justin's warning, the barb on the tail only managed to hook the sallet of one of the Shield Knights, knocking it off her head. Her golden blond braid whipped quickly out from underneath as Justin pushed hard against the beast with his shield. The sudden forward retaliation caused the wyvern's second tail strike to fly wildly off course, plunking into the deck harmlessly. The sallet crashed at Justin's feet a second later, invigorating him. He began to pray.

"Sword of Justice, guide my hand. May these creatures learn the laws of nature and order," he whispered to Invictus.

A pale, purple aura covered Justin's longsword. His answered prayer emboldened him. At that moment, he activated his uncanny magic, causing his skin to harden and become stone. Using an agile kick, he popped the sallet into the air, catching it with his sword. He offered it to the paladin, whose mouth was softly parted in a look of shock. She took it quickly and placed it back over her head, tucking her braid underneath it. Justin shouted as he rolled from behind his shield and plunged his sword into the beast's neck. It hiss-roared wickedly in response to the critical wound, its tail retaliating directly at Justin. It struck his neck, but it deflected off ineffectively.

The woman whose sallet Justin returned stood there in further amazement. His hardened skin easily resisted the puncture of the venomous barb. Justin pulled his shield close and bashed it into the face of the beast. It hissed and snapped its maw into the shield, repeatedly striking like a snake. It continued to try and prick Justin with its deadly tail, but between the shield and his hardened skin, the wyvern had no such luck. The woman started to engage but was forced to defend against the wyvern's slashing claws on the ends of its wings. It easily had a twenty-foot wingspan, allowing it to fend off multiple attackers in a large diameter with the claws on the ends of its flexible wings. Justin took the momentary distraction to pull his shield to his left and strike the beast. The beast lunged when the shield opened, but it was a ruse. Justin quickly snapped the shield back to center, connecting hard with the wyvern's snakelike head. It unfurled its neck further, the deflection leaving it vulnerable. Justin did not hesitate, striking a mortal blow at the base of the wyvern's skull. It made a shrieking-hissing noise and then began to sputter.

The adrenaline rushing through Justin was the most incredible sensation he had ever felt. Today, he had slain a terrible beast, one intent on killing his brethren. He immediately dreamed of further glory, ready to engage with the other beasts. After a moment, the wyvern before him collapsed onto the deck. Justin turned to see that the other Shield Knights formed similarly sized groups, using their numbers and defensive position to keep one wyvern flapping frustrated over the water and the other dead on the deck. The Shield

Knights regrouped, causing the remaining wyvern to beat its wings faster, granting it altitude. Before Gamnir could issue any orders, the beast looked up and gave a shrieking hiss. Seemingly out of nowhere, a paladin mounted on a pegasus darted in for a swift, decapitating blow. The beast splashed into the ocean below before anybody could size up the situation.

In a beautiful parade, more pegasus followed, flying northbound like *The Valiant Sailor*. The Pegasus Knights scattered through the Sea of Undine, quickly dispatching the wyverns accosting other vessels. One of the pegasus landed on the upper deck of the ship. Justin looked to the lieutenant for further orders, the immediate threat eliminated. Gamnir examined the skies before ordering the Shield Knights to stand down. They retired their shields to their backs. The lieutenant commanded, "Await here for further instruction. I will go speak with the commander."

The lieutenant scurried up the stairs to the upper deck. Four of the Shield Knights were looking at Justin intently, his skin still appearing to be made of stone. The woman whose helmet he recovered spoke first, "Well, you're a wild one, paladin."

Justin's face contorted with confusion. He had not committed to either path yet and started to correct her, "I'm sorry to mislead anyone. I have not yet chosen a path within the church," he replied.

The woman took her sallet off, as did two other Shield Knights. "Well met, Justin the Watchful. I am Valarie the Persistent, Shield Knight of Invictus, Judge of Retribution," she introduced, a smile growing on her lips. Justin just now noticed that she looked determined, tough, and beautiful. The hair on the back and sides of her head had been shaved clean, and her remaining golden blond hair had been pulled into a tight ponytail braid. Her skin tone was a warm brown. Her features were strong, and her brown eyes seemed perpetually narrowed and scrutinous. She was only an inch shorter than Justin, wearing a field plate similar to the commander and lieutenant minus the mithril shine and ornate decoration.

"Has my name passed through the ranks so quickly?" Justin replied.

One of the other Shield Knights nodded," And for good reason. You just slew a wyvern with as little effort as breathing. I am Tavi the Permanent, Shield Knight of Invictus. This is Dolan the Unseen," he introduced, gesturing to the other knight who had removed his helmet. All three of them were humans, their armor similar enough. The shields were all the same. Justin realized they must be standard issue for this group of knights within the church.

"I couldn't have done so without the solidarity of the Shield Knights," he explained, trying to maintain a front of humility. Inside he was swelling with pride. Justin's experiences over the last three days were drastic, from near death to slaying a deadly wyvern. Suddenly, circumstances aligned in his favor, and the other clergy noticed him. This was a new feeling to Justin, having always worked under Selasine, who was incredibly tough and experienced. Among his peers, however, he stood out.

"No need to be modest," Valarie replied, still smiling. "You can turn your skin to stone. You'd make an incredible Shield Knight."

Justin breathed swiftly with excitement. "What are the requirements for becoming a Shield Knight?" he asked.

Tavi replied, "Only those that walk the path of paladin can be welcomed as a Shield Knight. As many groups do, we undergo different training than the rest of the paladins. There are around ten thousand of us within the church. We specialize in defensive combat strategies that allow maximum opportunity with our shields."

Justin nodded, feeling his heart shift. The massive shields were impressive and enabled a different fighting style than he was accustomed to. He wanted to know more. Though paladins in the church walked a more military-focused path, the ultimate philosophical and spiritual goals were the same. Not all paladins had to be born imposing; he had realized that many of them found their overwhelming presence through the discipline and training they endured. For the first time in his life, he also felt large and imposing. August always seemed to best him in one-on-one combat. But to be fair, Justin had assumed the outcomes of those matches before they began. He realized he was his own worst enemy in those fights. He assumed victory over the wyvern. Just like he assumed defeat against August. Perhaps he was strong and valiant enough. He finally responded, "Very well. On this day, I claim the path of the paladin. I will wield my sword as an instrument of justice. I will wear my armor to defend the weak. The might of Invictus is my strength, and his will is my will. I devote myself to his laws, to his ways, and to his mind. I bind myself to the brotherhood of paladins within the Church of Invictus. My blade is your blade, my shield your shield. May order and prosperity light the path before us," he swore, reciting the pledge made by paladins as they joined the path.

Valarie's smile had grown, shifting from a small lip curl to a broad grin. "Then welcome, Paladin Justin the Watchful. May Invictus shower you with his strength," she replied.

Tavi and Dolan smiled as well, replacing their sallets. "Here comes the lieutenant," they warned.

"Shield Knights!" they heard Gamnir call for their attention.

In unison, they turned, standing at attention with their shield hands on the hilts of their swords. Justin joined the stance out of habit more than any presumptions.

"The Pegasus Knights have made some interesting reports. High Priest Carulus has stopped responding to correspondence from the archbishop. The girl has been whisked away to the Isles Known for Nothing. Two church members, a bishop and an acolyte, are in pursuit. We are changing our course for the Isles Known for Nothing. This will possibly require four to six days of sailing. We will return to our normal training schedule as we sail. Until then, you are dismissed. At ease," he explained, the line of well-armored paladins relaxing.

Valarie then spoke, "Lieutenant! I wish to notify you that Justin the Watchful has publicly declared his paladinhood in service to Invictus. I wish to formally invite him to train with the Shield Knights."

Gamnir looked from Valarie to Justin slowly. "Is that so, paladin?"

Justin nodded with confirmation. "Serving Invictus by your side has been an honor, one I wish to carry with me through my future years. I, too, humbly petition to be a part of your division."

The lieutenant inhaled sharply. "Do you swear to use your shield to defend the innocent and to block the onslaught of chaos?"

"I do," Justin replied, then saluted.

"Then it's settled. I declare your admission to the Shield Knights of Invictus. Report for training on the deck this evening after the sun has completely set. Understood?"

Justin relaxed to attention again, "Sir!" he replied.

That evening, Justin reported to the deck as required. He exited the forecastle, the sun directly in front of him. The ship's trajectory had changed to the southeast, which put the forecastle's exit facing directly northwest. The sun was nestling its way beneath the horizon. He knew he was on time. He was not the first to arrive, either. Valarie was already on deck, polishing her sword. Her sallet was sitting beside her, the gold braid on her head shimmering in the last vestiges of the sunlight. She was seated on a crate in front of the forecastle. When Justin emerged, she smiled at him, "Hey, paladin, come and talk."

Justin nodded and approached. Her smile was contagious, prompting him to return it. "So where did you learn to fight like that?" she began, reaching over to a rag nearby with several sharpening and polishing tools. She took a whetstone and began to sharpen her blade, emphasizing the casual nature of her questions.

"My teacher is Thomas Selasine. A most capable warpriest," Justin replied.

Valarie's tongue jutted out between her teeth, expressing concentration and precision. The whetstone made the steel of the blade chime as she made a grinding pass along the side of the blade. "I don't know this Selasine, but I'm jealous of your training. You are already an expert monster slayer," she commented.

Justin shook his head authentically, "Oh, no way! That was my first monster kill. Bishop Selasine always handles the violent part. Says he wanted us to train a little more before moving from defense to offense."

Valarie scowl-smiled again. "So, your first kill is a *wyvern*? Some sergeants have never even seen such a fierce beast," she retorted.

Justin backpedaled, "Oh, goodness. I've just trapped myself between modesty and showboating. My apologies. Please, I mean it when I say I couldn't have fought the beast without your help. Tavi's too. Too many targets and a beast has little reasoning in a fight."

"But you predicted the wyvern's movements and responses perfectly. Your mind is truly amazing," she replied, pausing her focus on the blade of her sword to look Justin in the eyes.

"August always teased me for ensuring I trained and studied equally. I've read Kzar's *Wyrm Ecology* and *Wyverns: Anatomy and Behavior*," he commented, feeling vindicated.

Valarie blinked for a moment. "August? Kzar's? What?" she bumbled in return.

Justin smiled and looked back at Valarie, his green eyes shimmering with excitement. That was the sign that he was about to begin a lecture. Unfortunately for Justin, he realized the sun had set, and the rest of the Shield Knights were beginning their training. He loosened the shield on his back and brought it forward. It cast an eerie shadow over his entire body. He stood, canceling his lecture. "It looks like it's time to start," he lamented.

Valarie smiled, "You can tell me about those names later. Come, I will be your training partner tonight and show you the ropes." She stood, put on her sallet, and picked up her shield, which had been propped nearby. "You've obviously used a tower shield before, so I don't need to show you any basics, do I?"

Justin's shoulders went up into an embarrassed shrug. "Second time. Part of Bishop Selasine's training was to be adaptable. I've had to fend off hydra heads with nothing but stones and a steel shield! The bishop wanted me to keep the heads busy while he got close to destroy the hydra's body. All I had to do was toss stones at the heads to keep their attention, and I blocked its strikes with the shield I was given."

Valarie huffed. "A hydra killer too, then, eh?" she said, her voice severe but teasing.

Justin smirked, "The wyvern was definitely scarier." They moved to some open space on the deck. *The Valiant Sailor* was quite large, easily accommodating this search party. He strapped his arm into his shield and set it firmly before him. The lightweight mithril was roughly the same weight as the much smaller steel shield he used while helping Bishop Selasine. He could bash as easily as block. "But not knowing what I am doing, that's the most terrifying thing to me. Please, start with the basics."

Valarie laughed. "You know, I think people are so impressed with you because you're so disciplined and authentic. The world can see your faith in the Sword, and we can't help but be inspired by it." She then stepped her body between him and his shield. She pulled his arm out of the leather shield strap and slipped hers into it with a tighter grip toward her elbow. "You can move it faster if you use your whole arm."

Justin felt his cheeks flush. Something about Valarie seemed different to him. She was strong and interesting. As she slipped her arm out of the shield brace, he replaced his arm, sliding it further than he was used to. He tightened the leather around his elbow and gripped the brace for the shield. He murmured, "Like that?"

She smiled. "That's perfect. Now, pivot," she ordered, her armor rustling as she firmly planted her left foot behind the shield. Shifting all her weight to that foot, she rotated her posture away from Justin by stepping with her right.

He complied, and the light mithril shield pivoted easily with his stance. He found himself tucked behind her again, that feeling returning. He stepped away after practicing the pivot. He smiled back at her, trying to make sense of his feelings. "So, can you dance across a battlefield with this technique?"

She chuckled. "If you do it right and know where the enemy fire is coming from, sure."

Justin pivoted on his right foot, tightened his shield to him, and stretched out his other leg. He then made another pivot, the shield moving at an angle that would cover him from most directions had his movements been fast enough. He smiled broadly. "Wow, this really is a powerful tool!"

Valarie beamed. "Yeah, and the best part? We look pretty badass when we get together on the battlefield." She winked at Justin, making his cheeks flush again. He had to admit the Shield Knights were a sight to behold on the battlefield, even though he had only seen them in action a few hours ago. Nevertheless, he was happy to be training with Valarie. She helped him slay a wyvern! Previously, he had been sad he was separated from his comrades. He understood now what Maréli meant about destiny. He then wondered if Valarie and the Shield Knights were part of his destiny. They also trained together the following night; Valarie showed him formation tactics commonly used by the Shield Knights when they fought as a division.

On the third day of the voyage, Justin was assigned to help on the gun deck. He awoke an hour before dawn as per his routine. He said his morning prayers, groomed, and dressed in the set of field plate armor given to him the day before. Gamnir met with him, officially giving him the spare armor and the mithril shield he borrowed from the top of the forecastle. Justin was grateful and swore to use them with pride as a Shield Knight.

After grabbing a serving of cold, stale bread and vegetable paste from the mess cabin, Justin reported to the gun deck as expected. When he walked up from the third deck, the early morning sun eerily illuminated the dusty space. He twisted his lips, wondering what kind of tasks they would have. A voice interrupted his internal questions. "So, you are going to add cannons to your arsenal of tricks?" Valarie asked, also emerging from the third deck.

Justin smiled big as his new friend greeted him. "Not exactly by choice, but new knowledge and experience never hurt."

She chuckled, her voice always lighter than her expression. "Well, sadly, gun deck duty is the most boring assignment on a ship like this. Usually. We'll probably have to clean the cannons, but beyond that, there won't be much to do unless there's a fight."

The new paladin continued to smile. "Guess it's a good thing I brought something to read!" he laughed.

"How are you so insightful, valiant, intelligent, and handsome at the same time?" she teased.

His shoulders raised into a shy, embarrassed shrug, staying there until he was finished speaking. "I had an excellent teacher," he responded, but the inflection in his voice made it sound like a question.

Valarie smirked and walked across the open space of the gun deck. She sat on a stool in front of a cannon hatch on the starboard side. Justin followed and stood close to her, pushing the hatch open slightly. It opened to the outside with a hinge at the top, letting gravity keep it closed when not in use. It squeaked thanks to the deterioration of the metals in the hinge. Opening the hatch let in more light, so Justin affixed the latch that would leave it completely open. They could see the calm waters of the Solar Sea glowing a fluorescent pink in the early morning light.

Looking at the glowing water, Valarie commented, "The Solar Sea is so much more beautiful than the Sea of Nulodia."

Justin tilted his head curiously. "Is that where you are from?" he asked.

She nodded, staring at the water. "What about you?"

"Devitus," he replied.

Her eyes broke away from the water, and the grin on her lips made Justin's heart skip a beat. "So, you're a frontier guy. That explains why you're so wild," she giggled. She was glad he'd be with her for gun deck duty.

He smiled in return, "Well, August is the one who always wanted to hunt, fish, and stay out in the woods. It's not that I don't like those things, but I've been very committed to my success in the church."

Valarie thought it was cute that he always tried to dodge compliments. "You promised to tell me about August, yes?"

Justin laughed, finding another stool nearby and pulling it close to the hatch. In the meantime, the king's gunners and other paladins assigned to gun deck duty had arrived. Nobody gave any orders, so Justin and Valarie remained by the hatch on the starboard side.

"August and Miranda both. My friends from Devitus. I always thought August would become a paladin. He's a big guy, tough as nails. Not very disciplined, though," he explained.

She pursed her lips in thought. "It takes great discipline to be a paladin, usually. Not all of us are so uptight, though. There's no law against being a fun person and learning how to relax when the situation doesn't require protocol," she continued.

He nodded in agreement. "I used to think the only things a paladin needed to be were strong and brave. I also didn't think I was either of those things."

Valarie's eyes widened, the brown orbs inside glinting in the sunlight. Her mouth was fixed in a rounded look of disbelief, "Oh, Justin," she huffed. "The way you kicked my helmet up so casually the other day. You not only looked strong and brave to me but smooth too." She shrugged, the slightest hint of shyness in her body language. "And I can't help it; I'm totally drawn to smooth people."

Justin blinked for a moment, absorbing her words carefully. He leaned toward the hatch, which opened conveniently at chest level for a seated adult human. He rested his arms on the opening, casually propping his chin in his hand. "I've always been lost when it comes to what kinds of people I am drawn to. My friend Miranda is totally beautiful and the kindest person I've ever met, but she's always felt like a sister to me. August is a total macho guy who can sometimes be difficult to deal with. Still, he's astute underneath that macho exterior," he stumbled through his words a little bit, the topic unsettling for him.

She also leaned forward, resting her chin in her hands on the opening, propped on her elbows. "Where are your friends?" she asked, curious about them.

Justin let out a soft breath. "It sounds like they all went to the Isles Known for Nothing. Miranda's healing powers seem to have gotten her into some trouble. Got me killed, too," he laughed casually.

Valarie's expression twisted into horror. "Wait, what?" she asked, shocked.

Justin nodded in return. "Miranda can heal beyond what

any priest has ever seen or done. I'm unsure why or how, but she's been amazingly blessed by Invictus. The pirates we were sent to fight kidnapped her right out of the camp. I was guarding her tent when suddenly I was on the ground, losing consciousness. I'll never forget the stinging sensation in my neck." He paused, subconsciously raising his hand to touch his neck. He swallowed and continued slowly, "The world went black, and all I can remember after that were golden swirling clouds. The next thing I really knew, two days had passed, and Miranda, August, and the bishop were long gone. That's why I came with the search party. I got killed and left behind."

Valarie's normally scrutinous expression was soft and sympathetic. She placed a hand on Justin's arm. "Do you know who brought you back?" she asked gently.

His eyes lingered on the beautiful colors in the water. He shook his head. "No, but I've felt free ever since I've been back. The temporary nature of mortality no longer feels like a weight. I felt no fear facing that wyvern because there were only two outcomes. And I knew before we began that destiny had already chosen the victor." Justin smiled after his explanation, clasping her hand on his arm with his other hand, still watching the pink light dance on the ocean's surface below.

Her concerned look washed away to an expression of comfort. "Just so you know, that only makes me twice as lucky to have met you."

His eyes cut from the water to her, meeting her gaze. "A month ago, I would have never thought somebody was lucky to know me. I'm just the middle child in a poor farmer's family. Agriculture was boring to me, so I joined the church. Now that I've glimpsed the other side," he said but then paused. "Now that I've seen it, I feel like I have to make the most of this gifted time."

Valarie took a deep breath and rested her head in a single hand on the hatch. "Your story sounds like the beginning of a legend. It's almost too good to be true."

Justin laughed, thinking to take a look around the gun deck. Everyone else was lounged or relaxed, and the king's gunners were napping in hammocks that had been strung up between the framing of the ship. "I'm sure your story is great, too," he continued.

She gave a half smile. "Not quite. I ran away from home at sixteen. My father wanted to arrange a marriage for me with a man I didn't like. It was a business decision or something."

Justin looked concerned. "The law in Alabaster allows a person to object to an arranged marriage, no?"

She shrugged. "It's about the same as running away if you back out of something like that. I just wanted to leave it all behind and find something to make my own. My mom left our family while I was still a baby, and my dad became more involved with shady business dealings. So, I ran away. That's when I met a priest of Invictus who helped me find my place in the church there in Nulodia. Fighting against the forces of chaos gives me a purpose I can stand by," she explained.

Justin smiled, "That's a pretty exciting story to me!"

Valarie laughed, "That was a whole four years ago. I've arrested a hundred lawbreakers and managed to join the Shield Knights last year. And you joined just a week ago and already have more monster kills than I do." Her lips twisted into a smile, which Justin found increasingly and deviously alluring.

He still held her hand under his, and he squeezed gently. "Like I said, it's an exciting story to me."

She wrinkled her nose in disbelief. "Why?"

His smile was wild, and he felt his heartbeat in his entire body. "Because it means you didn't get married yet. And what kind of legends have you ever heard that didn't have at least one good love story?"

She tilted her head. "But! I said your story was a legend, not mine," she objected.

Justin suavely responded, "I know."

Valarie's smooth, brown cheeks seemed permanently fixed into a smile. "So, is that how it's going to be?"

He shrugged his shoulders, with his lips twisting into a smirk. "I wouldn't mind it at all," he retorted.

She scooted her stool closer to him, so close that their legs touched. "If you were any smoother, I could skip you over the top of the water there," she teased, returning her gaze to the beautiful Solar Sea in the early sunlight.

They watched the water's color change from pink to blue,

holding hands silently for another half hour. They then spent the rest of their gun deck duty picking on each other, talking about nothing and everything, and complaining about how bored they would be if they had been put on duty with anybody else. From that moment on, Justin and Valarie were practically inseparable.

The following day, Justin learned more about defensively and offensively using a tower shield. Lieutenant Gamnir filed the necessary paperwork for Justin's promotions and accolades and sent it to Nulodia by messenger hawk. Throughout that day, Valarie worked with Justin to teach him new prayers unique to the Shield Knights. She was a fierce training partner, and if Justin tried to slack off, she made him pay for it. Thanks to his commitment to disciplined training, she found that he was an adept fighter and a quick thinker. They challenged each other to reach the next level of form and fighting wit. On the fourth day of their voyage to the Isles Known for Nothing, they reported for their evening training as they had every day.

Lieutenant Gamnir stood atop the forecastle, looking down at the Shield Knights as they trained. He noticed that Justin had made significant progress over the previous four days. The commander's instincts about him were correct; with his sharp mind and his honed discipline, he would make one of the most impressive paladins the church had ever seen.

Justin crouched slightly behind his shield as Valarie unleashed a series of attacks against him with her sword. Most clergy trained with wooden or fake weapons, but Justin had insisted that Valarie use a regular sword. His ability to turn his skin to stone made it safe for him and better, more accurate training for her. As Justin heard the sounds of the attacks on the outside of his shield, he used the sounds to formulate a plan. He pivoted with his right foot and swung his shield heavily to his left, the same direction Valarie was moving with her attacks. His sudden movement caused her to try and redirect, but she took the feint. As she thought she had found an opening in Justin's defenses, she expected her sword to connect with Justin's stone skin. However, she found herself outsmarted and trapped. Justin was waiting, spaced away from the shield, feigning a mighty blow with the wooden sword he had used for practice. The field plate mostly protected her neck, but some vulnerable flesh was still exposed between the bottom of the sallet and the top of the armor's collar. Valarie stood with wide eyes as she fell for it.

Gamnir smiled to himself. If somebody else had told him that Justin joined the Shield Knights less than a week ago, he would have cursed them for lying. Well ahead of schedule, thanks to favorable winds, *The Valiant Sailor* would arrive in Yendralia the following day, and their arrival worried the lieutenant. Rumored to be a haven for pirates, he did not expect a warm welcome. However, the more concerning situation was that Carulus had not communicated with the search party in the last three days. His most recent correspondence insisted that finding the girl, dead or alive, was critical to prevent an international incident. Correspondence from the archbishop agreed with those fears. Justin insisted he had a personal connection with the girl they sought. Gamnir decided to talk to Justin before they tried to dock in Yendralia.

Valarie, panting from the exertion of the training, started to laugh. "What a dirty trick," she joked.

Justin smirked. "Deception for personal gain is a chaotic act. The penance is to tell the truth twice as many times as you lied. One feint, two truths. One, your footwork gets predictable when your opponent moves. Two, an obvious opening against an experienced fighter is always a trap."

She scowled back with a smile in her eyes, "Yeah, *experienced* fighters."

Justin lowered his wooden sword and relaxed his grip on his shield. "This is true. I had never fought a deadly creature without my mentor until we fought those wyverns. I still have much to learn. I guess that leads me to a third truth," he smiled. "You're cute when you're caught by surprise."

Valarie's smiling scowl turned into a broad smile. Lanterns hung overhead, lighting the ship's deck, making it the perfect low-visibility condition for training. "Don't get too cocky, paladin." She stood tall for a moment. Ever since yesterday on the gun deck, she couldn't get Justin out of her head. She would ask the gods for help sorting out her heart, but those matters were outside Invictus's purview. Lexcord would just tell her to follow her heart. Which she planned on doing anyway. "Besides, I know your greatest weakness," she taunted.

He raised his sword again. "And what is that, then?"

She pursed her lips seductively, her eyes flickering wildly behind her helmet. "Me," she mumbled mischievously. With a quick strike, she initiated the second phase of their training: no shields. They both dropped their defenses. Justin was smart, but Valarie was fast. Her sword clinked off of his hardened skin once before he began parrying her strikes into his armor. He never found the footing to return to the offensive, perpetually fending off her attacks with little success. Her assault was so precise and quick that Justin soon found himself backed against the forecastle. Valarie pushed him against it, disarmed him, and pressed the side of her sword against his stone-protected neck. She leaned in very close to his face, her lips hovering mere inches from his. That seductive look was back. She could see the emotions in his eyes; his body tired from the sudden onslaught and a curious twinkle of excitement. "Too bad. The lieutenant is watching," she giggled, pulling away and returning to the center of the deck.

Gamnir peered down the forecastle, the brutal display having caught his attention. Valarie's style was hypnotic, and her uncanny magic helped her unleash more attacks than any foe could ever block. He could see the chemistry between the two, causing him to chuckle. They were good kids. It looked right to him. "Lexcord, smile on them," he prayed, deferring to the Silver Maiden, whose blessings were more whimsical and romantic than Invictus's.

Justin laughed, elated by Valarie's playfulness. His disciplined nature was starting to relax. He loved his friends dearly but never had fun like this. It was easy to be disciplined when he grew up on a farm, where the routines and the chores kept him perpetually busy. Serving the church in a bigger context really opened his eyes to the size of the world and the diversity of the people in it, even within the church itself.

Lieutenant Gamnir called from the top of the forecastle, "Adûnzha!"

The Shield Knights training on deck dropped what they

were doing, sheathed their training weapons, and stood at attention. Gamnir smiled at the crispness of his fellow Shield Knight's form. He began to speak, "Tomorrow, we arrive at the Isles Known for Nothing. At the very least, we expect tension between ourselves and the residents of the pirate capital Yendralia. This is not a mission to arrest pirates, nor is this an island vacation. We have one goal: locate the girl. She is to be treated as brethren, contrary to previous orders. Understood?"

The Shield Knights snapped into a salute. "Sir!" they replied in unison.

"With that, you are dismissed. Enjoy your last night at sea," Gamnir commented, turning to climb down into the forecastle.

Valarie's eyes went straight from the forecastle to Justin. Her excitement was palpable. She reached out and grabbed him by the hand, "Food?" she asked.

Justin nodded, gripping her hand in his. "Now you're reading my mind," he laughed. They collected their training equipment and went down to the third deck, where the mess cabin and several sleeping cabins were located. They put their things away and met in the mess cabin. They took some warm, citrusy soup supplemented with jerky and cheese for the late evening meal. Though the mess cabin had long benches for entire crews to eat comfortably at the tables, there were also smaller tables around the room, probably for the ship's officers. Most of the other clergy had already eaten, so the cabin was sparsely occupied. Justin and Valarie selected one of the smaller tables.

"If I had to guess, you've never been to an island before, have you?" Valarie began.

Justin shook his head. "The geography texts that I have read talk more about the islands in the Twin Seas, more than anywhere else. Based on what the lieutenant said, though, it looks like we won't get to enjoy the islands."

Valarie nodded in return, greedily enjoying the soup. The wooden spoon protruded from her mouth as she paused, looking at Justin. He chuckled softly; she looked like she had expected him to continue talking. Instead, he had passed the conversation back to her mid-bite. She withdrew the spoon from her mouth and put it back in the bowl. "Sorry, I'm not really used to eating with company," she apologized. She was a free spirit but valued her discipline and manners.

Justin smiled. The butterflies in his stomach made it hard for him to eat right now anyway. "I don't guess there's a book that can tell you exactly what to expect when you meet a person you never expected," he commented.

She looked at Justin with adoration and a hint of trepidation. "If tomorrow gets crazy," she started.

He nodded, the same thoughts already running through his mind. "It won't," he said confidently.

A shy smile replaced her concern. They finished their meal quietly and walked around the ship together, hand in hand. The midsummer air near the Isles Known for Nothing felt crisp and warm. They found themselves on the forecastle, looking out over the bow. The black waters churned beneath The Valiant Sailor. "Justin?" Valarie asked, breaking the silence.

"Yes?" he replied, not snapping to attention at the sound of his name for the first time in as long as he could remember.

"Can I hold you under the stars tonight?" she asked, her heart racing.

His cheeks flushed in the torchlight, and he squeezed her hand. "Protocol only dictates that we rest, not where we rest," he said, a grin spreading across his lips.

Her brown eyes twinkled with excitement. She pulled his arm, leading him toward the storage area Justin had found earlier that week. They piled some crates and cloth together, making a comfortable place to rest on the deck. They sat, putting their backs against the crates. Though they were supposed to be watching the stars, they couldn't take their eyes off each other. Valarie held Justin close to her, an arm around his waist. It caused a profound, comforting feeling in Justin's soul. Valarie ran her fingers through his hair, her touch making his entire body tingle. The young paladin saw the same wildness behind her eyes, her lips resting slightly open as she relished having him so close. He also had an arm draped around her shoulder. Sitting in such a way might have been uncomfortable under normal circumstances, but he could only feel the fire in her touch.

Valarie leaned in close as she had done during training.

"The lieutenant isn't watching anymore," she whispered, her body instinctively sucking in a quick, deep breath. She boldly pressed her lips into his, kissing him with every fiber of her existence. Justin's right hand instinctively reached up to cup her face, kissing her back with the same energy. She continued to run her fingers through his hair as their kiss ignited feelings deep within them that neither fully understood. After some time, she pulled away and laid her head on Justin's shoulder. She brought her arm from around his waist to under his arm, reaching through for his hand. She interlocked her fingers with his. Their hearts beat in unison the entire night, holding each other close like they were holding the most precious treasure known to the world.

The Shield Knights stood assembled on deck as Yendralia came into view about an hour after sunrise the next morning. Though the ocean glowed in the early morning light, the mountains surrounding the island city cast a long and ominous shadow over *The Valiant Sailor* as it approached. Their assignment was simple: defend the gangplank once the anchor was dropped. Justin and Valarie stood together, fully armed and armored. Gamnir paced along the length of the deck for a while until the ship rounded the island's west side, heading straight east to the docks and the tide wall that made this island an easily defensible position.

"Shield Knights!" he ordered.

They all snapped to attention, their sword hands dropping to their hilts. The lieutenant made a quick inspection. "Justin the Watchful, a word, please," he asked.

"Sir!" he responded with a brief salute and then stepped forward.

Lieutenant Gamnir lowered his voice so that only Justin could hear, "What is it that you know about the girl beyond her healing capabilities?"

Justin made a grim face. "Miranda was an orphan raised by the monks of Lexcord near Devitus. I know very little about her family. She pledged service to the Sword of Justice a year ago and worked with me as a peacekeeper. She is kind and gentle, and she prefers to resolve conflict without violence," he explained.

Gamnir nodded. "According to our intel, she peacefully removed Claston's navy from their watch points. This matches your description perfectly. Please, continue," the lieutenant commented.

Justin combed his mind for information that would be helpful to the lieutenant. "Oh!" he suddenly remembered. "She didn't seem to have full control over her gift. Our teacher is Bishop Thomas Selasine. He is pursuing her as well, according to Chief Healer Maréli. I would advise seeking their assistance and counsel if we locate him or his other pupil, August Burchard." His posture returned to attention, indicating that he had no more useful information.

"Excellent. Thank you, paladin," he concluded. "Rejoin your brethren."

Justin complied as ordered. The Shield Knights stood attentive as *The Valiant Sailor* approached the docks. They were flying the colors of Invictus, a royal purple flag with the golden scales of justice stitched into the center. A lone figure stood at the end of one of the docks observing the ship. He might have been five hundred feet away, but he still seemed huge. Everyone on the ship heard words twisted into an eerie melody with no discernable source.

"The holy men came to town and told me how to pray. The holy men came to town and told me where to stay. The holy men built a church and asked me to pay for it." The singing sounded ominous.

Justin immediately recognized what was happening. He shouted, "Cover your ears!" when he had the realization. The Shield Knights close to him let go of their shields and plugged their ears.

The singing continued. "The holy men started a war and asked me to die in it. The holy men promised my soul would be safe in their care, but who looks after the holy men? Sleep now and rest your weary burdens, holy men. Sleep until your soul is made whole." the words rang out across the deck of *The Valiant Sailor*, clergy looking around confused.

The lieutenant turned toward the Shield Knights and began to ask Justin about his outburst, but the officer fell to the deck. One of the other Shield Knights, who Justin had come to know as Trevor the Swift, rushed forward to check on the lieutenant, but he, too, collapsed. Valarie looked at Justin, a fearful look in her eyes. Justin mouthed, "It's going to be okay," leaving his hands firmly pressed against his new sallet, blocking his ears. Within a minute, most of the crew and the clergy had fallen into a deep, magical slumber. Both the commander and the lieutenant had succumbed to the magic. Justin, Valarie, and Tavi had all covered their ears before the words had their intended effect. A cleric that Justin had seen around the ship stood nearby, bewildered.

Suddenly, the boat lurched. The captain had fallen asleep at the wheel, causing it to turn dramatically. Valarie and Justin quickly grabbed for each other to keep steady as the deck dipped and tilted to port side. *The Valiant Sailor* was in the middle of a turn far too sharp, aiming it directly at the docks. Justin acted quickly, hoping the song had ended and lowering his hands from his ears. He sprinted into action, running up the stairs to the upper deck, gripping the railing and rigging with all his might. Arriving at the helm, he pulled the sleeping captain away from the wheel. He then pushed the wheel hard in the other direction causing the ship to buoy in the wake caused by their previous sudden turn.

A handful of other paladins and clerics either resisted the effects of the song or covered their ears as well. As Justin tried to steady the ship, an acolyte burst out of the forecastle in a panic. The song echoed throughout the ship, putting almost everyone working below deck to sleep. About fifteen of the two hundred people on *The Valiant Sailor* remained awake. The boat rocked hard in the other direction, causing a couple of people on deck to fall. Valarie and Tavi grabbed onto some rigging to keep steady. Justin could tell the ship was on course for disaster at this speed and trajectory. He shouted, "Hold on!" to the rest of the deck as he tried to let the rudder steady and return to a neutral position. The already choppy waters caused *The Valiant Sailor* to bounce on a wave as it turned hard back to starboard. The sudden reversal caused by Justin's last push of the wheel created a new gush of waves not even two hundred feet from the docks. The previous waves crashed hard against the ship's hull, pushing along their initial course. *The Valiant Sailor* began to tip to its left, causing a renewed panic to grab onto something on the deck. Unconscious paladins and clerics were strewn about the deck, their bodies rolling hard with each lurch of the ship.

Justin could see the man on the docks smiling and backing away slowly. *The Valiant Sailor* bounced in the water again, tilting somewhat less drastically to the right. However, its course was still sideways as the inertia from the first sudden change had yet to dissipate fully. The ship slowly slid into the hardily constructed docks, causing their planks to shatter. The first set of posts burst into splinters from the weight of the ship, but they slowed its trajectory significantly. The sudden crash caused another wave of people falling on the deck, fueling the desperation of being somewhat forcibly docked while nearly the entire crew was asleep.

Running down from the upper deck, Justin's eyes furiously scanned for the highest-ranking person who avoided the enchantment. He could see the acolyte that had emerged from the forecastle, Valarie, Tavi, another paladin, and two recently promoted clerics. "Valarie," he said, calm. "You're a Judge. It looks like you might be in charge," he added as she, too, was already calculating their next move.

She smirked at him briefly before snapping into her well-disciplined role as highest ranking paladin. "Anybody know how to drive this thing?" she asked, shouting. The acolyte who had emerged from below raised her hand and rushed to the center of the deck.

"Acolyte Ondi, at your service," she introduced herself as she approached. An auburn braid hung down her back, and she wore a white cloak over her armor. "My father is a fisherman; I've never driven one this big, but I know the general idea."

Valarie nodded. "We need to get some space between us and the docks. Is there anything that can be done?" she asked, the role of leader coming naturally to her.

Ondi shook her head, "I'm afraid the boat is in a very compromised situation. We're not properly docked, so we are at the mercy of the tide." The ship lurched again as a wave pushed its weight against the docks. Justin winced; these docks were very well constructed, which was fortunate. The man who had been singing now had a crowd gathered around him. Justin cursed and began to pray.

Valarie turned to Justin, who was actively praying with his holy symbol in his hand. She listened to the words he whispered to their god, "Sword of Justice, remedy this accursed sleep. The laws of nature dictate our rest, not the machinations of chaos. Wake and be healed." A faint glow surrounded his symbol, but it abruptly returned to normal. He wrinkled his nose in frustration. "Looks like I'm not ready yet."

Valarie was going to ask Justin if he knew any prayers that might lift the magical sleep, but he was one step ahead of her. His knowledge kept him perpetually ahead of everyone else, especially their enemies. She had a sudden, terrifying thought, "Do you think that the perpetrator could cause harm in the same way they put our forces to sleep?"

Justin shook his head confidently, "No, this seems like the working of a very powerful bard. There are many different songs of power, but I have never heard of anything able to cause bodily harm." He looked over the port side of the ship to the docks below. The crowd seemed to be a variety of pirates, common folk, and adventurers from many different paths. This could be a slaughter. Justin pointed out his concern.

Valarie's face darkened with frustration. "So, this is how they keep the law at bay. We don't stand a chance," she spat.

Justin looked at the forecastle and thought about the cannons. "Can anybody man the gun deck? Scattershot should keep would-be boarders at bay!" he shouted.

Justin recognized the paladin on deck as he approached. They hadn't spoken personally, but Justin had seen him on the gun deck before. "I'll see what I can do," he said, rushing below deck. Looking out over the side, the man that loomed on the docks previously had approached.

"I see that some of you didn't enjoy my song!" a melodic voice called up to them, clear as if he were standing beside them.

Justin stepped to the side of the deck and looked down at the probable culprit of the sleeping song. "I can't say that I'm a fan of taking naps. It shows a lack of discipline," he replied sarcastically.

The man began to laugh and laughed a little more than he should have. He continued, "You have a sense of humor for a lawman. That you would paint yourself with such a caricature is but music to my ears! Please tell me, holy man, why have you come to the shores of Yendralia flying the colors of the one who would see us flayed?"

Justin turned to look at Valarie, who would have to answer a question of that nature. He gave her a deferent nod, and she stepped toward the side. "We have no desire to flay anyone; we merely seek to prevent a tragedy. A girl was probably brought to this port a few days ago by one called Erk. Her testimony and presence are needed to prevent an international incident between Claston and Alabaster."

The man smiled in such an eerie way that it made Valarie shiver. His voice sang out, "I don't think she's here anymore, lawwoman. I am Cantalus, He Who Sings at the Gate. I am also here to keep the gates closed to ones who would disturb the balance of the island. Do not think you are awake because you are clever. You were chosen."

Valarie and Justin looked at each other. Tavi had joined them to look out over the side at Cantalus. Justin looked back to clarify, "Chosen by whom?"

Cantalus began to sing again, "The verse of a tragic song beginning in the seas to the northeast. One thousand souls held over the depths. Their lives in your hands; how will you save them? Only time will tell if you have been tempered enough for your destiny." He stopped singing. "One comes that I must bid farewell. He will be your guide," he finished, walking away. Those previously gathered with him followed. Justin noticed another crowd had gathered about a thousand feet up the tide wall behind Cantalus at the city's gates.

It took He Who Sings at the Gate a few minutes to fade into the crowd, and after he did, the sounds coming from the crowd quietened. He assumed this Cantalus person must have had something to do with that. Justin also realized that the ship had drifted a little way out from the docks. Fortunately, the wind seemed calm and southern, making the ship stall with its sails at this angle. He asked Valarie, "Any ideas? Maybe try to wake up the others?"

Her lips were drawn tight in thought. Before she could respond, the crowd began to cheer, easily audible even a thousand feet away. It caused their attention to return to the crowd rather than the ship's situation, fearing a return of the singing man and his rough-looking crowd. After a few moments of watching, a distinct party emerged from the crowd. Justin squinted, trying to get a close look at this small group. As they neared the docks, they seemed to be coming straight for *The Valiant Sailor*. He noticed the leader was a rather tall orc with a massive sword strapped to his back. He wore a captain's hat. With him were three others: an elven woman with light blue hair and a gnarled staff in her hand, a gnoll with reddish-brown fur and two menacingly large scimitars on his back, and a human man with no obvious weapon.

As they approached, Justin began to worry these four would be more trouble than a mob. Their trajectory was obvious now, and a few peculiar things happened as they got close. The elven woman stamped her staff into the ground, causing a pillar of water to rise out of the ocean. She then slung the water into the opened cannon hatch, effectively nullifying the cannon as a defensive option. The gnoll cupped out his hands, causing several discs to form in the air. They then spaced themselves out and multiplied in a way that looked like a series of stairs. Justin felt his heart skip a beat and got his shield ready. He shouted, "State your intent!"

The orc replied loudly, "Fear not! I am Pirate Lord Ut'wah the Magnificent, Harbinger of Lexcord. We board peacefully. For now."

"Then why did you disable the cannon?" Valarie retorted.

"We didn't want any accidents," the elf shouted back.

Justin frowned. Their approach was quick. The Shield Knights grouped together, shields ready just in case.

Ut'wah made a final bounding leap from a disc that dispersed a bit higher than the deck. His entourage joined him, standing close together. The Shield Knights' hands were on the hilts of their swords. The boarders made no further movement. Ut'wah began to speak, "It looks like Cantalus has denied your vessel entry to the port. Sorry about that. We'll handle the repairs."

Valarie replied, "Does this mean we can't even dock and purchase supplies?"

Ut'wah laughed. "Yes, it does, but do not fear," he said as he pulled his holy symbol into clear view. Justin breathed a deep sigh of relief, and Valarie relaxed.

"Welcome, brethren," Valarie commented. "Is there a way to break the bard's magical sleep?"

Ut'wah nodded. "Affirmative! We simply need to push your ship out to sea somewhat, and the enchantment will break," he explained.

Valarie twisted her lips in thought. "It seems we have no choice but to accept your terms to prevent conflict with the citizens of the island."

The elf that had arrived with Ut'wah turned her staff sideways and began to chant. She closed her eyes, and the Shield Knights could feel the ship begin to move out to sea, a fast-moving current pulling it around and away from the docks. The rushing water beneath them put them on a course where the wind caught in the sails and started to push *The Valiant Sailor*. After a few hundred feet of distance were between the docks and the ship, the crew began to awaken. The elf relaxed and opened her eyes.

The lieutenant sat up, looking around, confused. Justin heard the echoes of "What happened?" and "What's going on?" begin to sound around the deck. They were lucky nobody had gone overboard in the near disaster at the docks. They definitely felt the impact of their sleeping bodies being tossed around on the ship. Justin winced and feared for anybody who fell asleep below deck where something could have potentially crushed them.

Ut'wah began to speak. "You have been denied entry to the island paradise of Yendralia. My apologies again." His voice was commanding but still pleasant. "I am Ut'wah of the Silver Maiden, Pirate Lord of Yendralia, and I implore your assistance."

"What gives you the right to deny our entry into the port?" a voice bellowed out from the upper deck. It was Commander

Aguila.

Ut'wah replied, "It is not I who rejected you. It was Cantalus, He Who Sings at the Gate. Again, apologies for the inconvenience."

The commander was clearly not pleased with Ut'wah and his companions. However, he had hurt his leg being tossed around the deck, gripping the railing hard as he descended the stairs. "And what gives this Cantalus the right? We mean no harm and have a critical mission," Commander Aguila replied indignantly.

Ut'wah stood tall. "Cantalus was one of the eight original pirate lords. He is the guardian spirit of Yendralia and a god that perpetually walks among mortals. You would do well to heed his judgment. He could have kept you away for your own sake. Yendralia can be a dangerous place for people of Invictus's cloth," he explained. "Do share your mission. I would like to know your goal."

The commander finally whispered a healing prayer at the bottom of the stairs from the upper deck. "We seek a girl with a magnificent healing gift. The King of Claston threatens war with Alabaster if the girl is not found and has questions about Erk and the sudden transport of the Claston blockade. Our intel says she may be on the island," Aguila replied.

Ut'wah frowned, his tusks pointing down. "Your intelligence is a little slow, then. The girl you speak of, this Miranda, correct?"

The commander nodded. Justin listened intently, the deck tense. He was concerned that violence might erupt between the clergy of Invictus and a holy warrior of Lexcord. He had no rank to voice his concerns, but he could interrupt with knowledge of what happened while the commander was unconscious. Finding the correct protocol, he strapped his shield on his back and stomped his foot into an attention stance. With a loud voice, he shouted, "Commander Aguila, Justin the Watchful, Sir! I wish to report what transpired while the commander was under the influence of a sleeping enchantment!"

The commander started to rebuke Justin but then realized the wisdom. If anybody had remained conscious, more than being pushed out to sea might have transpired. "Report, then, paladin."

"Sir! A mighty bard used a song of power to put nearly everyone on the ship to sleep. I was able to put the ship into a slide that minimized damage to both our vessel and the docks. These four boarded our ship while you slept, using uncanny magic. They did not threaten violence and claimed to be a peaceful envoy. They instructed us on breaking the enchantment, and thanks to their help, we are safe," he reported, hoping that was enough to dispel tension.

"Very well, thank you, paladin," the commander replied. "How did you resist the attack, Justin the Watchful?" he further questioned.

"I covered my ears as soon as I realized it was a song of power and instructed my fellow Shield Knights to do the same, sir!" he explained with a salute.

"Excellent work, then. Can anyone confirm Justin's version of events?"

Tavi and Valarie stomped at attention. "Sir!" they shouted in unison.

"His report is accurate?" he asked.

"Yes, sir!" they replied in salute.

"It seems we all owe you again. Your quick thinking shows your promise. Though it's uncommon, you would make an excellent Judge. If you will accept the title, I shall promote you to Justin the Watchful, Judge of Action," the commander said with a broad smile.

Justin's eyes widened in shock. Valarie beamed. "Sir! I gladly accept the title," he replied.

Commander Aguila turned his attention back to the orc, who was still watching. "Tell me then, brethren, why have you boarded our ship without clearance? I hope you understand this creates additional paperwork for me," the commander continued, withdrawing another badge from a pouch, and handing it to Justin as he walked from the stairs toward Ut'wah with Justin standing between them.

Ut'wah nodded, "Our Silver Maiden's brother is particular about processes, and I apologize for the additional burden. However, we do implore you to change your task."

Aguila's face twisted, confused. "We simply seek the girl Miranda. Do you have news of her?"

Ut'wah gave another nod. "She is on *The Nebula* with Dread Pirate Lord Erk, Pirate Lady Naomi, Bishop Thomas Selasine, and Acolyte August Burchard. I fear the Miranda you seek seems to be affected by a magical condition. Erk and his entourage are sailing to a potential solution. Their journey could take a couple of weeks, maybe longer. However, there is a more pressing matter for you," the orc explained.

Commander Aguila tilted his head forward a bit, "And what is that?" he asked, still somewhat hostile.

"A week ago, I had a terrible premonition that was confirmed to me when Erk was here. I dreamed that I would meet a woman with pure white hair. When I did, I found the King of Claston to have risen as a great demon. In this form, he committed many atrocities, including drowning one thousand of our brethren in the Church of Invictus," Ut'wah explained, raising his hand to scratch his chin in thought. "Erk is directly in opposition to Claston's usurper, as am I. Erk's end goal is likely to work with that girl to end Claston's oppressive rule. From what I understand, even Invictus would accept such a result."

The commander nodded, "Indeed, that would be acceptable if a ruler of appropriate caliber were prepared to replace them."

Ut'wah sighed. "Of course, I understand the end goal is to preserve the rule of law. But right now, I fear for the paladins in my dreams. They drowned in the conflict because it came to violence. I know my mission now that I have seen the white-haired girl. Delivered to me by the Silver Maiden herself in the form of a premonition," he explained.

"You believe that we can save them?" the commander queried.

"Not just you. Together. I have a magnificent fleet that we can use to coordinate the rescue of so many people. I assure you, the international conflict you fear will be much worse if the King of Claston acts violently against the church," Ut'wah reasoned.

"You are correct in that sense; what was your name,

brother?" the commander asked.

"Call me Ut'wah." The orc looked at the three Shield Knights prepared to defend the ship on their own. "I would like to know your name and the names of these three paladins willing to die defending their brethren."

The commander stood tall, "I am Commander Aguila, currently the officer overseeing the work of this search party. I would need authorization from the archbishop to join your mission. However, I would be authorized to accompany you if you are a merchant vessel providing us with supplies we could not purchase in port," he explained, pointing out the loophole allowing him to begin the journey before authorization was acquired. Justin loved the strategy. "These three: Justin the Watchful, Judge of Action, Valarie the Persistent, Judge of Retribution, and Tavi the Permanent. All three Shield Knights of Invictus, defenders of the innocent and the weak," the commander introduced.

Justin was annoyed that the orc assumed the outcome of their defense of the ship. However, he also realized that his assumption was made from a place of confidence, not cockiness. Ut'wah replied, "I propose that we sail at once. My crew will provide you with supplies and additional manpower if you will accept it. I have fifteen vessels under my command. My flagship, *The Silver Corsair*, could accommodate another hundred people easily, but we may have a thousand people to save. The more space we provide, the better."

Commander Aguila inhaled deeply. "I will write the appropriate correspondence and get these actions sanctioned by the church. I do hope your premonition and confirmation are of value to us. We are taught by the Sword of Justice to trust his sister's will in times of doubt. Thanks to recent events, I am full of doubt. Can you corroborate your theory, Pirate Lord Ut'wah?"

The orc smiled. "Members of the Sword's flock, Selasine, and Burchard, are on *The Nebula* as we speak. I am sure you have ways to confirm that fact."

The commander sighed and nodded. He touched his finger to his temple. "High Paladin Damil," he thought loudly.

"What is it, commander?" Damil replied.

"I am speaking with a Harbinger of Lexcord. He has reason to believe that the rest of us dispatched with Carulus may be in danger. He says that he had a premonition. He further asserts that Selasine and his pupil are in the company of Erk, who we were dispatched to fight. Is there any way to confirm these claims?"

Damil replied, "Give me a moment, friend." There was silence in the commander's mind. He left his fingers pressed against his temple, willing the telepathy to continue. He sought the high paladin's voice as fervently as he could. After about three minutes, there was a whisper, "Commander Aguila?"

"Sir!" his mind saluted.

Damil's laugh could be heard through the telepathy. "No need for a salute, commander. Listen, I do have confirmation; Selasine and his student are sailing north with Erk and some other pirates. They believe they can revive the girl who is currently under a sort of enchantment. Also, please be wary. I have heard in the last hour a rumor that Carulus may be dead or missing. The situation is escalating, and I am not excited about the potential outcome." There was a pause in Damil's thoughts, but then he continued, "Under my order, you are to accompany the holy warrior of Lexcord. I am very concerned about the possibility that those entire battalions could be lost. Keep an eye on Claston for us."

"Sir," Commander Aguila replied, letting the telepathic contact dissipate. He looked around at the people around him. "Ut'wah. We will join you on the rescue mission. I have orders from the high paladin that your words are true. I apologize for my insistence on confirmation; however, this entire situation could have been prevented by more careful planning on behalf of leadership."

Ut'wah laughed. "Very well, commander," he concluded. He then turned to Justin, Valarie, and Tavi. "You three. If your commander permits, I invite you to serve as the first officers on three of my ships. Your determination in the face of an unknown, overwhelming threat tells me everything I need to know about you. Your strength and commitment are more valiant than many paladins I have met across several faiths."

Commander Aguila laughed. "I'm sorry, pirate lord, but

these three are too precious to share. They will work in their ranks as Shield Knights, protecting the innocent on the ships you've seen in your dreams."

Justin and Valarie thought the ambitious appointment would have been beneficial but also dreaded being separated. They agreed with the commander's choice.

Ut'wah pointed to a different dock in front of the port. "That galleon at the end there is *The Silver Corsair*," he indicated. Justin was struck by the size of the ship, almost quadruple that of *The Valiant Sailor*. The crew could easily include four hundred people, a massive ship indeed. For Ut'wah to have fifteen total ships at his disposal was also impressive.

The commander continued, "Very well. We will join in formation with you. Captain?" he shouted toward the upper deck. The captain and crew, technically vassals of the King of Claston, might resist such a course.

"Where to?" he asked.

"Beriton. We may have business with the king at this point," Aguila ordered.

"Good. I'm ready to go home," the captain mumbled. If he and the crew objected to the church, they were simply too outnumbered to resist. If they ended up rescuing the people the king wanted dead, the king would have to remedy that problem himself.

Justin's mind started to race. Miranda was under some kind of enchantment? He wondered if she was okay, but Valarie's hand rested on his shoulder. "Hey, those are your friends, right?" she asked.

He nodded. "Whatever they are doing, I know that I'm going to see them again," he said as if he were ordering destiny.

Valarie smiled. "And I know I'm going to get to meet them," she added.

Justin smiled, too. From the sound of it, this rescue mission would be an important part of stopping an international conflict.

As *The Valiant Sailor* drifted slightly to the north, waiting, a fleet of ships emerged from the waters surrounding

Yendralia. The ship joined the fifteen other vessels under the command of Pirate Lord Ut'wah on a journey rooted in their shared faith in good and justice. Justin looked up at the night sky, Valarie's hand in his. "Please be okay, Miranda," he whispered.

Valarie squeezed his hand. "Your friends are going to be fine; I can feel it in my heart."

He smiled. "This is what Maréli meant by destiny. I can feel it in my heart too."

Chapter 19
Under the Blossoms of the Solisberry Tree

elasine and Erk stood close to the bow of *The Nebula*. The journey to the Glacier Gulf only took ten days, the end of The Flourishing quickly approaching. The course to this remote location required them to sail around the southeastern tip of the Claston kingdom and then straight north. *The Violet Blur* seemed to speed along behind *The Nebula*, never struggling to keep up with the massive galleon. Three days ago, the Astral Spire had come into clear view while using a spyglass. It was a massive natural stone formation that rose far above Espa's surface. At night, the top of the spire shone like a star, albeit much brighter. Now that they were less than fifty miles from their destination, it was easily visible to the naked eye. What troubled Erk, however, was not what they could see above but what they could not see below.

"Icy water is more dangerous than an enemy fleet," Erk explained as the two of them cautiously examined the increasingly frigid conditions in the water.

"Ice is my sworn nemesis," Selasine replied absentmindedly as his eye scanned the frozen shores.

In such conditions, docking was an impossibility. Erk had considered several strategies but decided on the simplest course requiring the least time spent crossing the water. Once the top of the Astral Spire was clearly observable from the decks of the ships, Erk's quartermaster, Jacques, would use his uncanny magic to teleport Miranda, Selasine, Erk, Evan, August, and Naomi to the top of the geographic anomaly. From there, they would wait as the arcane stream flowed through Miranda at an accelerated rate. Her hair had already begun to regain color, turning a light pink after about a week of travel. Selasine breathed a deep sigh of relief the day they realized the magic passing through was starting to restore her. Erk, too, felt the uncertainty about this course of action melt away. Others that Miranda had touched, like Shalo and Evan, whispered a prayer of thanks to Lexcord and whatever other gods would listen to them. August cried tears of relief in private. Naomi insisted that she wanted the acolyte's hair and makeup to look nice when she awakened, so the pirate lady carefully combed and redid Miranda's braids. Erk told her that the only makeup Miranda ever used was the blue pigment on her cheeks. Naomi decided to wait for the girl to awaken before figuring out what Erk meant.

As *The Nebula* and *The Violet Blur* arrived in the Glacier Gulf, Erk had the crew reduce the number of open sails to slow the ships significantly. Slow, precise movement was required to navigate this area. Erk and Naomi collaborated with maps from several different eras to plot their course. The Glacier Gulf was southeast of Osgood, an independent human nation that relied on the cooler, crisper climate for their way of life. The frigid seas of the north butted against the northeastern boundaries of Osgood, and the coastline on this side formed a five-hundred-mile semicircle with a large, imposing, inactive volcano jutting up from the sea on a separate island in the center. The island mass around the quiet, cone-shaped mountain was about one hundred miles in diameter, making it easily visible from anywhere along the coast of the Glacier Gulf.

Small settlements dotted the coastline, but none had the docking infrastructure to support *The Violet Blur*, less so *The Nebula*. Those settlements were constructed along the Draikin Peninsula that stuck out from the continent of northern Osgood to the east. North of those settlements, hundreds of miles of towering glaciers floated at a tectonic pace in the sea beyond. The peninsula's south side had smaller accumulations of glacial mass, threatening vessels navigating the water.

The sun was setting, casting a beautiful aurora of reds and greens across the northern sky. Time seemed to move differently this far north because the nights were never as dark as elsewhere, and the days were exceptionally long this time of year.

Erk raised a spyglass to his eye and peered up at the Astral Spire. He grunted with frustration. "Jacques can't get us there if we can't see it. His power is safest if he goes to some place or somebody he knows," he complained. The frozen air caused each word he spoke to manifest simultaneously as a wisp, swirling and dissipating ephemerally. "Or, at least, if he can see it, he can get us there."

Selasine grimaced. The two pegasus that Damil had loaned them could potentially fly them up, but it would be perilous to transport Miranda by pegasus in her condition. Besides, such a high flight risked spooking the beasts and creating additional safety hazards. The best course of action was to find a magical method to reach the top of the Astral Spire. Most texts about the mysterious location described a magical entryway at the spire's base. Ancient devices would teleport their users to a higher level with another device. Some texts also described the guardians of the Astral Spire as unsleeping watchmen that warded off evil in that sacred place. Each level possessed a guardian, but the number of devices and chambers in the spire was unclear. That path also seemed dangerous due to the travel through harsh, frozen conditions and mountainous terrain. He shook himself out of his thoughts. "Maybe we'll have better luck after the sun fully sets?" he replied.

Erk nodded optimistically. "We will be a little closer by then, as well. I wouldn't want to move the ships at night with these conditions, but, fortunately, this will be about as dark as it gets. If we can get within five miles, I think we should be able to glimpse something useful to Jacques," he explained.

Selasine reached for his holy symbol. He and Damil had been communicating more frequently over the last week. He was pleased to learn that Justin had found his place among the Shield Knights that had initially volunteered for Carulus's mission. He was also proud that Justin was participating in a rescue mission for the paladins the King of Claston had officially taken hostage in the last week. When the king's ships transporting the soldiers arrived in Beriton, they dropped anchor approximately a mile out to sea. The crews had done all this stealthily, slipping into lifeboats and going to shore in the middle of the night. Before they left, they dumped all the gunpowder near the cannons and sabotaged the ships' defenses and sails. They also had massive reserves of gunpowder in the cargo decks. It made the vessels especially vulnerable to cannon fire, and the hostages had been threatened that those stores of gunpowder would be their end. Upon awakening to discover the treachery, the paladins were informed of their fates as hostages. It seems one of them got a message to the archbishop, who then disseminated this information to Selasine. The paladins would have had no escape, and the king's navy sat nearby to ensure they did not try to repair the ship. The king demanded Miranda in exchange for the hostages. This was deeply troubling to Selasine. The first task, however, was to reach the spire and get Miranda back to normal.

"Alright, then. Get some rest, bishop. I'll send for you when we have something workable, alright?" Erk offered. He could see that Selasine was weary. The closer they got to the Astral Spire, the more anxious he became. He stayed up later than usual, offering to watch Miranda longer than anyone else.

Selasine started to object, "Nonsense, I should relieve August so that—"

Erk interrupted him, "We need you rested. Who knows what waits for us at the top of this thing?" He gave a sincere glance at his brother-in-law.

Selasine let out a deep sigh and waited a moment before nodding. "You're right, friend." He placed a hand on Erk's shoulder and gave him a friendly shake. The journey had been good for both of them. They traded stories of Iria that filled each other's hearts with joy. Thomas told him more about Telisi and shared more about Farzg and the smuggling ring in Nulodia. Erk opened up about Iria's, Evan's, and his childhood and the terrors of living through The Unbinding. He gave a full account of the king's descent into corruption and tyranny as a worshiper of Na'agamlor. He also described his realization that his sister left because his heart was darkening. His crusade against the king was a righteous one, even though he had taken a dark path. Selasine had not only forgiven Erk, but he now saw him as family.

"Goodnight, Erk," Selasine finally said.

"Goodnight, Thomas," the pirate lord replied.

Selasine went down to the officers' cabins on the first deck and found his room, the last of six doors on the right. August's room was across from his. He looked around the small room; there was space for a desk, a bed, and a small, circular dining table with a thin stool. He shed his armor and crawled into the bed. His thoughts continued to anxiously bounce from possibility to possibility. He worried about Gelidor's pursuit of Miranda. He also worried that Carulus's death or disappearance was a bad omen. He prayed silently for peace and comfort. Sleep overtook him as he recited the prayers repeatedly.

Jacques looked through the spyglass. "I can't really make anything out, captain," he grumbled.

Erk sighed, his breath visible in the dim glow of the polar night. The pirates lit several large and magical torches to help light the arctic waters. They had dodged glacial masses all night. The sailing crew was so exhausted that they started two-hour rotations, and Jax had been glued to the wheel for most of the night. Shalo finally relieved him, being one of five people allowed to pilot *The Nebula* besides Erk. The tundra shores looked crisp and bland. A blanket of white coated the landscape, with hues of purple and black creating a dynamic contrast that made the night feel eerie and beautiful. Ice made the water impassible near the shore. "Does the light in the spire give you any hint as to what's up there?" Erk asked, growing worried.

The top of the Astral Spire was reminiscent of a defensive tower with large, stone crenellations cupping around it in even increments. These structures spired above and then turned inward, partially covering the top of whatever rested there. Though the stone was natural and unhewn, it was still perfectly shaped like the finest architecture. The legends said that an eldritch god used to watch the world from here before the gods discovered the primordial place.

Jacques squinted. "I'm afraid not, captain. In fact, the light is making it difficult to see." He still looked the same as he did all those years ago on the night Erk's sister, Ilyia, had been murdered. After Erk fled to the Isles Known for Nothing, Jacques found him by concentrating deeply on Erk and teleporting to him. He joined the crew of *The Nebula* about a decade ago, serving as the ship's quartermaster. However, he sparingly used his uncanny magic as it grew unstable with frequent use.

Erk nodded. "Right. And due to the magical nature of the place, I'm sure it would be impossible to see any better in the day," he replied. He also knew if they got any closer, their line of sight would no longer give them the angle to view the top. Though the legends said it towered to the stars themselves, it only looked about five thousand feet high. The spyglass was sophisticated enough that it could see that far away, but there seemed to be a bright light radiating from that place. It almost looked like a world without shadows. Erk frowned. Their options were beginning to narrow, and he did not like the implications.

They could feel the sun's light on their backs as they gazed at the Astral Spire. Their current course was northwest, the same direction that the sun passed through the sky. The planet's tilt meant the sun was never fully set this far north. Though the world seemed to light around them, the light in the spire started to turn shades of purple. Erk raised a finger. "Look!" he exclaimed.

Jacques returned the spyglass to his eye. As he peered up, he could make out distinct shapes of rock in the space now covered in shadows. They seemed to move as if they were alive. "I can see it clear as day, captain, but it does not look like a place I'd want to go," he cautioned, offering the spyglass to Erk.

Erk looked closely at the shadows dancing across the rock. "The sunlight probably changes the atmosphere up that high. It's good for us, though; I can see a rock formation that would be a great place to land," he said, excitement in his voice.

"Alright then, boss. Let us gather, and I will move us there," Jacques replied, compliant.

Erk ran back to the dressing room and opened the door. August was asleep on the lounge while Miranda rested on the bed as she had done for the last eleven days. "August, it's time," he ordered.

August stood and gathered himself. He ensured his armor was strapped on well and collected Miranda from the bed. "Right. Let's go."

Erk went to the captain's quarters and slipped inside to wake Naomi. August descended the stairs to the first deck where the officers' cabins were. He used his boot to kick on the doors as a knock. He woke Evan and Selasine, the first poking his head into the hallway as August opened Selasine's door, balancing Miranda in his arms. "Erk says it's time, everyone," the acolyte explained.

Evan replied, "Right." He then disappeared back into his room.

Selasine stirred quickly. "Already time? Thank Invictus," he commented, strapping on his armor as quickly as possible. August laid Miranda on the bed and assisted his mentor. As soon as they were finished, Evan returned from inside his cabin, waiting for the two in the hallway of the first deck. Once he was ready, Selasine scooped Miranda from the bed. Ever since this part of the ordeal began, somebody else had managed to pick her up before he could reach her. The more he realized that he thought of her as a daughter, the more anxious he became. He understood others had their attachments to Miranda, and he shared their love for her. August perhaps could see a sibling in her, and Justin would probably feel the same were he here. Erk had become a mentor to her in his own right, and Evan felt deeply grateful for her gift. But then there was Selasine. A girl that would have been approximately his own daughter's age had been working with him as a peacekeeper. He hadn't realized how much the girl and the two young men had become his new family. This morning, though, it was his turn to carry Miranda. He would protect her from now on.

They all united on the deck. Naomi was armed to the teeth as usual. Selasine wore the full plate armor he had been wearing since the beginning of this journey. August wore a resplendent, silver-scaled dragon plate that Erk had gifted him at the beginning of this journey north. Erk and Evan both wore elegant chainmail that seemed extraordinarily light. Jacques, not in fighting shape, wore only a fine red jacket with silver stitching that looked quite old and comfortable leather trousers. Miranda was still dressed in most of her mother's battlemail, the mithril breastplate and golden-colored skirt glinting brightly in the early morning light. Naomi had taken off parts like the ring mail and the shoulder pads to help keep her slowly recovering body comfortable. "Are we ready?" Erk asked.

Selasine and August nodded. Evan gave a grunt of affirmation. Naomi took Erk by the hand. Selasine stepped close with Miranda in his arms. "Let's go," the bishop ordered.

Jacques placed his hands together and took a deep breath. As he did, a bright circle of light appeared underneath them all. In the radiant field, the others could make out something that looked like the rivers of the world emptying into the seas. They could see mountains, deserts, tundras, and plains. In the very next second, which seemed to take an hour to arrive, they found themselves gently placed on a rock formation near the side of the top of the spire. The world beneath them seemed immensely small, which was extraordinarily unsettling. August stumbled backward from the edge about twenty feet in front of him. He tripped on a root that had grown into the raised slope beneath him, causing him to tumble onto his bottom on a flat rock behind him. Naomi crouched instinctively, her agility canceling any height-induced dizziness she might have felt. Erk bounded quickly over some low-laying rocks to get closer to the center. Evan also crouched but moved much more carefully and warily than Naomi. Selasine had been placed near the back of the rock formation. Jacques made doubly sure that the girl and her mentor would be placed far enough away that they had less chance of falling. Erk's quartermaster stood beside the bishop and his pupil.

They took a look at their surroundings. It was a beautiful place. The top of the spire looked out over the Glacier Gulf, and so much of the coastline was visible from here. They could see nearly the entire kingdom of Osgood to the west. The Tuzin forest stretched to the southeast as far as the eye could see. The glaciers to the north loomed dark in the distance. The rock formations that rose up from here stretched up and inward as they had observed, hovering over the interior of the disc-shaped top level. They seemed like massive fingers gripping around this space protectively. The internal area of this level resembled a summer meadow, and the air was much warmer than expected at such a great height. It stretched almost half a mile across, the terrain descending into a grotto. In the center, a small rock wall rose above a shimmering pool of purple water. From the rock wall, a waterfall poured, feeding the small body of water below. However, a massive, resplendent tree grew around and far above the grotto. Its roots looked huge and furled out from the tree's base, reflecting earth-toned colors in the bark. Above the grotto, an umbrella of purple blooms sparkled in the morning light. The solisberry leaves were spear tipped and looked to be velvety.

The group walked down the gentle slope, amazed by the purples, blues, and reds that painted this meadow an ominous and beautiful spectacle. Boulders and small thickets of vegetation were dispersed throughout the area. It took about five minutes to arrive at the center of the disc-shaped summit of the Astral Spire. Selasine took Miranda straight to the tree. The water splashed nearby as the waterfall that fed the magical lake caused it to slosh like the ocean as the tide changed. The roots of the solisberry tree were towering, with the leaves hanging dozens of feet overhead. Under those leaves, the companions could see the beautiful, purple, glowing blossoms that had earned this tree such admiration. The blossoms lit the entire area, which gave it an eerie, violet glow. The shadows danced in the shimmer of the blossoms, but they felt dark and oppressive. Erk, Selasine, and the others traded knowing nods. They could feel they were not alone in this place but were unsure why.

Selasine found a root at an easily reachable height and placed Miranda's body on it. A golden, dusty light covered her body as she came into contact with the tree. It shimmered brightly in the purplish radiance of the solisberry tree. He stepped away from her, and the arcane stream became visible as it surged through the tree. It began to pass through Miranda as a funnel point as it spewed out of the tree's roots back into the universe. The sight was marvelous, and it filled Erk with hope.

They watched intently as the stream poured into Miranda at an incredible speed. It seemed that her presence on the solisberry tree had excited the arcane stream in such a way that it flowed with much more swiftness than they estimated. She served as a catalyst of some kind to the whole of magic. Selasine's heart fluttered when her hair began to glow, changing slowly from a soft, pastel pink to light red. The stream continued flowing, and the darker tones of her hair began to restore.

As the magic of this place raced through Miranda, the shadows encroached more urgently. August and Selasine whispered a prayer, and they could detect that an entity hovered in the shadows. That ominous presence began to make itself apparent. They cursed as drops of black liquid oozed out of the shadows of the overhead rocks that cupped around the tops of this tiny paradise. Creatures made entirely of shadow splashed out of the drops. August and Selasine unsheathed their weapons. Naomi sprinted and jumped onto a boulder in the sloping meadow. Flames engulfed Erk's wrists, and he drew Iria's sword. Evan brandished a magical sword constructed of elaborate gears and a distinctly bronze-colored metal that was unusually reflective. The gears in this sword turned as a crystal glowed in the center, wrapping the blade in pink hues. Jacques stood near the water's edge close to the root where Selasine had placed Miranda, bewildered by how quickly the others responded to the threat. The shadow creatures stalked from all sides, growing in number alarmingly fast. Erk wondered if the darkness in his own heart had brought these shadows upon them.

The shadow creatures approached initially with a modicum of caution. One shaped like a large cat of prey broke rank, however, rushing at Selasine, who slashed his sword horizontally through it as it leaped through the air at him. When the blade made contact, it flashed bright white and caused the shadow to dissipate. Looking back at the others, Selasine gripped his holy symbol. Selasine yelled to his companions with a loud blessing, "This is where we stand against the forces of chaos together. We have been brought together by the gods for this purpose. This is a fight for dear Miranda and our kingdoms."

His blessing ignited a fury within each of them. They each had their own reasons for saving Miranda. Selasine saw her as a wonderful pupil and an adopted daughter. August wanted his sister back. Erk wanted to make things right with the girl who changed his entire world in the last month. Evan was grateful for her healing gift. Naomi pitied her for getting mixed up with Erk's machinations, but she wanted to see the girl's gift for herself. Jacques stood back, unequipped and unready for serious conflict. He realized he was the only one watching the girl. His importance had just grown a thousand-fold, and he meant to do his duty with fidelity.

The shadow creatures succumbed easily to the magical weapons and prayers wielded by the companions. Still, an endless stream of them seemed to pour from the rocks above. Erk channeled the sun's brilliance into a powerful beam that blasted entire ranks of the shadow creatures from existence. They took so many forms that it was hard to distinguish a pattern. Some were animals, some were humanoid like giants or halflings, and others still were elven and human. But a single slash from magic, a blessing, or an Unbinding power made them dissolve. They were so fragile, in fact, that Erk began to question if they were illusory creatures. To test his theory, he allowed himself to be tackled by a charging shadow person. The impact and the pain were real. He then destroyed the shadow with a swift stab of his blade. He stood up and dusted himself off, glancing around to check on the others. "They may be naught but shadow, but their attacks are true. Don't let them reach Miranda!"

Selasine, who had been struck full-force by one of the shadow creatures shaped much like a reptilian monster with a large, ram-shaped head, croaked back, "Yeah, I think we get that."

Jacques noticed the shadows seemed to draw in on the space around Miranda. The arcane stream certainly generated a lot of light, but the darkness thickened around her despite its glow. "Uh, fellows?" Jacques shouted.

August heard him, running from a group of shadow creatures intent on consuming the acolyte. He prayed, "Grant me light, Sword of Justice!" His holy symbol glowed brightly, much like the daylight prayer that Selasine had used to light the way on Olvidado. The core of the ominous shadow retreated, creating more creatures of darkness and dropping them into the meadow around Miranda. August and Jacques picked up a defensive position close to Miranda, but neither had weapons to stop the otherworldly creatures. August began to pray again, this time for a protective barrier. Naomi suddenly appeared atop a tall root nearby as the barrier activated. She leaped swiftly through the air, hurling her stiletto-style throwing daggers at an incredible rate. Each throw hit a shadow creature, causing it to dissipate. The daggers magically returned to the bandolier strapped to her thigh. With such a deadly armory and the agility to execute such a vicious assault, it was no wonder that Naomi had climbed to the rank of pirate lady.

"That was quick," Jacques huffed.

Naomi smiled, "Gotta watch out for the girl." She then turned invisible after she twisted a ring on her right hand.

Evan returned to the side of the tree where Miranda rested, having wiped out a wave of shadow creatures on the other side of the massive trunk. Evan's sword was brightly aglow in a pinkish light. "Let me keep light on Miranda, go and fend off the darkness around my brother." The gears on the sword were turning quickly. The light coming from the blade of the sword destroyed the shadows easily with a blast of intense light once they entered the brilliant globe.

"Right," August responded. He rushed back up the hill toward Selasine and Erk, who were fighting various shadow creatures.

Selasine had activated his uncanny magic. Known formerly by wizards as the spell Redundant Mirage, illusory copies of himself mimicked his every movement with perfect timing. The decoys helped Selasine deal with smaller numbers of creatures at a time. They did not seem capable of identifying which Selasine was the true threat, so they attacked the illusions in gangs, finding a clone more often than the true Selasine. However, when they did find him, he would call upon the power of Invictus to shroud his body in holy fire. That divine magic, Flame Shield, easily caused the shadow creatures to disintegrate.

Erk was wielding his sister's sword. He had taken it back from Miranda temporarily. He knew he would need it to honor his sister's memory and to save the young woman. The enchantment on the sword generated a substantial amount of holy power. He knew the blade as Holyfang; its magic was much more destructive than he remembered. It easily obliterated the shadows that attempted to encroach with a single swipe. August's prayer of light weakened the creatures more, and it pushed the pursuing shadows back.

Selasine looked at August, "That light!"

August raised his brow, "What do you mean, teacher?"

"You're wielding the light of Invictus himself. I've seen it before when he came to see Miranda."

August tightened his jaw. Was he truly wielding the light of his god? This felt like an important moment to him. He stood tall against the shadows and pushed them away by holding his holy symbol toward them. However, the light had a limited range, and the shadows filled in around him, almost like wolves waiting for their prey's fire to extinguish. As August wielded the light to keep them distracted and at bay, Selasine and Erk slaughtered the shadows en masse. "There's just no end to these guys," August complained, worried he would lose the light before this was over. They continued fighting the shadows without respite in sight.

After an hour had passed, Jacques called out, "Hey! The girl's hair! It's getting darker! She's breathing again! You can see it!"

Erk turned back toward the grotto in the center, "Quickly! Everyone! Regroup!" he ordered. August and Selasine backed into the center, the collective light helping keep the shadows at a safe distance. However, they continued to pour out endlessly, creating a palpable darkness outside the bubble of light that had about a one-hundred-foot radius, giving them a little space between Miranda and the shadows. They decided to play a tighter game of defense, with Erk and Evan standing atop the ten-foot rock face from where the waterfall emerged, feeding the lake of the grotto. August, Selasine, and Jacques stayed close to Miranda on the ground level. Naomi served as swift backup anytime the shadows seemed to surge into the light.

As they defended Miranda, it became apparent that the source of the shadow creatures dwelt within the shadows themselves. Furthermore, though the shadow creatures could enter the light, they were not eager to do so. They seemed to attack in waves, waiting for an unseen pressure to convince them to enter the light. However, the shadows that created these creatures would not approach the light. This quickly turned into a game of endurance.

After almost six hours of defending the center of this place, Selasine, Erk, August, and Evan were exhausted. Naomi was not visible; one of her tactics relied on a ring of invisibility that seemed limitless in its capabilities. Jacques had only seen Miranda in passing on *The Nebula*. Still, he was quite confident that her red hair was almost the correct rich, crimson hue he recognized. Evan was the closest person he could see, so he asked, "Hey! Master Evanthalus! Is she looking better?"

Evan looked down at her from above the waterfall, holding his interesting sword into the air, repelling the shadows like a magnificent torch. "It's hard to tell from here, Jacques! Her skin's color is restored. Her hair is normal. Shake her; try to wake her up!" he insisted.

Jacques shook Miranda gently. "Lady Miranda, please

awaken. We need you here; we are outnumbered," he explained hurriedly. She did not respond, so he shouted, "It's no use! She seems fast asleep still!"

"Do you have any salts or chemicals to wake her?" Erk shouted back, the magical sword in his hand stabbing through a shadow creature as it braved the light and attacked. He had fatigued himself by overusing his uncanny magic. It was highly efficient, blasting entire swaths of shadows back into oblivion. Even with that support, they still only controlled a small portion of this place, leading to fears over how and when to escape. Erk could barely move but continued wielding his sister's sword. He would not fail Miranda now, not this close to setting things right.

"No, nothing!" Jacques replied, feeling panicked.

August turned to look at Miranda, the light from his holy symbol still burning bright. Of all of the lights, his was the one that kept the creatures from attacking the most effectively. He had kept Erk and Selasine safe as they destroyed countless shadow creatures. As he observed his friend, Miranda looked exactly like he remembered before that terrifying moment in Erk's study when he thought he had lost her for good. "Hey, Jacques! She's a healer. Check her pouches; I can guarantee there's something in there that will help," he explained, turning his attention back to the shadow creatures surrounding them.

Jacques nodded, opening the leather bag designed to carry potions and sundry healing items. As he rummaged through the bag, he found cloths and bandages, a few vials of various liquids, and a small jewel-encrusted music box that fit in the palm of his hand. Without much thought, he wound the music box and set it on the root with Miranda. He finally found the salts that were commonly used to wake people. He started to open the jar when something caused him to scream.

The lullaby that echoed from the music box was a familiar melody throughout the world, and it was the same melody that Cantalus used when he sang his farewells to this group. Though it had many names and different words, this music box seemed to capture the essence of the ancient lullaby. It was a haunting but pretty melody, the notes lining up to sound forlorn and bittersweet. As Miranda's essence had been pouring back into her body, she had shown more signs of life. As the music played, Miranda's eyes opened, glowing with a vivid blue aura.

Jacques's scream caused a semi-panic among the others. Selasine leaped backward, turning to rush toward the sound. August turned his full attention to Miranda, causing the shadows to encroach closer. Evan and Erk leaped down the short cliff with the waterfall, splashing their way through the shallow grotto. Naomi appeared close by, unleashing a barrage of knives against a wave of shadows that tried to take advantage of the companions closing their distance between each other.

Selasine shouted, "Miranda!" when he saw how much healthier she looked. Then he noticed the bright, glowing blue in her eyes clashing with the vivid purple color of the solisberry blossoms above.

Before anybody could make sense of the situation, Miranda sat up. The intense glow in her eyes began to subside, leaving her cool, sapphire stare in its place. Her lips were parted in wonder as she looked around at everyone protecting her. She also took note of the shadows that seemed ready to devour them whole. "Bishop?" she replied, looking to him for his order. Time seemed to stand still as she was surrounded by those she loved the most, but they were surrounded by a terrifying force ready to consume them.

Selasine rushed to her side and clasped her firmly in his arms. She was still sitting on the solisberry tree root, putting her at about waist level for him. "Thank Invictus, you're okay. It's all going to be okay now. No more of this; you're safe now, understand?" he said, his heart finally releasing the emotions weighing on him. He shed several tears from his eye but maintained his composure.

Miranda giggled in his arms. "You're right; it will all be okay now!" She squeezed her mentor but broke away from his embrace, tossing her legs over the side of the root and jumping down. "August!" she piped, watching him hold shadows at bay with nothing more than a light. "Do you need some help?" she asked.

August looked at her with a look of relief. "I have all the help I need right here with me, Miranda," he said with a smile.

She turned to Erk. "Well, captain?" she asked innocently.

The pirate lord beamed, almost forgetting the shadows were there. Evan stood back, smiling broadly to see the girl healthy again. Naomi crouched nearby, and Jacques stood slack-jawed, still holding the smelling salts.

Miranda nodded. "Thank you. All of you. Now it's my turn to help." She inhaled deeply and began to pull the mana into herself. Those who had seen her gift before knew that the light alone would have been enough to destroy the shadows. They also knew there was a possibility they could be transported elsewhere. Either way, they were relieved that the quest to save Miranda had finally reached its next phase.

She then pressed her hands directly out from her sides, standing in a deep-centered fighting stance. The ether she had absorbed then burst as a wave of purple luminance radiated from her as the epicenter. Her companions closed their eyes as the light became so bright it could pierce even magical darkness. The army of shadows melted away as the light washed over them. A lone shadow remained visible after the light pushed past the boundaries of the Astral Spire. It looked to be human or elven, and it was not very large at all.

Miranda took a deep breath and opened her eyes. Everyone's gaze was silently fixed on her as she approached the lone remaining shadow. The substance of the arcane stream was still visibly flowing through her at high speeds. The more experienced adventurers of the group wondered if that meant her gift would have unlimited potential here. Her movements led her to kneel close to the shadow, and she exclaimed, "High Priest Carulus! What has happened to you?" She was about fifteen feet away from it, keeping a healthy distance.

Selasine rushed beside her, placing a hand on her shoulder from behind, "Be careful, Miranda. You've just woken up from a near-death experience; please take a moment—" he explained, but she interrupted him.

"I know, bishop." She turned up to face him, a sweet smile on her lips. "I know this sounds strange, but I was still here the entire time you cared for me. I could see you and hear you. But I was trapped in the magic. Thanks to you all, I'm back. And I know what I must do now." She turned her gaze back to the shadow, which had begun to distort and grow darker. "Right now, there's a more pressing issue, though," she murmured.

Carulus's shadow form turned its appendages into blades. Spikes burst out of it in every direction, firing out of his shadowy body as projectiles. With little more than a thought, Miranda gathered a bit of mana and created a magical, glowing shield that deflected the spikes harmlessly. The bladed appendages began to whip wildly, so Miranda took more mana and created a series of solid bars out of light that caused the appendages to become twisted and stuck. She drew them in the air with her mind and finger, the will of the universe immediately bending to her wishes. The shadow shrank back and fired itself at her like a bullet launched from a pistol.

Miranda raised a finger, and the shadow stopped, inches from her face pressed into a faint, glowing disc. She could still see Carulus's form inside this shadowy abomination. "What happened to you, high priest?" she asked, her voice full of sympathy and true concern. The light disc kept the shadow stuck. The others gathered close behind her, unwilling to allow Carulus to hurt her as the lich had done.

The shadow began to thrash, no sounds escaping. It tried another burst of shadow spikes, but the disc expanded and flashed brightly, causing the spikes to dissipate immediately. Here, where the mana flowed freely, Miranda truly was like a goddess. Her mind only had to ask for it, and it would happen.

"High priest, can you hear me?" she asked the shadow. It stayed stuck on the disc that separated them. She reached through the disk to touch the shadow, but the darkness burned her hand and caused it to wither. She looked at her hand, and it healed itself instantaneously. "I can feel you in there, Your Holiness. Please say something," she pleaded with the creature that silently fought with the disc of light.

"Miranda?" Erk asked her. "This is the high priest?"

Selasine let out a deep, disappointed sigh. "It seems that the darkness within him has turned him into a creature beyond our understanding. He was once a respected priest, but now. . .," his words trailed off as he shook his head in disapproval. "Now he himself is an agent of Chaos, a victim of foul magic."

August shuddered. Naomi had daggers at the ready. Jacques was ready to teleport them away but had been too overwhelmed by Miranda's revival that he said nothing. Erk reached up and placed his hand on Miranda's arm. "Miranda, what are you thinking of doing?" he asked, concerned as she stared calmly at the shadowy abomination.

Evan smiled. "It's easy, brother; I know that look," he explained.

Miranda nodded in agreement with Evan, but her expression was still bewildered. "Carulus didn't do this to himself," she whispered, using the mana to analyze the magic working within the high priest. At that moment, she leaped backward from her crouched position, using the abundant mana in the environment to press the shadowy figure forcibly into the ground. A black circle formed above the shadow, and a large, deformed hand crawled out, its fingers wiggling out of the blackness. The hand looked to be ten feet long from wrist to fingertip. It was covered in boils and pustules, blood and pus oozing from the many maladies covering the scabbed hand.

The voice of a small child began to cry, "Why won't you play with me anymore, Miranda?" The hand pointed a finger at Miranda with a horrifying mouth in the fingertip. Rows of rotted, razor-sharp teeth opened up before her.

Miranda shook her head, "I . . . I don't know who you are," she hesitated.

Selasine cursed loudly, "Gods be with us; that's the mortal avatar of Indervill! Quickly, look away, run! You'll be driven mad!" He stumbled backward so quickly that he tripped, finding himself on the ground in a panic.

Indervill's voice transitioned to the polyphonic, angry register, "You are an abomination! You should not exist! I want you for my collection! Please!" The hand rested on the butt of its palm, all four fingers stretching toward Miranda, more unsettling mouths in the fingertips.

Miranda took a deep breath and closed her eyes. Her voice changed to sound as it did when she was a small child. "I'm sorry, Indervill. I don't have time to play; I have to do my chores and help my mommy and daddy."

The horrifying hand froze, and the fingers curled slowly into a fist. "Can you play after?" the voice had changed to that of a little girl.

Philotrax's voice boomed from his daughter's mouth, "I'm afraid not, Indervill. However, you are welcome to join us for dinner. Do you like venison?" Erk, Selasine, August, and Naomi traded confused glances. Jacques trembled in fear in the presence of a god. Evan fixed his eyes on the shadow Miranda had pressed into the ground. Despite her divided focus, her attack still had it firmly pinned.

The hand began to dance on its fingertips. "Oh, goody! Goody! An invitation to stay! This is all we needed!"

Miranda opened her eyes, licked her lips, and channeled more mana. Her deep breaths in this place instantly caused her magic reserves to overflow. Her eyes then closed again in concentration. Her mother's voice then echoed, "Yes, Chaos, please, come stay with us here. We wait for you in the world between worlds."

Unpredictably, the avatar of Indervill reached into the sky and opened a new, black portal. "We will have dinner with Miranda in the world between worlds! This is the greatest news!" Indervill celebrated as it climbed through the portal. "Aren't you coming, Miranda?" it asked, the index finger looking down at her.

Miranda opened her eyes. "Sorry, I still have chores to do," she spat and then used the mana in the air to seal the god's portal, cutting off a fingertip that disintegrated into miasma before it could reach the ground. The shadow she had forced down with mana looked small and weak. It seemed to be fading from existence after Indervill teleported away.

Everyone stared in disbelief. Coming to this place was already something beyond understanding, but watching Miranda diffuse a conflict between herself and an actual god really emphasized the degree to which this journey had changed her. Selasine and Erk turned their attention back to the shadow. Evan, August, Naomi, and Jacques waited further behind, witnessing things they could have never imagined in this magical place.

Miranda approached the shadow that looked to be slowly vanishing. "You're in pain, Your Holiness," she commented, squatting on the ground where the vaguely half-elven shaped shadow lay in the process of disappearing. She smiled. "Here," she said, taking another deep breath, inhaling the ether that flowed here so prolifically. With an instantaneous flash, the divine enchantment placed upon Carulus was broken. There he lay as he did several days ago, wearing the robe of his station as high priest in Nulodia.

Carulus looked at his hands and touched his body to make sure it was solid. A look of true terror was in his eyes as they met Miranda's gaze, watching him reorient himself with a solid existence. The high priest's eyes were filled with tears flowing sporadically down his aged cheeks. "Have I been saved?" he asked.

Selasine took a step forward. "Saved from what?" he asked, hostility evident.

Carulus replied, the fear of Indervill's power making his voice shake, "From the madness. I became a shadow and felt myself dying just now."

Miranda continued to smile at the high priest. "Yes, you are safe, Your Holiness. I've sent Indervill away."

Carulus started to stand, but he was met by Selasine's drawn sword at his chest. "High Priest Gaius Carulus, on behalf of Archbishop Renault, I place you under arrest for the crimes of insubordination, misappropriation of church resources, and desertion," the bishop explained, his voice dripping with disdain.

Erk started to protest but realized he had no reason to do so. August smirked as justice unfolded in front of him. Naomi smiled broadly, the girl's powers more impressive than anything she could have dreamed. Evan made no expression, and Jacques breathed a sigh of relief. They all hoped the conflict had ended.

"I would like to turn myself in," Carulus offered, raising his hands to be shackled.

Selasine paused and looked at Miranda, who was still crouched as she was when she had chosen to heal Carulus's affliction. "With no protests or scornful words?" he asked the high priest. Miranda's lips were pursed into a small, mischievous smile.

"Yes, bishop. Indervill came to me at a moment of weakness and offered me the power to prevent war between

Claston and Alabaster. I had not prayed to the Sword of Justice in nearly a month. He had turned his ears away from my prayers. Only Chaos himself answered me, and in my desperation, I betrayed the very law I once swore to uphold. I deserve whatever fate the archbishop decides," the disheveled half-elf confessed in defeat.

Miranda tilted her head, the braids Naomi had woven anew into her hair bouncing with her movements as everyone was accustomed to. "High Priest Carulus?" she asked in a soft voice.

He replied with a glance at her, "Yes?" He was unsure how to respond.

"You didn't mean for anyone to get hurt, did you?" she asked. The question sounded naïve on the surface. She would not have been offended if Selasine or Erk had questioned her. But in this mysterious place, she seemed ethereal and overwhelming. The meekness of her question was on purpose.

"Truly, girl, I didn't care. My only objective became victory, and I lost myself in the madness of obsession. I've been losing myself to that ambition for a decade. I understand the penance that must be paid for such failures," Carulus admitted.

"You didn't mean for it to happen this way, but you accidentally gave me a priceless gift," Miranda added.

Carulus started to object, "The power was already within you, girl. I should have listened to the archbishop instead of trying to use you as a pawn."

Miranda shook her head, "Not this gift, sir." She opened her hand, and the magic visibly swirled in it, bursting into a cloud of colors and sparkling mana butterflies. She continued, "That's something my parents might have caused unintentionally." She smiled serenely. "But thanks to you, I got to meet them. And I know they are happy, safe, and proud of me," she started but stopped, feeling a tear catch in her voice.

Selasine's eye widened with concern; Erk stepped behind her and touched her shoulder. August looked between the four of them wildly while the others stood, quietly watching all of this unfold.

She stood up and looked at Bishop Selasine. "I'm so happy and so sad at the same time, bishop," she started to cry. He breathed deeply and was instantly at her side. Erk's hand rested on her shoulder, and the bishop covered the girl in his embrace, her mentors giving her their understanding and silent affection. "Bishop?" she sniffled and held him close, her arms tossed around his torso.

"I'm here, yolasha," he comforted.

Erk smiled gently. He thought the word was appropriate.

Miranda continued between sobs, "Thank you for coming to rescue me again. Being trapped in the arcane stream was strange, but I met my mom and dad there."

Selasine said nothing; he just let her talk. He glanced at Erk, who now had a watchful eye on Carulus, who remained on his knees.

She continued after composing herself, releasing the bishop from her tight squeeze. She looked up at him, "They taught me a lesson." Her eyes sparkled; Selasine knew she always enjoyed discussing what she had learned. He partially wondered if that lesson was the reason why here, in this powerful place, she had seamlessly learned to use the power within her that convinced the god of madness to leave without conflict.

"What was the lesson?" he asked, drying his eye.

"The future is too unpredictable to leave the things you feel for people unsaid. And things can never return to how they were before we started this journey. I guess that's really two lessons," she stumbled over her words a bit, getting ahead of herself. "Which is why I can't wait to say it anymore. August?" she chirped at the end of that sentence. "August, I need a hug from you too," she requested, turning to the acolyte.

He looked at her, tears now pushing their way out of his eyes. Naomi gave him a gentle nudge on his shoulder, and he stepped forward. Miranda tossed herself into his frame. He overwhelmed her, but not to the same degree as Selasine. "You always know how to make me laugh. You're such a kind soul, and after this last year, I've come to love you like the big brother I never had. Justin, too, but he's not here to tell." She sniffled, August holding her in his embrace as she rambled. "I don't ever want any of you to not know how much I care about you."

Thomas had not felt the grip of such emotion in almost a decade. Miranda let go of August, who stood speechless. She then turned to look at Selasine, a big smile on her lips through her tears. "And you," she started, taking five long steps to throw her arms around him again. "I'm so lucky that you are my teacher. I hope it's okay if I've started to think of you like a father, and—" she was interrupted by a big, squeezing hug from him.

"Miranda," he said happily. "The fates and gods can be so cruel, but you're a treasure in my heart that can never be replaced. I called you yolasha, the elven word for daughter. Your unspoken feelings are in the open, where they belong."

She squeezed him again, her heart over the moons. August smiled at Selasine, wiping the tears from his eyes. "Guess that means you've got one more confession to make, yeah?" he teased.

Miranda glared at him playfully, but her face suddenly expressed shock. "Oh! I have to find Justin!" she started to rush off but realized she had absolutely no idea where they were. She saw the grotto at the bottom of the disc. She saw the solisberry tree. "Well, if he's not here, I can just go to him," she laughed. As she closed her eyes, the mana swirled around her furiously, causing a faint glow.

"Miranda, careful!" Erk cautioned as she started to concentrate. Wind began to blow through the Astral Spire. It blew straight up with such force that the pirates lost their hats, causing them to scramble and catch them. After a moment, the wind died down, allowing Erk and Naomi to replace the tricorn hats on their heads.

"He's safe," she whispered. "And he's saving others! Without us! That's not fair," she protested.

Selasine laughed but then realized she had clairvoyantly used the magic to see Justin. "What did you see, Miranda?" he asked, growing nervous for Justin's sake.

She opened her eyes. "He is with Pirate Lord Ut'wah. They make way to rescue," she trailed off, taking a moment to think. Her face twisted into further confusion, "Paladins are being held hostage in the seas outside of Claston. When did this happen?" she asked, worried.

Selasine and Erk both gave Carulus a stern look. Selasine responded, "As soon as the high priest went missing. There was a report that he had been killed, but only three witnesses could testify to seeing the body. Damil has kept me abreast of the situation," he explained, realizing that Miranda may not know who that was.

Miranda frowned. "If I turn myself over to the king, will he let those paladins go?" she asked.

Everyone's faces turned horrified. There was a unanimous "No!" even from Carulus.

"Gelidor is not to be trusted," Erk reasoned. Selasine nodded in agreement. "You know he is in league with The Shadowed One. The hostages are more likely bait for the heroes among the pirates. Like Ut'wah."

"Then we have to go to Claston and help save those paladins. From what I could see, Justin and Ut'wah will arrive at the port, ready to make war against the king's navy. They'll be there in two days," she spoke her thoughts out loud.

"I'm confident in Ut'wah's forces," Erk began.

Miranda interrupted him, "And I am confident I can make this rescue safer for everyone, even the people of Claston. Your people, Erk. Why should they die for a king seeking to harm them without consideration?"

Erk was in utter shock. She was, of course, right. The people of Claston were his people, even if they made allegiances and decisions rooted in survival under a tyrannical usurper. He had done the same, leading him down a path almost as dark as the usurping king's. Her confidence in herself and her cause shocked him the most, as he felt the trepidation she once exuded was gone. As a master manipulator and cut-throat pirate, this kind of attitude from the onset would have changed their entire relationship. He had no reason to manipulate the naïve, faithful, optimistic Miranda. Now, he had no reason to manipulate anyone. The cause of justice would speak for itself, and people would fall on the side of their choice. Erk smiled, proud of her newfound confidence. "It will take at least a week to sail back to Claston. By the time we get there, the bulk of the fighting will be over," he asserted, fully expecting her immediate objection.

Miranda nodded, "Erk, do you remember when I sent the king's blockade away?"

Erk replied, "Of course. It was the moment that reminded me I am fighting for the people on those ships too."

She smirked. "Just let me replenish my energy so I can work one more miracle today."

Jacques butted in, "Pardon, Lady Miranda. I have some things that belong to you." He held out his hand, the salts and the music box there in his palm.

Her jaw slacked, "Oh! My music box!" She reached out and took them from him. "My mother used to sing this lullaby to me. I can't remember it clearly, but I know in my heart that's why I know this melody so well." She smiled at Jacques. "Thank you, quartermaster."

He chuckled happily. "You're welcome, Lady Miranda," he replied, turning to Erk. "Say, captain, shall I transport us back to the Neb?"

Erk nodded, "Come, everyone. Close!"

Miranda inhaled deeply, closing her eyes. She stored so much mana in her that she began to glow with a golden aura. Selasine started to worry, but then he considered the ease with which she had been controlling the magic here. Jacques put his hands together as before, and the white circle reappeared beneath them. Before they vanished, Naomi reached up into the air using her uncanny magic to snatch several handfuls of solisberry blooms with her telekinesis. They passed through the gates of time and space, reappearing on the deck of *The Nebula*.

Miranda looked around, happy to be in a familiar place. Her body still glowed from the magical energy she had stockpiled under the blossoms of the solisberry tree. "Erk, Naomi!" she shouted. They looked in her direction, having not fully regained their sense of balance after teleporting. "Warn your crews! This might be a little bumpier than Jacques's teleport!"

As soon as they felt they could move without stumbling, they rushed to the upper deck of *The Nebula*. Erk rang a bell four times, a loud clanging that alerted the crews of both *The Nebula* and *The Violet Blur* that the waters would be especially turbulent soon. Naomi gave a wave to Annaia on the deck of her ship.

Miranda joined the captains on the upper deck. Jacques had run below deck to resume his duties as quartermaster. Evan followed Miranda toward his brother. August looked at Selasine, who had his arms by his side and was conversing with Damil. August waited for his mentor's eyes to open. The bishop smiled broadly, "Damil will meet us in Beriton in two days. He wants his birds back, he said."

August chuckled but still asked, oblivious, "I thought they were pegasus?"

Selasine's smile never broke. "They are, son. They are."

Miranda's light engulfed the two ships as the magic within her transported them within visual distance of *The Silver Corsair*.

Chapter 20
Only a Plank Between

*T*he *Nebula* and *The Violet Blur* now sailed in formation with *The Silver Corsair*. Three pirate nobles joining together was a rare occasion, and a rescue mission of this caliber would be an incredible display of solidarity between the pirates and their new allies within the Church of Invictus. If they were successful, the Church of Invictus, and, therefore, the Kingdom of Alabaster, would have no reason to act against the King of Claston. If Gelidor retaliated for Miranda's intervention at the blockade or for the rescue of the hostages, the archbishop, Damil, and Selasine reasoned that his demise would be brought by his own hands. As it stood, the church would consider an invasion due to the revelation of Gelidor's worship of Na'agamlor. However, a proper invasion would take longer to mobilize, and it would be more difficult if the usurper could mobilize a counter-offensive.

Additionally, after the events at the Astral Spire, Carulus surrendered himself for arrest. Erk agreed to hold him in the brig of *The Nebula* until he could be transported by church officials to Nulodia. Though Miranda severed the connection between Indervill and the fallen high priest, Erk ordered multiple crew members to always watch over Carulus. The pirate lord did not want to risk another battle with Chaos, especially not on his beloved ship.

August and Justin could see each other with spyglasses. They waved and ran along the decks of their respective ships, *The Nebula* and *The Valiant Sailor*. Miranda caught sight of August's excitement from the upper deck, where she discussed her gift with Shalo, Evan, Jax, Erk, Naomi, and Selasine.

"If I transport all of us straight to Beriton, it might take me several hours, even days, to recover enough magic to be of much help," she explained. "While at the top of the Astral Spire, I had an unlimited flow of magic. The arcane flows differently here," she smiled at Evan. "I can't see it like Evan could, but I can feel how it flows. When it passes through me, it stays trapped within me. Now that I've been inside the arcane stream, I have even learned how to draw excess mana flow into me," she continued.

Evan confirmed her explanation. "It flows through all of us, but those with uncanny magic can turn that flow into manifest power. When I would activate my power, I could see the stream reach out and destroy the moisture in the air around me. It would then send it into my essence, a never-ending thirst that could not be quenched by water," he shuddered as he spoke, a true torment in his memory.

Selasine followed up, "So, after spending some time in the arcane stream, you can control the magic within you?"

Miranda smiled. "Yes, and I'm more comfortable telling it what to do. Just don't expect any big miracles back-to-back. If I use all of the mana within me, I might be pretty useless for a while. It's why I had so much trouble staying conscious after using my gift at first. But I can use smaller amounts of the magic now to help more than just one big gesture at a time," she explained, still craning to see August on the lower deck.

Erk laughed. "I will have Jacques take Naomi and myself

over to Ut'wah's ship for a while and discuss strategy. With that in mind," he looked at the people around him and paused. "With Miranda's power and limitations understood, I believe we can make a plan that doesn't involve Miranda using all her magic at once." He then took Naomi by the hand, "Bishop Selasine, would you accompany us to Ut'wah's ship?" he asked.

Selasine's face was serious. He had hoped to have a moment to get in touch with Justin on *The Valiant Sailor* nearby. He looked at Miranda. She was obviously distracted by August's loudly announced discovery that he had visual confirmation of Justin. Still, just to be sure, she needed an invitation to the strategy meeting. "Yes. I will join you. And Miranda?" he commented, looking at his pupil.

Erk shook his head. "She's our wild card. Right now, I think she has more pressing matters to attend to," he indicated with a gesture. Miranda was staring at August, who looked a bit silly, running up and down the port side of *The Nebula* with a spyglass. Erk wanted desperately for her to have a 'normal' day today. She deserved at least that.

Selasine smiled, understanding the pirate lord's reasoning. "Very well. Once we have a larger picture painted, we'll be able to give Miranda and August the specifics."

"Miranda," Erk said, catching her attention. She looked back at the pirate lord like she had been pulled out of a daydream. "I have something that belongs to you," he said, handing Iria's sword and scabbard over to her.

She took it in her hand with a smile, "I love how the mana flows through this. It's a beloved treasure, and I'm honored to carry on its legacy."

Erk felt unusually touched at her gratitude, which he had expected. It was the peculiar way she described the sword that disturbed his balance. It was almost like she could now see things that the rest could not. He shook off the feeling and continued, "You are dismissed until dawn. Please don't lose your life essence again," he teased.

She scrunched her nose sarcastically, "I'll make sure not to get kidnapped by pirates either." Naomi looked at Erk incredulously, but Erk's eyes and mouth expressed that her quip caught him off guard. The other pirates traded cheeky glances, and Selasine smiled broadly. There was a round of laughter at Erk's expense.

"You're lucky that she's forgiven you," Naomi pestered.

"The thing I deserve the least," Erk replied, smiling at Miranda.

"Where are my manners?" Miranda interjected. She gave a full Invictus salute to Erk and Selasine. "I will report at dawn. Does this mean I can see Justin?" she asked excitedly.

"How much magic will it take to teleport two people twice?" Selasine asked, concerned.

She chewed on her lip in thought as she felt for the intensity of the stream here, then replied, "Probably about two hours' worth, but it will ultimately depend on how much mana is flowing as we move."

Erk nodded. "Just be careful. That's one of Gelidor's ships, and the original crew is likely loyal to the king and biding their time to escape or worse."

Miranda's lips broke into a broad smile, "I will, I promise!" She hugged Selasine, a violation of church protocol while receiving orders.

Selasine squeezed her back, protocol be damned. He was still thinking about what she had said in the Astral Spire when she said things would never go back to the same as before. She was right, and for the first time in a while, Selasine felt ready to face the future.

Miranda looked over to Erk. "Can I hug you, too?"

Erk smiled, which was all the affirmation she needed before overwhelming the elf with her taller stature and abundant hair. He returned her hug gently. As she stood, she made eye contact with Naomi, and her cheeks flushed. The pirate lady was so beautiful that Miranda lost her words.

Naomi smiled back, "When this is all over, I've got room on *The Violet Blur* if you want to learn what it's really like to be a pirate!"

Miranda's head was caught somewhere between a nod and a shake. "I'll have to check with the bishop first!" she promised noncommittally.

Shalo could not look her in the eyes since she had awoken. She playfully punched the pungent pirate's shoulder. He looked up from the deck, his sorrow and shame evident. "The fates and the gods saved our friendship, Shalo. Just be a kinder person and avoid violence. You'll never have to worry about something like this happening again," she lectured.

He nodded solemnly and reached into a pouch. He withdrew a symbol of Lexcord. "Ya told me the gods would favor me if I gave them a reason to, Miss Miranda. I mean ta make ya proud, lass," he explained.

She smiled in return. "Your heart has found the right place. May your actions tell the world what's in there."

Jax was next, but the two of them had not really interacted much. Though his background was that of a more traditional pirate, Miranda had gotten the sense that Erk's philosophy began to change him into a better person. He dined with her and the captain every night of their first journey from Port Undine to the Isles Known for Nothing. He smiled and offered his arm out for a clasp. Miranda took his forearm in her hand, and he returned the grasp. "Have fun, kid," he ordered.

She nodded, "I will," she promised, releasing their handshake.

Evan complained, "It's like you're saying goodbye. Stop that. You're just going over there for a minute." He couldn't help but smile as well, everyone happy that Miranda was back to her normal self.

"I'm thankful you're okay, Evan," she commented. His smile softened.

"And I'm thankful that you are who you are, Miranda. You're going to change the world," he challenged in return. She, too, understood that her destiny would be much bigger than just this awesome power she possessed. Until she had to seek that destiny, she really just wanted to see her friends and forget the worry of the looming threat of war between Claston and Alabaster.

She hugged Evan anyway. "It's not goodbye; it's see you soon," she promised. With her one day of leave already burning, she scurried down the stairs of the upper deck, the pleats of the skirt of her battlemail clinking softly as she ran.

August was still staring off port at *The Valiant Sailor* about a thousand feet away. "August!" Miranda called out with her musical voice, singing his name.

He lowered the spyglass but did not look at her. "Justin is over there; I can see him!" he said excitedly.

"Do you want to go see him?" she asked, walking up to him and grabbing his hand before he could answer.

August stopped, looked at Miranda, and then at his hand clasped in hers. "Oh, for sure!" he replied, excited.

She took the spyglass from August and looked through it. She scanned the other ship's deck length, finally locating Justin, who also had a spyglass and was waving. "Oh wow, he looks way different," she commented. "Let's go find out why," she sang in her most mischievous voice.

August closed his eyes and inhaled deeply. Miranda felt for mana in the air, but the flow was slow this far out on the sea's surface. It was more likely to be abundant deep below them in the oceans teeming with worlds and kingdoms of their own. She used some of the magic stored within her to teleport them from *The Nebula's* deck to *The Valiant Sailor's* deck. The sudden appearance of two more clergy caused the paladins and clerics running the ship to pause. They paid little attention to the newcomers as they were also clergy.

As they appeared, Justin furiously looked around *The Nebula* and audibly complained, "Val, I can't see them anymore. I think they turned invisible."

Miranda and August looked around the ship, making sure they had their balance oriented. Valarie began to shake Justin's shoulder, which caused him to lower his spyglass. He looked up at her, "Is everything okay?" he asked. She pointed to Miranda and August silently with a smile on her lips.

Justin's eyes widened with excitement, flashing bright green in the morning light, rushing toward his friends. Before he reached them, he gave a harsh "Adûnzha, acolytes!" and snapped himself to attention.

The two scrambled into a salute, not in their best form. "Wait, Justin?" Miranda asked, confused.

Justin laughed, "Ah, c'mon. I'm just kidding," rushing out of his attention stance and grabbing them into a group hug.

Miranda's heart swelled with joy. August was happy, too, but suddenly felt that Justin had also grown a lot over the last month. "I thought I'd never see you again," Miranda finally confessed.

Justin said sarcastically, "Well, it looks like your luck ran out!"

Miranda glared at him, "Hey! Not funny." She squeezed him harder.

August laughed. He had missed his friend's wit.

Miranda sighed deeply and finally released Justin and August. "That's one massive shield," she commented, looking over Justin. Valarie had approached, her shield towering over her as well.

Justin looked behind him and extended his arm, and the woman that neither August nor Miranda knew took hold of Justin's hand and stood beside him, smiling. Justin began, "This is my girlfriend, Valarie. If this were a church introduction, I would also tell you that she is Valarie the Persistent, Shield Knight of Invictus, Judge of Retribution." He smiled at his friends broadly, August reaching out to give her a handshake.

"August Burchard, Acolyte of Invictus. At your service," he said as they clasped hands up to the wrists.

Miranda's lips were twisted into the most ecstatic smile. "Well met, Valarie," reaching out to shake her hand in greeting. She sarcastically remarked to Justin, "I think the most important title I heard in that list was girlfriend?"

His cheeks flushed a bit, but he smiled. Valarie interjected, "And you're the woman the whole church is talking about? Miranda?" she asked, grasping Miranda's hand for a lingering moment.

"That's me!" she giggled.

Valarie smiled at her, "I am honored, Miranda. Justin has told me so much about the two of you; I feel like I already know you. Which isn't fair, but . . ." she trailed off, smirking and looking at Justin. "Well, you know how it is once a lecture starts."

Justin made a silly, angry face, "Hey, somebody sticks around listening to me."

Valarie lifted her hands to her mouth and pretended to speak so that Justin was being excluded, "I usually have no idea what he's saying. I just listen because he's cute when he talks."

The ladies giggled. August was actively looking around the deck of *The Valiant Sailor*, "So, Shield Knights? Even you, Justin?" He eyed the shield strapped onto his friend's back.

Justin saluted, "Paladin Justin the Watchful, Shield Knight of Invictus, Judge of Action. Reporting for duty, sir!" he replied to August.

August's jaw slacked. Miranda's eyes widened, her mouth making that distinct, round shape that expressed wonder in her own way. She replied, "Oh, Justin! That's so wonderful! You've already earned accolades!"

Valarie, still all smiles, "He deserved both of them. His quick thinking has saved lives twice on this voyage. And I'm a sucker for heroes," she commented, her left hand still in Justin's right. She squeezed his hand with adoration.

August started to grin, "So you took the oath of the paladin? I thought you said that was my future and you'd be happy enough to push papers."

Justin smirked, "Guess the future is a little more unpredictable than we thought, yeah? Besides, I've learned a lot, and I've been training nonstop. Valarie is an incredible combat instructor," he added.

August puffed his chest out a bit, "Oh yeah? Wanna show me some of those new moves?"

Justin laughed and stepped away without hesitation; Valarie reluctantly let his hand go. He grabbed some wooden training swords from a crate nearby. Tossing one to August, he pulled his shield off his back. He sank into a fighting stance, his eyes shimmering with excitement. He had already decided he would beat August in a training match, here and now.

August hefted the sword, tested its weight, and then zipped into action. With his uncanny power, he moved faster than Valarie would have predicted. It only seemed to affect the agility in his footwork rather than his attacks. August tried to use speed and brute force to charge directly into Justin's shield to push him back. Justin used the tower shield to misdirect August's weight with a pivot tactic. As August tried to regain his balance after Justin's shift, Justin used the flat side of the wooden sword to give August a hard swat on his rear. It made the chainmail around August's waist clink.

"Oh hey, hey, that's a dirty trick!" August protested.

Justin smiled as they turned to face each other. "As it turns out, monsters don't fight fair. Neither do real enemies." He then leaped forward at August, unleashing a series of strikes, with August only parrying the first. The rest connected with his plate armor in varying locations. The tower shield made it impossible for August to try and fight offense with offense. After a few moments of clanging against August's armor with the wooden sword and mithril shield, Justin's leg suddenly appeared behind August's ankle, causing the bigger fighter to tumble backward. As he crashed on the deck, nobody seemed to even notice. The Shield Knights had so normalized training on deck that such events had become commonplace and casual.

August gave a hardy laugh. He laid back on the deck and stretched his arms to the sides. "Yeah, okay. I haven't really had much time to train lately, you know. I'm a little rusty; I've only fought a giant manticore, an eldritch dragon, an evil lich, and held a light against a buncha shadows. Doesn't teach me much about the regular battlefield, I guess, right?" Justin shouldered his shield, reaching down to help his friend up.

Justin replied, grinning and making eye contact for a lecture. "It might not help teach you tactics to fight against another person, but those battles made you wiser and braver. The same methods we always use against a certain type of foe must change if the old ways are not working. That's why I could trip you because I changed my strategy against you. But the wisdom you have acquired on your journey is incredible. You've seen the universe's secrets peeled back, a future I could only hope for as a cleric."

August stood easily with his help. Miranda was shocked at how adept Justin had become in such a short time. Valarie was beaming with pride. She bragged, "I taught him the leg sweep. A backpedal is the only time you can make an opening big enough with the shield to make a trick like that work."

"Woooooah." Miranda said in a deep, awed voice, a long raspy sound carried on for much longer than necessary.

Justin laughed. "Miranda, I didn't think you would be so impressed. I heard you can teleport stuff, and I've seen you bring people back to life."

She grinned, "I can do much more than that now!"

Justin tilted his head, "Oh, is that so?"

August had a bloodthirsty look in his eyes. "You should spar her, Justin. See what she's made of."

The paladin shook his head. "No way. Not until I have a full accounting of my opponent's capabilities."

Miranda flipped a braid with her hand and let out a huffing breath. "That's kind of impossible when I can do pretty much anything. Within limitations, I mean," she contradicted herself, causing her voice to waiver in confusion. "I mean, I can only work with magic stored inside my body and essence. It takes time for the mana to accumulate, but after it's there, I can shape it into whatever I want," she explained.

Valarie's normal, scrutinous expression excitedly softened, "Oh, like a shield made out of magic?"

Miranda nodded excitedly, "That one is actually easy!" She held her arm up and created a tower shield out of pure energy.

Justin instinctively tapped his training sword against it. "Solid as mithril," he commented.

Miranda gave a wicked grin. "Try it again," she prompted.

Justin struck the shield a little harder this time, and an arc of electricity burst from it, zapping him with as much force as a static shock after walking across especially plush wool rugs.

He yelped out of surprise more than pain. "What in the Abyss?" he protested.

Valarie was in awe. Miranda let the ethereal shield vanish. August looked very concerned and asked, "How in the world did you go from big, uncontrollable miracles to precise control over your gift so much that you can change the stuff you summon?"

Miranda rolled her eyes and sighed with humorous exaggeration. "August! I explained that. I literally had to make an entire body out of this stuff. I was part of this magic for a while, and now that I'm back here, I still feel like I'm in the mana. It's like an extension of my body at this point."

August looked aghast. "So, you could literally just use all that mana and kill somebody if you wanted?" True to his nature, he might have accidentally killed the conversation instead of moving it forward. He cursed internally, realizing how horrible his question sounded. Still, he needed to know her response.

Miranda's eyes shot open in horror, "August!" she shrieked. "Why in the Infernia would you even think of something like that?"

August didn't retract; he just looked intrigued. "Well, like, the whole King of Claston deal. Couldn't you just will him out of existence? That would end a great deal of this conflict, right?"

Miranda shook her head. "Even if I could, why would that be the right thing to do? All entities deserve an accounting of their actions. Though I'm sure his atrocities outweigh his acts of justice, it must still be done according to the law of the Sword of Justice," she replied, somewhat annoyed. August was smarter than that.

"Good," he replied. "You know, they say power sometimes goes to your head and all that. I just wanted to make sure this whimsical teleport-here, save-the-world-there, Miranda was still up to speed on her catechisms."

Justin punched August's breastplate playfully. "Hey, not cool. She is too smart to fall into a dark path like that."

Miranda smiled sweetly. She understood August's fears and was glad he voiced his concern honestly. She continued, "I'm glad you have faith in me, both of you." She breathed deeply, pride for her friends swirling in her heart. She couldn't have manipulated the universe enough to give Justin the things he had earned pursuing after her. That was his own doing. He forged his own destiny, and she was amazed and happy for her other brother. "You mean so much to me, and I hope I never let you down. I can't say whether it's older or younger, but you've become like a brother to me, and I cherish that."

Justin looked puzzled, but then he smiled big. "I'd say we were twins, but your hair is way too different."

August leaned in, "You know, that's a good point."

Valarie pursed her lips, thinking, "I don't know; not all twins look the same." She almost spoke it like a question.

Miranda laughed. They spent the rest of the afternoon talking and working together. They helped carry out some duties on *The Valiant Sailor*. Justin repeatedly reminded Miranda and August to maintain discipline while conducting official duties. The friends were reunited and had new friends to add to their number. Miranda smiled internally as she realized the wisdom of things never returning to how they were. She no longer wondered about her parents. Actually, she learned a great deal about them just by finding them in the arcane stream. Since their return from the north, she found that her mother's memories were present in her mind beside her own. Seeing the world through somebody else's eyes was odd, but she had all the earthly wisdom she would ever need in those memories. The girl of fire and lightning was finding her place, and so were those she cared about. As the sun set in the northwest.

"August?" she said as they stood together gazing off the starboard. They could easily see *The Nebula* and *The Violet Blur* from here, both large ships for their categories.

"Right," he agreed.

Justin placed a hand on both of their backs. "Hey, we're on the same mission. So, we're still together, okay?"

August beamed. "Got it. I've got your back, brother."

Valarie was smiling. "I'm there with you too. You're just as wild as the frontier boy. You inspire me," she said to Miranda.

Miranda smiled back. "Let's save those paladins, yeah?" and reached out to give Justin and Valarie a hug. They all embraced, and then, with a blink of her mind, she and August were back on *The Nebula*. They retired comfortably, their hearts whole and peaceful once again.

***

Ut'wah scratched his smooth chin, his obsidian skin reflecting the soft sunlight that filtered throughout his captain's quarters. Erk, Naomi, Selasine, and his first officer Raz were all present with him. Raz was a gnoll, a humanoid people reminiscent of hyenas. He was napping in a reclining chair while the others collaborated. They gathered to plan the rescue of approximately one thousand paladins held hostage in the open waters outside Beriton, the largest port city in the kingdom of Claston. Erk was notorious for dominating meetings, but that did not bother Ut'wah. The orc and Naomi had worked together in the past. She seemed to be the only pirate noble who could keep Erk in check.

Today, however, Erk seemed different. He was always methodical but seemed strangely focused with even greater precision than Ut'wah expected. He was pouring over maps while the priest, Thomas Selasine, examined some reconnaissance reports that Ut'wah's pirates had compiled. The first time Ut'wah had seen the bishop, he was in the Fortress of Lords seeking help to restore his pupil Miranda from a magical coma caused by Erk's "Master." He seemed to have a natural rapport with Erk and Naomi, and their recent journey to the north increased their urgency for their current mission.

Erk finally grumbled, "I really don't see any possibilities for a stealthy approach."

Naomi frowned. "The Blur can turn invisible, but she's the only ship that can."

Ut'wah continued to scratch his chin in thought. "The intel suggests that there are only three gunships positioned to obliterate the hostages on the king's order," he commented, contemplating removing the threat before executing the rescue.

Naomi winced. "I can outrun any ship in the open water, but there's no way in the Abyss my girls could sink three gunships, even with our advantages."

Selasine, who had been seated with the intel documents, suddenly stood. "If these reports are to be believed, the entire Claston navy is mobilized. But where are they? We'd stand no chance in open conflict, and neither would the hostages," he added.

Erk nodded in agreement. "Do you think it's part of an attempt to trap us? Dangle hostages before the heroes and wait until they come running?"

Naomi licked her lips in contemplation. "Say, maybe that's what they're hoping for. Use the hostage ships to burn up Miranda's power, and then we're left overwhelmed by the navy."

Selasine continued, "I would agree, but they don't have the same knowledge that we have. Perhaps there is another moving piece that is meant to account for Miranda's role in this." The lack of information meant they would be basing their decisions on faith. The bishop had faith in the gods, not in decisions made with only partial knowledge.

Ut'wah let out a deep, contemplative "Hmmm." He tapped the holy symbol hanging around his neck. He, too, was seated but was still the largest presence in the room. He stood and gripped the holy symbol tightly, whispering prayers in a language nobody else understood. It glowed faintly for a while, then Ut'wah smiled. "Fog," he said suddenly and without explanation. The room fell silent, all eyes turning to Ut'wah, anticipating his plan. He continued, "One of my ship's officers, Elmadyn, is a druid of incredible skill. She can harness the power of nature to create a fog screen big enough to cover our fleet and then some."

Erk's eyes lit up with excitement, "That could get us in close, but the ships are surely anchored. Raising anchor on three ships in foggy conditions would take too long."

Naomi had withdrawn a dagger, biting on it as was her habit. "What if we just cut the anchor chains?"

Selasine and Ut'wah furrowed their brows in contemplation. Erk spoke, "It would require incredible strength and precision to break the anchor chains. Who could we rely on for such a task?"

The bishop almost laughed, "Who, indeed? Do you think that's a good time to use our wildcard?"

Ut'wah nodded in agreement. "If she can cut the chains, we can tow the ships safely away. Then, there's only a plank between the paladins and freedom," he finished, his plan becoming concrete.

Naomi put her dagger away. "I could pull one ship with telekinesis, but we'd have to actually grapple and tie the other two. *The Nebula* and *The Silver Corsair* could easily pull two ships, but their size would make us easier to spot in the fog. A smaller ship might be a safer option," she contributed.

Erk gave an affirming nod. "The usurper's ship, *The Valiant Sailor*. Commander Aguila confirmed that the king's crew, including their captain, is currently in the brig. After the treachery in Beriton, I can't say I blame them. It sounds like the law makes faster decisions on the open water, doesn't it bishop?" he asked, turning to Selasine.

Selasine's expression remained grim, and he did not answer Erk's question. "*The Valiant Sailor* and *The Violet Blur* make the rescue. *The Nebula* and *The Silver Corsair* provide cover, first with fog and then after, firepower. The king's gunships wouldn't dare threaten the two of us together, not with Pirate Lord Erk the Radiant's ever-watchful light, would they?"

Erk smiled. "You're sure you're not a sailor, Selasine?" the pirate asked, a playful tone in his voice.

The bishop laughed, "I just want my kids and those paladins out of there safe. And if I have to become a sailor to make that happen, then as Invictus wills it, so shall it be."

Naomi's lips twisted into a smirk. "We'll have another day to prepare before we arrive. I'll take Miranda to *The Violet Blur*," she explained, finding a justification to spend a day with the girl. "I'll work with her on finding the perfect amount of magic to break chains. Then, she can cut the chains, and my crew can grapple one of the hostage ships. I'll pull one with my power, and *The Valiant Sailor* can tug the third ship. We'll want to move in at an hour that's natural for foggy conditions. That way, we stand the best chance of the ruse working," she elaborated. "But how close does Miranda need to be to cut the chains?" she asked.

The others looked around, concerned, until Erk spoke up, "We can use Jacques if we need to. His gift seems to be working well lately. Or, maybe Miranda can cut them from the deck of The Blur. We can make a final decision after you work with her tomorrow."

The others agreed. An early morning fog screen would be believable this time of year. They could probably execute the rescue in under an hour, depending on how much assistance Miranda needed to locate and cut the anchors' chains. Selasine would brief Aguila through Damil. Erk would brief his crew and Miranda, and Naomi would then take her to *The Violet Blur* for preparations for the mission. With a solid plan in place, Ut'wah dismissed the pirates and Selasine.

Jacques waited for them on deck. "My lord?" he greeted. As

those in the strategy meeting left, two others entered, an elven woman with light blue hair and a human pirate. They smiled kindly at Selasine and Naomi. Erk avoided eye contact with them but waved cordially, hurrying to Jacques by the center mast.

Erk gave a single nod. "Back to The Neb, friend," he replied, Selasine and Naomi standing close.

Ut'wah stuck his head out of the captain's quarters, "Captains!"

Erk and Naomi looked at him quickly. "There may be storms tonight, according to Elmadyn. Please, sail with caution," he advised.

"Thank you for the warning, Pirate Lord Ut'wah. May the Silver Maiden shed her light on all of us," Erk replied as Jacques clasped his hands together.

Naomi clicked open the door to her dressing room, slipping inside quietly. A gentle thunderstorm bellowed sparingly outside. She heard Miranda sleeping in the bed, and a single magical candle left barely enough light in the room for Naomi to find the armored corset she was looking for in the wardrobe. After retrieving it, she heard Miranda stir. "Naomi?" her voice whispered.

The pirate lady smiled, corset in hand, and replied, "Sorry to wake you. We've got a big day tomorrow."

Miranda sat up. She looked different, with her hair unbraided and tossed wildly by sleep. She was a beautiful young woman; her endearing personality drew everyone to her. Naomi didn't know the girl as well as she wanted to, so she sat on the side of the bed closest to the door. "It's okay," Miranda replied, her eyes reflecting deeper tones of blue in the sparse light.

Naomi could see her exhaustion. She thought she must have had a great day with her friends. She wanted to give her another great day on *The Violet Blur* as they reviewed and rehearsed the rescue plan. There wouldn't really be enough time for wine and makeup. From what Naomi understood, it was unlikely that the girl had many women to look up to. Then again, she only knew about Selasine, August, and Justin. Still, everyone loved Miranda greatly, and Naomi was no exception. Her reasons came from seeing how people changed after meeting Miranda. Most notably, Erk. He and Naomi had been together for twenty years, but in the last decade, she had seen him spiral out of control. Naomi correctly blamed Evan's worsening condition for Erk's increasingly desperate tactics. She was glad that Miranda was both a solution to Evan's affliction and returning her beloved's feet to the path of good.

"Did you enjoy your day with your friends?" Naomi asked, her voice soft and effortlessly rich.

Miranda's eyes lit up immediately as she turned onto her side to face Naomi more comfortably. "We had a lot of fun with Justin today!" she started, taking very little time to wake enough so that her excitement shone obviously. "He's had such a busy journey that he already outranks August and me. He's even got a girlfriend now, and she's fun and beautiful. I think Justin beat August in a training duel for the first time ever. I'm so happy for them; they've gotten to see and do so much since we left Devitus." She spoke so excitedly that she had to pause to catch her breath.

A smile stayed on Naomi's lips, the dim light stretching the shadows in the room comfortably and sleepily. The gentle thunder added to the atmosphere. "You seem so happy for everyone else, sweetheart. What about you? Are you happy, too?" she asked, reaching out and gently brushing Miranda's hair out of her face.

Miranda giggled, "I am happy seeing my friends happy. They have such kind hearts, and I care for them more than anything else."

Naomi's smile melted a bit, the danger of the rescue mission weighing on her mind. She normally had a worldly speech about being unable to save everyone and that reality could sometimes be crueler than anyone imagined. She, herself, had escaped from the horrors of slavery, and she protected girls and women who had run away from any kind of threat, usually a threat created by greedy and violent men. Somehow, she knew that Miranda had learned the realities of the harshness of life in a way that made her optimistic rather than naïve. Selasine truly was a wonderful teacher, Naomi realized. He had taken a beautiful person with a pure heart and cultivated that rather than stomping it out in favor of the empty, heartless way many people viewed the world.

Naomi let the silence sit for a moment before continuing. "You have a kind heart too, darling. They are lucky to have you as a friend. Erk had no idea he was kidnapping his savior," she explained.

Miranda yawned a bit and laid her head down on the pillow. Her eyes had adjusted well to the darkness. Naomi's beautiful features and skin made Miranda uncomfortable, but she didn't understand why. The pirate lady was so sweet. Miranda knew it couldn't be that she disliked or distrusted Naomi. Maybe it was something else? She thought that Naomi reminded her of her mother in some ways. They were both incredibly beautiful and strong women. "I didn't save Erk. He just listened to what I had to say and made up his own mind. I could see the good in his heart when I met him. I could also tell it was buried underneath more burdens than one heart should have to bear," Miranda said, trying to avoid the credit.

Naomi smirked. "Well, you saved *my* Erk. For the last ten years, he has been losing himself to the darkness, and The Master only fueled his anger and aggression. If you hadn't come into our lives and saved Evan, I don't know what would have happened to my darling Erilkaiden. You helped bring him back to me. And now I see why everyone loves you so much."

Miranda blinked in a moment of disbelief. "Me?"

"Yes, you, beautiful, sweet, sweet Miranda." Naomi sighed contentedly. She got her answer. The girl was just too pure. Naomi chuckled, realizing that Miranda's gift in anybody else's hands could have ushered in a new age of chaos and war. All the world should be grateful that this girl had the power to shape the world to her will. "You're going to be on *The Violet Blur* tomorrow. The women in my crew," she began and paused. "Don't be afraid to just be yourself around them. Annaia is going to love you. Rose will probably try to steal your hair; she loves everything red. Most of them have had complicated lives. Being around you will be all they need to lift their spirits."

Miranda nodded and pulled her arms up under the pillow

to raise her head a bit more. "I don't really know how to be anybody else, so I promise you'll get the one and only Miranda to help however I can," she assured the pirate lady.

Naomi's lips pursed up in a smile that turned into a gentle laugh. "Sleep well, darling. Erk will tell you all about it in the morning," she commented, tugging the covers tight around Miranda's shoulders. "Good night."

Miranda whispered back, "Good night, Pirate Lady Naomi." It sounded to Naomi like the girl began to whisper a prayer that turned into the sound of light sleep before the pirate lady even stood.

Naomi quietly slipped back over to the captain's quarters, where Erk sat alone at his meeting table. He glanced up to confirm it was Naomi and met her eyes, giving her his handsome smile. "You woke her up, didn't you?" he interrogated.

Naomi walked to a mannequin and laced her armored corset around it. Looking back at Erk as she worked, "Not on purpose. And you were right; she wasn't the slightest bit perturbed." Her silver hair was tied back into a simple, mid-shoulder length ponytail, shining brilliantly in Erk's well-lit cabin. The corset was a fine piece of armor made from a metallic mesh much like the long skirt of Miranda's battlemail. The most important part was the enchantment upon it. It enhanced Naomi's telekinesis so that she could use her powers precisely and defensively. She continued, "In fact, she seemed happy to see me. I tucked her in. Talk about a weird mom moment. I've never even once tucked any of the girls in. Maybe I should start doing that," she rambled.

Erk laughed at her motherly digression. "That's a long answer to a short question," he quipped.

Naomi tilted her head and smirked at him from behind the mannequin, "You said she'd get to me. I guess that means you were right."

He simply smiled and returned his eyes to a tome he was studying.

After Naomi tightened the corset, she glided across the cabin, around Erk's table to stand behind him. The chair was high enough that she could comfortably drape herself over the back and around Erk's shoulders. She purposefully flipped her ponytail over her shoulder and into his face. "What book in the world could be more interesting than me?" she teased.

Erk shook his face to knock her hair out of his way nonchalantly. "Just reading up on magical fog and naval warfare. It's only been done on rare occasions; druids and wizards capable of such feats are hard to come by," he answered.

She tossed her head to get her hair back behind her. "Oh! Sorry, I didn't realize you were still working. You haven't cared about a mission this much in a decade." Her tone shifted from playful and coy to serious and engaged immediately. Everything she said to Miranda a moment ago was so true. This was the Erk she had fallen for twenty years ago. Naomi seemed like an exceptionally tall and toned elf, but her grandmother on one side was an earth giant, making her a quarter giant. Her lifespan was likely double that of the average human. At fifty years old, nobody would have guessed that she was a day over twenty-five.

Erk smiled. "That's because we have hope again."

Naomi gave him a sad smile, "I always had hope because I always had you. I almost lost you to the darkness, too. Miranda has saved a lot of people in a lot of different ways."

Erk closed the tome and put it on the table in front of him. "Which is how I knew she'd get to you, too," he commented as he stood. He was dressed in a set of indigo sleeping trousers made of silk and a plush, black robe made of fur. As he approached middle age for an elf, his body still rippled with youthful muscle. His golden hair spilled down his back in shimmering waves.

She smiled back at him, wearing a similar dark robe. The only other thing she wore was a ring on her right hand and a bandolier of magical throwing daggers on her right thigh. "I'm looking forward to spending the day with her tomorrow. Some of my girls need another ray of sunshine. Right before all of this started, I nailed another slave ship. Some bastard named Farzg has been smuggling slaves into Nulodia like a madman for the last six months."

Erk's face twitched with incensed fury. Naomi stepped

back, a look of terror gripping her face immediately. Erk's expression softened as soon as he noticed her horror. "Oh, by the gods, I'm so sorry, Naomi."

"Did what? What did I say?" she stumbled over her words, never having seen Erk's face twist in a manner that terrifying, even at his lowest.

He took a deep breath. "Farzg is the hak-koth that murdered my sister Iria and my niece Telisi."

Naomi's expression went from horror to loving sympathy. Hak-koth was a powerful insult in elven that would have roughly translated to common as "devil's bastard child." She rushed forward and took him into her arms, pressing him against her, "Oh, darling." She held him with all the love she had.

He sighed deeply, calmed, and wrapped his arms around her waist. "Rest assured, once this is resolved in Claston, Farzg's slave trading days are over. And we'll hunt every slave trader in the Nulodian Sea to track down every last one of the people they have taken. The Frozen Death will know the sunlight," he swore.

Naomi kissed the top of his head. Erk had shared news of his sister's and niece's murder, but he did not name a culprit. She knew this also meant Bishop Selasine would have a debt to repay to this Farzg. Naomi, too, would bear such a grudge against the slaver. The giantkin had spent a year with Iria in Alabaster, and in that time, they had grown quite close. Naomi squeezed her pirate lord. She hoped a change of subject would calm him further. "Well, a couple of girls from that last ship were scared to return to their homes. I think their own families sold them out. It's disgusting. I think someone as sweet as Miranda would be comforting to them."

Erk smiled and looked up at his beautiful partner. "She is going to take her role over there way too seriously," he warned.

She laughed, "Of course, that's why I just asked her to be herself tomorrow."

He continued to smile, albeit tired. "She is wise beyond expectation. I blame it on her draconic heritage," he commented.

Naomi nodded, dropping her fur robe to the cabin floor

and slipping under the silk sheets of Erk's bed. "I'm just happy Erk the Kind has decided to listen to her wisdom. Now he can be a hostage-rescuing, king-toppling mastermind again."

Erk slipped out of his robe and dismissed his magical candles, darkening the room immediately. His elven eyes were still able to see in the faint moonlight. "And I've got you, and Evan, and now a brother-in-law. And, well, Miranda, too. And that is more than I deserve." He also slipped into bed, wrapping his muscular frame around hers even though she dwarfed him in stature.

She let out a deep, content breath and closed her eyes. "Then you better work harder, bad boy. Naomi doesn't give her love to anybody that doesn't deserve it."

He laughed gently, relaxing and drifting to sleep. "I'll be your hero tomorrow, and every day after, I promise."

She thought, "You better," but she didn't manage to say it as she began to drift. Erk's embrace was so comforting that sleep came easier with his gentle but strong arms around her. Besides, tomorrow was going to be a pretty big day of preparations. They needed their rest.

Chapter 21
Complications

lmadyn stood on the bow of *The Silver Corsair*. The sun was about an hour away from peeking out from the southeastern horizon. She took a deep breath and gripped her gnarled wooden staff. She could feel the power of the earth mother, Gaiater, coursing through it. Druids were similar to clerics in that they did not draw their energy from the arcane like a wizard, but instead of praying to the myriad deities for borrowed power, the druids worked their miracles with the magic inherent to nature itself. She focused on the water around them, feeling its ebb and flow. A solitary, waxing, silver half-moon hung overhead. In this part of Espa, this was an indication that summer was getting ready to let go, and the chill of autumn would soon be in the air.

A dense cloud of mist began to form around the hull of *The Silver Corsair*. Elmadyn continued to focus her energy on turning the top layer of ocean water into a thickening fog. She began whispering a prayer in the druidic language, a tongue of power that could bend the will of nature much like magical languages allowed wizards to bend the arcane stream. As she spoke, the waters beneath Ut'wah's ship began to bubble, and steam began to rise. As the fleet sailed northeast, a blanket of fog began to sweep across the front line of the ships. *The Valiant Sailor* sailed in front, prepared for its mission to grapple and tow one of the hostage ships. *The Violet Blur*, with its powers of speed and invisibility, was sailing close by. Naomi could have used the magical device installed in the center mast of the ship to turn the vessel invisible but was waiting until they were very close to activate it.

Naomi had ordered her crew to have sails ready for the escape plan. Once the ships were in place, Jacques would jump with Erk, Selasine, and Miranda to the two hostage ships that *The Violet Blur* was preparing to tow. They planned to cut the anchors' chains using Miranda's power. Naomi had been practicing with her, helping her figure out exactly how much mana it would require to cut such a sturdy object. Meanwhile, Ut'wah would wait for Miranda and Jacques on the third vessel, the one to be pulled by *The Valiant Sailor*. Selasine, Erk, and Ut'wah were to stay behind on each of the three ships to keep a telepathic link open between at least two of the vessels. Since Erk and Selasine would be on the ships pulled by Naomi and *The Violet Blur*, everyone involved would be at least within shouting distance of a connection to the telepathy. Damil's pegasus battalion laid in wait off the coast, planning to serve as air support in case something went awry.

As the fog's density grew, Elmadyn prayed the wind into a gentle north-easterly breeze that was not strong enough to disperse the ever-thickening cloud, but it kept the ships moving slowly. Even with her wisdom and skill, using the right balance of the elements would be difficult and delicate. However, she was confident in her power, continuing to create billowing fog to disguise Ut'wah's fleet, *The Nebula*, and *The Violet Blur*. They would arrive at the hostage ships in less than an hour.

As the end of that hour approached, Damil could see the rolling fog easily to the southwest. The sun began to rise above the southeastern horizon, lighting the Bay of Beriton in an ominous, golden light. The high paladin addressed his telepathic contacts, "Rescue team, the fog is close to the hostage ships. *The Violet Blur* is clear to infiltrate. Three gunships remain positioned in the bay; it looks like they're anchored."

Selasine's nod could be heard through the telepathy. "I'll let Erk know," he replied.

Ut'wah remained on standby. Aguila's thoughts then came through, "*The Valiant Sailor* is ready to move into position as well."

As a caravel, *The Violet Blur* sat closer to the water than galleons like *The Nebula* and *The Silver Corsair*. It still had a raised deck for the captain to steer the ship, but it was not quite as high. It only had three decks counting the top deck. Naomi had chosen the ship thanks to the fine magics involved in its construction rather than its size or firepower. Furthermore, the ship had a consciousness of its own and had chosen Naomi as her captain. The pirate lady shouted from the helm, "Annaia, now!"

Standing with Naomi on the upper deck, Miranda watched as *The Violet Blur*'s first officer ran to the main mast and placed both hands on a glowing, yellow crystal that was built into it. To the women aboard the ship, nothing changed. However, the ship was completely invisible to the rest of the fleet. Now, they waited for Erk, Jacques, and Selasine. They would be the first men aboard *The Violet Blur* since Naomi acquired the ship; even Erk had never been aboard.

The fog continued to roll forward while the rest of the fleet furled sails to slow their approach. Only *The Valiant Sailor* and *The Violet Blur* would approach the hostage ships. After a few minutes, Erk and Selasine suddenly appeared alongside Jacques.

Naomi turned to them quickly, instinctively drawing out daggers in each hand. She let out a quick, relieved breath when she realized who it was. Miranda had also drawn Iria's sword, but she sheathed it quickly.

As Erk oriented himself with his surroundings, his eyes quickly found Miranda and Naomi next to the helm. The teleporting group had appeared near the stern of the ship, the high railing at the back keeping Selasine from toppling out backward. "Excellent," Erk commented, noting that everyone was here.

Naomi replied, looking at Miranda with a caring, motherly look, "Miranda, darling, are you ready?" Miranda confirmed with a nod. The wind may have slowed for the other vessels, but *The Violet Blur* did not need wind to move at high speeds. The magic mast in the center provided invisibility and a continual favorable wind for the ship. Blur's consciousness could move the ship freely with that enchantment. They pulled ahead of the fog, Naomi escorting the group to the bow.

Jacques had a spyglass in hand, peering out at the hostage ships. "Visual confirmation for a landing point, three ships, no signs of life."

Erk raised a brow, "Come again?"

Jacques shook his head. "Nothing. Have a look, captain." He handed the spyglass to Erk.

Naomi frowned. "We have to wait for the fog to cover our activity so that we can investigate. Those gunships are armed to the teeth. I can count ten cannons, a single broadside from one of those could sink The Neb even."

Selasine was also not pleased. "The last report I saw on *The Silver Corsair* had visual confirmation of the hostages, but that was almost a week ago. Is it possible they are below deck due to the early hour?" he asked, concentrating on possible explanations.

Erk shook his head. "It's hard to say. Jacques, would you be able to take us below deck? Just you and me, a quick in and out."

"If we go without Miranda, I'll run low on strength and accuracy by the end. That will mean four extra teleports if we go for a look," he explained.

Selasine winced. "What about cutting the chains from here?" he asked, feeling trapped with a missing puzzle piece. Certainly, there should have been at least one paladin posted as watch.

Miranda breathed deeply. She closed her eyes, gripped her holy symbol, and whispered a prayer, "Invictus, give us wisdom. Give us strength. Protect us from evil and light our path." She felt the warmth of Invictus's response and opened her eyes. "I could just teleport the ships to safety or cut the chains from here. It will take about the same amount of mana. If the hostages are somehow below deck, we win. If not, then we'll have to take some time to recover. It wouldn't deplete the magic within me; it would just take a lot," she explained.

Selasine cursed. "Let's go, just the four of us for now. If possible, we can investigate, cut the chain, and then decide what to do."

Miranda nodded in agreement. Naomi and Erk looked uncomfortable with the prospects but had no alternative recommendations. Erk took Miranda and Selasine by the hands. "Alright, Jacques. Below deck. Be as precise as possible."

"As you command, sir," he replied, pressing his hands together. The circle of light surrounded them. Instantly, they felt their surroundings change. It was now dark, with a putrid smell filling the air. It was harsh and acrid. It was also strangely quiet for a large ship that should have had around three hundred people on board.

Erk's eyes adjusted first due to his elven eyesight. "By the gods," he swore. "Nobody move. Don't even think about fire."

Selasine whispered the daylight prayer, his holy symbol glowing gently. They had appeared in the cargo hold of the ship. They were surrounded by barrels of gunpowder, some of them open and some with their lids sealed far too tight, creating dangerous pressure in the barrel. "This isn't just a hostage ship. This is a planned execution," Selasine growled.

Erk's eyes widened, "We have to warn Naomi and get The Blur away from here."

Miranda objected, "Wait! What about the paladins?" She impulsively ran toward the stairs that probably led to the upper decks.

Selasine hissed, "Miranda, wait!"

Several pairs of eyes met them at the stairs leading up. Miranda froze. "I found the hostages," she mumbled.

A murmur spread through the people above. "Who are you?" one woman asked.

"I'm Miranda. We're here to rescue you. Why is everyone

hiding below deck?"

"You mustn't stay; this is a trap!" a different voice called back. More voices began to call out in panic, some asking the interlopers to save them, some telling them to run.

"Calm, everyone," Bishop Selasine commanded, raising his holy symbol high. The murmuring quieted a bit. "The Sword of Justice does not flee from the threat of chaos. We are going to cut the anchor chain and tug the boats away. Do not fear. Invictus has heard your prayers and has sent the combined forces of the church, the pirates of Yendralia, and the followers of Lexcord among their number. We must know why nobody is on deck before proceeding," he explained.

"They'll blow us to the sky if we dare show our faces above deck. Please, help us; the conditions are becoming unbearable. The waste is piling up, and the water has almost run out," the woman who questioned Miranda stated. "I'm one of the sergeants on board. The last week and a half have been a nightmare straight from Indervill's bowels."

Selasine nodded with sympathy and understanding. "Miranda, can you try to cut the chain from here? This deck is likely somewhat submerged. It's not as easy as cutting a chain you can see, but is it possible?"

Miranda nodded. "I won't have to extend the magic so far this close," she commented and looked around the cargo hold for the shaft that should lead up to the windlass and capstan. She approached the bow side of the ship, finding a metal pipe that loomed overhead about eight feet up. It opened up outside the ship, leaving the anchor safely tucked away on the front of the ship while it was in motion. The day she and August had gone to see Justin on *The Valiant Sailor* was also a partial reconnaissance mission; while there, Miranda carefully analyzed the structure of Gelidor's ships. She did not know if the plan would require such knowledge, but she wanted to be prepared for anything. "Or we could just knock a hole in this, and I can destroy the chain from here," she teased.

Erk smiled. "That's the way. Here, let's find something—" he started, but Miranda had taken a bit of mana out of the air and simply punched a hole in the pipe with pure energy. "Or, I mean, she technically could have done this alone," he finished, chuckling.

Suddenly Selasine felt a psychic shock. Damil was contacting him. "Your fog has covered the hostage ships. The gunboats seem to be raising anchor. How goes the plan?"

Selasine replied, "Better now that we know the hostages are alive." He felt a sigh of relief from Aguila and Ut'wah. "We should have anchors cut in the next ten minutes," he commented. "I will stay with this ship to save Jacques a jump and to coordinate with the paladins here."

Miranda focused on the chain. She stared intently at a single link and felt the mana inside her compress and take form. The single link of the chain began to glow red as it began to heat. She tried to pull magic from the arcane stream, but the flow was still quite weak in this area, having used most of the excess energy to open up the chain shaft. Having a lot of miserable hostages nearby probably did not help, either. Her concentration intensified, conserving as much energy as possible.

"Thomas, you have to hurry," Damil replied. "I have a terrible feeling," he pleaded, the communication only between Selasine and himself.

"Don't worry, my love. This will soon be a story we share with the rookies," he tried to stay lighthearted.

He felt Damil's worry until the paladin opened his mind back to Ut'wah and Aguila. "Report from *The Violet Blur*?"

Selasine responded, "Last known status, Naomi is in place. The women are ready with grappling hooks."

Damil's nod of affirmation could be heard through telepathy. "Good. *The Valiant Sailor*, report!" he ordered.

"Sir!" Aguila's voice saluted. "We are sailing blind, but we are prepared. Ballistae armed with hooks at the ready. We just need word on the chains."

Miranda smiled as there was a harsh snapping sound, and the entire boat lurched. "Got it!" she turned around. "Let's not waste time!" she said, hustling back to Erk, Selasine, and Jacques.

Erk agreed. "Thomas," he started. "See you soon, nulestotejin," he finished, adopting Miranda's promise to reunite after parting ways.

Selasine clasped his shoulder. "You too, brother. Get Miranda to the next ship." He paused to tell Damil the first chain was broken. Before he could finish, Miranda, Erk, and Jacques were gone.

Selasine then approached the stairs up to the next deck. "Servants of the Path of Justice. Prepare yourselves for war. I know that you are sickened and fatigued, and the conditions on this ship have been foul. The King of Claston is a usurper who follows The Counselor of the Corrupt," as the bishop explained, voices ranging from terrified to excited began to rumble above. "It is our duty to the Sword of Justice that we work with the pirates of Yendralia to eliminate this scourge. Though we hope to avoid conflict, please, prepare yourselves for a fight!"

The sergeant smiled at the bishop. "Our swords will be at the ready, Bishop Selasine."

*

Jacques, Erk, and Miranda appeared on the first deck of another ship, immediately struck by the smell of humanoid waste and decay. "My apologies, captain, I missed the mark. I couldn't see, and my accuracy is already declining. There's something strange happening in the astral tunnels," Jacques explained. The first deck had a large center hallway with smaller hallways extending to the left and right.

Erk shook his head, "Save your strength, Jacques. Look!" he pointed to the stairs leading up. "We have some cover now. We can go straight to the windlass." The fog billowed thick at the top of the stairs to the deck.

A voice suddenly interrupted, "Hey, who are you?" It was a weak voice, but it caught Miranda's attention.

She shrieked in surprise but composed herself. "Erk," she said with a tremble in her voice.

They turned to see a couple of paladins that looked somewhat emaciated. They had walked around the corner of one of the adjoining hallways. The pirate lord quickly sprang into action with his most charismatic voice, "We are friends, here to rescue you under the auspices of Lexcord and Invictus. I am Pirate Lord Erk," he introduced himself, purposefully leaving off the dread title that he wished to shed. "This is

Miranda, Acolyte of Invictus, and my quartermaster, Jacques."

The paladins traded glances. They were stripped down to their undergarments. The smell overwhelmed Miranda, "I need to get to the windlass," she said and started for the stairs.

As she ran, one of the hostages cried, "Wait! There is gunpowder in the cargo hold! The gunships will fire if we go above deck."

Erk held up a hand, "Do not fear; we have summoned a dense fog that will shield Miranda's activity on deck. She only needs to cut the chain to the anchor, and your ship will be rescued," he explained. However, numerous clinking sounds were heard above deck at that moment. Some of them sounded like they echoed off the side of the ship. "Do you hear that?" he asked.

The paladins nodded in fear. Miranda did not hesitate as she ran on deck. She saw grappling hooks grabbing the sides of the ship. She could see ropes running down them, but she saw no source. They immediately seemed to disappear into the fog. She ran straight to the windlass and found the chain wrapped around it. As before, she focused on a single link of the taut chain, superheating it.

Erk smiled, "That's the sound of a rescue crew grappling the ship. Miranda has gone to cut the anchor at the windlass. Soon you'll be in tow behind one of the finest ships you'll never see," he warned.

Miranda had been above deck for around a minute, and the hostages looked relieved. "We have to warn the others. We have had many casualties due to depleted resources. There's only around two hundred of us left," one of them said with a saddened expression. It seemed this ship's decision-makers were not as effective as on the other ship.

"Please, as you carry your warning. Prepare the righteous of Invictus for battle. We hope to avoid conflict, but if something unexpected happens, we may need to fight for our lives and freedom!" Erk explained.

The two turned and started announcing the impending rescue and the threat of conflict throughout the deck, down the hallways, and into the cabins.

Above deck, Miranda could see the sun's light reflecting

wildly off the fog around them. She knew the rising temperature would destroy their cover as the air warmed with the day. She had to hurry. She used more mana to heat the chain faster to compensate for a shortening timeline. She still had plenty left if she had to teleport everyone away simultaneously or do something huge. She realized that this kind of mission was exactly what she needed. She did not want to rely too heavily on her gift all the time and sincerely wanted to continue following in Selasine's footsteps as a cleric of Invictus. Learning to use the mana more efficiently would help her more than leaving herself vulnerable by expending all the magic at once. Still, she wouldn't hesitate to use it to save everyone else.

She gritted her teeth and focused until she heard a snap. Miranda inhaled deeply, the mana flowing more abundantly out here than below deck. The ship immediately buoyed in the water. Taking in as much of the stream as she could quickly, she turned around in a dead sprint back below deck. Erk and Jacques were watching the hostages rejoicing quietly. Rescuing paladins was definitely easier than townsfolk that tended to overreact. Erk turned to Jacques and Miranda, "This time, it should be easier. If the fog is over us, that means Ut'wah is already in position. Teleport straight to him, and you'll be fine," he ordered.

Miranda smiled, "Thank you, Pirate Lord Erk. See you soon!"

Erk laughed. "You too, Lady Hyacinth." Miranda and Jacques vanished before his eyes. He turned from a loving mentor to the captain of a tight ship. "Ladies and Gentlemen!" he shouted. It brought the disciplined soldiers to attention despite their current state. "Have any of you ever piloted a boat with no sails before?"

There was murmuring but no volunteers. Erk continued, "Then I, Pirate Lord Erk, hereby claim the office of captain of this ship. I have piloted a ship twice with no sails. Who here is in charge of these brave paladins?"

"I am!" a strong voice replied. "Paladin Yolosqui Nohamar! Second in command to Carulus in this operation."

It made sense. No wonder these hostages did not fare as

well as the others. Selasine had described Carulus's operation in detail; it was likely that Nohamar had attained this post by playing yes-man to Carulus. "Very well. You will retain all of your rights and responsibilities. My only duty is to sail you away from here safely. Understood?"

"Sir!" Nohamar saluted.

*

Miranda and Jacques appeared on the deck of the third ship where Ut'wah was waiting. Somehow, the imposing orc's uncanny magic had caused magical, ethereal wings to sprout from his back, reminding Miranda of her time in the arcane stream. She then realized that his power was probably some kind of magical flight which only added to the reasons why he made the perfect priest for this mission. "Miranda, Jacques," he greeted.

There were paladins hard at work all around them on the deck. They looked to be preparing for battle. The murky shadow of *The Valiant Sailor* could be seen through the fog. "Pirate Lord Ut'wah, where's the windlass?" Miranda asked immediately. This ship seemed a little different than the others, as it had no forecastle.

He pointed across the foredeck, still toward the bow. She wasted no time, drawing in as much magic as possible in the open air. She focused hard on a single chain link, the mana compressing and allowing her will to manifest. It only took so long because she was using hardly any magic. Naomi's training had helped her establish refined control over the power swirling within her. Being able to use such small amounts meant that it would be no serious problem to replenish.

Ut'wah followed her but ten paces behind. She had already begun concentrating when he said, "Brace yourself, Miranda. We are about to enter conflict with mortal stakes."

She lost her concentration and looked up. "I-I'm sorry," she sputtered.

"Apologies," he replied. "Please, hurry with the chain. I have a message from Selasine."

Miranda felt impatience swirl within her heart, and, contrary to her normally disciplined nature, she instantly willed the chain to snap. Such impatience had cost her maybe three or four percent of the mana she had stored within her. It would take half an hour to recover that much if the arcane stream remained this thin in their surroundings.

Ut'wah looked a bit shocked, "That was faster than anticipated."

Miranda's cheeks flushed with embarrassment at her lapse in discipline. "I'm sorry, I grew too anxious; please, give me the news from Selasine."

*

About ten minutes before, Selasine had made his way to the foredeck of the hostage ship. The rigging was in shambles, and the sails were all torn viciously. One of the masts looked ready to topple. It would be nearly impossible to repair a ship so severely impaired. He had already begun to issue orders, discovering that he technically outranked all of the paladins on the ship. It was no surprise that Carulus was given so many green paladins; the archbishop and the Council did not recognize the magnitude of the events that would unfold due to Carulus's actions.

Though he was no sailor, he was a warpriest. He immediately went to the helm and began praying a specific prayer he had learned to repair siege engines. "Oh, Sword of Justice, hear my plea. This construction that could be used as an instrument of righteousness has been sabotaged by those seeking to thwart the hand of the law. Hear my prayer, Invictus, and turn your ear to our desperate need. Heal this vessel."

The air swirled around the ship, causing a bubble to form in the fog cloud; however, the damaged parts of the ship began to repair. The fibers of the wood in the mast fused back together. The sails stitched themselves shut; the ropes in the rigging seemed to swirl and tie themselves whole. On the gun deck, the cannons were reconstructed, and they even looked polished and new. The waste stored on the upper deck dissipated into the air. However, the bottom of the anchor chain was deep beneath the ocean's surface and too far out of Selasine's reach with this prayer.

The bishop felt his heart hiccup and fell to a knee at the helm. The rest of the ship marveled at the sudden and inexplicable repairs. Naomi could see it all happening from *The*

Violet Blur and watched in amazement. This was the ship she had planned to pull with her telekinesis. Their odds of success increased if these repairs could move the ship.

Selasine felt Damil's thoughts, "Thomas, are you okay? I sense a weakness."

The bishop shook his head, "Don't worry. Just an old prayer I haven't recited in a couple of decades. Can't believe it worked. Took a lot out of me, but I think I just gave us a major advantage."

There was a moment of silence. He no longer felt Damil. Suddenly, Thomas's heart filled with dread. He understood Damil now and his history with the beautiful paladin. The wavelengths of their minds and souls were so aligned that their emotions and even physical feelings could not be totally separated. Damil broke the link with him in their youth because their missions had become increasingly dangerous. Maintaining such a close connection would have been unsafe when the line between success and failure could be as small as their heart rates or adrenaline. He had restored it now out of necessity. Still, Selasine knew the person he cared for was suddenly filled with the darkest fear possible.

Damil's voice returned, but it brought the presence of Ut'wah and Aguila. "Brethren," he began. Everyone's mind seemed in tune. "Another fleet just appeared from seemingly out of nowhere. They all look to be frigates with black sails. I can't quite make out the white there; give me a moment." Nobody spoke. There was only a sense of shared anxiety. "Okay, so I can see a skull clearly, and—" he cut off abruptly. "Oh, a cutlass? No, that's not right," he continued.

Ut'wah scanned his memories for variations of the jolly roger. Only Dread Pirate Lady Lascha had a skull on her flag among the Yendralian pirates. He doubted she would have planned such a betrayal. He thought back, "That other element is important, and so is its color. Please be as specific as possible, high paladin."

There was another momentary silence that seemed to last forever. His presence returned wholly to the telepathic conversation. "It's the symbol of Hoxark, the God of Wanton Decay. There is a scythe dripping with blood; the blood is green. Green is the only coloration on the black and white here. It was hard to make out the color in this lighting, sorry," he added.

Ut'wah cursed, "Silver Maiden be with us. It's the Death Pirates."

There was an almost unanimous confusion returned to Ut'wah. The pirate lord continued, "Pirate lords target the worst of society's elite or other lawbreakers. Dread pirate lords act as they see fit and weigh the consequences of their actions on a case-by-case basis. But the Death Pirate Scythes and their ilk?" His shudder was telepathically perceptible. "They cause harm for harm's sake. They are the slavers of the seas, the scourge of all that is righteous. Indiscriminately violent. They burn coastal crops to force people into starvation, only to taunt them from the sea with perfectly good food in abundance aboard their own ships. If the King of Claston has forged an alliance with the Death Pirates, we have a serious problem."

Selasine's thoughts pushed back, "What do the colors tell you, Ut'wah?"

Ut'wah replied, "It sounds like Death Pirate Scythe Ba-le-ba-ne. A Death Pirate with the most horrifying pet."

There was a pause in the communication altogether. Damil's consciousness had completely broken away. The three of them waited silently, Selasine finally finding a moment to stand straight. As he did, he felt his heart drop to the bottom of the Rift. Damil's heart just sank lower than it ever had, he was sure. After about three minutes of silence, Damil returned. "Everyone, I have dreadful news. The king's ship, *Her Royal Majesty the Sirenia*, has just come into view. Our vantage from this mountainside is not great enough. There is a royal port twenty-five miles to the northeast. The Death Pirates and the king must have sailed from there. This is a gross oversight on my part. I did not expect pushback of this size."

Everyone cursed in their own way. The holy men prayed for the safety of the hostages in their care. Ut'wah began to speak, "Somebody needs to let Erk and Naomi know immediately that Death Pirates are sailing with the King of Claston on their way toward the fog. Those pirates are especially vicious. *The Violet Blur* is exactly the target they would love to get their hands on." His thoughts echoed in his own mind as if his presence and ego had begun to increase. He could feel the impending battle and was already preparing himself.

"What do you mean?" Aguila echoed back. Selasine winced, but Damil just listened.

"They're the ones responsible for the slave trade on this continent. And The Blur is a crew full of women that specifically targets slavers. Do the math. The Death Pirate bounty for that crew is astounding. Naomi needs to know, and she needs to know now."

Selasine's voice reinserted itself, "Ut'wah when Miranda arrives to break your ship's chain, tell her to tell Naomi what's going on outside the fog. I've repaired this vessel with an old prayer I haven't used in years. Sailing without so much of Naomi's help should be a bit easier. We can make this escape."

Ut'wah's consciousness echoed back, "Alright then, she's just arrived."

*

Miranda blinked a few times. "Death Pirates?" she quizzed.

"And that's all Naomi needs to know. Please, tell her to prepare for battle. The Death Pirates have arrived with thirty vessels. However, Ba-le-ba-ne's pet will make all the difference in this battle. She will know what I mean," he explained. He combined his own knowledge with Selasine's message. "We have to hurry."

Miranda nodded and thanked Ut'wah. She then called out, "Jacques?"

There was no response. Suddenly a voice wailed out in horror. It was abruptly muffled and then stopped with a disgusting crunch.

"What's going on?" Ut'wah commanded loudly. The fog made it nearly impossible to see, but it was also their only hope of escape. "By Lexcord, no!" he blurted.

Miranda looked around in the fog and saw several shadows raised above the hostage ship. She felt the power swell within her, but instead, she prayed an earnest prayer of protection for the entire ship. Invictus heard her voice loud and clear in the primordial place, and he smiled broadly as he granted her prayer. Her essence had been strengthened so greatly by her time in the arcane stream that she could even channel more incredible prayers.

The shadows began to whip and swipe at the people on the deck. Having recovered their weapons at Ut'wah's command, some paladins lashed back at the shadows. Miranda realized they were tentacles of some kind. Ut'wah had the ship mobilized for violence before it was even anticipated. She admired his foresight and leadership skills. Miranda's protection prayer fended off the tentacles as they tried to swipe as many paladins off the deck as they could. She could hear their cries of joy as they praised Invictus for his protection. Their swords kept the beast's tentacles at bay.

Ut'wah's wings burst with vivid, varied colors as he leaped into the air. He withdrew the six-foot sword off his back and hurtled through a tentacle, sundering it off completely without hesitation. He shouted back to the ship, "This is Ba-le-ba-ne's pet, Tiny. A colossal squid."

Miranda's eyes widened. She had to get that message to Naomi, but Jacques was nowhere to be found. She called his name again, "Jacques! Where are you? Can you hear me?" She was not surprised that she heard no response as the air filled with the din of paladins fending off the tentacles of a kraken. She started to call on the power within her but hesitated. She thought carefully and began to pray. "Please, Invictus, speed a message to my friends. I have news of impending chaos," she whispered as she clutched her holy symbol.

The mana that stirred within her actually increased her importance to the universe. Her aura brimmed with strength as she held as much of the magic inside her as she could. Now that she fully understood and could control that flow, Invictus could more easily hear her prayers. He listened to her words and carried them across the winds of Espa, anyone she called friend hearing her words. "Hey, everyone, Ut'wah said there's some Death Pirates in league with the usurper. It's Ba-le-ba-ne if that means anything to you, Erk. I think we have their pet, Tiny, distracted right now. With Invictus by my side, it shall not take this ship. Selasine wanted you to know he repaired one of the ships, and with a favorable wind, it should carry him and his ship out of here with the hostages. That should help Naomi focus her efforts on a retreat. And it looks like the creature is determined to have this boat, but it's full of gunpowder too, so if it swallows us, make sure to give it a little fire."

Selasine, Erk, Naomi, August, and Justin heard that message. Naomi's complexion darkened with anger as she realized her recent targets, the Death Pirates, were involved in this fight. She squinted her eyes and activated her uncanny magic. She started to pull hard on the grappled vessel, and the enchantment of *The Violet Blur* pushed them quickly away from the impending threats. She also tugged the other vessel with her mind, and it began to catch the wind. Though his time as a sailor had been minimal, Selasine's wisdom helped him identify what was needed to get the ship moving. Erk frantically looked through the fog, the hostage ships barely five hundred feet apart previously. He felt Naomi's power as the tow of *The Violet Blur* began. The grappling hooks all slid into a corner along the ship's bow as the ships' gravity in the water caused them to shift. They dug deep into the wood, thanks to the vessel's weight.

Still on *The Nebula*, August held a scimitar Jax had loaned him. It could enhance his strength to let him pierce mithril with the blade's tip. He was ready for the coming fight. After all, August was the only one hearing the message that could see that the entire navy of Claston had appeared on the horizon behind them. This trap had been laid quite well, and August was itching for a fight. He didn't like to lose, and Justin had given him a reason to fight harder.

Justin needed to hear Miranda's message the most. Justin held on tight to a massive ballista mounted on the deck of *The Valiant Sailor*. He had used it to shoot a grappling hook onto the hostage ship. As their vessel began to catch wind, it began to tug hard on the other ship. They started to move in the water, which was problematic. The hostage ship was currently under attack from strange tentacle-shaped shadows that seemed to be gaining the upper hand against the vessel. The colossal beast beneath the water swung a tentacle at *The Valiant Sailor*, which was roughly the same size as the hostage vessel. A paladin on the stern was struck by the kraken's swipe, and two clerics rushed to his side to help.

At that moment, Justin felt the rope in the ballista tighten dramatically. He could see just enough of the shadows through the fog that it looked like four tentacles had grabbed onto the hostage ship. There was a sudden jolt, and the vessels began moving. The grapples held tight, but the rescue target was now dragging *The Valiant Sailor*. The Shield Knights were prepared thanks to their rigorous training and held onto the ropes. Valarie's face was scrunched in the intense struggle to hold the line. Tavi was also holding onto a rope with force. The other clerics and paladins aboard *The Valiant Sailor* latched onto the ballistae and their ropes on the upper deck. Those who could not find a place to grab began to pray prayers of strength and power. *The Valiant Sailor* held on tight as the hostage ship was hurtled through the water, both skipping in the air, causing many people on both ships to fall.

Miranda tumbled to her knees and then was pressed flat by another bounce. "Yeow!" she yelped as her body bounced on the deck.

Suddenly, Ut'wah was at her side, his magical wings shedding brilliant colors as he slid into place. "Lady Miranda, are you hurt?" he asked true concern in his voice.

She shook her head, using his help to stand. They were moving fast and bouncing through the water, but it was not too fast that she couldn't balance herself with a little help. "Thank you, pirate lord," she said as she gripped his strong hands.

"I am honored, Lady Miranda. I think we have been summoned to dine with the King of Claston," he commented as the kraken beneath them came to a skidding stop. Their speed reduced dramatically as the tentacles suddenly slid away from the ship back into the water. Ut'wah had been unable to dice off enough tentacles to stop the beast from dragging them within range of *Her Royal Majesty the Sirenia*. Their ship seemed like a tiny skiff next to the king's galleon. It could have been a floating mountain. It had around twenty decks, and it was several hundred feet long. It was truly a king's ship, and the wood sparkled with a golden shimmer. Miranda marveled at it internally, her love of beautiful things overshadowed by her current predicament.

Again, her mind turned to her draconic heritage and the power imbued upon her. However, she decided to trust in her newly refreshed faith. Perhaps even Gelidor could be saved by a miracle. He sought her, specifically, after all. She did not want to rely on her gift, but she felt comfortable knowing it was there if she needed to save lives. If things turned south, she had that as a chance to reset. Or so she hoped. She hoped she had not overestimated her capabilities like she did when facing Vortex. The mana within her churned, and she looked up at *Her Royal Majesty the Sirenia*. This would be the next important moment of her destiny as the girl of fire and lightning. Daughter of Philotrax and Reshiria, Mir'thax Toi'landra felt it was time for the rebellion in Claston to come to a just and righteous end.

Chapter 22
Destiny's Force

t'wah stared up at the king's ship, *Her Royal Majesty the Sirenia*. It looked like a floating castle that could easily support a crew of over three thousand sailors, five thousand passengers, and a royal entourage. The kraken that carried them away from the rescue mission easily dragged their ship the mile between the billowing fog and *Her Royal Majesty the Sirenia*. The morning sun was now climbing in the sky, the air warming quickly. Ut'wah had high hopes for the two vessels tied to *The Violet Blur*. It would be up to him and Miranda to see this third vessel to safety.

Miranda seemed much less concerned about the hostages now. She had fully turned her attention to the magnificent ship that loomed at least one hundred feet above them. Her cool, blue eyes shimmered with determination as she weighed their options. Her beautiful red hair, tied into the braids of Invictus's healers, draped her face like curtains, tossing gently in the ocean wind.

She looked to Ut'wah. "Pirate lord, would you be willing to fly me to the top of that ship?" she asked. The way the kraken had left them here seemed like part of some kind of plan; however, she wasn't sure if the plan was of her own machinations or of Gelidor's. A beast like that would require magic to control. She was unsure what kind of magical talents Ba-le-ba-ne possessed. Justin was on *The Valiant Sailor*; she knew the hostages would be okay.

The orc looked at her momentarily with disbelief, but then he understood her question. Because the king had demanded Miranda in exchange for the hostages, perhaps she intended to negotiate or use her incredible power to diffuse or resolve the situation. He stood tall and smiled broadly, admiring the girl's bravery. "Lady Miranda, are you sure this is the course of action you wish to take? It won't be easy to retrieve you if you are captured directly by the king's forces."

She looked away from the massive ship with a smile to Ut'wah. "I am certain that part of my destiny is up there. I can feel it. The magic flows through this vessel with incredible speed. Not like the solisberry tree, but much more than is in the air here. I am confident I can use my gift as needed, so there is no need to worry." Her blue eyes sparkled with determination in the morning light.

Ut'wah looked at *Her Royal Majesty the Sirenia*. The golden wood that formed the hull of this juggernaut looked beautiful in the warm rays of the morning summer sun. The unbelievably large vessel cast a looming shadow behind it to the northwest. Ut'wah was sure that this ship was built from a magical type of wood because it would be physically impossible for a vessel this size to function. He had no idea that a ship so massive could even exist, and if it did, he would expect it to belong to Umiaigén, the goddess of the sea. He tilted his head up, their proximity to the ship making it impossible to see the top. Paladins on the hostage ship fighting the gargantuan squid were now somewhat panicked, the king's vessel charging through the water a mere four hundred feet away. Its trajectory was similar to that of The Death Pirates, moving straight for the fog. His allies were in for an Infernia of a fight, and Ut'wah did not want to leave them without support. It seemed fitting that the girl would confront the king, interceding on behalf of her friends. With a big smile, he stretched the ethereal wings behind him and gave a handsome smile. "Well then, we fly together."

Ut'wah stepped behind her, his stature overwhelming. Wrapping an arm around her waist, he bent his knees. She gripped his arm firmly, holding on tight. With a jump, Ut'wah and Miranda spiraled straight up, their armor creating a visible glint in the morning sky. The pirate lord took them up about two hundred feet to survey the deck of *Her Royal Majesty the Sirenia*. That's when they both noticed that, to the southwest, a mass of ships loomed on the horizon. One hundred of them could have easily been sailing behind Ut'wah's fleet. Miranda and Ut'wah realized that their decisions at this point affected much more than the hostages; all their friends and crewmates depended on them to bring a swift end to the conflict between the church, the king, and the pirates of Yendralia.

On the deck of *Her Royal Majesty the Sirenia*, almost fifty soldiers had lined the ship's bow with longbows. Ut'wah started to curse, but as they began to fire, their arrows reflected harmlessly off the barrier Miranda had prayed for when the kraken emerged. Suddenly, their bowstrings began to break. Ut'wah looked at the girl in his arms as she was actively snapping her fingers, focusing on one bowman at a time. Shouts of confusion began to echo across the foredeck of *Her Royal Majesty the Sirenia*. The pirate lord grinned; this is why she had been so careful to conserve her mana. Prayers for defense, her power for offense. Her kind nature led her to disable her enemies rather than kill them outright, which she could probably do easily. Ut'wah felt his confidence in her grow, flying with fury toward the foredeck where the enemy had been firing their bows until Miranda snapped all their strings.

The Claston sailors ran away quickly as Ut'wah's towering form hurtled toward the area near the ship's bow. His wings accentuated his massive stature. He landed much more gently than expected, slowing the last twenty feet and descending vertically onto the deck, gently putting Miranda down and stepping back.

The soldiers on deck, mostly elves with a few half-elves and humans, were all dressed in the armor that bore the symbol of Na'agamlor. Miranda frowned. She had so much faith in Erk's story, but part of that naivete in her hoped that only part of the royal forces were somehow servants of The Counselor of the Corrupt. She realized that many of these people were probably forced into the servitude of a god they neither liked nor understood. Miranda wanted to cry for the soldiers, as the Silver Maiden was a natural goddess to elvenkind, having ascended from their own number. Na'agamlor was a human merchant at one time. He abused democratic systems so efficiently that he accumulated so much wealth to "purchase the world and still have enough left to buy a castle in the Abyss." Or so the legend stated. Miranda hoped these elves would never serve such a greedy, power-hungry god unless their lives depended on it.

There was a shout as the bowmen from before drew weapons. "Get them! The girl matches the description!" Miranda and Ut'wah heard.

Miranda smiled and gripped her holy symbol. "Sword of Justice, bind that which would do your faithful harm!" she prayed in a powerful voice. The curse took immediate effect, the entire group of warriors finding their bodies suddenly bound by red, crackling energy. The bindings caused them to trip and drop their weapons onto the deck.

Ut'wah tilted his head, impressed. He would have made Miranda the captain of a ship in his fleet in a heartbeat if she could learn to sail but did not seriously consider poaching the girl from Erk and her friends.

Still smiling, Miranda approached a sailor who had tripped because of the curse. Though they were on the deck of *Her Royal Majesty the Sirenia*, this part of the ship seemed more like a city's streets than a ship's top deck. Various buildings created maze-like paths on the deck, probably cabins for the king's royal entourage. She knelt beside a bound Claston soldier and politely began, "I'm sorry I had to bind you. I didn't want to hurt you, and I didn't want you to hurt my friend or me. I hope it's not very painful," she said in a small, sweet voice.

The soldier looked at her, confused and speechless. She continued, "Is Gelidor on board? I think he wants to see me."

The soldier nodded profusely, a terrified look in his eyes. All the sailors here were completely at her mercy, and she wasn't even the one that looked terrifying with Ut'wah standing nearby. "He's in the king's suite, where you would probably expect to find the captain on a normal vessel," he supplied information, hoping it would convince her to spare him.

She smiled, "You're so helpful, thank you." She stood and turned to Ut'wah, "Maybe it'll be easier to fly over all this and go straight to the captain's quarters?" She gestured toward the upper deck where the helm was located, almost six hundred feet away. This ship was truly massive. Even the cabins were built out of the magnificent golden wood. The mana flowed so fast through the ship that Miranda was fully replenished.

"Right!" Ut'wah replied. He stepped behind Miranda, took her in his arm, and together they blew over the top of the buildings on the upper deck. A series of loud bangs echoed from below, several pistol shots deflecting off Miranda's protection prayer. The pirate lord gritted his teeth, thankful for the girl's faith.

As they flew over the distance of the deck, Miranda and Ut'wah realized that this ship had no masts. The sails that hung overhead were entirely illusory and designed to make the already impossible ship look even more imposing, the tops stretching almost five hundred feet into the sky. Below, a city sprawled out before them. People marveled up at them as they flew overhead. Ut'wah's power of flight helped make him the pirate-priest he had become. Evil feared his name, and Gelidor Claston showed his true colors to the pirate. A follower of The Counselor of the Corrupt could not be afforded the possibility of a pardon by the law. Death was his only possible fate.

They landed about a minute later in front of what they would have assumed to be the captain's quarters. A regiment of twenty powerful, elite guards waited, weapons already drawn. They did not move as Ut'wah and Miranda landed in front of them. Miranda spoke first, holding no weapon, "I come in peace to seek an audience with King Claston."

An elf stepped forward from the king's guard. "Are you the one responsible for the disaster with the naval blockade and various acts of piracy?" he asked. All these elves were dressed in the plate mail with Na'agamlor's holy symbol etched into it. Their armor was also inlaid with gold and black trim, making these soldiers stand out. They were the usurper's personal guard and probably some of the clerics that helped him seize the throne in the first place.

Miranda nodded in response to the question. Righteous indignation burned deep within her. She felt the impulse to use the somewhat boundless power within her to flay these dark clerics with impunity. These were the types of servants that likely murdered Erk's sister Ilyia, their fates wrought by their own hands. As those angry thoughts swirled within her, she felt a peaceful, calmer voice from the lessons she learned over the last month. Her actions would affect so many, and she did not want the legacies of Bishop Selasine and Pirate Lord Erk the Kind to be a girl who murdered those she knew to be guilty of horrendous crimes. She trusted in the structures of law and order, and even the gods were puzzled by her power. Still, she wanted to make Invictus and those closest to her proud and planned to handle this conflict with the least amount of violence possible. Then, she heard the lead guard's command and felt her indignation turn to malicious creativity.

"Take her alive, kill the orc," the elf commanded and turned away. He then walked to the double doors of the captain's quarters, opened one, and stepped inside. The doors towered up twenty feet, the upper deck above almost the same size as the entirety of *The Nebula*. The golden wood glittered brilliantly in the early morning sun. Instead of a practical, straight staircase up to the helm and stern, ornate rounded steps curled around the sides of the ship to the upper deck. They seemed as grand as the steps in a beautiful palace. Miranda wanted to marvel at this place, but the threat before her demanded her attention.

The other guards gave a shout and started to charge forward. Ut'wah's massive sword was in his hands instantly. He acted before the enemy's attack materialized with any purpose. With a single sweep, he knocked two guards over, his sword cleaving into the heavy full plate armor of the first and the force of the swing slamming the soldier into another. Their momentum allowed the pirate lord to wrench his sword free of the armor, causing the metal of the breastplate to shatter, the elf wearing it shouting in shock as he flew.

Miranda's eyes flickered with light as the magic within her began to swirl. Three guards charged at her, wielding magical cudgels instead of swords. The bludgeon of those clubs would be more dangerous than swords and knives with her battlemail, and it was the favored weapon of Na'agamlor. They undoubtedly had special training with them as she had with the longsword, Invictus's chosen weapon. She repeated the binding curse, gripping her holy symbol. Though Invictus honored her wishes, the willpower of the charging guards was too firm, and the curse did not stop them. Her eyes widened, quickly scanning for a way to evade the charge.

The three elves crashed into the invisible barrier of protection that surrounded Miranda, making a metallic crunch and causing a grunt of surprise as each hit the barrier within the same second. Miranda thanked her god for the protection and stepped forward, the recently fallen guards scrambling backward, trying to stand. She tried another curse, "Justice incarnate, weaken these interlopers so that they may not raise their weapons against those that follow the Path of the Sword of Justice." A swirling purple mist surrounded the three on the deck as they felt their energy sapping away. After a moment, they became so exhausted their bodies entered a magically induced sleep. Miranda winced as the clouds disappeared from around them. She hoped the curse was not as horribly painful as it was when Vortex the Lich ripped the magic out of her.

Miranda turned to see Ut'wah surrounded by a dozen elves. On average, they were literally half his size. A few were abnormally large for elves but still not as tall as Miranda. She looked around her immediate surroundings and counted five incapacitated guards. She became worried, counting the guards surrounding Ut'wah again. There were at least two unaccounted for.

Ut'wah saw one of the elves raise a hand, and a blast of fire spat out, stopping at the protective barrier surrounding him.

Another guard hurled a barrage of deadly icicles, clinking and shattering loudly off the prayer. They were beginning an onslaught with their uncanny magic, which would surely destroy the divine barrier quickly. He needed to make quick work of this troop before they could coordinate their attacks against him.

Miranda shouted a prayer she learned from one of Iria's books that she discovered in Erk's small library on *The Nebula*. When Erk found her reading it, he specifically showed it to her so she could mess with Shalo if he was invisible. "The eyes of Justice see all and know all. Invictus, we implore thee; show us that which is hidden!" Suddenly, two more guards appeared, their invisibility melting away. They were approaching Miranda directly with their cudgels and a length of rope. She felt her nose crunch with a bit of anger and did not like how that emotion felt. She didn't have time for a prayer; she had to act quickly. Closing her eyes and drawing on the mana inside her, she inhaled deeply and stretched her arms to the side. This caused the deck to rumble slightly. In that same moment, numerous vines shot out of the golden wood, binding every enemy appendage it could reach. She kept pouring magic into what she wanted: a beautiful, massive vine cluster with red and blue flowers. The vines wrapped up the two guards that were previously invisible and continued growing, wrapping around the ankles of the elite guards that had Ut'wah surrounded. He reacted to two of them leaping at him, their furious attacks causing the protective spell to visibly crack when impacted. Their uncanny magic must have been some kind of enhancement that made them deadlier in hand-to-hand combat. He pushed back with a fierce chop from his greatsword that could easily cleave through metal. This bought him enough space to fly about ten feet in the air. He returned his sword to the sheath on his back and, like a bird of prey, targeted the two clerics using physical enhancements with a diving attack. Using the spiked gauntlets on his fists, he curved his dive from vertical to horizontal at the last possible second, his forearms connecting with their faces at high speed. He clotheslined them so hard they fell unconscious from the impact.

Ut'wah then noticed the vines growing, enveloping the small royal guard and expanding rapidly. This looked exactly like something Elmadyn would have done, but even her magic didn't work this quickly. He looked at Miranda, who was glowing with a faint green aura. Within a minute, the vines had wrapped together and coalesced to form a stem for one massive flower. It bloomed up high, reaching maybe one hundred feet into the air. It was magnificent and beautiful. Claston's elite guard was wrapped throughout it, effectively tied up in the girl's mana flower.

Miranda's eyes opened. She smiled and walked over to what she had created. It towered high above the upper deck even, covered in blooms of red and blue flowers. However, a beautiful stream of hyacinth petals opened at the top of the vines, eagerly greeting the morning sunlight. "They're even more beautiful than I had imagined," she hummed, touching one of the soft petals on a blue flower.

Ut'wah landed beside her, marveling at her creation. "Are you alright, Lady Miranda?"

She nodded absentmindedly and reached into a pouch Naomi had given her the night before. She withdrew a single solisberry blossom and placed the purple leaf in her mouth. She could feel the magic that caused this very bloom to exist. It quickly helped replenish the mana she had expended creating the flower and then some. She felt invigorated and powerful. She would be at full strength again in seconds between that and the magic coursing through this incredible ship.

"A magical herb?" the pirate lord asked.

She nodded, but her face was slightly contorted. The leaf had a distinct bitter taste; it would not have made an appealing snack if it weren't for the magic in its very fabric.

Ut'wah turned to look at the door. "Well, Lady Miranda. The King of Claston is rumored to be very dangerous. His curse can destroy a person with their own power."

She smiled at him. She tried to speak eloquently and bravely, but the leaf on her tongue caused her to sound more like a young person who talked far too loud with food in their mouth. "I know. I can sense his evil presence from here. I am not afraid. My powers come from The Unbinding. Not like everyone else, though. I'm sure his curse will not work as he intends. Nonetheless," she paused, finally gulping the leaf down. Now she could sound brave. "Mir'thax comes calling in the name of Invictus. What say you, pirate lord?"

He grinned, his tusks curling even further upward. "And Ut'wah comes calling under the banner of Lexcord. Come, let us confront the king as children of the just and the righteous."

She beamed, recognizing a shared catechism between their faiths. She took a moment and looked out as the fog had dispersed in the morning sun. A mile away, fighting had commenced between Ut'wah's ships and the Death Pirates. She hoped her friends were okay. She whispered a prayer for them too, but the distance between them was so great that Invictus could not bless them on her behalf.

Miranda and Ut'wah turned to the door of the king's suite. The ornate double doors were plated in gold and bronze. A large, hanging ring adorned each of them, and the symbol of Na'agamlor was etched into the doors. On closer inspection, Miranda suspected the etching was not in the original design. Ut'wah stood to Miranda's right as they each stepped to a door and took a ring in their right hands. They nodded at each other as they pulled them open. Inside the doors, they saw a massive room resembling a royal court. An aged elf sat on an ivory throne at the end of a fifty-foot carpet. It must have been carved from the tooth or tusk of some massive creature. It was encrusted with rubies, diamonds, and pearls, red and white making up the colors of Claston's coat of arms now that it had been corrupted by the influences of Na'agamlor.

Miranda presumed the elf on the throne was the usurper called king. He looked to be well over three hundred years old, living his last century. He seemed frail and weak. Grayed hairs billowed from under a silver circlet crown with a jeweled crest in the front, reminiscent of a peacock's feathers. He wore a white mantle that looked to be made of soft fur. Beside him stood the guard that had excused himself a moment before.

Miranda and Ut'wah contrasted each other much like Erk and Selasine. Though their statures were very different, their presence was very similar in that their power was indisputable. Still, they walked confidently toward Gelidor. They did not walk with hostility or deference to the king's station. They merely approached as representatives of their faiths to plead their case to a king who had fallen short of the ruling standards according to Invictus and Lexcord.

"King Claston!" Ut'wah commanded with his voice. "You have sought audience with this girl for some time now, even taking and abusing hostages. Lives have been lost, and your actions have caused great suffering within your own kingdom. I represent the Hammer of Righteousness, the Silver Maiden, Lexcord, and I am here as a reckoning for your crimes against elven, human, orcish, and draconic life." The authority in his voice seemed to come from a source outside of this realm. He was a paragon of power and faith, Miranda thought.

The aged elf's lips parted in a somewhat terrifying smile. Miranda felt her blood turn cold. She had felt this aura before; it was very similar to Vortex's. The king started to reply, "No, I have committed no crimes. You see, I am the king. I can't commit a crime when I decide what is wrong or right within my jurisdiction."

Miranda's face scrunched together at the king's perverse way of thinking. "Gelidor Claston," she spoke confidently, standing at attention. "The way you view your authority has created misery among your subjects. Erilkaiden and his followers protest your harshness and lack of mercy. They lament the living conditions of those you exploit for their labor. They shed tears for the many you have killed in your name and nothing more," her voice started to waver as she became emotional. She thought of Erk's family, and the other nobles purged as the king executed his vision after The Unbinding. Nevertheless, she continued, trying to sound brave, "The Sword of Justice, law incarnate, Invictus deems your actions unfitting for a king. In the name of all that is just, I declare your laws void and your authority stripped." Though she was neither a high priest nor a high paladin, she made demands equal to one. Invictus would have approved, she hoped.

His evil smile stretched further. Miranda was sure Vortex would have looked like this person if he had still been elven. "You clerics and paladins are all the same. You think that just because you follow a god, you have the authority to tell me, a king, what to do." He began to run his fingers through his hair. "You can make all of the decrees you like; it won't change the fact that I am still king. The only way you will take me off of this throne is if you have the power to do so. And you, girl, are the miracle worker that sided with the pirates instead of me, the king!"

Miranda expected the accusation. She had a formulated response but paused to give everyone's thoughts time to settle. "Erk the Radiant would have sunk those ships to save the people of this kingdom that fled your tyranny. I saved the lives of those sailors that you would so hastily throw away," her lips trembled with her passionate speaking. She knew her god was stirring in her. Perhaps she would not need to use her gift to resolve this conflict. "Every single person in your kingdom should matter to you. As a king, they would have all looked up to you. But you chose cruelty and control over the lives of your people," she finished, fully turning his accusation around.

Ut'wah smiled broadly on the inside. Miranda was perfect for this. An arbiter indeed, but between the mighty and the weak. She had the strength to defy kings, maybe even the gods. He discovered through her actions and words what Naomi discovered through her demeanor and sincerity.

King Gelidor Claston frowned. If Miranda's blood chilled at his smile, her heart sank with his frown. His eyes were entirely black. She had felt Ezelbrecht's evil aura. She was a victim of the hideous darkness born from Vortex. But Gelidor's eyes showed that not only was his soul already devoured by the darkness but that his actions had no purpose beyond malice. Things could get very ugly. She drew in the mana from around her, testing its flow.

"For your crimes against the crown and defiance of the king's will, I curse you, miracle worker. May your own power eat away at the very essence within you. Begone from me," the king spat.

Ut'wah unsheathed his sword. The guard beside the king suddenly lunged forward. He struck at Ut'wah with a double-headed ax coming from nowhere. It glanced off Ut'wah's armor, but the second head swung back around and clanged against the pirate lord's helmet. Such dangers were why Ut'wah dressed as a holy warrior today instead of a pirate. Ut'wah staggered but started to engage. No wonder this elf was the king's personal bodyguard.

Miranda stood defiant. Nothing seemed to be happening to her at first. Gelidor Claston stared at her with a vicious smile again. She turned her attention to the guard that had dashed to attack Ut'wah. The elf was only five feet tall but wore a resplendent plate mail that seemed as light as silk. He jumped easily, giving Ut'wah as many strikes as the paladin could parry with his massive sword.

Miranda reached out with her hand and began to try a curse, but her vision blurred momentarily. She looked back at the king quickly as her vision unclouded. His smile was sinister and even more unsettling than before. Suddenly, the magic in her pulsed. She could feel it heating up and cooling back down. Her eyes started to glow a bright, vivid blue. A purple aura formed around her body but left a distinct black silhouette around her as if she were going to be drawn into some kind of void. She fell to her knees as she felt the magic begin to change inside her. It felt very familiar. She suddenly realized it wasn't just changing inside her; it was changing her! As the light grew brighter, she could clearly remember her parents. She could see their faces, their talons, their wings. Peering through the light, she looked up through the blurry vision and flashed her own knowing smile. Gelidor Claston's eyes widened in horror.

***

Justin looked up at the glinting light in the morning sky heading for the top of *Her Royal Majesty the Sirenia*. "Miranda," he whispered. He let go of the heavy ballista he had been supporting with his strength, helping *The Valiant Sailor* stay attached to the hostage ship after a kraken had grabbed the gunpowder-filled vessel and towed it close to the king's incredible galleon. It must have been part of the plan to capture Miranda. Still, Justin knew the king would bite off more than he could chew trying to confront her.

Looking around the deck, many other Shield Knights held onto the ballistae used to grapple other ships. Some of the clergy were pointing off the bow of *The Valiant Sailor* as many of the hostages were on the surface deck of the hostage ship, armed and ready to fight. Commander Aguila thought quickly at the helm, using the momentum left behind by the kraken's wild pull to route their course to board the hostage ship. Using the grapples the crew had sunk into the damaged ship, they pulled the other ship close to *The Valiant Sailor*. After a couple of minutes, the ship was within boarding range.

Justin and Valarie hefted a sturdy plank and laid it between the ships. The hostages quickly crossed, fleeing the explosive-laden hostage vessel. The two Shield Knights helped people cross quickly, extending their arms to help steady those with less confidence in their balance. Another group laid another plank further down the deck to speed the boarding. Word spread quickly across the deck of the hostage vessel, and the ship was soon abandoned.

As *The Valiant Sailor* began to put a little distance between itself and the hostage ship, Commander Aguila could feel the tug of *Her Royal Majesty the Sirenia*'s great wake in the water around them. The massive galleon loomed over them as they stared up at the ship's port side from their own. Justin had a wild thought and smiled at Valarie as they put the plank into storage. She grinned back, "Got an idea, paladin?"

He nodded and motioned for her to follow him. He ran to the upper deck and saluted. "Commander Aguila, Sir!"

He smiled, "At ease, paladin. You have my attention."

"Would it be worthwhile to detonate the hostage ship and potentially damage the enemy vessel?"

Aguila's eyes lit up. "Dammit, Justin. You will be a high paladin by the end of the week. Let's give it a try. I'll leave you completely in charge of that operation. Use the cannons as you see fit."

Justin turned to face Valarie. "Paladin, with me!" he ordered.

She saluted, "Sir!" rushing through the crowd of rescued paladins down to the gundeck.

The crew was at the ready as Justin entered. "Sir!" a familiar voice greeted. Paladin Ekol had been awaiting orders since they ceased firing at the kraken minutes ago.

"Fire upon the hostage ship at my command. We want to try and detonate it and maybe slow down that big galleon out there. Don't target the other vessel; it's too large. Understood?" Justin ordered.

With a resounding "Sir!" the entire gundeck came alive with activity, loading specially designed cannonballs magically enhanced to burst into fire after impact. Justin waited another minute, making sure the explosive ship was far enough away. Aguila had realigned the ship for an attack against the abandoned vessel floating in the water.

Justin gave the order, "Fire!" The gundeck erupted with cannons booming. Their aim was excellent, and within a minute, a dense explosion rocked the water and sent debris flying. The blast disrupted the water enough that *The Valiant Sailor* could break free of the wake caused by *Her Royal Majesty the Sirenia*.

Justin and Valarie rushed back to the upper deck. People still had their hands in the air, covering themselves or ducking behind crates. Debris from the hostage ship had rained down on the deck of *The Valiant Sailor*, causing some minor injuries easily healable with prayers.

As the dust from the explosion began to settle, the crew of *The Valiant Sailor* could see a massive, beautiful red and blue flower growing from the top of the king's ship near the upper deck. It was a hyacinth bloom but had more petals than expected. It shimmered brightly as the sun soaked it in rich, warm tones. Justin smiled. That was definitely Miranda's doing. They turned their attention back to the hull of *Her Royal Majesty the Sirenia*. The explosion had caused no damage.

Justin commented, "Even if it didn't work, maybe the explosion will keep the crew's attention while Miranda is up there playing gardener, you think?"

Aguila replied. "It was a fantastic idea, paladin. Besides the debris. But we broke free of the royal vessel's wake."

After a few more moments, there was a disturbance on the highest deck of *Her Royal Majesty the Sirenia,* which was audible on *The Valiant Sailor*. It sounded like a roar of some kind. They had no time to investigate as the kraken's tentacles burst from the water around them as they tried to distance themselves between *The Valiant Sailor* and *Her Royal Majesty the Sirenia*.

Justin and Valarie heard Gamnir's voice, "Shield Knights! Assemble!"

Justin smiled at the woman who had so quickly stolen his heart. "Ready, city girl?"

Valarie gave him a determined grin in return. "Ever had fried squid, frontier boy?"

With a nonchalant shrug, he replied, "I'm not really into seafood or becoming food at sea."

They kept the squid's tentacles at bay, fighting a slow, downhill defensive battle for the next few minutes. They did not see the shadow that flew over their heads as they fought.

***

The fog around them broke quicker than Erk would have liked. He was glad they were already in tow behind *The Violet Blur*. He kept praying for Naomi's strength and safety. Though he could not see her, he knew she was working hard to pull the hostage ships away. With Selasine having repaired the other ship, Naomi could focus her telekinesis on the damaged ship and take advantage of *The Violet Blur*'s unmatchable speed. Every once in a while, Naomi would pull hard at Selasine's ship to keep it from falling too far behind The Blur. When the ships were even, Erk and Selasine could shout to each other.

Selasine looked behind them at the fog as it continued thinning significantly. They were moving incredibly fast. Naomi steered them toward the ships of Ut'wah's fleet, lowering her speed and using her telekinesis to stop the other two ships. *The Violet Blur* became visible to announce the mission's partial success. Selasine frowned as, behind Ut'wah's fleet, many Claston warships approached. He looked through a spyglass to confirm. They'd be in engagement range within the hour.

Erk was still looking off the stern and saw the Death Pirate frigates closing in quickly. Naomi saw it, too, as she shouted to her crew, "Full speed ahead, ladies. Death Pirates closing quick!" They looked to be around two thousand feet away.

There was a loud popping sound from one of the Death Pirate vessels. Red, glowing spheres followed the sound, rising up high into the air, arcing their way toward the hostage ships. *The Nebula* charged forward from the right flank of Ut'wah's ships, which were all still facing northeast. The Death Pirates' formation had broken as they looked to be attempting to target the flanks with ten frigates each. The other ten, however, were still moving toward *The Violet Blur* and the hostage ships.

A sudden flurry of activity from *The Violet Blur* signified that Naomi was preparing for a countermeasure. Erk's eyes widened, and he yelled, "Everybody get down!" and dove for the deck.

Selasine heard Erk's warning and repeated it for the people on his ship, "Get down, quick!" He got down a little less gracefully than Erk.

A moment later, there was a deep booming sound as a telekinetic wave blasted forward, shaking the masts of the hostage ships and rocking their hulls in the water. The surge went forward to the glowing spheres as they seemed ready to rain down on Erk and Selasine. Naomi's wave impacted them, causing them to detonate in the air harmlessly over the water. The exploding sound was terrifying as they popped with several loud blasts in short succession.

As everyone stood up, it was hard not to notice that Gelidor's vessel loomed behind the Death Pirates. It was so massive that Erk and Selasine could easily make out details on the ship from a mile away. Still, they had no time to wonder what was happening to Miranda, Jacques, and Ut'wah as the Death Pirates encroached quickly. *The Silver Corsair* was also surging forward with three smaller vessels, coming to defend their allies. A thundercloud began to form in the sails of the enemy ships. Erk smiled, "Elmadyn." For a moment, the ships floundered wildly in the water. It bought them just another minute or two, which might have been all the time they needed to prepare for open combat.

As *The Silver Corsair* approached, a massive disc of light formed between the two ships, taking up the entire space between the hostage vessels. Now that there were Death Pirates involved, the rescue team had to change their priorities. Erk shouted to the hostages, "Get in!" and jumped over the ship's railing onto the disc. He ran to the center and shouted to Selasine, "Hey, let's get off these rafts and get on a real boat."

Selasine smiled. Erk had some powerful allies among the

pirates. The bishop commanded his ship, "Everybody on!" Within a few minutes, the disc was full, and Raz pulled it up to the deck of The Silver Corsair about three hundred feet away. He returned another disc until all the hostages, Erk, and Selasine were rescued.

Meanwhile, Naomi had her crew cut the ropes attached to the grappled hostage ship. They activated *The Violet Blur*'s powers, speeding right back into action. Suddenly, the ship that Selasine had been piloting began to turn in the water and came astern to face one of the Death Pirate frigates directly. Though nobody could see *The Violet Blur*, it became obvious that Naomi intended to use the enemy's own ammunition against them.

Erk and Selasine clasped hands when they were reunited. The bishop smiled broadly as he spoke, "You've done a wonderful service for the Church of Invictus, brother. Many lives are saved today by your actions. The church sees your cause as just, and we will support you to our fullest."

"Look! The king's ship!" a voice echoed from the upper deck. It was Elmadyn. Her keen eyesight had helped her spot the blossoming flower atop *Her Royal Majesty the Sirenia*.

Selasine got his spyglass back out and looked. Erk's jaw slacked. "That's our Miranda, bishop." Part of him worried that whatever she was currently facing could be more dangerous than Vortex or even Ezelbrecht. The rest of him had faith in her and the gift her parents bestowed on her. This was part of her destiny.

Selasine smiled, looking through the device. "She does love the simple beauty of nature," he replied. He spent so much effort getting Justin and August not to be overprotective of the girl that he hadn't evaluated his tendency to shield her from conflict. He wanted to run to her and protect her. She had become a daughter to him, and after all they had been through just to have her as part of their lives, he wanted to ensure she was still safe. He prayed to Invictus for her safety and knew he would simply have to trust her judgment and wisdom.

***

August stood at the helm of *The Nebula* with Jax and Evan. Jax had a spyglass trained on the fog. "There!" he exclaimed as the two hostage ships became visible in the deteriorating fog. Their current concern was that Miranda's voice had warned August of Death Pirates on the other side of that fog, so they were ready for battle. As *The Violet Blur* became visible moving toward *The Silver Corsair*, Jax shouted, "Full speed ahead, gents!"

The sailing crew set to work immediately. *The Nebula* caught a good tailwind within minutes, quickly hurtling it through the water. Ten Death Pirate frigates were now easily visible as the fog continued to lift. They had broken formation and seemed ready to target the right flank of Ut'wah's formation. "Not on my watch," Evan grumbled, evaluating the situation through a spyglass.

They could hear the Death Pirates firing on the rescue team and heard the explosions as Naomi detonated the spheres in the air. Jax looked up at the king's ship sailing behind the enemy. He let out a deep sigh of envy. "Now that's a beaut," he commented. After a moment, he noticed some strange activity, and he watched as a beautiful red flower blossomed in a short minute atop the highest deck.

Jax lowered the spyglass. "Is 'at what ye was lookin' for?" he asked August, offering it to him.

The acolyte raised it to his eye, "That looks exactly like something she would do." He laughed and returned his attention to the enemy in front of them. "Hey, Evan?" he asked.

Evan jutted his chin up, "Yes?"

"Have you ever flown on a pegasus before?" the acolyte asked.

Evan lowered the spyglass and smiled, "I have."

"Want to give these Death Pirates some Infernia?" August asked, grinning wide.

"You don't have to ask me twice," Evan laughed. They headed to the stable cabin and began to saddle up the pegasus.

***

Damil shouted to the Pegasus Knights perched in hiding to the north of the battle, "Quickly! Defend the left flank." Their team did not see Miranda's flower. A swarm of pegasus leaped from the rocky cliffs to the direct west of Beriton.

***

Miranda began to heave. She knew this was going to be a strange sensation. As the king's curse tried to expel her essence, she held it tightly within her. As the magic swirled and churned, her body began to glow. Ut'wah kicked the king's guard square in the face, causing him to fly across the room. He landed with a sickening crunch at the king's throne. "Lady Miranda!" he shouted.

She looked up at the usurper, her glowing blue eyes creating an eerie expression unusual for someone with such a normal and pleasing face. As she spoke, she sounded much like the combined voices of herself and her mother and father. "You can't rule by force when you don't understand the force you wield. You are your own ruin," she warned.

Gelidor rolled his eyes. "Can you die with a little less bravado, please? It bores me so."

Miranda's hair also began to glow until the room was filled with a radiant, piercing blue and red light. It grew too bright for anyone to see. At first, it was silent, but then Ut'wah heard loud crashing and banging near him. This lasted for a moment, but then he felt his body lift. He felt something solid and grabbed onto it. It lifted him higher in the air. Debris smacked around him until he could feel the warm summer morning air. When the light eased, he opened his light-sensitive eyes to see he gripped onto what looked to be a massive, purple spine. He looked around and saw two leathery wings on either side of him and a tail whipping through the air in front of him. He turned around quickly to see the head of a colossal purple dragon. It was turned to look down the dragon's back. It seemed to smile, which was the most terrifying thing Ut'wah had ever seen.

"Are you okay, Pirate Lord Ut'wah?" Miranda's voice asked, though now it sounded like it boomed with power and authority.

Gelidor sat back on his throne, his face twisted into a wretched visage. He now understood why he needed to end this girl. She was too powerful to exist!

Ut'wah smiled broadly and rose into the air on his own. "Indeed, Lady Miranda! I've only incurred a few flesh wounds."

She snapped her head back around to Claston. Controlling

this draconic body was as easy as controlling the mana within her. "As I was saying, you cannot rule by force. You are not the only force in this realm that must be considered." Her words echoed loudly, much like Ezelbrecht's. The booming sound could be heard throughout the bay, causing everyone to turn their attention to the top deck of *Her Royal Majesty the Sirenia*. There, they saw a majestic purple dragon. Scales of such color had never been recorded in the history of mortals. They glinted vividly as the morning sky turned warmer. The beast stretched out its wings as the booming sound continued.

"There are people out there like Bishop Selasine and Erilkaiden that will fight for both what is good and lawful. Your heart is hardened; you would expend the lives of so many to hold on to your power," Miranda chastised Gelidor. She could feel the curse consuming her essence, but she knew that she had some time. This is why she was saving the magic within her. She continued, "Abdicate your throne and allow the church to oversee your successor," she demanded. There was so much power behind her voice that it spoke with destiny's force.

The king snarled and began to spit another curse, but Mir'thax opened her mouth and exhaled a crackling bolt of lightning. It blasted the raised steps leading up to the king's throne, shattering the marble. Claston froze. His hair stood out wildly from his proximity to the incredible, shocking blast. Dragons had been unable to use their breath weapons for nearly a hundred years! This was beyond outrageous.

She inhaled deeply and forced the air out her nose, causing a gust to wash over the king, his grayed hair flailing. "I will give you a minute to decide. I have lives to save." She flapped her wings with great force, taking a few beats to lift into the air. "I will return for your answer," she warned, then flew off from the shattered top deck.

Ut'wah had spiraled upward to watch the confrontation unfold, hovering high above the top deck of Gelidor's ship. He watched in horror as the king's body began to fuse with the deck beneath him.

Mir'thax looked around the bay. She could clearly see the Death Pirates' frigates. They were broken into a weird formation, so she started with the ones closest to her, the center ships. She sped through the air at an incredible speed, feeling at home in this form. As she neared the ten ships, she readied her breath weapon, spraying a jet of fire into the sails of a nearby frigate. Then, without hesitation, she charged a bolt of lightning and spit it into the main mast of a different ship, destroying it utterly. Ahead of the enemy vessels, Mir'thax could see *The Silver Corsair*. She hurried her approach, zipping by the Death Pirates before they could react to her disabling their ships.

On the bow, Selasine and Erk stood close. They looked in awe as the dragon before them changed the angle of its wings to slow to almost an immediate stop, hovering in the air with cautious, repeated flaps. "Hey, everyone!" she boomed across the deck. "I'll disable as many enemy ships as possible, and you all can arrest the Death Pirates!"

She heard numerous voices shouting back, mostly Erk's and Selasine's, frantically asking, "Miranda, is that you?"

She smiled, still a terrifying expression for a dragon. "Of course, it's me. Now stop wasting time!" she flapped hard and sped off over the water toward the ten Death Pirate frigates approaching *The Silver Corsair*. As she did, the enemies had prepared a counter-offensive. They were, however, unprepared to deal with a fully grown, fully powered dragon. Bursts of uncanny magic swirled up in the forms of fire, lightning, acid, and darkness. They reflected harmlessly off of Mir'thax's magic-resistant scales. In retaliation, she fired a bolt of lightning into the hull of one of the frigates and washed the deck of another in a hungry flame. She was being more violent than she wanted, but these were Death Pirates. She wanted to protect Selasine, August, Justin, Erk, and Naomi from these fiends. She understood the necessity of her brutality, as Death Pirates were not known for their mercy.

After disabling six ships in the fleet's center, Mir'thax flew northwest to the next ten enemy vessels where Damil's Pegasus Knights were engaging with the frigates. The Death Pirates fought with Ut'wah's fleet. "Watch out!" she warned as she blasted another round of fire and lightning into one of the frigate's masts and sails. It rocked the ship incredibly hard, knocking several Death Pirates overboard. Cries of terror came from the ship's deck, but Mir'thax needed a place to land and catch her breath. She could feel her essence slipping away, the curse affecting her much more slowly and in a very different way than Gelidor's normal victims. She had to end this quickly.

Mir'thax crashed onto the deck of one of the undamaged frigates, her colossal draconic body sweeping with talon and tail to clear the deck of the enemy. They seemed like insignificant insects beneath her. She finally understood why her mother had been so bitter about losing this form. Miranda only thought of the Death Pirates as insects, thanks to their alignment with Gelidor and the religious teachings of Hoxark. They had currently engaged the forces of justice and righteousness in battle; their lives were forfeit from the beginning. Still, the less blood she had on her hands, the better she would feel.

Mir'thax used her breath weapon repeatedly from her temporary perch for a minute. The Pegasus Knights withdrew high into the air. Damil peered down at the massive beast that had commandeered one of the Death Pirate vessels and was using it as a place to catch its breath and destroy the other nearby ships like a powerful turret of destruction. He raised a finger to his temple, establishing a telepathic connection with the creature. "The enemy of my enemy is my friend, I hope. Master dragon, I am above you on a pegasus; please do not be alarmed. I can communicate—" he was stopped mid-communication.

Miranda's thoughts pushed back, "Damil!" The paladin sat in shock momentarily, the voice sounding human and friendly. Plus, she already knew his name. "It's me, Mir'thax! Or Miranda, I guess."

Damil beamed. Of course. Selasine had told him about Miranda's peculiar heritage. "By the gods, girl, what's happened to you?"

The dragon, far below, looked up with another terrifying smile. "I'm dying because of the usurper's curse. Please tell Bishop Selasine to be ready with the Sixth Catechism of Curse Breaking when I return. I don't have much time," she insisted.

Before the high paladin could question her, she spread her

wings. Mir'thax ascended anew, prompting Damil and his knights to regroup. They gave Mir'thax their unique salute, raising their swords that glinted in the sun shining from the southeast. Mir'thax gave them a nod and flapped higher, turning toward the sun. *The Nebula* was moving to engage the Death Pirates that broke away to attack the right flank of Ut'wah's fleet. She built up a massive amount of speed and stretched out her talons in front of her. The masts of two separate ships splintered like toothpicks with the unstoppable force she became. Her attack came in so fast that even the pirates with attacks ready could not respond. Instantly, they were forced to dodge debris from the shattered masts. The dragon was past them before they could retaliate.

She swooped around by *The Nebula,* which was at arms, watching her in the air. She floated higher, dropping her speed. Gently, she let herself descend within range of the ship, making no hostile movement. "Don't worry, Jax, it's me!" The entire crew seemed relieved and lowered their weapons.

August and Evan struggled to control their pegasus as Mir'thax's presence spooked them a bit. "Hey! Miranda! You're a little scary now, you know," August shouted, wrangling the pegasus under him in the saddle.

Her eyes widened. "Don't be mean, August. I could eat you if I wanted to," she teased back.

He laughed, "It really is you!" He spurred his pegasus up. "We'll take care of the Death Pirates!"

Evan lifted into the air behind August. "Let's end this war, then, yeah?" he shouted to Miranda.

She smiled, again a terrifying sight to behold. "Right!" she agreed, flapping harder. Her body lifted up into the air as she turned back toward the north in the direction of the usurper's massive galleon. *The Nebula* had the firepower and the resources to easily overpower a few of the much smaller frigates, but Miranda still worried about her friends. With another brutal display of her draconic might, she set one of the enemy ships ablaze with her fire breath, destroyed the main mast of a second with her lightning breath, and smashed the central mast of a third as she swooshed by. She saw the face of the Death Pirate in the crow's nest of that final ship. She heard the curse he spat at her as she utterly destroyed the mast supporting him. It didn't bother her. His wicked fate was his own.

Satisfied that her friends would only have to deal with five seaworthy vessels, she started to return to *Her Royal Majesty the Sirenia*. It was time to hear the king's response. Far below the massive ship, however, was a vessel currently in combat with a severely wounded kraken. Mir'thax recognized the beast and changed her trajectory. She dove straight into the water, causing an epic splash to rock *The Valiant Sailor*. Under the water's surface, Mir'thax felt her talons pierce the flesh of a spongy, giant squid. She attacked the head directly, a vulnerability of krakens that was not easily targeted by humanoid-sized creatures that lived on the land. With a hideous squishing sound, Mir'thax slayed the beast. Using her wings and legs to swim back up to the surface, she struggled a bit to fan her way out of the water. The Shield Knights stood at the starboard side where the dragon was emerging. Her purple scales caused a murmuring among the clergy. "Are you Invictus?" a voice called.

She giggled, but it sounded like a rumble. "No, it's just me," Miranda's voice echoed with all of the power and authority of a formidable dragon.

Justin shouldered his shield. "Miranda?" he shouted to the beast hovering nearby.

"Of course!" she replied with a jovial tone. "I couldn't let you deal with this alone. Please, put yourself as far away from the big ship as possible!" she warned.

Justin marveled. Valarie put her shield away as well and waved to Mir'thax. "Thank you for your help, Miranda!"

With that terrifying smile, Mir'thax nodded and then bounced through the air back up to *Her Royal Majesty the Sirenia,* only six hundred feet away.

The king stood motionless, his countenance sullen. She landed directly in front of him. "Your forces will be defeated. The approaching navy will face the same fate unless you abdicate," she demanded.

The usurper's black eyes were filled with burning anger. He looked directly at her and shouted defiantly, "No."

Mir'thax could not understand why he would not listen to reason. She was left somewhat speechless at his obstinance, but at this point, she realized she had no other recourse. Gelidor had signed his own death warrant. Suddenly, the dragon heard Ut'wah's voice, "Miranda, watch out!"

A wicked smile crossed Gelidor's lips. Without warning, a large, wooden beam punched at the dragon with incredible force. It knocked her into the air. She instinctively flapped her wings to slow her tumble, turning the momentum into flight. Miranda wondered if the bruise would carry over between her forms as a searing pain spread through her chest. This form was not invincible.

"What have you done?" Mir'thax demanded.

"You claim I do not understand the power I wield. Behold, fool! I have become one with *Her Royal Majesty the Sirenia*. Her form is my body, and her power is mine!" he cackled madly. She recognized that the king's legs were clearly fused into the ship.

Suddenly, the ship began to creak loudly as it underwent a horrifying transformation. The beautiful, golden wood twisted into a humanoid colossus, shaping into a construct with a head, two arms, a torso, and legs. One arm formed into a sharp wooden blade instead of a hand. Cannons pointed haphazardly in random directions out of the strange aberration's form. Screams could be heard throughout the ship as the people aboard were thrown out of the ship or were crushed by the transformation. Gelidor's callousness made Miranda's blood boil.

"You would curse yourself so you can cling to power?" Mir'thax growled in anger. This time, the emotion felt correct. She let the righteous fury burn within her, and she prayed to Invictus for the wisdom and strength to end this conflict with the least amount of violence possible. She prayed for the people trapped inside Gelidor's abominable form.

The usurper's new, massive avatar laughed. He was about fifteen times bigger than Mir'thax, thanks to the absolutely unimaginable size of the vessel. The curse fused his essence throughout the magical wood that once gave form to the exquisite ship. "You were correct when you warned me that I am not the only entity to consider. However, I was selected by the universe itself to be an arbiter of who should wield their powers and who should not. My law is absolute and should have been obeyed worldwide." The towering construct began to levitate slightly above the water. The king's voice sounded like a sharp, raspy hiss that echoed through the air.

Mir'thax took a moment to evaluate the new *Her Royal Majesty the Sirenia*. Shaped like a three-hundred-foot-tall humanoid, its features were haphazard and unsettling. A gundeck had been converted to a mouth, while large windows had been formed for the eyes. The golden wood sparkled still but was no longer fascinating or beautiful. The right arm had been sharpened into a blade. Its weight alone would have been enough to sink a ship, and Mir'thax did not want to test her fortitude against it. Her best strategy would be to use its own size against it.

***

Erk, Selasine, and Raz rode on one of Raz's transportation discs over the open water. Miranda had disabled enough of the enemy vessels, creating confusion among the Death Pirates. As they scrambled to respond to the damage left behind by Miranda's sudden assault, Erk and Selasine decided to take maximum advantage of the situation. Partnering with Ut'wah's first mate Raz, they used his uncanny magic to make a mobile assault unit over the open water.

Selasine stood in the center of the disc with Raz. The disc, a translucent manifestation of light capable of supporting significant weight, was slightly concave. It provided no cover from enemy fire, which is why Selasine's task would be so important. He began to pray, "Sword of Justice, shield us from the enemy's attacks. Allow us to pour out your judgment safe from the spears and arrows of the wicked." His holy symbol glowed with a golden, brilliant light.

As the disc came within range of the Death Pirate frigates not disabled by Miranda, cannon fire echoed around them. As the deadly scattershot neared the disc, each individual bullet was deflected harmlessly by Selasine's prayer.

Erk began to smile and channel the sun's heat into his hands. "Your descent is my atonement!" he shouted to the

Death Pirates. The three of them could see the frigates beginning to change directions to pursue the disc. It was a little late, Erk thought as his smile melted into a frown. Pointing his hands at the hull of the closest ship, he focused a radiant beam of sunlight on a single spot near the bottom of the hull. Within seconds, he had burned a significant hole into the ship's hull, causing it to immediately begin sinking.

Raz growled with a pleased intonation. Selasine began to pray again, enhancing the barrier around them as it fended off another round of cannon fire. They were somewhat reckless, positioning themselves amidst ten enemy ships with nothing but their bravery and prayers. Erk began to bore a hole into another ship when they all heard an explosion.

Naomi clenched her hands as if they were gripping the former hostage ship. *The Violet Blur* was invisible, but the floating bomb was obvious to the Death Pirates on a nearby frigate. Their cries of panic could be heard as Naomi stood safely over nine hundred feet away, using her telekinesis to push the gunpowder-laden ship on a course directly for the nearest frigate.

Unable to maneuver their vessel quickly enough to evade, some pirates abandoned ship. The Claston naval transport was a bit larger than the Death Pirate ship, and as it collided with the frigate, the gunpowder in the cargo deck exploded in a bright flash. The explosion destroyed the front half of the enemy vessel, causing it to quickly dip and begin a swift descent to the bottom of the bay.

Naomi's face remained expressionless as she watched the pirates sink helplessly, the undertow of the frigate creating additional casualties among the Death Pirates who had abandoned ship.

Between Miranda's initial assault, Erk's uncanny magic, and Naomi's brilliant strategy, the four remaining seaworthy vessels were quickly sunk, and the other damaged ships floundered helplessly. As Selasine looked around at the wreckage, a sharp sensation called for his attention, "Thomas, have you spoken with Miranda?"

He inhaled a deep breath before replying. "No, but I'm

worried for her. She only stopped briefly at *The Silver Corsair*."

Damil's voice returned, "She seems to think she is dying. She said the king cursed her."

Selasine's eyes lit up with realization. Erk had explained to him with far too much detail how Gelidor's divine curse worked, causing a person's essence to simply evaporate into the arcane stream. Miranda's unique heritage and relationship with the arcane stream seemed to backfire, creating an impossible curse that turned Miranda into an incredible, purple-scaled dragon. For her essence to dissolve and disperse into the mana, the curse probably had to burn through the excess stores of magic she could hold within her. "Did she say anything else?"

"She said the sixth curse breaker should work. I have no idea how she knows that, but she shared that with me before she flew back your way," Damil finished.

Selasine turned to Erk and Raz. "We have to get back to *The Silver Corsair*. Miranda will be looking for me there. She's been cursed by Gelidor, and I have to be there to break the curse," he insisted.

Erk's eyes widened with fear. "Cursed? Is that how she has become a dragon?" he asked.

Selasine nodded. "Just like Evan, her essence is pouring into the arcane stream. However, without the hand of Invictus to hold it back, she likely only has as much time as she had mana stored within her."

Raz gave a nod and reversed the trajectory of the light disc. "Back to the Corrrsair, rrright away!" he growled.

***

August and Evan rode over the top of a Death Pirate frigate, just out of range of most abilities and weapons. Looking at the deck below, they began counting enemies. August shouted over to Evan, "Around a hundred, right?"

Evan confirmed with a nod, grinning with excitement. "I used to be able to bring that many down in one shot," he shouted back.

"We still can," August replied with an increasingly devious smile. He had noticed something that neither Evan nor the Death Pirates below had seen.

As they prepared their assault, they heard the explosion caused by Naomi's attack with the former hostage vessel. They watched in awe at how quickly the vessel sank as the bow of the frigate was obliterated by the larger, exploding vessel. Evan let out a laugh. "We don't have an exploding ship though," he voiced his objection.

The pegasus bounded through the air in circles above the frigate closest to *The Nebula*. The pirates were so distracted by the threat above that they did not notice Jax had veered just enough off course to ram into the starboard side near the frigate's bow. The Death Pirate ship was only about half the size of Erk's magnificent vessel, and it smashed into the smaller ship, the sound of planks shattering, filling the air with screams.

Evan looked at August, "Well, that makes our job easy." The two laughed but then noticed a lone pirate had taken flight off the ship's deck they were attacking.

The young acolyte replied, "Just gotta keep this mess clean." The two of them spurred their pegasus through the air. The flying pirate had no hope of outrunning the pegasus. The two riders used their mounts to trample the enemy as he sped through the air. The hooves of the pegasus kicking him as they flew hurt bad enough that it caused him to dive straight down, splashing into the surface of the ocean with incredible speed. He emerged a moment later, flying directly at August. With the scimitar that Jax had loaned him, August pushed his mount forward into a downward, spiraling trajectory. His heart raced with excitement as he met the pirate in the air, using his strength and size to disarm and mortally wound the pirate with two, firm, passing strikes. The pirate hovered momentarily before gravity yanked his lifeless body back into the water.

The two of them regrouped near *The Nebula*, creating a four-fold threat. August and Evan supported the main crew with airstrikes while the gundeck of the massive galleon promised a watery grave to anyone foolish enough to approach one of its sides. *The Nebula* was large enough to ram any other vessel except Gelidor's otherworldly huge ship, and the uncanny magics of Erk's crew were varied and potent. This would be an easy game of cleanup.

As they moved to destroy the next frigate in the formation, *Her Royal Majesty the Sirenia* began to undergo a terrifying change. August and Evan watched in shock as the ship's planks rearranged magically. August felt his heart drop to the Rift. "Miranda," he grumbled.

Evan looked to the young acolyte. "Have you ever hit yourself in the face trying to swat a mosquito?" he asked, not letting the sudden change demoralize him.

August's brows raised. "You know, Erk is pretty awesome, but it seems like you're the idea guy. How did he make it thirty years without you?"

Evan smiled broadly, "He almost didn't. Come on, let's get close and see what we can do."

***

From the deck of *The Silver Corsair*, Erk and Selasine watched in horror as Gelidor's ship began to transform. It became a massive, humanoid-shaped colossus that towered far above the ocean's surface. They could see Miranda flying nearby, the twisted ship dwarfing her draconic silhouette in the morning sky.

"By Invictus, what manner of foul magic is that?" Selasine cursed.

Erk stood in awe. He breathed slowly. "I'm afraid the usurper's vows of faith to Na'agamlor are more depraved than any of us imagined. There are only two possible outcomes today, and I believe in our cause." He stood tall, looking at the towering colossus as it flailed its sharpened arm wildly at Miranda in the air. "And I believe that Miranda's pure heart will extinguish the evil present here today."

The two of them watched as the fight between Miranda and Gelidor unfolded. Here, good would confront evil. Justice would challenge the usurper's corrupted law. And a pure soul would face a dark one. The future of Claston hung in the balance.

***

Justin and Valarie stared up at the creature that formed out of the golden wood. Valarie reached out to take Justin by the hand. They said nothing as *The Valiant Sailor* sped out to sea away from the colossus. Justin prayed fervently for Miranda's safety facing such a foe. From here, there was nothing they could do.

***

Mir'thax looked back at her friends and saw the Death Pirates were faring poorly against her allies. Ironically, the pirates of Yendralia would be enforcing the will of law today when they were initially the targets of Invictus. She turned her attention back to the abomination that Gelidor had become. "I am afraid violence is my only option to protect my friends. Invictus, guide my talons," she prayed; a glowing purple aura further enhanced her presence. She was thankful she did not need her holy symbol to call for her god's aid. She could feel his eyes on her, watching this historical moment.

Time seemed to freeze for Miranda. Mir'thax's body felt ready to give out. She did not have much time. She needed to return to the bishop before her magic expired. She felt the magic bleeding out of her slowly and could feel her soul shrinking. She wondered if this was what Evan felt as he knew his time was running out. Even if she couldn't return to Selasine in time, she knew she had to stop Gelidor's reign of terror. If she had been chosen by Saraix like her parents and was truly a dragon, she knew the dragon mother would call her name back to the mortal coil eventually, maybe even in her natural form as a dragon rather than her human self. It's not that she disliked being a human, but somehow this body felt right. As a young girl, she knew something about her was incomplete. She felt trapped in someone else's body, but after recent events, she understood. She would be happy to continue her destiny as Miranda, but Mir'thax was who she truly was in her soul.

Time seemed to restart as the colossus hurtled itself through the air. It flew directly at her, turning its body parallel to the water's surface. Its bladed arm was outstretched and aimed directly at the dragon. Fortunately, the construct was much slower than Mir'thax, especially because its sheer size would have made a high-speed swipe immediately fatal and difficult to evade. Mir'thax dove into the water, using gravity as an additional accelerant. As she dove deep, maybe one hundred feet, she turned upward and jetted quickly into a new ascent. She burst from the ocean's surface, using her significantly smaller size to latch onto the construct around its torso. As she made contact with the magical wood, she realized she could detect the mana flowing within it.

Gelidor began to use the massive vessel to try and ensnare Mir'thax. Vines of wood started to whip out of the former galleon, reaching toward the dragon with incredible speed and flexibility. As they did, Mir'thax could detect the mana that directed their movements. As a result, she was easily able to evade them. She scurried along the torso of the construct still facing the water as it flew through the air. The wood chased her like a lizard up a tree, her wings pulled tight to her sides for maximum agility on this surface.

Frustrated with his strategy, Gelidor commanded the colossus's body to tilt upright, diving the feet and legs straight into the water with significant depth. It created furious waves that immediately surged eighty feet into the air, the weight of this colossus unimaginable. The sudden shift in momentum threw Mir'thax off the construct, her body hurtling back into the air into the range of the usurper's weapon. He had disturbed the water significantly enough that Mir'thax was unsure if she could use the ocean for cover again if she needed to. It also caused a miniature tsunami that wrecked the docks of the port city and sent the ships locked in combat into violent lurches.

Suddenly, Gelidor felt a chipping sensation.

A loud, cracking sound echoed as Ut'wah dove entirely through the construct's right arm, splinters of magical wood gloriously rupturing around him. A protection prayer shattered around him as he blasted himself through the twisted ship, sparing his body from harm. He dove with full force into the former hull of the ship at a speed that should have broken every bone in his body, but Lexcord also poured her full effort into this fight. People began to look out of the hole created by Ut'wah's attack, confused and terrified. Ut'wah thanked Lexcord he did not accidentally injure anyone in his hasty blast through the construct. With a deep growl, Gelidor rearranged the decks and cabins again, twisting them at his will to serve as different appendages and tools. He formed three more sharp, bladed arms, some of the cabins narrowing so much that it crushed the people inside. The tips of the blades seemed to soak with the blood of Gelidor's most recent, immediate victims.

Miranda's heart broke, watching inside from the eyes of Mir'thax. She knew they were one and the same, but her draconic form was capable of the violence she was not. Miranda could not live with the role of executioner of even the people that deserved it. However, Mir'thax was the daughter of Reshiria. Her mother's heart was cold for so long before it was warmed by Philotrax and Miranda. She drew from her mother's ruthlessness and her father's brutality. "You who murder your own people with impunity deserve neither crown nor country. Nor do you deserve to reach the afterlife. May the primordial place lose your soul to the Abyss!" she boomed, her voice commanding and dripping with disdain.

Gelidor spat back, "My authority is absolute. I am a god. You will yield to me, and you will suffer! Die, now, abomination." The ship-turned-avatar moved toward Mir'thax, making wild swipes at her with the four, sharpened arms. She evaded as gracefully as possible with such a bulky weight to carry with her wings but found that dragons used as much magic to fly as they did physical exertion. She spiraled skyward with a swift series of upward flaps of her wings. She came even with the top of the colossus, where the king's elven manifestation remained rooted to the top of the makeshift head. As the colossus swiped, it looked like it was trying to attack a bug or bird in its face. The fight was easily visible throughout the bay.

Just then, Ut'wah burst through another section of an arm, hoping to target where bystanders would not be injured. Two pegasus also appeared to be flapping in and out of the range of the blades formed by Gelidor's construct. When they could make contact with the transformed vessel, they galloped alongside it through the air, tearing it with long strikes of their swords. After a moment of watching, Mir'thax recognized that Evan and August were there to help her face Gelidor's depravity. Her heart swelled. She was not alone in this fight at all.

As a result, the usurper began to grow more arms, shrinking the central torso of the colossus. "You will all face my judgment!" he shouted, the voice forcefully echoing throughout the Bay of Beriton.

From up here, Mir'thax could see that the Claston navy was no longer a threat. It seemed that Ut'wah's connections in Yendralia knew no limits. Almost three hundred pirate vessels had emerged from across the horizon or unseen places. She didn't know how she knew, but she could see Dread Pirate Lady Lascha's banner, Dread Pirate Lord Oorzgo's colors, and the rest of Naomi's and Erk's ships. The distance between them was great, but their hearts beat for the same purpose. Gelidor had gone to war with Erk, which put him at war with all of Yendralia. She knew why Erk was so loved because, until recently, his heart had been so strong and his conviction focused. Even the darker pirates of the island were here to see an end to this tyranny.

Miranda caught a glimpse of a raft sailing among those pirate vessels. On it stood Cantalus, He Who Sings at the Gate. The god of the pirates. She smiled, her heart swelling with pride and excitement. Her tiny little world seemed to hold its breath for this moment. It was time to end this.

Gelidor shouted at her, "Your authority is not recognized here, priest. Leave my kingdom at once!"

Mir'thax snarled her teeth and roared. The usurper's countenance changed when he realized he had been too slow bringing up a vicious swipe, as the dragon suddenly shot forward toward him. He was so massive; why couldn't he easily obliterate her? The new arms that he was trying to sprout flailed around wildly, trying to sharpen fast enough to cause maximum damage. Mir'thax would not let this monster break Miranda's heart anymore. She only had to take one life to save the lives of the people on the former ship.

As she soared straight toward the top of the head, Gelidor started to call up planks from the ship to try and pound her away again. She flew evasively and swerved around the planks as they punched. He started rolling the head down the back of the construct, forcing him to withdraw the numerous, spinning tendrils he was trying to attack with a moment ago. Mir'thax used her mana sense to detect the movement in the construction of the magical ship, allowing her to evade the usurper with ease. Furthermore, she could see where he was trying to move and protect himself. He had accidentally chosen a body that would telepathically warn Mir'thax of any impending attack, making her spirits soar despite the feeling that she was about to perish.

The usurper tried to create a cover of thick wood. Ut'wah again pierced the growing planks, shooting himself and his incredible sword through the golden colossus right where Gelidor was trying to hide. Every time he impacted the ship, a protection prayer shattered around him, saving him from unimaginable pain. Mir'thax knew repeating that prayer so quickly could be extremely draining. Ut'wah did not have much time, and she had even less.

August and Evan suddenly landed on the larger, upper arms of the colossus, using their incredible weapons to distract and damage the construct. They targeted the shoulders and biceps of the arms, the pegasus adept at maneuvering out of the way of flailing opponents. Tendrils of golden wood continued to lash out from the larger surfaces of Gelidor's avatar, creating a maze of deadly spikes and entangling vines. August and Evan seemed like natural Pegasus Knights, easily avoiding the threats.

Gelidor's multifront attacks worked against him and required him to divide his concentration. At this rate, he knew he could not continue to outrun the dragon and fend off the smaller attackers even though they were no more than insects to him.

He resigned himself to his fate. His reign had been one of order and true justice. His will was law, and Na'agamlor had given him the power to realize his goals. He gave the last of his cursed essence to try and stop the dragon.

He had no way to counter, however. Mir'thax was still pursuing the head as it rolled down the construct's back. As the dragon's maw opened, Gelidor's heart skipped a beat. He quickly covered himself with a massive shell of magical wood, but it splintered incredibly as a blast of lightning demolished the thickening carapace. He should have expected interference from the gods. And now, he had to pay the price. The dragon caught up to the retreating head with a fierce, downward swoop. Mir'thax chomped hard around the elven figure protruding from the top.

As soon as the dragon crushed the source of the enchantment on the ship, the colossus shattered, and the various cabins and decks spilled down into the ocean below with incredible speed. Mir'thax inhaled deeply, finding a third breath weapon: the mana stream. She sprayed a blast of magical energy at the breaking ship, slowing the descent of the various pieces and scattering them safely apart. They landed without harm in the water below. She breathed a sigh of relief, noting that *The Valiant Sailor* had changed course to investigate and help.

Mir'thax's mana breath reshaped the falling pieces of the ship so they would float until help arrived. She would have gone down to rescue them all if she could have, but using that attack had nearly exhausted the magic within her. She had less than a few minutes of life left. Her mission was accomplished, and she could rest in peace if she didn't return to Selasine in time. She slammed her wings hard, creating a shockwave behind her. If she couldn't stay Mir'thax forever, she still wanted to be Miranda. She loved the people in her life and wanted to see their stories unfold. To her, life's gift came in the form of happy experiences and sharing them with those she loved. Selasine, Erk, August, Justin, Naomi, the women on *The Violet Blur*, the people of Devitus, and all of the people she had yet to meet. She wanted to live for them.

Mir'thax's trajectory took her straight to *The Silver Corsair* in less than a minute. The massive galleon had begun to rush toward the fight between Gelidor and Mir'thax. Selasine and Erk had cleared a spot for her to land on the deck. She slammed into it hard. She looked very sleepy. "Bishop, please pray," she whispered slowly.

Selasine gripped his holy symbol and began praying loudly and confidently. "Oh, light of Invictus, the justice guiding our path. Take pity on our restless souls as we have been cursed to the root. This doth plague us with affliction, pain, and chaos. Destroy that which causes our souls to seep so sourly," he recited. A brilliant light enveloped Mir'thax. Much like when Miranda used her gift, the light became so bright that everyone had to look away. It glowed for what seemed like an hour.

Chapter 23
To Far Away Places

Miranda stood on the bow of *The Nebula*, her hair loose and wild. It blew out behind her, a sea of red tendrils waving without care or worry. She did not wear her mother's battlemail today. Instead, she was in a relaxed, flowing sundress Naomi helped her pick out from the wealth of plundered, fine clothing in the dressing room. It was a pastel yellow dress with a purple floral pattern along the hem. The warmth of summer was starting to wane, but Miranda never relished the feeling of the sun on her skin as much as now.

Almost a month had passed since she had been cursed by Gelidor, turning her into an impossible dragon with brilliant purple scales. Though she could use that form to ensure a swift defeat against the usurper and the Death Pirates, the nature of Gelidor's curse had nearly taken her life. Each moment she spent in that form burned the capacity of the mana to store within her. After Selasine broke the curse, Miranda still lived.

However, her ability to accumulate and control the arcane stream's flow diminished significantly. She relied more on her prayers now, which is all she would have asked for in the first place.

Thomas stood behind her. He was relieved Miranda's gift had changed in such a way. The unlimited power and potential she previously possessed would have made her a permanent target for those seeking her power for their own selfish reasons. He could breathe easier knowing his adopted daughter would be freer without such a heavy weight on her shoulders. And when he thought of her as an adopted daughter, he meant it. Together they had filed the paperwork necessary to declare themselves as a family in the eyes of the church and the law. He also filed the deeds and titles necessary so that Lady Mir'thax Toi'landra Miranda Hyacinth could fully claim the material inheritance left to her by her parents. She could live a comfortable, peaceful life among the people of Devitus.

He laughed to himself. Devitus was such a sleepy town where cattle escaping was the most exciting thing to happen. He wondered if she could return to simple times, but he already knew the answer. She had said that things would never return to how they were. He supposed that's why she was still on *The Nebula*. Erk offered her an official position in his crew, an officer whose only duty was to pray for the safety of Erk's crew and brighten their lives with her presence. Naomi countered the offer by promising Miranda her own ship. The poor girl's face was red from embarrassment as the pirates praised her. She turned them down with tears in her eyes. She clearly wanted to keep them close to her heart and promised to sail with them occasionally.

Erk and Naomi had ambitious plans following their conflict with Gelidor. Though Erk wanted to ensure a smooth succession of nobility in his kingdom, that plan had a major problem. Currently, Archbishop Renault took up residence in the Claston royal palace. Those fiercely loyal to the king were surprisingly eager to see major changes in their kingdom after the tyrant had been removed from the formula. Though he should have had heirs, the king's madness and thirst for control had driven him to even have his own children exiled or executed. By anyone's estimates, a lone runaway princess should have been out there somewhere. She would have had Invictus's full blessings to take her rightful place as the queen of the elves of Claston. She was Gelidor's niece but the daughter of the rightful king, Eisen. That was now Renault's problem. Erk had no interest in looking for a unique needle in the haystack of the world of Espa. There were Death Pirates to stop.

Which is partly why they were on the long journey to Nulodia. Miranda turned from the bow, the late summer air salty and refreshing. "One more day, Your Holiness!" she teased.

Thomas laughed. "One more day *until* you can call me that, yolasha." He smiled broadly at her. Damil took Carulus into custody shortly after the battle with the Death Pirates. As punishment for his crimes, he was stripped of all authority and rank within the church. He was offered prison, exile, or servitude. He chose the last option. He would work at the lowest level of the church hierarchy for the rest of his days, which, in an ironic sense, was the best outcome for everyone involved. His extensive knowledge of church regulations and bylaws would be put to full use. However, that meant an opening for Invictus's High Priest in Nulodia existed. Archbishop Renault and Brigadier Major High Paladin Otto, Damil's direct supervisor, insisted Selasine take the position.

The two of them would have never convinced Thomas to take the position. Damil persuaded Thomas to take the position in the city where they spent their youth. As soon as the Council of Four extended an offer to Selasine, Damil announced his retirement as the High Paladin of the Pegasus Knights. But not before he invited a young man named August Burchard to join the ranks of those elite soldiers. August and Evan commandeered pegasus to use in the fight against the Death Pirates. August's displays of bravery and strength impressed Damil more than Thomas anticipated. After that battle, the young man left his mentorship with Selasine to travel with Damil to Nulodia for training. He hoped this visit to the largest port in Alabaster would allow them to see August. However, he knew from experience what it was like trying to keep in touch with a Pegasus Knight. Even the ones that can talk to your mind directly stay far away as soldiers of the sky.

Miranda's voice interrupted his thoughts. "He just doesn't give up, does he?" she asked as there was an uproar of laughter on the foredeck. Thomas turned to face the rest of the deck, seeing Justin, Evan, and Erk, all three literally pinned against *The Nebula's* main mast together. Naomi wielded her knives with such precision that she could pin their silhouettes against the mast while Valarie kept them impossibly busy parrying with her efficiency in melee combat.

Naomi magically recalled her knives and dropped the three men to the ground. Thomas and Miranda traded mischievous glances and walked down the short platform leading up to the ship's bow. "Is it girls against boys?" Miranda piped, her voice still musical and enthusiastic.

Justin groaned, "It's already unfair! They don't need any more help!" His protest caused another wave of laughter to permeate the deck.

Erk lay panting, the training difficult but rewarding. He had become more of a sailor than a soldier but saw the value in the routines of the Shield Knights. Years ago, he and Evan had both undertaken the most intense physical training regimen among the followers of Lexcord. He missed the days of his prime physique, even though he was still fit from fighting and sailing. Longing for those older days, he invited Justin and Valarie to train his crew. He also wanted them to instill in his crew the virtues of discipline and acting justly. Though the pirate lord leaned toward Lexcord philosophically, some of his greatest treasures in life were followers of the Sword of Justice. He even committed himself to fighting for those causes more openly. Hence, this mission in the Sea of Nulodia.

Just before the battle with the Death Pirates, Naomi had discovered that a notorious smuggler named Farzg had increased the traffic of slaves in the port city of Nulodia. As a former victim of slavers, she was working tirelessly to set free everyone she could. Though Naomi never asked for compensation for her work, in many cases, noble and wealthy families would pay hefty sums for the safe return of their loved ones. It was one of the ways that Naomi managed to fund her fleet. Erk stood and looked off the starboard side, where *The*

Violet Blur sped alongside *The Nebula*. He left his thoughts and seconded Justin's sentiment, "We're no match for them alone, Miranda. I don't think it'd be fair to add the most powerful dragon in Espa to the mix," he smiled.

Miranda's lips crunched up into a smirk. Everyone had told her how terrifying she was as a dragon. Still, she didn't remember making a face that looked like she wanted to devour everyone she talked to. Miranda insisted she only smiled, and everyone was afraid because they didn't know it was her. Though that experience weakened her gift, she remembered those moments fondly. It was like getting to experience more of her parents' memories, and she was grateful it was part of her destiny. "Rawr!" she growled and tried to snap menacingly. It was awkward in an adorable way, with Valarie and Evan laughing the loudest.

Erk looked to Thomas. "Brother, join us for dinner again tonight? There is much to discuss about the future before our paths separate."

Naomi smiled and ran to grab Miranda's hand. "Oh, please, you simply must! There's still time for hair and makeup and dresses. We'll make an evening out of it!"

Valarie helped Justin stand as she frequently did in these training bouts. "And you too, Justin the Watchful and Valarie the Persistent," Erk added, gazing and smiling at them.

Thomas replied, "Of course, we will join you, nulestotejin." Thomas and Erk would have been the last pair of people to make friends in almost every possible scenario. Their shared love of Iria made such an impossibility a reality. The bishop found it ironic that the journey to destroy Erk had made him so many unlikely friends and allies. And he was glad to have them. He planned to use the full resources of the church to help Naomi and Erk on their quest to crush Farzg. Whatever machinations The Frozen Death had working in Nulodia, the three of them would chase him to the darkest corners of the underworld and put a permanent end to him.

Erk shouted, "Shalo! Make it a grand feast."

The pungent pirate appeared at the entrance to the lower decks. "On it, cap!" he shouted, descending the grand stairs below.

Naomi excitedly tugged Miranda's arm, pulling her toward the dressing room. "We have to get ready!" she insisted.

Valarie took off her sallet, her blond braid spilling out. "Pirate Lady Naomi?" she asked.

Naomi pursed her lips, and Miranda complied with a giggle, following Naomi's insistent pull. The pirate lady took Valarie's hand, "If you even have to ask, I'm not doing my job." They shared a mutual smile as the three of them went into Naomi's dressing room.

Erk shrugged playfully, "She takes care of so many girls in bad situations; it's no wonder she's so doting."

Thomas laughed. Justin smiled. He didn't take Valarie for the kind of woman that would be into makeup, dresses, and general pampering. Then again, how would she know if she liked it if she didn't try it? She was a city girl, and life there was very different. He felt butterflies in his stomach. It seemed like they had grown so close in such a short time, closer than he had ever been to anybody else. He could only see a future with her and hoped she felt the same. Even if she didn't, he was happy to have her in his life as long as she was happy to be in it.

Inside the dressing room, Valarie was echoing the same sentiments in her heart. As a runaway, she never had the opportunity for pampering. As a paladin, she followed a disciplined path that didn't leave time for such activities. As a younger girl, however, she used to play with makeup and clothes all the time. She felt nostalgic. Plus, she wondered if it would keep Justin's eyes glued to her all night. It seemed like fun to her.

Erk, Evan, and Thomas entered the captain's quarters to prepare for their last shared meal. They tidied up the various tomes and scrolls strewn about while conducting research for the day. They then set out Erk's finest mismatched plates and cutlery. It took them a couple of hours to get everything ready. Shalo reported back that the food would be ready in another hour. Erk invited him to stay, and the four of them sat at the table, relaxing silently. There was a knock at the door. Justin went below deck to change out of his armor into a comfortable, white cotton shirt commonly worn by young noblemen. He wore leather trousers that Evan had but were always a little too big for him. Erk wondered how he could find anything since he and Valarie volunteered to share an officer's cabin instead of taking one for each of them. Naomi always insisted on keeping her stuff separate, and he found it strange that Valarie did not make the same demands. He smiled. Naomi's boundaries did not make Erk uncomfortable. He concluded that he shouldn't question the expectations other couples set for each other.

"Justin! Come in, friend," Erk welcomed warmly.

"Thanks, captain," he replied, sliding in to take a seat. Erk was sitting at the head of the table, Evan on his right and Thomas on his left. Shalo was sitting on a lounge behind the head of the table. Nobody had told Justin who had brought him to the edge of the mortal coil, but seeing how important this young man was to his mentors and peers, Shalo made a vow. He would follow the young paladin secretly for the rest of his days if necessary, helping save him from danger in any case that he could.

Justin sat beside Bishop Selasine for the last time. He would be High Priest Thomas Selasine tomorrow, and the young man was proud of his mentor. He proved that staying determined and fighting for the right thing would lead to true righteousness. The five of them now sat together, telling stories. Eventually, Shalo scampered out, dismissing himself to the kitchen to check on the food.

At one point, Erk asked Selasine, "I am curious about the scar." The pirate lord made a gesture to his own right eye for a bit of awkward emphasis.

Thomas laughed and gave Justin a nudge. His peacekeepers had never asked, mostly because Miranda was probably terrified it would upset the bishop. "The first fight with Farzg. I caught a glacial attack with my face pushing Damil and Iria out of the way. The injury was so cold that no healing prayers would fix the wound. I had to be treated for a curse before my injuries could recover. The time between the injury and the prayers was too long. The sight that remains is more of a detriment than a help. So, I keep it covered." He laughed, but then his countenance fell. "Farzg's debt with me is large. His punishment will be worse than imprisonment in the Infernia."

Erk also frowned. Evan scowled. Selasine would not let them turn this into a mission of vengeance at any cost. They knew they would need to rely heavily on his wisdom, patience, and planning. The best fate for Farzg was one that was a consequence of his own doing.

After a little more time reminiscing, Shalo and several of the cooks arrived with the meal. As usual, the fare was great for a long ocean voyage, even if it would have been considered mediocre in a magnificent city like Nulodia. After everything was set, they looked around the room. Erk let out a laugh, "Not me!" he insisted.

Shalo said, "Nope, I've spent too much time guardin' that door to go bang on it now!"

Justin's eyes widened, "Uh, I'm just a guest on the ship, right?"

Selasine groaned and stood. Evan was getting ready to stand but relaxed when the bishop got up. "Fine. It's not like they will bite your head off if you follow protocol." He left the captain's quarters and turned to his right. He dodged a crate as he went to the dressing room door. He gave three solid knocks as protocol demanded, hearing a shriek from within. He must have startled Miranda. Poor girl. Selasine wondered; three solid, loud knocks seemed slightly too formal and frightening. No wonder the others didn't want to fetch the women. Even protocol failed sometimes.

A moment later, the slat in the door window opened, and Naomi's piercing eyes looked out. "Oh, hey! It's Selasine!" she called back to Miranda and Valarie.

"Well, don't just make him stand there," Miranda insisted.

Naomi smiled and opened the door. The three were dressed in elegant gowns, their hair fixed in wildly different than typical styles. Valarie's sat in a long, tight ponytail with ribbons, while Miranda's was fixed into an updo resembling Naomi's. Bangs draped her face where her braids usually hung, which was the primary difference. Naomi insisted the girl no longer looked right without something around her countenance. The sapphire comb was fixed beautifully into her hair. Thomas smiled and announced, "Dinner is ready!"

The women nodded and passed before Selasine on their way to Erk's cabin. He closed the door to the dressing room behind them and followed. They entered the captain's quarters unannounced, violating protocol in Selasine's mind. However, as he noted the brief moment of silence that fell when the women entered, he realized that Naomi laid equal claim to Erk's space as the pirate lord himself. She entered unannounced on purpose, her statement one of authority. Selasine respected that, causing him to smile. Miranda looked like she fit the role of a noblewoman for the first time. Naomi had truly given both Miranda and Valarie the works.

Everyone at the table rearranged as the rest of the guests arrived. Erk insisted that Selasine sit at the head of the table, as his wisdom would lead them through their next ordeal. The soon-to-be high priest reluctantly agreed, realizing he would need to adjust to such protocol with such a high station. Erk sat to his right and Miranda to his left. Naomi sat to the right of Erk, and Evan sat to her right. Shalo sat in the fourth seat on the right, while Justin and Valarie sat to Miranda's left.

They talked more than they ate.

"So, where is the first place you'll take Miranda to see?" Erk asked to Selasine.

"Probably the grand cathedral," he replied, knowing that duty would call him there immediately.

Miranda added, "I plan to stay there for a day with the healers. I want to talk to Maréli. After that, I'm returning to Devitus. I need to evaluate my parents' estate."

Erk nodded, understanding her plan. He hoped her next step would be to stay there and live comfortably and happily, but he wanted to know her heart's wishes. "And after that?"

Naomi interjected, "She's going to find The Blur, and she's going to be my ship's priest." She had a coy grin on her lips, making Miranda giggle.

"I know that one day, I'll sail with you, Naomi. I just don't know when it will be," she promised. The pirate lady grinned and poured wine into a glass. "But, I don't think I'll stay in Devitus long. I'll probably give most of the wealth to the monastery. I was thinking of," she paused and sighed deeply. "I was thinking of going on my own adventure. I always wanted to see the world. I've seen the ocean now. I think it's time to see the world between here and Devitus," she finished, taking a drink from a glass Naomi had placed in front of her.

Erk smiled broadly, and Selasine breathed a sigh of relief. There truly were plenty of adventurers in that region of the world, and surely she would gain useful experience being a priestess for people from all different walks of life. The best part was that adventuring in that part of the world meant she would be relatively close to home. With his new station in Nulodia, she could visit her adopted father anytime. At the other extremity, she was technically a noblewoman in Devitus now. The people there knew and loved her and would welcome her home, too. "Will you take church jobs as well?"

She smiled, "Of course, bishop. Especially the ones that take me to faraway places to see as much of the world as a girl hopes to." Her hair was radiant in the warm light of Erk's cabin.

Erk grinned, "You know, that just might mean you might end up helping us take down Farzg."

"As Invictus wills it, so shall it be," she replied, but she had an almost evil grin on her lips, the thought of taking down Farzg a little too exciting for her. Erk felt the same energy as when she had become a dragon and smiled at them. The Frozen Death had made some enemies even he would not be prepared to face.

There was a brief chuckle. Selasine then asked, "And you, Justin?"

The paladin sat up straight, reaching over to hold Valarie's hand. "We will finish all the paperwork to be declared an official couple with the church first." Thomas agreed that was the most pressing move for them to make.

"What does that mean?" Miranda wondered, never having heard of such a procedure.

Thomas explained, "It means that any conscripted assignments have to be made together, and they are to be placed in battalions with other groups of partnered soldiers. Otherwise, they're free to take missions together as they wish."

Miranda understood. It was a romantic practice, she thought.

"After that, we hope to be assigned to work under the high

priest on a special task force to destroy slavers within the city," Justin hinted with a smile.

Erk and Selasine laughed. Naomi poured some more wine, then opened another bottle. Both her and Miranda's cheeks were a little flushed from the effects of their beverages. Evan smiled and listened. Shalo had finished eating and was dozing in the comfortable dining chair. Miranda suspected he might have had a bit of swill down in the kitchen before dinner. He deserved a nap, she thought.

"I think that can be arranged," Selasine promised. Damil was right. He could make a great difference with this kind of opportunity. He had seen so much promise in all three of his pupils. He was glad that August's skills and bravery led him to become an elite warrior for the church. Justin had also met that potential with his usual overkill. In a single conflict, he earned more accolades than some warriors over their entire careers. Furthermore, he had chosen the path more reflective of his heart's righteousness. Valarie had brought out the best in his fighting potential. And then there was Miranda.

She managed to keep her cheerful spirit through all these ordeals. She softened Erk's heart and brought him back to the side of righteousness and light. He had many crimes to atone for and would do so willingly under Selasine's supervision. Miranda's youthful wisdom was enough to return his heart to the light. And with Naomi by his side, he would find plenty of opportunities to fight for what is right. Though he was not as ambitious as Carulus with the position, Thomas knew the timing was right for this kind of step. He worried for the people of Devitus as all three of the acolytes he trained had so much more in their destinies than a sleepy life of simple pastoring. There would be nobody to represent the law in that frontier town. He knew he had to prioritize a placement for a promising bishop there.

Justin's voice brought his mind back to the conversation, "Besides, where else would I go? I still have much to learn from you." Valarie squeezed Justin's hand. He turned his eyes to her, his heart fluttering. She was already beautiful to him, but Naomi was an amazing cosmetologist. She used colors that made Valarie's brown eyes radiant yet darkened them enough to make her even more alluring. Everything that was changed accentuated what was already there, but honestly, that wasn't what Justin enjoyed the most. It was her company, her presence, her bravery, and her persistence that he loved. He could not wait to make port and file the paperwork to make them an official couple.

Selasine beamed. "My mind is made up, then, Shield Knight. Tomorrow you and Valarie shall find yourselves declared essential assets to the High Priest of Nulodia. Your presence will be demanded immediately."

"Sir!" they replied in unison.

They looked at each other with so much adoration and excitement that Miranda giggled. It was cute to her, and she was so happy for them. She enjoyed romances and fairy tales, but those paths never appealed to her. She saw a different kind of romance between Valarie and Justin, founded in building each other up rather than striving to meet some idealized notion of love. It was practical. And Miranda admired that and even longed for it. "You guys remind me of my mom and dad," she added in a pouty tone.

The table looked at her in unison. She flushed harder, the wine making her story easier to tell. "While in the arcane stream, I could see my mother's memories. When she met my father, she could hardly believe she had met somebody who shared her deepest secret. Being a dragon stuck as a human is a pretty isolating experience." She gave a bittersweet smile. "My dad made her life so much richer and happier. She went from a cruel dragon to a loving mother with him by her side. So, you remind me of my parents. And that's a good thing," she smiled.

Justin nudged Miranda with his right elbow. "Thanks, sis. You are the nicest dragon in history," he teased.

She flushed a bit more, "Hey, I'm still a human, too." Her protest was more for trying to be the nicest person in history. She liked that idea.

Erk chuckled and interrupted, "Either way, Miranda. We will miss you while you're off adventuring. Human or dragon, you'll forever be an honorary member of my crew."

Naomi hiccupped. "The Blur, too. Seriously you'd be great for the girls. They need a mentor like you to love them as much as you do."

Miranda shook her head, her bangs wagging along. "Naomi, nobody could ever love those girls as much as you do. You're the best pirate mother in the world!"

They enjoyed their meal with more small talk of hopes and dreams. Some were unspoken, as Miranda had many dreams for her friends and newfound family. She was going to miss them dearly. She knew she wouldn't be able to stay away for long. Besides, destiny could not have brought them together this way to tear them apart forever. There were still many secrets of her own heritage she wanted to understand. Her adventures would be for her own growth. She would make her loved ones proud.

After dinner, almost everyone was content to retire to their cabins. Miranda returned to Naomi's dressing room, but after such an eventful night, she could not sleep. The wine had relaxed her, but the effects began to wear off after a couple of hours. She had already undressed and cleaned off the makeup Naomi had spent so much time perfecting. She liked it, but it felt uncomfortable to wear for long periods. She brushed her hair out, and the rich crimson glowed in the candlelight. She dressed in a warm evening robe and went out onto the deck of *The Nebula*. Nobody needed to guard the door. Miranda wondered if Shalo's assignment to guard the door hadn't been superfluous in those early days on the grand ship. She felt safer on *The Nebula* than almost anywhere else. She walked to the starboard side of the ship and gazed at the glowing silhouette of Nulodia to the east. The city looked massive, and many grand buildings could be made out as shadows behind other glowing lights in the metropolis. She was so excited to visit a city she had heard so much about; that's probably why she couldn't sleep.

"You too?" a familiar voice asked from behind her.

Miranda smiled and turned to see Evan staring off starboard nearby. "I just can't wait to see the city tomorrow!" she explained.

The young elf lord gave a grin and stood beside her. "It seems like a lot will change for Selasine and your friends. You said you wanted to have your own adventure, right?"

She nodded, looking at him in his beautiful gray eyes. "Everything that happened last month was because of the gift, and now that it's not as strong, I hope I can find out what it's like to be normal," she explained.

Evan's grin melted into a sad expression. "Your gift drove the actions of others, but they don't deserve all the credit. It was you that healed so many people that I hurt personally. And then you healed me, too. Though it nearly killed many of you, you and your allies destroyed an ancient evil that had spent nearly a decade sending my brother down the wrong path." Evan paused, his sad expression turning warmer. "You saved countless people from violent deaths at sea and defeated an evil king who took nearly everything from my brother and me." Evan's eyes cut to the water as they filled with tears of relief. "Everything that happened last month wasn't because of your gift. It happened because of your heart."

Miranda paused, and her lips formed the round, bewildered shape she was well-known for by this point.

Evan continued, "You seem to have an infinite capacity for love and care. Even if your powers seem limited now, you'll discover that who you are is a greater gift than anyone could understand."

Miranda suddenly hugged Evan, a tear running gently down her cheek. "I am so glad that I healed you in time. Erk cares for you so much, and I've grown to love both of you," her voice was stronger and more confident. "And my greatest gift is having all of you in my life and the memories we've made," she finished with a smile.

Evan's expression twisted into a bit of a smirk. "Are you sure about that, Miranda?" he asked teasingly. She nodded enthusiastically, so he continued, "If you keep us around too close, you're likely to get tangled up in another one of these grand adventures. Is that what you really want?"

The young woman smiled again, this time looking determined. "Evanthalus! Of course, that's what I want. I'm sure that whatever adventures I find between here and Devitus will see our paths crossing again soon," her smile melted slightly as she spoke. "I can't imagine a future without all of you in it. I hope to do more to help next time, especially before somebody takes a tragic or dark path." She finished her reply with a resolve fueled by her deepest convictions.

Evan sighed gently and patted her gently on the back. "The stakes are a little different. We'll be fighting slavers with access to bizarre technology," he commented.

Miranda suddenly remembered Evan's interesting sword he wielded against the shadows at the Astral Spire and against Gelidor's abominable transformation. "Are you talking about your sword?" she asked innocently.

The young elf lord nodded, withdrawing it from the scabbard on his belt. It was covered in gears, with a central chamber in the cross guard glowing bright pink. "I may not have access to my old power, but these kinds of weapons seem to be able to harvest magic somehow." He offered the sword to her, and she took it in her hands. "Naomi gave me this one on our way to the Astral Spire. There is some kind of crystal inside that powers the enchantment. Once that crystal is exhausted," he took a deep breath. "Once it's used up, the sword will be just a fancy-looking sword."

Miranda peered closely at the glowing gemstone inside. Though her connection to the arcane was weaker, she was sure that whatever powered these interesting weapons were connected to dragons somehow. "Is that so?" she finally asked, inspecting the weapon. Evan nodded. Handing the sword to Evan, Miranda continued, "I feel like whatever powers this weapon will be the next threat we face together."

Evan frowned a bit. "It's nice for us to reach the arcane through a tool, but we have no idea what the price is. And we both know," he explained, but Miranda interrupted.

"There's always a price," she said firmly.

He smiled at her in return. They both focused on the magnificent port city about four miles to their east, watching the lights silently for a moment. "I suppose I should try to sleep at some point. Tomorrow will be a big day," he explained with a smile. Miranda hugged him as he left her alone on the starboard side of *The Nebula*. Erk and Naomi were likely fast asleep in the captain's quarters. She had taken to calling Thomas her modai-rin, the formal title for father in elven. He was probably preparing for his speech and duties tomorrow if he was still awake. She did not want to interrupt him. She cherished the last month spent on *The Nebula* with him and Justin. And with everyone else aboard, it felt like she had a beautiful, huge family that she never would have had staying in that sleepy frontier town. She did miss August dearly but was proud he was on the fast track to becoming one of the Church of Invictus's most decorated paladins.

Miranda looked up at the early autumn stars, one moon visible and full and the other a waxing crescent. She smiled and thought of the day to come. She did not want to linger in the city for too long and knew traveling to Devitus would take two weeks on foot. Still, she had business there and planned to return there alone after tomorrow. She needed her rest as well. She returned to the dressing room, shed her robe, and wound up her music box. Though her mind was still racing, the haunting lullaby put her quickly to sleep.

They arrived in Nulodia the next morning. Brigadier Major High Paladin Otto and High Paladin Emeritus Damil Starstorm met them at the port at the docks. Otto's first act was to grant Erk clemency in Nulodia if he agreed to operate under the supervision of High Priest Thomas Selasine. He then adorned Thomas with the sash of the high priest, and Erk swore his allegiance to his brother-in-law and the cause of the church.

The crew of *The Violet Blur* were welcomed as heroines. Some girls on her ship were waiting to reunite with their families in the port city. Naomi's work was so prolific that many people worldwide would come to Nulodia looking for missing family members, hoping the Succubus of the Seas had rescued their loved ones. Miranda had not seen them, but children were also on the ship. Naomi's core crew would see them to the orphanage of Lexcord there in the grand city. They coordinated with other groups to locate the children's families. Miranda smiled as she watched the crowds cheering for *The Violet Blur*.

There was a parade that welcomed Selasine to town. They tried to get him into a palanquin, but he objected profusely. "I walked the path of a warpriest, and I still do to this day. There will never be a day when others must carry my weight when I can do so myself. Allow me to stay strong so that I may carry others to the safety of the Sword of Justice's arms," he insisted. As the high priest commanded it, nobody could really object. Naomi was going to offer to take the palanquin but decided that would be in bad taste.

Miranda's sense of wonder took over as soon as she disembarked. As they walked through the streets of Nulodia, she marveled at the grand port city. Though Yendralia was sprawling and populous, Nulodia was grand and beautiful. Buildings made of various kinds of stone were permanent and well-kept. The roads were paved with fine cobblestone and were not bumpy compared to the few paved streets in Devitus. She had braided her hair that morning, the red streams draping around her eyes as they soaked in the great city and its many inhabitants. Children played in the street, stepping aside to let the parade through as clerics and paladins welcomed the new high priest.

As they arrived at the grand cathedral, many bureaucrats and police sergeants welcomed them. Erk, Naomi, and Evan followed Thomas there. Justin, Valarie, and Miranda walked directly in his company. August awaited them on the top step leading to the beautiful church building. The new high paladin in charge of the Pegasus Knights had given August special leave to see High Priest Selasine welcomed to Nulodia.

Thomas and Miranda greeted the paladin with an overwhelming hug. Justin stood to the side, but he, too, hugged his friend. Valarie greeted him with a salute as per protocol, and he returned it and ordered her to be at ease, then hugged her as well. "My sister-in-law gets a hug, too, or we might face Miranda's wrath, no?" Everyone close by giggled. Erk and Evan offered him a bold handshake, and Naomi gave him a daring stare. August confidently extended his arm and shook her hand as a respected superior among the pirates, no longer flustered by her confidence and beauty. He had grown a lot in the last month.

The crowds gathered around the church's front steps, which served as an amphitheater of sorts. As per protocol, Selasine had prepared a speech. It was brief, but it was poignant. He delivered it from the steps of the cathedral, his voice echoing off the walls of the church complex and the magnificent building behind him. Miranda beamed with pride as her modai-rin delivered a speech that excitedly stirred her heart for her next adventure.

High Priest Thomas Selasine spoke with boldness and confidence. "Followers of the Path of the Sword of Justice. Recent events show that our role as peacekeepers is our first and foremost duty. We must learn ways to combat the chaos by strengthening our faith and communities. As high priest, I will see that the most egregious violators of the law are pursued fully and justly. As a result of those recent events, our church has forged an alliance with those who were once lawbreakers but now seek to make amends. Make no mistake, those who have fallen outside the law have much to atone for. I will see to it that their sentence is carried out dutifully. And thanks to our alliance with these former lawbreakers, slavery will know its end within our lifetimes." He paused for a moment to take a deep breath and continued. "In keeping with the laws of Invictus, I will see that the duties neglected by previous officials will be thoroughly investigated and examined. Any revealed injustices will be righted with diligence and haste."

He finished his speech with a well-known catechism, "May the Sword of Justice grant us the wisdom to make righteous and beneficial decisions. May Invictus grant us the strength to act on those decisions, and may he grant us the persistence to realize those goals. Blessings upon the faithful and the law of the Sword of Justice."

Those that managed to crowd around the grand cathedral cheered excitedly. Miranda clapped with the crowd but stared in admiration for the man who had volunteered to take care of her as early as the day of her parents' passing. Neither could have predicted what leaving Devitus would mean for them, but in hindsight, they were extremely grateful. Miranda stood behind Selasine to his right. She saw a familiar face from the corner of her left eye. Bureaucrat in Atonement Gaius Carulus, too, stood on the top step of the church, applauding his replacement. His robes were a stark red that indicated he must always be accompanied by other clergy members. Though he had hurt Miranda greatly, she had forgiven him. The value of what she learned due to his overly ambitious machinations had changed her world for the better. She hoped he, too, had learned something through his brush with Indervill.

After noticing Carulus, Miranda turned her attention back to the grand cathedral of Invictus. She could not get over how beautiful this building was. It was a gothic-style building with tall, pointed arches in the windows and doors. The stained glass was beyond anything she ever imagined. She always saw the simple stained glass at her home church with an imaginative eye; this artwork was much more elaborate. She liked it but missed the simplicity of the art in Devitus's church. She wondered if she could use her gift to make a grand church on the frontier. She decided that it might seem selfish, but she also wanted the people to have a captivating place to go and pay their tithes and petition the church. With a shrug at her thoughts, her eyes traced the buttresses surrounding the building and the massive complex of gardens and fountains surrounding the church. Just out front were ten statues of Invictus in varying poses. The statues were made of marble and bronze, creating an imposing colonnade of justice incarnate leading to the church's stairs. The stairs raised a solid twenty feet above the church grounds, and the sanctuary on the other side of the doors could have easily held a crowd of ten-thousand people gathered to hear the liturgy and homilies of Invictus.

She turned her attention back to Thomas. After his speech, he had many people he needed to meet and get to know. Miranda snuck up behind him and gave him a hug from the side. He looked down and proudly pulled her under his arm. There was another cheer, but neither was sure why. "I'm so proud of you modai-rin," she sang in her sweet, small voice.

"Yolasha'nides," he replied, the elven words meaning so much more than the common language could express. Her cheeks flushed with happiness, and she squeezed him again. Before they could say more, he was pulled away quicker than either had wanted. Still, he knew she sought a destiny beyond his wisdom. He trusted her. Although Gelidor's curse had significantly damaged her gift, she still had something nobody else could ever hope for. Her voice had been amplified in the ears of the Sword of Justice, making her the most incredible healer in history. She still used the arcane stream to bend the universe to her will, but she mostly used magic to make flowers and beautiful things now. Anything pretty usually fulfilled her whimsy. He didn't know if it would let her heal with the same capacity as before, nor did he hope it was excessive or noticeable.

As of now, the adventuring rumors described Miranda's encounter with Gelidor as a self-sacrificing strategy. Anyone who knew of Lady Miranda Hyacinth, Warpriest of Invictus, Judge of Hearts would know her gift of unlimited power was sacrificed to save Claston from the tyrannical rule of Gelidor. In turn, Alabaster acknowledged she also prevented war between the two kingdoms. Still, Selasine's thoughts contemplated her future. He loved her dearly and hoped she would find her own flavor of happiness. Miranda was not a replacement for Telisi no more than he was for Philotrax. Instead, they had helped heal wounds for each other that neither had fully understood were still present in their conditions before the ordeals they endured after Carulus arrived in their sleepy town.

In that interrupted moment before he could say anything else to Miranda, Thomas was approached by the head of the merchant guild, the guild of religious freedom, and Tai'n Taou, the representative of a fringe group of the Path of the Sword of Justice. Their ascetic ideals were promising, but their approach was too oppressive. He needed to meet with these people but just wanted to hug Miranda.

He turned around, and she was already gone. Her next adventure was already beginning. He had a new job and planned to do it much better than his predecessor. "May the Sword of Justice smile upon our meeting," he turned back to those that had approached him, beginning his formal introduction.

Miranda decided to explore the cathedral, spending almost eight hours wandering its halls and library. Though she was in a grand city with lots to explore, she found plenty of diversions within the magnificent church building. It had so many more resources than their little frontier church. She thought she would need at least a year here to see all of it. As the evening set upon the city, she prepared herself to retire to the guest wing of the church. With her new rank as a warpriest and a Judge, she would be welcome to stay as long as needed between missions. Before she arrived there, she found Maréli in the hospital wing of the temple.

"Hello, chief healer," Miranda greeted as Maréli looked over scrolls and recipes in her office. Her door was open, which made it easy to greet her.

"Miranda, dear, so nice to see you!" Maréli replied, answering the girl before seeing her.

The beautiful, young warpriest stood silently for a moment, a smile growing on her lips. "You were right about so much, and I wanted to thank you," she explained, feeling a bit emotional seeing the chief healer again.

"Of course, and I can tell by the look in your eyes you have glimpsed your destiny, haven't you?" the chief healer asked.

"I think so, ma'am. I can tell I'm still meant to heal something. And you taught me everything I need to know about what a healer is meant to do in times of great violence. I just don't want to have to heal because I don't want anyone to get hurt in the first place," she continued, choking up a bit.

"Don't think about it in terms of a who, but focus on the what. What is it that you can and cannot heal? The arcane stream flows through you in a way unlike any other person," Maréli explained.

Miranda contemplated the chief healer's words in a brief moment of silence. Eventually, she clarified, "My heritage makes me unique, but my fight against Gelidor has left me much weaker than before."

"All for the same purpose, my dear," Maréli replied. "It's not just your heritage. Your very soul is bent to making whole that which is broken." The chief healer's eyes looked heavy with worry. "Everything that you are is special, Miranda. There are still secrets you have yet to uncover."

"What does that mean? Should I seek answers through action or prayer?" she asked in response, excitement stirring in her rather than fear.

Maréli shrugged. "It's hard to say. But your immense

potential seems like it could correct the greatest wrong in our universe in the last century."

Miranda's nose twitched with agreement. "The Unbinding," she commented, reflecting on her conversation with Dalyn Tyrdrac. Her paradoxical nature was uniquely aligned with the arcane in a way that may provide more answers as she continued to learn about herself. "Do you think I can heal the arcane stream, chief healer?"

Maréli smiled, and her braids shook with her countenance. "Only you know the answer to that question, my dear. And if you do not know the answer now, you are the only one who can learn the truth."

Miranda's lips curled in thought. Based on what Dalyn Tyrdrac told her and what she witnessed in the stream, maybe she could. "Then I suppose I shall set off in search of answers," she said with a smile. Mir'thax Toi'landra had her next quest, but there were still some other matters to attend to before beginning that adventure.

The next morning, Miranda signed up for caravan work with a group of merchants heading back to the eastern reaches of Alabaster. As a warpriest, she was compensated at a premium rate compared to acolytes. She took the paperwork to the barracks for her assignment. The young cleric working the desk told her that her availability to take jobs was presently suspended by order of the high priest.

"I'm sorry, but you'll have to get this form and this waiver stamped by High Priest Thomas Selasine if you wish to take this job."

She gave the cleric a smile, "Of course, he would. He should know better than that. I wouldn't leave without saying goodbye!"

With a shrug, the helpful cleric gave Miranda all the paperwork, which she promptly took to the office of the high priest. She found three bureaucrats working hard outside the office, one of them Carulus. It looked like part of his punishment would be cleaning up the mess he left behind when he became obsessed with defeating Erk. As Miranda approached the doors to the high priest's study, Carulus turned and started to say, "Apologies, faithful, but . . . Oh, Judge of Hearts, my apologies for interrupting you. His Holiness awaits you inside," he finished, a half-smile to the young warpriest.

Miranda gave him a cordial nod and smile and entered the doors to the high priest's study. The study was massive, with towering bookshelves and numerous tables for study and collaboration. In the center sat a large, personal desk for the high priest's daily duties. Thomas was sitting at that desk, with papers stacked almost as high as himself while standing. He looked up from his work, his face immediately breaking into a smile, "Yolasha!"

"Modai-rin!" she replied, rushing to his desk as he stood. She gave him a greeting hug but shook the paperwork at him. "It seems I've been placed on some kind of suspension requiring the approval of the high priest to take a job!" she complained in a teasing melody.

"Surely there must be some mistake?" Thomas replied with a grin.

"According to the bylaws, the high priest can suspend anyone's authorization for church work for any reason. However, no reason was left in my file, so I only need your signature to lift the suspension!" Miranda explained, demonstrating her thorough knowledge of the necessary paperwork for adventuring under the church's banner.

Taking the paperwork from her, Thomas affixed his stamp. "The official reason is that you can't leave without saying goodbye, yolasha. Ever!"

Miranda scrunched her nose, "But modai-rin, I don't say goodbye. This is just see you later because I'll be back before you know it!"

Thomas smiled, his heart full and his pride for her overflowing. "Then, every time you take a new mission, make sure to come tell me I'll see you soon, alright?"

The warpriest smiled at him. "Of course, Your Holiness. I will see you soon," she said, her melodic voice heartwarming.

"Our steps forward bring the future," Thomas began.

Miranda completed the central line of the Catechism of the Traveler. "But our footprints are the evidence of our deeds," she finished with a smile.

Thomas knew she had already left grand footprints on the world. He was nervous about what might be in her future, but he trusted her. "Safe travels, yolasha," he finished, a tear streaming down his cheek.

She hugged him again. "See you soon, modai-rin." He stood, watching as she departed. She gave him a final, tear-filled stare and a wave as she slipped out the doors of the high priest's office.

Miranda stood in the grand parlor of her estate. The headmistress of the monastery and Bishop Alan Ekol stood with her. Ekol had received the appointment when High Priest Selasine heard of his disciplined and helpful actions on *The Valiant Sailor* while Justin was aboard. They began to go through the house room by room, pulling sheets off the furniture and checking for signs of disturbance. The townsfolk left this place alone out of respect for the Hyacinths and Miranda. Interlopers dared not bring down the wrath of the townsfolk.

"I think it's perfect!" the headmistress said to Miranda.

The warpriest smiled, happy to be back in this frontier town. "So, can we turn it into a school for the entire town?" she asked.

Ekol nodded with confidence, but the headmistress continued to speak. "Of course, it will strengthen the faith of both the followers of Lexcord and Invictus. By providing children here with access to learning, Devitus will be in an enviable position within the next century."

Miranda beamed with happiness. "I'm just glad we can put the estate to use for the whole community," she added, having learned from Erilkaiden and Evanthalus what true nobility should do for their communities. The two-week trip to Devitus was uneventful as she accompanied a caravan as far east as Eddiemont, the last city with over ten-thousand residents on the frontier. From there, she traveled northeast with August's cousin Samuel Burchard with his luxury fabrics and master-crafted tools and implements. They arrived in Devitus without having seen so much as a venomous snake.

Ekol spoke, "Though I am new to Devitus, I share your

passion and vision for building this community. I will petition the high priest for acolytes to assist in teaching the children of Devitus."

Both Miranda and the headmistress nodded in agreement. Miranda replied, "Then it is settled. I leave my estate in your hands as stewards, and whatever you must do to make this a thriving school, you have my full permission. However," she started, looking down shyly. "There is one room that will remain untouched and unused. The sitting room on the estate's west side is to be left unchanged down to the dust on the sheets." She finished her caveat with a nod.

The headmistress and Bishop Ekol replied with a bow and a salute, respectively. They spent the rest of that afternoon making plans and deciding what resources they would need to make the estate a school. After several hours, the headmistress and Ekol departed, but Miranda stayed on the estate while planning her next move.

In the sitting room, Miranda found the crystallized statue of her parents. She touched the gemstone statues and could feel the mana flowing inside them. Though she could not hear them the way she could while trapped in the arcane stream, she could feel them in her heart. She smiled and hugged the statue. "Mom, dad. I've got such a big family now. And I'm not scared. I think there's a lot of work ahead of me, thanks to you two," she teased them, giggling. "But," she sighed and stared blankly out the window of the sitting room. The evening sun lit up the fruit trees forming an orchard on the estate's west side, currently far out of season. Miranda continued, "But I'm going to heal the arcane stream. And when I do, I know that Saraix will call your names. When you make it back, please come find me. I love you both," she finished, her voice barely a whisper by the end.

She stood straight, touched the sapphire comb in her hair, and ran her hands along the skirt of her battlemail. She checked that Iria's sword was still firmly affixed to her belt and found a mirror. She painted two blue lines on each of her cheeks with the pigment she had taken from the dressing room on *The Nebula*. Looking back at the statue of her parents, she realized something. The gemstone in the center of Evan's sword gave her the same sensation as the statues of her parents. Her face twitched with a bit of fear.

"There's always a price," she said to herself.

She gathered as much mana as possible, allowing her to make a single wish. A white, glowing circle appeared underneath her, reminding her of Jacques's power. Nobody had heard from him since the fight against Gelidor. Everyone was worried about him, but nobody would assume the worst. They all prayed for his safety, hoping his uncanny magic had sent him elsewhere on his last attempt at teleporting.

As the white circle grew brighter still, Miranda felt herself transported through space and time. She looked at her surroundings and found herself in a quaint village of short, draconic-shaped figures. As she appeared suddenly in their midst, a crowd of these small creatures was immediately drawn to her. They began asking questions to each other and to her in the draconic language, which Miranda found she knew fluently, thanks to her mother's memories.

"Who are you?" "Why is there a human in our village?" "Is it here to kill the draikin?" were some questions floating around her.

With a comforting smile, she introduced herself in their language, "Greetings draikin, my name is Mir'thax Toi'landra. I've been sent by Philotrax and Reshiria. I'm here to help."

Epilogue

Eldon Farzg sat across from a man he knew only as Richard. The human was well dressed and sat comfortably in the chair across from the frost giantkin. He seemed too comfortable, so Farzg willed the air temperature in the room to drop, a natural talent gained from his heritage. The slaver tapped his chin, hidden underneath his flowing, white beard. "One hundred million gold coins invested, you say?"

Richard nodded, his blond hair bobbing freely. It came down to his shoulders but was well trimmed on top. "I'd like to ensure I'm doing my fiscal duty to ensure that my chief investor gets the returns he's looking for." He didn't respond to the dropping temperature.

Farzg leaned across the table with interest. "These new weapons, then. They're all connected to an enterprise you're bankrolling with the infinite wealth of The Shadowed One?" he asked, referring to Na'agamlor by a name more friendly to the god's followers.

The businessman smiled, greed and ambition evident in

his eyes. "He seeks a way to the primordial place, and we believe Santiago has the genius to reach it." He raised his hand to his nose, feeling the freezing temperature around him, causing it to begin bleeding. Still, he showed no discomfort as he continued, "For your participation in this venture, I will see to it that the merchant pays you for your full services rendered at double your normal rate." He clasped his hands and took a deep breath. A deep exhalation from the middle-aged human somehow neutralized the cold emanating from Farzg.

The frost giantkin narrowed his eyes with suspicion. "I cannot be paid in gold alone. I value irreplaceable artifacts above all else." It was unusual for someone to undo his temperature-controlling magic with just a breath. Farzg was further intrigued.

Richard nodded enthusiastically, "Oh, we are well aware of your fees, Eldon." His voice was like a casual salesman, plying his trade with eagerness. "Say, you know the story of the birth of magic, don't you?"

Farzg nodded, "The beginning of all things, Genesis, broke themselves into two halves, creating the Dragon Mother and Dragon Father. That shattering created a vacuum in the essence of creation. It formed the arcane stream, into which Gorthran and Saraix entered later as shards. Some say the stream is the sole reason life is capable in Espa." He shrugged. "I don't see how this has anything to do with my fee for supporting the wizard."

The salesman stood, smiling broadly. He reached into his fancy jacket and fumbled in his pockets momentarily. He twisted his lips with frustration until he pulled a thin sliver of silver metal from within. He placed it on the desk between them, and the fragment floated six inches above the surface thanks to an unseen pressure. It looked like a spike approximately a foot long, but one end had a design. It was shaped like a clover with a heart etched into the center with gold inlay.

"What is this trinket?" Farzg asked, his curiosity building.

"This, my friend, is the godshard of Saraix herself. It contains her literal essence, and it is only the first of many gifts Na'agamlor offers you if you would be willing to contract with us." Richard winked with a devious nod of his head. "I don't know what you can do with the heart of a goddess, but I'm sure you'll find something important to do with it!"

Farzg's jaw slacked in wonder. He possessed numerous wonderful items, many of which had significant historical importance. He was especially proud of the many religious relics he had stolen from the Church of Invictus. Their hypocritical codes allowed the church to seize possession of items deemed important. He wanted to demonstrate that a private collector was better at curating interesting objects. He tilted his head forward, making his long features look even more severe. "The heart of a goddess, you say. How did you acquire it?"

Richard shrugged. "She tried to break some kind of rule that was in place long before The Unbinding!" he explained with a laugh. "Apparently, she tried to birth herself into the cycle of draconic reincarnation. The remnants of Genesis did not like that." A sinister smile crossed his lips as he continued, "She ended up stuck like this." He gestured to the sliver of metal floating in the invisible globe of energy. "It took Na'agamlor a while to acquire it. It was previously protected by a cluster of good dragons living near Tanlin Falls. Na'agamlor had an agent slip in and acquire it before Santiago's henchmen could find it." The salesman returned to his seated position. "A unique object belongs in the hands of a collector like you, Eldon. You need this."

The frost giantkin licked his lips with frustration. "Don't tell me what I need, Richard. I don't know if I trust you." He looked back to the shard of Saraix and furrowed his brow. "If it is indeed what you say, you have purchased my full cooperation." His violet eyes glimmered with his lust for building the most unique collection of artifacts in Espa.

The salesman nodded politely. "Feel free to investigate it and confirm for yourself."

Farzg wrinkled his nose with disbelief as he reached his long arms across the table to touch the shard of Saraix. As his fingers contacted the invisible pressure around it, he felt a shock in his soul. He pushed his hand into the pressure, and his vision went dark. He could feel the essence of the Dragon

Mother pressing back against him; her voice filled his consciousness. "Vile creature, back from me!" she demanded.

Richard watched as Farzg's eyes began to glow, indicating he had made contact with the divinity within the shard. He remained seated, watching gleefully.

Farzg replied, "So it is truly the soul of a goddess. How deliciously rare. I wonder if I can bend you to my will?"

Saraix responded, "No, Farzg. I sense your bond with one of my brother's shards. The darkness of your heart is completely incompatible with the purity of my light. You would do well to put me in the hands of a dragon of good heart."

Farzg telepathically raised an eyebrow as he communicated with Saraix. His body did not respond in kind, preventing Richard from gauging the course of the conversation. The frost giantkin taunted, "You are a useless piece of metal, now. You cannot make demands, especially not of me. I am too powerful for you to resist."

The Dragon Mother laughed, "Oh, Farzg. You think your crusade is justified, but you're scared. I can taste your fear." The darkness around him felt the movement of Saraix's draconic tongue as it flicked past his face. "The Church of Invictus is closing in on you. You know it's only a matter of time."

Farzg felt rage building in his chest. "They will not destroy me! How dare you intrude my mind!" he roared.

Saraix let out a gentle sigh. "You shared all this with me when you put your fingers into my soul, Farzg. The longer you stay, the more I will influence your mind! You think yourself a god, but you are a mortal like everyone else. The only thing special about you is the pain and suffering you've inflicted on countless innocents. You know the truth in your heart, too," she rebuked.

Farzg's anger dissipated; a feeling of exhaustion replaced it. "Whatever, Dragon Mother. You are powerless; now you are just another trinket in my possession."

Saraix did not allow Farzg to withdraw his fingers from her soul. "I am not powerless, nor will I ever be, fool. You will find the strongest dragon of light you can and give them my godshard."

Farzg felt his heart seize with fear. He felt his connection to the cold cease as soon as Saraix gave him an order. His willpower resisted the command, but he felt his heart wavering with anxiety. He had never encountered a deity in person, and now that he had, he realized his true meekness in the role of existence. His deeds, ambitions, and decisions were replayed in front of him. He realized his wealth paled in comparison to that of Na'agamlor, the most illegitimate of all the gods. His evil was significantly overshadowed by Hoxark's depravity and had no way of consuming all those he faced, like Aylabrax the Devourer. Queen Cataclysta of the Thirteen Infernia had more loyalty among the devils serving her than Farzg of his mercenaries. Furthermore, eldritch deities lay beyond the reaches of history that would never even know his name. Farzg was nothing more than a speck, a momentary problem for mortals. His end would be unnoticed unless . . .

"Fine, Dragon Mother. The moment my death becomes clear to me, I will put your shard in possession of a dragon of light. You will be waiting a long time for me to fulfill that duty. Prepare yourself for captivity among my artifacts." He forced his soul out of the conversation with Saraix.

Richard leaned forward with an evil smile, his blond hair hanging over his shoulders. His features were sharp and severe, but he was very well-groomed and handsome. His smile was genuine and false at the same time. "So, what do you think, Eldon?" he asked.

Farzg glared as he smiled, "I agree to the contract terms, then. I will help this Santiago character acquire dragon eggs with my smuggling network. I will also increase the number of faekin that I am capturing."

Richard gave a humble nod and pushed the shard of Saraix across the table. His fingers did not enter the pressure, rolling it closer to Farzg. "I will send additional magic items and money as soon as Santiago receives the first egg from your efforts. And," he said, giving a dramatic pause. "For the record, Santiago is a bit of an eccentric character. He goes by the alias Doctor One. He likes to think himself a professor of magic."

The frost giantkin frowned. "I am not fond of mad scientists, Richard."

The salesman's smile returned as he replied, "His genius certainly outweighs his madness. The weapons your slavers have been using, the ones with the magic crystals. Those were his inventions."

Farzg tilted his head in disbelief, shuddering internally at what the Dragon Mother showed him. Perhaps the enhanced weapons would help keep the church at bay. Saraix was wrong. Farzg needed only to eliminate one target to prove his argument. He replied to Richard, "My smuggling network will benefit from them, no doubt, but I want something more tangible. Something personal."

Richard tilted his head, feeling the agreement terms changing in real time. "What is that?" he asked.

Farzg's expression shifted to disgust. "I want to destroy the Church of Invictus. I'll start with their new high priest in Nulodia."

The salesman gasped. "Nothing is outside of Na'agamlor's purchasing power, but Farzg, that's going to be more expensive than—" he objected, but Farzg interrupted.

"Nonsense. Just pit your brilliant wizard against them with my support. I won't have to find and kill him. He will come to me."

Richard's gaze was judgmental. "You have heard the rumors about the new church leader, haven't you?" he asked, his voice still smooth and convincing.

Farzg confirmed with a nod. "Thomas Selasine, High Priest of Invictus. Recently a hero in league with the Yendralians. He also adopted a peculiar girl as his daughter. She demonstrated incredible power at the Battle of Beriton by transforming into a . . ." he began but trailed off.

Saraix's godshard began to vibrate and emanate bright, golden light in brief pulses.

Richard's smile became sadistic, "That's right. A dragon."

Farzg stared at Saraix's shard, thinking about her words. "The ward of Selasine is an impossibility. Perhaps it's not the priest I should end, but the new symbol of hope for the poor, misguided clergy." He started to smile with malice. "Perhaps, indeed. Doing so would inevitably be a crushing blow to the church and Selasine's morale."

Richard seemed more comfortable now than before, which bothered Farzg. The frost giantkin wanted to see the salesman squirm but felt separated from the cold. Richard replied, "We'll have no problem putting the scientist against the church; they are, after all, the greatest threat to our operations. We'll help by accelerating our Death Pirate agents' progress on their invasion of Yendralia. The threat should be great enough to fragment our mutual enemies." The man glared angrily, "My ex-wife is important in the Church of Invictus. She stole my daughter from me, and I owe them a debt of pain. Divide and conquer, Farzg."

The frost giantkin gulped as his eyes lingered on the shard of Saraix. If Selasine's daughter was strong enough to defeat him, he knew Saraix was right. This was an argument he intended to settle with mortal stakes. If he was wrong, the girl would inevitably acquire the shard anyway. Farzg gave Richard an evil grin, "Then let us begin dividing and conquering."

Glossary
&
Liturgy

Glossary

<u>Old Common</u>

adûnzha - attention
mahalàkhas – praise and blessings
talirix volïs - unhallowed chaos

<u>Khantongue</u>

Errvin gol'tdon, Cantaloos - "Now is not good, Cantalus."
Marg'farked, ahlzbögendad - "Weary travelers, what ails you?"
MettosUndigne, fadwai noznogro peneeto - "Fleeing the violence in the Undine Sea"
Nyokto - Damn

<u>Elven</u>

Eba-zim - Cousin, ungendered
Edmi yulesta tek yolasha. Afirfin't lotz gerindalthus - "My wife and daughter. Far too soon, stolen."
Hai-rin - Mother, formal (Hai-n, informal)
Hai-yashir - Aunt
Modai-moshir - Uncle
Modai-rin - Father, formal (Modai-n, informal)
Molen - Nephew
Moshirin - Little brother, formal (Moshi'n, informal)
Moshirote - Little brother, formal (Moshte, informal)
Mosh-zim - Cousin, male
Mu-zim - Son, formal. (Muz, informal)
Nes'ni - Come here.
Nulestotejin - Brother-in-law
Yashirin - Little sister, formal (Yashi'n, informal)
Yashirote - Big sister, formal (Yashte, informal)
Yash-zim - Cousin, female
Yolasha - Daughter, formal (Yoli, informal)
Yolen - Niece
Yulesta - Wife, formal (Yula, informal)
Yulestotejin - Sister-in-law

Suffix - 'thi: Plural marker. For example, moshirin'thi = Little brothers (formal).

Suffix - 'nides: Expression of unconditional love. Example: Moshirin'nides = I love you, little brother.

Liturgy

The Catechism of the Peacekeeper

Humanity finds itself on the precipice between law and chaos. Those who find refuge at the feet of Invictus welcome order into their hearts. Those that embrace order are protected by the Sword of Justice. Those that are protected by his holy might rejoice, for the hour of delivery is upon us. Deliver them from chaos and shield them from anarchy. And may we, peacekeepers, stand firmly at the precipice, keeping the darkness at bay.

The Catechism of Greeting

We harvest the bounty of law: Peace and prosperity, the blessings of the Sword of Justice.

The Catechism of Dawning [Greeting]

Prompter: The Sword of Justice reveres the harmonious music of the morning.

Respondent: The awakening dawn a paragon of order and beauty.

The Catechism of the Traveler

The Sword of Justice guides our path! Let us set out with order in our step and righteousness in our heart. May Invictus shine his holy light upon us and pour out his judgment in abundance. Our steps forward bring the future, but our footprints are the evidence of our deeds. Silver Maiden, guard our hearts; Sword of Justice, guide our hands. Together we depart, and together we shall return.

The Catechism of Grief

We are bereft, Sword of Justice. Though Invictus is mighty, the destiny of mortals reaches beyond the sands of time. From creation to end, comfort our hearts, rest our minds. May we walk the Path of the Sword of Justice with solemnity and humility.

The Catechism of Balance

Beings of good heart need no laws, beings of no heart cannot be bound by laws. It is the essence of balance and the emergence of natural order that law binds our inclinations to do others harm. In this, morality and the law intertwine, each guiding the other toward the goal of righteous order.

The Catechism of Gratitude
The Sword of Justice pours out his bounty with mercy, love, and righteousness. We are grateful for his ever-watchful eye and his provisions of protection and law. We are grateful for the laws that bind us together as a society, and together we strive for a greater future. May Invictus part us from chaos, forevermore.

The Catechism of Gratitude [Reprisal]
Part us from chaos, and let us drive evil into the light so that the Silver Maiden and The Sword of Justice may purify them. Our gratitude is justified by the actions of our gods, and may those be reflected in our own actions.

The Catechism of Diligence
Times of peace and prosperity flourish when the faithful are diligent. Chaos ebbs and flows like the tide, may our children know days without struggle.

The Catechism of Decisiveness
May the Sword of Justice grant us the wisdom to make decisions that are both righteous and beneficial. May Invictus grant us the strength to act on those decisions, and may he grant us the persistence to see those goals realized. Blessings upon the faithful, and upon the law of the Sword of Justice.

The Catechism of Welcoming
Examiner: These peacekeepers have a firm foundation in the tenets of the faith. But do they have the traits necessary to serve the Sword of Justice as acolytes?

Mentor: May you test them in their strength and resolve. Let us hear the voice of Invictus and obey the will of order.

Examiner: Then let us temper their wills in a trial by combat. May they demonstrate the finesse to arrest lawbreakers, the strength to overcome the depraved, and the willpower to face overwhelming threats with conviction.

(Upon Passing) Examiner: Your resolve to defend law from chaos is commendable. With your guidance, these acolytes will shine as beacons of hope for those that cling to the Sword of Justice. May Invictus guide your hand against chaos at every turn.

The Catechism of Meeting Again

The Sword of Justice smiles on this reunion. May we follow the Path of the Sword of Justice with righteousness and humility.

The Oath of the Cleric

On this day, I claim the path of the cleric. I will wield my sword to defend my brethren. I shall wear my armor to stand against chaos. The might of Invictus is my strength, and his will is my will. I devote myself to his laws, to his ways, and to his mind. I bind myself to my kinsmen within the church, and I serve society to bring order and justice. My prayers are your prayers, my sword your sword. May order and prosperity light the path before us.

The Oath of the Paladin

On this day, I claim the path of the paladin. I will wield my sword as an instrument of justice. I will wear my armor to defend the weak. The might of Invictus is my strength, and his will is my will. I devote myself to his laws, to his ways, and to his mind. I bind myself to the brotherhood of paladins within the church of Invictus. My blade is your blade, my shield your shield. May order and prosperity light the path before us.

The Prayer of Healing

Restore to order what was damaged by chaos.

The Prayer of Protection

Protect us from harm and guide our hands against chaos.

The Prayer of Hardiness

Sword of Justice, lend us your aid. Fortify us against the onslaught of chaos and let us lay low the enemy.

The Prayer of Revival

Order, grant your faithful the blessing of another chance. A life ended too early is the work of chaos; let us set the universe to right in the Path of the Sword of Justice.

The Prayer of Curse Breaking #6

Oh light of Invictus, the justice that guides our path. Take pity on our restless souls as we have been cursed to the root. This doth plague us with affliction, pain, and chaos. Destroy that which causes our souls to seep so sourly.

The Prayer of Cleansing
Light of righteousness, Sword of Justice. What chaos has sullied, cleanse with your purity. Extract the filth from the blood, restore this body, and heal this mind.

The Prayer of Daylight
Sword of Justice, pour out your light and righteousness. Push back the darkness with your holy daylight.

The Prayer of Greater Protection
Sword of Justice, hear my plea. Shield myself and my companions from all harm as we seek to dispel the chaos that has manifest. We ask you, justice incarnate, to cover our bodies with your hands, our minds with your wisdom, and our souls with your righteousness.

The Prayer of Disguise
Invictus, let our travels pass unnoticed. Keep our identities secret so that we can expose the forces of chaos from within.

The Prayer of Awakening:
Sword of Justice, remedy this accursed sleep. The laws of nature dictate our rest, not the machinations of chaos. Wake, and be healed.

The Prayer of Reconstruction
Oh Sword of Justice, hear my plea. This construction that could be used as an instrument of righteousness has been sabotaged by those that seek to thwart the hand of the law. Hear my prayer, Invictus, and turn your ear to our desperate need. Heal this vessel.

The Curse of Implosion
To purify what has been sullied, Sword of Justice take the air away from this place. Suffocate the chaos with your righteous fury.

The Curse of Misfortune
Invictus, shield us from the fury of chaos, grant us your light, and curse those who would sully your legacy.

The Curse of Binding
There is peace in a just society. Allow me to be an instrument of that peace, Sword of Justice. Bind that which sews chaos and pour out your judgment tenfold.

The Curse of Exhaustion
Justice Incarnate, weaken these interlopers that they may not raise their weapons against those that follow the Path of the Sword of Justice.

The Curse of Revealing
The eyes of Justice see all and know all. Invictus, we implore thee, show us that which is hidden!

Espa Historical Timeline

The Rifting – A long-forgotten calamity, known as The Rifting, destroyed the southern hemisphere of Espa. Genesis, the beginning of all things, used its essence to preserve the northern hemisphere. It broke its consciousness into two entities: Saraix and Gorthran. Genesis's latent power became the arcane stream. The Rifting is considered the beginning of time.

The Age of Awakening – 1000 Years. This period saw the emergence of intelligent life in Espa. Many powerful entities struggled for dominance over sentience. Many of the eldritch gods whose names have been lost to history rose to power during The Age of Awakening. Humans, elves, dwarves, orcs, and giants built empires across Espa, but many were destroyed in the following epoch.

The Dracon Wars – 1000 Years. A time of great conflict in Espa's history. This period began when Saraix the Dragon Queen shattered herself into the arcane stream, the remnants of Genesis. Gorthran also shattered his essence into the stream to counteract her, though he reserved several shards to maintain his autonomous strength and sentience. The birth of dragons around Espa began a millennium-long conflict between the dragon gods. Gorthran's shards were eventually overpowered by Saraix's, especially after she further broke her shards into a powerful people known as the Drakinskäld. To punish the dragon gods for the destruction wrought on reality, Genesis exiled Gorthran to the island of Olvidado and Saraix to the island of Escondido.

The Rebuilding – 1000 Years. The Drakinskäld accompanied mortality until they reconstituted the dragons of light throughout Espa. This epoch was one of great prosperity and growth in which Espa's capitals began to flourish: Alabaster, Yendralia, South Port, Nishumi, Buenmar, Breckinshore, Gabah, and Thaliston exploded in population and wealth. The eldritch gods born during The Age of Awakening reemerged, but their differing philosophies began to drive a wedge between factions of mortals. Luxsol, Deridaña, Dimittena, Gaiater, and Umiaigén found themselves divided against Aylabrax, Hoxark, Grunax, Ultria, and Cataclysta. Their conflict led to the next great calamity: The Legion of Hoxark.

The Legion of Hoxark – 1000 Years. As the division among the eldritch gods widened, the hearts of mortals became their source of life. Though the gods could grant prayers previously, faith had little to do with the connection between mortal and divine. However, Hoxark, Lord of the Abyss, realized the evil and hatred in people's hearts could be physically weaponized. Hoxark created demons that could walk on the central plane of existence using those aspects of mortality. The destruction wrought by those entities began a new calamity that shook Espa to its core. Drawing upon the power of Genesis and The Rift, mortals and gods fought against the demons that plagued reality as they knew it. Genesis further divided itself to circumvent future conflicts, creating the primordial place. Luxsol and Grunax were slain during this conflict. Deridaña, Dimittena, and Ultria entered into long, deep sleeps. Luxsol was replaced by Invictus, a human man that fully believed in the purpose of order, and Deridaña was replaced by Lexcord, the strongest of the elves. A vacuum of power was left in several other places, permitting mortals to flirt with godhood and gods to flirt with mortality.

Epoch of Novo Deum – 1000 Years. Lexcord and Invictus champion the causes of order among mortals, but other powerful entities begin their rise to godhood during this time. Na'agamlor, The Counselor of the Corrupt, used the peace and prosperity of the era to accumulate wealth by manipulating mortal systems and governments. By the end of the era, the merchant had destroyed the growing Kingdom of Claston to fund his search for a way to the primordial place. His puppet, Gelidor Claston, funneled the enormous wealth of the elves to The Shadowed One. As a result, Na'agamlor's high priests came in contact with a wizard known as Santiago Eb'lin. He promised that he could help Na'agamlor reach his destination by using crystallized magic. However, their plans were wrecked by the next calamity.

The Unbinding – 100 Years. Though the Drakinskäld had gone extinct as the dragons of light were reborn, some dragons continued to use magic to take mortal form and mate with the various peoples of Espa. The mighty dragon, Tyrdrac the Silver, ignored the warnings of his brothers, Excelsior and Solarus, and married an elven woman in the Kingdom of Claston during the Epoch of Novo Deum. Their great-great-grandson, Dalyn Tyrdrac, possessed his ancestors' immense power and curiosity. That led to him fusing his soul with the arcane stream. Genesis was unprepared for the fractured, draconic soul, and the entirety of magic broke. Mortals and immortals could no longer use Genesis's essence to manipulate Espa's reality. Two dragons trapped as humans, Philotrax and Reshiria, found themselves in a symbiotic relationship of comfort and validation. Their union resulted in the birth of a dragon that was neither a shard of Saraix nor Gorthran. Gods and mortals continue to seek a way to repair the fabric of magic.

Place and Character Profiles

Devitus – The Frontier Town

Year: Unbinding, 100

With a population of approximately five thousand people, Devitus is a growing frontier community. They produce raw materials for advanced economies elsewhere in the Kingdom of Alabaster, but the region's wine is well-known across Espa. Wine, timber, temperate fruits, grain, fish, and ore are their primary exports.

Miranda Hyacinth was born in Devitus in the year Unbinding 80. Philotrax and Reshiria Hyacinth purchased titles of nobility from Baron Carson Devitus. Though remote, it is one of the most secure locations in the eastern reaches of Alabaster.

Yendralia – Capital of The Isles Known for Nothing

Year: Unbinding 30

Yendralia is a haphazard metropolis known as a refuge for persecuted or displaced peoples. Thanks to the strong presence of Cantalus, He Who Sings at the Gate, and Alaina the Pirate Queen, Yendralia was spared the worst effects of The Unbinding: decades of civil war and unrest. Their leadership kept the island unified and relatively stable during the transition.

Year: Unbinding 100

The Eight Pirate Nobles of Yendralia are beginning to stretch their influence beyond the borders of their sacred island. Erk the Radiant targets the usurper of Claston, and Naomi targets a new wave of slavers in league with the Death Pirates of Cassack. Simon the Astral Scathe is currently engaged in weakening the growing threat of Gabah's multicontinental empire.

The Fortress of Lords – Erk's Study

Year: Unbinding 81

Erilkaiden Lancethinas discovered the bonding crystal of an ancient entity he came to know as "The Master." Though Erk was once a wizard, his formal education ceased at the onset of The Unbinding. He thought it resembled a soul prism, a conduit for holding the life essence of an entity in a safe location. Thanks to Erk's lack of experience with the process and his desperation to save his brother, The Master convinced him that he was trapped in the prism as a result of Gelidor's curse.

Year: Unbinding 100

Miranda Hyacinth used her poorly understood powers to force The Master out of the soul prism. Vortex, formerly known as Alamar Ortega, was a wizard that reached the peak of his power during The Rebuilding. He placed his life essence in the soul prism to become a lich. He grew in power century over century. Shortly before The Unbinding, he was preparing to assist a promising wizard, Santiago Eb'lin, for the ritual necessary to become a lich.

The Astral Spire – The Solisberry Tree

Year: Dracon War 999
Genesis's consciousness awoke near the end of the Dracon War.
It planted seven seeds of pure magic around Espa in remote
locations. The Astral Spire in West Espa and The Lunar Spire in
East Espa were among the chosen places. Those seven seeds
bloomed into magnificent solisberry trees, creating anchor
points for the flow of the arcane stream. Genesis intended for
the trees to stabilize the flow of mana around the planet,
making magic more accessible to mortals and dragons.

Year: The Rebuilding 912
Legendary wizard Kzar was the first mortal to visit the Astral
Spire after the Dracon War. He rediscovered the solisberry tree
and wrote two academic texts about the blooms. Like many of
his works, that knowledge was lost to mortals through the
terrors of the Legion of Hoxark. In his work, he theorized that
solisberry trees could serve as a physical gateway to the arcane
stream.

Miranda "Mir'thax Toi'landra" Hyacinth

Birthday: Winter Solstice 4

Miranda might initially strike others as awkward, but her kind demeanor and eagerness to be helpful mitigate her idiosyncrasies. She is aware of her tendency to bungle social cues and expectations but uses that awareness to navigate those situations. She is disciplined but impatient. She is also easily distracted and frequently finds herself trapped in her thoughts. Her favorite animal is the butterfly, and her favorite treat is fried dough sprinkled with sugar and chocolate.

Thomas Selasine

Birthday: The Festival 22

Thomas was promoted to the bishop of the Devitan region after destroying the smuggling ring headed by Eldon Farzg. He prefers fishing over hunting, and his favorite flower is the tulip. As a massive human, he is imposing but is much more passive than his stature suggests.

Justin Elzen

Birthday: Fall Equinox 11

Justin is highly disciplined and rigorous in all he does, holding himself to a standard much higher than he should. He is very fact-oriented and prefers to make decisions cautiously. His favorite leisure activity is the game of Xanadu because "it sharpens the mind through strategy."

August Burchard

Birthday: The Fallowing 23

Though August comes across as brash and undisciplined, he is a kind person at heart. His brother, Marcus, was killed by bandits when August was young. Since then, August has vowed to do whatever it takes to prevent such tragedies from happening to other families. He takes his duty as a peacekeeper very seriously. His favorite beverage is warm tea.

About the Author

Jory Neff is an author, educator, and scholar by trade. He spent his childhood in Texas, Arkansas, and Oklahoma, but he began his academic endeavors at a small, religious school in Arkansas. He has pursued various disciplines including history, linguistics, art, and literature. He serves at a rural high school as a teacher of Spanish, social studies, and art.

Jory graduated with his Ph.D. in Education from Texas Tech University in December of 2021. He used that experience to pursue creative endeavors that exemplify the phenomenological journey that has shaped his perspective of reality. He enjoys videogames, anime, manga, books, tabletop roleplaying games, memes, and music (especially if it came from videogames!). He also holds two bachelor's degrees (Spanish Education and History) and a master's degree (History). His love of languages and stories have heavily influenced his vocabulary and artistic tendencies.

Jory married Janell in November of 2013, and she has been with him every step of this journey. Her love of stories and reading offered the critical lens necessary to create a narrative of this style.

The World of Espa Community Resources

If you enjoyed this story and setting, we are working on bringing Espa to life! Follow Jory's Facebook page for updates directly related to the books or follow his Instagram as he continues to learn how to create illustrations that will help bring characters and settings to life. If you are on Discord, hang out with us and talk about the book!

Facebook: J. Neff - Author

Discord: discord.gg/uuRS3DPm6b

Instagram: @J_Neff_Artexperiments

Email: author.unbindingchronicles@gmail.com

Scan the QR Code for my LinkTree!

Super special thanks to the cover artist, Emily Verkamp. Check out her socials for more of her creative projects:

Insta: @emiv_photography

Website: emilyverkamp.weebly.com

www.ingramcontent.com/pod-product-compliance
Lightning Source LLC
Chambersburg PA
CBHW022008300726